the earth legend

academy of magical creatures book three

MEGAN LINSKI & ALICIA RADES

We the authors acknowledge that the United States of America is a country formed on stolen land. We respect and honor the indigenous peoples who have lived here for centuries, and we recognize there is still much work to do to make reparations and heal the damage caused to the many indigenous nations who were first here, both in the past and today.

May we remember the atrocities once committed, create a better world in the present, and look forward together for our future.

A special thank-you to our sensitivity reader Kris Riley of the Cherokee tribe for her invaluable feedback on indigenous life and culture, as well as her commentary on living with chronic illness.

This book features a character with depression and suicidal thoughts. Depression is one of the most common mental disorders in America and affects over 264 million people world-wide. Symptoms may include fatigue, insomnia, and suicidal thoughts or actions. Suicide is the tenth leading cause of death in the United States and affects people across race, age, and gender identity.

Liam

ONE

I could recall the day I'd bonded like it was yesterday— and I knew I'd always remember it that way.

I'd been walking in the forest on my own in late September, during the afternoon around sunset. I was in my second year at Orenda Academy, and had been feeling pretty isolated from everyone else.

I felt different and alone. I couldn't understand why. My life was pretty good. I was happy, overall. But I couldn't shake the feeling that someone... something... was missing. I couldn't figure out who. There was just this gap in me that had always been there and that I could never explain. I always felt like my purpose, my destiny, was somewhere out there... not here. I wanted to go look for it, because I was restless without it.

When I got far enough into the woods, I heard a cracking sound and looked up. My heart skipped a beat, and then froze when I saw a pair of amber eyes peering out at me from the trees.

There was a large black wolf standing there, his coat deeper than night and shadow. He held himself tall, head high, his ears perked forward as he looked at me. Some people don't believe animals can have expressions, but this one did. His look was completely serious, and though we were at least twenty feet apart, it felt like he was pulling me in, further and further to him.

The gaze we shared was unbreakable. I couldn't wrench my eyes away if I tried. Time faded away, and so did everything around me. A soft flute played a solo melody in the background that only we could hear. Nothing else mattered. The only thing that meant anything anymore was the wolf. My body felt light and airy as I began walking toward the wolf, my feet moving not of their own accord.

My ears seemed to block out all sound as I approached the wolf. He turned, glancing behind himself once before he broke into a run.

I followed. I leapt into a run, but I wasn't chasing him. I was sprinting beside him. We weaved throughout the trees together, matching stride for stride. His paws touched the ground each time my foot did, and we moved seamlessly, in unison. Everything was fast, yet it was also in slow motion. I'd never felt so connected to something in my life. What I had known before, it hadn't ever made me feel this way.

Finally, the wolf stopped running. He came to a halt beside a cascading waterfall and allowed the spray to mist his black fur.

I took a few deep breaths before I sank to my knees before him. He didn't move, but remained standing, and kept staring back. I raised a shaking hand to touch his fur. The moment I did, shock waves were sent pulsating through my body.

My entire existence was rearranged. Saying that my life was different wasn't enough. This bond went beyond the short time I would exist on this plane. Everything I thought that had mattered didn't matter at all. The only thing that mattered was the wolf in front of me. He consumed every part of me, rearranged my thoughts about myself and created a mirror that I could use to reflect who I was. Every connection in my life— my family, my tribe, who I wanted to be— came loose and tied themselves tightly on to the wolf. Whatever I cared about or loved, if it didn't relate to the wolf, it was no longer important.

We were the same. There was nothing different about us. It was like we shared the same body, the same mind. All I cared about was his beating heart, his breath. Without it, *I meant nothing*. He carried all the best parts of me within him, and I was just the body that moved throughout this earthly realm. He was me— who I really was, not who I pretended or wanted to be. I would die and be buried, but he would live on with the ancestors forever.

The connection I felt between us was like golden threads twisting and binding around each other, creating a thick rope that tangled up the two of us so I couldn't distinguish where myself ended and he began. Because that would be impossible. Cutting us apart, trying to untangle the interwoven strands that bonded me and him, would be something not even the ancestors could do. I felt warm strands wrap around me like a thick blanket, and I could no longer resist and pull away from who and what this wolf was. The missing gap in my heart filled, and for the first time in my life, I truly felt like this was where I belonged. My purpose and my meaning in life had been filled up. It was like satisfying something that could never be satisfied. Whatever I'd been looking for, I'd found it, and now I was finally at peace.

"Nashoma," I whispered, and I wrapped my arms around the wolf and held him tight. The wolf buried his snout into my shoulder and huffed. I ran my hands through his fur and over his ears. He was perfect. A scar ran over his right eye, and he had a hardened look that said he wouldn't give up, no matter what happened.

He was tough. I liked it. I stood, one hand still wrapped firmly in the fur that ran across his shoulder blades. "Come on, brother. Let's go back and tell everyone I've found my Familiar."

My whole family had celebrated with me that day. Back then, I thought Nashoma would be by my side forever.

He was, in a way. But at the same time, he wasn't. The most unbearable part of it was that I didn't just *lose him.*

I'd lost Sophia.

sophia
TWO

Nausea slammed into my gut as the tall, twisted spires of Orenda Academy came into view. Normally, the sight would send a warm, fuzzy sensation in the pit of my stomach, as if arriving home to a comforting bed after a long trek through the Arctic.

But now... it felt like entering a graveyard after a massacre. The castle classrooms and halls remembered every kiss, every touch, every whisper Liam and I had ever shared. Orenda Academy was where our love had blossomed... and where it had died.

Going back was more painful than I'd imagined. I thought I could block it all out, forget it had ever happened and move on with my life, but I would never forget a single moment I shared with Liam Mitoh. He was once the very air I breathed.

Now it felt as if I was suffocating.

I turned my gaze away from the carriage window and stared down at Esis in my lap. The knot in my chest eased only slightly. I felt numb enough to almost forget it was there.

That's what this past summer had been like. I ate. I slept. I read. Everything else was numbness. I tried to forget Liam, and I almost thought I had... until the moment I spotted Orenda Academy. All those feelings— all those memories— came rushing back.

All I have to do is make it through the day without crying, I told myself. If I could manage that, I could make it through the rest of the semester.

"Are you going to be okay, Sophia?" Imogen asked from beside me.

I lifted my head to see her bright eyes on mine. She wore a tight blue top that showed off all her curves, and a purple tulle skirt she'd made over the summer. Her strawberry-blonde hair was tied into two buns, each with a daisy hairpiece attached to the top. She softly petted Sassy's red fur between us with a look of concern on her face.

I stroked Esis' horns for something to do with my hands. They'd grown an inch over the last few months. They were slowly transforming from the cute, nubby horns I liked so much into longer, more mature horns. The book in Imogen's library showed male kurbles grew ram-like horns once they reached full maturity. I wasn't ready for my little buddy to grow up. It seemed like everything in my life was changing, and I couldn't handle it.

"I'll be fine," I lied.

"Are you sure?" Imogen pressed. "I know it must be hard going back after the break-up, and seeing Liam today will only make things harder."

"I said I'm fine," I snapped. Imogen raised her eyebrows. I didn't intend to take such a harsh tone. It just slipped out.

I took a deep breath to calm my nerves and spoke softly. "I need to face him eventually. I might as well get it over with. Besides, we need to get everyone together to talk about the prophecy. After three months reading through every book in your family library and coming up with zilch on the Earth piece, we need more ideas. The boys should know we've been looking, at least."

"I can talk to Liam and Jonah alone," Imogen offered. "You don't have to come with."

I knew Imogen and Jonah had spent time together over the summer, but I'd always refused to tag along. I worried that I'd run into Liam. The only time I'd seen Jonah was right after the break-up, when he'd come to chew me out for breaking Liam's heart. I'd told him to go screw himself and threatened him with a fireball.

Liam was just as much at fault as I was. Besides, he'd been the one to dump me, not the other way around.

The fact was, I'd spent three months trying to avoid reality, and it hadn't done me a lick of good. Even revisiting our waterfall and burning out the initials on our tree hadn't helped me get over him. Avoiding him longer than I already had wasn't going to help, either. The fact was, this prophecy stuff was more important than a relationship I'd known was doomed from the start. As impossibly hard as it was to admit, I was going to have to swallow my pride and face him. That was the deal I'd made with myself. I'd take the summer to grieve, then put on my big girl panties when school started.

Fuck. Why did summer have to end? I wasn't ready for this.

Instead, I just told Imogen, "You don't have to do that. I'll come with you. Maybe it'll be good to see him again."

Imogen smiled, though it didn't mask her concern for me. "I'm glad to see you're feeling better."

"Thanks," I said, as if her statement were true. It was so far from the truth that it bordered on the absurd.

The carriage slowed as we reached the front of the castle. Imogen and I gathered our bags, then stepped out into a warm summer breeze. The sun shone brightly down on the castle. All throughout the court-yard, Elementai smiled cheerfully, and Familiars frolicked through the grass, playing with one another.

None of it felt right. How could everyone be so happy right now? It was like they couldn't hear the castle walls screaming at them that this was no longer a joyful place— that too much pain and anguish had taken place here. Would they ever hear it?

Imogen tipped our carriage driver, then started across the courtyard to the main entrance. "Do you realize where we were a year ago?"

I cracked a smile. "Yeah. You were over there sticking your head between some random guy's legs."

I nodded toward a corner of the courtyard and laughed as I thought back to my first day here, the day I'd met Imogen. My laughter quickly died when I remembered that Liam was there that day. Just thinking of him crushed my heart.

"Hey." Imogen swatted at me. "You make it sound dirty. I was just trying to keep Sassy from getting trampled. She's a lot better about running off now, at least."

I looked down to Sassy, who strutted proudly next to Imogen as we ascended the stairs. When we stepped into the the Great Hall, it was like walking right back into a life I thought was over. The golden accents on the chandelier, the massive fireplace next to the main doors, the hallway that led to the grand ballroom... none of it had to do with Liam, but all of it reminded me of him.

"Speaking of dirty, I need details from last night," I said, to take my mind off him.

Imogen blushed. "Nothing happened."

Cade had stopped over. He and Imogen had sat on the bridge between the Nivita treehouses for two hours, dangling their feet over the forest floor and talking. I'd snuck a glance toward the end and caught them making out.

I raised an eyebrow. "Really?"

"Really," Imogen stated. "He just wanted to talk about the Elemental Cup. I think he's nervous about being in this year's tournament."

We started up the grand staircase, lugging our bags behind us. My heart skipped a beat each time my eyes passed over a Toaqua guy, like it might be Liam waiting for me. But none of them were him. I turned my gaze to my feet.

"I think anyone would be worried," I told her.

We turned to our right, and Imogen followed me down the hall toward my dorms.

"Yeah," she agreed, "but Cade seems extra worried. Not that he'll do bad in the tournament, but it's like he's concerned about me. Like he's afraid of what I'll think of his performance or something."

"You told him not to worry, right? I mean, as long as he survives, that's all that matters."

Imogen dropped her gaze. "I know. That's what I told him, but he's like, '*What if I don't? I want you to go on if I don't make it.*' I told him that's not going to happen, that he's strong and he'll survive."

"He *will* survive," I assured her. I didn't see how he wouldn't.

"Right," she said. "And if he doesn't— which isn't going to happen— I told him we have to enjoy the time we have."

I wiggled my eyebrows at her. "This semester should be fun for you."

Maybe Cade would finally make *the move.*

Imogen smiled as we reached the wide doors with the golden flame handles that led to the Koigni dorms. "You've got that right. I'll wait here for you."

"I'll only be a minute."

I entered the dorms and passed through the common room into a long hallway that led to my dorm. When I stepped inside my room, I finally felt like I could breathe again. A fire burned in the fireplace, making the room feel warm and cozy. The bed had been made with fresh sheets, and the red curtains were open, allowing the sunlight to spill into the room. The cleaning staff had thrown out the dead, dried flowers Liam had given me for Valentine's Day. I'd followed all the other cleaning guidelines before I'd left last spring, but I just couldn't bring myself to touch the bouquet. It was a reminder of Liam's betrayal— how he'd tried to sabotage my magic in secret.

I was grateful they were gone. It felt like I could enjoy this room without a reminder of Liam every two seconds. This was one of the only places in the castle that I'd never been with him. It felt like my one quiet corner of Orenda Academy, where I could be myself without him. And the ancestors knew I needed that right now.

Esis hopped off my shoulder and onto the bed. I set my suitcase upright beside it, tossed my backpack onto the floor, and fell to the mattress beside him. All I had to do was drop off my stuff and head back to Imogen, but she could wait another minute. I just needed a moment to breathe.

Esis approached me slowly, until I could feel his soft fur against my cheek. He gently stroked my hair, then lowered his head to mine. I reached up my hand and ran my fingers through his fluffy tail. Esis had no idea how much his affection meant to me.

"I love you, buddy," I whispered.

Esis purred against my face. I took several moments to soak it in, but I knew I had to get back to Imogen.

Sighing, I pushed myself up to a sitting position and stared down into Esis' big blue eyes. "Well, should we go? We can unpack later."

Esis crawled into my arms, and I rose from the bed. On my way out, I caught sight of Vanessa, Lindsey, and Miranda in the common room. Aisha had grown to the size of a small car. Lindsey's basilisk Familiar, Medusa, was curled up at her feet.

"So you aren't living in the dorms this semester?" Miranda asked Vanessa.

Vanessa shook her head. "No, I'm just here to visit. Since Bren graduated and we got married, I have special permission to live off campus with him. We got an apartment in Kinpago."

Lindsey squealed in excitement. "Show us the ring again!"

Vanessa held her hand out, but her eyes caught mine a second later. "Sophia!"

The girls turned and rushed over to me. Vanessa pulled me into a hug. "It's been so long! We missed you."

I hugged her back. "I missed you, too."

I hadn't seen Vanessa since her wedding. After we'd gotten close last semester, she'd asked me to be a bridesmaid. It was a beautiful ceremony on the beach, and I'd loved every minute of it. It was one of my favorite parts of last summer, apart from visiting my parents and Amelia. Vanessa had left for her honeymoon the next day, and we hadn't had a chance to catch up since.

"We should hang out," Vanessa said.

"I'd like that," I said. "I'm kind of busy now, but we'll catch up soon."

"See you," Lindsey said with a wave.

I waved at the three of them, then headed out the door to meet up with Imogen. She was leaning against a wall opposite the doors, fiddling with the bracelets on her wrist. She immediately perked up when she saw me step into the hall.

"You ready?" she asked.

No.

"Yep. Let's go," I said.

Imogen tipped her luggage and began rolling it down the hall. Esis hopped out of my arms and jumped on the back of the suitcase for a ride.

The Nivita dorms were on the next floor all the way across the castle. Imogen dropped off her bags... and then came the moment I was dreading.

"I asked Liam and Jonah to meet us in the gardens," Imogen said when she and Sassy came out of the dorms.

My heart hammered at the sound of his name.

"Are you absolutely sure you want to come?" Imogen asked.

I wanted to see him... but I also didn't. I couldn't make up my mind.

"I'm glad you care, Im," I said, "but it's really no big deal. Liam and I are adults. We can talk without the world imploding."

"Okay." She sounded uncertain. "Maybe we should come up with an excuse in case you need to leave."

"I don't need a cop-out," I lied. "It'll be fine. I can handle it."

Ancestors, I hoped so.

My heart slammed against my rib cage, and my hands began to shake the closer we came to the gardens. I pulled Esis tighter to myself just to steady my fingers.

And yet none of it— *none* of it— could prepare me for the moment Liam finally came into view.

His long black hair fell over his shoulders and waved slightly in the warm breeze. He wore a burgundy Orenda Academy t-shirt and jeans that hung from his hips at just the right angle. They made my eyes travel downward. Beside him, Jonah was doing an impression of Squeaks, and he tripped and fell on his face. Which, incidentally, was the perfect impression of Squeaks. Liam threw his head back and laughed, and it was as if time had slowed. That smile, the crinkle around the corner of his eyes... it was all so beautiful.

Every nerve in my body betrayed me. My heart lifted, and for a moment, it was like the last three months had never happened. I was back at the waterfall, my legs wrapped around him and his lips on mine. It was the last good moment we had together... before everything fell apart.

Reality came crashing down on me like a ton of rocks. It felt as if all the air had been sucked out of the world. I came to a halt, but the rest of the world sped up to its normal pace. Tears immediately sprang to my eyes, but I forced them back. It felt like I was choking on them, like it didn't matter if the air came back because I'd suffocate anyway. I was kidding myself if I thought I could face him again.

"Sophia?" I barely heard Imogen's voice past the pounding of my own pulse in my ears. She grabbed my shoulder and shook me.

Esis jumped out of my arms, and he and Sassy took off to greet Squeaks. Jonah stood to brush the dirt off his jeans. Liam glanced up and spotted our Familiars headed his way.

Then his eyes met mine with an expression I couldn't quite read, and I knew there was no turning back.

Imogen tugged on my arm, and I forced myself to put one foot in front of the other. Liam swooped down to scoop Esis up, and he tickled him under the chin. I looked around for Nashoma, but I didn't see him. I noticed Imogen glancing around, too. I was too nervous to ask if the Water Elders had fulfilled their promise. Liam had done what they'd asked, hadn't he?

"Hey, little guy," Liam said. "It's been a while, hasn't it?"

Esis snuggled into Liam's chest. I'd nearly forgotten how much time they'd spent together this summer. Esis had gone on his own to visit Liam every chance he got. He'd even stayed in Kinpago for the few weeks I'd gone to visit my family in Utah, so Liam wouldn't have to go all that time without treatment. At first, I thought Esis spent all that time with him because I'd encouraged him to go heal Liam. Now seeing them together, it was clear they'd formed a special bond.

Jealousy twisted in my gut. Esis was *my* Familiar.

But what was I going to do? *Forbid* him from seeing Liam? From healing Liam? That was akin to murder, and I wasn't going to stoop that low, no matter how badly Liam broke my heart.

That didn't stop me from snatching Esis out of Liam's arms. I cradled him to my chest, avoiding Liam's gaze the whole time.

Jonah pushed himself between Imogen and me and rested an elbow on each of our shoulders. "So, ladies. How was your summer? I heard it was pretty lit."

I shot Imogen a questioning glance. "If you call reading through Imogen's family library all summer lit, sure. It was *lit*."

"Did you find anything?" Liam asked.

I finally looked at him, and it freaking tore my heart in two. I couldn't bear to look him in the eyes, so I dropped my gaze to Esis instead. "No. That's what we need to talk about."

Imogen lowered her voice and gestured toward the forest. "Should we go somewhere more private?"

Sassy and Squeaks led us away from the castle. Jonah and Imogen stayed ahead of us to walk by their Familiars, leaving Liam and me in the back. Jonah and Imogen talked enough for the whole group, but there was an agonizing silence hanging between Liam and me. I was sure he could feel it in the air. The tension was so thick you could cut it with a dragon's claw.

Finally, I cleared my throat. "You don't have to do this, you know."

"Do what?" Liam asked.

I caught his eye for barely a second before we both looked away from each other. "Help with the prophecy stuff."

Liam shrugged. "I promised you I would."

It felt so strange to talk to him like this. I thought the first time we saw each other we'd be screaming and throwing things or some stupid shit like that. Ancestors knew I'd pictured it a thousand times. But he talked like nothing had ever happened between us. Which frustrated me even more. Couldn't he at least *look* like he was upset by the breakup? I played nice because... well, because it was the only way I thought I might get through this.

"It's okay if you break this promise," I told him.

A beat passed between us, and for a second, I thought he was actually considering it. It would be both a relief and a disappointment if he stepped back.

"I still want to help," Liam finally said.

Relief flooded through me. I hadn't realized until he said it that was the answer I'd been hoping to hear. This time when he looked at me, I held his gaze. I didn't take a breath until he looked down at the path again to watch his footing.

"I'm glad," I said.

"You are?" He sounded surprised.

I hadn't meant to say it out loud. "Yeah," I said quickly, to cover. "You know, for Imogen and Jonah's sake. They'd probably go insane if we weren't all working together on this."

"Agreed," Liam said, though I couldn't read his tone.

We stopped when we entered a secluded section of forest where we couldn't be overheard.

Imogen turned toward the rest of us. "It's been three months since we agreed to look for the prophecy pieces together, and so far, we've found nothing. Did you two come up with anything?"

Liam shoved his hands in his pockets. "I, uh, didn't really have a lot of time."

That sounded like a lie, but whatever. I didn't expect him to help much anyway after what had happened between us.

Jonah sighed. "You know I love you, Im, but stuff just got in the way."

"Stuff?" Imogen asked with a raise of her eyebrows. "You mean Renar's dick."

Liam snickered beside me. I couldn't help but let out my own chuckle as well. It was so accurate.

But it was weird sharing a laugh with Liam again. So I stopped.

Jonah dropped his shoulders. "Come on. Don't be like that. I looked into the Air piece. I didn't find anything."

Imogen bit her lower lip. "Sophia and I went through all the books in my family library. We didn't find any mention of the prophecy at all. So we need other ideas on where to start."

"What about the school's library?" I suggested. "I never found anything about the prophecy my first semester, but I'm sure there are a lot more books to look through."

Liam pressed his finger to his chin, like he was thinking hard. "Maybe the library isn't the best place to start."

All eyes turned to him.

"The library books only cover stuff from our classes," Liam pointed out. "There isn't a class that teaches Hawkei prophecies. The old stuff— the legends— sure, you can find a few mentions of that here and there, but this prophecy is more recent. Until Sophia showed up, most of Kinpago thought it was just a story. Hell, most still feel that way. Only the Elders are really worried about it, and now we know why. They've had the pieces all along. They've known this was coming and let everyone else believe it was only a story to keep people from investigating. I bet each of the Houses played along to make the others believe they were clueless."

"It sounds like you've put a lot of thought into this," Imogen said.

Liam shrugged.

"What are you suggesting?" I asked.

"It's simple," Jonah said. "We have to talk to people. Have you tried talking to the Nivita Elders?"

Imogen scoffed. "Seriously? You think they're just going to *hand* me the piece of the prophecy?"

"Doesn't hurt to try," Jonah said.

Imogen placed her hands on her hips. "Did *you* try talking to the Yapluma Elders for your piece?"

Jonah bit his lip. "I thought about it, but..."

"But what?" Imogen pressed.

"Come on," Jonah whined. "The Elders are scary."

Imogen cocked an eyebrow. "The Yapluma Elders? The party House? Scary?"

Jonah nodded eagerly.

"Knowing Yapluma, the Elders probably left their piece sitting around," I said with a chuckle.

"Yeah, okay. You're probably right," Jonah admitted. "But I'd have to get a meeting with them first, which is basically impossible. I'll talk to my Elders if you talk to yours."

"I can't," Imogen insisted. "The Elders haven't been kind to my family since our hearing to authenticate my great grandfather's journal. They turned us down, and since then, the Nivita think my family is crazy. They won't listen to me in the first place, and even if I got an audience with them, I'm certain they wouldn't share the Earth piece with me."

Imogen took a breath. "Honestly, I don't think we should talk to *any* of the Elders. We don't want anyone to know we're searching for all the pieces. It could put us at risk. I wouldn't put it past any of our Elders to threaten us for the pieces we already have."

"Imogen's right," I said. "No Elders. At least, not now."

"Good point," Jonah agreed.

"So if the library isn't going to do us any good and we can't talk to anyone, we're stuck?" I asked.

"If only we could talk to the ancestors Showana gave the prophecy to," Jonah said hopelessly.

Imogen inhaled a deep breath, like she'd just had an epiphany.

"What?" Jonah asked quickly. "I was kidding. We can't get in contact with them."

"No," Imogen agreed. "But I have an idea that's close enough."

We all gave her a confused expression, and she hurried to say, "I can check the Nivita Elders' Scrolls!"

"Elders' Scrolls?" I asked, though Liam and Jonah looked like they knew what she meant.

"The scrolls are transcripts from the Elder meetings," Imogen explained. "They've been keeping records for centuries. The records are open to the Nivita public."

Liam looked skeptical. "Something as valuable as the prophecy, Im... they wouldn't just write that down for public consumption."

"Agreed," she said. "But they might've let something slip through. Or there could be some sort of code to their meetings. I'll start with the scrolls dated right after the prophecy was given. There might be a clue."

"That's a good idea," Jonah said thoughtfully. "I'll check the Yapluma Scrolls."

Imogen smirked. "Good luck. Yapluma keep terrible records."

Jonah shrugged. "We've gotta start somewhere."

"What about me and Liam?" I asked. "Is there anything we can do?"

Liam shook his head. "Not until we have those other two pieces. We just have to be patient, *pawee*."

The entire forest went silent when he called me that. Even the birds had stopped chirping. Sassy and Squeaks had stopped playing to look at us, and Esis blinked in shock. Imogen and Jonah glanced to each other like a bomb was about to go off. It felt as if even the ancestors had gone silent in their celestial abode.

I completely froze. Had I just heard him correctly? He called me *pawee*... as in *cherished one*. As in his soulmate.

As in, he loved me.

But he didn't, did he? Not anymore.

Liam ducked his head, like he'd realized what a horrible mistake he'd just made. "Sorry. Habit."

"No. It's okay," I heard myself say. "You can still call me that if you want."

I kept my cool, but inside, I was screaming. To be honest, it'd be weird if he stopped calling me that. Anything else would sound strange on his tongue. But to hear him say it again... it was like a confession— like he still cared about me.

And that tore my heart to fucking shreds. Because it didn't matter how much he cared. It didn't matter how much my heart yearned for him and how much I wanted to reach out and pull him back into my life like nothing had ever changed. Because we weren't getting back together. Ever.

Fire and Water just didn't belong together.

Liam stared at me like a deer in the headlights. This was getting too freaking uncomfortable.

I cleared my throat. "Well, uh, we all have lots of work to do. Scrolls to read and stuff."

Liam finally found his voice again. "Yeah. And me and Jonah have that thing."

"Thing?" Jonah asked, oblivious.

"Yeah, that *thing*." Liam grabbed Jonah by the arm and started dragging him back toward the castle. Squeaks followed behind them.

"Catch you guys for dinner?" Jonah called back.

"Sure," Imogen answered for the both of us. "See ya later!"

As soon as they were out if earshot, she turned to me. "That wasn't so bad, was it?"

I swallowed the lump in my throat as I watched Liam walk away into the forest. "No."

But it was. It *so* was.

Esis and I returned to my dorm shortly after to unpack. As soon as Imogen and I parted, I couldn't keep my mind off Liam. Seeing him again brought back feelings I thought I was done with. I wanted to touch him and hold him again. I wanted things to go back to the way they were, before all our secrets came out.

But I also never wanted to see him again. I was so conflicted.

I took to unpacking to take my mind off it, but it only made me think of him more. It was worse when I found the camera he'd given me buried at the bottom of my backpack. I hadn't touched it all summer. I'd wanted to get back into photography, but I couldn't bring myself to do it. It was a gift from Liam. I knew he said I could keep it, but it didn't feel like mine anymore. It felt like I was borrowing it, and it had overstayed its welcome.

I hid the camera in the back if my dresser drawer behind a pile of t-shirts. Out of sight, out of mind.

And it almost worked... until I reached the bottom of my suitcase. Folded up beneath my jeans was the leather jacket Liam had let me wear last Valentine's Day. I still hadn't returned it. I'd pretty much forgotten I still had it.

Esis stood at the side of my suitcase and glanced between me and the jacket.

"It's not a big deal, buddy," I lied.

The flowers were different. I'd left those because Liam had betrayed me with them. But the camera and this jacket... those were signs that we used to be something more.

I forced myself to reach into the suitcase and pull the jacket out. Without consciously deciding to, I put the fabric to my nose and inhaled its scent. It still smelled like him— hints of ocean and pine forest. Every touch, every hug, every moment, came rushing back to me all at once. I couldn't take it anymore.

I curled into a ball on the bed. As soon as the tears came, I couldn't stop them.

So much for making it through the day without crying.

Tears streamed down my cheeks and soaked into the red comforter. Esis placed a gentle paw to the top of my head, and it only made me cry harder. I pressed my face into the jacket to muffle the sounds, but it didn't stop my shoulders from heaving uncontrollably. I thought I'd cried it all out over the summer. I didn't know I had any more in me.

I stayed like that for over an hour. Each time I thought I was done crying, I caught a whiff of his scent on his jacket again, and it started all over again. Esis remained at my side the whole time, stroking my hair to comfort me.

"I just miss him so much." I sobbed into the mattress.

Eventually, the tears stopped coming, no matter how much I wanted them to. Letting them out helped ease the ache squeezing my chest. Now that my eyes had dried, it felt as if an elephant was sitting on my chest.

I stared up at the ceiling as thoughts raced through my head. I was such a mess. I barely knew who I was anymore. All I wanted was to find myself again, to be okay without Liam.

I wished that my parents or Amelia were around. Visiting them helped take my mind off Liam. They were a reminder of the life I had before him. Imogen was wonderful and supportive, and she was always there when I needed her, but my family was different. Imogen was part of this Orenda Academy life, the part of my life that involved Liam. All I wanted to do when I was around her was talk about him, because I knew she'd understand. With my family, I could separate myself from Liam, if only for a little while.

I wished I had family in Kinpago. It didn't have to be my parents or even my sister. Just someone I could talk to and spend time with without thoughts and memories of Liam getting in the way. If only I had extended family here, like a cousin or something.

I sat upright in bed.

I was Hawkei. I was born in Kinpago. Of *course* I had family here. I just hadn't met them yet.

I quickly jumped to my feet and scooped Esis up. I hurried out of the room and power-walked to the Nivita dorms. I let myself inside, ignoring a few glances Nivita shot my way, then knocked on Imogen's door.

The door swung open a few moments later, and Imogen looked me up and down. "Are you okay? You look like..."

"A wreck?" I finished for her. I hadn't bothered to fix my makeup before coming to find her.

Imogen opened the door wide to invite me inside. She'd mostly unpacked but was still working on decorations. Esis jumped from my arms to join Sassy on the bed.

I turned back to Imogen once I was inside the room. "I know what I have to do."

"What do you mean?"

"I don't know why I didn't do this the second I came to Kinpago."

"Do what? What are you talking about?" Imogen sounded a bit concerned.

"My grandparents, Imogen!" I said in excitement. "My biological ones, I mean. I want to meet them. I'm going to the Koigni village to find them!"

Liam

THREE

Sophia was kissing me.

We were by the waterfall in the middle of daytime, tangled up in each other's arms, and everything had a golden glow to it. The sun was brighter than it ever had been, and colors seemed more vibrant and pure. In the background, soft music played. My hands were tangled in her long brown hair, and her beautiful hands were running up and down my chest. Her touch was something I craved and needed, and no matter how blissful it felt, my body demanded more. It was agonizing each time her body drifted slightly away from mine, and I begged her to come closer.

I was kissing her like I didn't want to let her go. I was afraid to pull my mouth away from hers, because if I did, I knew the moment would end and she'd vanish from my life forever.

Eventually, she stopped kissing me. She pulled away and blinked her brown eyes a few times. "Liam?"

Without any warning, the dream ended, and I woke abruptly to a pair of big blue eyes two inches away from my face.

"Agh!" I screamed, and fell out of bed. Esis jumped off my chest and onto my desk before I could crush him beneath me. He chittered in a pleasant way, as if to say *good morning.*

"Holy hell. Don't scare me like that." My heart was still beating out of my chest. I got up off the floor, and Esis chortled, as if he was laughing.

I rubbed my face, trying to bring myself out of it. The feel of Sophia next to me was still loudly resonating. It made made my throat go tight. I reminded myself the golden scene by the waterfall had never happened. It was just something my head made up. Another stupid dream.

The stupid dreams that wouldn't end.

Esis reached out and slapped my face a few times, as if to bring me out of whatever stupor I was in. I shook my head, but it was hard to clear the fog of the dream away. It'd been so real.

During the summer, Esis kept on showing up in my room to heal me. I didn't know how he got to the island by himself, until I figured out that Squeaks kept flying him over. Now he was creeping in my dorm. I knew he'd been following me for months, and I put up with it.

I also knew Sophia was sending him to heal me. It hit me hard that even though we'd had the shittiest breakup ever, she still cared enough to make sure I was doing okay.

You have a rule. Don't think about Sophia.

Right. I'd promised myself when I got back to school, unless I was directly talking to her, I would stop torturing myself with thoughts of our relationship, what had been and what could've been. I had been doing it for the past three months. That was more than enough time to move on. I should be okay by now.

I am totally over Sophia Henley.

I'd broke it off. It'd been my choice.

"I think these sessions of ours need to end, buddy," I told Esis as I reached for my dresser. I grabbed a shirt and jeans, not caring what they were, or even if they were clean or not.

Esis crossed his arms and gave a few noises of protest as I dressed, obviously pointing out I'd die if he stopped coming to see me.

"You're Sophia's Familiar. It's a conflict of interest," I told him. It was okay that he'd stopped by every so often during the summer, but Sophia and I had no contact then. We'd be forced to see each other now, so it was inappropriate for Esis to keep healing me when all it would do... for me and her... was bring back memories of the past.

I hardly cared if I died anymore. I was walking around mostly dead these days, anyway. And it had nothing to do with my illness.

I extended my arm to Esis. He grabbed on to my hand with his little paws, and I felt a familiar warmth flow from where his paws were, flowing up my arm and coursing throughout my entire body. When he touched me, the migraine I'd been dealing with since last night faded away, and the various aches I had dulled. I straightened up and walked a little better. I'd been feeling tired when I'd woken up, but now, energy was pulsing through me.

The longer Esis kept treating me, the stupider I felt for not noticing his powers sooner. I could literally sense his magic working on me. I would've been able to back then if I had paid attention. The answer to why I'd been getting better had been right in front of my face all along, and it'd been pretty obvious in some places.

But I shouldn't have had to guess. She should've told me.

Yeah, well, too bad. Things didn't work out that way.

Esis chittered, pleased with himself.

I waved my hand. "Go on, go back to Sophia. This is the last time. I don't want to see you anymore."

Esis rolled his eyes and grumbled a few incoherent noises.

"I'm not being dramatic. I'm being reasonable."

He crossed his arms and raised an eyebrow at me.

"Look, the situation is already complicated. It would be a lot less complicated if you backed off," I said.

I was having a conversation with a rodent. Still, it would really suck to lose the consistent treatments from Esis. I'd been better physically than I had been since before Nashoma died. I was still sick, but it was less like riding a rollercoaster and more like knowing when the highs and lows would arrive... and when they did, they weren't nearly as bad as they used to be. The pain had become a dull, constant ache that I could deal with on a daily basis, instead of coming and going in a cycle of unbearable torture and sudden relief.

But I'd hurt Sophia enough. I'd seen the look in her eyes yesterday when I was petting Esis. I couldn't keep doing this to her, no matter how much it benefitted me.

Esis made a pleasant sound. He tugged at my wrist, like he wanted to give me something.

"All right, what is it?" I held out an open palm. Esis dug in his fur, then placed something small in my hand.

It was one of Sophia's hair ties. Esis looked at me hopefully, twitching his tail.

I stared at the hair tie for a full minute. It made me think of her ponytail... which made me think of her... which made me think of us... which made a gigantic, gaping hole open up in my guts and swallow me up.

"Would you stop? It's never gonna happen." I gave Esis the hair tie back, along with a glare. "We tried, and it didn't work. Give up."

Esis let out a huff. He'd been doing this all summer— bringing me small things of Sophia's, like it would remind me how great things were, magically make everything better, and reverse all the bad shit that had made us split up in the first place.

"You gotta let that go, buddy. I have," I told him as I packed my things into my backpack. "It's over. Time to move on."

I sighed as I hefted my bag over my shoulder. "Besides. She's long over me by now."

Sophia had looked so happy yesterday when we'd met up to talk about the pieces of the prophecy. It was obvious she was doing well. She'd clearly missed out that I was miserable. That, or she didn't care— which was fair game, because I'd been the one to break her heart.

She hadn't contacted me at all over the summer... not that I blamed her... but I thought what we'd shared was special enough that she'd at least check in a few times, say hi. I didn't feel like I could reach out, because I'd been the one who'd done the damage. But three months came and went, and nothing. I figured she was too busy having fun and enjoying an amazing summer to bother seeing what I was up to. I bet there were tons of Koigni guys who'd been more than happy to be a shoulder for her to cry on over the summer. She was too pretty to stay single for long. Most likely, I bet she already had another boyfriend.

A boyfriend that isn't me.

I needed to stop torturing myself like this. Sophia could date whoever she wanted. I'd chosen to be single, and it was obvious she'd forgotten all about me. It was for the best.

"Our meetings are over, little guy," I told Esis as I started for the door. "I hope you have a good life."

Esis stuck his tongue out at me, then gave me the finger before he scampered to my window, slid it open, and slipped out. I had a feeling he wouldn't give up that easily and would be back to heal me again in a couple of days.

Well, screw him. I wouldn't let him.

It was a Sunday, and classes didn't start until tomorrow, so I didn't have anything to do. I figured I should help Maddie move in. This would be my little sister's first year at Orenda and she was bound to be overwhelmed.

I went looking for her in the Toaqua dorms, but couldn't find her anywhere. She had to be somewhere in the castle. I didn't want to leave the Water dorms, as I was afraid I'd run into... *her*... but this had gone on long enough. I couldn't be afraid of walking around the castle just in case I ran into Sophia. So I headed in the direction of the entrance hall to look for my sister.

When I got outside the school, freshman were swarming the area. Tons of new students hauled suitcases and furniture across the lawn toward the great doors. It made me remember my first day here. I'd been pretty scared, but I didn't need to be. Orenda Academy had been great from the beginning.

It hit me that this was my last year, and it was hard to deal. I didn't know what I was going to do after graduation. I'd ruined my chances of working for the tribe by messing up my relationship with my dad. Orenda Academy was my home. I didn't feel like there was anywhere else to go after that.

A large shadow loomed overhead. Jonah was in the air riding Squeaks, barking orders at various kids. Over the summer, she'd gotten big enough for him to ride. He had a megaphone, and was shouting instructions over the crowd. I think he was confusing the new students more than he was helping them learn where to go. An orange t-shirt he wore said *Welcome Committee*. Squeaks was wearing a matching orange headband, an orange kerchief tied around her neck.

Jonah saw me and landed Squeaks. He slid off of her back and said, "Hey, buddy. How's it hanging?"

I didn't need to answer that. "What are you doing?" I asked.

"I'm an advisor for the freshman. It's for my major," Jonah said. "If I'm going to be a professor, I need to learn how to advise kids. Plus I'm, uh, a little short on cash lately."

I resisted giving myself a face-palm. If Jonah had already blown through all his tournament winnings, it had to be a record. Money burned a hole in his pocket, but still, that was an impressive number to waste. The reward for winning the Elemental Cup had been in the six figures for each of us.

"Are you sure you're good with kids?" I wouldn't want Jonah advising me if I was a freshman. He'd probably tell me to major in booze and dicks.

"I'm a natural," Jonah said, before he noticed some guy trying to sneak beer into a suitcase. "Hey, hey, hey! No alcohol for minors!"

Jonah reached over and grabbed the six-pack out of the dude's hands and handed it to Squeaks. "Here, Squeakers. Take this to.. uh... *contraband.*"

Squeaks gave a twitter and grabbed on to the six pack with her beak. She flew away in the direction of the Yapluma dorms.

"Are you sure you didn't just take this job because you wanted to confiscate stuff?" I asked.

"Of course not!" Jonah leaned in. "Not gonna lie, though. This one kid had a crapola-ton of weed in his suitcase. Which is mine now, if you want to come over later."

I shook my head. Stuff like this made me wonder what kind of teacher Jonah was gonna be when he was older. The cool kind, probably.

Jonah's attention was drawn away by someone at the doors of the school. Renar— *ick.* Jonah's on-again, off-again boyfriend. He was still as hideous and rude as ever.

Renar's cockatrice Familiar, Alvarice, was having a good time scaring the new students. The half-rooster, half-dragon monster even made one girl cry when she got too close and he lunged out. Renar laughed, like he enjoyed torturing people.

Jonah gave him a longing look. I suppressed a giant *ugh.*

"How was living with Renar?" I said, not really giving a shit but figuring I should ask anyway.

Jonah stuttered a bit before he plastered on a smile. "It was... uh... it was really great. Yeah."

Like that was fucking convincing. "Not as *great* as you thought?"

"Oh, no, it was cool," he hurried to add. "He was just gone a lot, and... yeah."

No wonder he'd been at my place all summer. I'd known Jonah had hung out with Imogen whenever he wasn't around me, which meant that Renar didn't spend time with Jonah unless he wanted sex. I knew moving in with him had been a bad idea.

"Anyway," Jonah said. "We're back in school now, so that's over with. And we're officially dating now! Which is cool. He's such a good boyfriend."

I'd seen Renar flirting hardcore with some dude I didn't know on the way over here. I opened my mouth to tell Jonah, but I knew he wouldn't listen, so instead I just said, "Yeah. I bet."

Jonah gave me a sympathetic look. "I'm sorry you and Sophia didn't work out. But you two seemed like you were on good terms yesterday."

I didn't know. "I guess. I'm not really mad at her anymore."

And I wasn't. I had ceased to be upset that she hadn't told me about Esis, as well as her mission given to her by the Koigni Elders months ago to figure out more about the prophecy. That was all water under the bridge. I wasn't pissed anymore.

Just... hurt. And not so much about the secrets and lies. More so that the lies had happened between us in the first place. I'd believed we were closer than that. But that was calling the kettle black. I had lied, too.

"You don't have to be mad. I was mad enough for you," Jonah said. "It was total crap that she dumped you last semester, bro. But don't worry. I gave Sophia hell for you."

Absolute mortification spread through me. "You did *what?*"

"Yeah. I told her off really good," Jonah said, proud of himself. "Nobody breaks my buddy's heart!"

It was like ice was spreading all over my entire body. "You didn't."

"Of course I did," Jonah said. "I wasn't gonna let her get away with hurting you like that. You were holed up in your house all summer. I couldn't just stand by and—"

"She didn't dump me! I broke up with her, you idiot!" I shouted.

Jonah's mouth dropped open. "What? But I thought she—"

"No! It was my idea! She wanted us to stay together," I insisted.

And she did. She'd wanted us to try and work it out. Take a break instead of break up. Why hadn't I listened to her?

Jonah still seemed shocked. "You broke up with... wait a second. It should be *you* I'm yelling at, then!"

"What did you say to her?" I asked. I put my hands on either side of my head. This was really bad.

Jonah hesitated. "Uh... it wasn't very nice."

"She probably thinks I *told* you to talk to her." I buried my head in my arms. This whole thing just got a million times more embarrassing.

"No, she didn't think that. I promise." Jonah shook his head. "She knew if something happened I'd yell at her. I told her that."

"But it's not your business, and even more than that, it wasn't her fault." I rubbed my face. "I thought Imogen would've told you how we broke up."

Jonah frowned. "Imogen and I can't really... talk about you guys without fighting. She takes Sophia's side, I take yours, and, well..."

Jonah made an exploding sound, along with hand gestures. I rolled my eyes.

"You need to apologize to Sophia," I started. "That wasn't right."

"It happened months ago," Jonah said, and he waved his hand. "She's probably forgotten about it by now."

"So what? Say sorry," I demanded.

Jonah gave me a curious look. "Why do you care so much about what Sophia thinks? She's your ex."

Those words seemed so wrong. Ex-girlfriend? That name was reserved for people you couldn't stand. Mia was my ex. But Sophia?

Aw, shit. She *was* my ex now. I'd never thought of it that way until now, but...

I cleared the thickness in my voice. "It doesn't matter. Please just do it. For me."

"Fine." Jonah let out an aggravated sigh. "I'll do it, but only cause you asked."

Thank the ancestors. Getting Jonah to apologize, let alone even admit he was wrong, was about as easy as putting a dragon in a headlock.

"Anyway, I've gotta go. Need to get back to work." He waggled his eyebrows. "See you around, Liam Baby."

Jonah headed back into the crowd, shouting more orders with his megaphone. I didn't have the heart to tell him he needed to stop calling me that.

I searched the crowd for my sister, knowing she was here somewhere. I finally spotted Maddie with a bunch of suitcases, which were being hauled by Ezra. Maddie had insisted taking all of her alchemy stuff with her for her dorm, despite the fact there were plenty of alchemy supplies in the school to use.

Even though it was freaking hot out, Maddie was wearing an ankle-length skirt and a long-sleeved blue shirt with the word *Toaqua* on it. She had a look of brilliance on her face as she turned in place, her expression filled with wonder as she took in the castle and all the creatures.

She spotted me, and her smile got even bigger. "Liam, this is amazing! You guys didn't tell me Orenda Academy was *this* cool!"

"There really isn't any way to describe it," I said.

I noticed Ezra was really struggling with those bags. His Familiar, Dyami, was doing his best to help. The thunderbird was over six feet tall now, but even he struggled to use his talons to yank the heavy bags along.

"You've got that right." Maddie's smile beamed. "I can't wait to start classes. See you around, big brother."

I needed to talk to her quick. "Maddie." I grabbed her arm and pulled her to the side. "If things get too overwhelming, you come talk to me, okay?"

She rolled her eyes. "I'm *fine*, Liam. Ancestors."

Maddie yanked her arm from me and stomped away, acting every part the hormonal teenager. I knew I was pulling the whole overprotective brother act, but Maddie wasn't the type of person who could handle a lot of stress. I had good reason to look out for her. She wasn't just a *naderei*— an Elementai who could see the future— she was also my little sister.

I didn't know how she would do without her Familiar, Eirakari, for a month. We were keeping her at home until tournament summons were over and we could stage a bonding, since Maddie had bonded early in life and if anyone knew, it would look suspicious.

Ezra was already participating in the tournament this year. My family couldn't handle if Maddie was in it, too.

I looked at Ezra. "Need some help?"

"No." He was panting. "It's all good."

"I can—"

"Liam, we've got this," Ezra said roughly. "You're going to overexert yourself again. Just let me handle it."

I backed off. "Oh, okay." I looked down. "See you around, I guess."

I walked away before he could say anything else. I knew Ezra didn't mean to snap at me, but still, it bothered me. Did my own family not even want me around?

There were too many people around here. It was too loud. The noise was giving me a headache. I needed to be alone.

I headed to the one place I could go when things got to be too much. The ocean.

There were quite a few people on the beach having back-to-school and end-of-summer parties. I hid myself in the woods and walked along the shoreline until I got to a part of the beach where there wasn't anyone around.

When I couldn't see a person in sight, I walked into the waves fully-clothed. I rocketed myself forward and kept the stream of water pushing me out to sea until my element could no longer feel the shore.

I came to a slow halt and looked around. In every direction, there were only giant blue waves— the sky was overcast, and the sun had been blocked by the clouds, making everything dark. It'd been sunny when I left the beach, but now a storm was starting to roll in.

I floated for a minute, letting the sea rock my body as I kept aloft over the white caps that churned me up and down.

I thought that the ocean might help my mind become more stable, but I could barely string two words together right now. My thoughts felt incoherent and jagged. Nothing I could fathom made sense. It was like there was this weird buzzing in my head, a static that made everything foggy and hard to hear.

Everything just felt so... hollow.

The thought came to me to see how long I could hold my breath. I inhaled deeply, then plunged downward. I counted seconds as I sank slowly to the bottom. Minutes later, when I got there, I sat on the ocean floor and curled my arms around my knees, waiting.

My record for holding my breath underwater was six minutes and thirty two seconds. I could beat that. I sat on the ocean floor and mentally counted as the minutes ticked by.

When I passed the six minute mark, my body started protesting. It wanted to go upward for air. But I wouldn't let it. I wanted to go farther. I made myself stay put and concentrated as I kept myself at the bottom of the ocean.

At seven minutes, my lungs started to burn. Black dots swarmed my vision, and a sharp ache grew in my temple. My limbs started to shake, and my chest felt like it was going to burst. My very limbs were on fire. I finally relented and pushed myself back up to the surface, though my magic was weak from not having enough oxygen.

It took longer than I thought to make the water raise me up for air. Each second was agonizing, painful, long-suffering as I looked onward toward the surface.

When I finally broke the crested waves, I took in huge, gasping breaths, trying to recover. I felt woozy and weak. My head spun, and my limbs were as watery and loose as the waves around me.

I felt like crap. But I was used to this kind of shit. I knew how it went. The feeling was familiar. Almost safe.

When the ocean stopped spinning, I took a few more deep breaths and dove downward. I tried holding my breath again, two more times.

On the third time, I reached eight minutes and nearly passed out. I almost allowed myself to before I shot to the surface again.

I barely kept myself afloat once I reached the surface. Still, I had the feeling that I'd accomplished something.

But I wasn't sure what I was trying to prove.

❧

I DIDN'T COME BACK to school until nightfall, when my body was literally too tired to swim anymore. I think I went farther from land than I'd ever been by myself— at least thirty miles.

The halls were mostly quiet and empty now. The freshman had long since moved in and were likely attending celebrations in their own dorms.

I spotted Imogen when I passed the Commons. She was carrying a huge stack of heavy textbooks and was struggling to see around them. She wavered back and forth, trying to keep the book tower balanced. It was comical, watching her try to avoid spilling the books all over the place.

Sassy was at her feet, dancing around nervously and watching the books with a keen eye, as if she intended to dodge out of the way if one of them fell.

The book tower dangerously wavered, and Imogen stumbled. The books went teetering. I ran forward and caught the stacks of books before they tumbled out of her arms. I helped to right them and barely avoided causing an avalanche in the hallway.

Imogen was breathless. "Oh, thank you, I almost dropped—"

Imogen peeked her head around the stack. When she saw that it was me, her eyes narrowed. Her friendly tone turned deadly. "Oh. It's you."

Didn't need to be a genius to know she was mad at me. "Yeah. Me."

Imogen turned her nose up and clutched to her books. "Well, we don't need help from *you*. Do we, Sassy?"

Sassy made a little *yip* to indicate she agreed, though the fox eyed the books in Imogen's arms warily.

"Would you at least let me take some?" I asked. "I don't want you to make a mess."

"I've been cleaning up your messes all summer, thank you very much," Imogen said. She put the books down on a nearby chest of drawers and stood upright. "But if you're that insistent, fine. You can take the heavy ones."

"Thanks," I said in relief. I didn't know why I was thanking her when I was the one lending a hand, but it made me feel ten times better that she was at least willing to let me help out.

I took half the stack, and Imogen took the other half. She set off in the direction of the Nivita dorms. I noticed she kept silent. She didn't want to speak with me.

"These are a lot of books," I said, trying to make small talk.

"I'm double majoring. Hawkei Fashion and Familiar Zoology," Imogen said fairly. "I need all of these for class."

"Double-majoring? Wow. That's impressive."

Imogen made a disgusted noise and didn't answer me.

When we stopped in front of the Nivita dorms, Imogen found a small greenhouse cart with wheels on it. She put her books on the cart, then grabbed the ones I held, placing them beside her original stack. "There. Thanks for the help."

Sassy jumped on top of the books. Imogen went to push the cart inside the Nivita dorms.

"Wait, Im…" I called to her, and she turned back around.

I was scared to ask the next question. But it was something that had been eating me up all summer.

"We're still friends, aren't we?" I blurted out. I couldn't lose another friend. Orenda Academy was already getting to be unbearably lonely, and it was only day one of senior year.

She looked me up and down. "Yes, Liam, we're still friends, but…" Imogen let out an angry huff. "I kind of hate you for breaking my best friend's heart. You have no idea how much I'd *love* to punch you in the face right now."

"I know I deserve it, believe me," I said quietly.

Imogen's face cleared. She tilted her head at me, like she couldn't believe I'd just said that.

"I thought you'd be defensive after what happened," she said. "I figured you'd blame Sophia."

"No. We both did bad stuff." I shook my head. "The breakup… it was just what had to be done."

"I thought you'd be angry." She frowned, but it was more a look of sympathy than anything else… which was fucked up, because she was supposed to hate me, not feel bad for me.

"I don't think there's any anger left in me." The words felt so weak coming out of my mouth. Nashoma had been gone a year. I'd been sick for an equal amount of time. I'd never get over either, but I'd gotten used to both. I was no longer pissed off that bad things had happened to me. They had happened, and there was no changing it. I just had to accept it.

To be angry, you had to care. And I didn't care about shit anymore.

Imogen's face looked conflicted. "You wore red on purpose to the meeting yesterday."

"I did not."

I totally did. It wasn't meant to be mean. More of a gesture that I was still here for Sophia, and I was behind her no matter what was going on. Now I realized it'd probably been seen as an insult. Stupid, stupid.

Imogen gave me a look that clearly said she didn't believe me before she tapped her chin thoughtfully. "I think you guys need to talk," she said. "Have a heart-to-heart."

"I highly doubt Sophia wants to talk to me. We're on speaking terms because we have to be, due to the prophecy," I said.

"Things can't be like this forever," Imogen pleaded. "She misses you."

I scoffed. "Yeah. Sure she does."

Imogen was quiet for a moment before she said, "Sophia spent her entire summer at my house cooped up in her room. Or in the library. Jonah and I couldn't get her to come out."

"Really?" I was shocked. "I thought—"

"You thought wrong." Imogen's tone was harsh, before she realized what she was doing and it became kind again. "How was your summer?"

I shrugged. "More or less the same. I helped my mom with the new baby a lot."

Truth be told, I didn't think I'd left the house except a handful of times. Mom had yelled at me for babysitting my newborn brother too much. Said a young person like me needed to get out and have fun. She'd been worried about me all summer. Dad wasn't around much, thank the ancestors, so we hadn't spoken either. Ezra was too busy partying with his friends to be home, and the rest of my siblings all had stuff going on. Unless Jonah was there, it was mostly me alone.

And it had gotten old. Fast.

Imogen ran her fingers over the spines of her books, thinking. "Maybe things would be better if you guys tried to be friends again. I don't want to rush you, but it's been three months. You're going to have to work together because we have to find the pieces, but I think your friendship is even more important."

"I don't think we're friends anymore." Admitting that out loud was exceptionally painful. It was like one of my father's hunting arrows had pierced my heart and come out the other side of my body.

"Then start over. Reach out," Imogen encouraged. "I know she'll listen. She's in the library if you want to talk."

Imogen headed off, pushing the cart of books through the Nivita doors. Sassy waved her tail in farewell.

I thought about talking to Sophia. Was it possible to feel like your heart was shriveling up and exploding at the same time? Ancestors, it was fucking terrifying to think of facing her, especially alone. At least the last time we'd talked to each other, Imogen and Jonah could serve as a buffer.

Yet I had to resolve this somehow, and there was no time like the present. Might as well get it over with.

My heart thudded out of my chest with every heavy step I took toward the library. It felt like my feet were made of stone. When I got there, I peered around the door to search for Sophia.

She was bent over a few open books at the nearest table to the door, her brunette hair fanned out on her back. Esis was sitting on the table, idly turning pages like he was bored. Her brown eyes were studying the pages in front of her in deep concentration.

She was wearing sweats, which shouldn't be sexy, but holy fuck, they were. Had I ever noticed that she had really nice skin? And those lips— holy shit. My dream came back to me in full force, and I told my dick to quiet down. *Not supposed to be attracted to her anymore.*

Seeing her felt like my insides were being ripped out. Slowly.

The library was a rough place for us to talk. She'd blown me a few rows back from the table she sat at. What I'd give to relive that memory.

But what was worse than losing Sophia as a girlfriend was losing her completely. We weren't close anymore. We weren't even friends. We were bigger strangers now than the night we first met.

It royally sucked. And I knew I couldn't live the rest of the semester this way. Hell, I couldn't stand it for five more minutes. I didn't want to — couldn't live— with avoiding her again. I'd done it before, and it ripped her up inside. I'd vowed to never do that to her again. Just because we weren't dating anymore didn't mean I could break that promise.

Imogen wanted me to reach out. It seemed like the right thing to do.

Well, we at least needed to talk about one thing. These sessions with Esis needed to stop. They wouldn't unless Sophia told Esis to quit seeing me. I gathered all my courage and forced myself out from behind the corner, because if I didn't, I'd be there all night studying her and being super creepy.

I shoved my hands in my pockets and walked forward. *Hey, Soph, how you doing? Nope, that's too casual. Hi Sophia? No. Dude, think of something!*

I came to a stop at her table. She looked up, seemingly shocked to see me standing there. I tried to force a smile, but my lips wouldn't move.

Use English! I was practically screaming at myself now. Thirty seconds had passed, and neither of us had said a thing.

I went to say hi, but that didn't work. Instead, I blurted out the first thing that came to my mind.

"Please stop sending Esis to heal me," I said out loud. And immediately regretted it.

Sophia gaped at me.

You fucking idiot, I told myself.

Sophia shut her mouth, and her eyes narrowed in anger. Then she said, "That's non-negotiable."

Aw, shit. I was entering a pissing match with a Koigni. What the hell had I gotten myself into? "I'm just letting you know that if you don't want Esis to heal me anymore, I'm cool with it," I started. "It's not a big deal."

"I'm not going to become a murderer because this makes you uncomfortable." Her tone was flat.

"You don't have to worry about it. Seriously, it would be okay to let me die," I said. What the hell was going on with me? It was like I could only say the worst-possible thing right now.

"Would you stop it with that fucked-up shit?" Sophia snapped, and she slammed the book she was reading closed. I was momentarily shocked. Sophia had never spoken to me like that.

Esis grabbed his ears and pulled them down, to block out the sound of her swearing. Sophia glanced around to make sure no one was listening, then continued ranting at me. "Do you know what it would to do me if you died, *especially* if I could've done something to prevent it? It would ruin my life if you were dead and I was the reason. I can't force you to let Esis heal you, but I know that you want him to, and that you asking me to stop sending him is your way of trying to spare me. So stop trying to be a martyr. I can handle myself."

I realized my mouth was hanging open. I quickly shut it. "Fine. Okay, then. You're right. I don't want Esis' treatments to stop. We should keep them going."

Then, because I was insane or because I had suddenly grown balls of steel, I sat in the chair next to her. She stiffened for a minute, but I kept my distance, and Sophia eventually relaxed beside me... though her expression continued to be suspicious.

"His healing magic has been helping a lot, by the way," I said. "I'm feeling better. Glad you talked me into it, *pawee*."

Motherfucker! Why in the name of the ancestors couldn't I stop calling her that? Esis gave me a sly look.

Her lips briefly tilted up. "You were always too stubborn for your own good."

Sophia looked around. "Where's Nashoma? I thought he'd be with you, but I haven't seen him yet."

My stomach bottomed out. Jonah hadn't told her. I should've guessed, due to their argument.

"He, uh... the Toaqua Elders used me," I said quietly. "They never had the ability to bring Nashoma back in the first place."

"Oh, Liam. I'm so sorry." Sophia actually looked sad for me. I figured she'd laugh at me or something, say I deserved it, but Sophia wasn't that kind of girl. She was too nice. She still cared.

"It's my own fault for falling for it. Do you remember Carter and Tiara? The Elementai and Familiar that died last year in Flight class, before the Elemental Cup?" I asked.

"Barely." Sophia scrunched up her eyebrows. "What do they have to do with it?"

"The Water Elders staged their deaths. They used Carter and Tiara to make me believe they could raise people from the dead, when really, he never died at all," I told her. "The Toaqua Elders saved his and Tiara's lives. Then they imprisoned them, and used them to get to me. Carter managed to escape and told me the truth. He's on the run now."

"You mean... your dad lied to you, too?" She put a hand over her mouth. Esis copied the gesture.

"Yeah." I shook my head. "But I don't really want to talk about that. What's done is done."

I reached into my pocket. "By the way, I wanted to return this to you."

When I showed her the Spirit Totem in my hand, the one we'd found in the cave during the Elemental Cup, Sophia's eyes widened. She snatched the totem from me and held it close to her chest, like it was something incredibly precious to her.

"Where did you find it? I never went back to look for it," she whispered.

"You dropped it in the temple on Ancestors' Day," I said. *Fuck that horrible night.* "I picked it up. I forgot to give it back to you, you know, because we were fighting. I'm sorry I didn't return it sooner. I just... didn't know if you wanted to see me."

I rubbed the back of my neck awkwardly. Sophia clung to the totem and said, "Thank you for keeping it safe. And for giving it back. I know you're not particularly fond of it, but it means something to me."

"No problem. I'd do anything for you," I responded without thinking.

Fuck my stupid words. My cheeks were burning. I couldn't read the expression she gave me. Esis, however, looked about two seconds away from cheering.

Her eyes wandered. "Is there anything else...?"

Yes. No. Everything. "I was thinking," I began. "Maybe we could put the past behind us and move forward. There's stuff going on that's a lot bigger than us."

I winced when I said the word *us*, because there wasn't an us anymore. But if Sophia noticed, she didn't give any indication.

She nodded somberly. "We do need to get along. For the sake of figuring out the prophecy."

"It's not just the prophecy," I started. "Jonah and Imogen are both our friends. It's not fair to mess things up in the group just because we..."

I couldn't finish that sentence. Sophia wasn't giving me anything in response. It's like she was refusing to speak to me as much as she physically had to, and it hurt.

I couldn't live like this. I had to take a risk. "Look," I said. "I know things aren't going to be what they used to. But I think this would be a lot easier on both of us if we decided to be friends again."

Sophia waited a moment before answering. Every second hurt to hear her answer. "Friends trust each other, don't they?"

Ouch. She was pointing out the obvious. She didn't think we could ever be friends, because that trust between us was gone now.

"We'll have to rebuild that. And there's no way that'll happen if we don't at least try," I said. "How are we going to work to find the pieces if we don't trust each other?"

She bit her lip and looked away. "I don't know."

I could practically hear the gears turning in her head. She was trying to figure me out, determine if this was some sort of trap or mind game.

But I wasn't playing mind games. I just wanted Sophia back in my life. I'd missed her. I hoped she'd missed me enough, too, to put the past behind us. "I think it's best if we start over," I said. I held out my hand to her. "Friends?"

She looked at me for a moment before she slowly extended her hand to shake mine. "Okay. Friends."

It was just a handshake. But when her skin touched mine, a million sensors fired off all over my body. All my reserves failed. I'd forgotten how she felt, how warm and soft she was. Dreams weren't enough. I remembered every touch, every moment. I wanted to hold her. I wanted to kiss her. I wanted to throw myself on my knees and beg for her forgiveness.

Stop, Liam, stop.

Esis chittered, and I pried my hand away from hers at the sound. "I knew you'd be cool with it," I said. "You're such a sweet girl."

Sophia's face turned sour. "Yeah. Sweet."

Esis gave me a scathing look. I was trying to compliment her, but apparently, that'd been the wrong thing to say. I had to get out of here... before I put my foot in my mouth again and said something even dumber.

I stood up. "Anyway... I gotta go. See you around?"

She nodded. "Sure." Then her eyes went back to what she'd been reading. She didn't give me any other sort of goodbye.

I headed off. When I glanced behind me, I noticed she'd raised her eyes from the book and was watching me go.

I waved goodbye. She waved back. It was the smallest gesture, but it made my heartbeat pick up again.

I let out a sigh of relief.

Okay, that was a bit awkward. No— really awkward. But at least it was over with. Hopefully Sophia and I could stand to be around each other now without things being super weird.

And hopefully my feelings would stop getting in the way. Though at this point, I severely doubted it.

sophia

FOUR

I took a deep breath to calm my nerves, but it didn't help. The paper in my hands shook as I stared down at the address Vanessa had given me, then back up to the house in front of me.

1345 Firebrick Lane. Yep. This was it.

The house was huge and stylized in red brick and a black roof. Sharp peaks, a large wrap-around porch, and a two-story turret accented the Victorian-style architecture.

I was starting to notice a trend in the Koigni village. Every house I passed shared the same color scheme, as if the village had been forged in Koigni Fire. Even the buildings back in the main square had *Koigni* written all over them. On my walk through town, I'd passed by endless high-end fashion stores, fancy day spas, and about a dozen financial investment firms. It was obvious the Fire Tribe had a lot of money and wanted to show it off. The Koigni village was high up in the mountains, overlooking the forest and the rest of the villages below. For the lack of nature they had up here, the Koigni more than made up for with high-rise penthouses and designer labels.

As I reached the residential area, I found that each house was more elaborate than the last. The higher I climbed the mountain, the richer the families seemed, as if those with money had to sit at the top, where they could lord over everyone else. I figured the mansions I'd caught a

41

glimpse of higher up the mountains were reserved for Elders, like Madame Doya and Chieftess Annette.

The house I stared up at belonged to Alan and Betsy Weber, my biological grandparents. It sat in the middle of the village, which I assumed said something about their status. It should've comforted me knowing I wasn't headed all the way to the top, but I couldn't bring myself to take another step toward the front door.

Esis didn't freeze up like I had. He hopped off my shoulder and pushed open the wrought-iron gate surrounding the property. He gazed up at me expectantly and chittered.

I let out the breath I'd been holding and tucked the paper in my pocket. "You're right. I can do this."

I still hadn't been able to get Liam out of my head. He wanted us to be friends, but I didn't know if I could. I barely knew myself anymore. I needed this.

Esis bounced down the walkway and up the porch steps before I'd even taken a step. I forced my shaking knees to steady and pushed forward. Two mahogany doors with elaborate iron handles and thick door knockers stared back at me, as if daring me to go through with this.

Visions of what I might find behind those doors assaulted me. What if my grandparents were like Doya, cold and cruel? There had to be a reason they hadn't contacted me since I'd arrived in Kinpago. What if I reminded them too much of their daughter, my biological mother?

I turned around. "I can't do this, Esis. This was a bad idea."

Esis scurried in front of me and blocked my path. He placed one paw on his hip and waved the other at me, clicking his tongue. It was like he was saying I'd come this far and couldn't turn back now.

I sighed. "Okay. But if they turn out to be anything like Doya, we're leaving."

Esis scurried up to the door, waiting for me to knock.

Hope pushed me forward— hope that I'd find something worthwhile behind those doors. After all, these people had been friends with my adoptive parents. They'd given me away to protect me. That had to count for something. I reached up and curled my fingers around the door knocker, then knocked.

Several seconds passed, and nothing happened. I glanced down to Esis. "Maybe they're not home."

It was Labor Day, the day before school started. Who knew whether they'd be home mid-day on a Monday?

Esis scowled at me, then pointed up to the knocker again, encouraging me to try once more. I did, and a few seconds later, the heavy door swung open.

An older woman, at least in her seventies, stood behind the door. She had short white hair and wrinkles around her eyes, but other than that, she didn't look her age. Her bangs swooped to the side in a trendy cut, and her makeup was worthy of a fashion magazine. She wore a flowing white top and black slacks, a comfortable combination of modest and elegant. She had to be Betsy Weber.

Her face paled. She opened her mouth to speak, but nothing came out.

"Hi," I said timidly. "I'm Sophia Henley."

The shocked expression stuck to her face. "I know who you are."

I couldn't read her tone. We just stood there for several seconds, staring at each other.

Without warning, she threw her arms around me. It was then I knew she was definitely nothing like Doya. In fact, Betsy was the exact opposite. Her embrace was warm and welcoming, and she smelled of vanilla. I relaxed into her hug, as if we'd done this a thousand times before.

"I'm so glad to finally meet you!" Betsy drew away and swung the door open wider. "Please, come in."

The tension in my body eased as I stepped into the house. The interior was just as beautiful as the outside, with endless hardwood floors and an elaborately carved banister leading upstairs. There were patterned red area rugs everywhere, which reminded me of the Koigni dorms. A beautiful golden light fixture hung from the entryway ceiling. Family pictures adorned the walls, along with various decorations that drew from our Hawkei heritage, like Familiar statuettes, dreamcatchers, and a collection of old arrowheads.

Betsy gestured to her left and led me into a red sitting room with a burning fireplace. A man relaxed on a recliner reading *The Hawkei Times*. Beside him sat a white Dall sheep with flames flickering where its large, curved horns should be. It sat in front of the fire, looking content.

The man lowered his paper, and shock flashed over his face. He sat upright and set the paper aside. He looked the same age as my grandmother, with white hair and lines across his face, but he had an air of class about him that had to do more with character than money. He had to be Alan Weber.

"Please, sit," Betsy said kindly.

I sat in a comfortable red chair across from my grandfather, and Esis hopped up on my lap.

"Sophia," Alan said breathlessly. "Can we get you anything?"

"Yes. Water, tea?" Betsy asked.

"Water's fine," I said.

Betsy left the room and came back a moment later carrying a fresh water bottle and a plate of chocolate chip cookies. They looked home-made. She set them in front of me on the coffee table.

"I'm Betsy, and this is Alan, but I guess you already knew that." Betsy offered a kind smile as she took a seat in the chair beside Alan.

The sound of a small bell jingled as a large house cat trotted into the room. It jumped to sit in Betsy's lap and curled up there, looking comfortable as she stroked its long white fur. The cat was large, at least fifteen pounds, with long ear tufts and wide paws. It could easily pass for a Maine Coon back home, but there was something mystical about its swirling, ruby-red eyes.

I felt it was rude to leave the water and cookies lying there, so I screwed the cap off the water bottle and took a sip, then began nibbling on a cookie. It was delicious.

Alan leaned forward in his chair and offered a welcoming smile. "We were hoping you'd find us."

My nerves began to wash away. "How long have you known I was in Kinpago?"

"Since you arrived last year," Betsy said. "We didn't want to overwhelm you with a visit. We thought it best if you came at your own pace — if you wanted to meet us at all."

It almost sounded like she was afraid of what I might think of her... like I might judge them for giving me away when they had a chance to raise me.

"I don't resent you giving me up," I blurted.

The two exchanged a glance. I thought I read sadness in their eyes.

"Oh, dear," Betsy said softly. "You have no idea how much we hoped you'd say that."

I straightened in my chair. Now that I was here, I had so many questions to ask them. I didn't know where to start.

"Why... why did you do it?" I asked. I knew the version my adoptive parents had given me, but I wanted to hear it from them. "Don't get me wrong. I love my parents, but..."

Alan cleared his throat. "You have to understand. It was dangerous to keep you here."

He hesitated and shot Betsy a wary look.

"It's okay," I encouraged. "My parents told me what happened. I know all about the prophecy and that the Toaqua wanted me dead."

Betsy frowned. "Yes. That's why we had to give you away. Not all Toaqua were a threat, of course. That's why we turned to your parents. Before Alan retired, he worked with your adoptive father— Robert— at City Hall. Despite House lines, they bonded over their love of chess. Used to play together every Sunday evening. Then Robert got the job in Utah, and we knew he could get you out of Kinpago."

"What about the other Toaqua?" I asked. "My parents said there was some sort of conflict between Koigni and Toaqua the night after I was born."

They both turned down their gazes.

"It was a riot," Alan admitted. "Right here in the Koigni Village. Toaqua came for you, said that your very existence was a threat to the Hawkei. Your father— your biological one, Tony— he left to join the other Koigni in defending you. It was a bloodbath." He cleared his throat, like thinking back to that night had stolen his voice.

"The Toaqua brought weapons," Betsy continued for him. "The Koigni retaliated. Dozens were killed. It almost started a full-fledged war between the Houses, but then you disappeared, and the Toaqua backed off."

"Just like that?" I asked.

Tears rose to Betsy's eyes as she recalled the massacre. "There was so much fire. When we told them we didn't know what happened to you, that you'd been lost in the chaos, they assumed you'd died along with hundreds of others."

My throat began to close up. I couldn't believe so many people had died in my name. It wasn't right.

"I'm sorry," I croaked, pulling Esis closer to me. "I shouldn't have brought it up."

Betsy sniffled and waved a hand. "Nonsense. You deserve to know."

"Can you tell me about them?" I asked, hoping to turn the conversation around to something more cheerful. "About Lucy and Anthony? What were they like at my age? Do you have any pictures?"

The two of them hesitated and looked to each other like they were sharing a silent conversation. Betsy gave a slight nod, then Alan stood and headed out of the room.

Betsy grabbed a tissue from the box on the end table beside her and wiped her nose. Her voice came out brighter and more upbeat. "Lucy was a lovely girl. Very bright, but very head-strong."

I smiled. "Sounds like me."

"She was very kind-hearted," she continued. "Friends with anyone, no matter their House. Tony was the same way. They're lucky they found each other, to be honest. It's rare for a Koigni to be as compassionate as those two were."

I thought of Vanessa and Bren. They were both Koigni, but you wouldn't know it by their personalities. I was starting to think Koigni traits weren't bred as much as taught from birth. There were more kind ones than there were cruel ones.

"Lucy must've got that from you," I said.

Betsy smiled. "That's very kind of you."

Alan returned, carrying a large book at least three inches thick. The cover was almost a whole square foot. He handed it to me. "This is Lucy's scrapbook from her time at Orenda Academy."

I went speechless as I took it from him. "My mom kept a scrapbook?"

It was so weird to think of this woman as my mother.

"Yep," Alan said as he took his seat again. "That was back before they banned cameras on campus."

I opened the cover to see a large picture of my birth parents smiling back at me. Their hairstyles and fashion were dated from at least twenty years ago, but they looked young, happy and carefree. They stood in front of the Orenda Academy castle. Tony had his arm around Lucy and was smiling at the camera, while she leaned in to kiss him on the cheek and kicked one of her feet up in a cute pose.

Lucy was blonde, with freckles all across her face and features that mirrored her mother's. Tony, on the other hand, had dark hair like mine, but more Native American features. I thought I might look like them, but I didn't.

I flipped to the next page, and my heart nearly stopped at what I saw. A red-headed woman sat on the back of one of the lion statues on the front steps of the castle. She held one arm in the air like she was riding a bull. Her nose was crinkled in laughter.

Could it be...?

Yes. It was definitely Madame Doya.

I gaped at the photograph. "My parents were friends with Madame Doya?"

Betsy stood beside my chair to gaze down at the photographs with me. "Oh, yes. She and Lucy were best friends."

"She was the instigator in their group," Alan mumbled.

"Eleanor wasn't that bad," Betsy scolded. "She was a nice girl. She just liked to break the rules every now and then. She had a wild streak."

I nearly choked on nothing but air. Madame Doya? Break the rules?

"She really was a sweetheart," Betsy said. "Always the life of the party, but very studious. She helped Lucy with her big breakthrough in their Third Year. Remember that, Alan? It wasn't long after Lucy bonded. She didn't know how to control her Fire tornados. Eleanor taught her how, and she used it in the tournament. I don't think she would've survived if it weren't for Ellie. I think that's why she decided to go into teaching. To think, she wasn't even bonded yet!"

I continued turning pages, but I couldn't find the words to respond. In what universe was Doya this kind-hearted, powerful, carefree girl Betsy was explaining? What triggered such a paradigm shift?

A photograph of Lucy and Doya hugging in the grand entrance caught my eye. They were smiling and laughing, clearly caught off guard at the candid shot.

Had Lucy's death changed Doya? Because she'd lost her best friend? I couldn't imagine how I'd handle it if I lost Imogen.

"What did my parents major in?" I asked as I continued to flip through the scrapbook.

"Lucy was majoring in political science," Betsy said. "And Tony... do you remember, hon?"

"General studies," Alan replied. "He never quite made up his mind."

"Oh, but the man was passionate about so many things," Betsy said. "Fishing, camping, photography, you name it. That's why you won't see him in most of these pictures. He was usually the one *behind* the camera."

I chuckled. "Well, I guess I inherited something from him. I love the outdoors, too. Did either of them have any siblings? Like, do I have any cousins out there I don't know about, or other family?"

"I'm afraid not," Betsy said. "Tony's parents died when he was young."

I was a little disappointed at first, but it was probably for the best. They'd probably be something like Haley. Then again, my grandparents were nice. I guess I shouldn't make assumptions.

As I continued to flip through the pages, I noticed that most of the pictures were of Lucy and Doya. It was like the two were joined at the hip. They took pictures all around the castle, always striking the silliest poses. They even had pictures from their classes, like one where Doya was petting a bright red dragon. The two of them reminded me of how Imogen and I were.

Toward the middle of the album, I noticed Familiars appear for the first time. Lucy had bonded with a white stag right around the same time Tony had bonded with a small golden puppy with red ears. Naomi was nowhere to be seen.

The following pages were filled with photographs of my parents' wedding. It looked like they'd gotten married in the Koigni village square. They looked so happy as they danced and celebrated.

"When was this?" I asked.

Betsy thought for a moment. "They got married the summer after their sophomore year. They wanted to do it before they faced the tournament. You were born a year later."

The breath left my chest. They hadn't even finished college. "They were so young."

I wasn't talking about their marriage or their pregnancy, either, but Alan took it that way.

"We were young once, too." He smiled up at Betsy, as if recalling their time together at Orenda.

I flipped a page and stopped dead in my tracks. "Oh my gosh! Is that *Baine?*"

He was missing the white hair and thick glasses. His brown hair was tousled, but in a kept way that made him look put together for once. His skin was smoother. I could almost see where Imogen was coming from when she talked about him being hot. In the photograph, he stood with his arm around Doya and presented her with some sort of certificate of achievement. She wasn't even looking at the camera. She was staring up at him with admiration in her eyes.

"Mm?" Betsy looked down at the photograph. "Elliot Baine? Oh, yes. That's him. The kids *loved* his class. You know, now that I think of it, he might be the reason Eleanor went into the teaching profession. She quite admired the man."

"Wow. I didn't realize Baine was Doya's professor," I said. "Didn't he do some sort of exploring before he became a teacher?"

"He took a few years off, if I remember right," Betsy said thoughtfully. "The year after the riot, I think. Came back a few years ago. I guess he never found whatever it was he was looking for."

"Yeah, I guess not." I continued to flip through the book, but I couldn't take my mind off that picture of Baine and Doya. They seemed like total opposites. I couldn't imagine them ever getting along. Apparently, I had more to learn about the past than I thought.

"Can I keep this?" I asked.

Betsy smiled. "Keep it as long as you want, dear."

Hours passed, and I began to loosen up the more I talked to my grandparents. They'd invited us to stay and eat. I couldn't refuse— especially with the way Esis looked at me with those pleading eyes. My grandfather showed me his collection of arrowheads, while my grandmother raved over her collection of decorative plates hanging in the kitchen. They'd told me stories of their time at Orenda Academy and made it sound even more magical than it was— which I didn't think was possible. My grandma showed me how to make fry bread, and my grandpa taught me a traditional Hawkei beat on the drum. It was amazing to learn about my heritage— both the Hawkei side and my direct relations.

By the end of the night, I felt like I'd found my new family.

I STEPPED out of Hawkei Legends the following morning still thinking about meeting with my grandparents. I'd spent the rest of the afternoon listening to stories of Lucy's childhood, and how my parents had met in high school and started dating in college. I'd even scheduled a lunch date with my grandparents for Saturday, just so I could hear more.

I was starting to get a real feel for who my birth parents were. They weren't just names on a genealogy chart anymore. They were real people, with faces I could picture and personalities that came to life through the stories my grandparents told.

My second class of the day was History of the Hawkei. It wasn't far from the Hawkei Legends, so I arrived early.

I took a step back when I entered the room. It was entirely empty, apart from Professor Baine shuffling through papers at his desk. Baine had been my mentor my first semester here. He'd helped our team get through the tournament.

But then he'd gone and betrayed me. I didn't know the whole story about what went down with the Toaqua Council last semester, but I knew he'd served on it— and that the council had asked Liam to kill me. I didn't care if Baine was the one to push it or not. I wasn't sure I even wanted to know. All I knew was that he didn't stop it.

I'd forgotten he taught this class. I'd signed up for it before I knew, before all the secrets came out.

When my eyes landed on him, it was like a knife was tearing through my guts. Baine was my mentor. He was supposed to protect me. And instead, he'd sent an assassin after me.

Screw this class, I thought. I was going straight to Doya to see if I could get my classes changed.

Baine looked up. "Sophia!" he called as he spotted me leaving the room.

I didn't turn back. Esis pulled on my ponytail to get my attention, but I kept walking.

"Sophia, wait!" Baine ran to keep up with me. He wasn't going to let me go. I had to face him.

I whirled around, ignoring the other people passing through the hall. "Do you want to explain yourself, *Professor Baine?*"

The blood drained from his face. "I owe you an apology."

"Damn right, you do," I snapped.

Ugh. I should've just kept walking. I could get in trouble for back talking a teacher, but at this point, I didn't care.

He glanced around. "Please come back to my room, where we can talk privately."

"Why? You don't want people knowing you and your Toaqua Council tried to kill me?" I hissed.

"Sophia, let me explain," Baine said softly.

Esis jumped from my shoulder to Baine's and crossed his arms at me, like he was taking Baine's side. My jaw dropped.

"I was against it the entire time." Baine sounded like he was telling the truth. "I had to go along with it because Elder Malison— one of the Toaqua Elders— was threatening Thalassa. Believe me, I never wanted any harm to come to you."

I gaped at him. I didn't know what to say. I was so torn. Would I do the same for Esis, in that situation?

Baine dropped his gaze, like he truly regretted playing any part in the matter. "I quit the council because of it."

I gasped. Quit the council? Could you do that?

My shoulders relaxed. "Really? You did that for me?"

Baine nodded, then reached up and pulled Esis off his shoulder. Esis curled up in his arms and began purring, while trying to chew the button off Baine's shirt.

"There is nothing I can do or say to express how very sorry I am," Baine said. "I just hope you can find it in your heart to someday forgive me.... and attend my class."

Baine handed Esis back, and I didn't know what to say. Baine seemed so gentle, so genuine. How could I tell him to fuck off now?

"It's, uh, going to take some time," I admitted. "But... I guess I can try."

Baine offered a light smile. "Thank you, Sophia. Take your time."

Baine turned and headed back into his classroom, where other students had started to flood in. I stared after him, but a giant lime-green hair bow blocked my vision, pulling me out of it.

"History of the Hawkei!" Imogen exclaimed. She twirled so that her matching green dress spun around her. Sassy danced at her feet in excitement. "I'm super excited."

Her expression changed to a scowl. "Though I'm still pissed at Baine for trying to kill you."

"It's fine," I said. Though I felt conflicted, I believed Baine was sincere in his apology. "He apologized, and quit the council. It's cool."

Imogen looked shocked, then said, "Well, in that case..." She wiggled her eyebrows.

"Ew, Imogen." I rolled my eyes at her. "Do you have to mention how hot he is every time you speak of the guy? He's a *professor*."

Imogen took my hand. "Come on. Let's get a good seat."

"Somewhere in the back this time, please," I pleaded.

Imogen looked offended. "The front row is best!"

"Not if you don't want to get caught staring," I teased.

Imogen sighed. "Okay, you're right."

We claimed our seats in the back corner farthest from the door.

"What's up?" Imogen asked. "You seem... I don't know."

"I had to get up early for Hawkei Legends," I told her, though that wasn't why I was acting weird. "I'm still tired."

"You're taking Hawkei Legends? Sweet! What else have you got?"

"Um... Intro to Child Development, Intermediate Koigni Magic, and Elementai Explorations."

Imogen wrinkled her nose. "Sounds boring. Jonah and I are taking a dance class together, and I'm in this wicked elective called Cryptozo-ology— in other words, an entire semester dedicated to alien Familiars! And the last one isn't as fun but still pretty cool— Magical Plants."

"Sounds great," I said flatly, though I didn't intend for my voice to come out that way. I thought my classes were way better than hers.

Imogen nudged me. "What's got you down, Sophia? This semester is going to be so fun."

I shrugged. I didn't want to tell Imogen I wasn't really interested in being in this class anymore.

I was saved from answering by Baine himself.

"Everyone calm down," he called from the front of the class. "I know we're all excited to be back, but we have a lot to cover today."

By the end of class, we made it through the syllabus. The class was centered on Elementai history, from the beginning of the original tribe to now. I was starting to think I might enjoy this class, despite Baine teaching. There weren't any huge projects, just a couple of essays, so that helped ease my nerves.

"What do you think?" Imogen asked as we left the classroom. "Same study place on the third floor this year? We can get a head-start on that first essay later this week."

My heart gave an involuntary jolt when I spotted Liam down the hall. He was leaning against a window with his arms crossed, talking to a girl I didn't know. He looked like he was enjoying himself.

She was pretty, with long black hair like his. Toaqua. They'd make a great freaking couple.

"Sophia?" Imogen prodded.

"Yeah, sure," I said absentmindedly. I couldn't take my eyes off him. "Sounds great."

Angry fire rose to my skin and manifested in tears. I choked them back and bit my lower lip to push my emotions down before they exploded— literally— right there in the middle of the hall.

Imogen followed my gaze and noticed Liam right away. "Let's go back to my dorm," she said quickly. "I redecorated and want to show you."

Imogen grabbed my arm and started dragging me away, but not before Liam's gaze found mine. Out of all the people flooding through the halls, his eyes landed on me, as if there was some invisible force connecting us.

Not anymore, I thought bitterly. The connection I thought we'd have forever was gone.

Liam turned his eyes back to the pretty Toaqua girl and shot her a smile. He didn't smile like that at me anymore.

Esis tugged on my ponytail, forcing my gaze off Liam. I brushed his fingers out of my hair. "I get it, buddy. I have to stop torturing myself."

Once we turned down the hall and Liam was out of sight, I couldn't take it any longer. Tears began falling down my cheeks, and I dashed them away. Imogen noticed, but she didn't say anything. She just increased her pace so we could get back to the dorms faster.

Inside her dorm, I fell down onto the bed and let my emotions run. I barely took one glance at her new decorations as I bawled, though I noticed almost everything was either orange or yellow. Sassy and Esis curled up beside me on the bed, and Imogen sat down next to me.

"I'm sorry," Imogen said gently. "I know how hard it must be to see him after everything that happened."

I lifted my head and wiped my eyes. "It sucks. We agreed to be friends, but I don't know if I can actually do it."

"You two talked, then?" she asked, sounding hopeful.

I gritted my teeth thinking back to that conversation. "He said I didn't *have* to send him Esis, like he thinks I was obligated to as his girlfriend, and now that I'm not, I shouldn't *care*. What the hell kind of person does he think I am? I mean, yeah, I feel bad for him, but that's not why I'm doing it. Did you know the Toaqua Elders didn't bring Nashoma back like they promised?"

Imogen dropped her gaze. "I was starting to wonder about that. Jonah never brought it up, though."

"Yeah. Apparently, they lied about the whole thing. I thought this summer he at least had someone to keep him company, so now I feel even worse about the break-up."

I was aware I was ranting now, but I couldn't stop. I hadn't even mentioned the Spirit Totem yet— how he'd given it back like it was some sort of bargaining chip in our friendship. Imogen didn't even know about it. Sure, I was happy to have the totem back. I'd intended to go back to the ruins to look for it over the summer, but I knew I'd never get through without everyone else's help. But it didn't soften the impact.

"I honestly don't know what to feel anymore. Half the time I feel bad for him, and half the time I hate him," I continued. "What makes it worse is that he keeps calling me *pawee*."

"I thought you said you didn't mind," Imogen pointed out.

I barely heard her. "And sweet! He called me *sweet*! Has anyone *ever* called a Koigni *sweet* in the history of all the Hawkei? It made me feel like I'm ten years old."

"Sophia, breathe." Imogen took my shoulders and shook me a little. "We're going to have to get you out of here one of these nights. Make you forget about him."

I sighed. "Im, I don't think that's going to help."

She shrugged. "What could it hurt?"

I could think of about a million things that could go wrong. But maybe Imogen was right. Maybe it was time to get Liam off my mind and live a little. I was sick of being upset over him. I wanted to be happy again.

Imogen smiled at me. "I think I have something that could help. Come on. Let's get back at that bastard."

FIVE

I'd just come back from a morning swim in the ocean when I heard screaming coming from the Nivita dorms.

Horrified yells lit up the halls at Orenda Academy. People stopped what they were doing and turned in the direction of the screaming, appearing bewildered. The screams got louder and took on a blood-curdling effect that made chills run up and down my spine. Whoever was screaming sounded like they were being tortured.

This wasn't my job. I didn't need to save anybody. I needed to stay out of it. The screams seemed to insist that I mind my own business and leave whoever was suffering to it.

But instead of making me run the other way, like a sensible person, danger had a way of making me go toward it instead. I dropped my bag and booked it toward the sound of the screaming, thinking some student had lost it or something and started shooting their magic off at everybody.

When I got there, there was a large crowd gathered around in a circle around the Nivita dorm doors. Professor Fawn was on her knees on the floor, and she was holding on to a Nivita girl who was sobbing profusely on the floor.

The student was a Fourth Year, like me. I knew her because she'd been in my freshman mentoring group my first year. Her name was Isabella. She had a filly-pixie Familiar, a miniature horse that had butterfly wings. I'd often seen the pink pixie on Isabella's shoulder when she walked around school, though now it was nowhere in sight.

Professor Fawn rocked the girl back and forth, trying to calm her down. Fawn's Familiar, a unicorn, stood nearby faithfully and nuzzled her nose into the girl's hair.

"Isabella, you need to calm down," Professor Fawn said, ignoring the circle of students around them. "We'll find her."

"She's gone!" the girl wailed. "Essarae's gone!"

"Familiars just don't wander off, my dear. I'm sure she's here somewhere," Professor Fawn said, though her tone seemed doubtful.

"She's been gone for three days, and she hasn't come home! That's not normal!" Isabella insisted.

"Where was the last place you saw her?" Professor Fawn spoke calmly and clearly.

Isabella took a steady breath through her tears. "She was sleeping on my pillow a few days ago. We took a nap together. When I woke up, the window was open. I figured she went to the greenhouses to get nectar, as she often does that. But she didn't come back that night, or the next morning. I've searched *everywhere*, and she's nowhere to be found!"

Isabella cried harder. "Someone must've seen what happened to her. Please, if you know anything, speak up!"

Professor Fawn looked to the crowd. "Has anyone seen a filly-pixie floating around? Pink in color, smaller than a hand, large purple butterfly wings?"

Everyone remained silent. Faces were blank and confused as Professor Fawn surveyed the crowd. She stood and lifted Isabella to her feet. "Very well. If any Nivita wish to help search, come with me."

A large group of students followed the two of them as they headed into the Nivita dorms. Students from the rest of the Houses dispersed. I noticed that, for some reason, a look of regret had passed Professor Fawn's face as the double doors of the Nivita dorms closed behind them.

I couldn't get Isabella's tortured face out of my mind. I couldn't imagine what it would be like for your Familiar to vanish. I knew I needed to eat, so I went to an early lunch, but food proved hard to swallow. It was difficult to enjoy anything while remembering Isabella's tortured sobs as she begged someone to find her Familiar.

By the time I left the dining hall, posters were being plastered all over the walls by Nivita students of the missing Familiar and where she'd last been seen, along with a reward.

I felt bad for Isabella. She would've already died if something bad had happened to Essarae, so that meant her Familiar was still alive. But if she hadn't come back in three days, that definitely meant someone had taken her.

I had no idea why anyone would want to steal a creature that was already bonded. Essarae would fight to the death to get back to Isabella, and she wouldn't bond or use her magic for anyone else. So why kidnap her?

It had to be something personal. But this crossed a line. You didn't mess with people's Familiars. That was beyond cruel.

I wanted to do something to lend a hand, but I knew they wouldn't accept my help, because I wasn't Nivita. So, with a lack of anything else to do, I went to the burial grounds and to Nashoma's grave. I left an offering and asked him and the rest of the ancestors to help Isabella find her Familiar. I didn't know if it actually did anything, but it was better than feeling worthless.

I tried to push Isabella and her missing Familiar out of my mind as I left the burial grounds and re-checked my schedule to see what I had later that day. I'd been at school for two weeks and should've known it by now, but it was like my head was still underwater. I couldn't remember anything these days. Stuff blurred together in a fog. I had Master Toaqua Magic and Basket Weaving III on Mondays and Wednesdays. Tuesdays and Thursdays had Senior Theory and Hawkei Home Ec.

Yes, I took Hawkei Home Ec. It was a blow-off class, and I was *so* sick of school. At this point, I was there to get the degree and get out. It counted for credit hours. That's all that mattered.

The only class that had any worth this semester was Hawkei Leadership on Friday mornings. It was a course I didn't think that I'd be able to get into, but applied for anyway. To my surprise, they let me in.

I didn't know what I'd use it for. Hawkei Leadership was a core class meant for people in Political Science, my old major. People couldn't just walk in there and take it unless they'd declared themselves to be future tribal leaders, which I'd been forced to renounce as a career choice after Nashoma died.

Baine must've pulled some strings behind the scenes to get me into that class. It was the least he could do after that disaster last semester. So far we'd been studying tribal law, something that sucked me in and demanded my attention. It was the only thing that kept my mind off of Sophia these past two weeks.

Not to mention it was the only class this semester that had, so far, held my interest. Even Basket Weaving was starting to get boring. I kept messing up all my projects because I couldn't focus. Ever since I had finished the present I was supposed to give Sophia last semester, everything else came out like shit. The gift was still in my closet back at home, gathering dust. It made me sick to look at.

I was supposed to go in to make my first appointment with Baine this afternoon for Senior Theory, which was a useless class. It wasn't even really a class. It was basically a mentoring session, where you went on your free time and talked to your House Head about what your career was going to be after graduation.

Not that I wanted to speak with him one-on-one. I sat in the back of the class in Master Toaqua Magic and avoided him as much as possible. But there was no avoiding it. I'd been ignoring him all summer, and now it was time to pay the piper.

I checked the classroom number on my schedule to see what room Senior Theory was in. I passed the Commons and turned down a familiar hallway. When I finally reached it, I double checked the number to make sure it was right.

It was the same room Sophia and I had broken up in. Figures Senior Theory would be held in there.

Fuck that classroom. I wasn't going in there. I turned on my heel and headed the other way.

I saw Jonah in the hallway. He waved me down, and I walked over.

"Hey, bro, first soccer game of the season is on Saturday," he said. "The girls are gonna be there. We're having a pre-game summer party on the beach at noon. You coming?"

Jonah had made the tryouts for Yapluma's Elementai soccer team. I wasn't very interested in going— I'd lost interest in everything lately— but Jonah was my best friend, and I knew that he wanted me there. I needed to support him. "Sure, I'll go."

"The party, too?" His eyes were pleading.

I sighed. "Yeah, party too." Sophia would be there, but I'd promised her we'd be friends again, didn't I?

"Great!" He clapped me on the back. "Glad to see you're returning to the land of the living."

Hardly.

Hawkei Home Ec was held in the highest tower at the school, and Orenda Academy didn't believe in elevators. So much for being disability accessible. I went in early, because I knew it would take forever for me to climb those fucking stairs, and just as long to recover. I got to my desk a half-an-hour before class started and buried my head in my arms on top of my desk, trying to catch my breath.

Esis could heal me, but he damn sure couldn't fix everything.

As time passed, the usual people came trickled in, followed by Professor Brown and his anteater Familiar. Then someone caught my eye. I recognized the spray tan, fake nails and designer purse without having to guess. Her canine Familiar, Taryn, followed dutifully by her side.

Wait a sec. *Mia* was in this class? Shit, she must've just transferred in. She took a seat at the front, and I kept my head down, hoping she wouldn't see me.

Didn't work. Mia noticed I was sitting in the back of the class. Instead of looking disgusted, though, like she usually did when she laid eyes on me, her eyes lit up and a broad grin spread across her face. She actually seemed... hopeful. What the fuck?

Professor Brown tapped the board, and Mia turned back around. "Pay attention, everyone. Today, we're going to be learning how to make Elementai-and-Familiar-safe brownies. These brownies are non-allergenic and are meant for treats, and have the ability to change the color of your Familiar. The effects last a few hours or so, though there's not a similar effect on Elementai."

He gave a brownie to his anteater to demonstrate. The anteater lapped it up before its gray fur changed into a bright, blazing orange.

I ignored everyone else and got cooking. The smell of chocolate soon filled the room, and all the girls were gushing about how great it smelled. Mia kept on making glances at me as she worked on her brownies, but I made sure my eyes stayed down.

The sound of hacking filled the room. Someone had got the recipe wrong and had fed it to their Familiar, who was now throwing up.

Professor Brown was making a ticking noise. "There now, Mr. Williams, if you can't make a simple brownie, how are you going to handle the Family Life Unit?"

Aw, fuck. If we had to take care of a plastic baby for a week, I was gonna lose my shit.

I got my brownies done early, but didn't have a Familiar to feed them to, so I put them into a plastic bag and stuffed them in my backpack before deciding to get started on a essay for Master Toaqua Magic. Now that Sophia was no longer around to do it for me, I had to write my own papers. Sucked.

I'd barely gotten started when a shadow fell over me. I knew it was Mia without having to look up. I smelled her perfume.

"Hey, Liam?" She fidgeted where she stood. "Can I talk to you?"

Had I landed on an alien planet or something? "Um... sure."

Mia took the seat next to me. I tried to summon some sort of disdain for my ex, the girl who I'd lost my virginity to, but I just couldn't do it. Mia had broken my heart, but Sophia had completely obliterated it. After everything that had gone down with the love of my life, Mia was an afterthought.

I could tell by the way she was looking at me she wanted something. "What is it?" I asked.

She knew I didn't want to fuck around. "It's about this." Mia unwrapped a thin scarf from around her neck. My eyes grew wide as they traveled across her neck and shoulders. Long and dark marks were there, like someone had put their hands on her to try and choke her or something. She'd tried to cover them up with makeup, but they still looked bad.

"Holy hell, Mia. Who did that to you?" I asked in a low tone. Disbelief spread throughout my form.

"It's Micah," she started as she wrapped the scarf back around her neck. "He's been hitting me for a while now."

She said it like it was everyday news. But this was anything but. My blood ran cold as rage spread throughout my form. I couldn't stand cowards who hit girls.

"That's not right, Mia. He's a total piece of shit," I spat out. It was all

I could say, because if she heard what was *really* going through my head, she'd think I was plotting murder.

Mia shrugged. "I can handle it. But today, he hurt Taryn." Mia put a hand on her Familiar's head.

Taryn held up her right paw. I realized that she'd been limping as she came in, though it was so slight it hadn't registered in my brain at first. My hands balled into fists.

"Do you want me to take care of him?" I asked in a low tone, and I cracked my knuckles. I knew Micah was shit at fighting— probably why he hit girls. Me, Jonah and Ezra could have some fun with him. Show him how much he felt like a man while he was eating dirt.

"No, no, please don't do that. Don't talk to him or anything. It'll just make it worse." Mia grabbed my arm and shook it, almost begging. "I don't want you to hurt him. I still love him. I just want him to change."

"Abusers don't change, Mia. You need to leave." Especially not Micah. That dude had been worthless from the beginning. Even as a kid he was a dickhead.

"I can't leave. We're meant to be together, I just know it." She shook her head. "I just need help on getting through to him, before the wedding."

"You still want to marry him?" I asked in shock.

"Yes. But not like this. Please, Liam. I need your help." Her brown eyes shone with tears.

Mia had played me so much over the years, but this time, I could tell she was being genuine. She did love Micah... whatever the reason... and she didn't want to end things with him even though he was beating her.

"Why come to me?" I asked. "We didn't exactly... end things on good terms." That was putting it lightly.

"Because you're safe. My friends don't believe me. I can't go to my parents. They'd freak out." She took a breath. "I don't know how to make it stop."

Taryn dropped her head and whimpered. Her ears were flat back against her head. I could tell that Taryn didn't think that Mia staying with Micah was a good decision. But Mia seemed determined to remain with him.

"Mia, this is really serious. He could kill you," I said, trying to talk some sense into her.

"He would never really hurt me. I deserve it most of the time," Mia insisted.

"No, you don't." I had to remind myself to count to ten and not blow my top. I didn't want to see Mia get hurt.

"Don't tell me to leave him, Liam. Please don't," Mia begged. "I just need someone to be there for me right now. Can you do that?"

This was a tough situation. The only way Micah would stop hurting her is if Mia took herself out of the relationship entirely. It would be dangerous, yeah, because Micah's family had a lot of power. But Mia's dad was powerful enough to protect her, and if she asked my family for help, my dad would offer his support, too. No one would go against the Water chief. She'd be safe.

But Mia didn't want to leave. She still wanted to marry the bastard, a concept I couldn't wrap my head around.

Yet for all the shit she'd done to me, I couldn't abandon her. "I'll help in any way I can," I said.

Mia smiled, and threw her arms around me. "Thanks, Liam. I knew you'd understand."

I hugged her back, though the gesture was stiff and distant. Class ended, and as if we'd never had the conversation at all, Mia left with Taryn on her heels, appearing cheerier than she had been when she'd arrived.

I was conflicted. I knew this wasn't really my business, and I needed to stay out of it. Mia was my ex. I had no obligation to her.

But at the same time, nobody deserved to get beat up, and she had asked for my help. I couldn't just abandon her after she'd reached out.

I didn't know how I could help Mia. But I at least wanted to try.

I was anxious about going to the beach party on Saturday. It would be the first time since last semester where we all hung out as a group, and not over anything serious.

But I'd made too many promises, and so on Saturday I headed down to the beach with my surfboard. As I left, I saw a large peacock sitting on a statue of a mermaid outside the Toaqua dorms. He had a note in his beak, and he cooed as I came near.

"Hello, Baxtor." I took the note from him and opened it, dreading what I'd find inside.

It was from Professor Perot, and it was unusually curt and short. He wanted to see me at the end of the month for another appointment. Baxtor fixed a suspicious eye on me before he fluttered his wings and flew off.

Perot was basically my doctor. I couldn't keep hiding things from him. Three months had gone by, and I was out of excuses as to why my health was getting better. He'd stopped all treatment as an experiment, and I'd only continued to improve. The man was about to pull his hair out.

He definitely knew something was up, but Esis' powers weren't my secret to tell. If I was going to tell Perot about him, I'd have to get Sophia's permission first.

At the same time, this was a big deal. I felt we could trust Perot, but still, if what Carter had said last semester was true, a war could begin at any time. And I wasn't sure which side Perot would be on. We'd be taking a big risk trusting him with Esis.

I'd leave the final decision up to Sophia. I hadn't seen her in a few days. The last time we'd locked eyes, I'd been talking to a Toaqua girl named Marcee a couple of days ago in the hall. She had a teacup pig Familiar named Daisy that had tiny feathered wings. Marcee wanted to know if my sister was interested in joining some sort of club for Toaqua girls. She didn't ask Maddie herself, because she said Maddie seemed so shy. I'd played along and told her I'd get my sister involved. I smiled and pretended to be friendly, just so she got out of my hair.

But Sophia had seen me talking to her, and she'd looked really upset. She ran off in the other direction with Imogen.

What, I couldn't talk to other girls now because we'd broken up? She needed to get over it. I didn't care that she talked to other guys...

The memory of her talking to a Koigni guy at lunch the other day surfaced, and a jealous rage surfaced in my chest. I think his name was Ben. She'd laughed at something he'd said. I wanted to punch him, because that was *me* who was supposed to make her laugh like that.

Yeah. I was a bad liar.

When I got to the beach, the party was already in full swing. Cade was barbecuing on the grill while his *alebrije* Familiar Arabelle rested at his feet. Ezra and Bren were playing frisbee with Dyami, and Bren's chimera. Vanessa was on a beach towel underneath an umbrella, chatting with Imogen and Jonah. Her Familiar, Aisha, sunbathed nearby. Squeaks and Sassy were by a stereo set up on a picnic table, dancing to rock music. Renar wasn't there, thank the ancestors.

My eyes fell on Sophia. It took every bit of self-control I had to not fall over.

Sophia's hair was curled, and she was wearing more makeup than I'd ever seen her put on. She was wearing a crop top that displayed her stomach and short shorts that, if she bent over, would show off her ass.

She looked amazing. And so not like herself. She'd told me last semester she'd rather be caught dead than wearing a crop top. They weren't her thing, she'd said. Apparently, now they were?

She was standing ankle-deep in the water and playing with Esis. I walked to the picnic table and dropped my bag on one of the benches. I'd brought it along to sneak beers to the beach, at Jonah's request. I stuck my surfboard in the sand with more force than needed.

Esis saw me and ran full-speed to the picnic table. He shoved my hand aside greedily so he could rifle through the bag. I unpacked the beer and put it in the cooler as Esis dove in to search.

Sophia noticed me. She walked over with intention, like what she had to discuss was serious. I practically read her mind as she came over.

"I need to talk to the three of you," Sophia said as she reached us. She shook Jonah and Imogen on the shoulder before looking at me. She dropped her voice as she said, "It's about the prophecy."

I suppressed a groan. This was supposed to be a party. We couldn't have *one day* without dealing with prophecy shit? That's all we ever talked about anymore.

Imogen nodded. She stood up and brushed sand off her clothes. "Baby, we're gonna go for a walk," she said to Cade. "We'll be right back."

"Okay, but hurry up," Cade said. "Food's almost done."

The four of us walked down the length of the beach, far enough away that we could still see the others but we wouldn't be overheard. Jonah was tightening his man-bun.

"Hurry up, babe," he said to Sophia as he fixed his hair. "I've got a game to win tonight. I can't be thinking about heavy stuff when we're going against Koigni."

"It's nothing that serious," Sophia said. "Just about this."

She took off the totem from around her neck and handed it to Imogen. "Liam and I found this during the tournament, when we were in the cave. You guys have seen me wearing it every day. It's—"

"A Spirit Totem." Imogen closed her eyes and shook her head as she passed it to Jonah. "I suspected, but never asked."

Jonah observed the tiny totem in his giant hand. "This puny thing? Doesn't look like much."

"But it is." Sophia took the totem back and put it around her neck again. "It amplifies my powers. Makes me stronger."

I said nothing as she blew one of the last secrets we had out of the water. She wanted to tell the others about the totem without consulting me first? It was supposed to be *our* thing.

There's no more our *anything*, I reminded myself, and I knew I was right. This was Sophia's secret to tell. It was her totem.

"You're a Spirit Warrior," Imogen said. Her tone was blunt and flat. "They're the only ones who can use these totems."

Sophia nodded. "Yes. Liam and I wanted to keep it secret from you guys, to keep you safe. But we're all in the line of fire now. It's best to know everything."

"Is there anything else?" Jonah crossed his arms. He wasn't happy about being left in the dark. Imogen neither.

"I think there's something about a weapon... the *Azaimperiai?* Liam can probably tell you more." Sophia looked at me. Jonah and Imogen turned to watch me with flat gazes.

"I don't know much about it myself," I confessed. "All I know is that it's a weapon that can control the ancestors and destroy the entire tribe. Baine told me about it."

"Oh, that's helpful," Jonah scoffed. "How many secrets do you guys have? I feel like I find out a new one every day."

"Don't act like you two aren't hiding something, too," I pointed out.

Imogen and Jonah exchanged guilty looks. Ha. Caught you. I *knew* Jonah and Imogen were keeping something from Sophia and I, but I didn't think it that critical, so I didn't bother to investigate to find out what it was. Secrets had wrecked my life already. Ignorance was bliss.

"You can't keep doing this to us, Sophia. We need to know what's going on at all times. We're too deep in this now," Imogen insisted. "Is there anything else we should know? More secrets?"

"That should be the last of them," Sophia said, with a wayward glance at me. "I thought everybody should know about the totem and the weapon before we proceed further with the prophecy."

Imogen seemed puzzled. "I've never heard of the *Azaimperiai*. Are you sure it really exists?"

I shrugged. "We don't know. But Baine was pretty sure it did. He was all over me to find it last semester."

"Well, anyway, can we *please* get back to having fun?" Jonah whined, his tone obviously annoyed. "This is kind of my day, and all this negative stuff is ruining it."

Sophia's face dropped. "Okay."

Jonah and Imogen kept to themselves on the walk back, talking in low tones. It was obvious they were irritated we'd never said anything about the totem until now.

Sophia and I remained silent. She kept her eyes on the ground, and mine fixated on the sea.

I was starting to wonder if we were heading in the wrong direction with this hidden weapon. If Imogen didn't know anything about the *Azaimperiai*, it really could be a myth. That girl believed in some wacky things. If even she was doubtful about its existence...

When we came back to the party, Esis was eating the brownies I'd made yesterday in Hawkei Home Ec. He devoured one, and his white fur morphed to bright blue. He scarfed down another, and his fur changed to pink. With every brownie he ate, he changed a different color.

Squeaks and Sassy smelled something. They stopped dancing and came over to sniff the brownies. Like a king guarding his horde, Esis hissed at Sassy and Squeaks, puffing his tail up and lowering his horns.

"Esis, play nice," Sophia scolded. "We need to share."

The Familiars fought over the brownies for a moment before Esis decided to divide them equally. Squeaks wasn't satisfied until she'd eaten a brownie that had turned her purple. Obviously it was for today's game. Esis and Sassy caught on to the idea and ate until Esis was a bright red and Sassy a muted green.

"Food's done," Cade said, and he started putting hot dogs and burgers out on the table. When Imogen passed by, he reached out and grabbed her by the waist, pulling her to his side.

"*Hola, chica,*" he said, and he gave her a quick kiss. She giggled and slapped his chest. She tried to pull away, but he refused to let her go. They fell in the sand together, laughing. Arabelle purred as she wove around the two of them.

Imogen and Cade made a really great couple. I was happy for them.

Ezra was piling food on top of his plate. Bren went to hand Vanessa some food, but she shook her head. "Not right now, hun. I'm not feeling very well." Aisha happily ate a burger for her.

Long after the rest of us were done eating, Ezra was still packing it in. The only one who ate more than him was Jonah. I was glad Cade had made extra, because whatever Ezra didn't take, Dyami ate.

"Wow, Ezra, you sure are good at putting those in your mouth," Sophia teased as Ezra scarfed down his fourth hot dog.

"I've had a lot of practice," Ezra said, and Jonah and I died laughing. Ezra took on a panicked look. "Not in *that* way!"

Sophia snickered before she looked at me. She caught sight of my surfboard in the sand a few feet away. "You know, you *did* promise to take me surfing last semester."

"Uh... I could teach you now, if you like," I said. Where was this coming from?

"Let's get in the water, then." Sophia pulled her crop top off and slipped out of her shorts. My jaw hit the ground.

She was wearing a bright red bikini that made the crop top and shorts look like a nun's outfit. The bikini top was a push-up, basically tiny triangles that barely covered her breasts. The bikini bottom, however, was practically a thong. It showed off her ass and only concealed what was absolutely necessary to avoid a public indecency charge.

If I didn't have a hard-on before, I did now.

"Damn, girl. You look *sexy,*" Jonah sang.

Sophia smiled. "Thank you."

I caught Ezra sneaking a glance. A steely glare from me made him turn around.

That bikini left fucking nothing to the imagination. First the shorts, now this. Was she *trying* to get under my skin?

Imogen kept sending me sheepish looks. I'll bet anything she had something to do with this. Damn it all if it was working.

Sophia waded into the ocean. I took off my shirt, threw it to the sand, and went to grab my surfboard.

"You were dumb for letting that one get away," Ezra said around a full mouth.

"Shut up." My cheeks were burning. I yanked my surfboard out of the sand and joined Sophia in the water.

Her eyes wandered over my abs as I came near. Yeah. Two can play at that game, honey.

We waded out farther, until our hips were submerged. "By the way, Soph..." I was nervous to ask this, but I needed to. "Perot's getting suspicious. I have an appointment at the end of the month with him, and I can't keep making excuses as to why I'm better. I think we need to tell him what's going on with Esis."

She hesitated. "Do you think it's safe?"

"I can't make any promises." I shook my head. "But I trust him. I don't think he'll tell anyone. He still thinks he owes us for saving his life, after we pulled him out of that tar pit."

Sophia nodded. "I trust him, too. All right. At your next appointment, we'll tell him together."

I felt relieved that she'd agreed so quickly and I didn't have to fight her on it. I tapped on the surfboard. "Anyway, you want to learn how to ride this thing?"

A couple of nice waves came in. I rode them as a demonstration, then gave her instructions. She still seemed mystified. It was like water was a foreign concept to her.

I tried something different. "Here. The only way you're going to learn is experience."

I put my hands on her hips to lift her up onto the surfboard. My hands fell on the bikini ties around her hips. She let me lift her up, as if it was no big deal we were touching.

My mind lost it as she flattened herself onto the board. I wanted to rip that bikini off of her and fuck her right here in the ocean. Didn't care if the rest of them were watching. *Don't look at her ass, DON'T look at her ass!*

She looked at me expectantly, and, I said, "Paddle to get some speed as the wave kicks up, then try to stand. Spring up, and to keep your balance." There was a lot more to it, but the basics were all my head could come up with right now. My brain was too preoccupied with how she looked.

Sophia paddled out to meet the first wave. She tried to stand, but tumbled off quickly. She attempted three more times, falling off each time before she ever got to her feet.

It became really clear really quickly that either I was a shitty teacher, or Sophia couldn't surf. She kept falling off, not to mention she was a bad swimmer. She had no balance.

I decided to make it easy on her. I kept most of my body submerged and controlled the waves around her board so she managed to stay standing. Her expression became delighted. It was obvious she believed she was actually doing it. I was satisfied with my work when a really big wave came her way, and I heard her laugh as I helped her to stay on top of it.

One time, a sea serpent came out of the waves next to her and swam at her side while she skimmed the water beside it. Her face lit up and got that magical quality to it that I loved.

That was one of the best parts about Sophia. She still saw the wonder in everything.

She was radiant when she hopped off the board. She guided it over to me, nearly glowing with pride. "I didn't know I'd be so good at surfing. I figured I would suck."

"Naw. You're a natural," I said. I dared to sling my arm around her shoulders as we walked toward the beach. That's what friends did, right?

She poked me in the ribs. "Well, you're always a good teacher."

"Don't poke me. I'll poke you right back." I tickled her sides. She cringed away and giggled, before she tackled me and we fell into the shallow water.

We were still laughing when we hit the sand. She was on top of me, and we kept teasing and messing around... like nothing ever happened.

We caught each other's eyes, and the smiles fell from our faces slowly. We had the same realization at the same time. We needed to stop. We were acting like a couple.

"Um... we should get going," Sophia said, and she rolled off of me. "The game's gonna start soon."

I nodded. "Right." I got to my feet, and stuck out a hand to help her up. She took it, but it was reluctantly this time.

Jonah and Squeaks had already left to get ready for the soccer game. Vanessa and Bren had apparently taken off early, too. I'd heard them talking about how they wanted to get good seats.

Ezra and Dyami swayed back and forth a little drunkenly. Apparently, they'd cleaned out the cooler.

"Hurry up. We've been waiting for you two forever," Ezra slurred as we came onto the beach. Dyami made a whistling noise.

"Yeah, yeah." I waved my hand and used my magic to dry Sophia and I off. She slipped her clothes back on over her swimsuit, and we avoided looking at each other.

Cade was talking to Imogen near the cooler. "Rumor is that Madame Laurel's Familiar is sick. She collapsed a couple of days ago and hasn't been able to get up since," Cade said. "The healers don't have any idea what's wrong with her."

That caught my interest. Madame Laurel was on the Nivita Council. Her Familiar was a centicore, an antelope-type creature with scales and moth wings. She'd gotten sick? That was unusual.

Imogen narrowed her eyebrows. "Familiars are usually hardy creatures. It's difficult to make them ill. Doesn't anyone have any idea what could be wrong with her?"

Cade shook his head. "No one knows."

He checked his watch. "Hey guys, we gotta go," he announced to the group. "Game's starting in less than an hour."

It had gotten a little chilly out, but everyone had brought extra clothes to change into. Imogen and Cade wore shirts that both said *Nivita*. Sassy and Arabelle were wearing matching green scarves. Ezra was wearing a douchey *Toaqua* tank top and had used blue dye and hair gel to form a mohawk on top of his and Dyami's heads. He had packed an extra Water t-shirt "just in case I forgot mine." I wasn't a team player and had "forgotten" on purpose, but Ezra knew me too well and harassed me until I put it on.

"Everyone told me to wear my House colors," Sophia said as she slipped a *Koigni* sweater over her cut-off tee. "Though I don't know why. Aren't Yapluma and Koigni the only ones playing?"

"Elementai soccer is different. It's played with four teams at once, not two," I explained. "All four Houses will be playing at the same time. That day we played last semester, we didn't have enough people for four teams. Any team can go for any House goal."

"Oh, I see." She nodded. A red-furred Esis hopped into her arms and bared his teeth, waving a tiny flag that had the Koigni House symbol on it. He was ready, apparently.

The game was held in the same arena the Elemental Cup began in every year. We took a carriage to the arena, which was bursting with thousands of Elementai and Familiars alike. It was hard to get around all the dragons, griffins, and monstrous Familiars that were crowding the arena. Every seat seemed to be sold out.

My heart fell as I looked at the ticket booth. Aw, shit. Marcee was selling tickets. Sophia noticed and took on a steely look. As we approached the booth, Marcee gave me a broad smile.

"It's so nice to see you again, Liam. How many today?" Marcee asked me. Daisy, her flying teacup pig, oinked happily.

"Um... five," I said. I paid for them as soon as possible. Sophia was currently making devil-eyes at Marcee and made no effort at all to hide it.

Marcee printed off the tickets and went to hand them to me. "Here you go."

Sophia's hand snapped out and tore the tickets out of Marcee's fingers before I could take them. "Thanks."

She turned around so quickly that her hair fanned out around her head, and the rest of us had to practically run to follow. Sophia was squeezing Esis so tight that his little tongue popped out.

I hurried to catch up. "Soph, we all need tickets to get in, you know."

"She seems nice," Sophia said in a sour way, ignoring my statement. "You know her?"

"Not really," I admitted. "She wanted me to talk to my sister about some club or something."

Sophia looked pleased when I said that. She stopped walking like her ass was on fire and handed the tickets out to the rest of us.

"Should we split up?" Imogen said, with a nervous glance at me. Cade looked similarly conflicted. I knew what they were asking, and I wasn't sure. The stands were segregated in a way that each of the four Houses had their own section. We were all supposed to be sitting with our corresponding Houses, but none of us wanted to separate.

Sophia was the one who answered for us. "Screw them. We can sit where we want. Let's go to the Yapluma section. Jonah will see us there."

None of us were Yapluma, but it seemed like a good plan. We got snacks and headed up to the Yapluma stands, taking seats in the middle. A lot of Yaplumas gave us weird looks as we passed by, like it was obvious we weren't supposed to be there. It was pretty uncomfortable, to be honest.

But Sophia was determined to sit there, and me and my friends were never very good at following rules, so we found an empty section and piled into it. The seats had long aisles and were wide, to make room for people's Familiars. Other Yapluma who passed by avoided sitting next to us, like we had the plague or something. We basically had a whole section to ourselves.

Sophia seemed bummed as we waited for the game to start. "What's wrong?" I asked her, hoping it had nothing to do with Marcee.

She played with Esis' ears as he ate a plate of nachos on her lap. "Jonah doesn't seem very interested in helping us figure out the prophecy. He acted mad earlier that I brought it up," Sophia said. Her tone was glum.

I leaned in to speak low. "He and Renar are having problems," I said. "He's been having a hard time dealing with it."

"He shouldn't take it out on me." She frowned.

"No," I agreed, "but he's going through a lot. His parents had a huge meltdown when they found out he got chosen for the soccer team. I think he found out that Renar's been cheating, too, but he doesn't wanna admit it. With that and the prophecy stuff... I just don't think he can handle it all."

"I didn't realize." She looked out at the field. "I'm glad we're here for him today, then."

I sat back. "Me too."

Sophia changed the subject to a more pleasant topic, thank the ancestors. "So, who do you think will win today?"

"It's usually a toss-up between Koigni and Yapluma," I told her. "Koigni has the record for the most championships, but if Yapluma wins the season this year, they'll be tied."

"What about Toaqua?"

I shrugged. "Toaqua does okay. We win sometimes."

"Toaqua forever!" Ezra shouted, and he raised his beer. It sloshed all over him, and I shook my head.

"Who's the worst?" Sophia asked.

"Nivita. Nivita always loses," Imogen said glumly, overhearing us. "Most of us suck at sports."

"We make up for it in brains," Cade said, and he tapped the side of his head. "Not all of us are meant to be dumb jocks."

"Hey! I take offense to that!" Ezra shouted, and Dyami squawked.

"Ezra, you're not Yapluma or Koigni," I reminded him.

A pleasant smile spread across his face. "Oh, yeah. Right."

"I think you're done." I reached across Cade and Imogen and took Ezra's beer away from him. He had a sad face, but too bad. He wasn't a freshman anymore. It was time he learned his limit.

A few minutes before the game started, whispers from behind us turned to loud-mouthed taunts. Some Yapluma was carrying on about it being "bad for Houses to mix" and people "keeping to their own" rather loudly.

It was obvious he was talking about us. He'd been going on for the past ten minutes. Sophia's mouth got thinner and thinner with every word. I was waiting for her to go off like a cannon any moment.

When his complaining failed to get our attention, the guy stood up. "Are these kids deaf? Don't they know they should keep to their own kind? This is *our* territory!"

"Dude, stop bothering them. They're Cup Champions," his buddy said, obviously embarrassed. He kept seated, though he looked mortified.

"I don't care if they're Elders! This section is for Yapluma only!" The guy was clearly drunk. He was older than us by at least ten years and was the type to brag that high school had been the best time of his life.

Sophia sprang out of her seat, handed Esis to me like she was looking for a fight, and faced the guy. "If you want us to leave, you're going to have to *make* us."

"You're probably one of those interhouse lunatics!" the guy said. "I won't sit next to a bunch of depraved weirdos!"

Sophia grabbed her drink and chucked it. It hit the Yapluma guy in the chest and went splattering all over him, soaking his front. He screamed in alarm. Cade, Imogen and Ezra watched the scene with open mouths.

"Sophia!" I shouted, shocked.

"You wanna get hit with a fireball next? Keep pushing your luck!" Sophia screamed.

"Crazy bitch!" the Yapluma guy yelled, but it worked. He left the stands in a hurry, with terrified glances back at Sophia. His buddy sank low in his seat and remained quiet.

Sophia plopped back down. Smoke was rising from her seat, making it smell like something was cooking,

"What's the matter with you? You can't just go around throwing things at people," I hissed at her.

"I'd had enough of that asshole!" Sophia erupted. "At least I *did* something about it! I didn't just sit there and avoid confrontation."

She was really pushing my buttons. "Would you chill out? You're catching the seat on fire."

Sophia's form simmered, until eventually the smoking stopped.

Cade leaned over. "Fun fact, the Koigni stands are fire-proof, so Koigni can't burn the arena down when matches get heated," he said.

That would've been a hell of a lot nicer to know before we sat down, Cade. But it was too late now. The game was starting. There was the sound of trumpets, and the lights in the stands went out as the field illuminated.

"Good evening, Kinpago!" an announcer's voice rang out, and the arena went wild. I recognized the voice of Eli, the announcer for the Elemental Cup. "Are we ready to play some college soccer?"

The entire arena shook as twenty-thousand Elementai and magical creatures roared intensely. Players flooded onto the field, wearing uniforms that sported numbers in each player's House. Magical creatures of all kinds ran onto the field behind the players, some taking to the sky with Elementai on their backs. They flew around the arena, performing tricks to show off.

The field was set up in a square fashion, a goal on each corner, with colored lines indicating which goal belonged to what house. But besides being on the ground, there were goalposts in the sky, too, square ones that winged creatures flew around to protect. If the ball passed through either of the goals, it counted as a point.

Eli introduced the teams as they flooded onto the field. Toaqua had a mediocre lineup compared to last year, because they'd lost all their senior star players and had to rebuild after graduation.

Nivita hardly got any cheers. Their fans were probably too busy hanging at the library to show up. Their top scorer had died in the Elemental Cup last year, and they'd had a hard time replacing him.

The Koigni team looked mean. They had the biggest and best players, and there were so many Koigni fans in here that every time a player's name was announced the seats shook. By the time the announcer got to the Yapluma team, most of the fans were bored and screaming to get on with it.

"Last up, newcomer to the Yapluma team, and, important to note, a Champion of last year's Elemental Cup, Jonah Chanee and his Familiar, Squeaks!" Eli shouted.

There was polite applause at Jonah's name, save for the group of us misfits, who were screaming our heads off as he came into the spotlight.

Jonah looked terrified out there on the field. He stared up at the stands with a pale face and wide eyes. Next to him, Squeaks shivered as she started upward at a Koigni dragon who was four times her size.

His eyes searched the stands for us. A bit of color came back into his cheeks when he saw us cheering for him in the Yapluma stands.

"Give 'em hell, Jonah!" Imogen screamed. Cade had to grab her to prevent her from falling over onto the person in front of her.

The four teams lined up in a square to begin. The stadium quieted down in breathless anticipation as a referee riding a manticore launched the ball into the air. He scrambled to get out of the way and all the teams attacked.

"Let the game begin!" Eli announced. The ball sailed through the air, and the Koigni fans cheered as one of the Fire team's griffins launched itself forward and grabbed hold of the ball. Elements went shooting every-where as Elementai used their powers to try and knock the ball in the direction of a goal. The Koigni griffin sailed forward toward the Yapluma goal, but was knocked out of the air by a strong gust of wind. As the ball hit the ground, a cheetah ran forward and sank its teeth in, darting out of reach of the other Familiars. It went toward the Nivita goal, before a large section of earth rose up out of the ground to stop it and the cheetah went sliding back downward. A rock mare galloped toward the ball intensely, but it was taken away from her seconds later by a mini-tornado caused by the Yapluma team. Jonah and Squeaks ran among the athletes, trying to keep up but failing to amid the more experienced players.

Not that I blamed him. It was hard to keep up as a spectator. Watching Elemental soccer was like playing a sport in itself. There was so much going on and so much chaos that you really had to pay attention to see what was going on. No player could retain the ball for more than a few seconds.

A flame ricocheted out of nowhere and pushed the soccer ball toward a dragon that was waiting on the ground. The dragon rushed forward to grab it, but a Toaqua riding a large eagle came in, and the eagle snatched the ball with its talons. The eagle soared upward toward the goal in the sky, did a loop and flung it out of his talons. The Toaqua player launched itself off of his Familiar and into the air to send a gushing stream of water at the ball so it would be rocketed into the Koigni goal.

But he wasn't looking where he was going, and Koigni was out for blood. The Fire dragon had followed them up into the air and launched itself at the Toaqua player. The crowd moaned as he crashed into the dragon.

"Ooh! That's gonna leave a mark in the morning, folks," Eli said.

The Toaqua player went careening toward the ground. He was bleeding from the impact. His Familiar dove down to try and save him, but he was too slow, and the player hit the ground in a sickening way.

The refs called a time out, and healers with stretchers came to carry the player off the field. His Familiar followed with a low head.

That was brutal. That player wasn't going to be walking for weeks.

The refs started up the game shortly after. One of the Yapluma players got the ball within seconds and had his alicorn Familiar launch it into a Koigni net before anyone knew what happened.

Koigni didn't like that. It was obviously payback time. They had their Familiars play rough and stampede whatever House was in their way. Jonah got too close and ended up getting slashed across the face by accident as a rhinoceros charged at him. He had to leap out of the way, and a wyvern with sharp claws accidentally hit him with its tail as it was aiming for the ball.

Jonah went down. Imogen gasped, and Sophia slapped a hand over her mouth in shock.

The game was paused. Jonah lay there for a moment, and the Yapluma coach ran onto the field.

Slowly, Jonah sat up, holding his head. Squeaks kneeled next to him, and he used her to get off the ground. He looked winded. The referee came over and asked him something, but Jonah shook his head, and the game started up again.

The game continued, but even though he was hurt, Jonah didn't stop playing. There was blood streaked across his face, but he didn't care. He kept at it, wiping the blood out of his eyes every so often and keeping his eye on the ball.

I knew why he was playing so hard. He had to prove to his parents that he belonged here. If he didn't score a goal, that proved that they were right and that he didn't deserve a spot on the team, so he had to show them that he was worthy of this. The notion was fucked up, but I knew that was exactly what was running through his head right now. He loved sports and wanted everyone to know he wanted to be here more than anything.

The match continued. Koigni scored four more points, while Toaqua got two and Nivita a measly one. Yapluma had to struggle to catch up, but once they did, it was like they were unstoppable. Jonah and Squeaks helped assist a goal, then blocked the other teams as the main scorers landed three in a row, all in the Koigni net.

Soon, it was down to the wire. There were only a few minutes left, and Koigni and Yapluma were tied. Toaqua had fallen behind, and Nivita had ceased to put any more points on the board. It was clearly a match between the two contenders.

Jonah was on Squeaks' back, flying up in the air around the Yapluma sky goal. He was using his magic to block the stream of Koigni shots, which were relentless. One time, Squeaks raised her wing to stop a goal, and she'd staggered while throwing it back. The hit had obviously hurt her, through determination kept her aloft.

Seconds left. The Yapluma were losing strength and having trouble keeping up. The Koigni fans roared, sensing a victory. The Fire dragon sent a shot hurtling toward the Yapluma goal on the ground.

Then something happened. A peryton from Yapluma intercepted and sent the ball sailing toward her Elementai, who sent it rocketing upward with her Air magic.

It was like ping-pong. Yapluma quickly sent the ball back and forth to each other as they worked its way up, playing keep-away with the Koigni. The Koigni players went to follow, but the Fire team was blocked by members of both Water and Earth. I was momentarily shocked. Toaqua and Nivita had no stake in this, yet they wanted to help Yapluma beat Koigni.

Jonah was the one closest to the net. The alicorn tossed the ball his way. Squeaks swung around and kicked it toward the Koigni goal, and Jonah used his Air power to put force behind it so that the ball was little more than a blur.

It was going so fast that it tore the Koigni net in half.

The buzzer went off, signaling the end of the game, and the stadium erupted in cheers. Me and the rest of our group sprang out of our seats, screaming at the top of our lungs. He'd done it! He'd scored the winning goal!

"Looks like the rookie has become our next top competitor! Winner, Yapluma!" Eli announced over the cheers.

Jonah and Squeaks trailed downward. He jumped off Squeaks' back, and the Yapluma team picked him up on their shoulders and carried him out of the arena in celebration. It was kind of funny, seeing a big guy be carried around by all those little people. The Toaqua and Nivita teams clapped in solidarity, while it was obvious the Koigni team was surly about losing. One Koigni guy started shoving his teammate, and it turned into a fistfight the referees had to break up.

I was really proud of Jonah. He'd done an awesome job today. And he'd shown his stupid parents what was up.

"Afterparty in the Commons!" Ezra announced to the rest of us. "Who's with me?"

It was too good of a night to end without another celebration, so we all agreed to head back to Orenda. Ezra and Cade broke off from us to go pick up some things at the store for the celebration.

As we left the stands, my mind wandered. Toaqua and Nivita had teamed up to help Yapluma win the game. If a war broke out, would the same happen?

Before we could take a carriage back to the school, we saw Vanessa crying outside one of the double-doors to the stadium. She was sobbing in Bren's arms, who seemed bewildered. Aisha was crooning next to her, looking sad.

What was wrong? Was she that upset Koigni lost?

No, that was silly. Whatever it was seemed serious. I hoped everything was okay.

"Vanessa?" Sophia headed over and laid a hand on her shoulder. "What's wrong?"

Vanessa came out of Bren's arms and turned around. She wiped her face. "My great-aunt Gwendolyn passed away," Vanessa said. "I just found out."

"Vanessa, I'm so sorry." Sophia frowned and rubbed her back. "Were you two close?"

"Not really. It's complicated." Vanessa cleared her voice. "She was on the Koigni Council."

"Oh." Sophia tried to keep the disdain out of her voice, but I heard it loud and clear. I knew Sophia had renounced any loyalty to her House, and the Fire Elders had been the reason for it. "What happened?"

"Apparently her Familiar had been sick for a while. She just never told anyone. She didn't want to seem weak." Vanessa appeared down-hearted.

"That's terrible," Sophia said.

"Yeah." Vanessa sniffed. "She wasn't really a nice lady, but she was still my great aunt. She was the one who made it possible for me and Bren to get married. She paid for the wedding. She didn't tell anyone, though. She knew the council wouldn't approve, because they hate me. Not even her own sister."

"Wow." Sophia's eyebrows raised. "I didn't know that."

"Yeah." Vanessa wiped her eyes. "Even the worst of people still have something good in them, I suppose."

Vanessa gave a watery laugh. "I'm being ridiculous. I barely knew her. Don't mind me. I'm just really emotional about everything lately. Anyway, see you guys around."

Vanessa gave a wave as she left with Aisha and Bren. Imogen looked at Sophia. "Do you know anything about her aunt? This story is too similar to what's happening to Madame Laurel's Familiar. She's sick, too."

"Her Elder name is Madame Chavis. She was on the Koigni Council. Her familiar was a tarantula," Sophia said. Her expression seemed concerned. "Do you think Madame Laurel's Familiar and Madame Chavis' got the same thing?"

"It's possible," I commented. "Though that doesn't explain what happened to Isabella's Familiar. Her filly-fairy went missing yesterday."

"Isabella Laurel?" Imogen piped up. "I know her. She's related to Madame Laurel— her daughter, I think."

I'd forgotten Isabella's last name. The theory that this was personal became more certain. "Maybe someone's targeting the family."

Sophia shook her head. "That doesn't make sense. The Laurels have nothing in common with Madame Chavis."

"Not that we know of," Imogen said. "But it *is* strange. We should keep an eye out. In case anyone else gets sick or goes missing."

I agreed. It was strange. First Madame Laurel's Familiar had gotten sick with a mysterious illness. Now Madame Chavis and her Familiar were dead. Not to mention Isabella's Familiar had vanished a few days ago, and no one could locate her.

Something weird was going on at this school. And I had an uneasy feeling it was the start of something bad.

sophia

SIX

The soccer game was the most fun I'd had in months. A week later, I was still smiling at myself for tossing my drink at that jackass Yapluma. I'd told my grandparents about it at dinner that week when they asked what I'd been up to. Grandma agreed the guy deserved it. Gramps said to throw a fireball at his head next time. It only made me love my grandparents even more.

I entered through the main doors of the castle on my way back from Kinpago. Esis was purring, unable to move after scarfing down almost a full plate of nachos my grandparents had ordered for the table. He rubbed his belly and closed his eyes, like he was at peace in my arms.

In an instant, his ears perked up, and his eyes shot open. He looked to the other end of the grand entrance, down a hall behind the stairs. My eyes followed, and I stopped in my tracks.

Liam was hiding behind the staircase with Mia, throwing quick glances each way. The two spoke in hushed whispers, as if they were worried about getting caught speaking to each other.

My blood boiled seeing them together. It wasn't the first time this week, either. I'd seen them talking in the gardens on Tuesday, and near the alchemy labs on Thursday. I thought it was a little strange at first, considering Liam told me he hated the pompous bitch, but this was just getting ridiculous. What was he doing hanging out with her? Were they back together or something?

Psh. He never got anything from me anymore, so he had to run back to Mia to finally get some again. I mean, why wouldn't he? She was freaking perfect as hell. Had a lot more boobs that I did, too.

Images of Liam and Mia fucking assaulted my mind, and hot tears rose to my eyes. That should've been *me*! Esis squeaked in my arms, and I realized I'd been squeezing him so tightly he couldn't breathe. I loosened my grip, and he sucked in a deep breath. He looked up to me with questioning eyes.

"I have to get out of here," I blurted. I hurried toward the stairs before Liam saw me.

I didn't know what it was about seeing those two together, but it set off some sort of trigger inside of me. Liam had said he never loved Mia the way he loved me. He was a filthy liar! He probably only said it to get in my pants. I was glad we never went all the way.

I didn't know where I was headed until I found myself passing by the study area on the third floor next to the Nivita dorms. Imogen and Sassy rounded the corner, and I nearly rammed into them.

"Sophia!" Imogen looked me up and down, and her face fell. "What's wrong?"

"Nothing," I lied. It felt as if I was being strangled, my throat closed up so tightly.

Imogen raised an eyebrow. "You can't lie to me that easily."

I dropped my shoulders. "Isn't it obvious?"

She frowned. "Liam?"

I nodded. "I saw Liam and Mia together again. Mia and her stupid fake nails and fake boobs and fake *everything*. I'll bet she has a fake vagina, too. How much you wanna bet Liam's been fucking around with her?"

"Sophia, that's ridiculous. Mia's engaged."

"So? The parts still work regardless." I set Esis on the ground so I wouldn't squash him again, or worse, light his fur on fire. "If Liam's going to be messing around, maybe I should, too. Clearly, the bikini you leant me didn't work. I'm going to have to step up my game."

"Sophia—" Imogen sounded like she was about to argue, but her words stopped in her tracks as a lightbulb went off in her head. "You know what? You're right."

Imogen took me by the arm and started leading me toward her dorm. Sassy and Esis followed. "We're going to do it the *right* way this time."

 ❧

AN HOUR LATER, my hair was in light tousled waves around my shoulders, and my face was so caked with makeup that I barely recognized myself. Imogen had gone all out with smokey eyes and contouring. I looked like I belonged on a modeling runway.

"Wow, Im," I said, looking at myself in the mirror. Esis sat on the vanity, brushing out his fur. "I'm going to break some poor guy's heart tonight."

Imogen smiled. "That's the idea."

She turned from the closet and held up a tiny black dress. "Try this on. I bought it for you over the summer in case of an emergency. I think it's finally time to use it."

I took the dress from her and ran my fingers across the fabric. "Thanks. That was really thoughtful."

"I'll be right back." Imogen grabbed another dress from the closet, but I didn't catch a good look at it before she disappeared into the bathroom.

In the privacy of her bedroom, I stripped off my clothes and pulled the dress on. It was skin-tight and hugged all my curves. The spandex fabric pulled my boobs together and lifted them, showing off my cleavage. It was so short that I was afraid someone might see my panties if I bent over too far.

Screw it. Let 'em see it.

I turned to the mirror, and I nearly dropped dead at what I saw. In the mirror was a tall, sexy girl with legs that went for miles and boobs that were so perky they even kind of turned *me* on. No way was that me.

Esis whistled. Sassy was nowhere to be seen, since Imogen had sent her out with a note tied around her neck a while ago.

"Can I come out yet?" Imogen called through the door.

It took me a moment to process what she'd said. I could hardly take my eyes off myself. I was still so shocked.

"Yeah, come out," I replied.

Imogen stepped out of the bathroom wearing a short, skin-tight dress that was strapless on one arm and had a full-length sleeve on the other. She wore hot-pink heels to match, and her strawberry blonde hair fell in loose waves around her.

"Imogen, you look great!" I said.

Her eyebrows shot up. "Me? Look at you!"

I twirled to show off my new dress.

"You're going to be the hottest girl in the room tonight, and that's saying something. All you need is some heels. I have the perfect ones." Imogen pulled a pair of heels from the closet so tall I wasn't sure I could walk in them.

"Before we go, I want to make something clear," she said. "This isn't about getting some revenge sex on Liam. I just want you to have fun. But if something *were* to go that far, I want you to have protection."

Imogen handed me a small foil packet.

"Imogen!" I snickered. "Where'd you get this? Cade?"

"Girl, no!" she cried. "I mean, yeah, I keep a few around just in case, but you know we haven't made it that far yet."

I handed the condom back to her. "Here. You keep it. I'm on birth control, anyway."

Imogen's eyes nearly bulged out of her skull. "*What?*"

I shrugged and turned to the mirror to smooth down my dress. "You know, just in case. After Liam and I got so close last semester, I figured I should go on it, just in case I meet someone."

She giggled. "You won't have any problems meeting someone tonight, though I don't know if anyone will be dating material where we're going."

"Where *are* we going?" I asked.

Imogen smirked. "The strip club."

My face turned bright pink, but it hardly showed beneath the makeup. "Wow. Jonah would be so proud."

A knock came at the door.

"And here's our DD." Imogen opened the door to Cade, Sassy, and Arabelle. She threw her arms around Cade's neck and drew him into a kiss before he could say anything.

He caught sight of the condom between her fingers and drew away. "Whoa. I didn't realize this was *that* kind of a night."

"We're having a threesome. Didn't you get the memo?" I teased.

Cade wrapped an arm around Imogen's waist and pulled her close to him. "Sorry, but I've only got eyes for one girl."

The way he looked at her was exactly how Liam used to look at me. I wanted to fling a fireball between the two of them.

Instead, I made a puking sound and said, "Someone gag me now."

Imogen flung the condom back at me, but it fluttered through the air to land on the ground between us. "Use that."

I snatched it up from the ground and pretended to shove it in my mouth and gag on it. I fell onto the bed and stuck my tongue out like I was dead.

Imogen kicked me lightly and leaned over me to grab her purse. "You dweeb. Let's go."

I sat up and tucked the condom in my bra. "Will you hold my stuff for me?" I asked Imogen, handing her a wad of cash and my ID.

"They're not going to check your ID, you know," she said, taking it. "We don't really have age limits in Kinpago."

I shrugged. "Whatever. Let's go get ourselves shitfaced."

Twenty minutes later we were pulling up in a carriage to a place called *Lucky Stars*. The building looked pretty big from the outside, but it didn't have any windows. I grinned more than I probably should've. I felt like such a rebel.

"See you ladies in there," Cade said as Imogen and I stepped out with our Familiars. He led the unicorn and the carriage around the side of the building to park it.

"It's girls-only," Imogen said as we approached the door. "The strippers, I mean. I hope that's okay."

"Totally. Honestly, I think I'm more comfortable with that than with guys in thongs. Gotta ease into it slowly." I giggled.

Imogen wiggled her eyebrows.

I swatted at her. "Get your mind out of the gutter!"

"Too late," she giggled. "I'm stuck."

She opened the door, and we were assaulted with the loud sound of music pumping through the building. We passed by a bouncer who barely gave us a second glance, then headed down a long hallway with flashing blue lights everywhere.

On the other side, the music was even louder. There was a long bar to our left and the main stage in front of us. Two dancers swung around poles with nothing but thongs and high heels on, while four others leaned over the corner of the stage to take people's money. Familiars danced onstage beside their Elementai. I didn't think a magical creature could be sensual, but the way they danced added to the performance. One Familiar looked like a purple hummingbird that rained glitter down on its Elementai while she danced. Another was a rainbow-colored snake that wrapped around its Elementai's body like a scarf. There was even a white deer that danced beautifully alongside a girl with dark hair. The magical creatures added to the atmosphere and amazement.

People crowded around the stage with drinks in one hand and dollar bills in the other. The place was so crowded that most people stood and danced along to the music. There was a smaller stage to our right that was less crowded, and a few seating areas that looked like you had to reserve just to get a seat. Signs everywhere advertised private lap dances and warned against touching the dancers.

I took a step back, trying to take in all the flashing lights and naked bodies. Esis didn't seem to care about the crowd. He just bobbed his head to the music from where he sat perched on my shoulder.

This was sort of intense. I'd never done this before. Maybe this wasn't such a good idea.

Imogen took my hand so we wouldn't lose each other in the crowd. "It's fine. You have nothing to be scared of. Let's get you a drink."

She dragged me up to the bar. The stools were all taken, so we had to squeeze in at a corner to even get noticed. She shouted over the music to the bartender. "Four beers and two margaritas, please."

"Thirsty?" I teased.

"They're not all for me." She giggled.

The bartender set the four beers in front of us and started mixing our margaritas. Imogen placed a few bills on the counter and took two beers. She handed one to Esis, then bent to Sassy to help her to the bottle.

I noticed a guy at the bar lean back a bit to check out her ass. "Eyes off, perv!" I snapped at him. "She's taken."

He shot me a dirty look and turned back to his beer.

Imogen looked flustered when she stood. "Was that guy really checking me out?"

"Yeah," I said, disgusted.

Imogen blushed.

"Ew. Don't tell me you're flattered."

She shrugged. "Kind of. I mean, I'm standing next to *you*."

She gestured up and down my body, as if to point out how hot I looked.

"Hey, ladies!" Cade reached between the two of us to grab the last two beers on the counter. He took one for himself and shared the other with Arabelle. "Thanks for ordering for us."

"You want another one?" Imogen asked.

"Whoa. Don't rush me, babe," he said. "Someone has to drive home."

The bartender set down our margaritas and took the cash off the counter.

"Fancy," I said, raising the margarita to my lips. I took a sip, and the god-awful taste of burnt cardboard entered my mouth. I spit the drink back into my glass. "Oh, God. Is this supposed to be *good*? What is this?"

Imogen snickered. "It's a margarita, Sophia. If you don't like it, I'm sure one of us will finish it off for you."

Esis was already on it. He set his empty beer bottle on the counter and leaned down to start sipping out of my glass. I tipped it back for him, and it was gone in under a minute. Esis let out a loud belch.

"Okay, buddy. You're going to have to pace yourself," I scolded. "Slow down."

He frowned at me.

"What do you want, Sophia?" Imogen asked. "You can order anything."

"I don't really know drinks," I said. "Maybe wine?"

Imogen flagged down the bartender and asked for moscato. It was definitely better than the margarita, but it was still lacking something.

"Hey!" Imogen shouted at us. "That group by the stage is leaving! Let's go claim that spot."

Esis, Sassy, and Arabelle took off sprinting beneath people's feet. Arabelle was the largest of the three and ended up tripping a girl, who spilled her drink all over herself. She was so wasted that she thought it was hilarious. Our Familiars claimed the seats before anyone else could, and we quickly followed behind them.

"Score!" I giggled as I fell into the seat Esis had claimed. He hopped out of the way and settled on the armrest.

Imogen shoved a pile of one-dollar bills in my hand. "Go wild."

I whooped and waved my pile of cash at the closest girl. Esis saw what I was doing and grabbed a bill from me and waved it, whistling at the girl.

The girl was tall, with a flat stomach, blonde hair, and big boobs. She noticed Esis jumping up and down on the chair and came over to us. She knelt on her knees and leaned over so that her boobs were practically in my face. My eyes stayed glued to them the whole time as a fluttering sensation danced throughout my stomach. She smelled really good, like cherry blossom perfume.

"Hey," she said kindly, offering us a nice smile. "I'm Jasmine. First time at *Lucky Stars?*"

I blushed. "Yeah."

"Don't be so nervous," she said encouragingly.

I didn't realize the dancers would come up and talk to us. I thought it'd feel weird to talk to her since she was practically naked, but it felt strangely natural— like she was just a normal girl doing her job.

"Here," Jasmine said. "I'll show you how it's done."

She leaned over and gave Esis a peck on the end of the nose. He looked totally starstruck and handed her his dollar. She took it and tucked it in between my cleavage. I leaned back in my chair, intrigued by where this was going.

"Just relax," Jasmine said.

I was vaguely aware of Imogen and Cade watching me, but I was more focused on Jasmine. My heart pounded as she leaned down and pulled the dollar bill out of my cleavage with her teeth. My whole body gave a shiver.

"See?" Jasmine said. "Easy."

I smiled up at her. "Easy. Hey, is it cool if I tuck a dollar in your G-string?"

Jasmine pushed her hip out at me, and I slipped the dollar into her thong. I glanced to Imogen and snickered.

"Have a great night," Jasmine said as she moved on to claim the dollar Imogen had trapped between her teeth.

I watched as Jasmine pressed her boobs to Imogen's face and squeezed them together with her hands. She pulled away with Imogen's dollar bill between her breasts. Cade stared wide-eyed at Imogen, like he didn't believe she'd do it. He looked slightly impressed, though. Imogen was laughing so hard she could hardly breathe.

"Oh, my ancestors. I've never done that before." Imogen laughed, like it was hilarious. Imogen cocked her finger at Jasmine and whispered something in her ear.

"Sure," Jasmine said.

I watched curiously as Imogen placed a dollar bill behind Cade's ear. Cade laughed as Imogen leaned in to kiss him on one side of his face and Jasmine kissed the other. Esis clapped. Arabelle looked totally at ease.

"You three have a great night," Jasmine said with a sexy wave as she moved on to the next patrons.

The three of us turned to each other and burst into laughter.

"Ancestors, Imogen!" I said. "I didn't know you were into girls."

"I'm not. It's just for fun." She laughed. "Besides, *you* looked pretty interested in her boobs, too."

"Well, yeah," Cade said. "They're *boobs*. Everyone loves boobs."

Imogen shimmied her shoulders and wiggled her eyebrows at him. He stared down at her breasts and grinned.

I leaned over to her. "That doesn't bother you? Cade being into the strippers?"

Imogen shrugged. "He can look at the menu. He just can't order. Plus, it'll make for a hot make-out session later."

I narrowed my eyes at her. "It sounds like you've done this before."

She bit her lower lip. "Well, you remember that night last summer when Cade took me out and I came home a little tipsy?"

"Im!" I cried. "Why didn't you tell me?"

"I thought you'd judge me."

"Never," I told her.

She lowered her voice. "They let me dance on the stripper pole."

"What?" I practically screamed.

She turned bright red. "It was a slow night. All you have to do is ask."

"Yeah, well, I'm going to have to get a few more drinks in me first." I threw my head back and downed the rest of my wine, then stood. "Save my spot. I'm going to get another drink."

Esis sat in my chair but didn't take his eyes off the dancers. He seemed entranced by the lights and the shadows flickering around the Familiars as they twirled around the room.

I pushed through a group of Yapluma college students at the bar and tried to get the bartender's attention.

"Where's Brock?" one of them asked the others.

"Brock?" a petite girl who clearly couldn't hold her liquor snickered. "Brock Lee? Get it? Broccoli?"

"He's sick," one of the guys answered. "Him and Maggie both. He's afraid it's contagious and didn't want to get any other Familiars ill."

My stomach sank. Another Familiar sick? Was there some sort of virus going around Kinpago?

I caught the bartender's eye just then. "Can I get a whiskey sour?"

I'd never had one before, but it'd been my parents' drink of choice. Neither of them were big drinkers, so I figured it had to taste okay.

The bartender returned with my drink, and I handed him a pile of bills. "Keep the change."

He gave me a polite nod, and I headed back to my chair at the stage. I sipped my drink as I went, and decided it was pretty good.

"Did I miss anything?" I asked as I sat.

Imogen and Cade were giggling.

"Nothing," Imogen said. "Just... look who's here."

Imogen pointed toward the doors. I turned to look and saw Haley in a tight red dress, her dark hair done up fancy. Anwara wasn't on her shoulder like normal, but was following along on the ground. She was trailed in toe by Kelsey and the rest of their posse.

"What's *she* doing here?" I snarled.

"Probably working," Cade joked.

Haley cocked her head to her group. They walked straight up to a group of guys at the side stage. She said something to them, and they immediately moved so the girls could take their seats.

"What the hell?" I said. "Why didn't they stand up to her?"

"She *is* the daughter of a chieftess," Imogen pointed out.

"Yeah, I guess," I said. "But you don't see *us* going around using our Champion status to intimidate people to give up their spots."

Imogen rolled her eyes. "Forget about her."

"Again, it's going to take a lot more alcohol." I raised my glass to Imogen and threw back a large gulp.

Imogen placed her hand at the bottom of my glass to keep it tipped back. "Drink. Drink. Drink!"

I let the alcohol flow down the back of my throat until the glass was empty of everything but ice.

Imogen whooped when I finished, and Esis cheered. I could already feel the alcohol buzzing through my system.

"Another round!" I shouted as I slammed my glass on the surface at the edge of the stage.

"Try this first." Imogen folded up a dollar bill and tucked it behind my ear as another dancer came our way. She had straight black hair and beautiful features.

"Hey, I'm Skye," the dancer said. "Girl's night?"

I glanced to Cade, but in his place sat Arabelle. I hadn't even noticed him get up. He must've gone to get more drinks.

I shrugged. "We're just out having some fun."

"Well, I hope you're enjoying yourself."

"We are!" I said eagerly.

Skye placed her hand over my empty glass and melted the ice inside. I watched, mesmerized, as she manipulated the water. It rose out of the glass like a mini tornado, then formed into a column and ran across the surface of my skin. It sizzled against my arm.

Skye chuckled. "You might be enjoying yourself a little too much."

"Just nervous," I admitted.

"Don't be." Skye leaned in and brushed her lips against my cheek. I shivered.

It's just the drinks talking, I told myself.

Skye drew away with the dollar bill in her teeth. By the time she moved on to Imogen, Cade had returned with a tray of drinks. Esis' eyes brightened, and he took another beer, while I grabbed a hard lemonade.

Now that's my kind of drink! It was super sweet and tasted like soda.

"You're not going to get drunk off that," Imogen scoffed.

"Depends on how much I drink," I argued.

She took my hand and tugged at me. "Let's get you some *real* drinks."

Imogen dragged me to my feet. Cade shot us a glance while Skye rubbed her hands over his chest, but he stayed put with our Familiars to save our seats.

"We'll be right back, love," Imogen said before placing a kiss on his cheek.

Up at the bar, Imogen ordered us shots that tasted like green apple candy. Another two shots later, and the alcohol was starting to hit me hard. I could feel my inhibitions falling, and I was starting to get a little dizzy. I was starting to forget about Liam, and I'd definitely already forgotten about Haley.

"Time to dance!" I took Imogen's hands and shook my boobs at her as we headed back through the crowd. She covered her mouth and snickered at me. The alcohol seemed to be hitting her harder than me.

By the time we made it back to our seats, another dancer had come around. She had long brown hair similar to mine, and looked like she might be Koigni.

"Can I dance with you?" I called to her.

She leaned down to hear me better. "What was that, love?"

"Can I dance with you?" I repeated. "My friend says all I have to do is ask."

The girl looked me up and down, then reached out a hand. My jaw dropped as I took it and climbed up on stage with her. She led me over to the pole and gestured for me to try it out.

Standing up on stage was so surreal. I was sure the announcer was saying something over the music, but I could hardly process it. I looked to my friends, and they were all clapping for me, including Esis, but beyond that, I couldn't process any other faces. I was really drunk.

Bravely, I walked straight up to the pole while swinging my hips in the sexiest manner I could. I grabbed hold of the pole and spun around. I was surprised when the pole moved with me, like it twisted around an axis. I always thought these poles were stationery. It made the movements easy.

I've totally got this! I felt like I was at the top of the world.

I jumped on the pole and spun around. The hummingbird

Familiar flew around my head and sprinkled me with glitter. I was acutely aware of the cheers growing from my side of the stage, so I decided to step it up. Dropping my legs from the pole, I sank down into the splits. The floor was slippery enough to keep me spinning around the pole. A group of people I didn't know in the front cheered for me.

"On the floor! On the floor!" they chanted.

"Abby!" the announcer called. "Let's get that girl on the floor."

The dancer who'd pulled me on stage— Abby, I guess— took my hand and guided me onto the stage floor. I had no idea what was happening, but I went with it. I lay on my back while Abby straddled me and danced above me. The cheers grew even louder. I glanced to Imogen momentarily. Her eyes were wider than I'd ever seen them, and she was struggling to pick her jaw up off the floor. I barely looked at her before my eyes were drawn back to Abby above me. Her skin looked so soft. I just wanted to touch it...

I found my fingers reaching out for her, but the second I touched her, I drew away. "Sorry, I forgot I'm not allowed to touch."

Abby smiled down at me. "Those signs are for the guys. Go ahead and touch, if you want."

The invitation sent a surge of adrenaline through my chest. I'd never touched a girl like that before. Every inch of my body was begging me to do it.

I placed my fingers on her stomach, then ran them all the way up her curves. I gasped when I took her breasts in mine. I never thought it'd feel so good, but I totally understood now why guys obsessed over girls' boobs. Second base was awesome.

For a moment, all I saw was Abby's breasts moving above me. It was incredible.

Then suddenly, all I saw as Liam. *Everywhere.*

What the fuck, loser? I'm supposed to be *forgetting* about you. Get out of my head!

Only, he wasn't in my head at all. He was there. At *Lucky Stars.* Pulling me off stage!

"Sophia, what do you think you're doing?" he hissed. His hand was around my wrist. What was going on?

I shook my head, trying to orient myself. One second I was onstage, feeling up the most gorgeous dancer I'd ever seen. The next I was on my feet and Liam was trying to steady me.

"Hey!" I slapped him in the chest. "What do you think you're doing? I was having fun up there!"

A security officer pushed through the crowd. He placed a hand on Liam's shoulder. "Sir, I'm going to have to ask you to step back from the stage."

"No, no, it's fine," I said. Why the heck was I defending him? "He's my boyfri— he's my friend."

The security officer stepped back. He looked me straight in the eyes. "Are you sure you're okay?"

"Yeah, totally," I lied. Liam was an asshole. Who did he think he was, dragging me off stage like that?

The security officer disappeared back into the crowd, and I turned on Liam. "You jackass! What were *you* doing?"

"Protecting you," Liam said. "Do you—?"

"Bullshit," I snapped back. "What are you even doing here? You didn't come to strip clubs when we were dating, did you?"

"Of course not." Liam sounded offended. "Jonah dragged me here."

I looked away from Liam for the first time to see Imogen, Cade, and Jonah all on their feet a short distance away. They looked conflicted, like they weren't sure whether to intervene or not. Squeaks, Sassy, and Arabelle were all on high alert.

"Whatever. Just go away." I scooped up Esis and the pile of bills I'd left next to our empty drinks, then headed toward the bar.

Liam caught my hand before I got far. I whirled around and summoned heat to my skin. Liam jerked away like he'd been burnt. "Sophia, you're drunk."

"So what? Fuck off, Liam. I don't need you to babysit me. I've got Cade for that."

Cade and Imogen had followed. I draped my arm around Cade's shoulders and leaned into him. Dang. He smelled really nice. Why hadn't Imogen banged him yet?

"Sophia," Jonah pleaded. "You *are* pretty far gone. Liam's just trying to—"

"I don't care what he's trying to do," I snapped back, even though I kept my eyes on Liam. "Leave me alone."

I turned back around and heard Cade say softly, "Maybe you guys should back off for the night. I'll make sure she gets home safe."

I stormed over to the bar. Liam thought he could control me? I'd show him who's boss.

"Another shot!" I called to the bartender.

Esis tugged at my shoe strap.

"And a beer," I added.

I glanced down to him and gave him a wink. He beamed back.

"Sophia," Imogen said from beside me. I hadn't realized she'd followed so closely. "You should slow down."

"Hell no," I said. "I have a long way to go before I drink Liam out of my mind. We're going all out tonight, aren't we?"

Imogen smiled weakly. "In that case, I'll have another margarita."

"One margarita, coming right up!"

I grabbed my shot off the bar, but I paused when I brought it to my lips. I noticed a Koigni guy a few chairs down eyeing me with interest. He was a few years older than me and hot as hell. Dark hair, piercing eyes, and a straight jawline. Not to mention the broad shoulders. I was certain there were endless layers of abs beneath that red t-shirt. He didn't have a Familiar at his side, but he was definitely old enough to have one. I pictured him with something big, like a dragon, that couldn't fit in the building.

I downed the shot and turned to Imogen. "Let's see how Liam likes *this*."

I walked straight up to the Koigni guy. He never took his eyes off me once. "Hi, I'm Sophia. This is my friend Imogen."

Imogen looked totally speechless. At her feet, Esis and Sassy were sharing the beer.

"I know who you are," the Koigni dude sang. My goodness, his voice was lovely. Better than Liam's stupid voice. "I saw you compete in last year's tournament."

"Oh, right." I slapped my forehead. "Tournament winners. I forget sometimes."

"You guys were awesome," he said kindly. "It definitely surprised everyone. You must've won a lot of money."

"Oh, yeah. Loads," I said.

He stuck out his hand. "I'm Landon."

"Hi, Landon." I shook his hand. "That's a hot name. *Landon*."

He chuckled. "I saw you dancing up there. *That* was hot."

I threw my head back and giggled. "Oh, stop it, Landon. I'm Koigni. You of all people should know how hot we are."

Landon's eyes flickered down to my cleavage. Imogen was laughing so hard she couldn't speak.

"So, look," I said. "This probably is going to come off a little crazy, but I'm pretty drunk, and I'm feeling brazen. You want to make out?"

Imogen's laughs grew until she couldn't breathe.

Landon paused for a second, then shrugged. "Sure."

He took me around the waist and pulled me into him. His arms were strong, and his lips were soft. But his breath... ick. He tasted like beer. I hated beer.

But I ignored the taste and stuck my tongue down his throat anyway, because I knew it would piss Liam off. I was vaguely aware of two things. One, Esis had crawled up Landon's leg and was in his lap, trying to push us apart.

And two, Landon's hands were inching further and further down my back, like he was about to grab my ass.

Let him, I thought. It was so worth it to show Liam he didn't own me anymore.

Suddenly, Esis wasn't the only one trying to tear us apart. Hands were all over me. So many hands. I couldn't keep track of them all. They were so strong that they tore me away from Landon, who was desperately trying to hold on to me.

We were ripped apart, and I finally sucked in a gulp of air. Landon shot off the bar stool and to his feet, taking a defensive stance. I whirled around to see that both Liam and Jonah had pulled me away from him. Cade looked conflicted, but Liam and Jonah were fuming.

Liam took a step forward, his angry eyes fixed to Landon's face.

I stepped in front of him. "What the hell's your problem? Can't you see I was enjoying myself?"

"Yeah, pipsqueak," Landon spat. "Fuck off!"

Liam's hands fisted at his side. "You know this prick?"

"Yeah," I lied. "You need to leave."

"I'm not leaving," Liam fumed.

Landon stepped forward and wrapped an arm around my waist. "The girl asked you to leave."

Jonah crossed his arms. "Not until we know exactly what your intentions are with her."

"Jonah—" I started to protest, but Landon answered before I could.

He shrugged. "Hey, I didn't come here for the drinks."

I tried to pull away from Landon, but he held me so close to him that I couldn't move. Okay, now he was freaking me out. Kissing him had been a mistake.

"Everyone needs to cool down," Imogen interjected. "Liam, Jonah, go home. Landon... find someone else to screw around with."

"I think Sophia can speak for herself," Landon replied.

"Yeah, I can." I tried to pull away from him again, but he wouldn't let me. I was starting to get very uncomfortable. "Liam, piss off. Landon, let me go."

"Come on, babe." He pulled me even closer and tried to plant a kiss on my lips. "I thought you wanted to make out."

I called heat to my skin, but I forgot he was Koigni. He wasn't completely immune to my Fire, but he could handle it more than others. It didn't faze him.

"Yeah, I did," I said. "And now I don't."

"Sophia, babe. I thought you wanted *them* to leave," Landon said.

"I want *all* of you to leave!" I exploded. "No, you know what. I'm leaving."

I ripped out of Landon's grasp. I wasn't even a step away from him before he mumbled *bitch* under his breath.

Before I knew what was happening, Liam was flying through the air toward Landon.

I whirled back toward them just in time to see Liam's fist connect with Landon's face. Landon's fingers tangled in Liam's shirt, and the two tumbled to the ground, nearly knocking three other people over in the process.

"Liam!" I shrieked.

A blur of white passed though my vision, then Esis was at their side, pounding Landon with his tiny little fists beside Liam.

"Stop!" I shouted. I tried to get between them to rescue Esis, but they didn't even notice me.

Landon rolled on top of Liam and nearly squashed Esis. He hopped out of the way just in time. Landon drew his fist back and slammed it into Liam's face. Blood spurted out his nose.

My hands slapped over my mouth, and I whimpered as Liam's head lolled to the side. In a flash, Jonah and Cade were on top of Landon, trying to pry him off of Liam. Squeaks stomped her feet and flapped her wings, keeping her eyes on Esis. It was clear she wanted to rescue him, but she also didn't want to hurt Liam, Cade, or Jonah. Landon threw an arm back, and it connected with Jonah's chest. Jonah gasped for breath.

Suddenly, four other Koigni guys joined the scuffle, trying to break everyone apart. Limbs flew everywhere, and I couldn't make sense of whose fists were flying where. Air swirled around us, and the area heated. Glasses on the bar shook as the ice inside of them swirled.

"Sophia!" Imogen cried, horrified. She held Sassy back to keep her from joining the bar fight.

I'd had enough of this. I threw myself forward and shoved two Koigni guys out of the way, then sank the point of my heel into Landon's stomach. Esis scurried out from the pile of guys, looking terrified. He jumped and scampered up my dress and to my shoulder, where he hid beneath my hair.

It'd been seconds since Liam threw the first punch. Three security officers arrived, and I couldn't make sense of what happened next. There was so much shouting, so much cursing. Before I knew it, we were being thrown out of the building and onto the street.

"Whoa," Imogen said, gasping. "That was intense."

I was still fuming so much that I barely heard her. I turned on Liam.

"You're an *idiot*, you know that?" I growled. "I can handle myself!"

"That fuckhead deserved it!" Liam snapped back while holding his bleeding nose.

Jonah stepped between us. Squeaks was flattening her feathers beside him. "Let's all calm down."

I pushed around Jonah to face Liam. "No. Liam totally overstepped his boundaries. You can't just go around punching people!"

"You can't go around *kissing* people," he barked back.

"Screw you!" I shouted. "I can do whatever the hell I want."

I crossed my arms and rubbed the goosebumps breaking out over them. Liam shrugged his jacket off and tried to wrap it around me.

"I was just trying to protect you," he said.

I shrugged the jacket off and threw it back at him. Imogen, Cade, Jonah, and their Familiars were too shocked to say anything.

"Let me make something *very clear*, Liam," I said. "I do *not* need you to protect me. You didn't have to pull me off stage, and you didn't have to punch Landon, either."

"Oh, so you're on first-name basis with the guy?" Liam fumed. "Are you dating him?"

"So what if I am?" I yelled. "It's none of your business!"

"Sophia, you're drunk. You're not thinking straight."

"That's the *point* Liam!" I screamed at him. "I came out here to have a good night, and you *ruined* it."

"You call that a good night!?" he exploded. "Do you have any idea how the guys in there were looking at you? You didn't see the lust all over their faces. You don't know what they were thinking."

"And you do?" I challenged. "Does it even matter? Maybe I *wanted* the attention."

"Did you? *Did* you!?" Liam yelled.

I curled my hands into tight fists. I was about to explode. "You. Do. Not. Own. Me."

"I never said I did," he shot back.

"You're acting like it!"

"I'm acting like I care. You can't just go around doing whatever you want, Sophia!"

"Like hell I can't!" Just to prove it, I grabbed the top of my dress and pulled the fabric down, exposing my breasts for the entire street to see. There weren't many people around, since most were inside, but there was a group smoking by the door and a few others coming and going from the parking lot. Jonah's jaw dropped, and Cade averted his eyes. Imogen was engaged in another one of her laughing fits.

"Hot damn, Sophia!" she whooped, like she was proud of me.

"Heeey!" I called loud enough for the entire parking lot to hear. "Check it ouuuut!"

Liam immediately tried to throw his jacket over me to cover my breasts, but I tossed the jacket to the side to keep everything exposed. Liam grabbed for my dress and tried to pull the fabric back up, but I swatted at him.

"Trying to feel me up?" I accused him.

Liam froze. "No, of course not. Sophia, stop it."

He took a step back. Satisfied, I covered myself again. The condom I'd shoved into my bra came dislodged, and it dropped to the ground at my feet. Liam's eyes went wide when he saw it. And I. Didn't. Give. A. Fuck.

If he thought I was screwing around, so be it. He was doing the same thing with Mia.

"Fine, Sophia," he growled. "Do whatever the hell you want. What are you going to do next? Steal a unicorn and get a tattoo?"

That was a great idea.

"Yeah," I said. "You know what? I think I will."

Liam's eyes nearly bulged out of his skull. "I didn't mean it!"

"Yeah, well, you can't say it wasn't your idea." I turned away from him. "Cade, get the unicorn!"

He hesitated, then hurried toward the parking lot.

"Come on, Jonah," Liam snarled. "We're leaving."

Jonah gaped at him, but he and Squeaks followed. "Really, Liam? You're not going to talk her out of this?"

Liam shrugged. "She's right. We're not dating anymore. She can do whatever she wants. See if I care."

He shot me a glare. He did. He totally cared.

"Sophiaaa!" Imogen sang once they were out of earshot. "You're crazy, you know that?"

"Good crazy, right?" I asked.

"Absolutely. Feel better yet?" she called out.

If I felt like I was on the top of the world up on that stripper pole, I was on the freaking moon right now.

"Never better," I answered. "Honestly."

Imogen clapped me on the back. "That a girl."

Cade pulled up in our carriage, and Imogen and I climbed inside with our Familiars.

"To the tattoo parlor!" I called up to Cade.

"You weren't serious about that, were you?" Cade asked.

"Hell yeah, I was."

"Sophia, I think we should just get you home," Cade said. "You've had a lot to drink, and I promised—"

"Cade, so help me, if you do not take me to a tattoo parlor *right now*, I will burn this carriage to the ground," I snarled.

Cade's jaw dropped.

"She's not kidding, babe," Imogen said. "You should probably do it."

The carriage started moving, leaving Jonah and Liam behind. I turned to Imogen. "What should I get?"

Esis began tracing out designs on my shoulder, like he was outlining a tattoo for me.

"I don't know," Imogen said. "A fire symbol, for Koigni?"

"Ew. No. That sounds like something Haley would get. I want to get something cool."

"Where will you put it?" Imogen asked, her eyes brightening.

"I don't know. My ankle? Maybe my wrist?" I twisted my arm around, picturing some sort of symbol over my skin. "I guess we'll see when we get there."

I was feeling steady on my feet when we arrived at the tattoo parlor. It was in the Yapluma neighborhood, not far from *Lucky Stars*.

"Are you sure about this?" Cade asked, looking worried.

"Absolutely." I strolled into the tattoo parlor with my head held high. Cade could worry all he wanted. I was going through with this

The place was quiet, with only the sound of a tattoo gun buzzing through the shop. The tattoo artist was bent over a Yapluma girl's backside, concentrating on the design he was drawing into her skin. She looked a little distressed as she squeezed her friend's hand tightly for support. A large scorpion rested on his shoulder.

"I'll be with you in a moment," the tattoo artist said, glancing up at us briefly. He was kind of cute, but way too old for me. He had a full sleeve of tattoos running up and down both arms. A scorpion Familiar the size of Esis sat on his shoulder.

Imogen pulled me over to a row of photo albums, which were filled with samples of his work and various tattoo designs we could choose from.

"Ooh, a dragon might be cool," Imogen said, pointing to a small design.

"Or a unicorn." Cade's eyes lit up when he saw the image, like he was starting to think this wasn't such a bad idea.

Arabelle and Sassy were both staring at the colorful images on the walls, as if they too were trying to pick out their favorite design. Esis tugged my hair as I turned a page, making me stop. He jumped off my shoulder and onto the table, then pointed at a small design of a daisy. It instantly made me think of Imogen.

"That one!" I pointed.

"Sophia, that's a Nivita tattoo," Imogen pointed out.

I shrugged. "That's the point. It's for my bestie."

I leaned over to her and pulled her into a hug.

"Aww. Really?" Imogen beamed. "For me?"

"Yes. Right here." I pointed over my shoulder to my right shoulder blade.

We sat in chairs lined up against the wall to wait. Cade flipped through one of the photo albums, and Imogen leaned against him to look too.

After a few minutes, Cade lifted his gaze. "Are you sure you still want to do this, Sophia?"

"Relax, Cade," I said. "My buzz has worn off. I know what I'm doing. I *want* to do this."

He looked skeptical, but he didn't say anything further.

"Maybe I should get a tattoo," Imogen said thoughtfully. "I think if I got one, it'd be of Sassy. I'd probably design it myself, though."

The artist finished up with the Yapluma girl's tattoo and gave her some instructions to keep it clean. The two girls thanked him and left.

"How can I help you?" he asked.

"I'm here to get a tattoo," I said, sounding more timid than I felt. "I'd like this one."

I held up the design and pointed to it.

He eyed me curiously, as if wondering if I was Nivita or not. "Neat. Have you ever had a tattoo before?"

"Nope," I admitted. "Virgin."

Imogen giggled.

"Tattoo virgin, I mean," I said.

The artist chuckled. "Don't worry. It's not as bad as it sounds. Follow me. You two can come along if you'd like."

He guided me to a seat in the back and helped me get comfortable. "My name is Luca. Feel free to ask any questions during the process."

Luca was really nice. It helped ease my nerves.

Luca took the design from me and looked it up on his computer. "Where are we going to go with this?"

"On my shoulder." I pointed for him.

"Perfect." He poked at a few things on his computer, then the printer started whirring. He held a sheet of paper out to me showing the daisy. "How's this for size?"

"That's perfect."

Luca fiddled with a few more things, and the printer spat out the design again, this time on transfer paper.

"The process is simple," Luca said. "We'll transfer this design to your skin and get it right where you want it. I can use the gun to trace it, or if you'd prefer, Dominique here can do it." He gestured to the large scorpion on his shoulder. He noticed my wary look. "I assure you we are a completely licensed facility, and use clean needles and new ink with each tattoo. If you go with Dominique, her stinger is naturally antibacterial. There's no risk of infection."

"Does it hurt?" I asked. Once I asked it, I realized I wasn't actually afraid of that. I was sure I'd experienced worse.

"Depends," Luca said with a shrug. "How's your pain tolerance?"

I chuckled. "Forget it. I can do this. Dominique's up."

"It's not bad. Really," Luca said. "Like a pencil drawing on the skin. Shall we get started?"

Luca placed the temporary stencil on my skin and handed me a mirror to get a good look at it.

"That's perfect," I told him. Esis looked pleased.

"Sophia, it's going to look great!" Imogen looked on the verge of tears. "Did she tell you it's for me?"

I wasn't convinced Imogen's buzz had worn off yet.

"Aw, that's sweet," Luca said.

"Yeah, just wait until morning," Cade laughed. "You might regret this, Sophia."

Luca placed Dominique on my back. "I'll tell you what. I've had hundreds of people walk in here, and I've never had a single one come back and tell me they regretted it. It's not as common as you think."

"They're not going to tell *you* that," Cade joked.

Luca shrugged. "Come on, man. You can't refute my data."

"Touche."

Dominique's legs tickled my back, and I relaxed into the table. I winced as her stinger touched my skin, but it wasn't as bad as I thought it'd be. Esis stood beside my head at the table, looking concerned. He reached out, but I pushed his paws away.

"It's okay, buddy," I told him. "It feels good."

It was true. The pain across my shoulder blade made me feel alive. I wasn't a sobbing mess, going numb curled up in my bed all day. I was out living my life. And if Liam had a problem with that, damn him.

"Imogen," I said as I let the burn spread across my shoulder.

"Yeah?"

"Thanks for taking me out tonight. I really needed it."

I'd shown Liam tonight I didn't need him. I was a free girl, and this was college. I was going to enjoy every moment of it.

Liam

SEVEN

o I *look* like the kind of guy who goes to clubs, let alone a *strip* club? No? Because I'm not.

I hate clubs. Absolutely fucking despise them. But Jonah freaking insisted on dragging me to one, because he'd claimed I was still depressed over Sophia, and it was time to move on and be happy already, all the way there complaining that this was a *great sacrifice* on his part, as we were going to a straight bar as opposed to a gay one.

Didn't work. No matter how many naked girls were around me, none of them compared to Sophia. I had no interest.

Then I saw Sophia on a literal stripper pole, and I thought I was hallucinating. Unfortunately, I was not.

She'd be safe in the club, but with the way all the guys were looking at her, and the way Cade was distracted with Imogen, I knew it'd be far too easy for one of those predators to lure her away and out of sight of the security guards. Several of them were plotting on how to do just that. That creep Landon was one of them. I'd been watching him, and he'd been looking for an opportunity to get Sophia away from Cade and Imogen before he cornered her. Jonah agreed with me, and once his hands were on her, we moved in.

I knew it wasn't my place and I should've backed off, but I just couldn't. Sophia was way over her limit, and she couldn't judge whether she wanted to sleep with anyone. That Landon prick would've totally taken advantage of her. Who knows what could've happened?

I was still thinking about it two days later on Monday. Jonah slid beside me in the booth at breakfast and elbowed me. "So, how's it going?"

I didn't like his casual tone. It was too much of a coincidence that Sophia and I had been at the same strip club on the same night. I was half convinced he and Imogen set it up on purpose.

"You two are ridiculous," I said. He didn't need context. He knew what I meant.

"I don't know what you're talking about." Jonah batted his eyelashes and pretended to look innocent. I scoffed.

I couldn't get that image of Sophia onstage out of my head. It was torturous, maddening.

By the look on her face, she'd liked how the stripper danced on her. I mean *really* liked it.

"Are you *still* thinking about Saturday?" Jonah asked.

"No." I crossed my arms and sank down in my seat.

"I think Sophia's a little bi-curious," Jonah teased as he took a sip of his drink. "She seemed to like having boobs in her face."

"Yeah, yeah." It was college. People experimented. She was single. I didn't care.

I really did care. Because at the same time, as envious as it made me that Sophia was all over the girl at the club... it was kinda hot, too. Something I hated to admit.

I checked my watch. I had an appointment with Perot, and it was about that time. "Gotta go." I got up from the table and grabbed my bag. I left my uneaten food on the table.

"Don't get too jealous," Jonah sang after me as I left.

Psh. I wasn't jealous.

I had to find Sophia. She said she'd wait for me after she got out of Elementai Explorations with Baine, in the hallway outside of his class. Baine was giving me a pass today for Master Toaqua Magic so I could make my appointment. I hoped Sophia still agreed to come, after the massive blowout argument we'd had over the weekend.

Then I saw her. And it was like walking into a brick wall.

If I thought the dress she wore last weekend was too revealing, it was nothing compared to this. She was wearing a black corset that was lined with red-hot lace. Her breasts were practically falling out of it. Over top of the corset, she wore leather shorts that barely covered her ass, and knee-high black boots that doubled as heels. Esis sat on her shoulder, his head held high and looking proud as anything.

A couple guys whistled as she walked past, but the fiery glare she sent made them all fall silent. When she stopped in front of me, I caught a scent of some sort of perfume that smelled really good. I liked it.

"Hi." She gave me a bright smile. "Ready to go?"

I was speechless. It was hard to say anything when I was presented with... *that*. But I wasn't fooled by her cheery attitude. This was Sophia's way of getting back at me after the club thing.

When I failed to respond, she giggled and said, "Like the outfit? Imogen picked it out for me yesterday. We went shopping."

Esis gave me a sultry gaze and played with his fluffy tail in a provocative way. I snapped myself out of it and said the first thing that came to mind.

"What, gonna flash everyone again?" I snidely commented.

Her smile faded. "If I want to print out a blow-up poster of my boobs and stick it in the Commons for everyone to see, I'll do it, Liam Mitoh, and you won't do a thing about it," she snapped back.

There was that Koigni attitude. It was getting worse every day. It didn't help that every time she yelled at me it *turned me the fuck on*.

I guess I had a fetish for feisty girls who liked telling me what to do. My mortal flaw.

Then I noticed something. Sophia moved her hair, and underneath it was *a literal fucking tattoo*. It was a realistic black-and-white composition of a daisy. It almost took up her entire shoulder blade. It was red around the area, as it was still healing.

I was in shock. I thought she was threatening me the other day when she said she was getting a tattoo. I didn't think she'd actually go *through* with it. I was ready to explode. She saw my horrified expression, and the grin was back.

"It's a daisy, for Imogen." Sophia bit her lip and looked up at me, holding back a laugh. "Isn't it cute?"

I didn't like tattoos, but I hated to admit it *did* look cute on her. I wasn't gonna tell her, though. And I wasn't going to give her the satisfaction of knowing she got under my skin. "Sure. Whatever. Can we go?"

"Certainly." She walked in front of me swiftly, swaying her hips. I gritted my teeth. I knew what she was doing.

We didn't talk on the way to Perot's classroom. I didn't want to. I was still internally bitching about her outfit. What purpose did she think that achieved? She made it pretty clear on Saturday that she didn't want to get back with me and was interested in dating other guys. Was she trying to rub it in?

You know, if she has that corset on, I bet she's wearing the panties to match...

I want her to wear something like that in OUR bedroom, for ME and not everyone else in the world to see...

It was like there were two different voices arguing in my head. Thankfully, they stopped when we entered Perot's class.

Perot glanced up as he saw us coming. Perot said nothing about Sophia's outfit, thank the ancestors. I don't even think he noticed it. He was too focused on Baxtor, who was sitting on a perch and dangling a limp wing.

"Hello, Liam," he said offhandedly. "I'm sorry, but I think we're going to have to reschedule. Baxtor isn't feeling too well. Twisted wing."

Baxtor drooped his head. Sophia walked forward and put Esis on the desk next to Baxtor's perch. "Here. Let Esis help."

Esis didn't hesitate or look to Sophia for a command. He simply stretched his paw out. Perot gasped when Esis touched Baxtor's hurt wing, but I held him back when he tried to move Esis away. Baxtor cooed, and we watched as the twisted wing straightened itself out. Baxtor flexed it, then took off his perch, taking a quick flight around the room before settling on Perot's desk. Perot slowly turned in his seat and looked at us, shocked.

I cleared my throat. "Esis is what we wanted to talk to you about."

Perot leaned back in his chair. "I hope you have a good explanation."

"We do. At least, kind of." Sophia glanced at me. "When I bonded with Esis, I didn't know that he had magic. But he does— healing magic. He's a creature from Anichi called a kurble."

Perot looked to me. "I'm guessing he's how you've managed to make a miraculous recovery?"

"Yes, sir." I nodded. "He healed me in the tournament and made it so I could finish the Cup."

"But he can't fix everything," Sophia hurried to add. "Esis can treat Liam, not cure him completely. At least, not yet. He's still a baby. I don't know what he'll be able to do once he's fully grown. But his powers keep Liam alive, and stop him from deteriorating... I think."

"Why on earth didn't you tell me this sooner, Liam? It could've drastically affected your course of treatment," Perot said, baffled.

"That was my fault." Sophia dropped her head. "I was sending Esis to heal Liam without his knowledge. He healed Liam in the tournament while he was still passed out. Liam didn't... find out... that Esis could heal until the end of last semester."

Esis chortled. I scratched him under the chin and said, "Esis has been healing me all summer. I thought it would be okay, since we pretty much stopped trying things at the end of spring. I wanted to tell you sooner, but Esis is Sophia's Familiar, not mine. She had to be the one to tell you."

Perot looked to Sophia. She seemed uncomfortable. "I wanted to come forward. But it was dangerous to. I was worried something would happen to Esis— that someone might take him."

Perot rubbed his chin. "You had good reason to fear that, child." He seemed thoughtful. "There have been no creatures that can heal— that I know of— since the days of Anichi. Many powerful Elementai would like to get their hands on him."

Baxtor ruffled his feathers, as if the thought was unpleasant. Perot reached out to Esis. The kurble crawled into his hand and sat there, looking up at him.

"I would much like to study him. Not take him," Perot said as Sophia went to object. "His powers are obviously working in Liam's favor, and if there's one of his kind right here, a group of some sort must still exist. This could change things for the tribe."

Sophia seemed nervous. "I don't want to let him go."

Perot shook his head. "You misunderstand me, Miss Henley. I believe I still owe you a debt, and revealing Esis now would be very foolish— for you and for him. It wouldn't be safe if people knew what he can do. We need to keep this quiet. But I would like the opportunity to research him as much as I can, so I can understand his magic. I'm going to need to, if there's any hope on finding a cure for Liam."

Sophia glanced at me. She was stuck between a rock and a hard place. Esis and me. "I can give you everything I know about Esis. And you can study how his magic works on Liam. But I can't let him be an experiment."

"That's all I ask for." Perot wrote some things down. "And don't be afraid that I'll reveal your secret. I understand that this needs to be kept quiet."

He sighed. "These are dangerous times we live in."

There was a rustling sound several feet behind him. Sophia and I both started. Perot froze. It was coming from a door on the other side of the room. I knew Perot was one of the few teachers that lived on campus, in an apartment adjacent to his classroom. Someone was coming out of it just now.

It was Head Dean Alric. He was still in his pajamas, like he'd just woken up. His grey hair was ruffled, and he was wearing fluffy slippers.

"Jacques, come back to bed..." Alric yawned, then froze when he saw us. Perot turned beet red.

Perot hurried to stand. Baxtor chirped in amusement as Perot put hands on both Sophia and I's shoulders and guided us to the hall door. "Yes, well, if you two have any questions or concerns that you want to run by me, feel free to stop by during my *office hours*. I'm always here."

Alric had slunk back into Perot's apartment. Esis raced after us and jumped onto Sophia's shoulder. Perot pushed us out of the classroom and said, "We'll discuss this in greater detail later, Liam. Make another appointment anytime."

Then he closed the door. Perot sure tried to hurry us out after Alric came calling. It was clear that "anytime" meant when the Head Dean wasn't around.

"Um..." Sophia tilted her head. "Do you think Alric overheard anything about Esis?"

I shook my head. "Nah. He would've said something. He was clearly out of it."

"Why... why do you think he was in Perot's apartment?" Sophia said slowly.

"I don't even wanna know." It wasn't my business.

Our meeting was so short that it was still around ten o'clock. Sophia and I didn't need to stick around and hang out.

But at the same time, neither one of us had class until the afternoon, and it was obvious we didn't want to part from each other, either. Things were complicated.

"I'm meeting Imogen in the courtyard. We have to go over some stuff from class. Wanna come?" she asked.

"Sure." I didn't have anything else to do. We walked in relative silence together. It was more than a bit uncomfortable.

Imogen was sitting on a large rock in the courtyard, Sassy beside her. Both were enjoying the sun, as it was a nice day. Sassy had a large monarch butterfly on her nose and was observing it with half-closed eyes. She sneezed, and the butterfly flew away.

Imogen closed the book she was reading when we approached. Her eyebrows knitted when she saw the two of us together, but she didn't say anything about it.

Her eyes ran up and down Sophia's outfit. "Hot damn, sexy! You're looking fine today. Who picked out your outfit?"

Sophia smiled, but didn't comment on it. "You never said why you wanted us to meet here," Sophia said as we came together.

Imogen slid off the rock and clutched the book to her chest. "I've been thinking. Maybe we've been looking for the Earth piece in the wrong places. Prophecies were passed down orally, for generations. Like stories. Showana told Nivita their part, but I bet she didn't allow them to write it down."

"But that lessens our chances of finding it, because we need to look for someone who not only knows about the piece, but is willing to tell us about it," I pointed out.

Imogen shook her head. "Not necessarily. I didn't find anything in the Nivita Elders' Scrolls, so that means it has to be somewhere else."

"Imogen, that doesn't make any sense," Sophia argued. "If someone doesn't tell us about it and the answer isn't in the scrolls, how are we supposed to find out what it is?"

"I have a theory," Imogen said. "Come with me."

Imogen started the long walk across the courtyard. Sophia and I followed curiously, not sure where we were going. It was so nice out that there were a lot of people in the courtyard, enjoying the sun with their Familiars and playing games.

Although most people wanted a pleasant day, Haley was there, and there was nothing pleasant about her. She wasn't happy unless she was making someone else miserable. Anwara sat on her shoulder, trying to get her Elementai's attention, but Haley ignored her.

Haley seemed bored. Her eyes lit up as her gaze landed on us.

Lindsey, Miranda, and Kelsey were with her. While Kelsey gossiped by Haley's side about shit that no one cared about, Lindsey and Miranda were tossing a beach ball back and forth.

Haley stepped forward as we walked past. "Dead man walking," she called out loudly, looking directly at me.

I didn't entertain her. Was that really the best she could do? I'd heard way worse.

Kelsey didn't laugh. She seemed upset that Haley had cut her off in the middle of her conversation. Miranda giggled, but she caught my eyes and stopped, looking guilty. I didn't hold it against her.

Lindsey was fuming. "That's not nice, Haley."

"Oh Lindsey, go blow it out your ass," Haley snapped at her. "Ancestors, when did you start feeling sorry for losers?"

I heard Sophia's knuckles crack as she tightened them into fists. Even though we'd been fighting earlier, she wanted to defend me. Which, at the same time was really endearing, it would get her into trouble.

"Don't," I told her quietly. I brushed her hand to show her it was okay. A simple gesture that sent rockets whizzing through my insides. Sophia relaxed slightly.

I kept my eyes forward and didn't react to Haley's taunt. When Haley saw she couldn't bother me, her cruel gaze went to Imogen. She started making *mooing* sounds.

Imogen's eyes watered and her lip began to tremble. Sophia and I noticed.

"Just ignore her, Im," I told her under my breath. Imogen looked away.

Haley saw that she was getting to Imogen and laughed harder. "I don't know how Imogen can keep a boyfriend. I bet he's cheating on her. She's such a fat ugly cow—"

Haley didn't get the chance to say anything else, because one minute Sophia was by my side, and the next, she was running toward Haley full-speed with a fist full of fire. Imogen and I both gasped as the hit connected and Haley went flying backward.

Haley hit the ground. When she sat back up, there was a large burn on her cheek from where Sophia had hit her.

Haley gritted her teeth, and she didn't hesitate. She got back up and slapped Sophia across the face. Before I knew what was going on, both girls were swinging punches and pulling hair, screaming insults at each other loudly. Haley's friends watched in disbelief as the two girls drew blood, sending flames and ash scattering everywhere. They were using a combination of fists and Fire to try and hit each other.

"All right! Girl fight!" some bro next to me shouted, and his entire square raced forward to huddle into a circle around Sophia and Haley. They chanted for them to fight, and it echoed throughout the courtyard. Esis stood at the edge of the fight and cheered for Sophia to win, while Anwara hovered anxiously above, looking worried.

I wasn't going to just stand around and let this happen. I rushed forward and grabbed Sophia by both arms, trying to wrench her away from Haley. By the ancestors, Sophia had a death grip on her. I don't even think she noticed me there, she was so focused on kicking Haley's ass. Some Koigni Second Year— Ben— saw me trying to pull them apart and went to help.

"Tell this crazy bitch to let go of my hair!" Haley screeched. Sophia didn't— only clenched her fists harder and brought her knee up to connect with Haley's face. I thought I heard her nose break. Blood splattered across my shoe.

We should've been able to pull them apart, but damn, both of them had their claws in each other and didn't want to let go. I had a hard time yanking them away without getting burned, and Ben, who could resist Fire, seemed anxious about doing so— either because he didn't want to hurt them, or because he was worried what the repercussions would be from Haley or Sophia if he did.

Out of the corner of my eye, I noticed an authority figure— a teacher. Thank the ancestors, it was Baine. He could put a stop to this.

I expected him to run over and immediately separate the girls, but instead, he stood at the edge of the circle and watched with a gaping expression as Ben and I failed to stop the brawl.

"Professor, do something!" I shouted to him.

Baine didn't. He just stood there like a dumbass, watching the fight with eyes darting from Haley to Sophia, not sure of how to step in. For the sake of the ancestors, he was a *teacher*. This was his job, to break up shit like this!

Then a miracle happened. Madame Doya came gliding in like a maniac from out of nowhere, her dress billowing around her with an expression that she was bringing all the fury of hell itself. Her lioness Familiar Naomi stalked at her side with a raised lip and fierce growls.

The chanting stopped, and the crowd immediately scattered in fear as Doya approached. Ben and I instantly let go of the fighting girls like we'd been burned as Doya came near, backing off several steps. With one hand on Sophia and the other on Haley, Madame Doya forcibly ripped them apart and sent them sailing in different directions.

"*Miss Henley! Miss Westfenix!*" she shouted. "How *dare* you embarrass me and bring shame upon your House in such a way!"

Both girls were sporting dirt and bruises. Sophia had a long scratch across her face from Haley's nails, while the burn Sophia had given Haley was turning an ashen color. Haley went pale underneath the blood coating her face, but Sophia stared up at Doya in a defiant way, like she regretted nothing. Because of course, she didn't.

"In my office! *Immediately!*" I'd never seen Doya so mad. She pointed toward the castle, and Haley and Sophia stalked toward it, giving each other hateful looks on the way. There went our morning research for the prophecy, I guess. Esis jumped onto Sophia for a ride. Anwara went to nuzzle Haley, to check if she was hurt, but the bitch swatted her away.

Baine had finally come out of his coma. He cleared his throat and said, "Thank you, Eleanor. That was sorely needed."

"Well, of course I needed to do *something*, Elliot, because when push comes to shove, you become *incapable* of doing anything but losing your spine!" Madame Doya shouted. Naomi snarled.

Baine's mouth dropped open. So did everyone else's in the square. Madame Doya seemed to realize she had lost her temper. She straightened up in a dignified way, brushed off her dress and smoothed out her hair.

"If you don't mind, Elliot, I have to discipline my students," she said. "If you find you're unable to do the same with members of your own House, please, send them my way."

She glamorously left the courtyard like a movie star afterward. What. A. Burn. Now that Madame Doya was gone, Baine was fuming. He grumbled unintelligible words under his breath as he stomped away.

I was anxious. Chieftess Westfenix would make sure Sophia paid for hurting her daughter. I was sure of it.

"Look, I got it on video!" Kelsey said. Looks like Jonah wasn't the only one who snuck a phone into school. She and Miranda rewatched the fight, huddled over her phone and looking awed it had happened in the first place.

Lindsey was blushing. I bet anything she thought Sophia fighting Haley was hot.

Imogen tugged on my arm. "We should get out of here. People are staring."

I could feel it. Imogen and I hurried out of the courtyard and into the castle before people could pepper us with questions about how nutty Sophia was. We didn't stop until we came to a secluded, dimly-lit section of the castle, near a mounted stuffed bear. Sassy kept glancing at it, as if she was afraid it would come back to life.

I didn't think either one of us knew what to say about the fight, so we didn't mention it. I turned to look at Imogen. "So... do you wanna show me what you think the Earth piece is, and tell Sophia later?"

Imogen shook her head. "Actually... I think it's best if I keep it to myself for right now."

It was like the fight had changed her mind. "Why not? You wanted to share a second ago."

"I don't want to get Sophia's hopes up if I'm wrong," she insisted. "She can't take anymore stress right now. It'll make her go over the edge if I give her all this build-up just to let her down."

"You're rarely wrong," I reminded her.

"I know. But it's kind of like a puzzle... I have the pieces, but I'm missing a few. I need a few more weeks to work it out. We don't need Sophia freaking out until then," Imogen said firmly.

"You don't think Sophia can handle it right now," I said bluntly.

"After that, do you?" Imogen asked.

I rubbed my eyes and sighed. "No."

"Exactly." Imogen's tone was certain. "She's like a bomb about to explode."

"Just show me, then. I can help."

"No. Because if I tell you, you'll run straight to Sophia, and that'll ruin the point," she insisted.

She hugged her arms to her sides. I could tell that what Haley said earlier had really hurt her.

"You know Haley's just trying to get to Sophia, so she went after us," I said. "What she said has nothing to do with you and Cade."

"No, but..." Imogen sucked in a breath and held it. "Even after dating him all this time, it's hard to believe that he's in love with *me*. Cade would never cheat, but I don't even know if I would blame him if he did. I'm not pretty."

"Cut that shit out. Of course you are." Cade was completely head over heels for Imogen. No other woman existed on this planet besides her, according to him.

Deep down, I knew I was the same way about Sophia.

"Jonah's always trying to get my confidence up." Imogen seemed deflated. "And it works, sometimes, but I still have doubts. And the way Cade's been talking lately... Liam, it's weird. It's like he's trying to prepare me for when he's going to leave or something. One minute he'll be all happy and everything will be perfect, and then..."

She shook her head. "He'll be distant. He keeps saying he doesn't want to hurt me. We'll be so in love, then he'll act like he wants to break up. We almost did the other night, before I talked him out of it. I don't get it."

"That's just the Elemental Cup talking," I said. "He's nervous about it, but he'll be fine. He's got Arabelle. Things will go back to normal once the Cup is over."

"I hope so." Imogen shivered. She gave me a steely look. "It didn't help that you freaked out about the strip club the other night. Cade feels guilty about it— like he didn't protect Sophia."

"I don't give a shit that you guys went to the strip club," I said, rolling my eyes. "I'm pissed that both of you went over your limit, Sophia *way* over her limit. She was completely wasted in a really unsafe place. How is that okay?"

"I was just trying to help her feel better." Imogen frowned.

"I get that. But you two crossed a line. Cade shouldn't have to babysit either one of you. He can't watch both of you at once," I pointed out. "A few drinks are okay, but that place was crawling with psychos."

"I know, I know." Imogen sighed. "Sophia's just... she's so different lately, Liam. I don't know what else to do. She's not happy. And it doesn't help that you're treating her like a yo-yo."

My heart skipped a beat. "What do you mean?"

Imogen gave me a scathing look. "You know exactly what I mean. You need to make up your mind. I'm starting to think it was a mistake for you guys to be friends."

She walked away. Sassy turned her tail up at me as she went.

I was left standing in the hallway alone for five minutes, contemplating what she meant. Imogen had just caved a hole in me I didn't even know was there.

I'D LEFT the castle shortly after that and returned around seven. I took a detour through the Commons to get back to the Toaqua dorms, but stopped when I witnessed the sorry sight in front of me.

Renar was lounging against Alvarice, his cockatrice Familiar, drinking a beer and watching as Jonah did his homework. I watched them for a full ten minutes. Whenever Renar asked for another beer, Jonah would hurry to get him one. When Alvarice made a cracking sound with his beak, Jonah would stop what he was doing immediately and go to feed him, too. The rooster-wyvern hybrid let out a menacing cackle when Jonah fell over trying to get it all done. It was pathetic. Jonah asked for a kiss, but Renar shoved him away. I didn't see Squeaks anywhere.

Whenever Renar told him to jump, Jonah asked how high. They were one step away from Micah and Mia. This needed to stop.

I walked forward. "Jonah, can I talk to you?" Renar's eyes narrowed at me, and Alvarice hissed, but I ignored both of them.

Jonah glanced up. "Hey, where've you been? I heard you weren't in class. Not at dinner, either."

"Skipped it, went swimming." And paid for it. I was having trouble breathing. Holding my breath too long again.

Renar scoffed. "This section is for Yapluma only. Beat it, asshole."

"Excuse me? You're talking to a Cup Champion," I growled. "Watch your mouth."

Renar shut it.

Jonah got up and looked between us worryingly. "I guess I can talk for a minute."

Jonah wanted to stay in the Commons, in eyesight of Renar, but I yanked him out into the hallway instead. "Jonah, what are you doing?" I asked in exhaustion. "Are you seriously okay with how he treats you?"

"I don't see a problem with it." He gave me a blank look. I could already tell this talk wasn't going anywhere.

"It's the start of the semester, and you're already failing all your classes," I told him. "They're not going to let you into the master's program for teaching if you keep this up."

"You're one to talk," Jonah shot back. "I'm not the only one who hasn't been going to class."

He had me there. I'd gone to Hawkei Leadership regularly enough, but that was it. I'd only been to the rest of my classes a handful of times. Baine had to chase me down and drag me into the "cursed classroom" for Senior Theory. I'd only gone once. I knew I was failing, too.

"We aren't talking about me," I said. "Do you really think they're gonna let you be a professor with a D average?"

"I'm thinking about changing my major," Jonah admitted. "Something easier, so I'll have more time to spend with Renar."

"*What?*" This was too unreal. What kind of hold did this jerk have on Jonah? "Don't even go there. You've wanted to teach since we were like, six."

"Things change. I'm not a kid anymore," Jonah insisted. "Renar needs my help a lot, and he doesn't like me studying all the time."

"A guy is never more important than your future. If Renar really cared about you, he'd be fine with you taking time to study," I said.

"No, he's right. I haven't been paying enough attention to him," Jonah insisted. "I do spend a lot of time in class, and when I'm not hitting the books, I'm with you guys. He barely has any time to spend with me."

That was a crock of bullshit. Jonah had barely been around in the past month. I don't even think he'd hit the gym in four weeks, something that would've horrified him a few months ago. This dickhead was even sucking up Jonah's hobbies.

I tried another way. "Sophia's counting on us. How can she expect you to find your piece of the prophecy when you're too busy fucking around with Renar to do your homework, let alone investigate?" I asked.

"Liam, this is *my life*. Let me make my own decisions," Jonah said flatly.

My mouth became a thin line. "Fine." But I wasn't about to sit around and watch Jonah jump like a dog for treats. I left.

There was a door to the Commons that led outside. I headed out. I took the stairs up to the next floor, and found Squeaks lying on a platform off the balcony, which observed the gardens below and the mountains in the distance. Her tail hung off of it, and she swished it as she watched the orange sunset. She chortled as I walked by.

"Hi, Squeaks." I rubbed her head. "Your Elementai's being a shithead."

She squawked in agreement. Squeaks was at the point where if Alvarice was in the room, she wouldn't be. Jonah was always with Renar these days, which meant that he and Squeaks probably didn't see each other except to go to class and sleep. The hippogriff and cockatrice were complete opposites, and Squeaks was apparently done trying to drag Jonah away from Renar.

I needed to be done, too, but no matter how much I knew you couldn't save people, for some reason, that didn't stop my masochistic ass from trying.

Squeaks turned her head and chirped. I looked her way and saw my brother sitting on a stone bench close by. He had his head in his hands and was taking deep breaths, like he was trying to calm himself down. Dyami had his head on Ezra's shoulder and was cooing, sparks flying off his feathers.

Something was up. "Ez, what's going on?" I said by way of a greeting.

He looked up. He tried to pull himself together when he saw me, and got to his feet. Dyami stood beside him. "Nothing. I uh... I got my tournament assignments."

"Oh." I hoped to the ancestors he got a good team. "Who are you with?"

"Cade, which is good," Ezra started. "And Vanessa. I'm happy about both of them."

Cade and Vanessa could both be trusted, and they were strong Elementai. They'd have his back in the Cup. "All right, good so far. Who's from Yapluma?"

Ezra frowned. "Fucking Renar."

"Fuck no." Why couldn't it have been literally anyone else?

"I know, right?" Ezra moaned. "We have Baine as our coach, which is good, I guess, but I'm just freaking nervous, man. I don't want to die out there."

"You're not going to die," I said sharply. "You three will take care of each other. I don't care what happens, take the other two and dump Renar. You won't regret it. He'll stab you in the back for sure."

Ezra nodded. "I know."

I wasn't sure my brother took my warning seriously. He was too good of a kid. He saw the good in everybody, even Renar. And he liked playing the hero.

If Ezra sacrificed himself in the Cup trying to save Renar, it'd be for nothing, because I'd kill the bastard the minute he got back.

On Friday, I left the forest after Hawkei Leadership and went to grab an essay that I'd forgotten to turn in. On my way back to Professor Cheveyo's office, I passed a group of students from mixed Houses having a hushed conversation.

"Did you hear what happened to Diana's Familiar?" a Nivita guy started. He seemed pale and nervous.

"She was right there, then Diana turned around and she was gone. She's distraught," a Koigni guy said.

"Just up and disappeared," a Yapluma girl whispered back. "No one can find her."

"Better than what happened to Davey's. His Familiar collapsed the other day and hasn't gotten up since. Symptoms are just like all the others. At least Diana's Familiar is probably well somewhere," the Nivita boy replied.

"We don't know that for sure," the Yapluma girl said.

More missing and sick Familiars. This wasn't good. I noticed as I walked around that the feeling around the school was edgy. People were on edge, and weren't laughing or talking like they used to. The school was mostly quiet instead of bustling with energy. It was like something big was about to happen— as if a bomb was going to go off any minute. People didn't quite know what it was, but it was there, and it loomed overhead, casting a dark shadow over Orenda Academy.

It made me want to crawl out of my skin. I had to get away from it. For the past couple weeks I'd been feeling pretty numb. It was hard to muster any sort of emotion about anything anymore, and the anxiety going around the school made it ten times worse.

I turned in my half-finished essay, didn't eat lunch (typical these days) and went to the hunting cabin. It was empty when I got there. I grabbed my compound bow and a couple of arrows, along with some magically enchanted ones blessed with my Water magic just in case I ran into something a little more powerful than a deer out there. It wasn't the right time for hunting— deer came out in the early morning or at dusk— but I just wanted to get my mind off things.

After a few hours, the nervous buzzing hadn't halted in my head, and I hadn't seen a single deer— or anything besides trees. I thought hunting would make me feel better, because it was something I liked to do. But all it did was remind me of my dad, and that made things worse.

I nearly fell out of the tree I'd been sitting in when a loud explosion rocked the area. I clung to a branch to avoid getting knocked off, and looked to my right. There were little black clouds of smoke rising over the tree-line about a hundred yards or so away.

Why did shit always happen when I was nearby? Couldn't it wait until I left— or even happen a little closer, so I didn't have to walk so far? Sighing, I grabbed my bow and headed toward where I'd heard the explosion, wondering what had caused it. I was a curious bastard, and it hadn't killed me yet, so apparently I had to keep tempting fate.

I expected the area to be decimated as I approached, but everything looked fine. The wildlife and foliage hadn't been touched. That meant it wasn't a real explosion, and must've been caused by some sort of magical backfire.

I reached the site of where I suspected the explosion to have come from. I was surprised to see Sophia. She was wearing normal clothes, a t-shirt and jeans, because apparently, she only dressed sexy when she wanted to piss me off, and lying on the ground.

I thought that she was just enjoying the day or something, until I noticed she had a large cut across her forehead. Esis was running around her in circles, giving loud and petrified squeaks. In her outstretched hand sat the Spirit Totem, still smoking.

My entire body went cold. Disbelief froze every particle of my being, and I felt like I was going to be sick. I got dizzy. I couldn't feel my limbs, or anything else. My breath was knocked out of me. Tears welled up in my eyes as I dropped my bow and sprinted forward.

She's dead, she's dead, she's really dead. She'd used the Spirit Totem, and it'd backfired on her. It had killed her. If she was dead, I wanted to die, too. Esis heard my footsteps. He seemed relieved to see me as I came to a stop at Sophia's side.

I skidded to my knees and lifted her up into my lap. *Please wake up.* But I knew she wasn't going to. I'd told her not to use that damn thing, and she didn't listen. The totem rolled away from her fingers as I cradled her against me.

"Sophia." I wiped away the blood that was still pouring from the cut on her head and whispered her name. My lips were trembling. I didn't know what to do. There was nothing left to do anymore. I would just stay here forever, holding her until I died and we both turned to dust.

Then, against all odds, her eyes flew open. Sophia blinked upward at the sky, then at me, trying to get her bearings on where she was and what was going on.

I was so fucking relieved I wanted to throw myself on the ground and thank the ancestors. She was okay.

Then worry turned to rage. I was *pissed off.* "What gives you the right to fucking scare me like that?"

"Huh?" She was still processing. Esis reached up and healed the cut on her forehead. It vanished slowly, leaving only smears of blood behind.

I was shaking, I was so mad. She rolled out of my arms, coming to, and I got up to pace a few feet away. She needed to back off for a minute. I was going to lose my temper.

Sophia slowly got to her feet. She shook her head, put the totem back around her neck, then picked up Esis as she asked, "Were you following me?"

Her nerve was unbelievable. "Following—" I took a breath. "As hard as it is to believe, Sophia, my entire life doesn't revolve around you."

That was mean. Sophia flinched like she'd been slapped, and said, "Well, it wouldn't be that much of a stretch, considering you were spying on me all last semester."

"Don't even go there." She had no right to bring that up right now. "What the hell were you thinking? You know better than to go playing with that thing." I gestured to the totem. I wanted to rip it off her neck and destroy it right then. It wasn't safe.

"I was just practicing. I've had this thing for a while. I might as well learn how to use it," she countered.

"Yes, but you don't know how!" I shouted. "You need to find some sort of information, or a teacher, or—"

"I've looked everywhere. Anichi didn't leave behind an instruction manual on how to use this thing," she said. "And all of them are dead, so the only way to figure out how to use it is by experimenting."

"By risking your life?!" I shouted. "Is that even worth it?"

"Would you calm down?" she asked. She was giving me attitude. "You're taking this too far."

"Believe me, I am angrier at you than I ever have been." I stuffed my hands in my pockets, because I didn't want her to see they were shaking.

She didn't understand. She'd be mad at me too if she'd found me unconscious in the middle of the woods with a dangerous item in my hands, after an explosion that had nearly caused an earthquake.

"Why are you so mad? Because I'm doing this without you?" she accused.

"Because you put yourself at risk! Worse still, you did it alone!" Shit, she didn't get it. If she died, she didn't know what that would do to me.

"I didn't ask you to come out here and save me. I was doing perfectly fine on my own!" she shouted.

I gave a skeptical sound. "Sure, that's why I found you passed out in the middle of the woods, with Esis freaking out."

She looked guilty at that. "You don't need to worry about me. We're not dat—"

"Newsflash, Sophia, *it doesn't matter*," I said harshly. "If you're in trouble, I'm *always* going to be there to save you. No matter what, *end of fucking story*."

Her eyes flared. "What if I said I don't *want* you to keep saving me?"

"You'd be a liar," I shot at her. "Didn't I tell you that thing was dangerous?"

She crossed her arms and turned away from me. "Whatever, *Mom*."

I hated when the team called me that. "Don't give me sass."

"I can take care of myself," Sophia snapped.

"It's not just the totem. You're out in the woods alone. Familiars are going *missing*. It's only a matter of time before people start vanishing, too," I spat.

"You don't know that. You're being over dramatic." She rolled her eyes. "Besides, you're out here alone, too."

"I was hunting," I said quickly.

"Like that's a good reason." She huffed. "What are those little arrows going to do if you run into a dragon or something, make it mad?"

"Yeah, because Fire works so well on dragons," I said sarcastically. "I don't give a crap what happens to me. I care about—"

I broke off and took several deep breaths. I grabbed my bow and turned away. "Come on. Let's go back to school."

"You're not the boss of me."

"*Come on*, Sophia."

I expected her to stomp her foot and refuse to go, like a little child. Ancestors, if *pawee* ever fit her now. Instead, she made a pissed-off sound and came after me.

I stopped at the hunting cabin to drop off the bow before we headed back. Sophia didn't follow me in, and I didn't blame her. Too many memories in there.

We were both still fuming by the time we got back to Orenda. I expected us to split the minute we walked into the entrance hall, but as we drew closer, we could hear loud noises coming from inside the school. It sounded like screams.

"What's going on?" Sophia asked. Esis perked up his ears, seeming worried.

"I don't know." We walked through the grand double doors, and our argument was forgotten. It was nothing in the face of this.

The entrance hall was in a complete meltdown. Hundreds of students and Familiars were milling about, and cries of people's names were drowned out by the various roars, squawks, and barks echoing around the room. Feathers fluttered downward from all the birds flying around the ceiling, and several Familiars got into fights out of stress that their Elementai had to pull them out of. Most of the students who went to Orenda Academy were packed into the space. There was hardly any room to stand.

There were a couple of Toaqua nearby. I noticed Wyatt huddling against the wall, looking scared. I went to him for information, and Sophia followed.

"What's going on?" I asked him.

Wyatt was super pale. "They were just there, man. They were there, and then they vanished."

"What are you talking about?" He wasn't making any sense.

"It's the Familiars." Marcee was nearby. She was clutching her teacup pig in her arms, who had her wings over her eyes. "A bunch of unbonded ones went missing yesterday. The Elders apparently tried to cover it up, but news broke this afternoon by local media. A bunch of dragons, unicorns, griffins, all kinds are just gone. Especially eggs. The Familiar nursery in Kinpago was raided of everything. Not one baby Familiar was left behind."

"Yeah, and now a ton of bonded ones are going missing, too. Familiars of Elders, powerful people, even a couple students," Wyatt said in a rush. "It's not just that Isabella girl's anymore. There's a few Familiars missing from almost every Elder Council. It's like a group of people came in and just took them all over the past few days. And more and more Familiars are getting sick, too. Some sort of plague has broken out."

This was bad. This was really bad. It was enough to incite the school into a panic. People were running around the entrance hall in alarm, clinging to their Familiars. Large Familiars were stampeding around the room. Dragons, elephants, unicorns and wyverns barreled over furniture and made the floor shake. The little Familiars, and some people, were in danger of getting crushed. There were more screams as people scattered out of the way.

"Sophia!" I called. I reached out my arm and brought her close to me. She didn't object and stayed tightly to my side as we were jostled around by the jumbling crowd. She put her arms around me and held tight, shutting her eyes. Esis stayed wedged between us and dug his little nails into my shirt like his life depended on it.

My eyes scanned the crowd. I caught glimpse of Jonah riding on top of Squeaks' back. He reached out into the crowd and grabbed someone. It was Imogen. He pulled her easily onto the back of Squeaks. Imogen clung to Jonah tightly with one arm while squeezing Sassy with the other. Squeaks kicked out and tried to bite anyone who came near, a glint in her eyes daring them to attack.

"SILENCE!" There was a loud, booming voice that echoed around the room, and everything came to a halt. Head Dean Alric was at the top of the stairs in the entrance hall, with Professor Baine, Madame Doya, and Professor Perot by his side. He held up his hands, and the room got quiet. The chaos dulled for a moment, and Head Dean Alric waited for things to settle before he spoke again.

"I understand that this news is very upsetting to you, but please, I ask for your cooperation!" Alric boomed over the crowd. "All sick Familiars have been moved—"

"Someone's poisoning them! We're all next!" a girl screamed. Shouts of alarm rose up all around the room.

Alric raised his hands, and the room fell silent again. "We cannot rush to any conclusions!" he announced. "The authorities are doing everything in their power to find those missing. All missing Familiars will be returned to their rightful Elementai! What is essential is that we *do not panic.*"

The room hung desperately on his words for some form of further instruction. "Now," Alric began, "a quarantine has already been set up for those Familiars who have fallen ill. If your Familiar begins behaving in a way that is strange, you are to take them to the hospital wing *immediately.*"

He cleared his throat. "As for the rest of you, the rumors are true. Someone is taking Familiars. We do not know how or why."

A nervous whisper went over the crowd. Alric hushed them. "We are taking measures to make sure that no more Familiars are abducted. All students currently have a curfew of being back in their dormitories by midnight. Students are to walk to classes in groups of two or more. Familiars are to stay at your side at all times, and not leave, not even to deliver messages.

"Those who have large Familiars who sleep separately from their Elementai, or Water Familiars who cannot leave the ocean, will be put into groups for their own protection. It is essential that every student follow these rules for their own safety. Those that do not will be punished."

Even though we were all college students, and of age, nobody whined about having to follow extra rules. The thought of having your Familiar taken was enough to make people get in line.

"In the meantime," Alric announced, "until the kidnappers are caught, members of the Elementai Task Force will be posted around school, for your own security. Be assured there is nothing to fear from them."

Shit. The cops were gonna be at the school? This was serious.

Alric looked at Perot. "Professor Perot and I are working to discover a cure for this strange disease. But it will take time. We beg you not to lose your heads."

This seemed to reassure people. A hopeful murmur took over the area. Alric was a master alchemist, and so was Perot. They'd find a cure for whatever this mysterious illness was, right?

I didn't know. Perot had failed to cure me yet, and this plague sounded even more serious.

Alric clapped his hands. "I suggest everyone go back to their dormitories and stay there," he said. "The Elementai Task Force is beginning their investigation. Classes will resume on Monday. With order, please."

People did as he said. The panic was gone. Students and their Familiars walked to their dorms, grateful to be given something to do. Imogen slid off of Squeaks, and she and Jonah went opposite ways back to their dorms.

Sophia was still holding on to me. We slowly let go of each other as we began the walk up the stairs back to our dorms.

For the first time, I was grateful Nashoma was gone. I didn't have to worry about him getting sick or disappearing, unlike the rest of these people.

We came to the hallway where Sophia and I would have to go in different directions to get back to our dorms. I looked at her, earlier argument forgotten. "Keep an eye on Esis," I told her lowly. "Whoever these kidnappers are, I bet they'd love to have him."

"I will. Be safe," Sophia whispered, and she disappeared into the group of Koignis nearby.

I followed the rest of the Toaquas. The dorm was quiet that night—most people were too busy clinging to their Familiars to do much else, except jump at every noise that was made, reacting as if the kidnapper was in that very room.

The Elementai Task Force wouldn't be setting up shop here if they didn't think Orenda Academy had something to do with the abductions. They'd search elsewhere. That meant the thief... and possibly, whoever had introduced the plague... was inside these walls.

sophia

EIGHT

Orenda Academy seemed to change overnight following Head Dean Alric's announcement. The entire castle became strangely quiet. Even the Koigni common room and the saunas stopped buzzing with their usual activity. Almost no one left their rooms except to go to the dining hall, and when they did, it was always in quiet groups. No one spoke higher than a whisper all weekend.

The eerie silence in the dining hall had shifted the entire tone of the room. Most people grabbed food from the takeout line and headed back to their dorms. Those who stayed barely spoke. The only sounds came from the clinking of silverware and quiet whispers at nearby tables. It was like everyone was worried that if they spoke, their Familiar would be next.

"This is all too weird," Miranda whispered on our way back to the Koigni dorms after dinner on Sunday.

Since we were required to travel in groups, I'd joined a small group of Koigni Second Years three times a day for meals. I had to admit, it made me feel a little safer, but I missed my usual group of friends. I hadn't seen them all weekend.

"I don't mind," Tabitha said. "It's good to take precautions."

"Yeah, but we shouldn't have to," Ben said. "Nothing like this has ever happened before. Orenda Academy is supposed to be safe."

"It's not just Orenda," Miranda pointed out. "It's all of Kinpago. At least we have the Task Force on campus, but people are acting... weird."

Lindsey stroked Medusa's head. "You guys don't have anything to worry about. You don't have Familiars yet."

I squeezed Esis tighter to my chest. At least he'd be immune from whatever illness was going around, but he was so small. He could get taken easily. I couldn't stand the thought of that.

"Hey," Miranda said softly as we entered the quiet common room. "We're not going to let anything happen to yours or Sophia's Familiar. Promise."

"Thanks," I said, but I didn't know how Miranda could keep that promise. She couldn't keep an eye on me twenty-four-seven, not when we all had different classes.

I took to braving the halls on my own Monday morning, since the only Koigni I knew in my Elementai Explorations class was Vanessa, and she lived off campus so we couldn't walk together. I wasn't far from the Great Hall when I heard someone calling my name.

"Sophia!"

I turned to see Mia rushing away from a group of Toaqua girls to catch up to me. Her canine Familiar followed at her heels.

What the hell did this bitch want?

"Um... hi?" I couldn't hide the disgust in my tone. Images of Mia and Liam together flashed through my mind. I tried to shut them out, but I couldn't stop their invasion.

"You shouldn't be walking alone," Mia said kindly as she fell into step beside me. "Didn't you hear what Dean Alric said?"

"I'm not alone," I snarled. It was like the girl was suggesting I couldn't take care of myself. "I have Esis."

Esis chittered proudly from my arms.

She twisted up her nose when she looked down at him, then said, "Either way, we're both headed to Elementai Explorations, so it doesn't hurt to stick together."

Her words rubbed me the wrong way. A wave of heat swept through me.

"Stick together?" I stopped in the middle of the hall and turned to her.

She blinked, looking stunned.

"You want to stick together? How about you stop fucking with my ex on the side?" I realized what I said a moment too late. No one was supposed to know Liam and I were ever together.

Mia's eyes went wide. "You think...? Me and Liam? Ancestors, no! Sophia, I would never. Liam's just helping me..."

"Helping you with what?" I demanded.

"That's not important," she said. "But you should know there is *nothing* going on between me and Liam."

That's exactly what someone who *was* screwing with him would say.

"Seriously, Sophia," Mia said. "Even if I *wanted* to, which I don't, Liam would never take me back. Besides, he's still hung up on you. He's not ready to move on yet."

I couldn't explain why my stomach flipped at the comment. I didn't care if Liam still wanted me, did I? I was getting over him. It wasn't like we were ever going to get back together. The whole stomach-flipping thing was just habit left over from our relationship— or so I told myself.

And then it hit me. How the hell did Mia know I'd been talking about Liam?

"What did Liam tell you?" I demanded.

Mia tossed her hair over her shoulder and started walking again. "He didn't say anything, but you just called him your ex, and you're not denying it. Clearly my suspicions are true. I know Liam, and I see it in the way he looks at you. He *never* looked at me like that, not even when we were dating."

I was practically sitting on cloud nine.

"Really?" I asked in giddy excitement. I caught myself and quickly added, "Not that I care."

Mia rolled her eyes. "Keep telling yourself that, girl. I know a crush when I see one."

My jaw dropped. "I do *not* have a crush on Liam. We broke up."

Esis made a noise that sounded a lot like a scoff.

"You're right," Mia said. "It's way more than a crush."

I opened my mouth to ask her just who she thought she was, making these stupid assumptions, but she spoke first.

"So, I've been really curious to ask. Does Liam still do that thing with his tongue when he's concentrating hard?" she said.

"What thing?" I asked.

"You know…" Mia stuck the tip of her tongue out to demonstrate.

"Oh my God!" I laughed. "I never noticed, but now that you point it out, yes!"

Mia chuckled. "I was trying to kick him of that habit. I thought it looked silly."

I scowled. Nobody insulted Liam like that. "Well, I think it's cute."

Mia's face paled. "Yeah, I just meant…"

We arrived at our classroom, and her words trailed off. Mia didn't step inside the room, though.

She stopped outside and faced me. "Liam changed after Nashoma died, but he changed again when he met you."

I suddenly felt very uncomfortable. "What are you getting at?"

"You were good for Liam," she said. "Don't give up on him, okay?"

I gaped at her. Was she suggesting Liam and I get back together?

Before I could ask, Mia turned inside the classroom, leaving me stunned. "See you around, Sophia."

By that afternoon, I joined my usual group of Second Years to walk to Intermediate Koigni Magic together. The classroom was almost empty when we entered, except for a small group in the training area.

"You're doing it wrong," Haley snapped at Kelsey, who was sustaining a flame in her open palm. Kelsey's jaguar Familiar let out a low growl that Haley didn't notice. Haley stomped over to the middle of the training section. "I'll show you how it's done."

Haley held her palm face-up. A burst of flame shot six feet high out of her hand. The two guys with them clapped, while Anwara ruffled her feathers from her perch atop the back of one of the couches.

Lindsey scoffed. She slid into her desk and mumbled, "Show off."

My brow furrowed as I took the desk beside hers. Esis curled up in my lap. "I thought you liked Haley."

Lindsey pursed her lips. "No comment."

Miranda leaned over and whispered, "Haley makes us hang out with her all the time. It's not like we can tell her no."

"Yes, you can," I stated firmly.

"She'd start someone's hair on fire," Tabitha said with a chuckle.

"So what?" I said with a shrug. "Start hers on fire first."

Ben burst into a fit of laughter so loud that it made Haley's group look our way. They shot us dirty looks, then turned back to their Fire.

Lindsey shook her head in amusement. "Maybe you can do it for us."

"Yeah, you already punched her in the face," Miranda said.

I smiled proudly. "Don't tempt me. I'll totally do it."

Everyone in our group laughed.

"What's so funny?" Vanessa entered the room with Aisha and sat in the far back corner with us, where there was room for the dragon beside her.

"We're plotting," I said with a chuckle.

Vanessa leaned in, her eyes bright. "Ooh, plotting against who?"

"Haley," I snickered.

Vanessa held her palm up to stop me. "Say no more. I'm in."

Tabitha shot a nervous glance across the room. "You guys aren't serious, are you?"

I shrugged. "Depends on whether she provokes me or not."

Another group of students entered the room, and we went silent. A minute later, Madame Doya breezed into the classroom with Naomi at her side. She snapped her fingers and headed straight toward the training area without a word. Everyone scampered out of their desks and quickly followed behind her.

Doya stood near the huge fireplace to address us all. "We're going to be doing things a little differently today. In Beginner Koigni Magic, we focused on our individual strengths. One of the lessons you'll learn before you pass Intermediate Koigni Magic is how to work with other members of your House. As you know, regular fire will not burn a Koigni. But magical Fire..."

Doya flicked her hand, and embers rained down on us. Students jumped and tried to put out the embers on their clothes. One landed on my pant leg, and I quickly patted it out with my palm before it could burn through. Still, I felt the burn from it on my skin. Was Doya allowed to do that? I was pretty certain she wasn't, but no one looked hurt, just really pissed off.

"Magical Fire *can* hurt another Koigni— whether it comes from another Koigni or a creature like Naomi." Doya gestured to her Familiar, and Naomi burst into flames to demonstrate. Heat waves pulsed off of her and over those of us toward the front.

"Tabitha, a fireball, please," Doya demanded.

The blood drained from Tabitha's face.

"We don't have all day," Doya pressed firmly.

Tabitha quickly formed a fireball and tossed it lightly into Doya's outstretched hands. Doya caught it and held it up for all of us to see.

"However, Fire does not *have* to burn you if two Koigni work in harmony," Doya explained. "It is only when that Fire is created with malicious intent that it will hurt."

My mind flickered back to the tournament, when I'd been stuck in the burning forest and the Koigni Elders' Fire had burned my ankle.

Doya continued. "To achieve this harmony, you must both *deliver* your fire with peaceful intentions and *receive* it with full compliance. Today, you will pair up and exchange fireballs. I don't expect to send anyone to the hospital wing, so I ask that you all be careful."

I turned to Vanessa to ask her to be my partner, but before I could say anything, Doya was barking orders again.

"Don't look so smug, Nicholas. It's not as easy as one might think, particularly if you let your emotions get in the way." Doya gestured to a girl on the other end of the room. "Piper, you're with Nicholas."

"You're kidding!" Piper protested.

Doya's lips pressed into a thin line. "I never kid. Now, partner up. Haley, you're with Sophia. Vanessa and Kelsey…"

I didn't hear the rest of the assignments, because I was already staring daggers at Haley. This was all her fault. When Doya dragged us to her office the other day after our fight, she'd given us a big lecture about how we had to get along because we were both Koigni. Turning on each other only made our House weaker.

Haley had kept her chin held high the entire time, like she thought she was off the hook and I was the one in trouble. "That's right, *Sophia*," Haley had sneered. "Koigni stick with their own kind."

Doya had cocked an eyebrow at her. "Now's not the time to go pointing fingers, Miss Westfenix. Sophia isn't the first Koigni you've had a brawl with. If you hope to be Chieftess someday, you'll have to learn how to respect the members of your House."

Doya was one to talk, but whatever. I was just pleased she was putting Haley in her place.

"I'm sick of this drama between the two of you," Doya had said. "Sooner or later, you'll have to work together in harmony, or you risk tearing this entire House apart."

Haley didn't take Doya's threat seriously. The truth was, Doya had a point. By the time Haley took over the council, she'd need to know how to play nice with others. She couldn't run the whole House on her own.

Haley had stood and crossed her arms. "Then that's a risk we're going to have to take. There's no way I'll *ever* work in harmony with *her*."

Those harsh words still rang in my ears as I stared Haley down in the training area. She shot back a hostile scowl.

"Let's just get this over with, okay?" she said as she tossed her hair over her shoulder.

"Fine with me," I snarled back. I lowered my voice to Esis, who sat on my shoulder. "Go sit on the couch."

I didn't want him getting hurt, but Esis held firmly on to me. His little nails dug through my shirt and into my skin, sending a clear message that he wasn't going anywhere.

Haley and I faced each other, as did the other partners. We both formed a fireball in our hands at the same time and prepared to throw them at each other. I would've slammed mine straight into her face if we weren't supposed to be getting along.

Haley's lips tightened. "*I'll* go first. Westfenixes always go first."

I clamped my fist shut, but the fireball inside begged to escape. "Fine, but don't go trying anything stupid. The sooner we complete this assignment, the sooner we can go back to fist fighting."

"Oh, you want another go?" Haley threatened. She took a quick step toward me, like it was supposed to scare me. I didn't even blink.

She narrowed her eyes and said, "Think fast."

A fireball shot out of her hands, and I reached out to catch it. Pain radiated across my palms, and I quickly dropped the fireball. It fizzled out on its way to the ground.

Esis gasped from my shoulder and reached out for my hand.

"Later," I whispered to him, then I turned on Haley. "What the hell? You weren't supposed to burn me."

Haley cocked an eyebrow at me. "It wasn't my fault. You heard what Madame Doya said. You must receive my Fire *willingly*."

And you need to go to hell. I was ninety-nine percent sure Haley had burned me on purpose.

"If it's so easy, let's see how you do." I threw a fireball at her face.

She threw up her hands to catch it but ducked at the last second. The fireball whizzed by her head and smashed into the stone wall behind her.

Haley pointed an ugly finger at me. "Madame Doya! She's provoking me."

Doya strolled over to us, looking completely at peace with her hands behind her back. She was totally expecting this. "In case you weren't listening, the task requires you *both* to work together harmoniously. You cannot blame your partner for your failure as a team, just as a chieftess can not blame the tribe for her mistakes. It's all or nothing, Miss Westfenix, and you'll do best to remember that."

Haley was fuming as Doya walked away. Like, literally. Smoke was rising out of her palms.

I sighed and lowered my voice. "Can't we agree to get along for one minute? Let's just prove to Doya we can do this."

Haley glanced over to Ben and Tabitha, who already had the task down and were tossing a fireball back and forth like it was a baseball.

"Fine." Haley gritted her teeth. "Try this!"

Haley threw her arms forward and blasted streams of fire so hot at me that it felt like I was sitting in the middle of a bonfire. Sweat broke out on my skin, even as I stumbled backward to avoid the flames. Esis clung tightly to me and quivered in fear.

Hell no! Haley was *not* going to hurt me or my Familiar. Time for some hair burning.

I dropped all my walls holding my emotions back and let my anger bubble up inside of me. Clutching the totem beneath my shirt, I tried to connect to its power to strengthen my Fire. Heat waves rippled across my skin, and my features contorted in pure rage. I thrust my hands out toward her.

Power exploded out of my palms so strong that it knocked both me and Haley off our feet. I landed hard on my back and went skidding along the floor, while Haley slammed into the wall. My vision blurred for a moment. I felt disoriented until sheer terror ripped through me when I realized I couldn't breathe.

I gasped for breath. Esis must've been knocked off my shoulder, because I heard his little paws scurry across the floor until he reached me. He placed his palm on my chest until a breath finally passed through my lungs. The whole room had gone silent, and everyone stared.

Doya stomped over to us. "What is going on here?"

Haley was on the ground shaking as Anwara flew to her side. "Sophia tried to kill me!"

"I did not!" I shouted back.

"This is the exact *opposite* of the task I gave you," Madame Doya snapped. "You two will learn how to work together. You'll not be leaving this classroom until you do."

We'll starve to death, I thought, but I held my tongue.

Haley and I were forced to face each other again. Everyone turned back to their partners.

"Let's start out small," I suggested.

Haley shoved her hand out toward me. A small fireball the size of a golf ball floated in her open palm. "Here. Take it."

I could already feel that it was hot enough to burn me. "Let's back up even further."

I reached out to touch her arm, and she jumped away from me.

"Relax," I said through gritted teeth. "I'm not going to hurt you. That's the whole idea."

Haley let me touch her. I took a deep breath and called heat to the surface of my skin. She jumped away from me, though I'd barely felt a thing.

"Ow!" Haley rubbed her arm. "What's your game, Henley?"

Forget it. This was never going to work if Haley couldn't stop being a bitch.

Nearly an hour passed, and we were still burning each other. Haley kept blaming me, but at least I was *trying*. She wasn't even pretending like she cared.

We were nearing the end of class, and Haley and I were the only team left who hadn't managed to share our Fire without hurting each other.

"Clearly, this is never going to work," Haley said in a low voice. "Let's just tell Doya we did it and get out of here."

"You mean lie?" I asked.

Haley shrugged. "Do you want to be stuck here for the rest of the night or not?"

Honestly, she had a point. At least we could agree on something. That was a step in the right direction, wasn't it?

"Follow my lead." Haley took a step back. When Doya wasn't looking, she conjured a fireball in her hands and let out a shrill of glee. "Look! We did it!"

I just stood there with a totally bored look on my face. Did she really think this was going to work?

Doya came over to inspect our work. "Good. Now let's see Sophia sustain one of your fireballs."

She totally knew we were lying, and she wanted to watch it blow up in our faces. The fact was, Haley was right. I didn't want to sit in this classroom with her another moment. But more than that, I never wanted to do this exercise with her again. If we didn't show Doya now that we could handle this assignment, we'd be partnered up for the rest of eternity until we proved ourselves to her. It was now or never.

"Okay," I shrugged. I stared Haley directly in the eyes, hoping she could read my plea to just work with me on this one. I readied myself to catch her fireball.

I accept your Fire willingly, I repeated in my mind. We could do this, as long as we set our pride aside.

Haley tossed a fireball at me, and I caught it. The Fire seared my hands, and pain shot up my arms, but I bit back a grimace and sustained the Fire in my palms.

Esis will heal me, I told myself. It was the only thing keeping me from shooting the fireball straight back at Haley's face. It hurt like hell, like the very sun was burning in my palms. It seared through my skin so hot that it felt as if it'd reached my tender muscles. I bit down hard on the inside of my cheek until I tasted blood. Esis tugged on my hair, begging me to stop, but I barely felt him.

Sweat broke out on my brow as I concentrated on holding out as long as I could. Finally, Doya tore her curious gaze from my hands. I breathed a sigh of relief and dropped my arms to my sides. They shook all the way up to my shoulders. The fireball went out.

"I must say, you two have impressed me," Doya said.

Haley gave a fist-pump. The bitch actually thought we'd done it.

Red-hot pain pulsed across my trembling hands, and I bit back tears. I looked down at them to see the skin was blistered and peeling off in places. I should've been rushed to the burn unit immediately. Doya followed my gaze, but I quickly shoved my hands behind my back.

Doya's expression remained stoic. I couldn't read her at all, and didn't know if she'd seen my hands or not.

"We'll be doing this exercise again," Doya said. "I suggest everyone practices outside of class. It will be part of your final grade."

She turned and raised her voice. "Class dismissed."

As soon as her eyes were no longer on me, I grabbed Esis off my shoulder. His soft fur eased some of the burning pain in my hands, and it helped to hide the burns from everyone. I could already feel his magic working on me as I headed back to my desk to grab my bag.

There was a traffic jam by the door as everyone tried leaving at once. Haley pushed past people to get out sooner.

"Would you let me through?" she snapped. "What is everyone's— ow!"

Haley tripped over someone else's feet and went tumbling through the doorway and into the hall. Anwara squawked and crashed into the ground beside her.

"Haley!" Lindsey cried. She reached out to help Haley to her feet, while Miranda helped Anwara.

"Get off of me, you whore," Haley snapped as she got to her feet. Then she saw who was helping her, and she relaxed. "Oh, it's you. I didn't mean that."

Lindsey crossed her arms. "I don't buy it. You always say stuff like that."

"Yeah, but not to you," Haley argued.

Miranda frowned. "That's not true. You called Lindsey a bitch just this morning."

By now, the traffic jam had thinned, but several people had stuck around to watch.

Haley rolled her eyes. "Yeah, but I didn't mean it like *that*."

"Then how *did* you mean it?" Lindsey challenged.

"I meant it as a *compliment*." Haley elbowed Kelsey. "Tell her, Kelsey."

Kelsey hesitated. "Yeah. She calls me a bitch all the time."

"And you think that's a compliment?" Lindsey asked in disbelief.

Kelsey gaped at her. "I— I don't mind."

"Well, I do," Lindsey said, taking a stand.

I found myself smiling as I stood back and watched the confrontation. I glanced over to Vanessa, who was also watching with interest.

"Fine. I won't call you that anymore." Haley huffed, like it was such a burden to take the word out of her vocabulary.

"No, you know what? Call me a bitch all you want. I don't care anymore." Lindsey turned on her heel and stomped away. Medusa slithered closely at her feet.

"Lindsey, come on!" Haley yelled. "You can't just leave."

Lindsey whirled toward her. "I can, and I will. And I'm taking Miranda with me."

Lindsey slipped an arm through Miranda's elbow.

"I think Miranda can speak for herself," Haley growled. "She wouldn't—"

"Fuck off, Haley," Miranda snapped, flipping her off as the two walked away.

Haley's hands balled into fists, and she stomped her feet like a little child. She became so enraged that she let out an earth-shattering screech and her hair went up in flames. Kelsey quickly tried to pat it out, but Haley swatted her away.

"You know what, I don't care!" Haley called after them. "I never wanted a *dyke* in my group, anyway!"

Lindsey whirled around, looking like she was about to gouge Haley's eyes out.

Doya cleared her throat from the doorway of her classroom, and the crowd quickly dispersed.

"They started it!" Haley insisted, pointing to Miranda and Lindsey.

Doya ignored them. She walked straight up to Haley instead and swatted her on the back of her flaming head. The flames quickly died down.

"You've been in two fights in the last week," Doya snapped fiercely.

"You're embarrassing your House. What would your mother think of you?"

Haley gaped at her.

"My office. Now." Doya started dragging Haley in the opposite direction without a second glance back at us.

I couldn't help but beam. "Oh. My. God!"

I squealed along with Lindsey, Miranda, and Vanessa. We all went dead silent when Doya shot back a scowl. We quickly hurried off back toward the Koigni dorms.

"That was insane," Vanessa said.

Miranda took a deep breath and smiled so wide it looked like she had a spoon in her mouth. "Ancestors, I've wanted to say that to Haley for years. I feel good. More than good. I feel great."

"Me, too," Lindsey said excitedly. "The only thing that would've made it better is if I actually set her hair on fire."

"Well, her hair *was* on fire, so that has to count for something," I said with a laugh. "I'd give anything to see that fight go down again. It was amazing."

"*Fuck off, Haley.*" Vanessa imitated Miranda proudly.

"*Call me a bitch all you want,*" Miranda said, repeating Lindsey's words.

Lindsey swayed her hips and snapped her fingers. "That bitch ain't got nothin' on me."

Miranda skipped forward and twirled around in the middle of the hall. "I feel so free!"

"You should," Vanessa said. "Being friends with Haley is like carrying around a hundred pounds of rocks. I'm glad you guys dumped her."

"You know what this means?" Miranda hopped up and down.

"Girls night!" Lindsey squealed, shooting her fist into the air.

I couldn't stop laughing. "That sounds amazing. Vanessa, can you stay?"

She grinned. "Absolutely. I just have to let Bren know."

"Well, I'm going to go into town to pick up some wine coolers," Lindsey said. "Anyone want to join me?"

"I have a class in an hour," Vanessa said.

"I'll come, and we can stop by your apartment and let Bren know you're staying for a sleepover," Miranda offered. "We'll even pick you up some clothes."

"Really?" Vanessa pressed her hand to her heart, like she was truly touched by the gesture. "You guys are so sweet."

"We'll meet back in the common room in a couple hours?" Lindsey asked.

"We wouldn't miss it for the world," I said.

Lindsey and Miranda headed for the Great Hall, while Vanessa and I continued toward the dorms. I still couldn't stop laughing.

"I wish someone would've recorded that," I joked as we entered the Koigni common room. It was completely deserted at this time of day. "I could watch that on repeat all day."

"I'm so glad I was there." Vanessa plopped down onto one of the chairs in front of the farthest fireplace from the door. She looked exhausted.

I would've offered to go back to my room, but Aisha was so big that she barely fit through the double doors anymore. She wouldn't make it into my bedroom without breaking the frame.

I sat beside Vanessa and kept Esis closely wrapped in my arms. The pain had significantly diminished, but the burns had been really bad. It'd take longer to heal than normal. The pulse in my palms had dulled until my hands became numb while Esis continued to heal me.

"Are you okay?" I asked Vanessa curiously. "You look a little drained."

She sighed. "I'm really fatigued lately. And just not feeling well in general."

"Why?" I joked. "Are you pregnant?"

Vanessa's cheeks turned bright pink.

I gasped and sat straight up. "Shut up! I was kidding. Are you serious?"

Vanessa tried to hold back a smile, but she couldn't. "I am! I totally am."

I shouldn't have been surprised since she was married and all, but I went totally speechless. Vanessa was *my* age. Nineteen. That was so young.

And yet, I couldn't stop the wave of jealousy that hit me. I wanted what Vanessa had— a husband, and a kid on the way. Her life was perfect. I couldn't stop images of Liam from invading my mind. *We should be getting married.*

I quickly pushed the thoughts away.

"I'm only six weeks along," she said. "Bren and I are waiting to tell everyone until our first ultrasound, to make sure the baby's healthy and all."

"I'm the first person you told?" I asked in shock.

"Besides Bren, yeah," she admitted.

My jealousy waned, but it didn't completely melt away. "I'm glad you told me. I'm happy for you. Is Bren going to be mad you spilled the beans?"

She shook her head. "No, he knows we're friends. I'm just contemplating whether I should tell Miranda and Lindsey. I can't exactly drink tonight."

I chuckled. "I'll drink for the both of us. How does that sound?"

She laughed. "Sounds good. Can we keep this between us for just a few more weeks?"

"Of course," I told her.

"You know what the weirdest thing is about being pregnant?" Vanessa asked. "How much my boobs hurt!"

She poked at her breasts, and I bust a gut laughing.

"I'm serious!" she laughed. "No one tells you how soon everything changes."

"That's a *good* thing," I told her. "Your boobs are going to get huge."

She stared down at her cleavage. "I know. I can't wait."

"So you'll be due..." I started doing the math in my head and suddenly realized something. "Oh my gosh! You'll be competing in the tournament when you're, what, five months along?"

Vanessa bit her lower lip. "Nineteen weeks," she said with certainty — like she'd already counted it out.

"They'll let you wait until next year, won't they?" I asked.

She shook her head. "No. They don't make exceptions."

My jaw dropped. "They can't let a pregnant woman participate!" That was just cruel.

She shrugged. "They have before. I'm nervous, but it's the second trimester. At least it's not like I'll be giving birth in the middle of the tournament."

I laughed, but I felt uneasy. If something happened to Vanessa or her baby during the tournament, the Elders were going to have to answer to me.

"It'll be fine," she said, but she didn't sound convinced. "As long as I make it to the end and my baby's okay, everything will be okay."

I leveled her with a serious glare. "Don't worry about winning. You finish that thing for your baby. No matter what."

Vanessa and I talked for hours— so much that that she lost track of time and missed her class.

Miranda and Lindsey returned from Kinpago carrying endless bags of groceries. Miranda also had a huge pizza box in her hands.

"We thought of everything," Lindsey said as they dropped it all onto a study table behind us. "Chips, dip, donuts, cookies, pizza, and... *booze!* I hope no one's on a diet."

Lindsey reached into one of the bags and pulled out a wine cooler. She popped the top off and took a sip. "Who's ready to get started? It's five o'clock somewhere, right?"

"It *is* five o'clock," I pointed out.

Lindsey smacked her lips. "Perfect."

Across the common room, a group of First Year Koigni guys eyed us curiously.

"Whose room are we crashing?" I asked.

"Actually, is it cool if we stay out here?" Vanessa asked. "I don't want to leave Aisha. Not with..."

"Of course," Miranda quickly cut in. "We wouldn't leave her out here on her own, would we?" She tickled Aisha's nose, and Aisha licked her back.

We resituated our area until our chairs were arranged in a circle and our snacks were piled on a table in front of us. We spoke in low voices and played with our Fire for hours as people passed in and out of the common room. Almost no one stuck around, since they were still on high alert. Haley and Kelsey passed through once and turned up their noses like they didn't see us.

By ten o'clock that night, we were completely alone. Darkness had settled over the night, leaving the only light coming from the burning fireplace next to us and a few dim lamps around the study tables.

I reached into one of the bags and pulled out the coconut rum the girls had bought. Between the four of us, we'd only made it through one six-pack of wine coolers in the last five hours, and I knew for certain Esis had drank two on his own. I didn't even feel a buzz.

"Ooh," Miranda teased. "Sophia's breaking out the booze."

"I think it's time to liven this party up," I said. "Who wants a shot?"

Lindsey's hand shot in the air. "Me!"

Since we didn't have any cups nearby, I took a swig straight from the bottle and handed it to Lindsey. It burned my throat, but left a sweet aftertaste.

Lindsey took a swig, then said, "I think I know how to liven things up. How about a drinking game?"

Vanessa exchanged a quick glance with me. I leaned over to her and whispered, "I'll drink for you, remember?"

"Yes!" Miranda said to Lindsey. "What kind of game?"

"Never Have I Ever?" Lindsey suggested.

Miranda hopped to her feet and squealed. "I'll be right back!"

She ran off down the hall and returned less than a minute later carrying a pile of plastic cups and a jug of orange juice. She set them down in front of Lindsey. "*Pace* yourself."

Lindsey tossed her red hair over her shoulder. "I have no idea what you're talking about."

Lindsey started mixing drinks. No one noticed when I only poured orange juice into a cup and handed it to Vanessa. Esis tugged at my arm while I was pouring rum into mine, encouraging me to add more. I filled the cup half full of rum and handed it to him. He looked positively pleased. I mixed a much weaker drink for myself.

Lindsey leaned her head against Medusa, who was draped over the back of her chair. "Here's how it works. We go around and say something we've *never* done. If you *have* done it, you drink. Easy, right?"

"We all know how it works," Vanessa teased. "The question is, is there anything you *haven't* done?"

Lindsey's jaw dropped jokingly. "Of course! I haven't... I haven't..."

Miranda leaned over and whispered something in her ear.

"I haven't been skydiving," Lindsey said, like that proved something.

I glanced around the circle, but nobody drank.

"Lame!" I snickered.

Lindsey raised an eyebrow. "If it's so easy, you think of something."

I raised my knees to my chest and pretended to hide behind them. "I don't want to go. I need time to think."

Lindsey turned to Miranda. "Okay, you go."

"Mm..." Miranda thought about it for a moment, then said, "Never have I ever... driven a car." She looked directly at me.

I took a drink. "Not fair. That was totally an attack. You guys don't have cars in Kinpago."

Vanessa shrugged. "Anything's fair game."

I sat up straighter. "Fine. In that case, never have I ever driven a carriage."

The three of them went silent as they took a sip.

"Okay, okay," Lindsey said. "We need to set some ground rules. No targeting other people."

"Fine," Miranda mumbled.

"Fair enough," Vanessa said. "I guess that makes it my turn? Never have I ever... watched *Star Wars*."

"Boo!" I shouted, tossing a potato chip at her face.

"Don't kill me," she begged.

The rest of us drank.

"Never have I ever..." Miranda started.

"Hey!" Lindsey stopped her. "It's *my* turn."

"It should go around in a circle," Miranda argued, gesturing to the circle.

"My bad," I laughed.

"It's all your fault, Sophia," Lindsey teased.

"Haha," I replied dryly. "Screw you."

Lindsey wiggled her eyebrows. "Careful what you wish for."

My demeanor quickly changed, and I became serious. "Okay, so I have to ask... that thing about you that Haley said earlier... was it true?"

"What thing?" Lindsey shoved a chip in her mouth, like Haley hadn't bothered her at all.

I hesitated. "When she called you a... d-word?"

Lindsey smirked. "Are you trying to ask if I'm a lesbian, Sophia?"

My cheeks turned bright red. "Um... yeah."

"So ask me." Lindsey shrugged. "I don't care."

"Are you a lesbian? I don't mean any offense," I added. "One of my best friends is gay. I was just curious."

Lindsey smiled. "Yeah, Sophia. And I'm proud of it."

I shrugged. "Okay. Cool."

"Speaking of which..." Lindsey said. "I have a good one. Never have I ever been with a guy."

Vanessa and Miranda both drank, but I didn't move an inch.

"Shut up, Sophia," Miranda said. "You've *never* been with a guy before?"

I looked down to my drink. Memories of Liam invaded my mind. I didn't want to think of that. "It depends on what you mean by *been with*. I mean, I've done *stuff*, but I've never gone that far."

Vanessa leaned forward. "What kind of stuff?"

I shrugged. "You know... everything but *sex*."

"Fooling around counts," Miranda insisted.

"No, it doesn't," I argued.

Lindsey straightened in her chair. "Let's make it easy. Have you ever had a dick inside any orifice of your body?"

I was suddenly back in the library with Liam. My gut twisted with emotions I couldn't identify. They were both good and bad.

"Yes," I admitted.

"Then you have to drink," Lindsey said.

"Drink, drink, drink," Vanessa started chanting, and Miranda quickly joined in. Even Esis started pounding his fists on the table to the rhythm.

I sighed and threw my head back, chugging several gulps until the chanting stopped. The girls laughed and high-fived each other.

Miranda's eyes brightened. "So, who was it? Anyone we know?"

The blood drained from my face. No way could I tell them it was Liam. "No," I lied. "It was a guy back in Utah."

"You're brave," Lindsey said. "I saw a dick once, and was like, '*Get that thing away from me.*'"

We all chuckled.

Lindsey took another sip of her drink, even though no one had said anything. "The real question is, which of you have ever been with a girl?"

We all glanced between each other, but nobody spoke.

"I *would*," Miranda finally said. "I just never have."

"You wou—? Mir. An. Da!" Lindsey swatted at her arm. "You never told me you were bi."

Miranda blushed. "I don't know that I am. I'm just saying, I'm not taking that option off the table. Guys are so... what's the word I'm looking for?"

"Controlling. Manipulative. Assholes. Take your pick," Lindsey offered.

"Hey!" Vanessa snapped playfully. "Not all guys are like that."

"No, you're right," Lindsey agreed. "Bren is great."

"You bet your ass he is." Vanessa chuckled.

"So, you're not even, like, curious about girls?" Miranda asked her.

"You see this?" Vanessa held up her wedding ring. "I'm faithful to my man."

"Doesn't mean you can't look at the menu," I teased.

"Do *you* look at the menu, Sophia?" Lindsey asked.

I eyed Lindsey up and down. She was really pretty, with long red hair, and freckles across her nose. She had bright red lips, soft eyes, and was all around worthy of a modeling career. She had the same build as me, but her breasts were at least a cup size bigger.

She caught my eyes on her chest. "You do!"

I bit my lower lip. "I danced with a stripper once."

"And you liked it!" Miranda accused.

An involuntary grin spread across my face. "Maybe?"

"Ooh!" Lindsey sang. "When did you realize you were bi?"

"What?" I asked in disbelief. "I'm not bisexual."

I looked to Vanessa for help, but she just said, "I don't know, Sophia. It kind of sounds like you are."

I gaped at the three of them. "No. I like dick."

"You can like dick *and* boobs," Miranda pointed out.

Slowly, the gears started to turn in my head. I *did* like watching the strippers at the strip club. And I *did* always kind of have a girl crush on Angelina Jolie. But that didn't make me bi, did it?

"It's okay, Sophia," Lindsey said kindly. "You don't have to admit it right now. Just think about it."

"I don't know," I said in thought. "Maybe I am. I think I would have to be with a girl to be sure, you know?"

"So kiss Lindsey," Miranda joked. "I dare you."

The suggestion took me off guard, but when I looked to Lindsey, she wasn't laughing like it was absurd. She was blushing. I found myself actually wanting to do it... if Lindsey was okay with it.

Lindsey shrugged. "I mean, I don't mind."

My heart was pounding so fast that I felt a little lightheaded. Was this seriously happening?

Vanessa nudged me.

Before I could question it too much, I set my drink on the table and stood up. "Okay. Purely for research purposes."

Lindsey got to her feet and wrapped her hands around my waist. Her body pressed into mine, and all I could think of was her breasts touching me. Heat pooled between my thighs.

What am I doing? I screamed in my mind. I hadn't even drank that much. Which meant I wasn't just doing this because I was drunk, like I had with the stripper. I actually wanted this. I wanted to be with a girl. It'd be so much different than Liam... maybe even *better*.

I closed the distance between Lindsey and me. Our lips connected, and a burning desire built up inside my chest. My hand came up to cradle the back of her neck as I deepened the kiss. Lindsey reached her hands around me tighter and kissed me over and over again. She was so soft.

When she drew away, I was breathless and in serious need of a new pair of panties. I was vaguely aware of the others clapping. Esis briefly looked at me wide-eyed and shocked, then joined in on the applause.

"O— okay," I breathed. "I think it's safe to say that I'm definitely bi."

Lindsey wiped at her lips and took her seat again. "I'm glad I could help."

For the rest of the night, I found it difficult to take my eyes off her. My gaze roamed up and down her body, wondering what it would be like not just kiss her, but to *be* with her. There was definitely some chemistry between us. I'd felt it in that kiss. I just knew I'd never be able to bring myself to make a move.

Besides, what would Liam think? And even then, why did I care?

We stayed up talking and laughing until at least one in the morning. Eventually, Miranda and Vanessa started nodding off.

"Should we call it a night?" Lindsey suggested. She was still wide awake.

I stood and started helping her clean up.

Miranda dragged herself to her feet. "You can stay in my room, Vanessa. I've got a balcony outside Aisha can sleep on."

"Quit bragging," I teased. "I don't have a balcony."

Miranda laughed. "Only special students get one."

"Don't listen to her," Lindsey said. "I don't have a balcony, either."

"Esis, come on, buddy." I poked him from where he slept on the coffee table. He was so full of junk food that he was as round as a ball. His fur stood up in all directions. He pushed himself to his feet and swayed a bit.

Miranda and Vanessa left, leaving Lindsey and me alone. We finished cleaning up, then I collapsed back down in my chair.

"Can't. Move," I said. The truth was, I wasn't very tired. I just didn't want the night to end.

"You can make it," Lindsey teased, kicking at my feet to get me to move.

"Ugh," I groaned. "My room's all the way at the end of the hall."

Lindsey reached her hand out to me, then whispered, "So stay in mine."

My heart was immediately tapping out a quick rhythm against my rib cage again. Was Lindsey suggesting what I thought she was suggesting?

"I..." I stared up at her, unable to find my words. I wanted to say yes and no at the same time. On the one hand, there was Liam, and it'd feel like cheating on him. And on the other...

No. Screw that. Why would it be like cheating on Liam? We weren't even together anymore. What was I even worried about? I was free to fly solo. That was what he *wanted*, wasn't it?

"Okay," I said breathlessly.

Lindsey took my hand and led me down the hall to her room, our Familiars trailing behind us. Her arms were full of leftovers, so I opened the door for her. It was dark inside, lit only by the light of the moon coming through her window. Her room was bigger than mine and set up differently, with the fireplace and bed on opposite walls and the bathroom in a different spot. The decor was the same, with red curtains and sheets and a gold bed frame. She had a small kitchenette in the far corner of the room with a countertop dividing it from the rest of the space. Lindsey headed across the room to set her stuff down on the chair.

When she wasn't looking, I ushered Esis and Medusa into the kitchen to give Lindsey and me a little privacy. I shut the door slowly, holding my breath.

I turned around to see Lindsey taking her shoes off and pulling her shirt up over her head. She had a camisole underneath, but it was low-cut, so I could see the shape of her breasts poking up out of her push-up bra.

I quivered in anticipation. Was I really going to go through with this?

Lindsey didn't say anything as she stepped toward me and took my hand. She cupped the side of my face and brought my lips to hers. All over again, that heat overtook me.

Hell yeah, I was doing this.

Lindsey guided me down onto the bed. She took control and straddled her body over mine, kissing me over and over. I didn't know what to do with my hands, so I settled them on her hips. Her cami rose up, and my fingers touched her bare skin. That alone was enough to turn me on.

There was something about a girl's body that was even more thrilling than a man's. Women were softer, gentler, but sensual in a way a man could never achieve, even though Liam had definitely been—

Nope. I shot the thought down before it completely formed. I wasn't thinking about Liam tonight.

Instead, I focused on Lindsey. She smelled amazing. Lindsey's hands roamed my sides, then down to my ass. I took it as an invitation to do the same to her.

Damn it, Lindsey was sexy. How had I never noticed how hot girls were, or at least never admitted it to myself?

"You're so pretty, Sophia," Lindsey said as she pulled away from me.

I smiled. "You, too."

"No," she whispered. "I mean, like, really, *really* pretty."

"I think *you're* really really pretty, too."

"I hope this doesn't freak you out, but I've had a bit of a crush on you for a long time," she admitted.

I shook my head. "That doesn't freak me out at all. I'm actually kind of flattered."

"You should be." She placed another gentle kiss on my lips, then pulled away again. "You seem kind of tense. You don't have to be nervous."

"I told you. I've never been with a girl. This is all so new to me."

"Just relax and go with it," she told me. "And if you ever feel uncomfortable, you can tell me. You know that, right?"

I nodded, but so far, nothing she'd done had made me feel uncomfortable. I didn't think she *could* make me feel uncomfortable.

"I'll let you know," I promised.

"Before we get into it, you should tell me how far you want to take things," she suggested.

I wrapped my arms around her neck and pulled her closer to me. My heart hammered just thinking about the words I was about to say. "I want you to show me what it's like to be with a girl, Lindsey. I want to know everything."

Lindsey's eyebrows shot up. "Everything?"

I nodded. "Everything."

"That's going to take more than one night, Sophia."

I shrugged. "I'm not going anywhere."

Lindsey grinned. "This is going to be fun."

Neither of us said another word as her lips connected with mine. Our hands roamed each other's bodies, but it wasn't until she drew away again that I took the invitation to touch her breasts. When my hands fell over them, a wave of pleasure washed through me. I *totally* got why guys were obsessed with boobs. My nipples hardened just looking at her curves, and she hadn't even taken her cami off yet.

Lindsey reached for the bottom of her shirt and pulled it over her head. Her bra was all black lace and pushed her breasts together to display the perfect amount of cleavage. I touched her there again, unable to take my eyes off her. She reached behind her back and undid the clasp, then let the fabric drop away. Now I seriously couldn't take my eyes away, even if I wanted. Lindsey's breasts defied gravity.

I just stopped and stared for several seconds, until she took my hands and said, "You can touch them, Sophia. It's okay."

She pressed my hands to her breasts again, and I squeezed. I couldn't stop thinking about how soft they were. Lindsey placed her hands on me, and I couldn't get my shirt off fast enough.

"Ooh, I *love* your bra," she said when my hot-pink bra came into view.

I'd bought it for Liam.

Damn it. What was he doing in my head again? I quickly removed it, so I'd stop thinking about him.

Lindsey leaned down and trailed kisses all across my breasts. Her nipples tickled my stomach, like she was purposely rubbing them lightly against me. I gasped when she brought my nipple into her mouth and sucked on it lightly. It reminded me of the time Liam—

Get out of my head!

I kissed Lindsey harder to push thoughts of Liam away. It worked, until she started stripping off my pants. I was reminded of the first time Liam saw me naked. I pulled off her pants to get him out of my mind... but it wasn't working. He was still there.

Lindsey shivered as we lay side by side, our hands trailing up and down each other's bodies. I focused my attention on her breasts against mine because... well... Liam didn't have boobs, and it was easier to forget about him when my mind was on that.

Boldly, I ran my hand down between her legs. Was this what it felt like for Liam when he touched me there?

Lindsey moaned, and I was grateful for the distraction. As I began to massage her, she drew away.

"Not like that," she whispered. "Let me show you."

Lindsey guided my hand to where she wanted it and pressed down, helping me rub her in gentle circles.

"Follow me." She placed her hand between my legs and showed me what to do. "Just like that. See? You're already a pro at this."

My breath came in shallow heaves. For the first time all night, I actually forgot about Liam.

If this was how I stopped torturing myself and got over him, I'd do it.

THE NEXT MORNING, I rolled over to find the bed beside me empty. Something crinkled beneath me.

I had to head to class and didn't want to wake you. Stay as long as you want. - Lindsey

I smiled, then checked my watch. Ten past eight.

"Crap!" I shouted.

Esis hurried out of the kitchen to check on me. Lindsey had obviously opened the door to let Medusa out and left it that way.

"Well, I guess I'm skipping Hawkei Legends today," I told him.

Esis scowled up at me.

"What?" I asked innocently.

Esis puffed his chest out and ran his paws over his bust, then turned his back to me. He crossed his arms over his body and moved his head around like he was imitating a couple making out. He turned back around and made gagging sounds.

"Who are you to judge?" I snapped at him.

Esis continued like he hadn't heard me. This time, he puffed up the fur on his shoulders and slapped his chest like a gorilla, then turned around and made the same make-out gesture. When he faced me again, he trilled and threw his hands in the air, like he was celebrating.

I shook my head at him. "Buddy, I have no idea what you mean."

He sighed and started the whole charade over again.

"Okay, I'll play along," I said. "You think it's gross I spent the night with a girl?"

He shook his head and started again. This time when he puffed his chest out, he sucked his stomach in and batted his eyelashes.

"You're a girl?" I guessed.

He nodded, then pointed to the red sheets I lay beneath.

"Sheet?"

He shook his head.

"Red?" I asked.

He pointed at me and nodded, then pulled his ears down around his face.

"Red hair? You're talking about Lindsey."

Esis nodded and made the gagging sounds again, then started pounding on his chest.

"Okay, now you're imitating a gorilla?"

He shook his head.

I sighed. "Buddy, I don't get it. A man?"

He nodded.

"Oh, I see." The offense was clear in my tone. "You don't like it that I'm with Lindsey. You want me to take Liam back."

He hopped up on the bed and nodded eagerly.

"Newsflash, Liam doesn't want me back," I growled. "He's the one who broke up with me. I need to get on with my life."

I stood and started pulling my clothes on, but Esis' little display was still going through my mind. "You know what?" I snapped.

Esis frowned.

I suddenly didn't know what to say. I softened my tone. "Never mind. Let's get ready for class."

I headed back to my dorm room to shower and put on a set of clean clothes. By the time I was ready, it was almost nine o'clock.

"Shoot. We have to hurry."

Esis climbed on my backpack and held tightly to my ponytail as I raced down the halls to History of the Hawkei. I entered the room just as Baine was telling everyone to settle down. I slid into my desk next to Imogen and Sassy and tried to catch my breath.

"Where were you?" Imogen leaned over and hissed. "I almost thought you wouldn't make it. I was worried."

"I'm fine," I whispered back. "Just slept in late."

Imogen frowned. "Sophia, you never—"

"I'll tell you about it after class," I promised.

"Ooh, the suspense." Imogen rubbed her hands together mischievously.

"Miss Henley. Miss Ahnild." Baine looked at us with a pointed expression. "Something you'd like to share with the class?"

"No," I said quickly.

"Then I suggest you pay attention." He turned back to his lesson, and Imogen and I went silent. Baine talked about how Arthur Cedrick had gifted the Hawkei this castle for the Academy. Almost no one paid attention, since we'd all heard the story before.

When class ended, Imogen practically dragged me down the hall. We stopped in a secluded corner between a big window and a suit of armor.

"Spill it," she demanded. "I can tell by your face it's something good. Did you and Liam—?"

"Oh, God," I groaned. "Does *everything* have to be about Liam? No. It was actually a Koigni."

Imogen's jaw dropped, and she stomped her heels excitedly. "You did *what* with a Koigni?"

I blushed so hard I thought flames might come shooting out my nose. "Made out a little... okay, a lot."

Imogen squealed, then quickly glanced around the hall to make sure no one heard. "Who was it? Any guy I know? Was it Ben?"

"Shh," I hissed. "No, it wasn't any *guy* you know."

Imogen's eyes widened to the size of saucers. "You didn't. Sophia!"

I bit my lower lip. "I did."

Imogen beamed. "I didn't know you swung both ways. I mean, you looked pretty comfortable on the stage with that stripper, but—"

"I didn't know either." I grabbed her hand and pulled her further behind the statue. Esis and Sassy squeezed in beside us. "But I... I kind of liked it. It was good to have a change of pace."

"Good," she said. "I'm happy for you. So, who was it?"

I chuckled. "You're always so curious. It was Lindsey."

"Ooh, I like Lindsey. One of the few Koigni I *do* like."

I punched her lightly in the shoulder. "You like me, don't you?"

"Ow. Of course. I said *one* of them."

I stepped out from behind the statue, and Imogen and I fell into step beside each other. "I missed you, Im. I wished we lived in the same dorms so we could spend more time together during this lockdown."

Just as I said it, two Task Force guys walked past. They wore all black, and helmets that covered their faces. Each one carried a big gun, like they were preparing for a terrorist attack or something. It made me uneasy, to say the least.

Imogen noticed me staring at the guns. "They're tranquilizer guns filled with noxite."

"What's noxite?" I asked.

"It's an enchanted metallic substance that can inhibit your powers," she explained.

A shiver ran down my spine thinking about it. I didn't like that the Elementai had weapons to use against each other.

"Where are their Familiars?" I asked.

"The Task Force has two separate units, one for Elementai and one for Familiars," she explained. "That way, if there's a dangerous situation, the Task Force members will be focused on getting the job done instead of protecting their bonded partner."

That was disturbing, but I shook it off. "What was it you wanted to tell me, by the way?"

Imogen dropped her gaze to her feet. "Oh, it's just a theory. I'm not sure it means anything."

"Come on, Im," I encouraged. "You can tell me anything."

She sighed. "I think our whole system for finding this prophecy piece is wrong. Toaqua are all about tradition. They're the ones writing down our history as it happens. Nivita... we're different. We're scholars, but we thrive on creativity. We don't just record history. We *experience* it. And we leave those experiences behind for our children."

"I don't get it," I said.

"I tried to put myself in the shoes of my Nivita ancestors," Imogen continued. "The Nivita Elders would never keep this to themselves. We know that'd be stupid because the prophecy could die with us if the Elders were ever challenged. If it were me, I'd make it a puzzle, one that only a Nivita could solve."

I slowed my step. "So, we have to solve a puzzle to get a piece of another puzzle?"

"Exactly." Imogen beamed. "It makes so much sense. If we can't talk about it or read about it, we have to find it from another source. That's exactly what a Nivita would do. They'd leave clues so that their children could find the pieces."

"Do you know where to start with this puzzle?" I asked.

Imogen bit her lower lip. "No, but at least we can stop wasting our time with history books and old scrolls. I think we need to look at Nivita songs and puzzles for clues."

"That's a good idea, Im," I told her. "But how can *I* help?"

"I'm still working on some stuff by myself, but let's get together on Thursday afternoon," she suggested.

"Okay."

Imogen quickly checked her watch. "Shoot. I'm going to be late for Cryptozoology."

"Do you want me to walk you?" I asked.

"Nah, it's just down this hall." She started walking in another direction, and Sassy followed. "See you soon. Be safe!"

"Bye, Im." I waved.

Esis and I started toward the dorms so we could get in some studying before Intro to Child Development. As we were passing a seating area, I heard a group of Nivita whispering. I slowed down to eavesdrop.

"Are you kidding me? Angelina *and* Sam are sick? Along with their Familiars?"

I gasped. I knew Sam. He had an alicorn Familiar named Zaria, and he often played ping pong with Cade in the Commons.

"Yeah," another whispered. "I guess they visited Kinpago over the weekend and their Familiars caught it there or something. They're all in quarantine."

"This thing is spreading too fast," a girl said. "At this rate, the entire town is going to be ill within a month."

"It won't be that fast," a guy argued.

"It's exponential," the girl said. "I can run the numbers for you. The fact is, if we don't find a cure for this plague fast, we'll have a full-fledged epidemic on our hands."

"That is if there are any Familiars left to get sick," someone added. "More and more are disappearing every day."

I scooped Esis up and held him tight as I hurried back to the dorms. I knocked on Lindsey's door, but she wasn't around.

"I hope she's okay," I said to Esis. She and Medusa had been in Kinpago yesterday. I hoped they hadn't caught anything.

Esis pointed to his chest proudly. His message was clear. Even if they were sick, he could help them...

I hoped.

"We'll check on them as soon as they get back from class."

I visited Lindsey that night, and she and Medusa both looked fine. I stayed in her room for a while— just to talk. It became our routine over the next few days, though it turned into more than just talking the following nights.

When I woke Friday morning, the sun was just rising and cast a beautiful pink glow across my room. I stretched, feeling well-rested.

"Okay, buddy. Who's up for Elementai Explorations?" I sat up and glanced around the room. It was eerily silent.

"Esis?" I stood and peeked under my bed, then checked the bathroom. "Esis?"

No response.

Sheer terror whipped through me. My voice became high-pitched and squeaky as I threw the bedding to the floor to see if he'd gotten tangled in the sheets. "Esis, this isn't funny! Where are you?"

I flung my door open and ran out into the hall in my pajamas. My whole body trembled.

"Esis!" I screamed.

Several doors opened, and people peeked out at me. I ran out into the common room and looked under the sofas, behind the tapestries, anywhere he might fit. A few people in the common room gave me strange looks as I frantically searched the area. I'd never felt so terrified in my life.

As people started to realize what was happening, they came to my aid— people I didn't even know. The common room buzzed as Koigni came out of their dorms and started looking for Esis.

I hurried out into the main hallway and ran from statue to statue. I peeked inside suits of armor— since I knew he liked shiny things and could fit inside one of them. But I never saw anything. I never heard the trill of his voice.

Reality came crashing down on me all at once. My knees buckled beneath me, and I fell to the ground as my shoulders shook in horrified sobs. I clutched my stomach.

Familiars were going missing, and now mine was gone, too. It was possible I'd never see him again. He'd been taken.

"ESIS!" I wailed. My voice echoed off the stone walls of the castle.

He was my life. My soul. My everything.

And he was gone.

Liam

NINE

I was on my way to Hawkei Leadership when I heard the sounds of devastated sobs coming from the Commons. It was still early in the morning, seven-thirty or so, and whoever was crying was screaming too, making wailing sounds that tore out the center of my chest.

It sounded like Sophia.

I fucking *ran*. I about knocked people over on my way into the Commons. I had to get to her. Her screams of horror made me have an immediate response, to fix everything and make it better.

My worst fears came true. It was her. Sophia was in the middle of the room, and she was bawling. She was still wearing her pajamas. Imogen was there, and she had an arm around Sophia's shoulder and was holding her tightly. Lindsey was by Sophia's side and was stroking her hair gently, as if trying to get her to calm down, while Medusa wove around their legs. There were a ton of Familiars and Elementai in here, milling around Sophia and asking if she was all right.

My eyes scanned the room for Esis, but I didn't see him. I immediately knew what was wrong, and my heart dropped.

"L-Liam," Sophia stuttered as I approached. She hiccuped, and said, "E— sis is— is gone! Someone t-took h— im!"

I could barely make out the words that were coming out of her mouth. She was more upset than I'd ever seen her. "Soph, where'd you last see him?"

Sophia let out some more garbled nonsense before she started crying even harder. It was hard to watch.

"Come on, *pawee*, you gotta talk to me," I said desperately.

"He went to sleep in her room, and when she woke up, he was gone," Lindsey told me quickly. "We've looked all around the Koigni dorms, but he vanished without a trace."

Imogen gave me a helpless look. Sassy's tail drooped, and her ears were back. She let out a few low sounds of sadness.

Sophia sniffled. "Wha— what if he's d-dead?"

"He's not dead, Soph. You'd know," I told her. "Trust me."

Her lip trembled. Every part of her was shaking. She looked totally helpless.

I put my hands on Sophia's shoulders. "We're gonna find him, okay? I promise. We'll get him back."

She nodded frantically, but I could tell she didn't believe me. Imogen made Sophia sit on the couch, and she put her head in her hands.

She was useless right now. She couldn't even talk. That meant it was up to the rest of us to locate where Esis had gone. But none of the other Familiars had returned since they'd been missing. If he really had been taken, he was probably long gone.

Fuck that. I wasn't going to let this happen to her. I was going to miss class, but I didn't care. I'd fail the semester if it meant helping Sophia find Esis.

"I'll be right back," I promised them. I dropped my bag in the Commons and left it.

"Take Sassy," Imogen said. Imogen motioned for Sassy to follow me, and the fox trotted at my heels with her ears up.

I walked toward the Koigni dorms, figuring that was just as good a place as any to start. I noticed my brother walking around, seeming worried.

"Esis!" Ezra called. He was literally roaming the halls, calling for him. Dyami flew overhead near the ceiling, peeking behind statues and places too high for most people to reach. Vanessa was nearby with Aisha, too, and the two of them looked behind shelves and wardrobes in their search. Cade and Arabelle were just down the hall, looking high and low.

"Any sign of him?" I asked them as I passed.

Ez shook his head. "Nope. It's like he completely disappeared."

Vanessa seemed terrified. "He was in the Koigni dorms last night. Someone must've snuck in and taken him."

Vanessa shivered and reached out to bring Aisha's head against hers, nuzzling into it. "I'm glad that I don't live on campus anymore. I couldn't bear to lose you, girl."

Aisha let out a low sound. She seemed sad that her friend was missing.

"We're checking around the Commons," Ezra said. "Do you think you can cover the west side of the castle?"

"Sounds like a plan." I left them behind to go the other way while I proceeded toward the Koigni dorms. I passed by an open window and noticed that outside, Jonah was flying overhead from Squeaks' back. Squeaks gave a couple of loud cries. She paused, waiting for an answer. When Esis didn't reply, she swished her tail and tried again. They were looking through the gardens.

On the way, I passed groups of students calling out Esis' name. There were a lot of people looking for Esis, of all Houses. It didn't matter that she was Koigni. This had become a big enough problem and scary enough to people that it wasn't an isolated incident anymore. The fact that he was gone from the Koigni dorms was frightening enough that everyone felt like their Familiars were in danger too and wanted to help.

Task Force members marched in uniform throughout the halls. I kept my head down and tried to ignore them. I didn't want to get the police involved unless we absolutely had to, but if we didn't find Esis soon...

I tried to think of all the places a kurble could be concealed, and it was a long list. It didn't help that he was so small. It was hard to hide big Familiars, but Esis could literally fit in the palm of your hand. If someone shoved him into a coat pocket, they could walk off with him without making a scene. There were a million places you could keep a Familiar his size.

The fiery doors of the Koigni living spaces came into view. I knew I couldn't head into the Koigni dorms, but that was useless to do anyway, since they'd already been cleared. I'd have to start my search from the outside and assume whoever had taken him had gone through the Koigni exit to do so.

I stopped outside the doors. I had to think. The Koigni dorms were on the second level, on the west side of the castle. There were multiple places of exit around this particular section of the castle, but you'd either need a flying Familiar, or you'd have to reach the ground floor to escape— or, you'd need to be a Yapluma to fly down. Not even a Nivita could make roots extend this high up in order to climb out a window, and a Toaqua wouldn't have enough water to get them up this high. I thought about the possibility of the thief being a Koigni, as they could easily get in and out of these dorms, but that didn't account for the Familiars that had vanished from other dorms, too.

Yet he'd been taken at some point during the night, and most of those exits were locked— and the ones that weren't were heavily guarded by Task Force security.

It was still early, and the Task Force was marching around like crazy. I bet if Esis really had been stolen, the thieves were still in the castle, and they were waiting for when the school would be more crowded, so they could disappear into the masses without being seen. Still, this place was huge. There was no end to the amount of places someone could hide.

Sassy was doing something weird. She was pawing at the floor, making yipping sounds and trying to get my attention.

"What is it, girl? Did you get his scent?" I asked.

Sassy yipped again and rose on her back legs to do a dance. I took that as a positive answer. "Okay, let's follow it."

Sassy kept her nose to the floor and led the way. She ran down the long hallway, to the other side of the castle. I had to jog to keep up with her. Eventually, she stopped at a staircase that led to the southernmost tower at the end of the castle. She climbed the stairs, and I followed her, going up to the third floor.

Once we got there, Sassy stopped abruptly. She spun in a circle, then laid down and put her paws over her ears, scratching at them and looking confused.

Looked like Sassy had lost the trail. I figured it would happen eventually. Some of the stolen Familiars could be tracked for a while until the scent went cold.

"Don't get frustrated. We're closer than we were before," I told her. She huffed at me.

I turned in place, feeling lost. There were tons of staircases in this corner of the castle, all leading downward. Esis could've been taken anywhere. But Sassy seemed to be sure that the trail went up. There was only one way to climb any higher, and that was by entering the southernmost tower.

There were four towers at Orenda Academy. The other three towers were used for classes, but the southern one was abandoned. It was closed off to students and teachers both, and had been for years. I didn't know why— professors said that it was unsafe and needed to be rebuilt. It was dangerous. Climbing it meant risking that something would tumble on you, or that part of the tower would collapse and you'd fall to your death.

Seemed like the perfect place for a thief to hide. I decided to follow my intuition. The door to the tower was locked. I slid against it and pretended to act casual as a Task Force group walked by. Sassy sat against my legs, playing the part.

Once they were gone, I looked around to make sure no one else was watching. Then I took some water from the air and sent it inside the lock that sealed the door. I froze the water and heard the sound of the lock breaking, though the doorknob remained secure.

I opened the door and hurried Sassy inside before shutting it behind us. It was super dark in here, only illuminated by the windows that were spaced out every now and then. I started climbing, keeping an eye on the steps beneath me in case one of them decided to give way. I kept a ball of water floating in my hand, to defend myself if someone decided to jump out at me.

As I climbed, I noticed something. This was weird. This tower didn't seem broken or unsafe at all. It looked just like the one I took almost every day to Hawkei Home Ec. As an experiment, I jumped up and down on the steps and pushed against the wall. Nothing happened.

So the teachers were lying— or didn't know the real truth. This tower was fine structurally. It was just hiding a big secret.

I looked down and caught a flash of something white. A small tuft of pale fur clinging to one of the steps. I picked it up. It felt a lot like Esis' fur. Sassy sniffed at it and yipped. I rubbed her ears and pocketed the fur.

"Yeah, that's his, all right." We were getting closer. Maybe when we found Esis we'd find all the other stolen Familiars, too.

At the top of the tower, I got to a door. I wanted to rush inside, but had to wait by resting on one of the steps and catching my breath. If I needed to fight someone, I had to recover some of my strength.

Sassy put a paw on my knee and looked at me. I stroked the fur on her back. "I'm good, Sassy. Just need a minute."

Esis hadn't visited me in a few days, and I could tell I needed another treatment soon. I felt really exhausted. If the little furball was really gone, that meant I'd be screwed, too. I'd die without his healing magic. I was gonna kick the shit out of whoever had taken him.

Eventually, I stood back up. I tried the door, but it was jammed. There wasn't a lock on it, which meant that something was behind it, barricading the way through. I stepped back to examine it. There was a jagged hole at the bottom of the door that was just big enough for a kurble to fit into, and Sassy was pawing at it, whimpering. I tried freezing the hinges and doorknob, and although they both fell off, the door stood in place.

"Well, gonna have to do this the old-fashioned way," I said. I took a few steps back, then rammed myself against the door. Pain exploded against my shoulder when I made contact, but the door splintered and gave way.

I kicked aside a few shattered wooden planks and cleared a way through. Looked like someone had barricaded the door with old wood and nails on the other side. Sassy scrambled through the mess. Once I got inside, I realized I was in a big, open area. My mouth dropped open as I observed the room around me.

A large window in the tower's ceiling cast sunlight into the space around me. Everything was decorated in various shades of white, though it looked darker due to all the dust collected around the space. There were tall bookshelves lined with ancient tomes, along with decorative pieces and artifacts of the tribe. Armchairs and couches were gathered around an empty fireplace, and threadbare rugs were placed carelessly around the room. Empty incense holders and crystals that had long lost their magic laid discarded all over the floor.

It hit me what it was. This was a dormitory. It looked really similar to mine. It took another minute to realize *what* dormitory it was.

The Anichi dorms. It had to be. This is where they were located. No wonder they were locked off. I bet the Elders had sealed them off years ago and everyone had forgotten about them, believing the lie that the tower itself was unsafe. I was probably the first person in here in a few decades.

I heard a chattering sound. There Esis was, sitting on a table and looking completely unbothered. He waved when he saw me.

"You little bastard!" I exploded. I stomped toward him. His eyes grew big, and he meeped. He turned tail and ran toward a wardrobe. He squeezed himself into it, to where I couldn't reach. Sassy went crazy at my feet and starting yipping like nuts.

"Come here!" I demanded. I reached for him and pressed against the wardrobe, where he'd run to the back in a scramble to get away from me. When I grazed his fur, he bit me and drew blood.

"Ouch!" I cradled my bleeding hand. "You're healing that!"

Esis stuck out his lip. He started shaking his fists at me like he wanted to box. I rolled my eyes.

"That's a fight you're gonna lose, pal. Let's go. Sophia is waiting for us."

Esis shook his head. He pointed at the ground, then crossed his arms, not wanting to leave.

"If you think I'm bringing Sophia up here, you've got another thing coming," I said sternly. "We can show this to her later. She couldn't even make the climb right now. Do you know how worried she is?"

Esis looked guilty. His eyes got big, and he mashed his little paws together in a nervous way. He looked sorry.

"She's been crying her eyes out. She thinks you're gone forever," I said harshly. "Why would you think of taking off like that when Familiars are going missing? Bad Esis."

Esis' eyes watered, but he didn't move. He made a begging sound and hopped up and down, pointing to the room around us.

I sighed. "Obviously, you really want me to show her this place. But it's not happening until later. I promise I'll bring her here tonight. But you need to come back *right now*."

I extended my hand into the wardrobe again. Esis looked down, mumbled something and kicked the dust at his feet. Then he squeezed out of the area he'd stuck himself in and tumbled into my hand. I brought him out and cradled him against my chest, in my bleeding hand. Esis put his hands on it, and the little bite mark went away, along with some of my fatigue.

Sassy looked cross. She hissed when Esis looked at her. Esis shook his little fist at her and said something that was probably really offensive, because Sassy snarled and jumped upward with her mouth open. I turned away and hugged Esis to my chest.

"You two can go at it later. We need to get back to Sophia." I kicked aside the debris that was blocking the way of the door and began the winding descent down to the third floor. I jostled Esis. "Hey, do you know where the other Familiars have gotten off to?"

Esis shook his head. That was disappointing. Esis didn't know where the missing Familiars had gone. He hadn't been taken. He'd wandered off on his own. Did the other Familiars do so as well?

When we entered the Commons, people gasped when they saw me holding Esis. Jonah was back with Squeaks, and both of them were standing next to Imogen and Sophia, creating a semi-circle. Sophia's head jerked up, and an expression of relief passed over her face when she saw that Esis was safe and sound.

"*Esis!*" Sophia shouted. She ran toward me. I put Esis into her arms, and Sophia squeezed him tightly. She kissed his head over and over and sobbed as she stroked his fur. "Thank the ancestors. I thought someone had hurt you."

I was relieved. I couldn't watch Sophia lose her Familiar. It would've been too much for me to bear— I'd have to teach her how to get along without Esis, like I did with Nashoma. Though I wondered... if Esis wanted Sophia to find the Anichi dorms, why hadn't he just shown her where they were instead of running off?

Esis put his arms against Sophia and leaned into her. He looked back and gave me a wink before he put his head onto her chest.

Oh. That's why. He had a plan for me to look like the hero. He knew that I'd go looking for him and wanted me to be the one to bring him back to Sophia. That little shit. He needed to stop interfering.

"Who took him?" Jonah asked as he approached. Squeaks observed Esis with a curious look. Esis ignored her.

"Nobody did," I said, making sure to elevate my voice so the crowd around us could hear. "He went off by himself."

People seemed disappointed by the answer. They'd thought Esis had been taken like all the others and that there was some sort of advancement in the case. They slowly filtered away. I think I caught a few resentful looks cast back at Sophia as students walked by.

"Where did you find him?" Imogen marveled.

I leaned in and dropped my voice so only the three of them could hear. "I'll tell you later. Right now, I should probably get to class. I promise I'll explain everything tonight. When people ask you, make up a story that he was in the gardens or something."

Jonah and Imogen looked confused. But Sophia was so grateful, she nodded and didn't ask questions. She said, "Sure. We'll wait for you in the dining hall at dinner."

"Meet you then." I headed off. I wasn't sure if the team would believe me if I told them face to face what I'd found— so I'd have to show them.

THAT NIGHT, I waited for Sophia, Imogen and Jonah outside of the dining hall. It was around six o'clock when I noticed the three of them walking toward me from inside the cafeteria.

When I caught sight of Esis, I nearly died laughing. Sophia had put him in some sort of red harness that ended in a backpack and was connected to a long leash that Sophia had in her hand. Esis yanked at it, trying to get it off, but he couldn't figure out the snaps. It looked like a child's leash— you know, the kind people put their toddlers in to prevent them from running away.

"Leashes are cruel for Familiars, Sophia," Imogen said. "Almost as bad as cages."

"That's what he gets," Sophia said. "I'll take it off when he promises not to do that to me ever again."

Esis crossed his arms and looked grumpy. Squeaks and Sassy were holding back hisses of delight at the sight of him on the leash.

"What did you want to show us?" Imogen asked. I motioned for them to follow, and we began climbing staircases up to the third floor.

Sophia put Esis on her shoulder so he wouldn't have to waddle after us in the leash.

We got to the southern tower. I pointed at it. "It's up here." I opened the door. Thankfully, most everyone was in the dining hall at this time of day, but there were still Task Force lurking about, so I didn't want to dick around.

"Liam, we're not supposed to go up there," Imogen said warily. "It's forbidden."

"That's what makes it fun," Jonah said cheerfully. He didn't even question it. Squeaks happily pranced inside, though her butt got stuck and Jonah had to push on it to get her through. I heard the sound of Squeaks' hooves tripping on stone, and her and Jonah crashing a few steps above us.

"Isn't it unsafe to go up there?" Sophia asked.

"It's not. You'll see why," I told her.

Sophia looked at Esis. He chattered at her, urging her upward. She shrugged, then said, "I might as well see what was so damn important that Esis decided to take off."

Sophia followed Jonah. Imogen looked nervous— she didn't like breaking the rules. Sassy was pulling at her tutu skirt with her teeth, to try and get her to climb the tower.

I looked at Im. "Unless you want the Task Force to catch us sneaking into an unauthorized area, I suggest you get in there."

That did the trick. She headed inside. Once she and Sassy were through, I made it a point to hurry up and close the door behind us.

I expected there to be a mess when we reached the top, but Jonah and Squeaks had already cleared away the broken door. Imogen and Sophia gasped in amazement when they entered the space. By this time of day, it was darker, but Sophia lit a fire in the empty fireplace so we could see. The room sprang to life underneath the glow of the flame, and I spread my arm out wide.

"The Anichi dorms," I said. "This is what Esis wanted to show us."

"Wow," Sophia said, looking around. She put Esis down on one of the armchairs and said, "This is really cool, but why did Esis want to show us this?"

"Don't you see? We can clean it up. Use it as a hideout," Jonah said. He was already catching on.

"What do we need a hideout for?" Sophia asked.

"It's always good to have a safe house," I said. "Just in case things go wrong."

Carter had told me last semester that things were getting dangerous at Orenda. I didn't know whether to believe him or not yet, but if shit did end up going down, it would be beneficial for all of us to have a safe place to come to in emergencies.

"We could make a new lock for the door that leads to the tower. One that looks identical to the old one, but that only us four have a key for," Imogen suggested.

"We should get a new door for the dorm, too, since this one is wrecked," Jonah said, kicking it.

Sophia nodded. "I guess it's a good thing to have a place for the four of us to hang out without being bothered."

"Agreed," I said. The fact that we were friends from four different Houses had caught the attention of the Task Force. I knew they were keeping an eye on us. Being tournament partners wasn't a good enough excuse to be around each other all the time anymore, even if we had won the Cup.

Sophia brushed off some dust from one of the chairs and coughed. "Although it's going to take days to get all the dust out of here."

"We can keep information about the prophecy in here!" Imogen said. She was getting excited. "I've been having to hide all my research. Here, we can leave it out without risking anything will be found."

"This is great. I can totally leave my gaming system up here!" Jonah shouted. Squeaks gave an excited squawk.

I was going to roll my eyes, then I realized Jonah had a point. Technology still worked on campus, it was just banned. It would be useful to have a computer and phones in here in case things got bad, or if we needed to check on stuff in the outside world. "Good thinking. When do we want to start working on restoring this place?"

"I say right away," Imogen stated. "My research has almost gotten discovered a couple of times by accident. I don't want people to know what we're doing."

"Me too," Sophia said. She stroked Esis' ears. "This was a good find, buddy. Though I wish you'd shown me yourself instead of running off."

Esis purred. Finally, I felt like we were getting somewhere. We hadn't found the next piece of the prophecy yet, but at least we had a home base.

❧

THAT SATURDAY, I expected to find Sophia waiting with the rest of the group in the Commons, like we'd planned. We had agreed to meet up and go to the Anichi dorms to start cleaning them up so they'd be useable for our hideout, but when I got to the Commons, I only found Imogen and Jonah, waiting with their Familiars.

"Where's Soph?" I asked as I advanced toward them.

Imogen shook her head. "She's sick. It's just going to be us three today."

"Sick? Can she even *get* sick with Esis?" I wondered.

"The flu's been going around. It's not the same illness as the Familiars are getting, just something common," Imogen explained.

"I know," I said. "I already got it." It hadn't lasted long, but it had sucked.

"Esis has been trying to heal her, but his healing magic doesn't seem to work the same with viruses," Imogen added.

That was interesting. Perot would want to know about this. But my first concern was Sophia. I said nothing, yet Imogen read the look on my face. She gave me a smile that was all too knowing. "Go, Liam. Jonah and I can take care of the cleaning for the day. We'll get a head start."

"I didn't want your input on *my* interior design, anyway," Jonah told me. "I want to decorate."

"We should keep things how they are. They're the Anichi dorms, after all," Imogen protested.

"Not anymore. Now they're Jonah's man-cave," he replied. "And possible dance studio with makeup room. I haven't decided."

Imogen and Jonah started walking up the stairs, arguing about whether a makeup room was really needed in a secret base.

I'd taken my ridiculous amount of free time over the summer to fix my bike, so I rolled it out from behind the secret place near the green-houses and fired it up to ride toward Kinpago.

I came back about an hour later with a bag full of stuff. I stood before the Koigni dorms and wondered how I was going to get in— and how I'd find Sophia's room without getting discovered and kicked out first.

After I'd stood there for fifteen minutes, the door in front of me opened. I came face to face with Lindsey. She looked like she was getting ready to leave. Her eyes widened when she saw me.

"Hi," I started. "Is Sophia around? I heard she has the flu."

"Yeah. That for her?" Lindsey looked at the bag.

"Yeah." I held it up. "Can I uh... give it to her?"

Lindsey stood tall. She glanced inside the Koigni dorms, looking around. "Sure. But be quick about it. If Doya finds out a Toaqua's been in here..."

"Yeah, I get it," I said. "I won't be long."

She didn't respond. Lindsey looked... really pale. And kind of off. I noticed Medusa wasn't around.

"You sick, too?" I asked.

Lindsey's eyes barely remained open. "Kind of. Here. Follow me."

She held the door open, and I stepped inside. Red was everywhere. It hurt my eyes to look at. And ancestors, it was freaking hot in here. What did they keep the heat at, ninety degrees?

Lindsey led me through the empty common room. I was on edge, but there was no one in here but us. Where were all the Koigni?

"Everyone's mostly gone for the weekend," Lindsey answered, noting my curious stare. "People have gotten scared. They go home now, because they don't want to risk their Familiars getting taken, or catching the plague that's been going around."

"It's like that in my dorm, too," I told her. Had to be the same throughout the school.

Lindsey led me down a maze of hallways, then pointed to a door. "She's in there. Please be quiet. If she's sleeping, I don't want you to wake her up. She needs all the rest she can get."

Lindsey really seemed to care about how Sophia was doing. I nodded to her. "Thanks. I won't be long."

Lindsey didn't acknowledge me again. She vanished inside her own dorm. I didn't bother knocking on Sophia's, just let myself in.

Sophia was awake. She was in bed, surrounded by a thousand tissues and looking miserable. Esis was on her pillow, brushing her hair. He squeaked when he saw me, dropped the brush and ran over, launching off the bed and onto my chest.

"What are you doing here?" Sophia asked. Her voice even sounded weak, like she had a bad sore throat. I put the bag on her dresser and started pulling stuff out of it.

"Lindsey let me in. I heard you had the flu." I took about ten different medicines and vitamins out of the bag and lined them up before I started opening them, counting out pills for her to take.

"Liam, you need to leave. You're gonna get sick." Sophia let out a weak cough. Esis jumped off my shirt and ran back to the bed to fan her face.

"I already caught it and got over it. You forget I catch everything that goes around this school." I put a hand to her forehead. I knew Koigni ran hot, but she was definitely running a fever. She shivered at my cold touch. "Has Esis been helping at all?"

Sophia nodded weakly. "Kind of. Like, every time he tries to heal me I get a little better, but not much. I think my immune system has to kick in and start fighting the virus before Esis' magic can do anything. His powers just enhance and speed up what my body can already do."

I nodded. "That makes sense." Esis hadn't visited me recently, so I couldn't judge the theory for myself when I'd been sick with the flu, but Sophia's idea was as close to an answer as we were gonna get right now. "Have you been throwing up?"

"Yeah, a bit," she admitted. "It's really bad."

"That's okay. I brought applesauce, ginger ale, and crackers," I told her. "Just eat what you can."

"How did you get so good at this?" she asked, before she gagged. I went to grab the trash can and held it under her, but she didn't throw up. She leaned back against the pillows again and closed her eyes.

"I'm a professional sick person." I brushed back the strands of hair that had fallen in front of her face. "It's kinda what I do."

Sophia gave a tiny sigh. "I'm a hot mess right now."

"Shut up. You're gorgeous no matter what," I said.

There was a bout of silence. Shit. That was awkward. But I think Sophia was so out of it she hardly noticed. I went back to counting pills, just for something to do. When I had a few, I gave them to her, along with a bottle of water. "Here. This should make things easier. Just keep taking these every twelve hours, and blast it with vitamins. You should be fine in a couple of days."

I rearranged the bottles. "If you're not, you need to go to the doctor. Stay away from the hospital wing. It's infected. Go to someone in Kinpago. I'll take you if I have to."

"Yes, Doctor Liam," Sophia moaned.

"Don't sass me. I mean it," I said sternly.

Sophia kept her eyes closed. "Being sick like this just makes me think of all those poor Familiars in quarantine. I know it's not the same. It's even worse. No one even knows what the plague is yet. But Esis could be the key to figuring all this out."

I sat on the edge of the bed by her legs. "If you send Esis to heal those Familiars, you risk exposing him," I reminded her.

"It might be worth it if it saves lives," she said.

"And what if his magic doesn't work?" I questioned. "What if you try, and the plague is something Esis can't heal? What if it *does* work? What will the Elders do when they learn how powerful Esis is?"

She sighed. "I know, Liam. But can I really let all those Familiars, and those Elementai, die when I could do something about it?"

I got off the bed. "Well, you can't do anything about it now until you're better. Just get some rest."

"Okay," she whispered. She was letting out tiny snores a moment later. The pills had already put her to sleep. Esis patted her head tenderly and curled up beside her, kissing her cheek.

I watched her for a few precious moments before I got the hell out of there. I was lucky enough that the Koigni common room was still empty when I left it. I was going to re-join Imogen and Jonah in the Anichi dorms so I could lend a hand with cleaning. It was a short walk to the tower, but on my way there, I figured I should pick up a few things from my own room that would help, so I ascended the stairs to go back to the Toaqua dorms first.

I found Ezra looking rather pissy by the pool when I got there. He was tossing a water ball back and forth at the wall and lying on the couch. Dyami stood on a wicker chair and was munching on a collection of burgers that Ezra had bought for him. Ezra didn't touch his own food.

"What's your problem?" I asked. I stopped beside the couch and looked down.

"Fucking Renar," Ezra snarled. "We had our first training session for the Cup today, and he totally made Vanessa cry about being pregnant. Said that she was going to slow us down and we were gonna leave her behind."

"Vanessa's pregnant?" Shit. That wasn't good. I mean, I was happy for her and all, but this was the Elemental Cup we were talking about. She'd have to walk for miles and fight for her life while carrying a baby inside of her. The Cup is why a lot of people waited to marry and get pregnant until after graduation— because of the risk something like this could happen.

"Yeah. Cade and I nearly knocked his lights out before Baine broke us up. His stupid cockatrice nearly bit Dyami's head off," Ezra said. "This isn't a good team, bro. Renar and I are gonna kill each other before the first task even starts. Can you please tell Jonah to tell his boyfriend to stop being such a fucking asshole?"

"I can try," I said, but my hopes were shot on that one. Jonah would do no such thing.

Ezra threw the water ball, hard. It turned into ice and shattered as it hit the wall, sending fragments everywhere. "I'm just done with it all." Ezra got off the couch. He called to Dyami, and the thunderbird left his chair to land beside Ezra. Ezra went to his dorm and slammed the door.

Geez. It must've been a bad fight. It took a lot to get Ezra in a bad mood, but when it happened, he went off like a bomb. I didn't know how to help fix the problem— Renar for sure wouldn't change, even if Jonah said anything to him. I was caught between my best friend and my brother.

I fantasized about taking Renar out before the tournament so my brother would have a better chance of making it through, but shot the idea down. I wasn't a murderer, and Jonah would never forgive me. I wanted to protect Ezra, but I knew he had to do this on his own.

I got a couple of cleaning supplies from my room and shoved them in my backpack, but before I left the Toaqua dorms, someone stepped in front of me. It was Marcee. Her flying pig oinked when it saw me.

"Hey, Liam, can I talk to you?" she asked.

I was never going to get to the Anichi dorms at this rate. "Sure, what is it?" I said, making it clear in my tone I was in a hurry.

Marcee took a breath. "It's about Maddie. She's not really...

connecting with anyone here. She spends a lot of time by herself. I'm worried about her. I've tried to do things to get the freshman girls involved, and your sister's the only one who still keeps to herself. She doesn't have any friends. Do you know if something's wrong?"

This was exactly what I feared would happen. A variety of responses ran through my head. *She's shy. She's a loner. She's a naderei who can't deal with her visions and thinks it makes her a freak, so she stays away from everyone else.*

I just shook my head and said, "No. It could be anything."

Marcee took a breath. "Well, I think you should talk to her. You're her big brother. She's acting... distant. It's strange. We're not like the other Houses, you know— we're a family here in Toaqua. I worry that if she doesn't start to reach out, the other Toaqua girls are going to pick on her. I'm the freshman RA, and I don't want anyone excluded. You're the oldest. I think she'll listen to you better than Ezra."

"I'll see if I can get her to come out of her shell," I said. "Bye, Marcee."

I ended the conversation there, and left before I could get sucked into another conversation. I imagined talking to Maddie about making friends would go about as well as trying to fist-fight Renar's cockatrice. Ancestors, what was up with my siblings lately?

I thought about my options. I didn't think me talking to Maddie would help the situation. But maybe there was someone that could.

"Liam, you have to pick *something*. Graduation is six months away. You can't do nothing for the rest of your life."

It was a beautiful Tuesday afternoon, and Baine was up my ass. He'd seen me trying to sneak past his classroom back to the Toaqua dorms after Hawkei Home Ec and dragged me back into his office for Senior Theory. I wasn't happy about it, but at least we didn't have to talk in that horrible classroom-that-must-not-be-named.

"Can't I just wing it?" I complained. I was sitting in a chair, balancing back on two legs while my feet were propped up on Baine's desk. Baine was pacing around his office, not caring if he stepped on the papers that were scattered around the room.

Baine made a face. "I've never had a student of mine *wing* their future."

"You've never had a student who outlived their Familiar, either, but here I am. Life's full of surprises," I told him.

"Don't get smart with me. You're extremely talented, and you're wasting your potential." He threw his hands up in frustration. "If you're not sure of a career, why don't you consider going forward with your Masters? There are plenty of programs here that would love to have you."

I groaned. "I am *not* going to one class more than I absolutely have to. A bachelor's degree is good enough for me."

"You're acting like a child." Baine narrowed his eyes as he looked at the classes I'd picked for next semester. "*Carriage Driving?* Ancestors, Liam, you're killing me."

"It's a credit hour!" I countered. I'd put down whatever I first saw, and whatever looked easiest for next semester. Why did it matter what I took? Didn't he realize I no longer *cared* what happened to me?

"You're not taking Carriage Driving, so help me." Baine rubbed his face. "How can you expect to support a family if you have no sense of direction?"

I made a skeptical sound. "Yeah, like that's going to happen. I'm single for life."

"Some of your brother's optimism would look great on you," Baine countered, shooting me a glare.

"What are you gonna do? Run to my dad?" I asked. I was kind of being a disrespectful brat, but oh well.

"Your father's got problems of his own," Baine responded as he shuffled through my file. "He doesn't need to be worrying about you more than he already does."

That caught my interest. "What do you mean?" I asked. I took my feet off the desk and set the chair back on all four legs, leaning forward.

Baine hesitated. He looked up. "There's been an... unfortunate reassignment to take my place on the Water Council," Baine said, mumbling. "Elder Oleander was sworn in days after I left. He's taken it upon himself to oppose Chief Mitoh at every opportunity. He's had some bad dealings in the past that have put Toaqua at risk. I don't know why he's there."

Elder Oleander sounded awful. How the hell had he managed to get on the council? Had my dad lost his mind and elected the first person who applied after Baine stepped down?

Baine closed my file. "At any rate, I expect you to come in here next time with some resemblance of a plan for your future. The past aside, your poor father is going through enough trying to keep the council in line. He doesn't need to worry about you, too."

Shame flooded me, and it was so unexpected that I didn't realize what it was until it'd taken over my body. I didn't know Dad was having issues with the council. I'd figured everything had been fine.

But why was I feeling guilty? Dad— and Baine for that matter, too— had totally screwed me over last semester. They'd told me they could bring Nashoma back, and lied to my face. How could I let that go? Baine was different— he was just my teacher. He wasn't my father. Dad had done irreparable damage between us, and I wasn't ready to forgive him yet.

Baine waved me off. I stood up and grabbed my bag, nearly tripping on an artifact as I left. *Could've broken my damn neck*, I thought sourly. Baine had no right to criticize anyone for winging anything. The man was completely disorganized.

The week wasn't even over with. I had a huge paper due that I needed to work on. My grade was so low at this point if I didn't turn it in, I'd fail the class, so I knew I had to finish it. I headed to the Commons to pick out a table by the window.

Sophia was already there, and she was looking a lot better. She was bent over her homework and working intensely on it, pencil flying as she wrote. Esis was no longer wearing a leash, and instead turned pages of the textbook for her as she read.

"Hey," I said as I came beside her. "Mind if I sit here?"

"No, I don't mind." She gestured to the seat next to her, and I slid in. I put my bag down and brought out my homework, though I lost all initiative to do it once it was in front of me. I had to push myself. This had to get done.

"You seem like you've recovered," I told her.

"Yeah." She closed her book. "I think our theory is right. Once I started to feel better, Esis healed me, and it was like I was never sick at all. My immune system must've kicked in, and his magic accelerated it.

Those pills you brought me really helped in the meantime, though. Thank you."

"No problem. I'll tell Perot about what we've found," I said, and I smiled at her. She gave me a small smile in return, one that stayed on her face as she worked. I had to force myself to drag my eyes away from her and back on my paper.

It wasn't just her being well, though. Sophia looked... happier. There was a kind of glow about her I couldn't put my finger on. Had something changed recently?

"Are you still thinking of taking Esis into the quarantine, to see if he can heal those Familiars?" I asked.

Sophia chewed on her pencil. "I don't know. Maybe."

I knew that answer meant that she was, she just didn't want to tell me. I hoped that whenever she did sneak into the hospital wing to try, she was very careful.

I was distracted from my homework by sequins glinting light into my eye. Imogen and Jonah had just gotten back from dance class. Imogen had on a tank top and yoga pants, but Jonah was wearing a sparkly purple gymnast leotard that was ankle length and I was sure no one wanted to see him in. I wasn't even sure how he'd found one in his size. I didn't care to describe it further, just kept my eyes averted.

"Hey everyone," Imogen said cheerfully. She took an apple out of her bag and put it on the table. "How's everyone's day going?"

"Fine," I said.

"Wonderful," Sophia said, with a bit of a sigh.

"I *love* my new dance outfit," Jonah said, and he skimmed his hands over it. "So I'd say it's going fabulous."

"Besides the fact that it shows off your junk?" Sophia asked, and she snickered.

"That's a plus, honey," Jonah said. "Shows off the curves of my ass, too."

Imogen crunched into her apple. "So, Sophia, how are things going with the new girlfriend?"

"It's not like we're dating," Sophia said. She turned bright red and snuck a look at me. "We're just messing around."

Imogen sent a glance my way, but I kept my gaze downward, even though I was interested. Girlfriend, huh?

"What's this I hear? Are you going out with someone?" Jonah asked coyly.

Sophia blushed. "Not really. Lindsey and I are just getting to know each other. It's not a big deal."

"Oh my gosh, yay!" Jonah squealed. "I'm so excited! Another gay in the group! Sophia, does this mean you're bisexual?"

Sophia bit her lip and started putting things into her bag. She wore a slight grin. "Yes."

My mind had gone completely blank. Sophia, bisexual? No freaking way. I couldn't believe it. And she was going out with *Lindsey*? Had she moved on from me already?

No. No way. She was just doing this to make me jealous. It was just another plot she and Imogen cooked up, I bet. Satisfied with that answer, I concentrated on my work.

"Is that why you and Lindsey have a date tonight at Kinpago, at the nicest restaurant in town? I know her parents own it," Imogen teased.

"Meeting the family," Jonah said. "That's a big step."

"Geez, guys, it's just dinner. It's not like I'm sleeping with her," Sophia said.

"Yet," Jonah added, and he and Imogen squealed. He was about to put on a gay pride parade right there in the Commons.

Sophia checked her watch. "I actually have to go get ready for that now. Are we cleaning the Anichi dorms this weekend?"

"That's the plan," Jonah sang. "See you later, you sexy minx, you!"

Sophia picked Esis up and waved goodbye. Jonah saw Renar coming into the Commons and dropped us like a hot potato. Squeaks stayed stubbornly put by my side.

Imogen was giving me curious looks. It's like she was practically poking me, waiting for a reaction.

"What?" I asked.

Her grin was huge. "Don't you think it's sweet that Sophia and Lindsey are thinking about becoming a couple?"

"I mean, I guess," I said offhandedly. I looked back at my paper.

Imogen stared at me. "I thought you were gonna freak out when you heard about her and Lindsey."

I shrugged. "No. Why should I freak out? It's not real, anyway."

Imogen's mouth dropped open. "Excuse me?"

"You guys can drop the ruse, because it's not working. I already know you've roped Jonah into it," I told her. "Good try, though."

"You're an absolute dick!" Imogen shouted. Several people looked our way, but Imogen didn't appear to care, because she kept yelling at me. "You think Sophia can't be interested in anyone but *you?*"

"I didn't say that. But Lindsey? Come on." I shook my head. "If you guys want to get back at me this way, it's really sad."

"She's trying to *pick* between you and Lindsey!" Imogen stated. "And right now, Lindsey's looking like a pretty good option, because you won't put aside your pride and beg her to take you back!"

"Im, what do you want?" I asked in exasperation. "Not that long ago you told me you thought it was a mistake for me and Soph to be friends, now you're telling me that you want us back together?"

Imogen took an impatient breath. "To be honest, I'm torn, Liam. *Of course* I want you and Sophia back together, but I'm sick of seeing her be sad. And I'm sick of watching you sit around and not do anything about it."

Heavy guilt settled around my shoulders. I dropped my voice and hissed, "Don't you get that *I* don't really know what I want, either?"

"Then you'd better figure it out, because she's not gonna wait around for you," Imogen snapped. "You need to hurry up and make a decision, and fast. Before she decides she no longer loves you."

I couldn't believe she'd do that. I wouldn't. I knew that was selfish of me.

"You know what I *really* want? For Sophia to be happy," Imogen shot at me. "And if you aren't willing to step up to the plate, Lindsey is more than willing to fill in for you."

"Yeah, right." I scoffed. "I know what you guys are doing. You're trying to make me jealous, like you did at the strip club, and it's not gonna work."

"You're an idiot," Imogen snapped. She gathered her things and stomped off. Sassy followed her with an upturned nose.

Who was she kidding? Sophia wasn't into girls. It was so obvious. The thought of her and Lindsey together made me laugh. Sophia liked guys, and only guys. So what if she got turned on by some stripper in a club? Didn't mean anything. She hadn't done anything with Lindsey except maybe talk to her. I didn't need to be worried.

I struggled with the paper all afternoon. I wasted a lot of time and got it half-finished. I figured it'd have to do. I took my things back to my dorm and looked out the window at the orange October sky.

It was a nice evening. Just warm enough for a bike ride, probably the last of the year. I decided it would be nice. Maybe it'd make me feel something.

For once.

On my way down to the greenhouses, I spotted Sophia outside the entrance hall. She looked really pretty. She was wearing high heels, and her makeup was done. She had on a pretty red dress that showed off her shoulders. She carried a tiny purse that Esis sat in like a little dog. She saw me and waved me down.

I walked over to her. "What's up?"

Her fingers clutched her purse. "It's Lindsey. She said she'd meet me here at five for our date, but she's a little late." Sophia looked concerned. "Do you think you could walk me there? She said if she wasn't here by six to go ahead and leave, and it's fifteen minutes past that now. She might be there already. Sometimes her parents call her in to help if the restaurant's really busy, but I don't want to walk alone, with how things have been lately."

"Sure," I told her. I'd really wanted to ride my bike, but making sure Sophia was safe was more important, especially with the Esis crisis last week. We started down the path to town. Her heels clicked on the stone as we walked.

"Thanks for doing this," she said quietly, after some time. "I know it's awkward, you escorting me to a date with another person."

"It's not awkward at all," I told her. "I'm happy to do it."

"Really?" Her face seemed a little crestfallen. "I didn't think you would take it well."

"I'm fine with it." Sophia couldn't fool me. This wasn't a date. This was just a dinner between friends. It was cute she was trying so hard, though.

"So... you don't care that I'm dating a girl?" Sophia asked.

"Why would I care? It's your life. Live it how you want," I said.

Sophia nodded. "Okay. Thanks for understanding. I think it's good that I'm moving on with other people. You should too."

"Sure," I said. Then I paused.

What did she mean by *moving on?*

"Have you been seeing anyone else?" Sophia asked. I barely heard the question. I was thinking.

"Liam?" She poked me. I started back to reality.

"Huh? Oh, no," I said. "I've been busy with school and stuff."

"Oh." Her expression appeared conflicted. It was like she was wrestling with a major decision, one that had two choices. I didn't get it.

We walked in silence for a few minutes. The wind blew, and she shivered. The sun was setting, and it was getting cold. I slipped my jacket off my shoulders and held it out to her.

"No, that's not necessary," she said.

"You just got over being sick. Take it. You can give it back later," I told her. I draped the jacket around her shoulders. She pulled it closer around her and wouldn't look me in the eye. Esis was giving me some major dagger eyes.

"Can I ask you for a favor?" I said.

"What is it? I think I owe you one after you found Esis for me," Sophia said. She snuggled her nose into Esis' fur, and he peeped.

"It's Maddie," I told her. "She's not adjusting well to living at Orenda. She's always been a little shy, but I think this is a bit much for her. She hasn't made any friends since she's been here."

"Have your parents staged a bonding with Eirakari yet?" Sophia asked.

I nodded. "Yeah, once the assignments for this year's Cup were over. She's on next year's roster. But even with Eira here, it hasn't been helping her confidence much. I could try to intervene, but she'd just think I was being an overprotective big brother. You know a lot of the younger girls. Would you mind introducing her to some people?"

Sophia tapped her chin and nodded thoughtfully. "Sure. I think there's a couple of freshmen she'd really get along with. I can introduce her to some."

"That'd be great. Thanks."

We came to a bridge. It was one of several that led to Kinpago, and went over two cliffs that were separated from each other. She stopped and faced me as we came to the middle of it.

"I think I can make it from here. The restaurant's just up ahead," Sophia said. "Thanks for walking with me."

"Anytime," I said. We stood on the bridge. Esis whistled, and a collection of bats came flying out of the trees— except these bats were purple, and had four wings instead of two. They flew overhead, to the castle in the distance where a moon was rising. There was the cry of a magical creature, and a chamrosh— half-bird, half-dog— flew out of the same tree the bats were nesting in. Soon, a whole family of chamroshs were fluttering through the sky, barking and playing with each other as they lifted toward the clouds.

Nature was incredible. Animals weren't bothered by any of the shit people couldn't handle. They just existed day by day and let things happen, death and life churning in an endless cycle.

"Isn't Orenda Academy beautiful?" Sophia asked quietly. "It's like the most wonderful place in the world." She looked so inspired by the sight of the chamrosh pack.

She still saw the magic in this world we lived in. I wanted some of that magic back.

"Yeah," I said. I couldn't stop staring at her. It was like my eyes were locked on hers.

Then I did something really stupid. I kissed her.

The kiss only lasted a few seconds, but it brought everything back. *Everything.* I remembered how much I loved her, what it was like to be together, what it was like to actually be alive. For the first time in five months, I felt something other than cold, dark emptiness. I felt a tiny breath of happiness that was so fleeting and brief, but it was enough to remind me what happiness was, because I'd completely forgotten it existed at all. I'd forgotten any other feeling breathed besides numbness.

My life had been so empty and hollow. It appeared so meaningless. Kissing Sophia made all that go away...

Then I felt her hands on my chest, shoving me back *hard.* All those feelings were gone, leaving me vacant again. The loss of emotions was gut-wrenching and painful. I could hardly bear it.

But what was worse was Sophia's reaction. I almost fell down from her push. I recovered my balance at the last second. Sophia's face was rageful. But beneath that was agony. It was worse than when we broke up. I knew that look, and it was complete devastation. Whatever decision she'd been mulling over, I'd just made ten times harder. I hated that

I was putting her through so much pain. I hated myself for doing this to her.

"What the hell was that?" she raged. Her fists were clenched. I didn't know how to respond to her. My mouth gaped, but no words came out.

Her face turned red. "You think you can just show up and come in and out of my life as you please? You think you can just continue to fuck with my feelings?" she screamed. She pushed me again. I stumbled backward. Her hands were so hot that they burned my shirt.

"No," I said weakly. It was so small that I don't think she heard it. Tears were streaming down her face, and it was ruining her makeup. Esis hissed at me from inside the purse, bearing his teeth and lowering his horns at me.

Sophia threw a fireball at me, which I had to dodge. It smashed against the bridge and created a hole in the siding.

"I *hate* you! Make up your fucking mind!"

"Sophia—"

"Get the *fuck* away from me!" She threw my jacket back at me, and I barely caught it. I didn't know Sophia could run in heels, but apparently, she could if it was to get away from me.

Ancestors, what had I done?

sophia

TEN

I needed a break. From everyone. From every*thing*.

I skipped class the next day and took the long walk to the Koigni village. It felt good to be out in nature. Esis chittered from my backpack as we ascended the foothills of the mountain. I turned to look out over the landscape. Orenda Academy was just a dot in the distance now, but it was beautiful.

I swung my backpack off my shoulder and set it down in the middle of the path. Esis sat inside, with his head and arms poking out the top. I felt more secure with him riding that way. I unzipped the bag, and he hopped out.

"You're right, buddy," I said. "This is a gorgeous view."

I dug into my bag and pulled out my camera, then removed the lens cap and snapped a few pictures of the landscape. For a moment, I just stopped and stared. I inhaled a deep breath and forced the tension out of my muscles as I focused on the scene before me. I was surprised to find it actually worked, considering the barrage of emotions I'd been feeling lately. I wasn't sure I'd ever be able to sort through them. But for now, I just wanted to forget all that.

Esis scurried in front of me and struck a pose in the middle of the path. I chuckled and took a photo of him. He hurried over to me and up my shoulder to peek at the screen. I turned the setting to playback mode and showed him the picture. He looked proud of himself.

I placed my camera back in my bag, then held it open for him to climb inside. He hesitated and jumped off my shoulder, bouncing a few feet away from me.

"Esis!" I cried, hurrying after him.

He stopped at the side of the path and picked up a shiny rock, then turned back to me with a proud look on his face.

I bent and took the rock, then picked him up and put him inside my bag. "Thanks, buddy. It's beautiful, but you have to be careful. We aren't supposed to be walking alone right now. I need you to stay by my side."

Esis' bottom lip stuck out in a pout, but he nodded.

"Let's keep going," I said. "It's not much farther."

It took only another ten minutes before I arrived at my grandparents' house. Betsy answered.

"Sophia, dear!" she cried, spreading her arms wide and coming in for a hug. "What are you doing here? I didn't expect to see you until next week."

"I missed you," I admitted.

"Come in, come in," she said hurriedly. Betsy opened the door wider, and I followed her down the hall and into the kitchen. The delicious smell of bacon and eggs hit my nose. "I was just getting started on a late breakfast. Sit."

She pulled out a chair at the table and guided me into it before I could respond. Alan sat across from me reading the paper. I set my bag on the table. Esis hopped out and onto the floor, where he sniffed my grandfather's Familiar curiously.

Alan folded his newspaper and set it aside. "Sophia, it's good to see you. What brings you to our neck of the woods?"

I shifted in my chair. "I just needed a break."

Betsy turned from the stove with alarm on her face. "Is something wrong?"

I shrugged. The truth was, that list never ended, but I didn't come here to discuss any of that. I came to get my mind off it. Plus, I didn't want to burden them with my troubles.

"It's nothing, really," I lied, then quickly changed the subject. "Hey, Betsy, can you tell me another one of those stories about my mom?"

She chuckled. "You don't have to call me by my first name, dear. You can call me Grandma."

She'd mentioned it at one of our lunch dates before, but I was still getting used to the name. Even though they already felt like family, I'd never had grandparents in my life before. It was still new to me.

"Okay, Grandma," I said, testing the word on my tongue. To my surprise, it felt natural, like I'd been calling her that my whole life. "Actually— I changed my mind. I'd like to know more about you two."

I smiled and glanced between them.

"Sure," Grandma said. "Help your grandpa set the table and we'll tell you anything you want to know."

Grandpa showed me where the plates and cups were. "What did you two do before you retired?" I asked.

"I was a midwife," Grandma said as she brought the food over to the table. "I delivered babies for forty-two years."

My eyebrows shot up. "Oh, wow. That's a lot of babies. Did you deliver me?"

The two of them exchanged a glance as Grandma sat. I couldn't quite read the look.

"Yes, as a matter of fact. I did," she said with a smile. "Your mother wanted a home birth. You were born right here in this house."

My brows shot up. "I was? Why didn't you ever tell me?"

"You never asked," she said simply. "Shall we pray?"

Esis hopped onto my lap and folded his paws in front of him, though he never took his big blue eyes off the pile of bacon in the center of the table.

"Ancestors," Grandma said. "For this food, this house, and the blessings you've bestowed upon us, we give thanks. *Akotee et veni.*"

"*Akotee et veni.*" Grandpa and I echoed the Hawkei phrase for "*let it come.*"

Esis unfolded his paws and reached forward, but I held him close to my chest.

"Patience is a virtue, buddy." I grabbed a piece of bacon and handed it to him, and he gobbled it right up.

"What did you do for work, Grandpa?" I asked. "I know you worked at City Hall with my dad, but I don't really know what you did there."

Grandpa cleared his throat. "I worked in several departments, but I spent most of my time cataloging and managing the inventory of ancient artifacts."

"Oh?" I asked curiously. "That sounds interesting. My friend Imogen would love that. It must've been fun studying them."

Grandpa glanced down at his food, not meeting my eye. "It wasn't exactly my job to study them."

"What do you mean?" I asked, looking between the two of them. Grandma wore a wide-eyed look, like there was something they weren't telling me.

Grandma reached over and placed a gentle hand on mine. "Grandpa's job was to identify artifacts and... destroy them."

"Destroy them?" I practically choked on my eggs.

"Not all of them," he said quickly. "Just the ones the Elders requested be destroyed."

Why would they destroy their own history like that? Suddenly, I remembered something Liam had said. The Elders had destroyed all Anichi totems, like the Spirit Totem I wore around my neck. They'd do anything to keep that kind of magic out of anyone else's hands.

"Why would you help them?" I had to believe he didn't agree with it. It wasn't right.

"It was my job," he replied. "Hawkei don't go against their Elders, Sophia. They're our highest authority, save for the ancestors and the Great Spirit."

"Do you ever regret destroying parts of our history?" I asked.

"Yes, of course," he admitted. "But if I didn't destroy them, the Elders would find someone else who would. If that person didn't know what they were doing, they could hurt themselves— or others."

I relaxed. It was clear Grandpa had respect for the totems and artifacts he worked with. Without thinking about it, I reached up and touched the Spirit Totem that lay beneath my shirt. It'd backfired on me twice now. Maybe Grandpa would know how to use it...

"What would happen if you discovered a totem, now that you're retired?" I asked curiously.

He tilted his head and swallowed a bite of eggs. "What do you mean?"

"Let's say you stumbled across an ancient totem in the woods. Would you be obligated to turn it in to the Elders, or would you keep it for yourself? Or would you just leave it there?" I asked.

Grandpa took another bite of food and thought about it for a moment. "I'd be under no obligation to turn it in. Truth be told, I'd never thought about it before."

Grandma nudged him and smiled. "You'd start a collection and go out every day to see if you could find more."

Grandpa chuckled. "That sounds about right."

I took a deep breath. My hands trembled as I reached for the chain around my neck and pulled it over my head. I knew I could trust my grandparents with this, but it was still nerve-racking to show it to them.

"I found this, and I was wondering if you could teach me how to use it." I held out the Spirit Totem for both of them to see.

Grandma gasped, and Grandpa reached for his reading glasses to get a better look. He took it in his hands and looked it over.

"This looks very old, Sophia. Where did you find it?" Grandpa asked.

"I found it in the mountains," I told him honestly. "I know it contains magic, because it helped me get through the Cup. My friend thinks it might be a Spirit Totem."

Grandma's eyebrows shot up. "A Spirit Totem? I thought those were all destroyed after Anichi died out."

Grandpa continued to inspect it. "We don't know that for sure. Several have surfaced throughout the years, so it's possible there are more out there. But Sophia, Spirit Totems only work if you're a Spirit Warrior."

Grandpa handed the totem back to me. Esis poked his head up over the table and tried to get a good look at it.

"I think I am," I admitted. "I don't know how. All I know is that the totem works. But... it keeps backfiring on me lately, like it's throwing my magic back at me instead of working *with* me. I know that Spirit Warriors have died because they couldn't handle the power. I don't want to be one of those people. I want to learn how to use it, in case I ever need it again like I did in the tournament."

Grandpa leaned back in his chair and pressed his lips together, thinking. "Spirit Totems themselves don't hold power. They only work to amplify the power already inside of you. So if it's backfiring on you, it's not a problem with the totem. It's a problem with how you're channeling your magic."

"What do you mean?" I asked, trying to keep an open mind.

Grandpa leaned forward and placed his elbows on the table. He seemed intrigued by my problem, like it was a puzzle he was excited to solve. "Think back to the times it backfired on you. What were you feeling?"

When I'd tested in the woods, I remembered feeling frustrated because it wasn't working, then... *bam!* It backfired. It was obvious what I was feeling in Intermediate Koigni Magic when it did the same thing. I mean, I was trying to work with Haley. That girl always sent my anger meter off the charts.

"I felt angry," I told him.

Grandpa nodded, like that made sense. "And when it *did* work for you?"

I thought back to the tournament. I'd been feeling... loved. Liam had been healed. We'd been reunited with Imogen and Jonah. I was ready to take on anything.

"I felt confident," I said.

"Exactly!" Grandpa slammed his palm against the top of the table, like he'd found his *eureka* moment. "The totem backfired on you because it rejected your anger. It's the totem's way of saying *you are better than this.*"

It sounded a lot like channeling lightning. Somehow, I had let those lessons slip from my mind.

"But anger is easy," I argued.

Grandma chuckled. "Yes, but anger is only the spark that lights a fire. It can't sustain magic the way other emotions can."

I slipped the totem back over my head. "Maybe our coursework needs to include a class on emotional intelligence," I joked.

Grandma and Grandpa both chuckled. Esis joined in, but I didn't think he knew what he was laughing at.

"It'd certainly help," Grandpa agreed. "Why don't you show us what you can do with the totem?"

I ate the last two bites of my eggs and stood with Esis in my arms. I hesitated before following behind him. "You won't tell anyone I have it, will you?"

Grandpa stopped and turned to me. "No, Sophia. Your secret's safe with us."

Grandpa led me into the sitting room and told me to stand in front of the fireplace. He used his magic to kill the fire burning inside, then told me to channel my powers into the fireplace and up the chimney. Grandma sat nearby and observed with curiosity in her eyes. Esis sat beside her and her Familiar.

Closing my eyes, I tried to picture my power channeling through the totem, then through me. Fire shot out of my palms and lit the logs, but it wasn't any stronger than normal.

Grandpa killed the flames again. "It's okay. Just concentrate and try again."

The second time, the same thing happened, and I started to get frustrated.

"We're not in any hurry," Grandma assured me. "Take your time."

I gritted my teeth and narrowed my eyes at the fireplace. *I can do this. I'm strong. I'm powerful.*

I willed flames to shoot out of my palms, but instead, a weight slammed into me and knocked me off my feet. I went flying back into the coffee table. Magazines and a pile of coasters flew everywhere.

Grandma gasped and quickly rushed to my side. Esis stood on his toes, looking on high alert.

I sat up and grumbled. "Ugh. This is exactly what I meant. Every time I try to channel my power through the totem, it tries to hurt me. Do you think maybe it's rejected me?"

"Mm..." Grandpa stood next to the fireplace, looking deep in thought. "It doesn't seem to be working how it's supposed to... you did look a little frustrated, though."

"I was," I said as I got to my feet. "Because it's not working."

Grandma checked me over to make sure I was okay. When she was satisfied, she took a seat again.

"I think I know what your problem is," Grandpa theorized.

I rubbed my elbow where it'd slammed into the coffee table. "What's that?"

"Do you trust the totem, Sophia?" he asked.

"Trust it? Like, how?"

"Do you trust that it's going to work?" he questioned.

"I..." I thought about it for a moment. "I guess not. I mean, it's back-fired on me several times now."

He nodded thoughtfully. "You're waiting for it to prove itself to you before you put your faith in it, but that's the exact opposite of how this works. You must put your faith into it *first*."

I bit my lower lip. "I— I don't know how to do that."

"You've done this before," Grandma reminded me. "What did it feel like then?"

"Yes!" Grandpa exclaimed, like Grandma had the answer. "Think about what it felt like when it worked the first time, and channel that feeling."

I adjusted my weight between my feet and nodded. "Okay, let's try this again."

I took three deep breaths to clear my mind. Tension eased from my shoulders. I took myself back to the tournament, how it felt to push the Elders' fire away and guide my team to the finish line. It'd been by far one of the most profound moments of my life— and I hadn't even known the totem was helping me at the time.

I pushed the totem from my mind and focused instead on my own power, what I knew I was capable of, what I had the confidence to do. If I'd done it once, I could do it again. There was no question about it.

Fire shot out of my palms with such intensity that it whirled up the chimney like a fire tornado. A wave of heat blasted across the room, then everything settled.

Grandma and Grandpa clapped in unison. A feeling of elation soared through me. I'd actually done it!

"That's what I'm talking about!" Grandpa cried. "See? You can do it, Sophia. You just have to trust in yourself."

Grandma rose from her chair and pulled me into a hug. "I'm so proud of you. Our little Spirit Warrior."

"WHERE *WERE* YOU YESTERDAY?" Imogen demanded the following day when I arrived at History of the Hawkei. We were early, so we spoke in low whispers at our seats.

"I visited my grandparents," I told her. "I needed a break."

I didn't tell Imogen about my most recent failure. When we'd gotten back to the castle, Esis and I tried to sneak into the hospital, but there were so many doctors and nurses around that we couldn't get in. The Task Force security set up around the quarantine was insane. There was no way I'd be able to sneak Esis past the cops to try and heal the sick without getting caught.

I felt insanely frustrated. Esis could be the cure to this plague, but how would we know if we couldn't reach the sick?

"I wanted to ask about how the other day went," Imogen said.

"You mean with Lindsey?" I asked.

"Yeah. How was the date?" Imogen wiggled her eyebrows.

I sighed. "Dinner was great. Her parents are really cool. It was what happened *before* that was a problem."

She furrowed her brow.

"Liam," I groaned.

"Oh," she said, like that explained everything.

I shook my head thinking back to it. "I just don't get him. Some days he'll act like he doesn't want to be around me at all, then the next it's like he's trying to win me back."

"Win you back?" Imogen's eyes widened.

I lowered my voice. "He kissed me."

Imogen squealed, but I quickly shushed her.

"And then I threw a fireball at him," I admitted.

"Sophia!" she hissed.

"It wasn't fair, Im," I told her. "Liam's the one who broke up with *me*. He's just making this harder on both of us."

I leaned back and shook my head. "What's even worse is that I'm worried about him. He's been acting different. He's losing weight, and not behaving like himself. I just want to take care of him. My stupid girl-friend instinct is kicking in again. It's like he's doing it on purpose."

Imogen leaned closer to me. "So, who are you going to pick?"

I swatted at her. "Can we stop acting like this is *The Bachelor* or something?"

Imogen chuckled. "I can't resist. I'm kind of rooting for them both."

I sighed. "I don't know. With Lindsey, it's easy. We're both Koigni, so we can be together in public. And girls are just not as complicated. We can talk about things easier, and we *get* each other. But with Liam..."

Where did I even start? Being with him was confusing as hell. That man was all over the place, and our relationship was just one miscommunication after the other.

But there was a passion there that I didn't have with Lindsey. Then again, there was the forbidden aspect, too. If Liam and I ever *did* get back together, we'd have to hide it for the rest of our lives— or face the Elders.

"Maybe I'll just start a harem," I deadpanned.

Imogen laughed so hard that a few students across the room turned to look at us.

"I'm serious," I said. "It'd be so much easier than having to choose."

"If only life were that simple," she said.

Baine entered the classroom just then, cutting our conversation short.

I leaned over to her and said quickly, "Hey, are we meeting after class like we did last week? To talk about prophecy stuff?"

We hadn't come up with anything last week, but maybe this week would be different. We *had* to keep looking, no matter what it took.

"Yes," Imogen whispered. "I found a few more things we can look at."

"Everyone settle down," Baine said.

It took him two more tries before the class went silent. I swore, he was one of my only professors who couldn't command a room. I felt kind of bad for him.

"Let's begin." Baine turned on the projector, and a photo of the tree in the Kinpago town square lit up the front of the room. The tree was one of the thickest I'd ever seen, and taller than any of the surrounding buildings. It had a large, twisted base and low-hanging branches. The leaves were all different colors year-round and reminded me of oak leaves, but the tree bore fruits that looked like a mix between apples and peaches. There was no other tree like it in the world outside of Kinpago. I was sure of it.

"We're all familiar with the Blessing Tree," Baine said. "But does anyone know *why* we call it the Blessing Tree?"

Imogen scoffed from beside me. "Who *hasn't* heard this story?"

Her hand immediately shot into the air.

"Yes, Miss Ahnild?" Baine said.

"Legend has it that anyone who eats the fruit of the Blessing Tree will receive great blessings from the ancestors," she said. "Of course, it has never been proven that its fruit contains magic."

Baine looked pleased with her answer. "Yes, but if we look into the history behind the tree, we will find that there is merit to these claims."

He continued, like he was reciting the story he'd told a hundred times. "Centuries ago, a Toaqua man was walking into town when a Koigni man beat him and stole his money. He left him in the path, bloody and bruised. A Yapluma woman passed by the hurt Toaqua man. When he asked for her help, she ran, afraid that the attacker might still be nearby. Next came a Nivita girl by the name of *Lyda Leve Nivaras*, or Girl Who Lives in Trees. She was only seventeen and still unbonded. She helped the man into her cart and brought him back to the Nivita village to nurse him back to health.

"The ancestors recognized her good deed and blessed her with great power. This upset the Koigni thief, and he murdered her in the square. The ancestors would not let her kindness go to waste, however. Where her body fell, a tree sprouted. This grew into the Blessing Tree. It is believed that her body still lies beneath the tree, that she has become one with it. Therefore, those who eat the fruit of the tree shall share in her magic."

I leaned over to Imogen. "I don't get it."

She pursed her lips, looking upset at Baine. "That's because he didn't tell it right. He totally butchered the story."

"Miss Henley. Miss Ahnild," Baine snapped. "Something you want to share with the class?"

I glanced around the room. All eyes were on us. A few shot me disgusted glares. Everyone had been a little cold to me since I got Esis back. It was like they were jealous my Familiar came back and no one else's did.

Whatever. Screw them. Esis started to growl, but I put a comforting hand on the top of his head.

"Yeah, I don't really get the story," I said.

Baine looked to me in question. "Which part is tripping you up?"

"What's the moral of the story? I mean, she helped someone and got killed for it. Besides *Koigni are murderers*, I'm not really sure what we're supposed to learn from the legend."

Baine blinked at me. "This is not a fable, Miss Henley. It's history."

"If the ancestors thought she was important enough to turn her into a tree, don't you think they were trying to send a message?" I argued. "So... what's the message?"

Baine thought about it for a moment. "It's a story about the ancestors and their will."

A collective mumble traveled around the room, like the students agreed, but it felt like Baine was taking a shot in the dark.

"He's wrong," Imogen whispered to me. "He left parts out. Don't feel bad. I agree with you. The message is a little ambiguous—"

Imogen sucked in a sharp breath and grabbed my arm. Her finger-nails dug in so hard that it broke skin.

"Ow!" I hissed at her. "What?"

"This is the story we've been looking for!" she exclaimed in a low whisper.

My jaw dropped. "*The* story? How can you be sure?"

"I'm not. Not yet," she admitted. "I need to find the exact wording, but I'll have to go home, and I can't go until tomorrow."

"Miss Ahnild!" Baine snapped.

Imogen leaned over and quickly said, "We'll meet on Saturday in the Anichi dorms to discuss."

AFTER CLASS, I cut through the Atrium. It was a large, open area bigger than a football field in the center of the castle, with stone walls and large windows on all sides and a modern glass ceiling over the top. The temperature and humidity was regulated year-round. Endless plants lined stone pathways that led to doors in and out of the Atrium. Most were so tall that it felt like a maze through a jungle. There was a big fountain in the center, and a koi pond with an artificial waterfall in one of the corners. Gazebos dotted the space, where students often gathered to study. I'd never spent much time in here, as it always seemed too crowded for my liking, but it was a shortcut back to the dorms.

On my way, I caught sight of Maddie at the edge of the pond. She had her jeans rolled up to her knees and her toes in the water. She bit the end of a pencil while studying an image in her textbook. Eirakari sat by her side, licking the water in the pond. The ice dragon swished her tail as she watched the fish swim by. Nearby, a group of First Year Toaqua guys were splashing each other with water. She didn't notice them until a big wave came up out of the water and splashed all over her jeans.

She squealed, then quickly gathered the water in her palm to dry her clothes off. It trickled out of her hands and back into the pond. She shot a dirty look at the guys, but didn't say anything. Maddie used her magic to clean up the puddles across the path, then turned back to her book. She looked lonely all by herself— like she could really use a friend.

I suddenly remembered Liam's request. I slapped my palm to my forehead. How could I have forgotten? Esis made a noise from my arms and pointed at Maddie.

"I know," I whispered to him. "But who am I going to introduce her to?"

Esis looked up at me and shrugged. I had to do *something*.

I hurried into the castle and up the steps to the Koigni common room. Inside, I spotted a First Year Koigni guy hunched over a pile of textbooks. At this time of day, he was the only one in the common room. Esis tugged on my hair and pointed.

"What?" I hissed at him. "No."

Esis tugged again, looking more insistent this time.

I sighed. "Well, I can't say I didn't try."

I slid into the chair across from him. He wore thick black-rimmed glasses and a *Star Trek* t-shirt. His hair was dark and a little wild around his face, but he was kind of cute in a nerdy way. He didn't really fit the usual Koigni stereotype, which meant I liked him already.

What am I doing? I asked myself. I didn't even know if this guy was Maddie's type.

What was I saying? Of course he wasn't. He was Fire, and she was Water. The two didn't mix. Yet for some reason, Esis thought I should chance it.

The guy looked up to me. "Uh, can I help you?"

"Hi," I said, sounding confident. I stuck my hand out in his direction. "I'm Sophia."

He hesitated, then took my hand, but he looked totally confused. "I'm Drew?"

"Is that a question?" I asked.

"Huh?" He furrowed his brow at me.

"Your name," I clarified. "Is it Drew, or was that a question?"

He eyed me like I was crazy. "It's Drew. No question."

I smiled at him, then leaned forward. "Hey, Drew. This might sound really weird, but I was wondering if you wanted to meet a girl."

He looked me up and down with like I was *so* not his type.

"Not me," I said quickly. "Blame it on my Familiar."

I gestured to Esis, who poked his head up over the table. "He wanted me to ask you."

Drew's eyes brightened. "Oh, wow. He's so cute. I've never seen anything like him. May I?"

I nodded.

Drew reached out and let Esis sniff his fingers. When Esis determined it was safe, he hopped up on the table and inched closer to Drew.

"Aw... you're such a friendly little guy," Drew said as he scratched behind Esis' horns. Esis purred. "You remind me a little of a tribble."

"Tribble?" I asked.

"Sorry," he said quickly, like it was automatic for him to apologize. "*Star Trek* reference."

"You don't have to apologize," I assured him.

He froze up, like no one had ever said that to him before. An awkward silence stretched between us before I said, "So, um, have I successfully intrigued you enough that you'll follow a complete stranger to an undisclosed location to meet a girl who may or may not totally creep you out?"

Drew chuckled. "I won't lie. You definitely have me intrigued. But, like... why me?"

I shrugged. "Because you look like you need a friend."

Drew looked skeptical, but in a fun way, like he was enjoying the mystery.

"I'll buy you dinner afterward," I offered.

He laughed in a friendly manner. "I can get free food anytime I want in the dining hall."

"I'll do your homework for you," I said hopefully.

He closed his textbook and smirked. "Nah, I'm good with that."

I didn't have anything left to bargain with. "I'm offering to introduce you to a really sweet girl. Do you really want to pass up the chance that she might be the *one?*"

He thought about it for a moment, then said, "I guess I'll try anything once."

"Awesome!" I jumped to my feet and gestured for him to follow me.

He seemed reluctant, but got to his feet anyway and left his textbooks on the study table. Esis jumped into my arms, and we entered the main hallway.

"You really have to work on your introductions," Drew said.

"What fun would it be without the mystery?" I teased.

"Just know, at the first sign of trouble, I'm turning back," he warned playfully.

"Trouble? What ever could you mean?" I feigned. "I'm a totally normal human being."

He shrugged. "You seem like it, but you could be leading me down to the dungeons to knock me out with a sleeping potion and harvest my organs."

"Ah," I said. "You caught me. The reason I chose you is because you're an exact match for my friend's kidney. She needs a transplant, stat!"

Drew laughed. "Seriously, though. No harvesting my organs."

"Deal," I agreed.

We entered the Atrium, and I led him over to the pool. I was relieved to see Maddie was still sitting there.

"You didn't say she was Toaqua," Drew hissed from beside me.

I shrugged. "I didn't say she wasn't. Is that going to be a problem?"

He didn't answer. His eyes were locked on Maddie. He looked her up and down curiously. Just by the look on his face I could tell he was attracted to her.

"Hey, Maddie," I said as we approached.

She looked up from her textbook and smiled when she saw me. She set her book aside and hopped to her feet, leaving wet footprints across the stone path. "Sophia! It's great to see you."

She gave me a hug, then drew away. "How have you been?"

"Good," I lied, before quickly changing the subject. "This is my friend Drew. Drew, this is Maddie."

"Hi," she said kindly. "I like your shirt. *Beam me up, Scotty!*"

Drew's eyes instantly brightened. "You're a fan?"

She shrugged. "I'm more of a *Star Wars* kind of girl."

Drew was practically drooling. It took him a second to compose himself. "Is that... is that an ice dragon?"

Eira stepped forward. The path was wide enough for several people to walk at once, but Eira took up almost all of it.

"Yes," Maddie said, stroking Eira's head. "Her name's Eirakari. You can pet her if you'd like."

Drew seemed too stunned at the offer to move. "No, no. I couldn't. She's too beautiful. A Familiar like that should be treated with nothing but respect."

Esis grumbled from my arms, clearly offended.

Maddie chuckled. "It's okay. She's friendly."

Maddie reached out for Drew's hand. He completely froze when she touched him, but she didn't seem to notice. She lifted his hand and guided his fingers over Eira's scales. I swore I saw him shiver.

Excited jitters welled up in my stomach. Esis really did have that one pegged. We were officially a kick-ass matchmaking team.

Drew and Maddie were laughing together when a familiar voice cleared his throat from behind us. I turned to see Liam standing there with tight eyebrows and pursed lips.

A weight instantly settled in my gut. I wasn't ready to see him again, not after how he treated me the other day. That kiss was still burned in my memory. I'd wanted to kiss him back, but I just couldn't. It was too much... too emotional.

"Maddie?" Liam said in a strained tone.

Maddie whirled around toward her brother. "Oh, Liam. Hi. I didn't expect to see you here."

His jaw tightened. "I was just passing through. I was headed to Senior Theory."

Liar, I thought to myself. Liam always skipped that class. Everyone knew it.

Liam stepped past me and walked straight over to Drew, like he was playing the big protective brother card. "Who's this guy touching your Familiar?"

Maddie looked to Drew, then giggled, like Liam's behavior amused her. "This is Drew. We just met."

Drew seemed to shrink under Liam's tough gaze. Liam looked to me, then back to Maddie. "Is that so?"

"Yeah," she said casually. "Sophia introduced us."

"Huh. Sophia, can I have a word?" Liam started walking away, expecting me to follow.

"I'll see you later," I said to Maddie and Drew. "You two have fun."

They turned to each other, but I didn't hear what they said. At least they looked like they were enjoying themselves. Liam led me down another path and behind a cluster of tall ferns.

I noticed he was wearing a new leather jacket, since I still had his from last semester. "Have you been out for a ride?"

He shrugged, like he barely registered the question. "Yeah. My last one."

I furrowed my brow. "What do you mean?"

"I'm giving the bike to Ezra." Liam shoved his hands into his pockets, not meeting my gaze. "He'll enjoy it more than me."

"But you love that bike," I pointed out.

Liam shrugged. "I don't need it anymore."

This was so unlike Liam. What was his deal? "But you're a total adrenaline junkie. That bike was a part of you."

He scoffed. "Yeah. I have a real death wish."

My stomach sank. I got a sick feeling in my gut from his words. I didn't like the way he said it... something about it just felt... really off.

But that was typical Liam. Always negative. "I was just trying to help."

"Forget it. You were supposed to introduce Maddie to *girls!*" he hissed. "I wanted her to make *friends*, not boyfriends."

I shrugged. "What's the big deal? Why can't girls and guys be friends?"

"They can. It's just rarely works out that way."

His words hit me like a punch to the gut. Was he talking about us?

He quickly added, "Plus, I thought you might introduce her to some girls from her own House."

"What makes you think I'm more qualified to do that than you are?" I asked. Esis chittered from my arms, like he agreed with me.

"I don't know. You have classes with some of them... don't you?"

"Well, yeah, but that doesn't mean I talk to them," I said.

The truth was, there were some girls in my Hawkei Legends class I could approach about befriending Maddie, but I didn't have the class again until Monday and wanted to help her before then. Plus, I was kind of enjoying watching Liam get so bent up about this. It wasn't a big deal. Drew and Maddie could talk without it turning into a warzone.

"I thought you said you knew some freshman you could introduce her to," he reminded me.

I rose a challenging brow. "Drew's a freshman."

Liam pressed his fingers to his eyes. "This isn't what I asked for, Sophia."

My stomach sank. He was really distressed about this, and I felt bad. "Look, I'll talk to some girls on Monday. In the meantime, I think Maddie can make her own decisions about Drew."

Liam took a deep breath, then said, "Yeah, okay. Just... please don't make me regret asking for your help."

I pursed my lips. "I thought you already did."

"No, Sophia, I—" He paused, and his tone softened. "I'm sorry about the other night. I never should've kissed you without asking first."

"Damn straight," I said.

Liam's features hardened. "Ancestors, Sophia. Can't you take an apology without rubbing it in my face?"

My jaw dropped. I hadn't realized that was what I'd been doing. "Liam, I—"

He held up a hand. "I don't want to hear it, Sophia. I'm sorry, and that's all I have to say to you right now."

Then he turned and stomped away from me. He didn't even let me finish. It was so unlike him. Why was he acting so weird lately?

As I watched him go, a little piece of my heart broke. And it was in that moment that I realized how much I still cared about him. I'd hurt him by not accepting his apology.

I never wanted to hurt him again.

❧

I SLUMPED into the Commons minutes later. It was closer than the dorms, and I just wanted to sit down somewhere. The room was quiet and deserted this time of day. I took my usual seat in front of the big TV and spread out over the full length of the couch.

Ugh. This couch. So many memories.

And they were good memories, too. No matter how much Liam had hurt me when he broke up with me, no matter how bitter I felt about everything, it didn't change the good times we shared together.

I pulled Esis to my face and pressed my nose into his fur.

I missed him. The Liam I used to know. The people we used to be. Before we hurt each other.

"Sophia?"

I sat up and glanced around for the source of my name. Lindsey stood in the doorway with Medusa at her side. She looked drained— like she hadn't slept in days. Her lips were void of color, and there were dark circles under her eyes. Her red hair was piled atop her head in a messy bun.

Yet somehow, she still managed to look hot. Ancestors, why couldn't I just make up my mind already?

Lindsey caught my eye and walked over to me slowly. I scooted over on the couch so she could sit beside me. Esis hopped into my lap.

I smoothed out my hair. "What's up?"

"I've been looking everywhere for you," she said as she sat. She didn't quite sound like herself. She sounded tired and worn.

I instantly sat up straighter. "What's wrong? Are you okay?"

"Me?" she asked. "What about you? You look upset."

"I am, kind of," I admitted. "But it's no big deal."

"It is," Lindsey insisted. "If you're upset, you should talk about it."

I shook my head. "I can't."

Lindsey sighed. "Sophia, you can tell me anything."

I sniffled. I knew I could, but it was just too hard to admit. Lindsey and I were sort of together now. She didn't need to hear all about how I was pining over my ex.

"Sophia," Lindsey said softly, placing a hand on mine. "Anything."

I bit my lip and gazed up at her. "Remember that guy I told you about from Utah?"

She nodded.

"Well, he wasn't from Utah. He was from Orenda."

Lindsey chuckled. "I know, Sophia."

I furrowed my brow. "You do?"

"I could tell you were lying, but it's okay. I understand why you didn't tell me."

"You're not mad at me? For lying to you?"

She shook her head. "I know you would've told me eventually. Besides, we weren't even fooling around when you told me that."

My gut sank. "Is that all we're doing? Fooling around?"

Lindsey looked at me sympathetically. "I don't know. I really like you, Sophia, and I'd like this to be more than that, but..."

"But what?" I asked, already sensing where this was going, and it broke my heart. I didn't think I could handle going through this again.

"But you're still hung up on him," Lindsey finally said. "Are you sure you're ready to start a new relationship— a serious relationship? Because if you're going to be my girlfriend, I want to know you're *mine*."

"I can do that. I can give myself to you." I heard the lie in my own voice. Lindsey was right. Part of my heart would always belong to Liam.

"Look," Lindsey said. "I don't mind fooling around— if that's what you want. But if you're doing this to convince yourself you're over him, maybe we shouldn't be doing this at all."

My chest felt empty and heavy all at the same time. Lindsey and I weren't even officially dating, but it definitely felt like we were breaking up. Tears rose to my eyes.

I choked them back. "Are you saying you want to stop seeing me?"

Lindsey hesitated. "I want you to make sure you know what you want."

I sighed. I couldn't give her an answer right now.

"We don't really have a choice right now," she said, dropping her gaze. "We should probably take a break."

"What do you mean we don't have a choice?" My voice cracked.

Lindsey twisted her hands in her lap. "Medusa and I are sick."

Worry shot through my chest. "Like, flu sick, or sick sick?"

She wiped her nose with a tissue in her hand. "I thought it was the flu, but it's lasted too long. We've got the plague. I came to tell you I'm headed to the hospital wing. Medusa and I are going under quarantine. You might not see me for a while."

My stomach bottomed out. I suddenly didn't care if we broke up or not. All I cared about was Lindsey's health.

"It could just be the flu," I argued. I had to convince her of this so Esis could heal her without suspicion. I nudged at Esis, and he hopped across the couch toward Medusa.

"No, Esis," Lindsey said, catching him and handing him back to me. "You could get sick."

"He'll be fine," I assured her. I let him go, and he scurried over to Medusa and placed his paws on her head. She looked too ill to notice or care.

"Sophia," Lindsey said. "It's okay for us to be by each other because the illness isn't passed between Elementai. It's passed between Familiars. Their Elementai get sick because of the bond. Esis shouldn't be touching Medusa."

"He has a really good immune system," I told her. I watched closely as Esis tried to heal Medusa, but I couldn't tell if it was working.

"Anyway, you should take some time for yourself while we're in quarantine," Lindsey suggested.

I sniffled again.

"If you decide this is what you want, I'll be waiting for you when I get out," she said. "But I'm willing to bet *he's* waiting for you, too."

Tears began to fall from my eyes. "I don't think so."

Lindsey reached over and wiped a tear from my cheek. "He'd be a fool not to."

My breath wavered under her touch. "I don't want to lose you."

I stole a quick glance at Esis. He looked like he was getting frustrated. *Not a good sign.*

"That's not what this is," Lindsey said.

I nodded like I understood, but it sure felt like this was goodbye. I looked to Esis again. He dropped his shoulders in defeat, like it was a lost cause. Whatever this illness was, his magic couldn't heal it. It only made the tears stream down my face harder. Lindsey and Medusa were going to die.

Ancestors, please let them find a cure for this soon.

"Can I... can I get a goodbye kiss?" I asked Lindsey.

She blinked the tears from her eyes and nodded. Cupping my face in her hands, she slowly pulled my lips to hers. Our lips connected in a soft, tender kiss.

The sound of shattering glass sent us reeling apart. My eyes darted toward the noise to see Liam standing near the door. A vase he'd stumbled into lay in pieces at his feet. His eyes went wide staring at us, like he didn't believe I was with a girl until now. He was in total shock.

The whole room went dead silent.

"I— I'm sorry," Liam stuttered. "I didn't mean..."

He whirled around and raced out of the room.

And just like that, I'd already hurt Liam again. Would we ever stop doing this to each other?

Liam

ELEVEN

"I turned Sophia Henley into a lesbian."

"You what?" Jonah laughed. "Naw, man. That's not how it works."

I'd just literally ran out of the room when I saw Sophia kissing Lindsey like there was no tomorrow. I really didn't believe her when she'd said her and Lindsey were a thing— now there was proof of it being shoved in my face. My ex-girlfriend liked girls, and I had never noticed.

I felt like a total idiot. Now I was commiserating with Jonah in the Anichi dorms, which were pretty much clean now— all we had left to do was move some furniture around and the common room would be ready for us to use.

It proved a worthy distraction. But I really hoped Sophia didn't come up here, because right now, I wanted to die of embarrassment.

"That is how it works. I dated her, and now she likes women. I'm a total girl-repellant," I said in horror.

"Liam, trust me, my gaydar works just fine, and Sophia *is not* a lesbian," Jonah said. He laughed again. Squeaks, who was lounging on top of one of the white couches, chirped in agreement.

"She kissed Lindsey."

"It's college. Everyone experiments," he said. "To be honest, I *know* she's bisexual. But I don't think it matters, seeing as how her heart is pretty much reserved for you."

He said that carefully, like he wasn't sure how I was going to react. I didn't know how I was going to react, either. It wasn't like I didn't know how to feel anymore— more that I didn't have any sort of feelings at all, about anything.

"We're broken up. It doesn't matter. We'll never get back together," I responded.

Jonah made a skeptical noise. "Sure. That's why it's been six months and you two are still pining away for each other."

"She's not *pining away* for me. She's dating Lindsey now," I mumbled.

All that talk about moving on the other day had been serious. Sophia had gotten tired of waiting for me, and had decided to go ahead and find someone else. I didn't even have the right to be mad about it. She was single. This was my fault in the first place.

Oh well. At least it wasn't a Koigni guy. It was so much better that Sophia had moved on to dating a girl. I didn't think my ego could handle the thought of Sophia getting banged by another dude. That was complete torture.

How far had Lindsey and Sophia gone? Had they done stuff other than kissing? Had they seen each other naked? Holy shit, I was getting turned on and upset all at the same time. As hot as it was the thought of Sophia messing around with another girl, it was also heartbreaking.

"I can tell you're conflicted, which is okay," Jonah said. "It's perfectly natural to want to be in a threesome with Sophia and Lindsey, because *ancestors*, those two are really hot. Like, I'm gay, and even I would consider—"

"I'm not thinking of having a threesome with them," I grumbled.

"Then you must not have a dick, because every guy would be at least tempted," Jonah shot back at me. "Bro, it's obvious why this is bothering you. You still want to be with Sophia. I think you need to man up and tell her how you feel. It's been long enough."

"If we were to get back together, do you know what would happen? We'd be in the same situation as we were before," I told him. "Interhouse relationships still aren't legal."

"Does it matter? What you're putting yourself through is worse than anything the Elders could do to you," Jonah argued. "This is self-torture."

"You don't understand," I said. "You don't know what it's like to be forbidden to love someone. For people to tell you that your love is wrong."

"Dude, are you kidding me?" Jonah said, flatly and with a little disgust. "People like me know *exactly* how that feels. Yeah, it's not a big deal for me to be gay in the Hawkei world, because it's what our tribe has been doing for thousands of years. Our religion accepts it, but out there in the rest of the world?"

He made a skeptical noise. "You forget that there are still parts of America where I could be killed for kissing a man in public. I'm safe here. In other parts of the U.S., not always. And even if I'm not in danger of losing my life, there are still people in our country who think I'm an abomination."

I hadn't thought of that. I'd grown up as an Elementai, so being anything but straight was more than tolerated, it was accepted. Different sexualities and genders were a part of Hawkei lore from the beginning of our culture. In some cases, it was even reserved as sacred. It wasn't weird to be gay or transgender in our community. Some were even called two-spirit, or *naa-anichi*, in Hawkei, and considered blessed by the ancestors. Jonah had only been afraid of coming out because he was worried about what his parents would think— but they'd disapprove of him either way, whether he was gay or straight. The rest of our society didn't care.

But it wasn't like that everywhere. It wasn't that long ago before gay people weren't even allowed to get married in the United States. But I'd never noticed, because I'd lived in a society that sheltered me from that kind of hate.

"Sorry, Jonah. I didn't mean it like that," I said.

"I know you didn't," Jonah said. "But don't act like I haven't been there, because I have."

"She wouldn't take me back even if I begged her," I said desperately. I'd burned that bridge long ago.

"You don't get it. This isn't just affecting you guys. It's ruining the entire group," Jonah pointed out. "You and Sophia are acting like divorced parents, and Imogen and I are the kids stuck in the middle. The four of us can't hang out anymore without it being weird or awkward, or you two starting an argument. It's not fair to anyone."

Jonah was right.

"I didn't meant to fuck things up this badly," I said. "Why can't we just be friends?"

"You and Sophia don't work as besties. You're either together, or you're not," Jonah said. "But if you aren't going to ask her to be your girl-friend again, you need to let her go, man. She's torn up over you."

I thought about that in silence for a moment. Could I really let Sophia walk out of my life for good, forever?

I was still pondering the question hours later. I lay in bed all night, staring at the ceiling and contemplating what the hell was going on. I didn't get any sleep. All I could replay in my head was the sight of Sophia kissing Lindsey, and Jonah repeating over and over that I had to let her go.

She was probably in Lindsey's bed right now, doing stuff I wanted to picture and block out all at once. Have you ever gotten hard and wanted to cry at the same time? Because it's really fucking weird.

On Friday morning, I gave up trying to sleep and went down to the dining hall to get some coffee, so I'd be able to stay awake for Hawkei Leadership.

I saw Imogen for the first time in days. She was at the drink station, mixing all different kinds of veggies and fruits together to make a smoothie. Sassy was beside her, balancing an orange on her nose.

When I came up beside her, Imogen narrowed her eyes at me. "I hate you."

"That's okay. I kind of hate me, too," I responded quietly. I poured myself some coffee in a disposable cup and kept my eyes on the floor.

Imogen seethed. She refused to talk to me any further. I decided to ask a question, to try and break the ice.

"How are Sophia and Lindsey doing?" I asked quietly.

"You shouldn't worry yourself about it. They broke up last night," Imogen said dismissively.

"What?" I was so startled I nearly dropped my drink. "Why?"

"Lindsey called it off because she knows Sophia's still hung up on *you*," Imogen said harshly. "She's never going to be able to move on unless you finally tell her it's over between you for good."

I remained silent, and Imogen said, "It's because it's not really over for good, is it?"

"I don't know," I answered hollowly.

"You need to make up your mind," Imogen snapped viciously. "Either beg Sophia to take you back, or don't. But quit playing with her, because it's obvious you two can't be just friends."

Imogen stormed off. Sassy followed her with her tail raised high. I fidgeted with my coffee and felt like shit. I was so confused.

I still had an hour before Hawkei Leadership. I decided to go for a walk, to try and clear my head. I just wanted some way to stop all the voices that were shouting at me. Maybe in the forest it'd be quiet. It felt like my mind hadn't been at peace since before I could remember.

I found myself returning to our waterfall. Sophia and I's. I hadn't been here since we'd left it on Ancestors' Day. I didn't know why I headed there, only that I was at the school one minute, and I seemed to blank out for a long time, my consciousness only returning when I heard the rushing of the water hitting the stones.

It looked the same as it ever did. Nothing had changed. But everything had. This time of year, the waterfall was surrounded by orange, red, and yellow leaves, and the grass was starting to die. There were no more butterflies or flowers, and most of the birds had migrated. It seemed like everything in our special place had died.

I noticed a black mark on one of the trees. The tree itself seemed familiar. I walked closer— there, where Sophia and I's initials had been, was nothing but blackened bark and a violent scar.

What the fuck?! She'd burned our initials off our tree!

The burn mark was old, as if it'd been done months ago. A couple of ivy vines and leaves had already grown over it.

I thought it was dorky and cute when Sophia had carved our initials, but I didn't realize how much those tiny letters meant to me until now. The fact that they were gone seemed permanent and final.

I also didn't realize how hard I'd been holding on to the hope that Sophia and I weren't over for good until I saw her kissing Lindsey last night.

I punched the burn mark with all I had in me. Of course, it was a tree, so it didn't give. Pain went in shockwaves through my hand, bending my wrist, and I thought I heard something crack. I might have broken a knuckle. But I didn't care. This hurt more than anything my body could do to me.

My back hit the tree, and I slid down it, cradling my head in my hands. What else had she done? Toasted my jacket? Thrown out the camera I had gotten her? Had those months meant *nothing* to her at all?

I was tired of living. This shit hurt too much. Every time I thought I hit my limit, there was always more for me to endure. How much more could the ancestors ask of me? What else did they want me to carry? I felt like I was being crushed under all this weight.

I just wanted it all to end. And I'd been thinking that way for months. I wasn't sure what I was sticking around for anymore. I had no purpose.

After a while, I got up off the ground and wiped my face. I had class. I couldn't sit around feeling sorry for myself. I caused this shit.

I heard the sounds of a bike revving in the distance. It was probably my brother. Ezra had taken my bike with nothing more than a, "Really? Thanks, bro!"

It was for the best. He'd appreciate it. It was a piece of me he could have when I was no longer around.

I arrived ten minutes late to class on the first floor. Professor Cheveyo had already started lecturing. He stopped when I entered. "Mister Mitoh, make it a priority to arrive to my class on time," he said. "The world doesn't wait on you."

"Yes, sir." Nobody paid attention when I sat down at the back of the class. They'd taken it upon themselves to make their own little group to exclude me. There were only six people in this class. It was extremely exclusive, open only to Political Science seniors and kids who already had internships or future job offers to work for the Elders. Naturally, I wasn't one of those people, so my attendance in this class had been a bit of a sore spot for everyone else who had busted their ass to get in here. Cheveyo probably owed Baine a favor.

Everyone else in this class had powerful Familiars. Maddox was a Yapluma who rode a huge white lion that had wings. Courtney, a Nivita girl who'd taken a particular dislike to me, rode a giant bird with rainbow feathers that made her magic ten times stronger. The others either had dragons or something else equally monstrous.

I felt really out of place among them. The only person who had gone out of their way to make me feel like I actually belonged here was Professor Cheveyo. He was Toaqua, and if anyone was a true Hawkei, it'd be him. His Familiar was a gray spotted Appaloosa stallion, and the man was so native it was unmistakable. He kept his long black hair in two braids, and rarely wore anything if it wasn't wool or buckskin made by the tribe. His face was tan and weathered, and his voice deep and gruff.

"Now, let's continue," Professor Cheveyo said. "Leadership is primarily the giving of self. One must be willing to volunteer yourself at all times for the tribe's welfare, even when it deems inconvenient or even costly to your own personal life."

I nodded. Being a good leader in our culture meant that you put the tribe first. You always sacrificed whatever you could to be in service of your people.

I looked around. I wasn't so sure the students in this room would do that. From what I'd seen of my colleagues, they were all selfish, and only interested in serving their self-interests or bolstering their position. The prophecy was right. The tribe was doomed.

"As we all know, a good leader doesn't have material attachments, at least, not any that he or she is unwilling to sacrifice for the greater good," Professor Cheveyo continued. "Weak leaders try to make themselves seem important. Great leaders are not great by themselves, but are exceptional at leading because they bring out the best in others. This is the most important quality of any good chief or Elder— to enable those around them to succeed."

Professor Cheveyo gestured to us. "We'll be doing a team exercise today to put these virtues into practice. Follow me into the forest."

We left the classroom. Professor Cheveyo led us outside, to a tall rock face that went about a hundred feet up. I heard a roar somewhere close by that shook the trees, over the rock face. That couldn't be good.

Around us, a river raged at the bottom of the cliff. Cheveyo climbed a platform that was taller than the cliff itself and began shouting down to us using a megaphone.

"All right," Professor Cheveyo said. "I'll be splitting you up into teams of three. Logan, Joanna, and Courtney, you'll be on one team. Liam, Maddox, and Angie, you'll be on the other."

Angie and Maddox sent me scathing looks. They were obviously hating that they'd been paired up with me. Logan, Joanna and Courtney were busy giving each other high-fives.

Cheveyo continued. "Somewhere beyond this cliff face is a flag, guarded by a certain magical creature. There is a finish line beyond it. Your task is to scale the cliff face and get to the end of the course. You are not allowed to use your Familiars— leave them behind with me. Whatever individual gets the flag from the magical creature first will receive extra credit."

People looked excited about that. Cheveyo was a hard grader. It was difficult for the best of students to get higher than a C in his class, if they passed at all, and you couldn't work for the Elders if you failed this course. That extra credit was sorely needed by a lot of students.

"I will be watching closely from the observation deck on who completes the exercise. On my count," Professor Cheveyo said. "Three... two... one!"

The other team raced forward and started climbing the cliff face individually. They didn't even stop to strategize. They really wanted that flag. Courtney, who was Nivita, wrapped vines around her body to lift her up as she climbed, and jutted out stones with her magic to grab. She could've done the same for her Koigni teammates, but it seemed like she'd forgotten about them. They didn't pay her any attention, climbing up the rock with sheer grit.

Angie looked at me. "Well, we already know we're going to lose."

"Ang, don't say that. Liam's a Cup Champion. That's got to count for something," Maddox argued.

They were talking about me like I wasn't even there. I ignored it and said, "We don't have rappelling gear. Is there another way up the cliff besides climbing it free-hand?"

"Yeah," Angie said, and she pushed her hands down toward the ground. She used her Air magic to lift her and Maddox up and over the cliff side, leaving me behind.

Fine. Be that way. It was clear the two of them intended to reach the finish line without me. I'd figure out a way up myself.

The other team had almost reached the top by now, but I knew I wasn't going to be able to climb up after them. I had about as much energy today as a limp dick. Try going up that way and it'd be a sure way to land on my ass.

I looked at the river. Looked like my one ticket up. I walked into it—I felt Cheveyo's eyes on me closely. I used the water to boost myself up—it wrapped around my waist and lifted me into the sky, then deposited me on the top of the cliff with ease. My lower half was soaked, but I'd made it up here before the other team did.

I didn't have time to dry myself off before another roar caught my attention. I looked up to see what the creature was. A typhon. It was an enormous reptile, green in color, with armor-like scales and snapping jaws. If I had to describe it simply, it was a big-ass crocodile with six legs that could breathe fire. It was twenty feet long and half as wide. One of its fangs was as big as me. One bite from that thing, and you'd be dead.

Maddox and Angie were currently trying to get around it. They came at the typhon separately, from different directions, but the monster was so big and quick that they couldn't get around to the orange flag on the other side. Angie barely missed getting snapped up by the typhon's jaws, while Maddox was sent flying by the creature's broad, flat tail. He moaned and struggled to get up once he landed.

The other team arrived, pulling themselves on top of the cliff. They seemed stunned at the sight of the typhon— Joanna even looked scared.

The finish was a separate white line in the grass a safe distance away from the typhon. I had the mind to say screw Maddox and Angie and just go there to wait. But my stupid nice guy instincts kicked in, so I ran around the typhon before it could eat me and kneeled beside Maddox. Angie had backed off to where we were, and the typhon was currently dealing with fending off the other team. They threw fire and boulders at it, but they bounced off the scales of the typhon without hurting it. The creature hissed. The other team was only making it mad.

"We should just say fuck the flag." I shook my head. "We'll never be able to outrun the typhon or get around it. The finish line is right there. Let's just complete the exercise."

"No way! I'm barely passing this class. I need that flag," Maddox growled.

"Of course *you* want to give up," Angie said, shooting me a glare. She had a long scratch on her arm that one of the typhon's claws had given her.

I rolled my eyes. Because ten extra points was worth losing a limb to that thing.

"This is impossible," Angie spit. "What a stupid lesson."

"How can I help?" I asked.

"Help? You wanna help, stay out of the way," Maddox snapped.

I stared at the typhon as it attacked. The flag was still far out of reach. But this was supposed to be a lesson, not some pointless exercise. What was the lecture centered around today? Self-sacrifice.

Then I put it together. There'd be no way for all three of us to get past the creature. Someone had to stay behind.

"You two go on ahead and get the flag. I'll distract the typhon," I said, and I stood up.

"Really?" Maddox got off the ground, raising his eyebrows. "But you'll fail."

"I'll take the losing grade. I'm probably not gonna pass this class, anyway," I told them. "You need the points more than I do."

"Why would you do that for us?" Angie said suspiciously, like I had an ulterior motive.

I shrugged. "Why not?"

Maddox and Angie looked at each other. "All right," Maddox said. "Tell us when."

I nodded. I got up and went to the right to face the typhon, while Maddox and Angie took the left. The other team had backed off, and two of them were sporting minor injuries. Courtney was screaming at Joanna— the Koigni girl was crying, holding her leg and refusing to get any closer to the creature. They struggled to recover their breath as they watched me approach the typhon.

The creature's yellow eyes fixed on me as I walked slowly toward it. I noticed there was a plot of sand beneath my feet. In seconds, I reached down and grabbed a fistful of sand, flinging it at the typhon's face. The typhon snarled as it became blinded, and I started backing away.

The typhon shook sand out of its eyes and growled. It lunged for me, and I fucking ran like hell. The typhon gave chase, just as I hoped it would. I glanced over my shoulder and saw Maddox and Angie running for the flag. The typhon ignored them to come after me. I heard the stomping of its giant feet as it stampeded behind me. I had to hustle, my eyes looking for an exit.

But there was nowhere to go, and I was no match in a foot race against a giant crocodile that had six legs. I couldn't climb a tree to lose it, or outrun it— the only route of escape was down.

I launched myself off the edge of the cliff, and barely avoided the typhon snapping its jaws down on me, its hot air passing me over as its teeth skimmed my jeans. I felt weightless as I began to fall downward, but I wasn't scared. I'd taken bigger jumps while cliff diving. The fall made me breathless. I turned in mid-air so that I faced the water, and shoved my hands outward.

The river rushing below me rose upward to catch my body. The water cradled me in a soft way, and landing on it felt like jumping on a pillow. Once it had caught me, I made the water rise so that it lifted me back up to the cliff again. This time, I had it deposit me on the other side of the cliff, where the finish line was. Maddox and Angie were already waiting there with the flag. Yards away, the typhon paced back and forth with its eyes on us, but didn't venture any closer.

Angie had a huge smile as I approached. "I did it! I got the flag!"

She'd forgotten that I'd done all the work. But Maddox nodded at me. "Thanks. That was a good idea."

"No problem," I gasped. I was still trying to catch my breath.

Courtney was giving me dagger eyes. Joanna was still crying, but it wasn't more than a few sniffles. Logan patted her on the back sheepishly.

Professor Cheveyo had left the observation platform. He was now walking toward us with his Appaloosa by his side.

"Thank you for the help, Titan," Cheveyo said to the typhon as he passed it. "Tell Professor Azalea her assistance is much appreciated."

The typhon bowed. Titan ambled off, probably to return to the school. Professor Cheveyo faced all of us, but he didn't seem impressed.

"Well done, Liam," he told me. "You're the only one that passed."

Everyone's mouths dropped open in surprise, including mine. Courtney stepped forward. "What? But he failed the course!"

Cheveyo ignored her. "Maddox, Angie, you came very close to passing the exercise. I'm willing to give you both half the credit," Professor Cheveyo said. "But if you had paid attention, you would've stuck with Liam and went immediately to the end of the course. The task wasn't to capture the flag, but to ensure that all teammates made it to the finish line safely."

Courtney gritted her teeth, outraged. "But you said that whoever got to the flag first would receive extra credit!"

"I did, but the flag wasn't the purpose. If you had paid attention closely, there was no possible way to get to the flag without losing a teammate, and that wasn't the objective," Cheveyo said firmly. "It was merely meant as an enticing distraction. Liam was the only student who was willing to put the needs of the group ahead of his own selfish benefit."

The rest of the class looked ashamed— except for Angie, of course, who didn't care, because she'd gotten the extra credit— and Courtney, whose face was turning red with rage.

"He *lost*," she demanded, and she pointed at me. I hated being put on the spot.

"There is no such thing as a losing side in leadership, Courtney," Cheveyo said. "If you are doing your job correctly and taking everyone into account, each one of your people should be on the winning side. We all must work together for the benefit of the group as a whole. If one fails, we all fail."

"But it was Joanna's fault we didn't get the flag!" she protested. Joanna hiccuped.

"Accountability is important. Any person worthy of leading has to be willing to take responsibility for the failures of their people, whether it is their fault or not," Professor Cheveyo told her sternly. "Only unworthy individuals place blame."

Courtney crossed her arms and refused to say anything more.

Cheveyo said, "The effort given here today was poor. I hope that the rest of you will pay more attention to my lectures in the future. Class dismissed."

There were mumbles of discontent and aggravation. I got more than a few nasty glances.

"You just got the points because you're the disabled kid," Courtney whispered viciously to me as she shoved past. Maddox sent me a shrugging gesture as he went by, as if he was sorry she'd done that but didn't want to confront her, either. I went to jump off the cliff and into the water again, so I could grab my bag and get out of here.

"Liam, hold on a moment," Cheveyo said to me. I held back and waited— I could hear his horse snort as he approached.

Professor Cheveyo stood before me and clasped his hands. "I've been meaning to ask. Have you given any thought to what the future might hold for you?"

"Not really," I said. "I'm kind of figuring it out."

"I think it's clear that you're designed for some sort of authority role," Cheveyo said. "I don't play favorites with my students. Though I will say this, and I expect you not to repeat it; you show more qualities of leadership than any student I've ever had under my instruction. Even with the minimal effort you've chosen to provide thus far. It's critical that you consider a career in government. The tribe needs people like you."

I said nothing.

"You seem hesitant," he added.

I mulled the words over in my head. "Well... to be honest, I don't know why you let me take this class in the first place," I confessed. "Besides that Professor Baine got me in."

"Mister Mitoh, I allowed you into my classroom because I saw the potential in you," Professor Cheveyo said. "You have certain talents that shouldn't go to waste, and both Professor Baine and I think you only need someone to believe in you. Your performance in class today was exceptional. I expect that kind of initiative to be shown by you for the rest of the semester, without excuses."

I drew myself up. "Of course I will."

"Good." Professor Cheveyo turned away. "Now please, never turn in a half-finished essay again, or I will make sure you fail this course. I don't give second chances often."

"I won't." I left before he could grill me more, though I was smiling when I got back to the castle. Cheveyo thought I was designed for leadership. He wanted me to get involved in tribal government. He didn't give praise often, if ever.

Screw it. Maybe there was still a reason for me to stick around. Maybe I was worth giving one last chance.

What the hell. I got inspired. I went back to the library and rewrote the paper that I'd already turned in. I didn't think I'd get any points for it, as the first paper was already graded and he didn't accept late work, but I wanted to show Cheveyo I had initiative.

If it worked, maybe it'd be enough to stop me from what I was already planning. I wanted some sort of sign— to help me make a final decision.

It took me all afternoon to rewrite the essay. When I was finished, I was actually hungry. I hadn't been hungry in freaking ages. I ate dinner, though it still wasn't much, and was ready to deliver the brand-new paper to Cheveyo's office.

Maybe I'd go for a swim in the Toaqua dorms later. I was so tired of being alone. I wanted to be around people.

I had to cross the Atrium to get to Cheveyo's office. The sun was almost set by this time. I walked fast, because I was excited, thinking about the proud look he'd give me when I handed the paper in.

"I hate Hawkei Leadership. It's like the only person Cheveyo has time for is Liam."

I heard someone say my name when I left the Atrium. It was Courtney, along with a couple of other people from my Hawkei Leadership class— Maddox and Angie. They were down a ways. I didn't want to run into them— I turned around to go the other way instead.

"You know why Cheveyo has to," Angie said. "It's because he feels *sorry* for Mitoh."

They were still talking about me. Something in my gut said it was horrible and not to listen in. My feet urged me to run the other way, but I didn't pay attention. I wanted to know what they were going on about. I ducked behind a statue to listen in. They hadn't seen me.

"Cheveyo only let Liam in Hawkei Leadership on a pity card," Courtney said. "Gotta have equal representation and all that crap. It's not like he *deserves* to be there. I mean, his Familiar died because of him, for ancestors' sake, and he lost the chief hood. His own father doesn't even want him anymore."

I clutched my paper to my chest.

"Won't Chief Mitoh give the tribe to his younger brother when he graduates? Always liked him," Maddox said.

"Yeah, Ezra's all right," Angie said. "Sucks for him having an embarrassing older brother, though."

"Liam's not that bad," Maddox said. "He shows up every day whether he's sick or not. I couldn't do that."

"Okay, the disabled hero thing is *so* overplayed," Courtney said scathingly. "Honestly, if I was like Liam, I'd want to die. I wouldn't want to live like he does. He's sick every class."

"Agreed. It's cruel to let him suffer like that. Society should just take care of those people. End their pain," Angie agreed.

"Guys, let's be reasonable," Maddox said. He sounded repulsed by Courtney's words.

"We're right and you know it. His parents should be ashamed of themselves, letting him waste away like that," Courtney said fiercely. The disgust in her voice was immense. "If it was my son, I'd get it over with and just kill him. It'd be a mercy. I'd abort my kid if I knew they were gonna end up like him. It's the humane thing to do."

Maddox sighed. "I guess you're right. If you don't have your health, what do you have?"

"Not to mention he's a burden to the tribe," Angie said. "We don't have endless resources to keep taking care of sick people."

"But he won the Cup," Maddox pointed out.

"So?" Courtney asked. "I bet his teammates got him there. He wouldn't have lasted on his own."

My paper was practically being crushed against my chest.

Maddox asked quietly, "Do you think he stands a chance of beating out the rest of us for job offers?"

Courtney scoffed. "I'm not worried about him. His life is over. At this rate, he's just making things harder for the rest of us."

The three of them walked off. I stood behind the statue for what seemed like forever and tried to breathe.

They wanted to put me down. Like some kind of animal.

The rational part of me said they were just jealous, and pissed that I'd passed the course today. Maddox's worry that I'd get a better job offer was evidence of that.

But I didn't want to listen to evidence or reason. Both of them paled against my stark reality.

All the anger was gone. There wasn't anything left but hurt. And it was so bad that it became overwhelming. It completely consumed me and made everything else look entirely hopeless. There was no more meaning. I didn't want to die, but I didn't want to keep doing this. I didn't want to keep living. I didn't want to be in pain anymore. Was it really fair to ask a sick person to keep fighting if they didn't want to?

I missed Nashoma. More than anything, I wanted to be with him. I wanted to go home. I pined for him so badly I didn't have a way to describe the pain, and Sophia was no longer around to fill the hole that he had left.

And so, I made my final decision.

I decided to stop fighting.

I threw my paper away. Wouldn't do me any good now. It was pointless. I hadn't done anything in my life except be a major fuck-up. Why did I think today would've made any difference?

I left the main castle and proceeded to the outer gardens. Maddie and Drew were there, playing some sort of nerdy board game. They were laughing. I smiled. I wouldn't have to worry about her. Maddie would be okay. She was starting to make friends, and Ezra would take care of the rest. He'd be the big brother now.

I'd hurt everyone in my life. My family, my friends... Sophia. Ancestors, I'd fucked things up with Sophia. Jonah and Imogen said I needed to stop hurting her, and they were right. The only way I'd be able to make everything better is if I was gone. Their lives would be so much better without me. I wouldn't be able to mess things up for them anymore.

Darkness fell. I wasn't sure where I was going, only sure that I'd never see another sunrise. I didn't have a plan. I didn't feel like I had control of my actions. It was almost like I was in a trance. My head felt like it was in a fog.

I ended up on the bridge where I'd kissed Sophia a few days ago, standing in the empty gap where her fireball had blown a hole in the railing. They hadn't repaired it yet. The moon was almost full, and it had risen to light up the bottom of the canyon below the bridge.

There wasn't any water down there. It was an eighty foot drop. If I fell, there wouldn't be a way for me to save myself. I glanced around. No one was nearby.

Courtney, Maddox and Angie's words replayed in my head over and over, like a mantra that I couldn't stop hearing. The way they'd said it... it was like they believed that my life wasn't worth living because I was sick. Like all that existed was my illness.

And not me.

Was my disability really all that was left? I'd always just thought it was just a part of me. Not the defining factor. Not what I'd become.

They'd all agreed that they'd rather *die* than be like me. I bet the entire tribe felt that way.

What if they were right?

I hovered my right foot over the edge.

What if I just...?

"Liam?"

I thought the voice I heard came from the ancestors— spirit guides, or perhaps some sort of angel. There was a beautiful girl standing near me, about six feet away. She glowed with the white light of the moon. I didn't recognize her. Not at first.

But it wasn't an angel. It was Sophia. She looked at me with a pale face. Esis poked his head out of the purse she carried and stared at me with big eyes, his tiny paws held over his mouth.

I quickly placed my foot back on the ground. "Hi." Fuck, I sounded empty.

She came up beside me. Her expression was equal to one who'd just had a heart attack. "You okay?" She kept her voice steady.

"Yeah." I looked back down over the embankment, then at the wooden platforms of the bridge. "I'm fine, *pawee*."

She grabbed my arm and led me away from the edge. Her grip was firm and tight. "I was just going for a walk. You want to join me?" Her voice sounded fake, like she was forcing herself to be casual and relaxed.

"Okay." I croaked out the last word. My mouth was dry. Esis reached out from her purse and laid a paw on the top of my hand. Things cleared up a little— my head got a little less foggy.

The forgetting-thing happened again. One minute we were on the bridge, the next we were on the pathway back up to the school. Her hand was still on my arm, and it felt warm and comforting.

"You shouldn't be walking around by yourself at night," I told her. Saying a simple, small sentence like that took all my energy.

"Why are you worried about me when you should be thinking about yourself?" she asked.

I didn't answer. Sophia was chewing her lip nervously. She didn't let go of me, not even when we got back inside the school. I expected her to drag me to the hospital wing, but instead, she guided me in the direction of the Yapluma dorms.

She knocked on the door. A tiny Yapluma girl answered. She stared upward at us in confusion. "Can I help you?"

"I need to speak to Jonah Chanee," Sophia said. "Please, let me in."

The girl must've heard the urgency in her voice, so she opened the door wider so we could enter. It wasn't weird for people of other Houses to come in and out of the Yapluma dorms— it technically wasn't allowed, but they were the party people, so their House Head usually looked the other way.

The Yapluma dorms were covered in different shades of purple. It was messy in here— Yaplumas weren't often neat— and remnants of parties from the night before were still scattered around the floor. The glass ceilings were super high— hundreds of feet— and students could be seen flying around high above, sitting on chairs that levitated and playing games in the air. The Yapluma girl pointed, and Sophia practically dragged me to the door she'd gestured to. A couple Yapluma gave us curious stares as we passed.

Sophia banged on Jonah's door. There was loud music coming from the inside, which stopped as the lock turned. When the door opened, I saw Jonah in workout gear. He seemed confused when he saw us.

"Hey, how'd you guys get in here?" Jonah asked.

"Liam's spending the night with you," Sophia belted out. Jonah looked to me. He could tell by the expression on her face something had happened.

It was like he instantly understood without having to be told. "Yeah, sure. Come in."

Sophia led me inside. She only let go of my arm when the door closed behind us. It felt like her fingers would leave marks. Squeaks was lying on an oversized couch big enough for her and Jonah, eating chips. She paused when she saw me.

Jonah was friends with the Yapluma RA's, so he'd gotten one of the biggest dorms. It had a small kitchen, and a decent sized living room as opposed to my dorm, which was just a bedroom. It looked more like an apartment. Protein shakes, sports trophies and dumbbells lined the walls, underneath posters of male models who were half-naked, or worse. A football game played on the big screen attached to the wall. Jonah turned it off.

Jonah went to his bedroom and came back a few minutes later with a blanket. "Squeaks can be your pillow for the night. You need a Familiar right now. I have this extra quilt. It's clean. Promise there's no jizz on it." He winked at me.

I couldn't even lift a smile. I fell on the couch and curled up against Squeaks. Sophia threw the blanket over me. Both she and Jonah glanced at each other. I closed my eyes.

"Jonah, can I talk to you?" Sophia asked. She wrung her hands nervously and glanced at me.

Jonah nodded. He went out the door with Sophia. I kept my eyes closed and breathed evenly. Squeaks chirped and nuzzled my hair with her beak.

"I'm sorry. I didn't know where else to take him. I didn't know what to do." Sophia's voice was thick and upset. She was crying again.

"You did the right thing. The hospital wing is swamped right now with sick Familiars anyway," Jonah said calmly. "They wouldn't have been able to keep an eye on him."

"Can I use your phone? I'm gonna call his mom."

"Yeah, sure. I have her number saved. Here. Just don't let anyone see you on it."

Their voices got quieter, and I couldn't hear anything after that. I chanced opening my eyes for a moment. I looked at the poster above me on the ceiling of a guy showing his bare ass and wondered what I'd gotten myself into this time.

After fifteen minutes or so, Jonah came back in. "You're sleeping here, bud. Squeaks is gonna stay with you."

Squeaks cooed. I didn't respond, just nuzzled further into her feathers. Jonah sat across from me in an armchair and turned the TV back on, glancing at me every few minutes. I couldn't take his concerned stares, so I closed my eyes again.

I drifted in and out of consciousness for about an hour before I pressed into the safe darkness of sleep.

I woke up the next morning to the smell of bacon and eggs. Sleep was an escape. Now the grim fact of what I'd almost done last night pressed in around me, but I'd nearly ceased to care. I was more concerned that it'd been Sophia who had witnessed.

"Rise and shine, Liam Baby," Jonah sang at the stove. "I'm making pancakes!"

It felt like there were concrete blocks attached to my body. I struggled to walk across the room and sit at the kitchen table. Squeaks got up when I did and happily perched before the table, where Jonah placed a stack of twenty pancakes for her. She licked her beak and chortled.

"Here you go," Jonah said, and he put food in front of me. "Overeasy, how you like it. Don't bitch."

Jonah was an amazing cook, but the last thing I felt I could stomach at the moment was food. "Not hungry."

"You're eating this, or I'm shoving it down your throat. Your choice," Jonah said, and he put a hand on his hip over the pink apron he wore. I knew I couldn't argue. I picked up a fork and did as he said.

A half an hour later, there was another knock on the door. It was Ezra. The area around his eyes was rimmed with red, as if he'd been crying.

"Hey, bro," he said hoarsely. "You need to come home for a while. Mom's waiting."

I nodded. I followed Ezra out. Jonah blew me a kiss as I left and said, "You'll feel better soon, darling. We're all here for you."

A bunch of Yapluma stared and whispered as Ezra escorted me out. I wondered if word had gotten around the school that fast. *Liam Mitoh tried to kill himself.* I kept my eyes focused on the floor, and soon carpet turned to grass as we left the castle and ventured into the courtyard. A carriage pulled by a pair of peryton waited for us.

"You're taking your bike back," Ezra said roughly. "You're not going anywhere."

Ezra sent a watery glance at me before he wrenched his eyes forward.

I gave a feeble nod. "Okay."

I didn't think I'd see another sunrise, but there it was. Today was the first dawn of a new morning.

sophia
TWELVE

The night I found Liam standing on the bridge ready to jump, I'd just returned from the hospital wing. I'd wanted to visit Lindsey and check on how she was doing, but they wouldn't let me in.

I'd just sat down on my bed and opened my Intro to Child Development textbook when a sickening sensation slammed into my gut. It came out of nowhere and was unlike anything I'd ever felt before. I immediately jumped off the bed made a beeline for the bathroom. I hunched over the toilet, waiting for my dinner to come spewing out, but nothing happened. Fear swept over me, though I didn't know why. Esis scurried into the bathroom behind me, looking worried.

"I'm fine," I lied, but my stomach continued to churn. "I just need some fresh air."

For some reason, leaving the castle was all I could think about. It didn't matter that we were supposed to travel in groups and that there were dangers lurking about. I just needed to go for a walk.

I scooped up my purse from the floor and opened it for Esis to jump inside. I hurried out of the dorms, then down the main stairs and out into the night. I didn't know where my feet were taking me. It was like they had a mind of their own. All I knew was that I had to get somewhere— and fast.

Then I saw him. Liam's form was nothing but a silhouette in the

231

moonlight. He stood on the bridge we'd fought on just days ago, staring down into the empty canyon below. His foot hovered over empty air, like he was ready to jump.

Oh shit!

My stomach bottomed out. Suddenly, I knew where I had to be. Right here. Right now. It was a message from the ancestors.

"Liam?"

His head jerked in my direction. I couldn't read his features or his tone of voice. It was all empty— like he'd completely given up. "Hi."

I pretended like I didn't know what was about to happen. It seemed like that might make it worse. I just had to get him away from there.

What do I do? What do I do?

My mind raced. Was this truly what I thought it was? Liam wouldn't try to kill himself, right?

What did I know? I knew he was depressed— had been since the moment I met him. But... ancestors, why hadn't I been paying attention?

Now wasn't the time to get into the gritty details. All I knew was I couldn't leave Liam on his own tonight. I thought about staying out in the woods with him, just to keep him company, but that'd be stupid considering Familiars were going missing. Instead, I dragged him to Jonah's dorm, where I knew he'd be safe for the night until we could figure out how to help him.

The following day, I still couldn't wrap my head around what I'd seen. It was Saturday, and Jonah, Imogen, Cade and I were gathered in our usual spot in the Commons. We were all squished onto a single couch, but we didn't care. It felt better to be next to each other.

"How is he?" I asked Jonah hopefully. Maybe last night wasn't at all what I thought it was.

Jonah dropped his head, and Squeaks looked as equally sullen beside him. "Quiet. He won't tell me a thing. He's taking the week off school to recover. He's gone back home."

"You're sure?" I pressed.

"Yes," Jonah said firmly. "I spoke to his mom. He should be safe there for the next few days."

"But.. what if he...?" Imogen hiccuped.

Tears brimmed her lower lid. She was dressed in a t-shirt and sweatpants, with her hair piled into a messy bun at the top of her head. She was almost unrecognizable. Cade sat on her other side with his arm around her, softly stroking her arm. His features were blank, like he couldn't believe what had happened.

"What if he tries to hurt himself again?" Imogen forced out.

Jonah leaned his head on her shoulder. "There's nothing more we can do right now. He's in good hands."

Our corner of the Commons went quiet. I could feel the tension in the air... like we all wanted to talk about it, but didn't know what to say. I couldn't take the silence.

"I feel awful," I admitted. "I mean, how could I have not noticed?"

"You?" Jonah asked. "You barely spend time with him anymore. If anything, I should've been the one to notice..."

Imogen buried her face into my hands. "It's my fault."

We all looked to her in confusion. Sassy nudged her head against Imogen's elbow, trying to get her to feel better.

"Your fault?" Cade balked.

"I yelled at him right before... before..." She sniffled. "I told him I hated him."

I shook my head firmly. "No, Im. It's not your fault. Liam's depressed because of me. Because we broke up."

Jonah put an arm around me, pulling me close. "Don't say that, babydoll. This is no one's fault."

I stroked Esis' fur in my lap. "I'm just glad I was there, you know?"

"See?" Jonah pressed. "Not your fault. He's alive because of you."

I blinked away the tears. "Yeah. I guess—"

I cut off when I heard a familiar voice clear his throat from behind us. I sat up straight and turned to see Ezra, with Dyami at his side. His face was fallen, and his eyes were red. He carried a backpack that looked filled to the brim.

"Hey, guys," he said flatly.

Jonah stood and rounded the couch to pull Ezra into a one-armed hug.

"Thanks for keeping him company last night," Ezra said.

Jonah patted him on the back. "Anything for my Liam Baby."

"How is he?" I asked desperately.

Ezra looked totally out of it. His eyes didn't even focus on me when he responded. "Better. Kind of. I had to come pick up a few things, but

I'm headed back now. I feel so *stupid*." Ezra slammed his palm into his forehead.

"Hey, hey, hey," Jonah said softly, reaching for Ezra's hands to calm him.

Ezra kicked the back of the couch, then stood up straighter. "He gave me his bike, dude. I didn't realize what it meant at the time, but now…"

"None of us knew," Jonah repeated. He looked between all of us to reinforce the statement. "At least now we can get him the help he needs."

Jonah was right. Liam was still here. We'd gotten to him before it was too late. All we could do now was figure out how to help him so that it never happened again.

Ezra took a deep breath, then looked to me. "Mom says you're the one who found him."

I nodded, but the words closed up around my throat.

"Thanks," he said. "Today would be a lot different if you hadn't been there. I should probably get going."

"Wait," I said, before I could stop myself. Ezra hesitated. "Can you… can you tell Liam we miss him? And let us know when he's ready for visitors?"

Ezra nodded. "I will."

Ezra left out the door that led to outside. Dyami just barely squeezed through it behind him.

Jonah took a deep breath and plopped back onto the sofa between me and Imogen. "I wish there was something we could do."

"There isn't anything we *can* do right now," I pointed out, feeling the weight of the truth in my chest. "We just have to wait until he's ready for us."

Jonah groaned. "Can we at least do something to pass the time? I'm going to kill myself with worry."

Jonah clammed up when he realized what he'd said.

Imogen checked her watch, then turned to Cade. "Love, you're going to be late for your meeting with your advisor."

Cade didn't move right away. He clearly really cared about what happened to Liam— and about being here for Imogen. "I can skip."

"It's okay," she said softly. "I'll be fine. We'll meet up later."

Cade seemed reluctant, but he gave in. He leaned in to give Imogen a peck on the lips, then stood. "Love you, babe."

"Love you," she replied. Her eyes followed Cade and Arabelle all the way out of the room, then she turned to look at us. "I went home yesterday and got the story we were looking for."

Jonah glanced around and lowered his voice. "About the prophecy?"

Imogen nodded.

"Should we talk about this *somewhere else?*" I whispered.

We quietly left the Commons and climbed the castle stairs until we reached the doorway at the bottom of the Anichi tower. A few students were passing by, so we waited until the coast was clear before we slipped inside.

I drew a breath when we reached the top. "Wow. You guys. This looks great!"

Jonah plopped onto one of the couches, and Squeaks spread out over the one beside him. She took up the entire thing. Jonah placed his hands behind his head. "Yeah, it's been a helluva time cleaning up this place."

Imogen swatted him. "Please. You watched while I did all the work."

Jonah flexed his biceps. "I'm here for the heavy lifting, babe."

Imogen frowned at him. "True. You did help move some of the furniture."

I bent beside the fireplace and started up a fire with some of the dry logs piled beside it, then I joined Imogen and Sassy on one of the couches. Imogen pulled an old book out of her bag and opened to the first page. Esis hopped over to her and settled onto her lap, like he was a kid getting ready for a bedtime story.

"This book has been in my family for over a hundred years," Imogen said. "It's filled with Elementai stories for children. I didn't think of this story until Baine talked about it in class. I did some digging, and look."

Imogen showed me the copyright page. "It's copyrighted in 1902, only a few years after the prophecy was given, but the Blessing Tree... it's at least two hundred years old."

"Yeah, so?" Jonah asked. "What's your point?"

"If the legend has been around as long as the tree, why is this the first account of it?" Imogen cocked an eyebrow at Jonah.

He shrugged.

"Because..." The pieces began to fall into place in my mind.

"Because the legend never was about the tree. It was written for the prophecy."

"Exactly," Imogen said proudly. "Nivita made it up to pass the wording of the prophecy down through the generations."

I scooted closer to her, feeling hopeful. Could this really be it? "What's the passage we're looking for?"

Imogen cleared her throat and turned the pages to the middle of the book. She began reciting the story.

> *"The day was bright and cheerful*
> *But not for this Toaqua man*
> *For this tale tells of something fearful*
> *A terrifying plan*
>
> *The Toaqua man was gentle*
> *He wouldn't hurt a fly*
> *But the Koigni man he met*
> *Left him there to die*
>
> *Blood splayed the path beside him*
> *Every coin was gone*
> *The Toaqua man prayed for help*
> *Through the night and into dawn*
>
> *A Yapluma woman crossed his path*
> *But she feared the attacker was nearby*
> *She hurried on her way*
> *And ignored his pleading cry*
>
> *Next came a Nivita girl*
> *Without a companion by her side*
> *Lyda Leve Nivaras approached him*
> *And set aside her pride*
>
> *She pulled the man into her cart*
> *And brought him back into the trees*
> *She nursed him back to health*

Until he was steady on two knees

The ancestors saw her courage
They knew what she had done
Great power was bestowed upon her
Great power, she'd become

But the Koigni thief was selfish
He wanted power for his own
So he took the woman down
In the center of their home

She wouldn't let her power
Be used in such vain ways
A tree would sprout years later
Exactly where she lay

In her last breath, she raised her voice
And forecast words that warned of end
'The future of the tribe is in Nivita's hands.
No Hawkei shall survive if the weakest refuse to bend.'"

We looked between each other.

"Don't you see?" Imogen said. "This is it!"

Jonah narrowed his eyes, like he didn't quite get it. "Which part?"

"*And forecast words that warned of end*," she repeated. "It's a prophecy. Don't you see? The entire story is a warning."

"What kind of warning?" I asked curiously.

Imogen sat up straighter. "They're warning Nivita about choosing sides. This is why you didn't get the moral of the story in Baine's class, Sophia. You were looking for the moral of the story in the kindness she offered the Toaqua man, but that's not it at all. The Elders who wrote this story are warning Nivita not to be too kind. It has led to consequences in the past. It could destroy us again."

Jonah looked skeptical. "How can you know for sure this story has anything to do with the prophecy?"

Imogen sighed, like it was obvious. "We've been divided ever since

Anichi died out, and this poem wasn't written until shortly after Showana created the prophecy in the first place."

She looked between me and Jonah, as if waiting for the pieces to click. "Why would all the Houses be against each other in the story if the story supposedly happened so long before that?"

"So it's another clue," I theorized. "It's a way to call attention to the story, to say that something's wrong with the legend."

"Exactly," Imogen said.

Jonah sat up. "I don't get it. What does the tree have to do with the prophecy?"

"Nothing," Imogen said simply. "It was only a way to keep the legend alive, to tie the story into our culture."

"So all that matters is what she whispered at the end?" I asked.

"Yes," Imogen said proudly. She glanced back down to the story and recited the words. "*The future of the tribe is in Nivita's hands. No Hawkei shall survive if the weakest refuse to bend.*"

I pressed my lips together. "What do you think that means? That Nivita is the most powerful House in this war?"

"In a sense," Imogen said. "I told you. The story is about Nivita choosing sides. We have to be prepared for the consequences of whatever side we pick."

Jonah inhaled a breath. "I think I get it."

A silent beat passed. "Care to elaborate?" I asked.

Jonah sat up straighter, looking like he was thinking hard. "During the last war, Nivita and Yapluma sat things out until it was too late. Nivita wouldn't be stupid enough to let history repeat itself, so they're going to choose sides this time. But if I know my House— and I do— Yapluma is going to wait until Nivita makes their move. Wherever Nivita goes, Yapluma will follow. They don't want to make the final decision and end up on the losing side."

"That's why the fate of the tribe is in Nivita's hands," I realized. "Because whichever side Nivita chooses will be the strongest. Their side will have three Houses fighting against one."

"Yes," Imogen said confidently.

"What about the second line?" I leaned closer to read it. "*The weakest must bend...* weak Elementai? Like, they have to give in, comply? Are they talking about Toaqua?"

"I don't know…" Imogen said in thought. "That's how I'm interpreting it, but it's a little ambiguous."

Jonah snorted. "Every piece we find is ambiguous."

"At least we have the piece now," I said. "And I think we all know what we have to do."

Imogen looked up from the book. "What's that?"

I held my head up high. "Whatever happens, we need to convince Nivita to join our side."

THE FOLLOWING DAY, I visited my grandparents' house for dinner, but I didn't feel present like normal. My mind was somewhere else entirely—on Liam.

"Is everything okay, dear?" Grandma asked while I poked at my food.

Esis reached up from my lap and snatched a piece of broccoli from my plate. He popped it in his mouth and made a face, then spit it back out onto my plate. At this point, I didn't care. I barely took notice.

I sighed, then looked up to my grandparents. "It's nothing," I lied.

They exchanged a worried glance, and Grandma turned to me. "Whenever you're ready to talk, we'll be here to listen."

My shoulders fell. I wanted to talk about it, but at the same time, I didn't. I found the words forcing themselves out anyway. "It's one of my friends."

Grandma and Grandpa looked at me with concern on their faces, but they didn't prod. They waited for me to come at my own pace.

I took another deep breath. "He's in a bad place right now."

"You're worried about him," Grandpa guessed.

I nodded. "That, and I'm afraid it's my fault. Like I'm the one who put him there."

"So, you're feeling guilty?" Grandma asked.

I looked back down at my food, poking at the mashed potatoes on my plate. Esis tugged at my arm, so I scooped some into his mouth. "I guess so."

When I looked up into my grandma's eyes, I could see that she really cared. Her tone softened. "Do you think you could've done anything to change it?"

I thought about her question for a moment. "I don't know."

She rephrased the question. "If you'd done everything in your power to change how you'd acted toward this friend, would the outcome be any different?"

I realized that they hadn't even asked what had happened. They were nice that way— not prodding or criticizing me.

The kitchen went silent for what felt like a whole minute as I contemplated her question. *Would* it have been any different? Liam was depressed before I met him. If our break-up hadn't triggered him, would something else have? Had this been inevitable all along?

I didn't know the answer to that, but I was starting to understand what my grandma was getting at. I couldn't blame myself.

Heck, I didn't think I could even blame Liam. This was nobody's fault. But that didn't stop me from worrying about him. I wondered what he was doing right now. I tried to picture him in his room, weaving a basket or praying to the ancestors. I wanted to believe he was healing— with or without me at his side.

"I don't know that I could've changed anything," I admitted. "I guess what's really bothering me is that I don't know what to do moving forward."

"What are your options?" Grandpa asked.

Another beat of silence passed. It seemed like I only had two options. One, I could get back together with Liam, because I thought that might make him happy, but I quickly realized that would only be a temporary fix. I couldn't give my whole life to him just because I was afraid of what might happen if I didn't. That kind of relationship would only be filled with resentment on both sides. Neither of us would ever truly be happy.

Or two, I could walk away. That option scared me more.

There had to be something else— an in-between, a way to help Liam without sacrificing my own future. No matter how much he'd hurt me, I still cared. I still wanted him to live. I still wanted to be his friend.

Even if I didn't know if I wanted to be with him anymore.

"I don't know what to do," I told my grandparents. "I feel lost, like I need guidance. Do you have any suggestions?"

Grandpa shook his head regrettably. "We can't tell you what to do, Sophia."

I groaned and playfully said, "Can't you just point me in the right direction and hold my hand until I reach my destination?"

Grandma raised an eyebrow. "And what destination is that?"

I opened my mouth to answer, but I stopped when I realized I didn't know.

Grandma smiled sweetly. "Dear, that is exactly why you feel lost. You need to find a sense of direction before you can know whether you're on the right path or not."

I scowled. "Can't I just figure out the destination once I get there?"

Grandpa laughed. "Is that what you want?"

I dropped my head. "No, it's not. I just wish there was a way to orient myself."

Grandpa smiled. "There's something we can do."

"Oh?" I perked up immediately. "What's that?"

Grandma quickly caught on to what Grandpa was saying. She turned to me. "We can perform a Naming Ceremony."

Excitement washed over me. "My friend told me about that! What is it, exactly?"

"A Naming Ceremony provides you with your spirit name, which we believe is your true name, as opposed to your legal name," Grandma said. "Your spirit name tells you about your personality and your path in life. It is very sacred and is rarely spoken outside the family."

"Why?" I asked curiously.

"So that it can never be used against you," Grandpa said. "No matter what happens, you will always retain a part of your identity."

I liked the sound of that. "How do you get a spirit name? I mean, how does the Naming Ceremony work?"

"A Naming Ceremony involves offerings and prayers," Grandma answered. "The ancestors will tell you what your name is."

"Do I need to ask the Elders, then?" I asked. "Since they're the only ones who can contact the ancestors?"

Grandpa shook his head. "A Naming Ceremony is different than traditional contacting ceremonies. We don't speak directly to our ancestors. Usually, it's performed by a parent, grandparent, or other elder family member, who guides the subject in the prayer process."

I felt restless in my seat. "That means you two can perform the ceremony for me, right?"

Grandma beamed. "Yes."

I started to stand with Esis in my arms. "Let's go! I want to do it right now."

Grandpa chuckled. "Not so fast, Sophia. We will need time to prepare the sweat lodge. Plus, you will need to prepare yourself before the ceremony begins."

I sat back down. I was eager to start this now. "How much time will we need?"

Grandma looked to Grandpa, then back to me. She seemed to sense my eagerness. "We can do it next Saturday."

I clapped my hands together. "That's perfect. What do I need to do to prepare?"

Grandma and Grandpa guided me through everything I'd have to do over the next week; how I'd have to fast for twenty-four hours before the ceremony, and how I had to prepare a gift to offer to the ancestors. By the end of the night, I couldn't wait for Saturday to arrive.

Maybe then everything would get better.

THE WEEK PASSED at a crawl as I eagerly awaited my Naming Ceremony on Saturday. I'd hardly been able to concentrate on homework all week, as I was focused so much on getting this done and over with.

Jonah, Imogen, and Vanessa climbed the mountain trail beside me early that morning. My grandparents had said I could invite whoever I wanted, and these were the people I'd decided I wanted to share this with. I'd tried to get word to Amelia, but I wasn't sure my letter had reached her in time.

"I'm so excited for you!" Imogen said as we climbed higher.

Sassy and Esis ran ahead on the trail, playfully nipping at one another. Squeaks and Aisha held up the rear.

"What was it like for you guys?" I asked, pulling Liam's leather jacket tighter around me. No one had asked why I was wearing it, which I was glad for. I didn't want to explain.

"It's different for everyone," Vanessa said. "Mine only took an hour. Bren's took all night and into the next day."

"Yikes," I said, biting my lower lip. I didn't want to be held up in a sweat lodge that long.

"You have nothing to worry about," Imogen told me. "It's a really spiritual, amazing experience."

"Yeah," Jonah said, clapping me on the back. "You've got this."

"How do you know when it's done?" I asked.

"There's no doubt about it," Vanessa said. "You'll hear your name from the ancestors."

"*I* hear it?" I asked. "My grandparents don't give it to me?"

"No," Imogen said. "They're just there to guide you, but you must find the name on your own."

We reached a clearing in the trees. I caught sight of the sweat lodge first. It sat at the base of a high cliff, with trees all around. It was a small hut about four-feet high and ten wide feet at its base, and was covered in all different colors of blankets. Grandpa stood just feet away from it beside a burning fire. He wore traditional Hawkei regalia, a robe that was stitched with all colors of the rainbow. The fire had been reduced down to nothing but coals. Large flat rocks lay in the middle and were just as red as the coals.

"This is it!" I cried, bouncing on the balls of my feet.

Two women emerged from the trees with their Familiars at their sides— a parrot and a small feline. They carried pails of water, which I assumed they'd gotten from a nearby stream. Grandma wore a similar dress to my grandfather, but it was stitched with endless beads.

The other woman was Amelia. She was in her normal jeans and tee. She was here!

"Amelia!" I shrieked, racing over to them. "You made it!"

I threw my arms around her neck. She chuckled, but her hands were full, so she couldn't hug me back. "I wouldn't miss this for the world."

"Here. Let me take those." Jonah came up beside us and took the pails out of Amelia's hands.

She drew me into a hug, burying her face into my hair and inhaling my scent. "I missed you!"

"I missed you, too." I squeezed her tighter, until she couldn't breathe. Her Familiar Kiwi squawked at me, and I let her go.

"How do you feel?" she asked.

"Good," I told her. "I'm ready for this."

"That's great." Amelia walked over to the fire where everyone else had gathered, and I followed.

"Amelia, why don't you help Sophia get dressed?" my grandma suggested. "We should be ready as soon as you return."

"Yes ma'am." Amelia bent and grabbed a backpack lying next to the fire, then gestured for me to follow her.

I glanced back at my friends as Amelia and I ventured into the trees. They'd already settled in cross-legged around the fire and eyed the flames curiously as my grandfather made the smoke dance. I left Esis behind with them, since he seemed intrigued at the display.

Amelia stopped once we were out of sight of the clearing. I could hear a small stream trickling through the mountain not far from us. She swung the bag off her shoulder and set it on the ground. Kiwi squawked again from her other shoulder.

"I have a present for you," she said as she reached into the bag.

"Really?" I asked in shock. "You didn't have to—"

Amelia pulled a large piece of fabric from the bag and held it up. It was a dress made of yellow, blue, and red threads that zig-zagged in a mesmerizing pattern. Small beads were stitched into the design.

"This was Mom's dress," she said. "I wore it to my Naming Ceremony, and I think you should wear it, too."

Tears sprang to my eyes. "Am... this is..."

She shoved it in my direction. "It's perfect. Take it."

"Thank you." I began to strip down in the middle of the forest. I wasn't embarrassed in front of her.

Amelia's eyes locked on the totem around my neck, and she frowned. The way she looked at it made me suddenly feel self-conscious... like it was giving her bad vibes or something.

"You'll need to take everything off," she told me when I started to pull the dress on over my underwear. "Everything but the dress."

The dress was lightweight, and I felt beautiful in it. I pulled my bra and panties off beneath it, then placed my clothes in the open bag she offered— all except Liam's jacket. I draped that across my arms to bring with me. I kept the totem on, but she didn't say anything about it.

Amelia looked me up and down. "Sophia, you look amazing."

I twirled around, giggling. "You think?"

"Just one more thing." She pulled a hairbrush and hair tie from her bag, then approached me and started brushing out my hair. She twisted it into a braid, then secured it with the hair tie.

I ran my fingers gently down the braid. "Thank you."

She smiled. "Anytime."

Amelia's features softened as she looked me over one last time. It was the same way people always looked at the bride in movies. "I can't go with you, but I'll be waiting outside the whole time. This is a big step, Sophia. Are you ready for it?"

I nodded. "How can I not be?"

She straightened the dress on my shoulders. "You've fasted for twenty-four hours?"

I nodded.

"You have your offering?" She glanced down to the jacket in my arms.

I nodded. My grandparents had explained that your offering must represent something important to you, something you were willing to give to the ancestors in exchange for your name. I'd wracked my brain all week trying to come up with something I could offer them— something that was important to me. I'd thought of one of the shiny rocks sitting on my window ledge that Esis had given me, but that didn't seem significant enough.

Then I thought of the jacket, and the answer was obvious. This jacket represented everything I'd been holding on to. It was the moment in the utility closet with Liam— and every moment after that. It was the kisses, the warm hugs, and the love I'd given to Liam. It was everything that was and everything that had been.

If I was going to truly get over him and move on with my life, I had to let all of that go— as much as it killed me to do so.

I had to let *him* go.

Amelia took my hand. "Let's go."

When we returned to the clearing, Grandma had joined Grandpa in manipulating the fire. They were laughing with each other, while my friends watched in amazement. They all quieted as we approached.

"It is time," Amelia said.

Grandpa nodded, then pulled a large pitchfork out of the ground beside the fire. "Then we shall begin."

Amelia went to sit beside my friends on the ground, and Esis hurried over to jump into my arms. My grandfather's ram stood beside him, and my grandmother's cat sat in her arms.

"A Naming Ceremony is an ancient tradition in the Hawkei culture," Grandpa started. "It dates as far back as anyone can remember. The lodge represents the womb of the earth. You must prepare for a new beginning when you step into the lodge. When the ceremony is complete, you will step out into a new life, with a new name."

I bounced on the balls of my feet. I was ready to find out what my spirit name was.

"The door of the sweat lodge faces east toward the rising sun, signifying the start of a new dawn." Grandpa turned to me. "Sophia Henley, are you prepared to start anew?"

I held my head up proudly. "I am."

"Then it's time to pray," Grandpa said.

He picked up stones with his pitchfork and began moving them into the lodge. When seven stones were placed inside a pit inside, he instructed my grandmother and me to bring in the water.

"Good luck, Sophia!" Amelia called.

I smiled back to her, then ducked inside the lodge behind my grandparents and their Familiars. It was pitch-black inside, with no lighting except that of the red-hot stones in the center of the lodge and the flaming horns of Grandpa's ram. I could already feel the heat coming off the stones in waves. I sat cross-legged on the ground with Esis beside me.

Grandpa started chanting something in Hawkei, while the sound of voices singing softly outside met my ears. It sounded like the song was in the original language, too. I found the tune and the sound of my friends' voices comforting.

"Your offering," Grandma said from beside me.

I held out the leather jacket, and she found it through the darkness. She placed it beside the burning stones. Grandpa sprinkled sage over the stones, then poured a pail of water over them. Steam immediately rose around us. Even for a Koigni, the heat was almost unbearable. But it was pleasant, too. I could already feel the tension in my shoulders melting away.

"Now what?" I whispered.

Grandpa joined in on the song from outside while Grandma spoke from beside me. "Your name must come from within you, Sophia."

"How will I know?" I asked.

"The ancestors have many ways of communicating," she said vaguely. "All we can do is guide you. Take a deep breath, and feel all the tension melting out of your body."

She took a long, audible breath to demonstrate. I followed her guidance. Damp air and the smell of sage filled my nasal passages.

"Focus on the elements around you," Grandma instructed. "Feel the earth beneath your legs, the air on your skin, the fire in the stones, and the water in your body."

I closed my eyes and tried to block out all my thoughts as I focused only on the elements and the harmonious sounds of singing around me.

"When you are ready, you must pray to the ancestors," Grandma said.

I opened my mouth. She must've heard me inhale a breath.

"Not yet," she said quickly. "And not out loud. This is your journey, Sophia. We need not know where you have been or where you're going. That is between you and the ancestors."

Fifteen minutes passed, and I continued to sweat more and more with each passing moment. I thought that I was ready to pray, but when I tried to speak to the ancestors, it felt unauthentic and forced. My mind began to wander.

Is it supposed to feel this hot?

What if I get dehydrated?

What are my friends doing out there?

Maybe I made a mistake with the jacket.

Liam should be here.

I forced myself to push all that out of my mind, then returned to focusing on my breath and the elements around me. Over and over again, I went through this process, until I couldn't count how many times I'd repeated the routine. There was no telling how much time had passed, since it was so dark we couldn't see the sun, but it felt like hours.

Grandma kept assuring me to take my time, but I felt like I was wasting theirs. Weren't they sick of this by now? Weren't they getting frustrated with me for taking so long? What if they gave up on me?

Finally, I just decided to go for it. *Ancestors?* I called in my mind. *Ancestors, I am here. I'm ready to receive my name. Please, help guide me and tell me where I need to go.*

Nothing happened. Were they even listening?

Tell me what I need to do, I begged.

I rephrased myself over and over again, but still the ancestors didn't answer. It was almost as if they couldn't hear me, like I'd been abandoned... or I didn't belong.

Shut up, Sophia, I chastised myself. *You belong here. You can do this.*

Hours continued to tick by, and soon, my thoughts turned to my empty stomach. What was taking the ancestors so long? I was hungry. I was tired. Couldn't they just get this over with and let me eat something already? At this point, I was going to starve to death. Is that what they wanted?

I gritted my teeth. *Tell me what I need to know!*

Nothing.

Please!

I kept trying to remind myself what Vanessa had said, how Bren's Naming Ceremony took him all night. I just had to be patient, but my patience was wearing thin.

"Why isn't it working?" I asked. The singing outside had died down. Had my friends abandoned me because they'd gotten sick of waiting out there?

"It takes time," my grandma said gently. "You must connect with the ancestors— *truly* connect with them."

"I'm trying," I said through gritted teeth.

I expected Grandma to tell me try try harder, but instead, all she said was, "I know."

Silence settled over the lodge once again, and I continued to push myself to clear my mind and listen to the ancestors. But the more I tried, the more frustrated I became.

What if there's something wrong with me? What if I rushed this and I'm not ready? Will I ever be ready? Maybe it already happened and I just didn't realize it. I should just take the first name that comes to mind. Surely that's how this works. The ancestors send you a name and you just feel it, right?

My teeth gritted tighter and tighter as I willed a name to come to me, but all I got was *White Buffalo*, and I could easily say without a doubt that wasn't my name. I was making shit up at this point. My head was starting to hurt.

"Sophia," my grandfather said softly. "I can sense that you're struggling. We are here to guide you— with whatever you may need."

"Then why isn't this working?" I asked.

It must be their fault. I did everything I was asked to do. They messed up somehow.

"Sophia, what is it that's holding you back?" Grandma asked.

"I..." I wanted to scream. None of it made any sense! I should have my name by now! Why wasn't this working?

It'd been hot in here for hours, but suddenly, it felt as if I was standing in the middle of an inferno. I couldn't breathe anymore, and I thought I might pass out if I spent one more second in here.

So I bolted.

I ripped back the flap of the sweat lodge and scurried to my feet. The air felt like ice on my wet skin. My friends still sat outside, but I ignored them as I let my feet take me into the forest. It was dark now, the last bits of sunlight leaving shadows over the ground. I could hear Esis' worried cries from behind me, but I didn't care. I pushed further and further into the forest until the sweat lodge was far in the distance.

"I'm done!" I cried to the ancestors. "I can't do this! Why are you making this so hard on me?"

I reached the stream I'd heard earlier and fell to my knees in the dirt at its bank. Tears streamed down my face and into the water. My shoulder shook as I buried my face in my hands.

I was briefly aware of Esis crawling onto my back to offer comfort, but it wasn't until I heard my grandparents' footsteps that I lifted my head. I dashed the tears away and looked up to meet their eyes.

"Go away!" I cried.

They both stopped in their tracks. They shared a fallen glance, then started in the other direction. I knew they'd never leave me. They were testing me.

"No... wait!" I quickly stopped them.

Grandma slowly approached, then lowered herself to the bank beside me. She took my face in her hands and guided my eyes toward hers. "You are angry, Sophia. I understand that."

"I'm not angry," I grumbled, tearing my face from her hands. I slapped the water in front of me. "I'm... I'm..."

Grandpa knelt on my other side. "It's okay, Sophia. You can tell us."

"All right," I caved. "I'm angry. I'm frustrated. I don't know why this isn't working."

I lifted my gaze to look at him, but I didn't dash the tears away this time. I let them freely fall down my face. "I don't know why the ancestors don't want to help me."

Grandma took a deep breath. "The ancestors cannot help you if you are not willing to help yourself."

"I *am*," I growled in frustration.

"Sophia, why do you think you're angry?" my grandfather asked.

I pulled Esis off my shoulder and snuggled him to my chest. He gasped for breath as I squeezed him tightly. I loosened my hold on him, but my tears continued to soak into his fur. "I don't know, Grandpa. All I know is that I don't want to feel this way anymore. How do I do that?"

Grandpa sighed. "Anger is a choice, Sophia."

"It doesn't feel like it." I sobbed.

Grandpa placed a comforting hand on my shoulder. "People choose anger because it's easier to be angry at a situation than to solve it. If you don't feel like you're ready, Sophia, we can do this another time. It's up to you. Whatever you choose, we will be there for you."

Nobody spoke for a long time as I contemplated what my grandpa said. Had I been choosing anger as a way to avoid solving problems? I never used to be this angry. Had I somehow lost touch with my own emotions since I came to Orenda Academy?

I thought back to the times when anger had screwed me over. It almost always resulted in me threatening someone with a fireball, and that never ended well. It was the reason Haley and I couldn't get past that assignment in class. It'd caused my fight with Imogen last semester and had sent me spiraling into a depression after Liam and I had broken up. Was it really that easy to just shut it off and everything would be okay?

No, I realized quickly. Letting go of my anger wouldn't solve everything, but it'd sure make it all a lot easier.

My anger had been a problem for me for a long time. It was ruining my life, and I was sick of it. I was *done* with it.

A sense of peace washed over me unlike anything I'd ever felt before. It was akin to bonding with Esis, but different too. My whole body relaxed, and my mind cleared. It was so profound, like a blessing from the ancestors.

Suddenly, the world was spinning around me. I felt my body tip to the side, then darkness enveloped me.

❧

I STOOD *at the peak of a mountain overlooking the ocean. Esis stood at my feet, looking over the landscape with me. The air was warm, but I wore a jacket around my shoulders. The dark sky was spotted with stars, and a single torch stood burning in front of me. I felt drawn to it and stepped forward. My fingers reached out and touched the flame. It flickered beneath my touch, but it didn't hurt me. It was warm and welcoming.*

"Sophia." My name sounded like a breeze in the wind, but it felt as if it was coming from someone I'd always known. I didn't know the voice, but it was like I'd been listening to it my whole life.

I turned to find four figures staring at me. Their faces were familiar. I'd met them twice before— the Hawkei warrior, the red-headed woman in the corset ball gown, the man in the cowboy hat, and the woman with beautiful black hair, dressed in traditional Hawkei clothing. My ancestors.

They bowed to me, and I bowed back. I didn't question how Esis and I got here. All I knew was I was right where I was meant to be.

"Hello," I said aloud.

They didn't respond with words, but I could feel their emotions in the air. It was peaceful, warm, and comforting. They didn't have to say anything. I already understood. No matter where I went, they would be there to shelter my burdens and support me in whatever path I decided to take.

"What path is that?" I asked them.

They each pointed in different directions. I suddenly understood. It was not something they could choose for me. I had to decide for myself.

"I know what I have to do now," I said, stepping toward them.

Esis followed and gazed up at me with proud eyes.

I shrugged Liam's leather jacket off my shoulders and knelt at my ancestor's knees. I offered the jacket to the woman with the red hair, and she took it with a proud smile.

"I let go of my anger," I said. "I choose to put my own desires aside and serve the tribe. I give my life to the Hawkei."

I'd known it for months, but there was something profound about declaring my intentions to my ancestors.

Everything was clear to me now. Liam would be okay. The ancestors watched over him last time, and I trusted them with every fiber of my being to ensure nothing bad would happen to him again. And if we never got back together, that was okay too. We'd be okay on our own. Our ancestors would make sure of that.

"I'm okay," I whispered.

For the first time in a long time, it wasn't just wishful thinking. I felt it deep within my soul.

The woman in the ballgown reached out and placed a hand on my chin, guiding me gaze up to hers. My ancestors' mouths didn't move, but I heard their collective voices in the wind, each one layering over top of another.

"Go forth and burn bright, Kyra Koignichi."

MY EYES SPRANG open to a dark canopy above me. My body lay upon cold, damp earth, and my head rested in someone's lap. I could hear the stream trickling down the mountain beside me. Various faces stared down at me, but it took me a moment to make sense of them. A fire burned in Vanessa's palm, casting shadows across each person's face. Everyone was here— my sister, my grandparents, and my friends.

"Sophia?" Amelia's voice sounded desperate. She was so close to me, and I realized it was her lap I rested in.

I pushed myself to a sitting position, and Esis hopped into my lap. I hugged him close.

Imogen knelt beside me, and Sassy nudged my hand with her nose. "Are you okay?"

I nodded as a comforting warmth spread throughout my chest. "Better than okay. I spoke to my ancestors."

My grandma inhaled an audible breath. "It worked? Did you get your name?"

I couldn't help but grin. "Yes. It's—"

Grandpa held up a hand. "You don't have to tell us. Not unless you want to."

I looked between each of their faces. They were so soft, and they felt like home. "I want to tell you. It's *Kyra Koignichi*."

Imogen gasped. "Sophia, it's beautiful."

"More than beautiful. It's..." Jonah reached out and helped me to my feet. "I don't have the word."

"Exquisite," Amelia offered.

I was still a little unsteady, seeing as I hadn't eaten in days, so I leaned up against Squeaks for support. Amelia stayed close, as if watching for signs that I might pass out again.

"I love it," Vanessa said.

"What does it mean?" I asked, looking between my grandparents.

Grandma stepped forward and brushed a strand of hair behind my ear that had fallen out of my braid. "*Kyra Koignichi*. Blazing Firespirit."

I beamed. I couldn't help it. Amelia pulled me into a hug, and suddenly, everyone's arms were wrapped around me. I felt cocooned in a safe embrace by the people I loved most.

Grandpa hugged me the tightest. "It fits you perfectly, Sophia."

"You're right," I said as they all drew away. Esis was the only one to stay close to me. He clung to my middle in a sweet embrace. "It doesn't just sound like me. It *feels* like me."

Liam

THIRTEEN

The days blurred together. A week passed without me even realizing it. It had been Sunday, then all of a sudden, almost two weeks had gone by.

I'd spent the majority of time in bed. I drifted between sleep and staring at the walls. Time didn't even exist. The only way I experienced it passing at all was when Mom came in to bring me meals and I occasionally heard Dad peek through the door to check on me.

We still hadn't spoken. But something was definitely different between us. The animosity was gone. I think he knew I'd finally been pushed over the edge.

There was a weight on the bed by my legs come Friday morning. Maddie was sitting there, watching me.

"Hey, big brother." She gave me a soft smile. Eirakari sat by the edge of the bed and hummed.

I sat up. I hadn't seen her since I'd left school. "Hey. What's going on?"

She shrugged. "Not much. Just thought I'd be in to check up on you, since Ez... you know."

Ezra wasn't speaking to me at the moment. I wasn't sure if it was because he was mad, or if he just couldn't handle it. I didn't blame him. I'd put him, and the rest of my family, though a lot.

I sighed. "Well thanks, Mads, but I'm fine."

"No you're not. You can't just sit in this bed every day and wait to die," she insisted. "I came here to tell you that I've been where you're at right now, and trust me, it only gets lower from there, unless you do something about it. You've gotta get up and start living your life. Dwelling on everything won't make the problems go away."

"I don't... know if I'm strong enough," I confessed.

"You are," Maddie insisted. "Liam, my visions of you are incredible. You're going to be doing some *awesome* things. But those things are never going to get done if you don't keep moving forward, or if you kill yourself before any of those things can happen."

"Suppose you can't tell me what those things are?" I asked, and I put my hand in my head.

She shook her head. "Sorry, no. *Naderei* secrets. You'll never go through with all of it if I tell you now. And even though I don't know *everything* that happens, or how it all connects, I can tell you that you're going to have an amazing life. The Great Spirit has a plan. You just have to get there."

I stared at her. "You know what happens between Sophia and I for good, don't you?"

She gave another quick nod. "Yes. But don't go trying to get answers out of me. It'll ruin the lessons and the journey."

"You're wise for your age," I remarked.

"It comes with the territory of being a seer," she told me. "But like I said. You can't sit around continuing to let life get to you. At some point, you've got to make a decision to move forward no matter the consequences, before it destroys you."

She dropped her head. "I should know."

She did. Last year I'd walked in on Maddie hurting herself due to her visions. She'd been doing it for a long time, and nobody knew. She'd begged me to keep it a secret. I hadn't told anyone, but I'd helped her learn how to handle her stress in a better way— though I was still worried being at Orenda would trigger her again, and I really wasn't giving her a great example to live by now.

"You helped me move on. Now it's my turn to help you," she said cheerfully. "Everything's going to turn around for you, starting today. Promise."

I scratched my head. "If you say so."

"I've gotta go. Drew and I are going to a cosplay contest." She popped up from the bed and gave a huge smile. "We're wearing matching *Lord of the Rings* costumes. He's Aragorn, and I'm Arwen."

"Cute." I waved goodbye, and Maddie skipped away with Eirakari at her heels. For the first time in days, I got up, took a shower, and got dressed. She was right. I'd sulked around long enough. Time to start living.

By this time, it was around lunch. Mom was making fish sandwiches and some sort of rice pilaf. She seemed surprised to see me come downstairs, and a huge smile lit up her face.

"Glad to see you up and around, honey." She gave me a kiss on the cheek before she went back to cooking, balancing my baby brother on her hip.

Mom had been like an iron rock throughout this whole process. If what had happened had upset her or made her cry, I'd never seen it. She'd just been there for me for whatever I needed.

Mom put food in front of me, and I made sure to eat it. It'd been made clear to me that not eating was no longer an option.

It was Friday. My classes were over with for the week, but for the first time, I thought about how far behind I'd be. "Mom, can I go back to school and get my assignments?"

Mom hesitated. "I think we agreed that you aren't going back to school until next Monday. If your father and I feel that's safe for you to do."

"Okay," I said. No way was I going to argue. I got up and put my empty plate in the sink. I then turned around and put my hands against it, leaning backward.

"You've got something on your mind," Mom commented. "I can see it written on your face."

I thought for a minute before answering. "I love her, Mom," I said. "I love her, and I don't know what to do."

Mom adjusted Jackson on her hip and said, "Love sometimes isn't enough, honey."

"I know," I said. "But it has to be this time."

"Oh, Liam." Mom took a hand and parted back the hair from my face. "If the Great Spirit wills it in his plan for you and Sophia to be together, not even the Elders will be able to keep you apart. But love isn't based on need. It has to be freely given."

I bit the inside of my cheek. "Can we go to the gravesite today?"

Mom put the rest of the dishes inside the sink. "Just give me a few moments to gather some things."

A half an hour later, we came to the burial grounds. Mom was a good distance away at my grandfather's grave, putting flowers on it and showing Jackson the marking stone, but not so far away I was out of her eyesight.

I sat cross-legged in front of Nashoma's grave and stared at the burial mound. "Bud, you gotta help me," I told him. "I have no freaking idea how to go on from here."

There was no answer except the whistling of the wind and the autumn leaves falling from the trees. I closed my eyes and started meditating. I was waiting for an answer— some sort of sign, or maybe a sentence that would give direction.

I didn't intend to fall into a trance. The burial mounds fell away, and the wind died down as I entered into a new world.

❧

Autumn had changed to summer. I was standing in the same green section of forest I had been over two years ago when I first bonded with Nashoma.

He sat in front of me, all intimidation and muscle. There was a slight breeze that ruffled his black fur. He was larger than I remembered— nearly the size of a small horse now. He didn't move an inch... didn't even blink as we locked gazes.

Seeing him knocked the wind out of me. I staggered backward— he continued to sit calmly and observe with cool amber eyes.

Hello, Liam, *he said.* It's been a long time.

His voice was deep and commanding. He sounded older than me, even though we were the same age.

"How is this possible?" I breathed.

The ancestors have permitted, in some circumstances, Elementai who are very near to death to speak with those who have passed beyond to the Ancestral Lands, *Nashoma said.* And Liam, you are dangerously close to the edge.

He and I stared at each other for a long moment before I spoke again. "You got bigger."

Yes. As you continue to grow on earth, I grow beside you in the afterlife, *Nashoma said.*

I wanted to touch him. I wanted to reach out and run my hands through his thick fur, but something in his stare prevented me from doing that. "Why are we here?" I asked.

Nashoma raised a lip and growled. I am here to knock some sense into that thick skull of yours.

Shock went through me— then something I didn't expect... resentment. "Me?!" I burst. "I'm sorry, but since you've been gone, I've been doing the best I fucking can! Sorry if it's not good enough for you."

It's not, *Nashoma stated bluntly.* Your performance has been rather poor.

I let out a disgusted noise. "Fuck this." I went to walk away from him, but as I turned around, there he was, sitting in front of me again even though I was facing the opposite direction.

You cannot run from this, *Nashoma insisted.* You must turn and face it!

"I don't have to do anything! I can do whatever the hell I feel like!" I shouted at him.

You can, but you won't. You are tired of running, *Nashoma said.* And I am tired of watching you run like a scared little deer. I have had enough of your dismal attitude toward life and everyone in it.

"You don't get it. I don't want to live anymore! I want to be with you!" I exploded. I kicked at a rock on the ground— my foot went right through it. Screw the Ancestral Lands.

It does not matter what you want. I did not want to leave my pack. I did not want to leave my mate. Most of all, I did not want to leave you. It changed nothing. *Nashoma's voice was monotone and emotionless.* I am still here, and you are there. So there we are.

I shook my head. "You know, most Familiars would be more comforting. They wouldn't have a bitch-fest after their Elementai tried to off themselves."

Do not expect me to coddle you. I know how you work, *Nashoma said coldly.* You are sorely mistaken if you think your life is about yourself. You are alive in service to others, nothing more.

"*But how is this fair to me? How am I the only Elementai that can stay alive without a Familiar? How am I the only person that's cursed with a fucking disease that no one can understand and that's killing me from the inside out?!*" *I was screaming at him so loud now it made my voice feel raw. Everything hurt, and I was tired of hurting. Why couldn't I just be done?*

Because the ancestors knew you were strong enough to take it, above all others, though you are currently proving them wrong, *he growled.* Your existence, my existence, is about sacrifice. We are apart from each other because you still have a job to do. There is a purpose beyond any you're seeing, and if you cannot understand, then so be it, but that does not give you the right to end your own life!

I crossed my arms and turned away, but not so much that I couldn't see him. "Don't you think I've been through enough?"

Did you ever consider that I have had a difficult time myself continuing in the Ancestral Lands without you? *Nashoma spat at me, and I heard a bit of bitterness in his voice as he curled his tail around his paws and looked away from me.* No. You have not.

"*How would I know? I've needed you so many times, and you weren't there!*"

It was I who was on that bridge, *Nashoma thundered.* It was I who heard your every thought as you were about to take that jump. It was I who sent Sophia to save you, before you made a decision you'd utterly regret!

He shook his head. And I was near you, powerless as I did everything I could to get you to hear me, to see me, my spirit in a panic because I knew that if someone did not intervene, your life on earth would come to an end. I gave myself up for you. And you are throwing that gift back in my face.

The guilt that pummeled me in the stomach nearly made me sick. "You heard what they said about me. The whole tribe feels that way, I bet. People don't think I have the right to live."

A wolf does not concern himself with the opinions of prey, and Liam, those people were prey, *Nashoma said.* They are frightened of you. They know you are a hunter.

"I know they were jealous, and yeah, they're probably worried I'll earn the tribe's favor and gain a higher position," I said. *"That doesn't mean what they said didn't hurt. Didn't matter that they were strangers. What they said got to me. I hardly know who I am anymore."*

Then perhaps you need to take some time out for yourself and reevaluate. An alpha is no good to the pack if he cannot lead, *he said.*

I made a scoffing noise. "Gonna keep throwing wolf metaphors at me? Got one about a rabbit next?"

Wolf metaphors are good metaphors. Wait, no, that isn't the point, *he said in frustration. He stomped his paw.*

"I'm tired of being trapped in a body that feels like a prison!" I shouted at him. *"Why isn't that enough?"*

Liam, I am sorry you are sick. *Nashoma's voice broke, and for the first time, he seemed to be getting emotional. He dropped his head.* And I am sorry I am not there to help you. But life goes on. And your story is more important than your suffering.

I threw my arms skyward. "I knew this wasn't going to be easy. I understood that from the first day I was told something was wrong with me. But I didn't know it was going to be this fucking hard. Excuse me if I want just a little reprieve from it all."

Your grandfather has been helping as best he can, but damn you if you see the signs, negative fool you are, *Nashoma spat.* You are acting like a child. Ancestors forbid if you ever looked on the bright side of things.

I grabbed my hair. I was about ready to pull it out. "Bright side? How the hell do you expect me to do that? The one person who meant everything to me isn't in my life anymore. Yes, I know it's my own fault, don't give me that look," I told him as Nashoma sent a scathing gaze *my way.*

An alpha proves himself to his she-wolf, and trust me when I say that you haven't done anything to inspire her to return to you. *If wolves could eye-roll, Nashoma would be giving me one right now.* Your attempts at wooing her back have been dismal, and at worst, embarrassing.

"Oh, sure, keep it up with the sarcasm," I told him. *"Not like it hurts or anything."*

I don't care if it hurts. You need to hear the truth.

"She doesn't want me back! She's tried to move on with someone else!" I burst.

Because your stubbornness pushes her away! Nashoma shouted. Great Spirit forgive you, Liam, but you are a selfish ass. For all the work I did sending her to you, you certainly are doing everything in your power to keep fucking it up!

"I know I fucked up. I get it," I said. *"But I don't know how to fix it anymore. I never had the power to in the first place."*

Quit acting like a victim for everything in your life. *His teeth began to show beneath snarling lips. It doesn't suit you.*

"Yeah? What are you gonna do about it?" I asked, throwing my arms wide.

Nashoma snarled. He crouched down and pounced, sailing toward me through the air. I expected him to back off mid-leap, but he didn't. He slammed into my body and forced me to the ground. His weight was like getting hit by a car. His massive paws pinned me to the forest floor as his teeth lunged for my jugular. I reacted out of instinct and dove out of the way, and his snout smashed into the grass.

Holy shit. I wasn't expecting that. "Nashoma!"

Are you an alpha, or a coward? Are you a wolf, or are you prey? Nashoma shouted. He went to go for my neck again. I grabbed his scruff and hurtled him off, staggering to my feet. He didn't stop his assault— he leapt again on top of me and pinned me down. We wrestled with each other. I did my best to hold him off, but he was strong, and freaking huge. We tumbled over and over on the grass as Nashoma barely missed drawing blood from me each time.

He wasn't going to stop. The rock I'd tried to kick earlier was lying nearby. I reached out to grab it, and this time, my hand connected. I used it to smash the rock against the side of Nashoma's muzzle. He yelped and jumped off of me— however, he had a thrill in his eyes as he saw the rock in my hand.

That's what I like to see! Fight back! Fight for your mate! Nashoma jumped again, but I knew what to do this time. I dropped the rock and spun out of the way as he made his attack. Then I grabbed the fur on the back of his pelt and tackled him into the dirt, holding him down.

Nashoma panted beneath me, and I struggled to catch my breath. So you struggle with me, you struggle with life, *he said. I let him up. He didn't appear hurt at all by the fight. Neither was there a scratch on me.*

I brushed my hair out of my eyes. "Was that really necessary?"

You wouldn't have learned any other way, *he said.*

It was then that I got it. I got what he meant. I'd given up these past few months— hell, I'd probably given up the moment Nashoma had died. I'd fought less and less until I stopped fighting at all. Even during the Elemental Cup, I'd more or less struggled to survive out of instinct, not a true desire to live. Afterwards, I'd pushed everyone who cared about me away and basically waited to die.

But that wasn't who I was. I was a fighter. Nashoma knew there was no other way to make me realize it except to drive me to be the best I could be. When push came to shove and life started throwing punches, he didn't want me to curl up and surrender. He wanted me to push back.

Lately, I hadn't fought against my illness. I hadn't fought for my future. And I definitely hadn't fought for Sophia. I'd become a victim of circumstance instead of taking charge. There were things about my life that I couldn't change— but I had power over the things that I could. I needed to stop letting life happen to me and start making decisions that I could stand by. He was right. Being a victim was getting really fucking old. I wanted to take back some power over my life.

Nashoma knew that I suffered. He knew that I was in pain every day and that I'd been through a lot. But he didn't accept it as an excuse to give up. And maybe he experienced just as much pain being apart from me as I did him.

Maddie said that I was going to do amazing things. But I bet those amazing things weren't going to get done if I couldn't buck up and be strong enough to take the resistance that was sure to come as a result of me making a stand. A great life didn't come without sacrifice and a lot of struggle. And if this war was really coming, and the prophecy was about to come true... I had to be strong enough to protect the people I loved, no matter what I was personally going through.

He stared at me for a moment— I had the feeling our conversation was drawing to a close. We stood there for minutes, drinking each other in, trying to take in every last second we had together before the end.

Finally, I asked, "What must I do?"

You know what you need to do. You've known it all along, *Nashoma told me.* You must return to your mate and beg for forgiveness. Beg her to take you back.

"*And if she doesn't?*"

He stared at me. Then you need to move on. And let. Her. Go.

I lowered my gaze. Nashoma paused. Tell me... have you seen Vitella recently?

I nodded. "*She comes around the house sometimes. And I hear her singing to you outside my dorm, every night.*"

He nodded. It is a comfort, then. She does not have long. Her time is coming. Our children will soon take up the pack. I will have her by my side once more.

He narrowed his gaze. Though I do not intend for you to join me anytime soon. Go now to your mate. End this doubt between the two of you, and let her final answer be the arrow that guides you forward.

I could feel the trance ending. The summer colors that were around us were slowly draining to fall again. "*I'll miss you, Nashoma. And I love you.*"

I love you as well, brother. And Liam?

I lifted my gaze. He stared at me with those yellow eyes.

I do not want to speak with you again until you are at the border of the Ancestral Lands, which I hope will not come to pass for a very, very long time. *His gaze was cold and steely.* I have protected you from everything else in this life, but I cannot protect you from yourself. I only hope that you can believe the Great Spirit has a plan for you.

THE TRANCE CEASED TO BE. I reached out my fingers to brush Nashoma's fur as I found myself sitting by his burial mound again, the autumn breeze giving me a slight shiver.

Maddie kept repeating it. Mom kept repeating it. Nashoma had drilled it into my head. There was a plan. I just needed to trust that things were going to work out. And trust that somehow, I could be happy again.

I stood up. I knew what I had to do now. I approached Mom. She had a smile on her face as I joined her at Grandpa's grave.

"Something has happened inside of you," she commented. "It nearly glows."

I nodded. "I feel like I've changed."

Mom gave a light little laugh. "We all change through the seasons of life. Though perhaps your dark season is nearly over."

I liked that. We stared at Grandpa's marking stone for a while before Mom said, "I have to go into town and run some errands. Won't be back until later tonight. I've told your brother to take you back to the house this afternoon."

"That's fine." I wasn't allowed to be alone for a while, but I was fine with being passed off to Ezra. It'd give me an opportunity to reach out to Sophia.

Mom and I walked up to the school grounds together. Ezra was waiting by the main gate for us— he avoided my gaze, and Mom spoke with him in hushed tones as I kept a distance. His expression was stone-faced as Mom continued to whisper to him.

With luck— or maybe, as if the ancestors planned it— Sophia was sitting on a stone bench with Esis nearby, doing her homework. I kinda felt like shit— I hadn't had Esis' heal me in a long time, so I hurt all over, but I ignored it. What I was about to do was far more important.

She looked up when she heard my footsteps. A brief expression of surprise crossed her face before it settled into a slight smile. "Liam. How are you?"

"Doing a lot better," I began as I took a seat next to her. "Thanks to you."

She looked away for a second and slightly frowned. She picked Esis up off the bench next to her and said, "Here. You haven't been healed in a week. You need this."

Esis squeaked as Sophia placed him on my lap. His eyes were big and sparkling as he looked up at me. He missed me. Esis placed his paws on my abdomen, and instantly, all the pain melted away.

This time, it felt better than ever before. Sweeter, even. More fulfilling.

Sophia seemed to shine as she watched Esis do his work. It was incredible watching her. It got to me that she might be something I'd have to set free.

"There's something different about you," I said. "You seem... happier."

"I am. I got my spirit name." She beamed. "My grandparents held the ceremony for me last weekend."

"Really? That's amazing." Awe overtook me, before a bit of regret settled on my shoulders. "I'm sorry I couldn't be there for you."

"It's okay. You needed time for yourself," she said. "I don't know. It just changed me. It showed me who I really was."

I nodded. "You don't come out of that sweat lodge the same as you went in."

She seemed hopeful. "It's been weird without you around the castle. Are you moving back into the dorms next week?"

I shook my head. "I'm supposed to come back next Monday, but I'm not staying in the dorms. Mom still wants me at home for another week while I get re-adjusted to classes."

Sophia nodded. "That sounds like a good idea."

There was the sound of birdsong for a minute before Sophia said, "Liam... we need to talk about stuff."

We were on the same page. "Yeah. There's some things we need to settle." I stood up. "Can you come to my house later? We can talk then."

"Sure. I'll take a peryton there." She gave me a weak grin. "See you around."

I nodded. My stomach was twisted up in knots as I walked away. How was tonight gonna go? I had hours before she'd arrive so we could talk. What if she said no? What if she rejected me?

At least it'd be over and I'd finally have an answer to what was between us.

Mom had already taken off to do errands. Ezra held his arms tightly over his body as he watched me approach.

"Come on." His tone was blunt. "Let's go."

I knew he was missing stuff at school to be home with me. I felt bad for taking that away from him. We took the main road to the beach and walked there mainly in silence.

Having Sophia and I be up in the air was one thing, but this tension between Ezra and I was another. It was unbearable. I needed my brother by my side, whatever happened moving forward.

When we got back to the house, Ezra went to lock himself in his room. "Ez, wait," I said, and he stopped. He paused with his hand still on the doorknob.

I took a deep breath. "I'm sorry," I started. "I didn't mean to hurt you."

He scoffed. "Yeah, well, you fucking did."

"I didn't mean to hurt anyone," I pleaded. "I just thought things would be better if I wasn't—"

"Bullshit, man." He turned around. "You have any idea how many people care about you? You know what their lives would've been like if you'd taken that jump? What *my* life would've been like?"

He punched the wall with the side of his fist. "I couldn't get over you killing yourself. Neither could Mom or Dad, or the rest of us, or Jonah, or Imogen, or Sophia for that matter. It would destroy a piece of me that would never be the same again."

He shoved his hands in his pockets. "I know I'm gonna be chief. It's not what I want, but I'll put up with it. But I don't wanna do it unless my big brother is by my side."

His eyes got watery, and his lip trembled.

"Aw, Ez, come here." I gave him a tight hug. I hadn't hugged Ezra in a really long time— probably since we were kids— but he needed it right now. He was a wreck. His shoulders shook a couple of times before he hugged me back, then pulled away.

"Are you okay, bro?" Ezra asked. "Like, really? I've been worried about you."

I nodded. "I'm in a better place now. Really."

"I'm sorry I didn't notice," he belted out. "I should've seen the signs. I'm a shitty brother."

"It's not your fault," I said. "I kept everything pretty well hid."

He bounced nervously. "I just... I'm really concerned that..."

"Ez." I put a hand on his shoulder. "I'm not gonna try it again. Honestly."

He seemed to relax at that. "What are you gonna do now?" he asked. "I mean, you can't go on living like this."

"I don't plan to. First thing is I have to know where Sophia and I stand," I said. "Then whatever happens afterward is based on that."

"You mean... you want to ask her out again?" His eyes widened.

"Yeah. I'm going to ask her to get back together with me, tonight," I said. "And if she says no... fine. I'm moving on with my life."

Ezra stared at me. "Sure you can handle that?"

I shrugged. "It's gonna hurt like hell if she rejects me, sure. But at least I'll have a fresh start. I can't live anymore not knowing if we're going to be together or not."

Ezra said nothing for a moment, then punched my shoulder. "Come on. The waves look pretty rad today. Let's get our boards."

I knew he was just trying to pass the time and keep my mind off of things until Sophia showed up. But I agreed, because surfing sounded like the one thing that could get my head straight right now. We rode the waves for a few hours, then went inside.

Sophia showed up shortly after. She stood outside my front door, Esis in her arms and seeming... apprehensive, but determined, as if she already knew what she was going to say to me.

I was worried about the answer I was going to get. But I wouldn't back away from asking the question. Sophia walked into the kitchen, looking apprehensive.

"I'll be on the beach. Give you two some privacy," Ezra said. He walked out. Sophia and I were left standing there, staring at each other in silence.

Esis was making squealing noises. He wanted to get on the counter. Sophia put him down, and he immediately started rummaging through the cupboards, finding a bag of cookies and ripping into it. He shoved one after the other into his mouth.

"Esis, that's not ours," Sophia scolded.

"He can have it. What's mine is yours," I told Sophia. I scratched the back of my head. Esis' chewing was really loud and distracting. "You wanna talk upstairs?"

She blinked. "Sure."

We left Esis in the kitchen, and she followed me up to my room. When we were inside, I closed the door behind us.

Sophia looked around, observing the decor. The walls were painted blue, and I had a queen-sized bed covered with an orange and teal comforter. The walls were covered with landscape scenes of various parts of California, posters of bikes, and surfers. Baskets and blankets were piled up in a corner almost to the ceiling. A large window with a sliding glass door led to a balcony that displayed the ocean. I'd cleaned up the clothes that were thrown all over before she got here and put them in a hamper. I didn't want her to know I was messy.

"I like your room. It's neat," she said, twirling around.

I gave a light laugh. "It's hardly ever this clean. You need to see my dorm."

She gave a slight smile. I gestured to the bed. "You can sit down."

Sophia sat on the edge of the bed, crossing her ankles. I sat on the opposite side of her and turned so we were facing head-on. The only sound that could be heard were the waves coming through the open sliding door that led to the balcony. It was like neither one of us wanted to speak first.

I decided to take the plunge. "I want you back."

Sophia stared at me. Then she gave a long, drawn out sigh, brushing her curls back from her face. "Liam..."

Not the reaction I was hoping for. I took a few deep breaths and tried not to panic. "I messed up. I really, really, fucked up," I said. "I know this isn't great timing. And that doing this right now is shit. But I want us to be back together."

She bit her lip and looked down. "I don't know if that's the best idea."

My heart fell. Had I already waited too long? Had she already made up her mind? "What do you mean?"

"Things are different now," she began. "I'm not the same person you met back in Utah."

"And I'm not the same person, either. I've changed," I told her. "We both have."

"Liam, you know I'd take you back in a heartbeat... before. But things have changed. I've been preparing myself to let you go."

It felt like I was being suffocated. "Let me go?"

She stared at the carpet. "You know that you have to offer a sacrifice to the ancestors, to get your spirit name?"

"Yeah?" I said, not sure where this was going.

"My sacrifice was you," she said, and my breath was swept out of me. "All the anger I've balled up over the past few months, all the hurt, I had to let that go. I burned your jacket and gave my love for you over to the ancestors."

I was momentarily speechless. "So... you don't love me anymore?"

"Don't say it like that." She put her face in her hands and rubbed her eyes before wrenching her gaze back up to meet mine. "You don't understand. I don't want you to not know who you are without me. I don't want myself to not know who I am without you. That's why we can't do this."

"That's not what this is," I insisted.

"Why do you want me back, then?" she insisted. "I want something more profound than you telling me you can't live without me."

"You aren't gonna get that, then, because that's not true," I told her quietly.

A little bit of breath left her. "Really?"

I nodded. "I don't want you back because I can't live without you. I want you back because you make my life better."

She seemed confused. "But... but you tried to kill yourself because we broke up."

"Ancestors, no, Sophia. That wasn't what that was about," I told her. My tone was horrified. "What happened that night wasn't your fault. It had nothing to do with you."

"Really? Then what *was* it about?" She acted like she didn't believe me.

This was embarrassing. "I, uh... I overheard a couple of people from my Hawkei Leadership class talking about me," I confessed. "They basically said that I didn't deserve to live, because I was sick, and that it'd be better for the tribe if someone just killed me."

"Oh my God. Liam." She put a hand over her mouth. "Why didn't you tell me? Or Jonah, or someone?"

"I didn't want to talk to anyone about it. It just... it really bothered me," I said, my words coming out in a jumble. "Stuff's been piling up forever now, and I didn't deal with it until it got to be too much."

"But how could you believe them? Nothing they said was true, and you don't really know them," she said.

"It felt true, at the time." I looked out at the ocean. "I know they're strangers, but what they said still hurt. I couldn't deal with it."

I looked at her. "But I can now. I'm in a better place. And I can promise you that I won't do anything like that ever again. But I wouldn't be here to say that if you hadn't stopped me. You saved my life."

Sophia slowly said the next few words. "But I don't want to have to keep saving you. Seeing you almost take that jump... it gutted me. Is that what our relationship is going to be like going forward? Me worrying about you at every turn, wondering if something someone said is going to trigger you?"

"No," I said firmly. "I've come to a realization that I've got to do better. I get it, Sophia. I know I'm fucked up." Her eyes flashed to my face. "Don't try to deny it. It happened after Nashoma's death, and I haven't been right ever since. A part of me is always going to be ruined for life."

I took a breath to continue. "But that doesn't mean I can't be better for you. And I'll never put you through anything like that ever again."

Sophia ran her hands through her hair. "I don't know, Liam. I just don't..." She took another breath. "I've wanted you back for so long. But now I'm so confused. I don't know if this is right for me anymore. Or healthy."

"I don't want it to be unhealthy," I said. I reached out and tried to take her hand, but she pulled it away. It felt like ice froze over my heart as she did that.

Her eyes showed fear. She was scared of me. She thought I was going to break her heart all over again.

I decided to take a chance. "Was it better with Lindsey?"

Her expression was thoughtful. "I don't know. Lindsey and I had fun together. I liked her, but I didn't have the same connection with her that I did with you."

She gave me a sheepish look. "I should probably tell you that Lindsey and I did stuff. Like, below the belt, naked stuff."

"I figured as much. I'm not mad about it." And I wasn't. She was single and trying to find her way. I had no right to judge.

She played with the loose strands on the comforter. "Lindsey and I had a connection, but it was more like a crush. I wish I could've followed it more, but I couldn't, because my heart was still set on you."

"And... is it still that way?" I dared to ask.

She remained still as she looked at me. "I need to know for certain why you want to do this. You never wanted to get back together until now."

"Because I'm a coward," I said. "Or at least, I was. I let my pride and my hurt get in the way of loving you. But Soph, I don't want us to be together because I need you to survive. I want us to be together because I think we bring out the best in each other."

I straightened up. "You push me to be the best I can be. You don't take excuses or allow me to sit around and suffer. You don't see me as some burden on the tribe, or a sick person that needs to be taken care of... hell, even though you take better care of me than I do myself most days. You just see me for me."

She smiled at that.

I went on. "You give me hope. You make me see that there's still joy and goodness in living. You show me all the wonder this world has to offer when I thought all the light had gone out of it. You don't give up. You inspire me to keep going, to keep doing better. And even though I hurt you, you still have my back. That's saying something for all the shit we've been through together."

Sophia twirled shapes on the comforter with her finger. "I've had to find my way without you, you know," she said quietly. "You're what makes Orenda feel like home, because for the longest time, you were home for me. You made me feel protected and safe. You introduced me to this incredible world, and stuck by my side through all of it, even when your life was at stake during the tournament... even when you didn't want to go through with the temple on Ancestors' Day, you still went. You're willing to sacrifice yourself for the good of everyone around you, and you love *so hard*, Liam. You've got the biggest heart out of all of us in the group. I just hated how you never let me in."

I didn't like how she was speaking everything in past tense. "Go on."

"Life was... ancestors, it was just so easy with you. Everything we wanted together seemed to match up. I always knew you'd be a good husband, and a good father. I think it's what attracted me to you in the first place," she said. "I never cared that you were whiny or sarcastic. I knew you were just trying to hide your true self under a mask, and that never bothered me, because I always saw the true you. You made me feel free. I never felt happier than when I was clinging to your back when we were on that bike, or cliff diving into the ocean. You were someone I could trust to lead me and take care of me until the very end."

Her tone turned dark. "I just couldn't take the secrets, or the lies.

And the worst thing about it all was that no matter how much I loved you, you still left me."

"That was a bad decision," I said quietly. "One I wish I'd never made."

Her lip trembled. "Well, you did. And you can't take it back now. I'm not so sure if I want to be with you anymore."

Heartbreak. So this is what it felt like to have your feelings totally torn in half. I held myself together even though I was falling apart on the inside.

But I wasn't done fighting yet. Nashoma wanted me to fight for her. I wasn't giving in unless there was absolutely no chance.

We sat in silence for a moment. Sophia said, "What are you going to do now?"

I held back for a moment or two. "I don't know. It depends on if you take me back or not."

"And if not?" she asked softly.

"I'm not going to tell you what my plans are, because I don't want it to affect your decision," I told her.

"All I ask for is honesty. I need to know," she insisted.

I put a hand on the back of my head. "Honestly... if you say no, I'm not coming back to Orenda Academy."

"*What?*" Her expression became shocked. Hot tears came furiously out of her eyes. "Are you serious?"

"Don't cry. This is why I didn't want to tell you." I reached out and wiped away some of the tears from her face.

"Why?" she asked. "Why would you not come back?"

"What's left for me here, Soph? That place holds too many memories," I said. "Nashoma, you, all my friends... it's just a constant reminder of everything I've lost. I don't have a place in this society anymore."

"We could find you one," she protested.

"That's not going to work. My reason for staying here is you," I told her gently. "But it doesn't work like that. If we're not together, we can't be in each other's lives. I'll need a clean break. I'll have to start over, or I'll never be able to get over you."

"You can't do that," she sputtered. "We still need you for the prophecy."

"You already have the Water piece. You don't need me anymore for that," I told her gently. "To be honest, I think if I'm around and we're not together, I'll just be getting in the way. We'll never be able to work on stopping the prophecy with all this history between us. It'll be a distraction from saving the tribe."

She knew I was right. Sophia fiddled with her fingers for a moment, thinking, before she looked up. "Where will you go?"

I shrugged. "I don't know. I'll probably take my tournament money and travel. Maybe do some charity work, join the Peace Corps. I want to help people. I want to help reduce some of the suffering that's in this shitty world."

"You can do that here."

"No, I can't. Not unless I'm by your side. I've tried, Sophia. And if we're going to be done, we're done forever. We can't be friends, and I can't stay here."

I shook my head. "And you can't ask me to do anything else. I owe it to myself to do what makes me happy. My whole life, I've put everyone else first. I haven't thought of me and what I need. I nearly died because of it. And for the first time, I need to save myself before I go saving everyone else. That means getting a fresh start if it comes to the end of you and me."

"So that's it? If we aren't together, you can't be in my life at all?" she said weakly.

I nodded. "It's what has to happen. I can't just be your friend, Sophia. I can't sit around and watch you date other people. I can't—"

I took a quivering breath. "It's been tearing me up inside. But I don't want it to change your decision. Whatever you decide, it has to be because *you* want it. Not because you're worried that I'll try to kill myself again if you reject me, or say yes to keep me from leaving. That wouldn't be fair to either of us, and we'll eventually end up in the same damn situation we're in now all over again. I couldn't live through losing you again. So if you're going to break my heart, let this be the last time."

"But if you aren't in my life anymore... Esis won't be able to heal you. You'll die," she protested softly.

"Then let me die," I said. "Let me go out on my terms. There's other things I can try for treatment. Perot's got some ideas. But Soph, if they don't work, you have to be willing to let me go."

"You're giving up on your life."

"Sick people decide to stop treatment all the time. This isn't any different," I told her gently. "If I gotta go, I want to be at peace. Esis' magic is no guarantee I'll live a full life. Time's always been running short for me. Which is why you need to let me do what's best, so I can make those months I have count."

"You could have more with me."

"Maybe, maybe not. I'm gonna die when the ancestors take me and not a moment before. But you can't base your decision around it."

I stared at her.

Sophia seemed contemplative. "If we're together, we need to be together because we make each other's lives better. Not because we depend on each other or need each other to get by."

"I wholeheartedly agree. Which is why I need you to make a choice. My heart has already made mine for me," I told her.

"Do you really mean that? I don't want us to have to go back into hiding again," she said.

"I don't either. Which is why if we go forward with this, I think we need to come out publicly," I said.

Her mouth dropped open. "What? You're willing to risk your life to be with me?"

"Yes. We need to make a stand and fight for this. Tell the entire world we're together, no matter what wrath the Elders bring down on us," I said. "If we have to run away, we run away. But I've counted up the cost, and if I'm imprisoned or executed for loving you, Sophia, it's a crime I'm guilty of and happy to pay the price for."

She began to stutter. "But... but you were so against it before. You never wanted to commit."

"Do you really think I backed off on committing because I was afraid of what the Elders would do?" I asked her. "Soph, if that was the only thing in our way, I would've gotten over it months ago."

"Then why...?" Her eyes widened as she slowly pieced it together. "Liam..."

I gave her a cold stare. "You know I'm right. It's not fair, but it doesn't matter. If you're with me, you're taking on everything. Days, maybe weeks of me in the hospital. Treatment after treatment. Watching me slowly deteriorate while you can do nothing about it. Picking up my medical bills if it's something Esis can't fix. Falling in love with me just to watch me die in the end, leaving you alone."

"You don't want me to become your caregiver instead of your girlfriend," she said, voice lightening with the clarification.

"Yes," I acknowledged. "Because I don't want to put that on you. Any way you look at it, this doesn't have a happy ending. You always get hurt in the end."

"We're all going to die, Liam. Like you said, there are no guarantees. I could even die before you," she said.

"Don't talk like that," I said harshly. "I could deal with you moving on, but I'd never get over your death, *pawee*. It'd ruin me."

"And how do you think I felt, watching you about to step off that bridge?" she asked sharply. "It felt like my whole world was ending right then and there."

"You're healthy. You'll be okay."

"You forget about the prophecy. Showana said that I'd lose everything, even my life."

"We can change the prophecy. You're not going anywhere," I said quickly.

Sophia made an angry noise. "This is such a double standard! If I have to be okay with losing you, you need to be okay with losing me. There's a war coming, Liam. It's getting closer and closer every day. We're doing our best to prevent it, but what if we can't? *Everyone's* life is going to be on the line pretty quick. The question is, are you willing to accept you're not the only one who might have a short life?"

"I don't want to talk about that."

"It doesn't matter!" she reached out for my hand this time. She squeezed it tightly as she said, "When I got my spirit name, I made a vow to the ancestors and to the Great Spirit that I would give myself up for the tribe. I'd lay my life down for the Hawkei if it came to it. And if the prophecy asks me to sacrifice myself to prevent our people from going extinct, then it's what I'll do. I'm not going to run. And you have to be okay with me making that sacrifice, because you're asking me to do the same with you. You of all people know that the best leaders are willing to do anything for their tribe."

My throat was dry. I fucking hated this. But she was right. "I don't want to have to give you up," I choked out. "But if it comes down to it, I won't interfere with your choice. I promise you that."

Sophia went silent. She clung to my hand and studied the features of my face... as if she was committing them to memory, losing herself in the moment.

"Sophia, please make up your mind," I begged her. "I can't take any more of this waiting. Let me know what you decide."

She finally let go of my hand and drew away. "When I was speaking with my spirit guides, I felt like there were two roads before me," she said quietly. "I think one leads to you, and other other doesn't. But I knew I would be happy no matter what road I chose."

"And that's all I ever want for you, Sophia, is for you to be happy," I told her. "I'll be okay with whatever you choose. This is in your hands."

She looked down. "I'm not sure. I feel like on the road that leads to you, I'd be... happier."

"Seriously?" Holy shit, there was actually hope. I was planning to start packing my bags to leave town the minute she left.

"Yes. But I'm still torn. I can see us having a great future together. But after everything we've been through, I'm scared to try again. You crushed me, Liam."

"And I never will again," I vowed. "I can't promise I'll never hurt you again, because people make mistakes. But I'll never leave again. I'll be committed to you until my lungs give out."

"Those are just words. How can I be sure?" she pleaded.

"*Da-ahi Mitoh Anichi*," I said.

"What?" She looked at me blankly.

"It's my true name. The one the ancestors gave me. It means Fighting Wolf Spirit. I've never told anyone what it is before." My heart was beating so fast I thought it was going to give out. I'd never felt so exhilarated before. What a rush.

"I thought Mitoh men didn't reveal their true names until they got married? You were supposed to save that for your wife," she said.

"And I want that to be you. Sophia." I took both of her hands in mine. "There's no one else for me after you. If you're not the girl I'm gonna marry, then I'm not getting married at all. It begins and ends with you."

She gave me a watery smile. "You're just saying that. You'd fall in love with someone else eventually."

"No. I wouldn't." I let go of her hands. "But you would. And if you think there's someone else out there for you that's not me, you need to follow that. I'll be fine. I promise."

She stared at me. "You keep asking if I want you back, and of course I do. But if things are going to end the way they did before... we can't do that to each other again, Liam."

"This time will be different, because we're different now," I said. "We're not the same people."

"That's the point. How do we know if it's going to work?" she asked.

"Nothing's ever a sure thing." I gave her the best smile I could. "But in my life, I know the surest thing I've ever been certain of is us."

She chewed her lip. "If we're going to get back together, there are going to be conditions."

"Name them." I'd do anything.

She held up three fingers. "First, this is the last chance I'm giving you. If we break up again, we're done for good. I'm never coming back to you."

"That's fair." I didn't expect anything different.

She put down a finger. "Second, no more secrets, and no more lies. We tell each other *everything*. I don't care how bad it is. I'll never hide anything from you again as long as you promise to do the same."

"Agreed." I was sick of the secrets, too. This one was easy.

She held up a final finger. "Last... you get some help."

I felt like I'd run into a brick wall. I was temporarily dazed. "What?"

"Come on, Liam." She gave me a look. "You've been depressed since I met you. You haven't been dealing with Nashoma's death at all. Hell, you just tried to jump off a bridge. I can't be with someone I don't know is taking care of themselves mentally. I don't want to have to worry about if you're stable or if you're going to be okay. I can't live with that kind of anxiety. I want you to be happy. Agree to go to treatment, or else this thing between us isn't happening again."

That was a hard bargain. I didn't want to go to treatment. I'd been avoiding it since Nashoma died.

Yet she was right. Perot was right. I was depressed. I had been living in denial about it forever, and it had come right up and bit me in the ass.

But if I had to talk to somebody to get Sophia back, that was something I was willing to do. "Fine. I'll go to therapy, or whatever. I'll even start next week."

"You promise?" she hedged.

"Yes. I will do everything you ask." I hesitated. "Just... please don't tell me this is over for good."

Sophia paused. The following seconds were agonizing, like waiting for someone to tell you if your greatest hopes had been realized or destroyed. A tightness wrapped around my heart and held my chest hostage, freezing me so I couldn't breathe, barbed wire cutting into my lungs. Those few seconds of tension were drawn-out, full of tension and worry. If she said no...

Finally, Sophia whispered, "It'll never be over, Liam."

"Thank the ancestors." I lunged forward and took her face in my hands as I kissed her passionately, unlike I'd ever kissed her before. I felt like if I didn't kiss her then, I would die, and there would be nothing left of me. Putting my lips against hers was like the first breath of life. I'd felt numb for so long, and now she was bringing me back from the dead. Warmth and light spread over my chest where a freezing cold had once been, and I realized for the first time how painful living without Sophia had been, and how much I loved her. She was crucial to my story. She was everything.

Sophia threw her arms around my neck and pulled me into her. We crashed together like two waves in the ocean. Her hands roamed over every inch of my body, like she needed to be reminded that I was there in the flesh.

I forced myself to draw away from her. To part from her was excruciating. "I'm not going anywhere, *pawee*," I whispered. "Not ever again."

Tears streaked her cheeks, and I brushed them away.

"Never again," she whispered back to me. "We're meant to be together."

Fuck yeah, we were! And I intended to show her how much. I grabbed the front of her blouse and pulled it open. Buttons went flying everywhere. Sophia started clawing at my clothes and yanked my shirt over my head. Her hands roamed my chest as I leaned forward to kiss her neck and the crook of her shoulder. I reached my arms around her and undid the clasp on her bra and threw it aside onto the floor. She gasped as the fabric fell away and the cool air hit her exposed skin. Her amazing breasts rubbed against my bare chest as we continued to make out more furiously than ever before.

I hadn't touched her in so long. I needed to touch her. One of my hands came up to gently roam over her breasts. She moaned quietly, and I got *so turned on.*

She started messing with the button on my jeans, and we leaned back on the bed. My dick was so hard it was practically straining to get out of my pants. Sophia unzipped my jeans and yanked them down. I kicked them off to the side of the bed and began kissing her again, but this time, we froze.

I was only in my boxers, and Sophia was half-naked already. She breathlessly gasped against my mouth, "Are we really going to do this?"

"Fuck yeah we are." I had a thought, and said, "Oh, shit. I don't have any condoms."

"It's fine, I'm on birth control," Sophia said quickly, like she wanted to get back to what we were doing.

Momentary panic swept through me. Sophia read my face and said, "No, it was just in case. I'm still a virgin."

Relief. I'd gotten *so* lucky on that. We'd been broken up for months — she could've easily slept with someone else, and she didn't. I had a feeling she was waiting for me.

Holy shit. I was gonna be the one to take Sophia Henley's virginity. That was so fucking hot.

"Not for much longer," I said under my breath, and Sophia blushed. I put my thumbs underneath the waistband of her yoga pants and pulled them off. Then I bent down and grabbed the top of her panties with my teeth, pulling them down slowly. She shivered as my mouth drifted down over her and slipped the panties away. I dropped them to the floor and came back upward, kissing her entire body, starting with her feet, her legs, drifting my lips up her stomach and over her breasts. I caressed her curves, letting my hands drift over her hips and thighs. Her body quivered, and she reached into my boxers to grab my ass. I stopped fucking around and yanked off my boxers so that we were both naked.

Sophia wrapped her hand around my dick and started pumping slowly. She guided me to my back and rolled on top of me as she continued stroking. Ancestors, this was fucking amazing. My mind went blank and became static as her fingers roamed across my length. I could barely even think right now. Every part of my body was firing off incredible sensors that made this feel like the most pleasurable thing I'd ever experienced. My body shook with the effort not to come already.

I'd missed her for so long. I missed everything we were and everything we did together. Ancestors, I'd been so stupid. How could I have destroyed us like that? I never should've left. And I was going to spend the rest of my lifetime making up for it.

Sophia lowered her head and placed her mouth around my dick. She gently licked it, and I shivered. She gave a few more slow and desirable movements before I pushed her away gently and said, "I'm not gonna last like that. Let me pleasure you."

I moved quickly. I grabbed her and flipped her over onto her back with one arm. She giggled, but her quiet laughs turned into gasps as I ran my tongue across the sensitive area between her thighs. Her back rose off the bed as my mouth continued to move over the most delicate parts of her. I put my finger inside her as my tongue worked, and it didn't take too long for her to come— loudly. I could let her scream as much as she wanted to, because we were alone and I fucking loved hearing it.

After she came, I hovered myself over her. I positioned myself and caught her eyes. All the bad shit that had happened over the past few months melted away and was replaced by a strong connection beyond anything I'd ever shared with anyone— deeper than our very souls.

"Are you ready?" I asked. Shit, this was really happening. After so long, after talking about it and thinking about it and hoping for it, the moment was finally here.

Sophia nodded and took a few short breaths. "Yes, Liam. I'm ready."

FOURTEEN

I hated all the time Liam and I had wasted apart. The last few months had been the hardest of my life. But in this moment, I realized that we'd needed that time apart to come to this point. Both of us needed to grow, and we did so on our own. Now it was time to grow together.

A week ago, I wasn't sure I wanted him back. Now I knew it was the right decision. Nothing had felt as right as it did in this moment, like this was where we were meant to be. Being here with Liam was like returning home after a long, hard journey. He gave me the comfort and stability I needed in this world where nothing was predictable. I felt safe in his arms, like he would protect me from whatever came our way— no matter the cost. I knew that come hell or high water, he would take care of me, and I him.

His hands rested on either side of me, but he lifted one to guide his erection against me. Gently, he eased the tip of himself inside me. I inhaled a sharp breath, expecting it to hurt, but it didn't.

"Is this still okay?" he asked.

I couldn't find my breath, so I responded with a nod.

"I need to hear you say it, Sophia. I won't do this without hearing yes."

"Yes, Liam," I moaned, begging for more. "Do it."

Slowly, Liam pressed deeper. I felt pressure, then all of a sudden, it was like something gave way. He fit perfectly inside me, and I completely relaxed. It hurt for only a moment before the most amazing feeling ever came over me. It was like stumbling upon a hidden meadow in the forest, like a brand new world I'd never explored. Colors in the room changed, becoming more vibrant and clear.

"Fuck, Sophia. You're so tight."

I looked up to him to see his eyes were shut, like this new world was too much to take in all at once. He had a blissful expression on his face, and my heart felt full knowing I was the one making him feel like that.

Liam's weight pressed down on me in a warm, safe embrace. I wrapped my arms around his neck, and he held on to me as he began thrusting. It started slow at first, until small, involuntary noises of pleasure passed my lips. Liam moaned and increased his speed. It was so hot that I couldn't help but claw at his back. There were so many emotions flooding through me in that moment that it was overwhelming. I wanted to slow down and experience each one on its own, savoring the incredible feelings one by one. But I couldn't think. I couldn't hardly breathe. All I could concentrate on was the motion of his body.

Liam shifted to take my hands in his, lacing his fingers through mine and pinning them to the bed beside my head.

"I love you," he said against the crook of my neck. His warm breath brushed across my skin as he went deeper.

"I love you, too." Tears welled up in my eyes as I tried to hold back all the love I had for him. I didn't want to cry and ruin the moment, but damn, this was so amazing. I was glad I waited for him. Nothing else could ever compare to sharing yourself with the person your soul belonged to for the first time.

Liam picked up speed, and I couldn't take it anymore. I called out his name as I spiraled into a heart-stopping orgasm.

Liam joined me seconds later. He whispered my name in my ear and squeezed my hands tighter. He let out three quick moans as we came together in this moment that would forever mark our new beginning.

Our eyes locked, knowing we were forever connected. A beat passed where I couldn't read his face, like he was trying to process everything that happened— almost like he didn't believe it. I could tell the second it sank in, because he gave me a huge smile, as if he could no longer contain his elation.

Liam rolled to the side and wrapped a strong arm beneath me. I curled into him and rested my head on his shoulder. We couldn't take our eyes off each other. Neither of us spoke as we struggled to catch our breath. I was still trying to gather my bearings. What we'd just done was unbelievable. A moment ago, Liam only had my heart. Now he'd claimed my body. I was no longer a virgin, and I was glad I'd given that part of myself to him.

"That was amazing, Liam," I whispered.

He pressed his lips to the top of my head. "That was fucking incredible, *pawee*."

His eyes suddenly left mine, and a blush rose to his cheeks. "Sorry I came in you."

I beamed. "Don't worry about it."

"I just couldn't help myself. I got lost in the moment."

"It's fine," I assured him. "It was what I wanted."

Liam held me tighter as I gently traced the muscles in his arms and torso. I didn't know how long we lay like that. All I knew was that I never wanted this to end.

Eventually, it did end, but it must've been at least an hour later. I'd nodded off and woke to Liam stirring beside me. I opened my eyes, feeling refreshed.

"What is it?" I asked as we sat up.

His gaze locked on my breasts, but I didn't care. He could look at me all he wanted. "I heard someone downstairs. Probably Ezra. We should... get dressed."

Liam stood, then dug in his dresser for clean clothes.

"Think your brother heard?" I asked as I pulled my pants on.

"Does it matter?" he asked with a smirk.

"No, I guess not," I admitted.

Liam noticed the missing buttons on my shirt and gave me a clean one to wear. It was way too big on me, but it smelled like him. He was never getting it back.

After we both were fully dressed, Liam sat beside me on the bed. He gazed into my eyes with such warmth that I felt it spread through me.

I ran my hands through the tangles in my hair and blushed under his gaze. "What?"

Liam smiled. "You just look... radiant."

I giggled. "Well, yeah. What do you expect after that?"

He chuckled, and I leaned forward to press my lips to his. Ancestors, I missed the taste of his lips.

"I love you, Liam," I said as I drew away and took his hands in mine.

He rested his forehead against mine and spoke softly. "I love you, too, *pawee*."

"*Kyra Koignichi*," I blurted.

He pulled away and shot me a confused look.

"It means—"

"Blazing Firespirit," Liam finished for me.

I nodded. "My spirit name."

Liam looked as if his heart was full. "It's beautiful."

I ran my hand across his cheek just to feel his skin on mine. "I thought you should know. Now that we're official again."

Liam beamed so wide that I snickered at him. "What?" I asked innocently.

He shrugged, still beaming. "I just like the sound of it. Official. Sophia Henley's my girlfriend."

Liam wiggled his shoulders in a happy dance, and I could hardly contain my heart. He was shining, which made me glow, too.

I kissed him, and it turned into a full-on make-out session again. I was ready to strip my clothes off again for another go, but Liam pulled away.

It took several moments for me to catch my breath. "So, when are we going to tell everyone?"

"Whenever you want, *pawee*," he said.

"Monday, at school," I answered automatically. I loved him so much, and I wanted everyone else to know.

I expected some resistance, but all he said was, "Fair enough."

I was speechless. Liam Mitoh really had changed. And I loved him now more than ever.

❧

Ezra knew Liam and I had sex. He *totally* knew. But worse than that, Esis had heard *everything*. The little perv had been sitting outside Liam's door the whole time eavesdropping. He'd even finished off a bag of microwave popcorn and had butter all over his paws. I had to give him a bath when we returned back to the dorms that night, after spending the day on the beach with Liam.

Saturday morning, Esis and I took another peryton to Liam's house. His mom answered and looked delighted to see me. She gave me a hug, then waved me upstairs to Liam's room.

Liam was still asleep. The curtains over the balcony doors were closed, and he was nothing more than a lump on the bed.

I set Esis at my feet and signaled for him to be quiet. He eyed me curiously as I tiptoed over to Liam's bed and crawled under the sheets beside him. Liam moaned and rolled over. I lightly placed my lips to his, and his eyes shot open.

"Sophia, what are you—?"

"Shh..." I placed an index finger to his lips. "No questions. Just enjoy it."

Liam's eyes closed again, and he wrapped his arms around me, relaxing into my kiss. I ran my hands up and down his shirtless torso, then slid my hand inside his boxers. He was rock hard.

"Is this a dream?" he mumbled against me.

I chuckled. "It's real. I promise."

Liam's eyes opened again, and he drew away to look me in the eyes. "Then maybe we should stop. My mom's home."

I kissed him again and whispered, "Then we'll just have to find someplace private to finish this."

Liam groaned. "Can't. I'm on house arrest."

"Not anymore," I said with a grin. "I just talked to your mom. You're mine for the day."

He furrowed his brow.

"As long as you don't leave my sight, she says we can hang out— go anywhere," I told him. "And you know I won't be able to keep my eyes off you."

Liam immediately perked up. He rolled out of bed and pulled on jeans and a red t-shirt. He pulled open the curtains to let the sunlight in.

"You look good today." I lay propped up on one elbow, my eyes roaming his backside.

He inhaled a breath of ocean air. "I feel good."

He took my hand and pulled me to my feet. He wrapped an arm around my waist and pulled me close. Another kiss brushed across my lips.

From our feet, Esis jumped and cheered, punching his little fists into the air. He looked happier than I'd ever seen him.

I laughed and scooped him into my arms. "I know, buddy. You've been rooting for us. You can relax now."

Liam and I started for the door. "So, where are we going?" he asked.

"Back to school," I said. "Dance studio."

"Dancing? Sophia, I—"

"Not us," I said with a laugh. "I agreed to meet Jonah and Imogen there this morning. They wanted to show me something. They'll be happy to see you."

"I miss them," Liam said as we descended the stairs.

"Have fun!" his mom called from the kitchen.

"We will," I told her. She had no idea how much *fun* we were going to have.

Liam glanced around when we stepped outside. "Where's your peryton?"

I kept walking down the beach. "One-way ticket," I explained. "I thought maybe we could take another way back."

Liam caught my meaning the closer we got to the motorboat parked beside the dock next to the house. "Ezra went boating this morning, didn't he?"

"Yep." I turned to him and jingled the keys in my hand. "I caught him just as he was done. He left us the keys."

Liam beamed. "How much time do we have before we have to meet Imogen and Jonah?"

I smirked. "Enough."

Liam couldn't get on the boat fast enough. It wasn't very big— maybe twenty feet long, with an open top, a couple of leather seats, and a cooler. He sat behind the wheel and had me undo the rope from the dock while he started up the motor. Esis stood at the front, spreading his arms out wide like he was on *Titanic*.

I shot Liam a nervous glance. "He's going to go flying into the water."

Liam chuckled as we pulled away from the dock. "He'll be fine. I won't let him fall off."

Esis looked pleased as the wind whipped through his fur. It was cool out here on the water, but I pulled my sweatshirt tighter around me and brought Fire to the surface of my skin. The chill left me. I couldn't take my eyes off Liam as he steered the boat out into the middle of the water. His eyes kept flickering over to mine. His features were so soft, and there was a permanent smile on his lips. I'd never seen him look so happy.

Liam stopped the boat when we were far enough from shore that no one could see us. This time of day, no one else was out on the water. He cut the engine, and the waves bobbed us up and down. Esis stared over the edge of the boat at the rising sun glittering off the water, totally ignoring us as he watched the fish that swam below the surface with interest.

Liam and I didn't have to say anything. It was like we were in tune now— to each other's bodies and minds. We connected like magnets. He pulled me onto his lap, and we began stripping each other's clothes off. Liam kissed me with so much passion that I thought my heart might beat its way out of my chest. I was breathless as his lips left mine and trailed down my neck and to my rock-hard nipples.

Liam and I removed our pants, until I was sitting stark naked on his lap, straddling him on the boat seat. He grabbed my hips and guided me over top of him. Slowly, I lowered myself until he was inside of me. I moaned loudly, but I didn't care. No one could hear us. My hands roamed all over his chest as I rocked back and forth. It was just as amazing as the first time, if not better. I'd never felt so in sync with anyone in my life. Liam and I knew each other better than anyone else. We moved together as one, the waves of the boat amplifying our shared movements.

"Oh my God," I cried out as we came together.

"That's right, *pawee*," Liam gasped against me. "Call me what I am."

I burst out laughing and swatted him playfully in the shoulder. "You're not a god. You're better."

Liam smirked, then kissed my nose. "You're full of it, *pawee*."

"Full of you," I joked.

He grinned. "Yeah. You are."

I leaned against Liam in an embrace for a long time, but eventually, I climbed off him and started dressing again. I caught Esis looking at us with wide eyes while I was putting my bra back on.

"Ew, Esis," I scolded. "A little privacy."

Esis quickly turned around and stared back out over the ocean.

Liam and I shared a laugh as he started up the boat again. It didn't take long to get back to the docks on the mainland, and it was only a short walk back to the school from there.

When we reached the dance studio on the third floor of the castle, Jonah and Imogen were already there. Imogen was fiddling with the music speakers, Sassy at her feet. Jonah stood in a blue leotard next to a wall of floor-to-ceiling mirrors. He held on to a railing that wrapped around the room and had one ankle propped up on it, stretching. Squeaks was trying to lift her back leg up to copy him, but she lost her footing and fell on her face.

Liam strolled into the room laughing at Squeaks. Imogen squealed when she saw him, and Jonah was so excited his ankle got stuck on the beam and he fell over beside his Familiar. The door fell shut behind us.

"Liam!" Imogen squeaked as she ran over to us and threw her arms around his middle. Sassy yipped and jumped up and down at his feet. Esis jumped out of my hands to join Sassy on the ground. "I'm so sorry! I never meant it when I said I hated you. I love you. I'm so glad you're okay."

Liam laughed, and hugged her back. "We're good, Im. You okay, bro?"

"Aw, hell." Jonah sat up and rubbed his face. "Think I broke a marvelous cheek bone. How's it look?"

"You look beautiful, as always," Liam joked.

Jonah got to his feet, then froze. "Beautiful? Me? Who are you, and what did you do with Liam?"

"Liam Baby's right here," he teased, gesturing up and down his body as he stepped further into the room.

I placed my hand over my mouth as I tried not to laugh. The new Liam was seriously impressing me. I loved seeing him so happy.

Jonah made a show of inspecting him. He sniffed him, then poked at his face. "I'll be damned. It *is* you."

Imogen stood beside me and lowered her voice. "Did something happen? Liam seems..."

"Renewed?" I finished for her. "Yeah, he is. So am I."

Imogen inhaled a sharp breath. "You guys...?"

I couldn't hide my smile. I nodded eagerly.

Imogen swatted me so hard it kind of hurt. "*Shut up.*"

"I won't," I said.

"Lucky," Imogen said. "Cade still won't get in my pants."

"Loser," I joked. "What's his problem?"

Imogen rolled her eyes. "Something stupid about my brother."

"Ew!" I cried.

"No, not like that," Imogen said. "Like, he wants to ask my brother's permission to be with me first or something, but like, I guess he doesn't get that he *can't do that.*"

"He'll come around," I assured her.

Imogen quickly changed the subject. "So, you guys really did it? You realize I *was* talking about sex, right?"

"Who's talking about sex?" Jonah strolled up to us and didn't mind butting into the middle of the conversation. Squeaks had finally rose to her feet and walked beside him.

I blushed bright red and glanced to Liam. He didn't seem bothered at all by the topic. He was probably bursting to tell someone. Typical guy.

"Um... me and Liam," I admitted.

Jonah's jaw dropped so far it was comical. He glanced between Liam and me like he was putting on a theater performance. I'd never seen such a dramatic show of surprise in my life. "You and Liam... Liam and you... you guys *did it!*"

Liam walked over to me and placed an arm around my shoulder, looking pleased with himself. I couldn't say I blamed him. I felt on the top of the world. Liam leaned over to Jonah and whispered, "Twice."

Jonah squealed, and our three Familiars joined in the cheering beside him. "O.M.G! I can't believe it. We have to celebrate."

"Ancestors, Jonah," Imogen complained. "They just had sex. It's not like they're getting married." She whirled toward us. "Wait. Are you?"

"No, God," I said, blushing harder than I thought possible. "Some-day, sure. But not now."

I looked to Liam to make sure that was the right answer. He gave me an encouraging nod.

"A wedding!" Jonah cried. He reached for Imogen's tulle skirt and held up the red fabric to my waist. "Tulle? No. We'll have to work on it. But you know you can't wear white now." He winked at me.

I swatted his hand away, and he dropped Imogen's skirt. "Shut up, or you're not invited."

"Yeah," Imogen sneered, placing her hands on her hips. "And who says you get to design the dress?"

"Slow down." Liam stepped between all of us. "No one's designing a dress. Sophia and I *just* got back together."

"Yeah, but it won't be long until she starts showing," Jonah joked.

I wasn't even mad. I found myself laughing along with him.

Imogen quickly came to my defense, but it was all in good fun. "Sophia's not pregnant, asshole."

"Okay, everyone calm down," I quickly said. "What did you guys want to show us?"

"We've been working on choreography for our dance routine for class," Jonah said. "But we need some feedback before we present it."

"You know we're probably just going to laugh at you, right?" Liam teased.

"You would never," Jonah teased. "Now sit down and watch the magic happen."

Liam and I sat on one end of the room with the Familiars while Jonah and Imogen set up their props and music.

"Ten bucks says Jonah falls on his face," I whispered.

Liam stuck his hand out to me. "Deal. I hope you win."

I shook his hand, feeling the electricity between us.

"Okay, lovebirds," Imogen said. "Pay attention."

The song started, and Imogen and Jonah began to dance. It was a soft, slow melody. It started with Jonah performing a graceful dance across the floor. Imogen came leaping onto the scene, and the two moved in harmony as they depicted a scene where Imogen beat Jonah. The music increased in intensity until he was lying on the ground.

Imogen twirled and ripped the top layer of her skirt off herself. The red fabric dropped away to reveal a purple skirt beneath. Imogen danced by Jonah's unmoving form, then continued on her way. I suddenly realized what they were depicting.

"The legend," I whispered under my breath.

"What?" Liam asked.

I shook my head. I was too mesmerized by their dance to look away. "I'll tell you later."

Their dance continued, and Imogen ripped off another layer of skirt until she was in a green one. The two moved in sync again as they depicted Lyda Leve Nivaras nursing the Toaqua man to health.

Imogen performed beautiful twirls and leaps as Jonah went offstage for a moment. He came back wearing a golden cloak with beads all over it. *The ancestors.*

Jonah danced around Imogen, depicting the blessing. The music became very happy and upbeat as Imogen did another solo dance. Jonah returned wearing a red cloak. The music shifted to an angry dogfight as they acted out a grueling fight between Lyda Leve Nivaras and the Koigni man.

The music shifted again, until it was almost inaudible. It grew again to a soft, beautiful melody as Jonah went offstage and Imogen was left alone. Jonah used his air magic to make leaves swirl around Imogen as she controlled her body in a way that made her look like a marionette. She rose to her feet gracefully, the leaves still swirling around her. Her hands reached above her head, and she stood in a beautiful pose. From somewhere within her skirt, vines grew upward and wrapped around her hands, growing leaves right in front of our eyes. The leaves Jonah was controlling slowed, then fell to the ground softly as the music faded to nothing.

I was left speechless. It took me a few seconds to absorb how beautiful and creative the dance was, before I rose to my feet and gave the two of them a standing ovation. Liam joined me, as did our Familiars. Imogen blushed and curtsied, then gestured to Jonah as he bowed.

"You guys!" I cried. "That was awesome. It's the Earth legend!"

"I know, right?" Imogen bounced on the balls of her feet. "We came up with it after we talked about the prophecy. So, you liked it?"

"Loved it!" I told her.

At the same time, Liam said, "The prophecy?"

"We think we found the Nivita part," Jonah told him.

Liam glanced between all three of us. "Why didn't anyone mention it to me?"

Imogen bit her lip. "We haven't seen you since we figured it out."

Liam relaxed. "Okay. So what is it?"

We sat on the floor in the dance studio and told Liam all about the legend, the prophecy wording, and what we thought it meant.

"I agree," he said thoughtfully. "We need to get Nivita on our side. It's going to be hard. Koigni has the most power, so they might be more inclined to side with them to save their own House."

"Right," I agreed. "But how do we convince them?"

"I'm working on that," Imogen said.

"You are?" I asked in surprise. She hadn't told me what she'd been up to.

Imogen held her head up high. "I'm the Nivita in this group. This piece of the prophecy is my responsibility, which is why I've decided to meet with the Nivita Elders myself."

❧

Liam and I spent Sunday together on the beach, but Monday came far too soon. I woke up late and skipped a shower, then tossed on a pair of old jeans, a sweatshirt with a hole in the sleeve, and my high-top hiking shoes. I was excited to finally be getting out of the classroom for Elementai Explorations.

We'd spent most of the semester learning about archaeology techniques. Though some of it was hands-on in the classroom, most of it came from our textbook. Baine often told stories of his travels while he worked for the Hawkei exploring the world for magical creatures and enchanted artifacts. I'd had no idea there was a whole career based on exploring magical history, myths, and legends. I could totally see Imogen doing it for a living.

I hiked my backpack up on my shoulder, and Esis climbed on for a ride. When we got to the classroom, Baine was speaking to a girl up front. He'd given up his usual button-down shirt and slacks for a pair of cargo pants and a long-sleeve sweater. The rest of the class sat in their chairs, waiting for everyone else to arrive.

"Miss Swanson, I'm sorry, but I can't let you go on our spelunking expedition dressed like that," Baine said.

The girl was Koigni, a year ahead of me. She was wearing a plaid skirt and high heels, with a white button-down top. A large raven sat on her shoulder, and she crossed her arms. "What do you mean I can't go like this?"

Baine pressed his fingers to his eyes, like he couldn't deal with the stupidity today. "You do know we're going into a *cave*, right?"

She huffed. "I don't see why I can't look good anyway."

A group of Nivita guys up front laughed at her.

Baine sighed in exasperation. "We'll be crawling through narrow tunnels on our hands and knees." When she didn't respond, he added, "In the mud."

"Yuck! No way am I crawling through the mud," she sneered.

"Then why did you sign up for this class?" He sounded more curious than anything.

She shrugged. "Someone told me it was an easy A."

"Not if you can't crawl through the mud," Baine pointed out. "If you don't come to the caves with us, you'll fail today's assignment."

She rolled her eyes. "Whatever. Then I'll fail. I'll make it up on the final."

She whirled around and stomped out of the room, nearly slamming into Vanessa, who'd just rounded the corner. My face fell when I saw her. She looked a little pale, and Aisha wasn't by her side.

"Are you okay?" I asked immediately, rushing to her side.

She waved a hand like it was nothing. "Morning sickness."

"Where's Aisha?" I glanced out into the hallway, but I didn't see her following nearby.

"She's back home with Bren. Baine said she was too big to fit in the caves."

"Are you sure you're well enough to do this?" I asked, though I already noticed color returning to her face.

"Are you kidding?" she asked. "This is my favorite class. I'm not missing this lesson."

Esis held a little paw up and gave her a high-five. He seemed excited, too.

"Okay," Baine's voice called from the front of the room. He stepped forward with a big white box in his hands. The class quieted, and all eyes turned toward him. "It looks like everyone's here. We don't have a lot of time, so let's make the trip to and from the caves as smooth as possible. Everyone follow me."

Baine led us outside to a bus-like carriage. It was pulled by two ox-looking creatures that were the size of elephants. Their fur glinted blue in the sunlight, and their horns shimmered a metallic silver.

"Everyone in," Baine said, ushering the class inside the long carriage.

Our class wasn't very big— about fifteen students— but we filled every seat. Vanessa and I took a seat beside each other, and Esis settled in on my lap.

Mia sat with her Familiar in the back and didn't even look my way. We hadn't talked since she'd insisted her and Liam weren't a thing weeks ago. I knew now I'd been wrong about them being together, but something seemed up with Mia. She usually didn't shut up during class, but this time, she stared out the window and kept to herself.

Baine gave a signal to the oxen once everyone was seated, and the bus-carriage began moving.

Baine stood at the front of the carriage in the center of the aisle. He reached into his box and began handing out headlamps. "Safety inside the caves is vital. There's a large network of caves all throughout Kinpago, and we don't need anyone to get lost."

Baine handed Vanessa and I our headlamps, then reached back into his box and gave a mini headlamp to Esis. Esis smiled and placed it on his head backward, looking proud of himself. I chuckled and readjusted it for him.

"You're all adults," Baine said as he finished handing out the headlamps. "I trust that you'll all stay with the group and won't go wandering off on your own. Can we all agree to that?"

A collective murmur traveled around the carriage.

"Good. Now, a few things before we enter the caves," Baine said. "Some of the things you see down there will tempt you, but you are not to touch them without my explicit permission. We do not want to disrupt this habitat."

A Nivita girl in the front seat raised her hand.

"Yes, Sandy?" Baine asked.

"What kind of things are we going to see?" she asked.

Baine smirked. "If I told you, that would ruin the surprise."

We stopped along the road beside a trail marker several minutes later. Baine led us about a hundred yards into the woods, then stopped beside a small cave mouth cut into the earth. The cave opening was nearly flat, so it was almost impossible to see until you were right on top of it. It was only big enough for two people to fit inside at a time.

"The interesting thing about this particular section of the caves is that it was only discovered a decade ago," Baine explained once we were all gathered around.

Esis was already trying to scurry out of my arms and into the cave. I held on to him tightly. "Calm down, buddy."

"There are still undiscovered and unexplored sections of the Kinpago caves," Baine said. "As you will see today, we have very good reason to continue exploring these caves and opening new passageways to see what we find."

Sandy shot her hand into the air.

"Yes?" Baine asked.

"Is that safe?" she asked timidly. "I mean, what if we uncover creatures that intend to hurt us?"

Baine raised an eyebrow. "What if we uncover those that intend to help us?"

The forest went silent, then Baine turned on his heel and said, "Everyone follow me. Watch your footing."

One by one, we crawled into the cave with our Familiars beside us. It seemed bigger when I got up close. I clicked on mine and Esis' head-lamps, then lowered myself into the cave feet-first. The cave wall was sloped at an easy angle, so all I had to do was watch my head when I ducked inside the cave. Esis went way ahead of me, scurrying down the rocks before I was even halfway to the bottom.

Vanessa came after me, and I offered my hand over the last few rocks to help her stay steady on her feet.

The cave opened up wide enough for the whole class to stand comfortably at the bottom. Three tunnels broke off from the main cavern— one crawl space to our right and an even smaller opening above our heads, then a wide tunnel straight in front of us.

"This way," Baine said, guiding us down the widest tunnel. It sloped downward, looking like it never ended.

I scooped Esis up and followed at the back of the group beside Vanessa. "What do you think the surprise is?"

Vanessa gazed deep into the cave in front of us, looking excited. She leaned over to me and said lowly, "Legend says there's an underground river somewhere in these caves."

My eyebrows shot up. "Really? Is it magical?"

"If it were ordinary, would it be legend?" She laughed lightly. "The story says that during the last Hawkei war, a group of Anichi hid down here for months before they were discovered by the Koigni hunting them. Legend has it the ancestors blessed the waters that ran through this cave to nourish any Elementai who drank from the river. That's how they survived so long."

"Wow. Do you think the legend's true?" I asked.

Vanessa shrugged. "Don't know. No one's ever found the river. If they have, they haven't told anyone else about it."

Mud squished at my feet. "Clearly water gets into the caves somehow," I pointed out.

"Yeah, from the rain," Vanessa said. "The river is different. It comes from high up in the mountains and goes through the cave and out into the ocean."

Baine stopped ahead of us, and the class slowed. The walls had narrowed around us, and the ceiling was just a few feet above my head. "Before we venture into the next section of the caves, I'd like everyone to turn their head lamps off and just listen."

I clicked off mine and Esis' lamps. After several moments, everyone else's lamps went off, and we were enveloped in darkness.

"I don't hear anything," Mia whispered toward the front.

"Shh..." Baine instructed. "Listen closer."

Everyone quieted. I paid close attention to the sounds around me, but all I could hear was Vanessa's breathing beside me. Slowly, I began to detect a second sound. I wasn't sure if it was in my head or not until someone said, "Are those wings?"

Baine clicked on his headlamp. "Precisely. Shall we go see what these wings belong to?"

We followed behind Baine single-file into a narrow tunnel that we had to crawl through. I kept my head low and went on my hands and knees, though the guy in front of me was so big that he had to army crawl on his belly. Esis stayed at my side, though he looked impatient.

The tunnel opened up to a huge cavern half the size of a football field and at least twenty feet high. Tunnels broke off in all different directions. Headlamps scanned the room, but the cavern didn't need it. All along the walls and most of the floor were bright sparkling crystals, giving off their own luminous glow. They looked electric, fading in and out in mesmerizing shades of blue, purple, and pink.

Above us, creatures that could fit in the palm of my hand flew around the cavern. At first I thought they were bats, but they were completely different. They looked like tiny dragons, with scales that shimmered all colors of the rainbow, but they had insect wings like dragonflies that were at least six inches in length. The light from the crystals shimmered through their thin wings and illuminated the ceiling, creating a dancing lights display above our heads.

My jaw dropped, and everyone else went silent in awe. Vanessa inhaled a breath of amazement.

"What are they?" she whispered beside me.

"I don't know," I said.

Esis batted at the air, like he wanted to play with them.

Baine reached his hand into the air, and one of the creatures gently landed in his outstretched palm. "They're called *dracavern*, or cave dragons."

"Oh, my friend is bonded to one of these!" Sandy exclaimed.

Baine petted the dracavern's tiny head as the class gathered around to hear him teach about them. "Yes, they're actually quite common Familiars. They're drawn to Nivita Elementai and are said to be some of the best emotionally supportive companions. But until this cave was discovered, the bonds they formed were strained."

"Strained how?" a Toaqua girl asked.

"Dracavern are cave-dwelling creatures for one reason and one reason only," Baine said as another dracavern landed on his shoulder. "The unique draco crystals around you give off an energy signature that calm the dracavern. Without the crystals, they become very irritable. It was once believed that this was in their nature, but the Elementai who bonded with them didn't understand why this was, as it didn't make for a good companion."

A dracavern landed on Esis' head. He relaxed and began purring. I stroked the dracavern's scales and found them soft and warm. It took my breath away to be in the presence of such beautiful creatures.

Baine continued. "At times, dracavern Familiars would wander off and come back with a completely different temperament. No one knew why. It's believed they'd come down into this cave to be rejuvenated with the crystals' energy."

Vanessa raised her hand. "So if they could run off and get rejuvenated whenever they wanted, why was this discovery so critical?"

"For two reasons, Mrs. Emberly." Baine held up a finger. "One, it taught us about these Familiars and allowed us to understand their nature. No longer was their irritability a mystery, because we were able to treat them. Two, we've been able to mine a small portion of these crystals specifically for the Elementai who bond with a dracavern. If their Elementai carries a piece of draco crystal with them, their Familiars remain their good-natured selves."

"It's like a medication for them?" Vanessa asked.

Baine thought about it a moment. "In a way. This is why Elementai Explorations is such an important field. The more we know about the world we live in, the better we can serve the creatures who live here."

Vanessa held her hand out, and a dracavern with a shimmering purple belly landed in her hand. She giggled and touched its outstretched wings. "I want to keep one."

"Aisha would get jealous," I teased.

"We have one more cavern to visit before we return to the school," Baine said. "If you'll all follow me, we'll meet the bats whose venom can be used in a potion that eliminates the hectra parasite from bovine Familiar intestines."

The class followed Baine single-file into a narrow tunnel. The dracavern on Esis' head seemed to have taken a liking to him and was hanging tightly to his fur.

I laughed. "Let him go, little guy. We're falling behind."

"Don't hurt him." Vanessa gently helped me pry the dracavern from Esis' fur, but by the time we got them apart, the rest of the class had already disappeared into the tunnel.

"Let's go—" I cut off as Esis' ears perked up. He jumped out of my arms and raced toward a tunnel to our left.

"Esis!" I cried. "That's not the right way!"

He didn't listen. Esis scurried down the wide tunnel, and I rushed after him. Vanessa hurried closely behind me. I could see Esis' light bobbing up and down along the cave walls in front of me, but he ran so fast that I could hardly keep up. Ancestors, when did he get so fast?

I cursed under my breath and called his name again. My voice echoed off the cave walls. Esis chittered back at me, like he thought he was hilarious.

"Esis!" I called firmly.

No use. He continued down the tunnel, then turned right when the tunnel came to a fork. This tunnel was even muddier than the last, and it was rocky. I ended up using my hands to stay steady on the rocks. I couldn't see Esis' light in front of me anymore.

Vanessa was panting by the time we reached another wide cavern filled with boulders and tunnels splitting off in various directions. I didn't know how far we were away from the rest of the group, but it seemed like a mile. I glanced around frantically, but I saw no sign of Esis or his light.

"Shit. Where did he go?" My heart was hammering, and I was beyond worried. It was like losing him all over again. "Esis! We can't risk getting lost down here!"

"Shh..." Vanessa held a finger to her lips.

I held my breath, and suddenly, I heard it. Esis' tiny claws scratched on the cave floor behind a large rock formation. I turned my headlamp off and took a cautious step forward so he couldn't hear me. Then I leapt. Esis squealed when he saw me, but I got ahold of his tail before he could get out of reach. I curled up beside the rock formation and hugged him tight to my chest.

"Bad Esis," I scolded. "You can't keep running off like that. I can't lose you!"

Esis pushed at my arm, like I was squeezing him too tightly, but I wasn't going to let go.

"It's this or you're going in my bag," I threatened.

Esis gave up, but he crossed his arms like he wasn't pleased.

Vanessa looked down at us with concern written all over her face as I turned my headlight back on. "We should get back. Everyone's probably wondering where we went."

"Agreed." I got to my feet. "You think we can find our way back, right?"

"I'm not sure—" she started, but she cut off, and her whole body froze.

My head snapped in the direction of her gaze. I noticed a shadow crossing our lights at the other side of the cavern. The figure went still and looked at us.

For a second, I was filled with hope. If it was one of our classmates, it meant we weren't far from the bat caves and didn't have to backtrack our way to meet up with the group. But I quickly realized I'd never seen the guy before. He was a few years older than me, with a strong build and blond hair. His eyes looked familiar, though I was sure I'd never seen him before. I just barely caught the outline of a gray fox with huge ears like Esis' standing at his feet before the guy quickly turned away and disappeared into another tunnel.

What the...?

"Hey!" I called, starting toward him.

What was some rando doing down here in the caves? Was he here to vandalize things, or could he help us get back to our group?

"Sophia." Vanessa reached out and grabbed my shoulder before I could make it far. "What are you doing?"

"I don't know," I admitted. "I'm suspicious."

"Which is exactly why we *shouldn't* chase a stranger into caves we're unfamiliar with," she argued. "That was creepy. Let's go, before he follows us."

I hesitated. There was something about the guy— about the mystery — that told me I had to follow.

"We can get back from here," Vanessa said. "But if we go any further, we could get lost. You heard Baine. These caves go all over Kinpago. It could take days before we find a way out."

She made a good point. I gave in. "Okay, let's go back."

We turned around, but I couldn't shake the irresistible curiosity pulling me back to that cavern.

Vanessa and I returned to the crystal cavern just as our group was passing through from the bat cave. Vanessa and I slipped behind them seamlessly, as if we'd never disappeared in the first place. My heart pounded, waiting for someone to yell at us for wandering off, but no one did. We reached the carriage and returned to the castle. My heart finally started to slow.

I thought we were off the hook, until Vanessa and I were climbing out of the carriage and placed our headlamps in Baine's box.

"How did you enjoy the field trip?" Baine asked.

"It was cool," I said. "I'm glad we went."

"Yes, indeed," he replied casually. "Next time, try to stay with the group. I've never lost a student before, and I don't intent to lose either of you."

My jaw dropped. So he *had* noticed.

"S-sorry," I stuttered. "My Familiar ran off."

Baine nodded once. "See to it that it doesn't happen again."

Vanessa took my elbow. "She'll make sure to have a leash next time."

I snickered at her. "It's true. I have one."

Esis grunted. He wasn't a fan.

"You should maybe consider that leash," Vanessa said as we started back toward the castle. "Esis could've been lost running off like that."

"Yeah," I said dryly.

The thing was, I was starting to wonder if Esis didn't just run off for kicks. Maybe he was trying to lead me somewhere.

Or to *someone*.

I WAS on my way to lunch later that day when Madame Doya stopped me in the hall. Naomi prowled at her side. Esis shot the lioness a glare.

"Sophia?" Doya called.

I turned to face her and was surprised to find that blazing heat that often surfaced when she was around wasn't there. Maybe it had something to do with her pleasant expression. I found it a little strange for a second, but it seemed genuine, so I relaxed.

"Yeah?" I said.

Doya strolled up to me. She wore one of her usual velvet dresses and had her red hair piled into a bun at the top of her head. She carried with her a stack of folders.

"I heard you went through with your Naming Ceremony," she said. It was almost impossible to read her tone.

I held my head up high. "I did. How did you know?"

"Your grandparents told me," she said.

I'd almost forgotten they were close to her. They seemed so different.

I suddenly felt a sting of betrayal. Was it normal to talk about other people's Naming Ceremonies? And to their professors, no less?

She noticed the fallen look on my face. "They didn't tell me your name, if that's what you're wondering. The right to tell someone that remains solely with you."

I relaxed a little, but I didn't know what to say to her. She wasn't insulting me, so I didn't know how to take her. "Um..."

"The reason I mention it is because I wanted to tell you..." Doya paused, like she was struggling with her words. It almost looked like she was choking on them. "I'm proud of you."

Now I was the one choking. Was Doya serious, or was this some sort of a joke?

Doya took a deep breath, like saying all this out loud was too hard for her. "Elementai often find strength in their spirit name. You've proven yourself to be capable without one. I'm intrigued to see how your magic performs now that you have your spirit name."

I blinked a few times, waiting for the punchline, but there wasn't one. Doya was being genuine for once.

So weird.

"Um... thank you," I said. "I'm excited to see what happens, too."

When Doya didn't say anything else, I turned back toward the cafeteria.

She hesitated, then stopped me again. "Sophia."

Here it comes.

"You have what it takes to be the chosen one," she said, but her tone came without feeling. "The magic, the power, the... courage."

Her gaze flickered down to my hands, and I instantly knew she'd seen what I'd done to pass the assignment with Haley. If she knew, why did she pass us? Had I— dare I say it— *impressed* Madame Doya?

"Thank you," I said honestly. "It means a lot to me."

"Yes. It should." Doya offered the slightest of smiles, then turned and strolled off in the opposite direction.

I stood there speechless as I watched her leave. "What... what just happened, buddy?"

Esis looked up to me and shrugged his shoulders.

"Sophia!" Imogen called behind me.

I turned to see her waving me toward the cafeteria. She was wearing a purple polka-dotted dress today, with her hair in a side ponytail that had beads hanging from it. Sassy swished her tail at Imogen's feet. Cade and Arabelle stood next to her, along with Jonah, Squeaks, and Liam.

My heart warmed at the sight of Liam. All the things we'd done that past weekend flashed through my mind. Maybe we could sneak away this afternoon.

"What's happening?" Imogen asked when I got close to them. "You look... shocked."

"Yeah," I said. "Doya was just being *nice* to me."

Jonah scoffed. "She would never. Must be a clone."

I laughed. "It would explain a lot."

"Shall we?" Liam said, turning toward the cafeteria.

We all started toward the doors, but I nearly lost my footing when he took my hand in his. I was so surprised, and my stomach did flips in my abdomen.

I looked up into his eyes, which were sparkling unlike I'd ever seen them. "Are you sure about this?"

Liam nodded. "I've never been more sure about anything in my life. I just got you back, *pawee*, and I want all of Kinpago to know."

Imogen and Jonah heard what Liam said and started whispering excitedly from in front of us. Esis clapped from where he was wrapped in my left arm. Cade gave a knowing smile, like we'd never fooled him in the first place.

I beamed and leaned into Liam. "They will."

We got our food and took a seat at one of the tables in the middle of the dining hall. Liam kept hold of my hand beneath the table. Esis sat on the table beside my plate, scarfing down donut holes like they were candy. Imogen and Cade sat close, and he shared a bite of cake off his plate. Mallory, Cade's ex, shot them daggers from across the room.

Jonah leaned forward and looked between us excitedly. "So, how are you going to do it?"

"Do what?" I asked.

Jonah rolled his eyes. "*Come out*, of course."

"Um... I don't know," I admitted. I'd thought of telling people a million times, but I never pictured how we'd actually do it. "I just kind of figured we'd let people assume."

"And deny us the pleasure of a spectacle?" Imogen asked, feigning offense.

Liam laughed. "It's not like we're going to get up on stage and sing Lady Gaga."

Liam shot Jonah an amused glance. It'd been how Jonah came out as gay.

Jonah huffed. "That was beautiful, and you know it."

"It was," Liam admitted reluctantly.

"So it's true?" Cade asked. "You two are together— officially?"

"Yes." I couldn't hold back my smile. It felt amazing to finally admit it to someone. "Did Imogen tell you?"

Cade blushed a little, then said, "No. I saw you two kissing by the stables last semester. It explains why you four always act so secretive."

We all exchanged a look, but I was the first to speak. "Um, right."

The truth was, our secrets were a lot bigger than Liam and me.

"Ew," a familiar voice sounded behind us. I turned to see Haley and Kelsey breezing by us with their Familiars at their sides. "It's the Loser Team."

Jonah shot out of his chair. "That's the Reject Team to you, bitch!"

He shouted it loud enough for the whole room to hear. Eyes began to turn our way. Cade bit his lower lip to keep from laughing.

Haley whirled around with her tray in hand. "What did you just call me?"

Jonah placed a hand on his hip. "You heard me, *biotch.*"

"Call me that one more time," Haley threatened.

I was half surprised her hair wasn't smoking yet. I was just sitting back enjoying the show. Imogen gave the same amused look.

"What are you going to do?" Jonah asked. "Throw a fireball at my head?"

Haley formed a fireball in her hand. Kelsey smirked from beside her.

"If I have to," Haley said.

"Try me," Jonah replied, gesturing for her to come at him.

I was on my feet in a split second, blocking Haley's path to Jonah. "Throw that fireball, and you'll regret it."

The cafeteria had gone silent, and all eyes were on us. Haley didn't seem to notice.

She chuckled, but her laughter quickly died down. She scowled at me. "I don't know why you hang out with these losers. It's like you're in love with them or something."

My glance involuntarily flickered to Liam. I couldn't let Haley threaten my friends.

"So what if I am?" I challenged her with a raised eyebrow.

Haley followed my gaze to Liam, then let out a loud, fake laugh. It was the only sound in the entire cafeteria. "Ancestors, you have to be kidding me." She clutched her stomach and doubled over in laughter. "You and Mitoh are back together? You fell for a Toaqua? And worse, a cripple?"

Liam shot to his feet beside me and clenched his fists, but I placed a hand on his chest to stop him.

"I've got this," I whispered.

I turned back to Haley. "Better a Toaqua cripple than a heartless bitch like you."

A chorus of *ooh's* traveled around the room. One guy even shouted, "Burn!"

"You wanna play that game?" Haley shoved her tray at Kelsey, who was already holding her own, but she took it anyway. Haley shot the fireball in her hand at my face.

On instinct, I threw my hands up and caught it. It seared my skin, but I held on because I knew Esis would heal me afterward. The pain was worth it for the utter look of shock on her face.

I squeezed my hands together, and the fireball shrank to nothing. Haley's face paled, and she looked speechless. But I wasn't done yet. I directed my fire across the space between us, and her hair went up in flames. She started screaming and spinning around in circles, trying to pat it out. Kelsey dropped their trays to the ground and tried to help her, while Anwara flew onto her head. Haley slapped them both away.

I let the fire burn enough to freak her out but not to hurt her. I pulled back on my magic. The whole cafeteria was bursting into a mix of cheers, laughter, and protests.

Haley looked relieved when the fire was gone, but her hair was at least half the length. Her hands curled into fists as she screamed at me. "Screw you, Sophia Henley. My mother will hear about this!"

She whirled around and ran from the cafeteria.

When I turned back to my friends, their jaws were practically on the floor. Esis' eyes had gone wide.

"Holy shit," Imogen said. "Sophia, the Elders are going to be pissed."

I shrugged. "I didn't hurt her. I think Doya would be proud that we're using our magic in a real-life setting."

Jonah laughed. "Not really what magic is supposed to be used for, but it was bad ass. Thanks, Sophia."

"Anytime," I said with a smile.

Liam gazed down at me with a smirk. I blushed.

"What?" I asked innocently.

"I thought you said you'd changed," he teased. "You said you let go of your anger."

I smiled. "We all know Haley's the exception. There's no excuse for the way she treats you guys."

Liam wrapped an arm around my waist and pulled me close. He whispered so only I could hear. "I have to admit, it was kind of hot. Turned me on a little."

I laughed. "Good to know. There's more where that came from."

Liam beamed down at me. "Ancestors, *pawee*. I love you."

"I love you, too," I whispered.

Then I stood on my toes and kissed him for all of Orenda Academy to see.

Liam

FIFTEEN

The dining hall was dead silent. Everyone's eyes were on us—and I mean *everyone*.

No turning back now. Shock was shown on every face. Where there wasn't surprise, there was absolute disgust. Nobody spoke. It was like a murder had been committed right in the middle of the dining hall, and everyone was unsure of what to do about it.

I took advantage of the silence and drew myself up. "That's right," I announced. "Sophia Henley and I are in a relationship. She's Koigni, I'm Toaqua, and we're together. Anyone who's got a problem with it should take it up with me."

"And me," Sophia said afterward, and she slipped her hand into mine, intertwining our fingers. People's eyes latched on to our locked hands.

"And me," Imogen said. She got up and planted herself in front of us. Cade stood faithfully at her side.

"Yeah," Jonah said. He cracked his knuckles loudly. "Anyone wanna argue?"

Nobody said a damn word. I decided it was time to make our out. Sophia and I left the hall holding hands, with Jonah and Imogen behind us. Squeaks and Sassy walked beside us, as if they were planning to protect us if anyone decided to pull anything. A couple of girls laughed and pointed, and Esis hissed at them from Sophia's arms.

One guy we passed called out, "Freaks! Fucking degenerates!" He went to go toward us, but Jonah raised a fist and Squeaks hissed at him. He sat right the fuck back down.

My heart was pounding when the doors to the dining hall closed behind us. I realized I'd been holding my breath, and let out a huge sigh. My chest was tight, and my stomach knotted in anxiety.

"So what now?" Sophia asked me breathlessly.

Jonah, Cade and Imogen looked between us, their brave faces falling. They were scared.

"I don't know," I confessed. We hadn't really come up with a plan—we just winged it. I think we were both afraid if we talked about coming out, it would never happen. "Wait for the Task Force to show up, I guess."

"Do you really think that they're going to come for us?" Sophia snuggled her nose into Esis' fur.

I nodded. "They're probably already on their way. Soph, if you want to leave now, we need to go."

She shook her head. "I'm not running. This is what's right."

"Then neither am I," I vowed.

"You guys can always hide in the Anichi dorms if you change your mind," Imogen suggested. "Jonah and I will be able to sneak you out of town."

"You guys are probably already being watched, since you stood up for us," I pointed out.

"Doesn't matter." Jonah shook his head. "We'll find a way. Come on. Let's go wait for the po-po."

We didn't have any other ideas except to go wait in the Commons. We took a couch by the window. People around us in the room whispered and shot us glances full of hatred, but Sophia and I hardly saw them. We were too busy watching the door, expecting the Task Force to come storming in any minute.

Ezra and Wyatt were there, playing ping-pong. Jonah went forward and whispered something to my brother under his breath. Ezra left the table and stood at the back of the couch, and along with Jonah, Cade and Imogen, formed a protective circle. Dyami, Squeaks, Sassy and Arabelle stood guard, and the gossip quieted, or at least moved to the other side of the room at the Familiars' sharp stares.

Minutes passed. It felt agonizing, even worse than it did when we were waiting to begin the Elemental Cup. The school was full of Task Force members who were here guarding the place due to the missing Familiars. They should've found us by now.

"I can't *wait* for them to walk in here," Ezra growled under his breath. He played with a ball of water in his hands, freezing it to ice and back to liquid again.

"Ez, don't fight when they get here. Let them take us," I said.

"Like hell," Ezra said.

"We have to show our side has reason," Sophia said. "If we react with violence, it's only going to end badly. We have to let the Elders know that we're doing this peacefully, and our relationship isn't going to hurt the tribe."

"I'm not going to let you guys become martyrs," Ezra said darkly. "I almost lost my brother. I'm not gonna risk losing him again."

"I'm not so sure the tribe has reason," Imogen spoke up. "Rationality might not work when there's unfair bias involved."

We quieted for a moment, and Jonah said, "Well, I hope the sex was worth it."

Several of us laughed, including Sophia.

Ezra smirked. "I'm sure it was. I heard the headboard hit the wall at least five times the other day. Liam was getting it."

"All right, guys, that's enough," I said, though I couldn't keep the grin off my face.

"Sophia, don't take this the wrong way, but *how* big is it?" Imogen asked, ignoring me. She held up her hands as if measuring something, and Cade snorted. Nervous snickers broke out around us.

Sophia grinned. "Let's just say it's not little."

"That big, huh?" Jonah teased.

"It's *legendary*," Sophia said. Everyone died with laughter, including me.

It was nice to be joking around at a time like this. I didn't know how much longer we'd have to laugh together.

As sunset fell and the Commons grew dark, we started to grow impatient with waiting. We'd even seen a few Task Force members walk past, but they didn't so much as peek their heads in the window before marching off. What was the deal?

"Shouldn't we have been arrested by now?" Sophia asked worryingly as the third patrol went by, and nothing.

"Yes, we should've," I told her. "That's what I'm concerned about."

It was weird to be bothered that we weren't yet in jail, but the fact that no legal action had been taken against us by the Elders was beyond weird. I thought that this would've been a done deal— they'd take us in immediately after we revealed ourselves, and we'd have a chance to make our case. The fact that we'd revealed our relationship and nothing had happened wasn't comforting.

It was like the Elders were waiting... biding their time.

Hours later, everyone looked exhausted. The Commons were empty by now, except for us. The other students had gotten bored of staring at Sophia and I like we were in a zoo. Jonah was snoring slightly on an armchair, and Ezra struggled to keep his eyes open as he leaned against Dyami. Squeaks and Sassy had curled up on the rug together, and Esis was sleeping inside of Sophia's hoodie.

Imogen had cuddled up in Cade's lap and was almost drifting off. He was the only one who didn't seem sleepy. He played with Imogen's hair and stared into the fireplace, his expression haunted, as if something was deeply bothering him.

Sophia and I were still awake. We were both silently freaking out, but at this point, it was like the tension had climbed to an unbearable level. Time kept on going and going, and nothing happened. I kept my arm around her as she nestled up to my side, tucking her legs underneath her.

"Should we... just go to sleep here?" Sophia wondered. "I don't feel safe going back to my dorm alone."

"I don't want you to. We shouldn't separate." I was supposed to be home right now— Mom was probably flipping out. But I worried that if Sophia and I parted that something bad would happen. I'd be safe at home, but there were probably plenty of prejudiced Koigni in Sophia's dorm that might try to break into her room and hurt her for being part of an interhouse relationship. But our friends had class tomorrow... and we did too, assuming that we weren't behind bars. Was it too much to hope for that the Elders were looking the other way, or simply didn't care about our relationship?

Around midnight, the doors opened. Our heads turned— I was

shocked to see my dad striding toward us, Tatum following. The grizzly bear had his head low and his teeth bared, eyes scanning the room as if looking out for any attackers that might spring out of the shadows.

"The rest of you must leave. Sophia and Liam will be coming with me," Dad told the group as he approached. "Ezra, get your sister and head home."

Ezra nodded and hurried off. Cade stepped in front of Sophia and said, "We can't just let you take them in like this."

"I'm not taking them in. I'm protecting them," Dad said firmly. "If the rest of you don't want to be in any more trouble than what's already been started. You need to move. Now."

Nobody else questioned him. Jonah and Imogen gave us lonely waves as they and their Familiars followed Cade and Arabelle out. Once the doors were closed, Dad turned toward us. He was all business.

"You two will be staying with us until all of this is over. Yes, Sophia, you too," Dad said when he noticed her stunned expression. "The dorms at Orenda Academy aren't safe for you presently. We need both of you in a place where we can be certain you won't be attacked."

"Dad... what do you mean by, *until all of this is over?*" I asked.

Dad stared at me for a moment. He sighed, and reached into his pocket. "I was hoping I wouldn't have to give these to you until later."

He handed Sophia and I two brown envelopes. We opened them slowly— my insides turned to water with each word I read.

Liam Mitoh,

You are hereby summoned by the Elders for committing high treason of willfully participating in an intertribal relationship. Such actions are forbidden by tribal law and are especially heinous, punishable by up to life in prison or (if the Elders shall find sufficient concern) the penalty of death.

Your trial date is December 23. Please arrive to the Intertribal Court no later than 8 a.m.

Sincerely,

The Elder Council

My legs were gonna collapse from underneath me. A cold, clammy feeling, like one of death, was crawling over me slowly and consuming me whole. I was gonna puke. I didn't know how we'd ever get out of this. It felt like a mountain had just crashed on me. Reality came upon me suddenly and quickly. This was real. The Elders weren't playing around.

I'd known all this already, but this letter made it all too real. We could go to jail for life, not just a few years. Worse, we could be killed. This was a severe crime we were being accused of.

The worst part of it all was Sophia and I could be torn away from each other. And we hadn't even done anything wrong.

Sophia's letter was identical to mine— except in hers, it had a note about Esis being removed from her if we lost. Her face had gone pale white, and she was shaking. Esis patted her cheek and had a determined look on his face, like he'd be damned if he allowed anyone to take him away.

Our trial date was set for the end of December. That was two months away. We had to sit and wait to know what our fate would be for *two whole months?*

"I was able to get you both a trial, with Madame Doya's help," Dad said as he glanced to both of our faces. "It's more than most interhouse couples receive. The two of you have caused quite a stir with the Elders."

I swallowed past the lump in my throat. "Dad, you can't let anything happen to us."

"I'll do everything in my power to make sure the two of you win this case," he said firmly. "But for now, let's move. It's not safe for us to talk in the open."

He waved a hand, and Sophia and I followed. He moved so quickly through the halls that Sophia and I practically had to jog to keep up.

"The Elders need time to deliberate before the case begins. You'll still be allowed to attend classes in the meantime, and Sophia will be able to keep Esis, for now," Dad said as we walked. "I've organized for a flying carriage to take the two of you back and forth to school on weekdays. Task Force members have been instructed not to harm you before the trial proceeds."

We stopped in front of the Koigni dorms, and Dad looked to Sophia. "Grab what you need, Miss Henley, and quickly. It's going to be a long stay for you."

Sophia nodded and headed inside. Dad and I were left waiting outside in the quiet. "Dad... why are you doing this?" I dared to ask.

He made a skeptical noise. "You're asking why I need to protect my eldest son?"

"But you don't agree with our relationship," I protested.

"It doesn't matter if I don't agree. You two have obviously made your decision, and I have to stand by you on it," Dad said.

"That's not where you stood last semester," I said slowly.

"Last semester was a mistake I fully regret," Dad stated. "It was wrong to send you to kill Sophia. I never should've put you up to that. It's on my shoulders that your mother and I nearly lost you."

"No, Dad, it's not," I said gently. I didn't want him thinking my suicide attempt was on him.

"Yes, it is. I pushed you too hard. I asked you to do something no father should ever think to ask," he insisted. "I knew you loved Sophia from the beginning. I didn't have to guess."

He sighed. "I just wish you two had handled the situation better. We've got a full-scale crisis on our hands."

"People had to know, Dad. We got tired of hiding," I told him. "Sophia and I just got back together, and one of our conditions was going public. We'd been broken up for a long time."

"I knew that. Something had changed in you after Ancestors' Day," Dad said, and Tatum rumbled in agreement. "I didn't realize how important she was to you until then... until I saw the hope go out of you. I want to see my son happy again. Even if it means sacrificing tradition."

A bit of warmth grew inside of me, warding off the coldness. I ran a hand over Tatum's head. "I forgive you, Dad," I said. "For everything."

Dad gave me a grim smile. Sophia emerged from the Koigni dorms, carrying a small suitcase and her book bag.

"Okay. I've got everything I need," she said.

"Good to go, *pawee?*" I asked. She nodded.

Dad noticed I'd called her that, but besides a side glance, he didn't say anything. He just gestured for us to move. We hustled to a carriage outside, one pulled by a pegasus that flew us all the way back to my house.

Mom had been pacing by the door. She looked worried for the first time since I could remember— Mom was usually the rock of the family. If she wavered, it was definitely a sign of a huge issue.

When we came through the entryway, she rushed toward us. She gave me a kiss on my cheek and brushed a hand over Sophia's hair. "I was so worried about you two." Thin lines had creased around her eyes in concern.

"Haloke, we need to talk," Dad said. His tone was serious. He took her hand and jerked his head toward his office. Mom nodded, then glanced back at us.

"You can stay in Liam's room, Sophia. Liwanu and I don't mind," Mom said as she followed Dad into the next room. I heard the lock click as the door shut behind them.

Ezra and Maddie's low voices came from somewhere down the hall. It sounded like a serious conversation, one we shouldn't interrupt.

"It's late. We should get some sleep," I told Sophia.

She barely reacted to my words. She was still scared— her letter was crunched up in one hand that wasn't holding the suitcase.

I took the suitcase and the letter from her. When we got up to my room, I shoved both of the letters in my dresser— as if putting them away meant that the Elders couldn't harm us.

Sophia sat on my bed with her head in her hands. Esis rubbed her lower back, trying to get her to calm down.

"Maybe we *should've* ran away," Sophia said in a weak voice, the sound muffled.

I shook my head and sat beside her. "No. I'm tired of running. The tribe has kicked me around for the past two years. It's time I started fighting back."

She lifted her gaze. "And if we lose?"

My insides curled inward, and I said, "We won't."

Sophia got up. She opened her suitcase and started pulling clothes out. "Where should I put these?"

"I have an empty drawer at the bottom you can use." I pointed, and Sophia started putting her things away. When her suitcase was empty, she took off her day clothes and tossed them to the floor. I watched her rummage for pajamas in just her underwear, no bra included, and felt myself getting a hard-on. It was weird— being on the verge of being put to death for loving Sophia just made her ten times hotter to me. If the Elders thought making a relationship forbidden would be any deterrent, they were dead wrong.

I tossed off my shirt and jeans and climbed into bed in just my boxers. Sophia slipped on a loose, short nightgown, turned off the light and slid in beside me. Esis became a ball on the pillow next to her head and put his tail over his nose to sleep. I put an arm around her, and she nestled her head up against my chest. Our legs tangled together. We lay there in the dark, just breathing.

After a few moments, she giggled unexpectedly.

"What is it?" I asked.

She snickered. "I have a drawer of things at your place."

"Gee, we're moving fast," I said sarcastically.

"I can't believe your parents are letting us room together," she said excitedly. "I mean, they know we're gonna do stuff, right?"

I chuckled. "We need to be careful. I don't think my parents would be super impressed if they came in here and saw us banging."

"Then we need to learn how to do ninja sex," she whispered. "And maybe get rid of the headboard."

I laughed lowly. "Yeah, like they wouldn't notice that."

She giggled again and let out a deep sigh. Soon, Sophia quieted. I heard the sound of her soft breathing, accompanied by Esis' snores. I stroked her hair and let my fingertips roam up and down her body so she could rest peacefully.

I couldn't. I was too pent up, too worried about what would happen in December. It felt like I had a ticking time bomb over my head that was about to go off any minute. I'd be freaking out right now if Sophia's body wasn't firmly pressed against mine, acting as an anchor to sanity.

The ancestors have a plan. Yeah, well, how was that plan working out now?

Well, at least this whole situation had one big perk. I got to fall asleep next to Sophia every evening, and she'd be there in the morning when I woke up. It was like a dream in the middle of one big nightmare. The first thing I'd see was her big brown eyes.

I just hoped it wouldn't be ripped away from us.

❧

THE NEXT MORNING, Sophia and I were all over the news.

Every paper, every Hawkei news outlet, had photos of us. I wasn't sure how they'd gotten them, but it was clear that reporters had pulled an all-nighter digging up any information they could find on Sophia and I, along with our relationship.

Some of the shit was insane. Most of it was made up, and the stuff that was accurate was grossly exaggerated. Someone had found an old photo of me riding my bike, and now I was apparently the leader of some underground Toaqua biker gang who was responsible for half the crimes being committed in Kinpago.

Sophia had it worse than I did. The news claimed that she was some outsider temptress who'd seduced me into giving up traditional Hawkei values so we could perform blood sacrifices in the wilderness together. They made it sound like I was some victim, and she was a wicked witch who'd enchanted me with a love potion to act against my own self-interest.

It got worse from there. A couple of reporters accused Sophia and I of trying to overthrow the Elders. One paper even reported that Sophia and I had an illegitimate baby that we'd given to wild dragons to raise.

It would've been funny if our lives weren't on the line. I hoped the Elders weren't stupid enough to be influenced by propagandist garbage, but who knew.

Reporters and paparazzi were waiting outside the school when we arrived. They rushed forward with microphones and cameras, trying to get an interview as we stepped out of the carriage. I put my arm around Sophia, and we rushed down the path to the safety of Orenda's campus. We kept our heads down, but they got a few shots of us before we were able to get into the gardens.

The reporters couldn't follow us onto school grounds, but what was waiting inside was almost worse.

Stares. Some from strangers, some from people we knew. So many people sneered at us, or turned away with revulsion when they saw us coming. They truly thought we were repulsive.

My shoulders sank in relief when we saw Jonah and Imogen waiting for us in the Great Hall. Imogen was busy flipping through a magazine, and Jonah eyed it over her shoulder. Sassy wound around Imogen's ankles, while Squeaks looked at the magazine with a careful eye as if she could read it, too.

Imogen saw us coming and snapped the magazine shut. She quickly stuffed it in her bag. "Hey, guys. What's going on?"

I wasn't fooled by her pleasant tone. Neither was Sophia. "What does that one say?" Sophia asked blandly, pointing to the end of the magazine sticking out of the bag.

Imogen's face fell. "Nothing. Nothing important."

"You guys are the story of the century," Jonah said. "I'd almost be jealous if it wasn't so serious."

Raised voices came from down the hallway. This time of morning, there weren't very many students milling around. Most classes didn't start until nine. It sounded like the voices were coming from the entrance of Head Dean Alric's tower.

Alric came out of the entrance of the tower, holding the door open. "I understand your concern, Jakob, but Professor Perot and I have the situation handled. Good day to you, sir."

An incredibly deep voice responded. "You think you can stop what's coming, Caspian, but I can assure you things are only going to get worse. You know where to find me."

A man stepped out from the tower. He was huge— six foot seven, with a strong jaw and thick arms corded with muscle. He had long blond hair that fell across his shoulders, and a beard trimmed short around his face. He wore a long black cloak that hung off his broad shoulders. I was surprised the floor didn't shake when he walked. He was older than me by at least five years or more.

The guy was bigger than Jonah. No, I really mean it. *Bigger than Jonah.* He had to be the tallest guy I'd ever seen.

Following him was a giant hippogriff, his feathers dark gray in color. The hippogriff was huge, eighteen hands or more, and towered over Alric as he emerged from the tower. Alric quickly retreated, and the stranger used Air magic to blow the door shut behind him.

"Oh my gosh, what hot stuff!" Imogen squeaked. "And he's coming this way!"

Sophia, Imogen and I pressed ourselves to the wall to make room, but Squeaks and Jonah stood in the middle of the hall like a couple of deer in headlights. Squeaks' eyes were on the hippogriff. The male glanced her way, and Squeaks fluttered her eyelashes. He observed her for a minute before planting his gaze forward.

The stranger seemed to be deep in thought. Jonah was acting too stunned to move, feet glued to the floor. They ended up bumping into each other. Jonah stumbled, but the stranger caught him before he could make a total face plant on the floor.

"Whoops," the stranger said. He smiled. "Sorry there, little guy."

He patted Jonah on the chest, gave him a wink, then walked away. The stranger turned the corner, vanishing with his massive hippogriff.

Jonah looked like he'd been hit by a train. His mouth hung open as he stared at the spot where the man had gone, dazed.

"Earth to Jonah!" Imogen yelled, and she snapped her fingers in front of his face. "Did you even *see* that guy flirting with you? He was a total hottie!"

"Huh?" Jonah was still dazed. He shook his head, as if he was coming out of a dream. It was like he couldn't comprehend English.

"Go after him and get his number!" Imogen insisted. "I'm sure he'll call you. He looked like he liked you."

"What? No," Jonah said, and he blushed. "He wouldn't give it to me, anyhow. Besides, I have a boyfriend."

I'd never seen Jonah get shy about talking to guys before. This was new. Squeaks made a clipping sound with her beak. She'd liked that hippogriff that was on the menu, if her behavior was any indication.

"Renar's a shit boyfriend. You need to upgrade," Imogen said.

Jonah seemed bothered. His forehead was creased, and his eyes were puzzled. "I've gotta get to Psychology, guys. See ya."

Jonah hurried off. Squeaks followed with a bit of a spring in her step. Imogen did a little dance. "Did you guys see that? Jonah has eyes for somebody other than his shithead BF!"

"Yeah," I responded, watching as Jonah vanished into Dean Alizeh's classroom. "We need to go chase that guy down and beg him to take Jonah out on a date."

"He's a little old," Sophia said disapprovingly. "He looks thirty."

I scoffed. "I don't care if the dude is eighty-five, if it gets Jonah away from Renar."

"What do you think he and Alric were talking about?" Imogen asked. "Sounded serious."

"I'm not sure," I mused. "Alric said he and Perot had it handled, so that must mean it's got something to do with the sick Familiars. But if this guy is offering to help, I don't know why Alric would be turning him away. He and Perot aren't making any process on finding a cure."

"Perhaps he's up to no good," Sophia suggested. "Alric knows where there's trouble, and I've never seen that guy around school before."

"Me neither," I said. It was weird. Someone like that I'd remember.

Imogen shrugged. "Well, I hope he shows up again. He and Jonah would be a cute couple."

Imogen bounced off to Magical Plants with Sassy strutting at her heels. It was getting late— I had to get Sophia to class.

Sophia and I had resolved to walk to as many classes together as we could, as it would be safer, and people would be less likely to confront us if we showed a united front. I didn't have class until that afternoon, but Sophia had Hawkei Legends right away at eight. We started walking down that way, only to be stopped by none other than Professor Baine.

He wore an anxious expression. He glanced down at our joined hands before saying, "Sophia. Liam. May I talk to you both for a moment?"

Great. A lecture. I resisted rolling my eyes as Baine led us behind a sprite statue that was right next to Doya's classroom. He fiddled with his hands nervously before he spat out, "You two don't understand what you're getting into."

I raised my eyebrow. "Really? Because we just got a letter yesterday telling us that we're being put on trial for being together."

"Yeah, and we're still here, *together*," Sophia said firmly. "So if you think we don't know the consequences, you're wrong."

Baine shook his head. "No. You truly don't. As your mentor, I need you both to hear me. This isn't going to work out in your favor. You both need to do what's best. You two need to end this and go to the Elders, to beg for mercy. If you're fortunate, your sentence will be reduced, and you'll be able to keep your lives."

"And never be able to be together again?" Sophia asked. "No way."

Esis made a chittering sound of agreement. Baine's expression grew hollow and thin.

"Listen. Don't go to court. Don't fight this. Take a deal," Baine pleaded with us. "Even if this *was* legal, it'd only end in disaster. Toaqua and Koigni don't work together. They're too different. You're both going to get broken hearts."

I got so tired of hearing that crap. It'd been repeated over and over to me and shoved down my throat since I was born, and I didn't believe a word of it. "It's our decision to make," I told Baine firmly. "So let us make it."

"What kind of children would you raise? A half-breed child could never be strong. It probably wouldn't be able to wield magic. They wouldn't survive in this society," Baine insisted.

Sophia's face got really red. "If Liam and I decide to have children, that's none of your damn business."

Damn, Sophia. She had a mama bear complex coming out, and she didn't even have kids yet.

Baine blushed, embarrassed, and he turned to me instead. Words came tumbling out of his mouth. "Liam, don't go through with this. I know you're happy *now*, but this type of thing can't last. One day, everything will be fine, the next thing you know, she'll be threatening to burn your house down."

"*Excuse me?*" Sophia asked, outraged.

"No offense to you, Sophia, I don't mean it like that," Baine rushed to say. "But I don't wish to see either of you get hurt, and it looks like it's heading that way. Please ask the Elders for forgiveness. Before they decide to take your lives."

Sophia's hand was so tight in mine, it was restricting circulation. She was pissed. I decided to end things before they could get worse. "We're not asking for forgiveness, because we didn't do anything wrong. That's the end of it," I said.

"See you in class, Professor," Sophia finished. She dragged me off before Baine could stop us.

"He's unbelievable," Sophia muttered under her breath. People cleared out of the way as we came down the hallway, shooting to the other side— like they couldn't stand to be near us.

"He's just looking out for us, even though he's wrong," I told her. "He doesn't want to see us get the death penalty."

Sophia stopped in front of the classroom that led to Hawkei Legends. She dropped my hand, and said, "Do you think we will?"

I stared at her. "I don't know. But after what I've been through the past few months, I think death's preferable to losing you again."

Her face softened. "We aren't going to die, Liam. We're going to win. Somehow, someway, we'll change the law."

She rose up on her toes to give me a goodbye kiss, then ran inside the classroom. Having her out of my sight made a sickening feeling churn in my gut.

I just got her back, and we could be separated all over again. Worst part about it was, there was nothing we could do right now. The only option we had was to sit around and wait for the trial to be over, to know for sure if the Elders would let us be together.

But we were together now, and I wanted to cherish that. I spun on my heels and left. If we truly were running on borrowed time, we had to make these last few months count.

ON HALLOWEEN, I got out of Hawkei Home Ec. early and decided to wait for Sophia outside of her Intro to Child Development class. It was held in a separate building from the school, but still attached to campus. It was a daycare where professors and students who were parents could leave their kids five and under for the day while they were in class.

I passed Mia on the way out of the castle. She avoided my eyes and kept her gaze down. Another bruise had appeared on her cheek, though she'd covered it with makeup. We'd stopped talking a couple of weeks ago, but it wasn't my choice. She wasn't following my advice to leave Micah, and I felt powerless. At this point, I felt like there was nothing more I could do.

The door to the daycare was open when I walked inside of it. Sophia's class should've been over, so I took a chance to step inside. It looked like any other daycare would, except that along with kids, there were also a ton of baby magical creatures running about. Tiny griffins, little dragons, unicorn foals and newborn fawns played alongside the infants and toddlers. A baby calf chased after a lion cub with leaves for fur, and a little boy painted the fur on a kitten with a watercolor paint set. It was all so adorably cute— along with loud and chaotic.

Sophia had fallen in the middle of the room, on an alphabet foam mat under a pile of kids, both Elementai and Familiar. She laughed as they tugged on her clothes and sat on top of her.

She was absolutely glowing. You could tell that this was her calling. My heart swelled watching her play with them.

Esis had taken a place in the corner of the room on top of a small table. He was showing a picture book to a group of toddlers who'd formed a circle around him. A baby wyvern let out a puff of smoke and accidentally set the book on fire. Esis rushed to put it out.

Sophia sat up and put a little boy on her lap. She saw me coming and immediately brightened up.

"You look like you have your hands full," I said. She had at least six kids on her— two girls, one boy, a phoenix hatchling, a newborn chimera, and a feline-looking creature with purple fur and big ears.

"Miss Sophia, who's that *guy*?" A little boy with black hair wrinkled his nose at me.

Sophia brushed her hair back and said, "That's Mister Liam. He's my boyfriend."

"You have a boyfriend? *Ew*," the boy said. "Do you kiss and stuff?"

"Sometimes." Sophia smiled. The boy stuck out his tongue, like he was grossed out.

"Are you getting married? Will you have a Koigni wedding?" one of the girls asked.

Sophia hesitated. "Oh... um... Camila, he's not Koigni," Sophia said slowly, and she looked up at me. "He's Toaqua."

None of the kids blinked an eye. "Oh, okay," Camila said, and she shrugged. "How old is he?"

Sophia laughed. "He's twenty-two, and I'm nineteen."

"You're so *old*!" the little boy burst. "Like my grandma!"

She poked him in the stomach. "*You're* old, Josiah."

"Yep. I'm five," Josiah said, very seriously.

The back door opened, and a tall, dark-skinned woman entered the room. I knew her as Professor Ambika— the head of the Child Development program.

"Everyone to the playground!" she announced. "It's recess!"

The kids scattered toward the door. Professor Ambika gave us a glare as she herded the kids outside, and shut the door with a snap. Esis put the book down and came running toward us, jumping onto Sophia's shoulder.

She laughed. "You know, when I signed up for this class, I knew I was going to be watching kids, but I didn't know I'd be babysitting baby Familiars, too."

"They kind of go hand in hand," I said.

I extended a hand to lift her up. She brushed off her clothes, which looked like they were covered in apple juice stains, graham cracker crumbs, and acrylic paint.

"It was kind of nice they didn't judge us," she said. "You know, for being interhouse."

"Kids don't care about that type of shit," I said. "They don't know hatred unless someone teaches it to them."

I tried to steer the conversation to more positive matters. "Anyway... I thought we could go out on a date tonight. You know, just the two of us."

Her eyes sparked. "A date, huh?"

"Yeah. Haven't had one of those in a long time, have we?" I teased.

Sophia looked down at her ruined clothes and said, "Can we run to your house real quick so I can change? I smell like babies."

"Smelling like babies isn't a bad thing," I said, and I nudged her. "But sure."

I noticed Professor Ambika watching us through the window. I put my arm around Sophia's hips and guided her outside. "How's that class going, anyway?" I asked, remembering the snotty glare Ambika had given us.

She frowned. "I don't know. A bunch of parents took their kids out of the program after they found out I was helping to teach. They're worried about me influencing their kids to be interhouse."

"Oh." That wasn't good. No wonder Ambika wasn't exactly warm toward us.

She huffed, and Esis copied her. "I don't get what the big deal is. Kids can't *catch the interhouse* just like they can't *catch the gay*. And even if they could, what's the big deal? Aren't we supposed to be encouraging kids to be who they are?"

She shrugged. "Anyway, I think I'm gonna get an A. I've changed more diapers than anyone else in that class, and Professor Ambika is impressed by that. At least I'm not getting kicked out of the program. I don't think I could choose a major besides Child Development."

"You'll be fine," I told her. We spoke no more about it on the carriage ride home. I wanted our date to be a break from all the bad stuff, so I didn't ask any more questions.

When Sophia came out of my bathroom, she was wearing skinny jeans that hugged her ass and a thick sweater underneath a tan leather jacket. She was holding something behind her back.

"Before we head out, I kinda have a surprise for you," Sophia said. She brought her hand around, holding a basket that was packed to the brim with all kinds of items.

"What's all of this?" I sat on the bed, and Sophia placed the basket on my lap. It was really heavy.

"I've never really gotten you anything as a gift. So I wanted to change that," she said. "I went to town while you were in class the other day and got a bunch of stuff. Imogen helped me pick some things out. I couldn't just get you one thing."

She sat next to me and started pointing. "I found you new headphones— the ones I caught you looking at a while back. There are some mineral salts and menthol oils for baths in there, and this pain relief lotion I found. Your meds are also *really* disorganized, so I got a box for that, along with some ibuprofen if you need it. There's this mini-sleep machine I got that makes noise— you toss and turn a lot, so I figured it could help. Also, I bought that new book you've been wanting— along with a book light, so you can stop keeping me up by leaving the lamp on while you read."

She snickered before she continued. "There's a heating pad for your muscles when they get sore, and a journal for you to start tracking your symptoms. I got you wrists and knee braces, to help your joints, too. Watch it, the basket is kind of heavy— there's a weighted blanket at the bottom, for your anxiety, along with a mini-humidifier to help you breathe. Oh, and I got us a subscription package for streaming movies, so if you don't feel well we can just chill together instead of going out."

She reached in the basket. "And I couldn't resist this little guy— he was too cute. But he's kinda more for me." Sophia held up a stuffed wolf by her face and smiled. "Isn't he adorable?"

I was stunned. Nobody had ever gotten me a gift like this before. It was so incredibly thoughtful. It was like Sophia had studied me and figured out everything that bothered me, so she could help with what I really needed.

Her face fell at my lack of a reaction. "You don't like it? Oh my gosh, I'm so sorry."

I put the basket aside and wrapped her in a tight hug. "I *love* it," I told her. "It's absolutely perfect for me."

Her body sagged in relief. "I'm really happy to hear that. I wanted to give you something that showed I care."

"I know you care." I ran my thumb over the corner of her mouth. "And it was incredibly thoughtful. Thank you."

I put the gift basket on my dresser and rummaged in my pocket. "Now it's my turn. I can't wait for you to see what I have planned."

I brought out a blindfold and put it around her eyes, tying it behind her head.

She giggled. "Where are you taking me?"

"You'll find out." I took her by the hand and carefully led her down-stairs, making sure to grab her purse. Esis launched himself onto my shoulder and sat there, making excited noises. We took the boat to the mainland, and I guided her through the woods by her shoulders.

"I'm starting to think you're kidnapping me," she joked as we walked up a hill.

"You're almost there," I said. When we got to the top, I untied the blindfold and said, "Okay. Now you can open your eyes."

Sophia did, and she gasped with delight. I'd taken her to the top of a cliffside that overlooked the ocean and the setting sun beyond. There was a large tree on the cliff that'd been decorated with tiny glowing lanterns. From the trees branches hung glass bottles with rolled up messages inside. Underneath the tree was a small round table, covered with a white table cloth, along with two chairs and a couple of candles. A bottle of wine sat in a bucket of ice that I'd chilled with my Water magic to stay cold, and two glasses stood next to it.

"Liam. How long did this take you?" Sophia asked as she

approached the tree, looking up in wonder. Esis jumped from my shoulder and started climbing the tree, scaling up its height.

"All morning," I said. "Take a look at the bottles."

Sophia reached up, took a bottle down from a branch, and uncorked it. "Reason number twelve why I love you— the way you smile when you catch me staring."

She reached up and grabbed another bottle, placing the first on the table. "Reason number eight why I love you— the sound of your laugh when you tell a corny joke."

Sophia gazed up at the tree with an open mouth. "Are all of these filled with reasons why you love me?"

"Every one," I said.

"There are dozens of bottles here!" she said, and her grin widened. She retrieved another bottle and read, "Reason number thirty-five why I love you— the way you dance like no one is watching."

"There were a lot of reasons. I pretty much ran out of paper," I confessed. "And that's not all." I reached underneath the table and pulled out a picnic basket, setting it on the table. "I made us dinner."

"This is all so amazing." Sophia put the bottles down and wrapped her arms around my waist. "I can't believe you did all this for me."

"Believe it. You deserve it," I told her, and I kissed her.

Sophia continued reading bottles while I got dinner set up. I set out pasta salad, chicken pesto, antipasto skewers, spring rolls, and strawberries for dessert. The ice that I'd surrounded the basket with was still cold, so everything had stayed fresh.

Sophia gathered the rest of the bottles from the tree and set them beside her chair on the ground. She sat down at the table while I poured the wine, and she asked playfully, "I thought we agreed not to drink around each other after last time?"

"Well, since I took your virginity last week, I say that rule's out the window. We can get as drunk as we want now and fuck later," I said.

She giggled. "Is *fucking* on the list for tonight?"

"If you want it to be," I said coyly.

She nudged my foot underneath the table and said, "We'll see."

We started eating. Sophia read notes from bottles in-between bites, and we worked through the wine pretty quickly. Both of us were buzzed, but the food helped offset some of the alcohol.

"You didn't tell me you could cook. This is delicious," Sophia said. "A man who can make food is like, a million times hotter than anything else in the world."

"My mom helped me a lot, but thanks," I said. "I don't like eating out, so I know how to make my own food."

Sophia read another note. "Reason sixty-eight why I love you— the noises you make when I'm kissing you."

She uncorked another bottle and read the note inside. "Reason number twenty-nine why I love you— the way you feel when I'm inside you."

She gave me a sultry look. I chuckled.

"Okay, some of them are dirty," I confessed. "You know I couldn't resist throwing a few of those in there."

She laughed, before slowly, a frown overtook her expression. Something was on her mind.

"What's wrong?" I asked.

Sophia looked down at her plate. "I have a confession to make. After we broke up, I was really upset. And so angry. I went back to the waterfall and burned our initials off of our tree. I hope you can forgive me for it."

"Don't worry about it. I saw that, and already took care of it." A grin played around my lips.

"Took care of it? How?" She looked confused.

I smirked. "While you were in class the other day, I used my Water magic to carve our initials into one of the rocks by the waterfall. Can't burn that. It's there forever now."

Sophia laughed. "Guess we *have* to be permanent, then."

"Guess so." The mood had definitely shifted. We'd finished up dinner, and the notes were winding down. It was obvious that there was only one thing on both of our minds, and we wanted to get to it.

Sophia was reading the last of the bottles. "Reason number one— you'll always, always, *always* be my *pawee.*"

"Always," I said. Her eyes were shimmering. She rolled up the note, then put the pile of them into her purse for safe-keeping.

Night had fallen, and it had gotten cold. Sophia shivered, and I said, "We should go back home. Just leave the stuff here. I'll come back and get it all later."

Esis came running down the tree when Sophia called for him. We both were a little tipsy. We staggered down the hill, but Sophia tripped. I reached out to catch her and ended up falling over, too. We rolled down the hill with Esis chasing after us, making loud squeaking noises.

We landed in a giant mud puddle that was at the bottom of the hill. Mud and water went everywhere as we splashed into it. Esis screeched to a halt before he could get covered in muck. Sophia and I, though, were soaked.

"Ew!" Sophia cried.

I laughed and grabbed her. I pulled her on top of me and started kissing her, not paying attention to the fact that we were covered in mud. She kissed me back. I felt her brush mud across my forehead as she swept my hair back.

She pulled her mouth away from mine with a giggle. "We're filthy."

"The hunting cabin isn't far," I told her. "We should clean up before we go home. Don't want my parents thinking we had sex in the mud."

Sophia laughed. She got to her feet and pulled me up so we could make our way to the cabin. Once we were inside, Esis turned on the TV, then sat on the living room couch, eating chips that he'd scavenged from the kitchen.

I started up the shower so the water could get warm. Sophia followed me to the laundry room, and slowly, we stripped off our mud-soaked clothes and put them in the washer.

We were completely naked, but still covered in muck. I took the mud that was all over her shoulders and smeared it across her breasts. I laughed.

"You're such a little kid." Sophia smiled and rolled her eyes. She dragged me to the shower. We stepped in, and she circled her arms around my lower back as she pulled me underneath the shower's stream.

The dirt slicked off of us, but we still needed to wash up. It was pretty clear the last thing on our minds was getting clean, though. As the water rolled down, we started kissing. My tongue moved around hers, and she moaned as her hands moved downward, grabbing my ass and rubbing herself against my dick.

My hands came up to massage her breasts, and her back hit the ceramic wall. I rolled her nipples between my thumb and forefinger as I continued moving my lips against her mouth. I trailed my mouth downward, sucking at her neck and down her shoulders.

"Leave a mark," she gasped. "I want everyone to see I belong to you."

I gave a throaty laugh. "I'm not gonna leave a giant hickey on your neck."

"Somewhere else, then," she pleaded.

I obliged. I leaned down and placed my mouth over the top part of her breast and started sucking. Sophia moaned in a combination of desire, pleasure and pain. My left hand went downward, and I started rubbing her. My fingers dipped in and out of her, and her hips moved in circles over my hand as she pleaded for more.

I finally pulled away. There was a large dark spot already forming, at least two inches across.

"Shit, that's gonna be huge," I said. "Don't wear any low cut shirts."

"Maybe I will," she whispered. Her hands started rubbing up and down the length of my dick, and my mind went completely blank. I could only hear the sound of water rushing and her soft breathing as she jerked me at a steady pace. She sat on the edge of the tub, then her hands grabbed my ass as she pulled me forward. Her mouth slid over me in one quick movement before her head started bobbing.

Fuck, fuck, fuck. This was incredible. Her mouth was warm and slick. I fisted my hands in her wet hair as she continued to make love to my dick. She took a deep breath and relaxed to let it in as far as it could go, and I felt my knees go weak. I whispered her name, and she started moving faster. Complete bliss spread all over my body. Colors merged together, and the rest of the world went numb. It felt like I was floating.

I was about to come, so I forced myself to pull out of her mouth. I didn't want to end things just yet. "My turn." I got her up off the edge of the tub and dragged her back underneath the water. I got to my knees and started licking the sweetest parts of her. She moaned, and I reached up to palm her breasts. My mouth focused on her peak, and I inserted two fingers inside of her. I continued my assault on her until she came, and as she did, I stood up and turned her around.

"I've got to be in you," I said breathlessly.

Sophia definitely made no complaint. She leaned forward, bracing her hands against the shower wall, and I inserted her from behind. Both of us gasped at the same time. I started thrusting, my eyes watching

Sophia's ass as it bounced, and the spread of her beautiful back, her wet hair scattered across her shoulders. I noticed her daisy tattoo glistening under the spray of the water, and it made me go crazy. I thought that it was *so hot*.

"Harder," Sophia breathed, and I picked up the pace.

My thrusts became hard and fast. My body started to shake. Sophia spiraled into an orgasm, and another one after that. I lost all control and exploded, only able to concentrate on the feel of Sophia wrapped around me.

The steam and exhilaration made it hard for both of us to breathe. Sophia turned around and fell into my arms. We stood underneath the shower's stream for a moment, heaving.

Eventually, Sophia brought her head off my chest and smiled. "Guess fucking was on the list, huh?"

"That it was," I confirmed. I gave her another quick kiss, because I couldn't resist, before I reached for the soap. "Though I think we'd better get cleaned up. Before my parents start wondering where the hell we are."

"Probably a good idea," Sophia confirmed. She turned around and turned up the heat. I yelped as the water hit my arm, and leapt back to a safer part of the shower.

"Holy shit, Sophia, that's hot!" I shouted.

"I like warm showers," she said. Her body turned red as the boiling water washed over her.

"That's not warm, that's frying your skin off," I told her.

She giggled. "Perks of being a Koigni." She turned the heat down and said, "Come on. It's freezing now, to me, but you should be able to stand it."

The temperature of the water was still a little too hot for my taste, but at least it was bearable.

Sophia started washing my hair. She took shampoo and began massaging my head, running her fingers through the long strands.

"I can wash my own hair, you know," I said.

"Not when I'm showering with you," she said pleasantly. The look on her face said she truly enjoyed doing it for me.

"Well, if you're gonna be that way..." I reached for the body wash. I started rubbing my hands up and down her entire body, sudsing her up. I put bubbles on her nipples, and she playfully smacked me away.

We spent the rest of our time in the shower taking care of each other. I washed her hair, and she washed my body, going slow and taking the utmost care. We both dried each other off. By the time we emerged from the bathroom, I felt closer to her than I ever had before.

It was so nice to be with someone who cared for you like that. Who made you feel loved.

❧

Monday afternoon, I came out of Basket Weaving with something in my hands.

"What's that?" Sophia asked me curiously as she waited outside the classroom. Her head tilted, and Esis copied her in his arms.

"It's a blanket," I told her. "I made it for you last semester, but I decided to add a little bit more to it."

I unfurled it, then wrapped it around her shoulders. It was made in the traditional Hawkei design, with blocks and triangles of red, orange and white intermingling together. Sophia pulled it tighter around her shoulders. Esis peeked his head out from inside of it.

"It's beautiful," Sophia said. "There are so many colors."

"I'm glad you like it," I said. A couple of people in the corner of the hallway looked shocked that I'd draped the garment around her, but fuck them. This was my decision, not theirs.

Sophia and I were supposed to be heading home. We'd moved our carriage to the back of the school, within the woods, so that the paparazzi and everyone else wouldn't see us coming or going.

But there was someone waiting by the carriage for us when we got there. It was a woman with a long blonde braid and glasses. She was short, but intelligent-looking... probably Nivita. How had she gotten on campus and past the Task Force?

The woman shuffled toward us with intent. "Sophia Henley, Liam Mitoh? Might I have a word with you?"

"We don't talk to reporters," I said quickly.

"I'm not a reporter," the woman said. "But I have information that might help your case."

333

Neither of us responded, and the woman hurried to add, "Sorry. I haven't introduced myself. My name is Jaymin Riske. I'm the lead organizer for the Interhouse Alliance."

Then it clicked. She'd been interviewed on TV last semester, when the last interhouse couple had been discovered and arrested.

"What do you want?" Sophia asked quickly. It was clear in her tone that she didn't trust her.

Jaymin sighed and adjusted her glasses. "Let me be frank, Miss Henley. This case... it doesn't look good for either of you. But we think you might stand a chance if you show the Elders there are people behind you."

Jaymin looked around, then gestured toward the trees. From behind her, all kinds of figures emerged. Men and women came out into the light, each of them holding hands.

Couples were gay, straight, and everything in-between. They were old, some looking like they could be grandparents, middle-aged, and young. But there was one commonality. They were all interhouse.

And some of the faces we recognized.

"Ben?" Sophia asked in astonishment.

"And Marcee?" I asked. Ben and Marcee were standing across from us, Marcee clinging on to Ben's arm— a Koigni and Toaqua, standing together as clear as day. Daisy flew beside Marcee, appearing proud.

"That's right. Marcee and I are in a relationship, and have been for months now," Ben said. "We're tired of hiding this. You guys have given us the courage to come into the light."

"We're *all* tired of hiding," Marcee insisted. "That's why we've all decided to come out, too, in support of you guys. The Elders can't arrest all of us and put us all on trial. At least not at once. This is the most important case of the century. We need to stand up and fight for our rights."

Sounds of agreement went up around the group. I shook my head. "We can't ask you guys to do that. It's not fair for you to put yourselves at risk for us."

"The protest has already begun. Many couples have already been arrested and taken into custody by the Task Force," Jaymin said. "There are hundreds of interhouse relationships all around Kinpago. And each of them are willing to come forward to support a movement. A movement to legalize interhouse marriages."

Sophia and I looked at each other. I was totally humbled. People were going to jail and risking themselves for us— for the right to be in love.

"We'll support you in any way we can," Jaymin said. "If the Elders know you have support behind you, they're more likely to decide in your favor, to avoid upsetting the general public."

"This case is the most important thing facing the fate of the Hawkei right now," Marcee spoke up. "It'll decide whether or not being in love with someone from another House is against the law. All of our fates depend on whether you guys win or lose. And we're not willing to let you lose."

"The Elders aren't going to be happy about this," I said.

"Let them be angry. I've been angry about not telling anyone how I feel about Marcee for months," Ben said. He wrapped an arm around her. "I'm willing to do whatever it takes to be with her. If that means standing up to the Elders, then so be it."

Sophia seemed awed. "I'm... I'm so glad there's people out there willing to back us up. For the longest time, Liam and I... we thought we were all alone."

"You were never alone. There's more people like you than you know," Jaymin said kindly. "You have a cause worth fighting for. Just know that we'll be behind you all the way."

There were footsteps behind us. "Liam! Sophia!" We turned to see Imogen sprinting our way, Sassy at her heels. She skidded to a stop beside us. "I was hoping I'd catch you before you left. Jonah—"

She cut off, blinking at the group surrounding us. "Who are all these people?"

"We'll tell you later," Sophia said quickly. "What's wrong with Jonah?"

Imogen bit her lip. "Come with me."

She grabbed our arms and started dragging us back toward the castle. I sent a glance backward at Jaymin and the others, but they'd already dispersed. How many more of them would get arrested tonight on Sophia and I's behalf? Not all of them had people in power like my Dad to keep them safe.

We looked around to make sure we weren't followed before we slipped into the tower leading up to the Anichi dorms. Jonah was pacing when we arrived— he stopped as we approached, and then looked down, seeming guilty. Squeaks was stomping her hooves in the corner of the room, gnashing her beak. She seemed pissed.

"What's up?" I asked. Jonah didn't answer, just kept his gaze fixed on the floor.

"Tell them, Jonah." Imogen crossed her arms. "Tell them what you just told me."

Jonah scratched the back of his head. "Well... the other night, Renar and I... we got a little drunk. Like, a lot drunk. Or at least, I did."

I could already tell this wasn't going to be good. "And?" I prodded.

He let out a sigh. "I might've... let it slip that we're looking for pieces of the prophecy."

"You *what?*" Sophia and I both said at the same time. Imogen gave a face-palm.

"I didn't tell him much," he hurried to add. "Just that we were looking for the Air piece. I wanted to see if he had any ideas."

"Jonah, Renar's *dad* is on the Air Council! This is serious!" I shouted.

"I know! I get it!" Jonah said. He rubbed his face. "But you guys, I don't think it's that big of a deal. I know we weren't supposed to chat about this outside the group, but Renar's a good guy. Really. I know he'll keep our secret."

"Like hell he will!" Sophia shouted. "Jonah, Renar's *not* a good guy."

"He is! He just needs to change!" Jonah protested. "He'll do what's best for me! We belong together!"

Holy hell, it was like talking to Mia. "Do you understand the situation you've put us all in?" I asked him. "We're all at risk now, because someone we can't trust knows we're messing with the prophecy!"

"I can trust Renar. I can," Jonah insisted weakly.

"Did you tell yourself that before you found out he was cheating on you, or after?" I asked. I didn't mean to let that slip— but out it came.

Everything got really quiet. Jonah's lower lip wobbled, and he said, "Renar promised he wouldn't do it again."

"Open your eyes!" I shouted. "He's probably out there fucking some other guy right now!"

"Liam," Sophia said, as a signal for me to calm down, but I didn't hear her. This was an emergency situation. Sophia and I were already in hot water due to this case. If the Elders found out we were involved in the prophecy on top of it, it was all over. All because Jonah trusted the wrong person.

Jonah's hurt turned to anger. He balled his hands up into fists, and he said, "Stop judging me for who I want to be with! It's none of your business."

"You're my friend, so it is my business. You need to realize that Renar is an abusive jerk, and start looking to the people who *really* love you!" I gestured to myself, Sophia, and Imogen.

"You guys don't get it!" Jonah screamed. "You and Sophia have each other, and Imogen has Cade, but I have *no one*. I'm completely alone!"

"Give it time, Jonah. He's out there," I said.

"I'm sick of being *lonely*!" Jonah's voice cracked, and tears started beading the bottom of his eyelids. "I am *so tired* of always thinking I'm never going to find someone. I'd rather be with someone who hurts me than be by myself!"

"You can't do that, Jonah. You need to learn how to be okay with being alone," I insisted. "You're twenty-one freaking years old. What the fuck's the rush?"

"Easy for you to say, now that you're not pining away for Sophia every hour of the day," he shot back at me.

"That's not fair," I responded viciously.

"You're so lucky. You have someone you'd risk everything to be with. You know what I'd give to have that kind of love? I'd *die* to have it," he said desperately.

"You've got to be happy with yourself first," I repeated. Jonah didn't understand— but he hadn't been through what I'd been through in the past couple of months. He'd spent his entire life being rejected by his parents, his sister, and everyone else around him. Imogen, Sophia and I were pretty much his only friends. If not for us, he truly wouldn't have anyone besides Squeaks.

But what he didn't know is that if he really loved himself, he wouldn't have to go seeking that approval from other people— the validation that he mattered. I didn't know what I had to do to get that through to him. He wanted to be liked *so badly*. And that need was killing him.

"How can I be happy with myself if I can't get Renar to love me? *Anyone* to love me?" Jonah asked.

"Love isn't fricken earned! When are you gonna get that through your head?" I asked.

"Just shut the fuck up, Liam," he snapped at me.

My temper broke. I was so done with this shit. "The only people you find attractive are the people who treat you like shit!" I yelled. "You're so used to your parents abusing you and pushing you around, you think it's love when your boyfriend does the same—"

Jonah swung. I acted on instinct, ducked, and swung back. Imogen and Sophia screamed as Jonah and I started landing punches. He kicked my legs out from under me, and I fell backward. Jonah got on top of me, but I grabbed him by the shirt and tossed him off. We rolled on the ground for a few minutes, tossing blows while the girls shouted at us to stop. Jonah and I usually fist-fought when we got into it, but this was different. I could really tell he was hurting this time. So I let him take his hurt out on the closest thing he could— me— while trading some of my own frustration back.

Eventually, he got me in a headlock. We stayed on the ground while I struggled to get out of it, but it was a no-go. My body didn't have anything left to give.

"Give up, Liam! I'm stronger than you!" Jonah shouted.

He had me. But I'd made my point. I kicked him, to let him know I was tapping out, and he let me go. I rolled away and onto my knees, while Jonah got to his feet. The two of us panted for air. We hadn't hit hard enough to really hurt each other, but there'd be bruises.

"You two are fucking ridiculous!" Imogen shouted.

I wiped blood off my mouth. Sophia looked between Jonah and I and shook her head, speechless.

There were the sound of heavy hoofbeats. Squeaks barged between us. She head butted Jonah until he was against the wall, then put her face at his eye-level.

They seemed to be communicating silently, which was surprising to me... I didn't know Jonah had gained the ability to speak telepathically with Squeaks yet. It had to have been recently. Guess that was one more thing he'd been keeping from us.

We couldn't hear what Squeaks was saying, but the message was clear. I could see the line being drawn in her expression, and how her form tensed as she continued to stare at her Elementai.

Jonah's eyes narrowed as he gazed at Squeaks. "Fine. You want me to pick between you and him? Done."

Jonah pushed Squeaks out of the way and stomped toward the door. He wrenched it open and left it hanging as he headed down the staircase.

Squeaks' head dropped low. She seemed completely heartbroken, her beak hanging open as she stared at the spot where Jonah had left. Esis jumped out of Sophia's arms and scuttled to her, laying a paw on her cheek. Sassy left Imogen's side and sat next to Squeaks' front leg, leaning against it. Thick tears dropped out of Squeaks' eyes and splashed onto the floor as she let out a mournful cry for Jonah to come back.

sophia
SIXTEEN

Over the next few days, the tension in the air seemed to wane, but it didn't completely go away. I didn't think it ever would, even after the trial— even if we won. But I had Liam, and that was all that mattered.

On Wednesday, I stayed behind after Intermediate Koigni Magic. Haley bumped my shoulder on her way out of the room, then lowered her voice to hiss in my ear. "It was only a matter of time before everyone knew about you and Mitoh. You owe me one for not ratting you out."

I didn't get a chance to respond before she tossed her dark hair over her shoulder and breezed out of the room. Haley spoke it like some sort of threat, but I did my best to ignore her. I approached Doya.

Doya sat at the desk at the front of the room, flipping through papers and acting like I wasn't there. Naomi sat curled at her feet.

I cleared my throat, and Doya finally looked up at me. She wore a sour look on her face like normal. Good. I could handle normal. I didn't need any more surprises.

"Madame Doya," I started slowly, unsure of how to say this to her face. Esis placed a comforting hand on my arm. "I just wanted to thank you."

She raised a curious eyebrow. "Thank me?"

I ran my fingers through Esis' fur. "I know you helped Chief Mitoh convince the council to give us a trial. So, um, thank you."

Doya stopped rifling through papers. She spoke in a cold tone I couldn't read. "Yes, well, unfortunately it's all I can do."

"So you... support us?" I asked.

Doya sucked her cheeks in. "I wouldn't go that far, Sophia. What you're doing is dangerous, but it's clear that nothing I say will change your mind."

I flashed back to the warning she'd given me before, when Haley told her something was going on between Liam and me. Doya was right. There was nothing she could say to change my mind.

She sighed. "That said, I don't believe this is worthy of a death sentence. You are not the first couple to challenge the rules, and you won't be the last."

She spoke in her usual harsh tone, but her words communicated something entirely different. It was hard to wrap my head around. Doya seemed like the kind of person who played everything by the book. To challenge the other Elders... well, maybe she had a bigger heart than I thought.

She leaned forward and folded her hands. "Just know this, Sophia. I helped get you this trial, but I cannot change the outcome of it. The rest of the Elder Council are very set in their ways. They truly fear the extinction of their Houses and their magic if interhouse relationships become mainstream. So I suggest you take your time between now and the trial to come up with a damned good defense."

I opened my mouth to tell her I loved Liam and that should be enough, but she held her hand up to stop me, like she could already sense what I was about to say.

"Love is not enough," Doya said. "Not for the Elders. You'll need to use logic with them."

I nodded, though I wanted to argue. Even the Elders had emotions, but what she was saying was clear. "Thank you for the advice."

Doya turned back to her papers. I expected her to say more, but several seconds of silence passed. She looked up to me with raised eyebrows. "I think we're done here, Sophia. I can't protect you any further."

"That's okay," I said honestly. "I'll handle it myself."

"I hope you do," she replied. "I'd hate to see your magic go to waste."

I left her room feeling conflicted. Her tone suggested she couldn't be bothered by any of this, but her actions and words were the exact oppo-site. She seemed like she actually cared, but didn't want to admit it... almost like she felt guilty to support me.

I shook it off. At least she'd helped us get the trial, and that was all I could ask of her.

&a.

A WEEK PASSED, and I was already feeling accustomed to our new routine.

Imogen met me after Intermediate Koigni Magic and walked me to the Commons while we waited for Liam to meet us after Basket Weav-ing. Squeaks curled up in front of the couch we sat in, but Jonah was nowhere nearby. He came and went with Imogen, but there was still some tension between him, Squeaks, and Liam.

"I miss you guys," Imogen said, resting her head on my shoulder.

Esis and Sassy chased each other around at our feet. They tried to get Squeaks to play, but she rested her head on the ground and stared off into the distance, like she didn't even feel their little feet bouncing over her.

"I know," I said to Imogen.

"You barely spend any time around the castle anymore," she complained. "And when you're here, you're in class."

"I'm here now," I said.

Imogen sat up straight and glanced around the room. No one was close enough to hear us. "I want to know what's been going on with you and Liam. Spare no detail."

I snickered. "I already told you about our date."

Imogen swooned. "And it sounded so romantic."

"I forgot to tell you he made me a blanket. It was really sweet. He wrapped it around my shoulders and everything."

Imogen wiggled her eyebrows. "I know what that means." Her eyes caught something across the room. I turned to see Cade had entered with a few of his Nivita buddies. They were headed straight toward the ping pong table. "Hold on. I'll be right back."

Imogen hurried over to Cade, who looked thrilled to see her. He wrapped an arm around her shoulder and brought her in for a kiss.

While they chatted, Liam entered the Commons and sat beside me. A few people looked our way, but we ignored them. I slid my fingers into his. He looked exhausted, but he squeezed me back.

"How was Basket Weaving?" I asked.

Liam shrugged. "Good, I guess. And Koigni Magic?"

I laughed. "Same as always. It gets pretty heated in there."

He smirked. "Pun intended?"

"Yep." I scooted closer to him. He didn't really look at me. He kept his eyes on the TV, like he had something else on his mind. I had a vague idea of what, but I didn't know how to bring up the topic. He'd gone to therapy earlier today, and he always seemed a little bothered afterward. I decided to just dive in. "How's therapy going?"

Liam took a deep breath and looked at me. His features softened as he drank me in. "It's helping."

My chest warmed. "Really? That's good."

"Yeah, I guess." He shrugged, like he wasn't really willing to talk about it. "It's helping me manage. But, Sophia..."

My heart sank, suddenly turning cold in my chest. I could feel whatever he was about to say wasn't good. My mouth felt dry when I said, "What?"

Liam took a deep breath. "There's something my therapist and I talked about that I think you should know."

"Oh?" My voice came out cool, but I was imagining the worst.

Liam dropped his gaze and lowered his voice. "I don't know how to say this... At the beginning of the semester, I swam out to the middle of the ocean and... I tried to drown myself. Like, a lot. Several times, as a matter of fact. I don't know if I understood what I was doing at the time. I just kind of... held my breath underwater and tried to pass out."

I inhaled a sharp breath. I was shook and didn't know what to say, but I didn't have to. Liam quickly cut in before I could get a word out.

"I couldn't do it, though," he said. "I just thought... it'd be nice, you know, if the ocean took me. But..."

He choked up a little. I could see how hard it was for him to admit it. I placed a hand on his and gently said, "It happened, Liam, but it's over. Thank you for trusting me enough to tell me."

He lifted his gaze to meet mine and nodded. "I just didn't want to keep any secrets."

I nodded back, but inside, my guts were sinking. How hadn't I seen how low Liam had fallen? Why hadn't I done something about it then?

I didn't press any further. "I'm glad you're doing better."

Liam resituated himself and wrapped an arm around my shoulder. He dragged me close and pressed a kiss to the top of my head. "I am. I really am."

Imogen returned and playfully kicked my foot. "Okay, lovebirds. Who wants to play a round of—?"

She cut off, and her eyes darted to the TV. She quickly grabbed the remote and turned up the volume. "Did they just say Elder Kim's Familiar died?"

"We have confirmed that two other Nivita Elders' Familiars are sick. Names are not being released at this time," the news anchor was saying.

Imogen's face went paper white. "Elder Kim is Nivita. If his Familiar died... he doesn't have long."

The room seemed to quiet as all eyes turned to the newscast. Even our Familiars stopped playing to watch. The screen switched to another area of the newsroom, where three people sat around a table, one women and two men. They looked like political commentators.

"Look," the woman said. "We've known for months that this is a problem. The question is, when is it going to stop? What are the Elders going to do about it?"

"I completely agree with you, but I think we all know what needs to be done," the man on her right said. "It's clear where this disease originated from. If we get rid of the source, we get rid of the disease."

"What exactly are you suggesting, Mister Brown?" the other guy asked.

"Isn't it obvious, Mister Foster?" Brown said, straightening his tie. He looked to be Yapluma, or perhaps Nivita— it was harder to tell without their Familiars on screen— but he had all the pride and confidence on his face of a Koigni. "Familiars such as these don't just fall ill, not without some sort of catalyst. It's obviously coming from the weakest in the tribe and working its way up."

My jaw dropped. Was he seriously blaming innocent people for this? Clearly someone was targeting Elders' Familiars, and the weakest Elementai were the ones being summoned to the gallows.

Foster opened his mouth to say something, but the woman in the middle cut him off. "You make a good point," she said. "Familiars every-where are getting sick—"

"But where's the evidence, Miss Rivera?" Foster cut in. "We'd have to track it back to patient zero before we could say for sure."

Rivera raised an eyebrow. "That'd be impossible at this point. What Mister Brown is saying makes sense, does it not?"

The table fell silent as Foster stared at the two of them. "Well, yes. I'm not saying that I don't agree with you—"

"So you *do* agree?" Brown pressed. "The fact is, some Familiars are more equipped to handle these kinds of things. Their bodies are just stronger, *better*. Those that aren't are out there running around, spreading this disease from one Familiar to the next. We need to invoke a herd immunity clause."

"Are you suggesting some sort of high-level quarantine?" Rivera asked, already looking like she agreed with the idea.

"Absolutely," Brown said proudly. "It would certainly be the best way to test this theory."

"He can't be serious," I hissed while the commentators continued to argue about the best course of action. Both Liam and Imogen looked horrified. "They're suggesting segregation, not quarantine."

"Can they even do that?" Imogen asked.

Liam huffed. "If the Elders buy into it, why not?"

Imogen crossed her arms and scowled at the TV. "It's ridiculous. Who decides which Familiars are weak and which ones aren't?"

"Not to mention Familiars of all species are getting sick," Liam growled under his breath. "Their theory is so off the wall, it's sick."

Foster spoke again. "If you're going to go that far, why not just blame the weakest Elementai for starting this whole thing out of jealousy, or some type of plot to overthrow the Elders?"

"Why don't we?" Brown said quickly. Foster's face fell. "A wonderful theory, Mister Foster. I think you might be on to something."

"That's not what I—"

"Someone's clearly behind it," Brown continued. "We just have to ask ourselves, who has the motive?"

I shot to my feet and scooped Esis up in my arms, then tossed my bag over my shoulder. "I can't keep listening to this. These people are idiots."

Imogen and Liam quickly stood and followed behind me out of the room, with Sassy and Squeaks close behind. Imogen waved to Cade before slipping out of the Commons.

I shook my head as I started up the stairs. "I can't believe they're blaming innocent people without any evidence."

Imogen held tightly on to Sassy. "I think I get it."

"What?" I asked, totally baffled.

"No, not that I agree or anything," she said. "But if you listen to Jonah talk about his psych class long enough, I get the thinking behind it. They're scared, and they need someone to blame, so they're going after the easiest target— people who aren't like them. It's not right."

"They shouldn't be allowed to say stuff like that," Liam said, fuming.

"They're political commentators, not journalists," Imogen pointed out.

None of us mentioned where we were going, but it was like our feet already knew where to take us. We reached the Anichi dorms and climbed the steps. Liam fell down onto one of the couches, and Squeaks lay on the floor beneath him. She nudged his hand so he'd pet the top of her head.

"I don't know what to think of this," I admitted as I sat with Esis in my lap. "It's... sick."

Imogen sat and petted Sassy. She chewed her bottom lip. "You don't think this is what the prophecy meant, do you?"

"What do you mean?" Liam asked.

Imogen knotted her hands together. "Well, the Nivita part said that *No Hawkei shall survive if the weakest refuse to bend.*"

The room went completely silent as we contemplated the words.

"That can't be it," I finally said. "Why would the ancestors want us to turn on each other like this?"

"We've already turned on each other," Liam mumbled, so quiet I barely heard him. He sat up straighter when Imogen and I looked at him. "Toaqua against Koigni. That's what the whole prophecy's about, anyway."

"So why would we divide ourselves further?" I asked. I refused to believe this is what the ancestors wanted. "There has to be a meaning we're missing."

Imogen pressed her lips together in thought. "Showana said we could change the prophecy, didn't she?"

I sighed. "Yes, but if this is really what it talks about, that means it's coming true. The question is, can we still stop it?"

Liam set his feet on the floor and rested his elbows on his knees. He stared at the floor, like he was thinking hard. "We can't stop now. We're too far in. There's only one piece left."

"Agreed," Imogen said quickly. "Showana said we needed to find all the pieces to get the bigger picture. You could be right, Sophia."

Some of the tension in my shoulders eased.

"We can still stop this, once we have the Air piece," Imogen said confidently.

I dropped my gaze. "That's going to be tough without Jonah."

Squeaks huffed at the sound of his name.

Liam scratched her head and said, "He'll come around. Meanwhile, we can still work on getting that meeting with the Nivita Elders."

Imogen frowned. "That's what I wanted to talk to you guys about." She paused before continuing slowly. "I... I tried to get a meeting with them, but they won't see me. I even approached Elder Kim while he was having lunch in Kinpago, but he brushed me off. No one's taking me seriously. Even if they did, the Nivita Council is down for the count right now..."

Liam's face paled. "So, what do we do?"

My stomach felt hollow, but I knew there was only one thing we could do. "We find that last piece. And then we change the fate of the tribe."

SATURDAY MORNING CAME, and I didn't want to move. Being wrapped in Liam's arms made everything feel like it would all be okay— if just for a moment.

Liam stirred beside me, then his eyes slowly fluttered open. His gaze traveled over my face, and a smile crept across his lips.

I pushed my hair from my eyes. "What?"

He leaned closer to press his lips to my forehead, warming me all the way down to my toes. "I love waking up next to you every morning. This is how it should be."

I curled up closer to him, resting my head beneath his chin. "It is. Liam, I don't ever want it to end."

"It doesn't have to," he whispered, but his voice cracked. I could tell he was thinking about the trial.

I drew away from him to look him in the eyes. "Liam, I think we need to talk about what we're going to do."

He titled his head in question.

"It's been a few weeks already since we were subpoenaed, and we still don't have a lawyer," I pointed out. "How did it go talking to your dad?"

Liam's face fell. "I've talked to him, but…"

"What?" I asked.

"It doesn't sound like his lawyer's going to take on the case," he admitted.

I sighed and plopped my head back on the pillow. "There have to be other lawyers in town. Someone will take our case."

Liam went quiet, like he was thinking. I didn't know the first thing about finding a lawyer. Maybe it was time to hit up all the law offices in Kinpago. Unless…

I pushed myself up to my elbows to look down at Liam. "We should talk to my grandparents. They know a lot of people."

Liam smiled. "You want me to meet your grandparents?"

I poked him in the side and giggled. "Yes. Besides, I need to see them. It's been weeks, and I need to talk to them about what's going on."

"Okay." Liam sat up, groaning a little as he did. Esis stirred from where he slept at Liam's feet. "We'll go see them today. Breakfast first?"

I ran my fingers through my tangled hair. "I'm going to take a quick shower. I'll meet you downstairs."

Liam nodded, but he made no effort to start getting ready for the day. I gathered a fresh set of clothes and slipped out of the room.

As I started down the hall toward the bathroom, Liam's dad stepped out of his room with Tatum, his grizzly bear Familiar, behind him. Liwanu's eyes caught mine, and a look of shock hit his face, like he was surprised to see me alone. I dropped my gaze and reached for the bathroom door, but he stopped me.

"Sophia, can I have a word?" he asked softly.

My hands started to shake a little, so I held tighter to my pile of clothes in my arms. "Sure, what's up?"

I was surprised at how steady my voice came out.

Liwanu took several steps and stopped beside me. He crossed his hands in front of himself and closed his eyes for a moment, taking a deep breath. "I wanted to apologize."

The words hit me like a tsunami. I swayed on my feet, but I kept my cool.

He looked me straight in the eye as he spoke. "What I did— what the entire Toaqua Council did— to you and Liam last semester was wrong. I was only trying to do what was best for my people. But I need you to know something, Sophia."

The hall fell silent.

He took another deep breath. "I know I may never gain your trust, but I'm speaking honestly when I say that you're a part of our family now. And I'm going to protect you, because my son loves you."

I was rendered speechless. Liam's dad always came off a little scary to me, and it was even worse after all those secrets came out last semester. But I couldn't find a shred of dishonesty in his tone or his features.

"Thank you," I said, though my voice came out smaller than I intended.

Liwanu and I stood there for another few seconds, just staring at each other, then he straightened, gave me a friendly nod, and continued down the hall. Tatum mimicked the nod, then followed behind his Elementai.

I hurried into the bathroom and shut the door behind me, then sat on the closed toilet lid to process what had just happened. I knew Liam's father had changed his mind about us. He had, after all, helped us get the trial. But I never thought I'd hear him apologize to me. Had he meant what he'd said? About me being part of his family now?

I hoped so, because I wanted to be.

LIAM and I arrived at my grandparents' by lunchtime. We came in the flying carriage, which helped conceal us so that no one would notice a Toaqua in the middle of the Koigni village. We didn't want to risk anything with the tension surrounding missing Familiars and our public relationship. Besides, we didn't need to give the media anything else they could twist into rumors.

We arrived in the back alley and hurried through the lawn toward the door. Grandma opened it before we even knocked, like she'd heard us arrive.

"Sophia!" she cried, throwing her arms around me and squashing Esis between us. She pulled away, then hugged Liam. He seemed shocked, but he hugged her back. Grandma dragged the two of us into the house, then glanced up and down the alleyway before she shut the door. "We're so glad to see you. We've been so worried."

"I'm okay," I assured her. "Grandma, this is Liam."

"It's so great to meet you. Why don't we all have a seat?" She gestured to the kitchen table.

Grandpa came into the room when he heard the sound of our voices. He had a worried look fixed to his face.

"I'm fine, Grandpa," I said, and he relaxed.

Grandma was already digging in the fridge for food. She never let me go hungry. Liam exchanged a quick glance with me, like he didn't know the proper protocol with my grandparents.

I sat, and he followed my lead. Esis bounded over toward the fridge next to my grandma to peek curiously inside. She handed him a deviled egg, and he smiled proudly. He brought it back to the table and sat in my lap while he munched on it.

"Grandpa," I said. "This is Liam."

Grandpa extended a hand out to Liam, and he shook it. "Alan," he introduced.

"Alan, sir. I've heard so much about you," Liam said.

Grandma smirked as she returned to the table with potato salad, deviled eggs, and a bag of dinner rolls. "And we've heard very little about you."

She raised an eyebrow at me, but I could tell she was only teasing.

I sighed. "You both know why I couldn't tell you about him."

Grandpa spoke gently from across the table. "Sophia, you don't owe us an explanation."

I relaxed. "I wanted to tell you guys, but things have been crazy."

"As long as you're okay," Grandpa said. "That's what matters."

Grandma placed plates, forks, and cups in front of all of us, then set a gallon of milk on the table. Finally, she sat. Since I hadn't moved at all, she started dishing up potato salad on my plate. Esis' eyes widened, and he licked his lips.

"We've heard so many rumors," Grandma said.

"Yeah, well, don't trust them," I said. I couldn't keep my eyes off Liam as I spoke. "The truth is, Liam and I are in love, and the rest of it is just..."

"It's shit," Liam finished for me.

Grandma and Grandpa both laughed.

"Oh, dear," Grandma said softly. "We never did trust a single rumor. So, tell us what really happened."

"Well..." I didn't even know where to start. "I guess it all started when I came to Orenda Academy."

I looked to Liam, and he stared back at me with soft eyes. He continued for me. "The school sent me to go pick her up, and the rest is history."

I chuckled. "Well, there were a few bumps along the way."

"There always are," Grandpa said, smiling.

"Liam thought I was a pain in the ass at first." I smirked at him.

He couldn't hide his smile. "Yeah, okay. Maybe a little."

"We tried to stay away from each other," I said. "But... we couldn't."

Liam gazed at me with such admiration that I could feel my heart melting in my chest. "That's because we were meant to be."

Grandma grabbed Grandpa's hand from under the table and pressed her other hand to her heart. She looked like she might be tearing up. "You can't fight those kinds of feelings."

"No," I agreed, understanding far too well. "You can't."

"This potato salad is wonderful," Liam said, digging in. I was glad to see him eating again.

Grandma smiled. "Thank you. If we can help at all, you just say something." I could tell she wasn't just saying it to be nice. She truly meant it.

"Well, there is one thing," I admitted. "As you've probably heard, our relationship is going to trial. And... we could really use a good lawyer."

Grandpa leaned back in his chair with a furrowed brow. He pressed his fingers to his lips. "This could be one of the biggest cases in decades. Most lawyers in town might be too cautious to take it on. If they don't win, it could ruin their career."

"And if they do?" Liam asked.

Grandpa sat up straighter. "If they do, it could change everything. We'd have to find someone who's willing to take that risk."

Grandma sighed. "You know who we have to call, Alan."

"No, no," Grandpa said. "No one will take this case seriously if he's on it."

"No one will take this case at all if he doesn't," she pointed out.

"Who?" I asked, glancing between the two of them.

Grandma turned to me. "There's a man by the name of Ludwig Vanderbilt. He retired from law about twenty years ago, but... he might be willing to take on your case."

"That's great!" I said, but Liam looked skeptical.

"Why wouldn't anyone take us seriously?" he asked.

Grandpa took a deep breath. "Well, the last case he fought... he lost. He was representing a boy who was said to be mixed House. The mother was put to death, and the child was excommunicated from the tribe."

"What about the father?" Liam asked.

"The mother was Nivita, but the paternity test showed the child's father was Koigni," Grandma explained. "Without the father's DNA, it was impossible to prove who he was, and the mother wouldn't give him up."

Grandpa lowered his voice, like just the mere thought of the trial perturbed him. "Rumor had it, Vanderbilt fathered the child himself."

I gasped. "He fought for his own son, and he lost?"

Grandma and Grandpa shared a nod.

"How come he was never convicted?" Liam asked curiously.

Grandpa shrugged. "By the time the rumors started, the case was already closed and the boy was long gone. They never reopened the case. Vanderbilt rarely comes out of his house now."

"Would he come out to help us?" I asked hopefully.

Grandma stood, then scribbled something on a piece of paper that was sitting on the counter. She turned around and handed it to me. "I guess you're going to have to find out for yourself."

I glanced down at the paper and saw that it was an address right here in the Koigni village. "Well, Liam. It looks like we might have ourselves a lawyer."

&

VANDERBILT'S HOUSE was on the outskirts of the Koigni village, nestled far back between two mountain peaks. It looked like one of the oldest houses in the area, but it still had the red brick of all the other buildings in the village. We climbed up rickety wooden steps, and Esis reached out to ring the doorbell.

Floorboards creaked from behind the door, but the footsteps stopped just on the other side. I expected to hear the sound of the doorknob twisting, but it never came. I glanced to Liam with a hopeless look. He sighed and reached past me to press the doorbell again.

I noticed movement in the window as the curtains were brushed aside, and I caught a blue eye rimmed in age lines staring back at us. As soon as I caught the eye, it was gone. Quickly, before we lost his attention, I pounded my fist on the door. "Mister Vanderbilt?"

An old, gruff voice came muffled through the door. "Whatever you're selling, I'm not buying."

"We're not selling anything," Liam replied.

"We actually have an offer for you," I said.

The floorboard creaked again. "I'm retired. I need nothing."

Heat began to rise to my skin. If Vanderbilt couldn't help us, no one would. We needed a lawyer if we had any chance of winning our case. I took a deep breath to calm my Fire. "What if you could change the laws regarding interhouse relationships?"

Silence.

"Also, a very large sum of money for your time," Liam added.

The door popped open a crack. All I could make out was that blue eye and a shag of gray hair atop his head. "You're that couple, aren't you?

The Toaqua and Koigni the newspapers have been talking about. You won the Cup last year."

"Yes," I said proudly, while trying to hold on to Esis, who was pushing out of my arms.

I lost my grip on him, and he jumped down and bolted straight for the door. Vanderbilt tried to block the crack with his foot, but Esis clawed at his pant leg and squeezed inside.

"Esis!" I cried.

Vanderbilt sighed and opened the door further. "I guess I have no choice but to let you in now, do I?"

Liam and I exchanged a gaping glance as Vanderbilt turned and left the door open for us. I finally got a look at him and saw that he wore a plaid shirt and gray suspenders. He was shorter than I was, and though he looked very old, there was something about him that suggested he was younger than he seemed— late fifties, maybe early sixties.

We stepped inside, and it was like walking into an abandoned newspaper factory. The shades were drawn on every window, and dust layered most of the surfaces. Stacks and stacks of newspapers filled his living room and lined his stairway. An old TV sat across from a tattered couch, and I smelled the faint scent of lemongrass tea.

"Ah, there you are," Vanderbilt said as he reached up to Esis.

Esis sat on top of one of the many stacks of newspapers, which seemed like skyscrapers piled next to each other. Some of the stacks were even taller than Liam was.

Vanderbilt held Esis gently in his hands, then extended them out to me. I took Esis and curled him up in my arms.

"Bad Esis," I said. "We don't run off."

He dropped his ears.

Vanderbilt took a seat on the couch, causing the hound that was lying there to perk up like he'd just been startled awake. The Familiar inched forward, until his head was rested on Vanderbilt's leg. He ran his hands through the dog's fur, then looked up to us. "Why have you come here?"

"We need a lawyer—" Liam started, but Vanderbilt held up a hand to cut him off.

"I'm aware of your situation," he said. "The question is, why did you come to me?"

I hesitated, then stepped forward. "Mister Vanderbilt, we can't fight this case alone, but other lawyers have already refused to take on our case. We need someone who understands our position."

Vanderbilt huffed. "And what is your position?"

"We're in love," I answered automatically.

Vanderbilt shook his head. "Not good enough."

"It should be," I said sternly, trying not to lose my temper. "Haven't *you* ever been in love?"

Vanderbilt frowned. "I never said it wasn't good enough for me. I'm not the judge of your case, Miss Henley."

My nostrils flared, and Liam quickly took over. "Look, Mister Vanderbilt. This case isn't just about us. It's about the entire tribe. We aren't the first interhouse couple, but we were lucky enough to get a trial. People have died for this kind of thing, and they shouldn't have to. If we win this thing, we *all* win."

Vanderbilt went silent, but his hands shook in his lap. "No, no. I'm afraid I can't help you. I'm retired."

"So come out of retirement," I pleaded.

"Laws have changed in the last twenty years," he said. "I'm not brushed up on anything current."

It was a total lie. He had every newspaper printed in Kinpago for at least the last two decades. He'd been keeping up. And I wasn't leaving here without a lawyer.

I shoved Esis into Liam's hands, then knelt beside Mister Vanderbilt. He looked into my eyes with emotions I couldn't read. I thought I spotted conflict, like he wanted to help us but didn't think it'd help.

"Mister Vanderbilt, this case can go one of two ways." I held up a finger. "One, we lose, Liam and I are imprisoned— or whatever the Elder Council decides to do with us— and everyone goes on with their merry lives. Or two, we convince the Elder Council that their laws are flawed. Interhouse couples and interhouse children will no longer be prosecuted for what they are. The ones who've already been banished can return."

A sparkle entered his eyes when I said that.

"Other Elementai have already shown their support," I said. "Now all we need is you. Because without you... we don't stand a chance."

Vanderbilt just stared at me, breathing in and out without a sound. I couldn't read his features anymore. At least a minute passed as I waited for his response, but it never came.

Finally, I stood, feeling frustrated. "Come on, Liam. We'll have to find someone else who can help us." I grabbed Liam's hand, but I stopped and whirled toward Vanderbilt before we reached the door. I couldn't leave here without saying what I really felt. "You know what? I heard that you fought for this kind of thing. If you've given up, you're a coward. I hope the ancestors are proud."

Just as we reached the door, Vanderbilt stood. "Wait."

Liam and I paused and turned back to him.

Vanderbilt dropped his head. "The ancestors are not proud. I already know that. And you're right. I have given up. But maybe... maybe I can make up for it."

"So, you'll take the case?" Liam asked breathlessly.

Vanderbilt nodded. "Yes, I'll take the case."

I squealed. I didn't even know what I was doing when I rushed over to Vanderbilt and threw my arms around his neck. "Thank you, Mister Vanderbilt! You won't regret it."

He frowned. "I hope not, Miss Henley."

ANOTHER WEEK PASSED, and we hadn't heard from Vanderbilt at all. It was the end of November and only a month until our trial.

"Do you think he was just trying to get rid of us?" I asked Liam. We were sitting in the Anichi dorms, chilling with Imogen, Sassy, and Squeaks the following Sunday night. I could barely focus on schoolwork all week because I was worrying about the trial. I wanted to help Vanderbilt build his case, but I didn't know what he needed from us.

"I'm sure he's doing all he can to prepare," Liam said.

"Yeah," Imogen agreed. "He won't just leave you hanging."

I frowned. "You didn't meet the guy."

Squeaks made a coughing sound from where she lay between the couches. I glanced over to her. She looked even worse than she did when Jonah and her got in that fight.

"Okay, has anyone talked to Jonah?" I asked, changing the subject. "Squeaks clearly misses him."

"I've tried," Imogen said.

"Me, too," Liam admitted. "But he made it clear he's not ready to talk."

Imogen frowned. "He seems to think I'm taking *sides*. I told him that wasn't true, but—"

Squeaks coughed again, this time more violently than the last. It turned into a full coughing fit, and everyone immediately jumped into action. We were all at her side in a second. Liam smacked her back to help her, but she didn't seem to feel it. She tried to stand, but her legs were too shaky to hold her up. She collapsed back onto the floor.

"Squeaks! Oh my God." I rested my hand on her, but I didn't know what to do. We didn't cover this kind of thing in Medical Care of Familiars.

Esis scrambled straight in front of her and took her beak in his paws. Sassy yipped in worry. Squeaks looked Esis straight in the eye, and her coughing slowed. We all breathed a sigh of relief and stepped back cautiously.

"Is she okay?" I asked warily, waiting for her to break out into another coughing fit. She didn't.

"She doesn't look well," Imogen said.

We'd all noticed Squeaks looking worse and worse since the fight with Jonah, but I'd assumed it was depression that she wouldn't recover from it until she and Jonah made up. But now I was starting to wonder...

"Do you think...?" Liam hesitated. "Could she have the Familiar illness?"

I bit my lower lip. "I don't know. Coughing isn't a side effect, is it? And Esis tried to heal Medusa, but couldn't. He's helping Squeaks."

Squeaks relaxed on the floor, looking on the verge of sleep, but she still seemed weak. I was worried. All I could do was hope it wasn't what we thought it was.

"We should check on Jonah," I suggested. "If Squeaks is ill, he won't be far behind."

"I'll go," Liam offered.

"We'll all go," I said, but when I tried to help Squeaks to her feet, she just fell back down again. She was so tired that she couldn't even walk. My stomach sank to my feet.

"Liam's right," Imogen said while she gently stroked Squeaks' feathers. Two of them fell out and drifted onto the floor. "Someone has to stay behind to watch Squeaks, and only one of us can get into the Yapluma dorms at a time without getting noticed."

"Okay," I agreed. "Be quick, Liam. I'm worried."

He nodded. "I will be."

Esis looked up at me with watery blue eyes. His face was fallen.

"Keep trying, buddy," I told him, and he turned back to Squeaks.

The minutes stretched into an hour as we tried to comfort Squeaks. My stomach felt hollow and worsened as each minute passed. Esis' powers seemed to help her at first, but they only took the edge off. Squeaks wasn't getting any better.

Finally, we heard the sound of footsteps on the stairs. Relief flooded through me, but my heart fell when I saw that Liam was alone.

"Did you find him?" Imogen asked.

Liam dropped his shoulders. "He wasn't in his room, so I asked around. I guess he went to stay with his parents this weekend."

"What?!" I practically screamed. "After the way they treated him last time?"

"Yeah, which means he's hit rock bottom," Liam said.

"We need to go get him." I was already on my feet.

Liam nodded and said firmly, "Hell yeah, we do. Let's go, guys."

We tried to get Squeaks on her feet again, but she couldn't get up. Her head hung low, and her knees wobbled underneath her. Her hooves slipped and wouldn't support her weight. More feathers fell from her neck and coated the floor, exposing pink patches of skin.

Imogen sent me a desperate look. "Squeaks isn't going anywhere. I'll stay. You guys go get Jonah without me."

Liam nodded quickly. He grabbed my hand and said, "Come on, *pawee.*"

I scooped up Esis, then followed behind Liam.

The media was still swarming around the school, but we managed to slip through the evening shadows and get to our carriage unseen. It felt like an hour later that we arrived at the Yapluma village, but it must've been only fifteen minutes. We pulled up outside a huge white house with endless windows and large, Roman-style pillars on the front porch. I was relieved to see it was on the ground— unlike some of the other houses in the Yapluma village. I could see their lights hovering high above us in the night sky.

Liam gave three forceful knocks on the door. It didn't open right away. Liam knocked again, harder this time. I was worried he was going to pound the door down.

Eventually, the door opened. Jonah's dad, Jacen, stood behind it. He immediately gave us a cold glare. "What are *you* doing here?"

"We're here to get Jonah," Liam said coldly.

"You can turn around and go right back to where you came from," Jacen responded. "He's not going anywhere."

Liam's face got red, so I decided to step in. "Squeaks is sick. She needs Jonah," I protested.

"And?" Jacen asked. "It's none of my concern."

"We need to talk to him!" I shouted. Lights came on from the houses next door. We were creating a scene, but I'd cause a riot if it meant getting Jonah back to school with us.

Someone else appeared in the hallway. "Squeaks is sick?" It was Jonah. He didn't look well. He had dark bags under his eyes, and bits of hair were sticking out of his bun. He froze on the marble tile, his face paling.

"Yeah, so you need to come with us," Liam demanded. "She can't even stand."

Jonah went to move toward the door, but Jacen blocked the way. "I thought I told you that you're staying home for the weekend."

"I have to go back," Jonah said weakly. "Squeaks needs me."

"She didn't need you all weekend, and suddenly you need to go running back? This is just a ruse so you can get fucked up with your degenerate loser friends!" Jacen shouted.

"Unless *you* want to get fucked up, move out of the fucking way!" Liam said, voice rising.

Jonah looked scared. His hands trembled at his sides.

"Look, we have class in the morning," I pleaded. "Just let Jonah come back now. Please."

Jacen still looked furious. Another figure appeared in the hallway— a woman. It was Jonah's mom, Joyce. "Are you going back to school, Jonah? Already?" she asked.

"I have to go," Jonah said. "Squeaks—"

Joyce sniffed, and she said, "Fine. Go. We're *only* your parents. We hardly see you anymore, anyway. It's fine if we're lonely. One day your father and I will be dead, and then you'll wish you'd spent more time with us."

Jonah didn't respond. He kept his head down and grabbed his coat on the way out. Jacen didn't move from the door, until Liam took a step forward. He obviously wasn't playing around. Jacen barely moved out of the way, and Jonah squeezed past him.

"You owe us, Jonah!" his father shouted from the door as we climbed into the carriage. "Don't forget everything we've done for you!"

Jonah mumbled something under his breath, but I didn't catch it. Esis' ears perked up, though, like he'd heard. He glanced back to Jacen and gave a low growl.

Liam paused with his hand on the carriage door. He stared at Jonah in shock. "Did you just say...?"

Jonah crossed his arms from where he sat in the carriage. "Forget it."

"No, I won't forget it." Liam climbed inside and sat beside me. He closed the carriage door, and we started moving back toward the castle. "You said you've been paying them back. Did you give them your tournament winnings?"

Jonah gazed out the carriage window, not meeting either of our gazes. "I said forget it, Liam. It's none of your business."

"Jonah, you can't let them use you like this." Liam tried to stay calm, but I could hear the irritation in his tone.

"It's nothing," Jonah said, like he actually believed it. "They just needed some help with some debt payments. If I didn't help, they were going to lose the house."

I couldn't believe it. His parents treated him horribly— and now they were taking advantage of his Cup winnings, too.

"Jonah, you need to—" Liam started, but Jonah cut him off.

"Don't tell me what I need to do," Jonah snapped. "I need to get to Squeaks."

The rest of the carriage ride was quiet. When we returned to the castle, we led Jonah to the Anichi dorms. Squeaks hadn't moved, and Imogen had stayed at her side. Sassy sat far across the room, eyeing Squeaks with concern. It was probably best she kept her distance. We didn't want Sassy to get sick, too. Squeaks' eyes brightened when Jonah walked in the room, but she barely lifted her head.

Imogen shot to her feet. "Jonah..."

He hurried across the room and knelt beside Squeaks. He pressed his face to the side of hers. "I'm so sorry, Squeakers."

Squeaks took a deep breath, but she seemed too weak to do any more than that.

"I never should've started that fight," Jonah whispered, like they were the only two in the room. "I wish I could take it all back."

Squeaks nuzzled her head into his shoulder. He ran his hand down the back of her head, whispering things to her we couldn't hear.

I slipped my fingers into Liam's and looked up at him. "Do you think they'll be okay?"

Liam looked unsure. "I hope so."

I did, too.

We spent the rest of the evening in the Anichi dorms, keeping watch over our friends. Imogen and I slipped out for a few minutes to grab takeout from the dining hall since none of us had eaten dinner. When we returned, Jonah and Liam were playing video games on the console Jonah had snuck in a few weeks ago. Jonah hadn't said much this whole time, but he seemed to be loosening up once he was blowing people's heads off.

Eventually, Liam and I had to leave. Squeaks couldn't move, so Jonah decided to stay in the Anichi dorms for the night. He spread out across one of the couches, where Squeaks lay beside him on the floor.

"Are you sure you don't want to get checked into the infirmary?" Imogen asked him.

"Nah, we're already feeling better. Aren't we, girl?" Jonah rubbed Squeaks' head. "It was just a side effect of being away from each other so long."

"Okay..." Liam said, but he sounded skeptical.

As soon as we made it to the hall outside the Anichi dorms, I turned to Imogen and Liam. "I think Jonah's lying."

"He's acting weird, that's for sure," Liam said.

"Look, all I know is I've only seen one thing Esis couldn't heal, and it's that disease that's been going around," I told them, squeezing Esis tight in my arms. "Jonah and Squeaks could be risking spreading it."

Imogen bit her lower lip.

"What?" I asked. "Something's on your mind."

"Well, I might have a theory, but we can't test it if Jonah and Squeaks are in quarantine," she admitted. "They should be okay for tonight, if they stay put. We'll meet after class tomorrow. Sound good?"

I frowned. I wanted to help them sooner. "Fair enough."

❧

Monday morning, I watched the halls for Jonah, but I never saw him. I shouldn't have worried, considering I didn't usually see him between classes, but I couldn't help it. When classes finished for the day, Liam and I met up like usual.

"How's Jonah doing?" I asked. I knew he'd checked on him this morning.

"I'm not sure," Liam admitted. "I think he's worse than he's letting on."

"Did Imogen say where we were supposed to meet?" I asked him.

"I don't think so," he replied.

Just then, I heard Sassy's yip down the hallway. She trotted ahead of Imogen and weaved between other people milling around the hall. Imogen was waving us down, a notebook in her hands. When Sassy reached us, she circled around our feet.

Imogen looked exhausted, like she'd been up reading all night. She was still wearing the same clothes she had on yesterday, and huge bags were underneath her eyes. "Hey, guys. I have information, but I need to grab a book from the library to be certain. It might have something that can confirm my theory about..."

She trailed off, then glanced around the hall to make sure no one was listening. "Meet me upstairs in fifteen minutes."

"Okay," I said. "We'll see you soon."

Liam was right. Jonah looked terrible. By now, half his hair was falling out of his bun. His eyes drooped, and his lips looked chapped. He could barely manage to keep his eyes open. We'd brought him and Squeaks food, but they both refused to eat. I checked my watch as we waited for Imogen. Fifteen minutes passed, then half an hour.

When my watch hit forty minutes, I'd had enough. I stood. Esis' eyes darted up to me. "Guys, I'm worried about Imogen. She said she'd only be fifteen minutes."

"I'm sure she's fine," Jonah said in a bleary tone. "It's only been like... twenty minutes—"

"It's been forty," I stated bluntly.

Liam shot to his feet beside me. "Let's go find her."

"I'm coming," Jonah groaned as he tried to get to his feet.

Liam rushed over to him and placed a hand on his shoulder. He tried to get him to lie back down, but Jonah pushed his hands away.

"You're not well," Liam insisted.

"I'm fine," Jonah lied.

There was no talking him out of it.

"Come on," I said quickly.

We left Squeaks behind, since she couldn't move. We only made it to the second floor when we spotted Baine climbing the stairs and heading straight for us. He looked relieved to see us.

"Where have you three been? I've been looking everywhere for you," Baine said breathlessly.

"What's wrong?" Liam asked, but I could already sense what Baine was about to say.

Baine's face went pale. "I need you three to come to the hospital with me. There's been an incident with Miss Ahnild."

Liam

SEVENTEEN

"Professor, what's going on?" I asked. Baine was walking down the hallway at a pace I'd never seen him take before. He was practically sprinting toward the hospital wing.

Baine didn't answer, which worried me. It was like every step I took increased the dread growing in my gut— like I already knew what had happened.

At first, I thought that Sassy had gotten the illness too and now we had two sick Familiars on our hands, but Baine turned away from the quarantine area as soon as we entered through the hospital doors.

"Stay as far away from the left side as possible. The quarantine is still being heavily enforced," Baine told us.

Through a clear plastic curtain, I could see the quarantine area. There were so many sick Familiars inside that they'd crowded all the rooms. Some of them, along with their Elementai, were in beds that lined the hallways. There just wasn't enough room for all the sick students. I couldn't imagine what the main hospital in Kinpago looked like right now.

Some of the Familiars and Elementai lying in bed had long white sheets draped over them. I paled at the sight. Had the morgue already run out of room for bodies?

Baine took a right and headed down a long hallway. I knew how the hospital wing was laid out. I'd been here enough. I was in here for weeks after Nashoma died, because Orenda Academy students were always sent here instead of the main hospital in town. Baine was taking us to the surgery ward.

He burst through the doors. I heard the wheels of a gurney first. Sounds of shouts and loud voices could be heard coming from down the hall.

"Everyone out of the way!" a doctor called at the head of the gurney. Two nurses on either side ran as they pushed the gurney toward the operating unit. We pressed ourselves to the wall to let the patient pass.

Then I recognized her. Imogen. She was stretched out on the gurney, with heavy gauze wrapped around her neck— except the gauze was soaked with blood. Long, jagged gashes ran from her cheek all the way down to her shoulder, as if something had tried to take her head off. Several puncture marks were littered throughout her body, and a nurse pushing the gurney held bloody gauze around her middle... as if trying to keep organs in.

On a smaller gurney being pushed behind her by Familiars was Sassy. She looked as bad as Imogen did, with ragged cuts running through her side. She was in her kitsune form— like she'd been trying to protect Imogen, and passed out in the process before she had time to change back to a fox. Blood dripped from both gurneys onto the floor, creating a trail.

"*Imogen!*" Sophia screamed. She went to follow the doctors through the operating doors, but Baine grabbed her and held her back. She fought against him as Imogen and Sassy disappeared into surgery, tears streaming down her face. Esis reached out his arms from within Sophia's grasp, as if he wanted to go after Imogen and try to heal her. He squeezed out of Sophia's arms and ran forward, but the surgery doors closed before he could get inside.

"Sorry, little one. We can't let you back there," a nurse said to Esis. She picked him up and put him back in Sophia's trembling hands.

Jonah was sobbing. He had his hands fisted in his hair and his back against the wall, as if he needed it to hold himself up.

I was speechless. Numb. My jaw hung open, and it stayed like that. I couldn't feel anything— couldn't hear any of the sounds of the hospital around me. I could only see things in one giant blur. It was like I was in shock.

When Imogen was gone, Sophia yanked herself away from Baine. "What. Happened?"

Baine gave us a sad look. "It appears that Miss Ahnild was walking alone in the halls when she was attacked, most likely by some rogue magical creature, possibly associated with whoever is responsible for the illness and the missing Familiars. Professor Fawn heard her scream before she and her unicorn arrived to help, but by then, her assailant had fled."

Baine shook his head. "I thought she would know better. No one should be walking alone in times like this."

"She had good reason to!" I shouted. Like hell, was Baine really blaming *Imogen* for whatever had happened to her?"

"Be that as it may..." Baine acted like he was about to launch into a lecture, but the murderous faces we were all giving him must've changed his mind, because he said, "The Task Force is investigating the crime scene now. It appears she was jumped near the library."

"Can we see her?" Sophia pleaded.

Baine shook his head. "Not until she's out of surgery, I'm afraid. That is... I'm sorry to say... if she makes it out. Her injuries were very extensive."

Sophia let out a sob. I reached my arm out and pulled her to my side. "What can we do?"

"There's nothing you can do but wait," Baine said. "Her family has been given a room. I suggest you join them."

Baine guided us into a small waiting room. Jonah was gasping behind me, as if trying to take deep breaths so he didn't lose it. Inside were Imogen's parents, along with all four of her brothers. Her mother and father were talking with a doctor quietly, with terrified expressions and frozen mouths. Her brothers, even the young ones, stared at the wall, completely silent and petrified.

"I think it might be best if we called in a medicine man or woman for your daughter," the doctor said gently, and he reached out and put a hand on Mrs. Ahnild's shoulder.

Mrs. Ahnild sniffed and put a tissue to her nose. "Yes... just... just in case."

Jonah's sobs picked up in intensity, and I felt a heaviness weigh in my gut. Sophia looked confused about what a medicine man would do if there were doctors around, but I didn't go to explain. I didn't want to.

The three of us jumped when the door behind us smacked into the wall. Cade was there, with Ezra behind him. He was a total mess. His hair was wild and crazy, and his eyes were large and puffy. His face was wet. Tears continued to streak out of his bloodshot eyes. Arabelle was at his side, though she looked just as upset as he did, with her gaze wide and hair standing on end. Dyami did what he could and put a wing around her for comfort.

Cade was rambling and shaking. Ezra was trying to control him, but it wasn't working very well. I couldn't make out a word Cade was saying. Imogen's parents startled when they saw him. As they watched him break down, they started to cry harder.

Sophia took initiative and launched herself on Cade. She held him tightly and didn't let him go, rocking him back and forth. Cade squeezed her and wept. From between them, Esis pressed his paws into Cade's side, working his healing power.

After a few moments, Cade relaxed. When Sophia finally released him, Ezra was able to ease Cade into a chair. He sat in it with his head in his hand, staring straight ahead with trembling lips. He knew he was about to lose the love of his life.

The horrifying reality that Imogen could die pressed in around me and made me feel like I was suffocating. This was real. She was in surgery right now, and if she didn't pull through...

I was terrified. I wanted to yell and cry and scream. I wanted to go out there and find whatever had done this to Imogen, and rip it to pieces.

But then I saw Sophia and Jonah's tearful faces. They were seconds from crumbling. They didn't know what to do.

My own feelings weren't important right now. I had to hold the team together, or we'd all fall apart. Somebody had to lead them in a time like this.

Jonah wasn't much help. He was still trembling. The only person I could depend on was Sophia. "Soph, I need to talk to you outside," I told her. I grabbed her elbow and guided her out, shutting the door to the waiting room behind me.

"What was that about?" Sophia asked. "A medicine man can help, right? Imogen will be fine."

I hesitated, before I decided to tell her the truth. "Medicine men often come in to deliver last rites," I said quickly. "So that the spirit can be prepared to join the ancestors."

Sophia put a hand over her mouth, like she was trying to hold in a scream. It barely worked. She let out an inhuman sound before dissolving completely into a fit of tears. I had to grab her before she collapsed.

"Hey, Soph. Soph, stop," I told her. I grabbed her shoulders and shook her roughly. "You need to pull yourself together. Squeaks is still sick. If we don't figure out what Imogen knew before she was attacked, there's a good chance we could lose both of them."

Sophia's voice was shaky. "I can't lose Imogen *and* Jonah. We need them."

"We're not going to lose either of them. Not unless we sit around instead of taking action," I told her. "But you can't be like this. You need to remain calm and be at the top of your game. For Imogen and Jonah both."

Sophia nodded quickly before she wiped away her tears. She managed to stabilize herself before she said calmly, "If we can get Esis near her and Sassy, he'll be able to heal them both."

Esis peeped, but I shook my head. "We can't get in there until after surgery. They won't allow us in. Think about it, Sophia. Why would Imogen be attacked, tonight of all nights?"

Sophia's gaze widened. "She must've found out a cure for the plague. And the person who caused it found out, and tried to stop it."

"Exactly," I said firmly. "We can't do anything about Imogen right now, but there might be a way to cure Squeaks. And we have to find it."

"Hey, you guys okay?" Ezra had come out of the waiting room. He looked between us, seemingly confused as to why we weren't waiting with the others.

"Imogen got hurt trying to find a cure for the plague," I told him. "We're figuring she must've found a cure; otherwise, why would someone try to attack her?"

Ezra nodded. "So you two are going to see what you can find?"

"Yes, and Jonah, too," I said. "He's not much use here. Can you stay here with Cade?"

"Sure. I'm not about to let my best bro go through this by himself," Ezra said. "I'll let you guys know if there are any updates."

"Thanks, man." I grabbed his hand and bumped my shoulder against his. Ezra sent Jonah out.

"Why are we leaving now? Im needs us," Jonah said weakly as we left the hospital wing and headed toward the staircase.

"She needs us to find a cure more," I told him. "Squeaks is still sick, and if she—"

Sophia and Jonah looked at me, and I took a deep breath. "If something happens, she'll have sacrificed herself for nothing."

"This is my fault," Jonah moaned. "If Squeaks hadn't gotten sick, she wouldn't have gotten hurt. And Squeaks wouldn't have gotten sick if I hadn't ignored her."

"You can't blame yourself. Squeaks got in contact with a sick Familiar somehow. That's the only way she contracted the disease," I said.

"We should start at the crime scene," Sophia suggested. "We can work our way back from there."

There was a large crowd of people gathered outside the library on the first floor. The library had been closed. About twenty yards from it, the Task Force had roped off an area with yellow tape. There were tons of Task Force members around, investigating the scene.

"Get the fuck out of the way," I growled at a couple of First Years as I shoved a path to the front. The crowd parted to let us through, though not without a lot of complaining about how rude I was.

The scene was a disaster. Pools of blood stained the floor. Broken ivy vines lay all over the floor, mingling with the blood— those were from Sassy. Large streaks of red across the floor indicated that a body had been dragged and played with. Along with the small, bloody handprints from Imogen littering the stones, there were also the footprints of a three-toed creature with long claws.

It was some kind of bird, one that walked on four legs. No hippogriff — there were no hoof marks. No griffin, either... these prints were too huge to come from one. The span of them was at least three feet long. Judging by the footprints, whatever had attacked Imogen had most likely come from behind, fought her and Sassy, then run off the moment they heard Professor Fawn coming.

"Hey, back off," a Task Force member said from behind their mask, and they raised their noxite gun as they approached us. "There's an investigation underway."

"Our friend was hurt here," Sophia protested.

"We can't risk anyone damaging the crime scene. Leave now," they said in a low voice.

We slowly backed off. I didn't feel like getting shot full of noxite and losing my magic for the next twenty-four hours, because at a time like this, it was a high possibility I'd need it. Esis gave a finger to the Task Force guy as we turned around and walked away.

We left the crowd. I felt a tinge of irritation at all the students surrounding the area. They were acting like this was entertainment. Didn't they understand someone's life was on the line?

Once we were far enough away from the crowd, I gestured for Sophia and Jonah to follow me into a secluded alcove down a relatively quiet hall.

"It was a bird," I said immediately. "It's obvious."

Sophia nodded. "I agree. No other Familiar I know makes marks like that."

I took a deep breath. "Guys, I know this is hard. But if we're gonna figure out what happened to Imogen, we have to examine her injuries."

Sophia turned a little green, before she took a few deep breaths and tapped a finger against her chin. "It looked like... I don't know. I didn't get too close of a look when she was being wheeled by, but it seemed like something attacked her with its talons. Like it tried to rip her apart."

"There were puncture wounds from a beak, too, in her and Sassy," Jonah added. "They look similar to the marks Squeaks makes when she's eating."

"But what kind of Familiar does that to its prey? From what I've learned in class, most creatures like to make quick blows, and end it quickly so that their meal doesn't struggle," Sophia said. "Magical creatures don't like to exert energy while hunting. They need to conserve as much as possible. It's a survival tactic."

"Not unless it's a creature that likes to toy with their game," I said darkly. "It's also a possibility that whoever ordered their Familiar to attack Imogen told them not to kill her. Not at first, anyway. To try and get some information."

I knew exactly what kind of animal made those injuries. I'd had the thought that Imogen had looked far too much like the deer my dad and I had found in the forest sometimes... ripped to shreds. But I didn't want to say what it was, because I didn't want to hurt Jonah.

"Do you think that Sassy might've wounded the creature?" Sophia asked.

I shrugged. "It's possible. Let's check the area around the crime scene, since we can't get into it."

The three of us avoided the Task Force and ended up on the opposite side of the hall— in the direction where we hoped the attacker had fled. We walked up and down the halls for over an hour looking for clues, and didn't find anything. Not at first.

Then Sophia called my name. I hurried over. She was kneeling by a traditional Hawkei statue. She pointed to show a small trail of blood droplets leading away from the crime scene. They were so minute, I wasn't surprised the Task Force hadn't noticed.

The statue of the Hawkei was carrying a spear. The spear tip was dotted in a tiny amount of blood, as if the creature fleeing had done so in a hurry and scraped itself against the spear, drawing blood. The droplet trail ended a few paces off, but collected around the statue were a collection of black and brown feathers, so sharp that you might cut yourself on the edges.

Cockatrice feathers.

I closed my eyes. I'd been right. I stood up and carefully grabbed one of the feathers between two fingers, handling it gently so I didn't cut myself. I placed it in Jonah's outstretched hand.

He stared at the feather blankly for a moment, as if he couldn't believe it. He closed his eyes, and a visage of utter pain crossed over his face.

Then he squeezed his hand shut, tightly as he could. The feather cut into his palm, and blood oozed out from between his fingers.

"What? What is it?" Sophia asked, not getting the point.

"It's from a cockatrice," I said bluntly. Jonah let the blood from his hand drip on the floor. Esis eyed it from his place on the ground, but made no move to heal.

"Are you fucking kidding me? *Renar* did this?" Sophia asked in outrage.

"How many people do we know have a cockatrice? They're not popular Familiars," I said. "And if someone else was walking around the school with a cockatrice besides one that had already been registered to a student, you can damn well bet someone would've bloody noticed. Head Dean Alric doesn't just let those things walk around. They're restricted on school property because of how dangerous and unpredictable they are, unless they're already bonded. Professors aren't even allowed to use them in class."

"This doesn't make sense, though. Why would Renar have a reason to bring a plague to the school?" Sophia protested.

Jonah was so quiet it was scary. He had this deadly, hooded look in his eyes, one I'd never seen before. I nearly shuddered when I glanced at him.

Sophia picked Esis off the floor. "So what do we do now? Do we report Renar as a suspect?"

"No. Not gonna work," I said dully.

"What do you mean it's not going to work? It's attempted murder!" Sophia shouted.

"Renar's dad is on the Air Council, and even if Imogen wakes up, it's her word against his. A couple of feathers and some blood droplets aren't enough evidence to pin him, even if they do a DNA test, and the Air Elders will back him up against the other tribes. No one will want to start a conflict with Yapluma over a Nivita girl, not even the Nivita Elders, with how tense things are right now in the tribe. He'll walk free," I said weakly. "And Renar knows it. That's why he didn't hesitate to attack."

"So he's just gonna get away with it? *We're* gonna let him get away with it?" Sophia asked.

Jonah swept past us. He moved with intention. I got a panicked feeling in my gut. "Jonah, where are you going?"

He didn't answer. Sophia and I rushed to catch up. He started climbing the stairs, two at a time. It was as if how he felt physically was temporarily forgotten as he stormed upward. Sophia and I rushed to keep up.

"Jonah, you don't want to do this," I said. I didn't dare to put a hand on him to try and hold him back. Sophia kept sending desperate glances at me, like she wanted me to do something.

Jonah kicked the doors of the Yapluma dorms down. Several people glanced our way, mouths dropping open as they watched Jonah storm forward.

Renar was lounging on a couch with his legs thrown up. Alvarice was nowhere to be seen. Where'd he send his Familiar off to?

Renar gave us a cocky grin as we approached. His eyes fell on Jonah. "Hey, *babe*," he said sarcastically. "Sorry to hear about your friend."

Jonah didn't ask any questions. He strode forward and wrapped his hand around Renar's neck, lifting him off the couch and slamming him into the wall. A bunch of kids screamed. Renar's feet dangled off the ground several feet, kicking out into the air as Jonah suspended him with one arm. Renar's face slowly started turning red.

"*You son of a bitch!*" Jonah shouted. Renar's hands scrambled at his neck, gasping as he slowly lost oxygen.

"Jonah, put him down!" Sophia screamed. It was like Jonah didn't hear. His fingers tightened, and Renar choked.

"You tried to kill my friend," Jonah said lowly. He wrenched Renar away from the wall and tossed him. He went crashing into a table, and it broke as Renar's weight fell on it. Jonah started for him again, and he fisted a hand in his shirt as he smacked Renar across the face.

This was terrifying. It wasn't like watching Jonah at all. It was like watching his dad. There was red in his eyes— like the only thing he desired was to end Renar's life.

"You went after her because you knew she could cure the plague, didn't you? *Didn't you?*" Jonah accused.

"What are you talking about?" Renar was bleeding. He clutched at his throat as he rasped, "It's her fault she got involved with the prophecy."

Jonah's eyes widened in realization, and I suddenly got what he meant. Renar didn't have anything to do with the plague. He went after Imogen because he thought she had information on the prophecy. His father was on the Air Council— he must've assigned Renar to get any information about the prophecy he could. Imogen was just the easiest target.

Jonah kicked Renar in the gut. "You knew better than to *touch* her."

Renar sneered as he clutched at his stomach. "She fucking deserved it. Poking her nose in places it didn't belong."

Jonah gave a loud cry, and he started punching Renar again and again. I launched forward and tried to grab Jonah's arm to hold him back, but he shook me off as if I was a fly.

He was really going to kill him, and I couldn't stop him. No one could. Sophia and I watched in terror as Jonah continued to brutalize Renar. Jonah grabbed his arm and wrenched it backwards. I heard Renar let out a cry of pain, and the room gave an audible gasp as we all heard something snap. Jonah tossed Renar to the floor, and he crumpled into a pile, cradling his hurt arm.

"Fuck you, Jonah," Renar snarled, and he spat on his boots. "You were always a shitty lay, anyway."

"Where's Alvarice?" Jonah bellowed. "Where'd you send him?"

Renar's eyes narrowed. "Somewhere he'll be safe. You can go to hell if you think I'm telling you."

Jonah yanked on Renar's hurt arm. Renar howled.

"You're a little bitch," Jonah growled. "No one messes with my friends."

Jonah stomped down, hard. Renar gave a loud cry and clutched at his leg. There was another snapping sound, and everyone gasped.

The tone in the room changed as Jonah started coughing, hard. He wiped blood away from his mouth and backed off as he hacked for air.

Sophia moved. She grabbed Jonah's arm and hauled him away as best she could. I dove in to help and took Jonah's other arm. He didn't resist as we dragged him away. He was too busy gasping.

We didn't stop until we were far away from the Yapluma dorms. Jonah heaved. He dove for a potted plant and threw up into it. When he wiped his mouth on his sleeve, I spotted blood.

Esis immediately got to work. He scampered up Jonah's leg and up to his shoulder, putting a hand on his cheek. A bit more color came back into his features, and he stopped coughing, though he still had to keep a hand on the wall so he stayed upright.

It was hard to acknowledge the feelings I had in that moment. I was terrified of Jonah. It was scary to think someone so gentle could turn so murderous. The only freaking reason Renar was alive was because Jonah was too weak to do any permanent damage to him.

Jonah took a few rasping gasps before he righted.

"I should've finished the job," Jonah grumbled. "Ended him, like he ended Imogen."

"Imogen's still alive. She's a fighter. She'll make it," I said. "But she wouldn't have wanted you to go to jail for murder on her behalf."

"I'll still get into trouble. I beat his ass in front of everyone," Jonah said.

"Not unless Renar wants to turn himself in for hurting Imogen," Sophia said firmly. "But that doesn't matter now. We need to keep moving forward."

Jonah's phone went off. He checked it, and his face paled. "Imogen's out of surgery," he said. He went to move forward, but staggered. The fight with Renar had taken out what little energy he had left.

I put his arm over my shoulders to help him walk as we headed back to the hospital wing. "Come on, bro. I'm the only one allowed to be sick around here. Buck up."

Jonah gave me a half-smile, but it didn't meet his eyes. I could tell he was thinking about not just Imogen, but Squeaks, too. We'd left her alone for hours back in the Anichi dorms. There was no telling how she was doing right now.

"I don't think we should tell Cade about Renar. At least not right now," I whispered quietly. "He's liable to go livid and hunt Renar down."

"Agreed. We say nothing," Sophia said. Jonah only gave a firm nod.

When we got back to the hospital wing, Imogen's parents were waiting outside of a room. "You can go in and see her," Mrs. Ahnild whispered quietly. "She's recovering."

"How is she?" Sophia asked.

Mrs. Ahnild shook her head. "The doctors have done all they can. It's up to her now. We've all visited. You can go in. We'll give you some privacy."

Jonah pushed open the door. The three of us filed inside. Imogen was lying in a hospital bed, her neck, chest, and middle tightly bandaged. She was on a ventilator, and remained still and unmoving. IVs, along with other tubes, stuck out of her arms and chest.

It was really hard looking at someone else in a hospital bed. I'd gotten so used to it being me that seeing someone else hooked up to machines was a real shock.

Next to her, Sassy was on a similar bed. She was breathing on her own, although she also was wrapped in bandages from head to toe. She was still in her kitsune form. Guess the secret about her was out.

Cade was sitting by Imogen's bedside, holding her hand, while Arabelle lay on the floor at his feet. Ezra was leaning against the wall with his arms crossed. Dyami wasn't in here. He probably couldn't have fit.

Sophia stepped up next to Imogen, biting her lip and holding back tears. She placed Esis at the foot of Imogen's bed.

"If you use Esis, the doctors will think something's up," I said.

"I don't care. Go, Esis," Sophia said. Esis scuttled upward, avoiding stepping on any of the tubes, or Imogen herself.

"What are you guys doing?" Cade asked hoarsely. Esis sat by Imogen's head and rested a gentle paw on her neck.

"Esis can heal," Sophia said. "We'd appreciate it if you didn't tell anyone. Watch."

Esis closed his eyes. Color began to return to Imogen's face as he worked his magic. Although we couldn't physically see the changes taking place underneath the bandages, we knew his magic had to be working— though I didn't know if Esis was strong enough to fix everything. I'd seen Esis do some incredible things, but Imogen basically had her organs rearranged and her throat gouged out. I wasn't sure if his powers would be enough this time.

When Esis was done, he hopped around Imogen and placed a paw on Sassy. Her labored breathing became calm and soft, and her body relaxed. Esis looked at Sophia and held his tail tightly, as if to tell her that was all he could do. Neither of them woke up.

"Good job, Esis," Sophia said. She observed Imogen. "That's it, guys. Esis did all he could. The rest is up to her."

Ezra's eyes were huge. He pushed himself off the wall. "Woah. Is this how you've been getting better, bro?"

I nodded. "Yep. Esis' healing powers have been keeping me alive."

Cade stroked Esis' fur, and Esis cooed. "I won't tell anyone. He helped Imogen. That's more than what I could ever ask for."

Ezra seemed thoughtful. "If Esis can heal, can't he stop the plague?"

"No." Sophia shook her head. "We've tried that, but what we've figured out is that the way Esis' powers work is that he uses the body's natural ability and energy to heal itself. He channels what's already there and boosts it with his own magic to speed up the healing process, but the plague is different. Whatever it is, it blocks his Soul magic from healing the victim. They get a little better, but not completely."

"That reminds me." Cade reached down. He ruffled through a plastic bag before handing us four books. "These were by Imogen when she was found. Professor Fawn grabbed them before the Task Force could. Do they mean anything to you guys?"

I looked at them. One of them was the notebook that Imogen had waved at us earlier. Could it contain any clues?

"They might," I said. I took the books from him and eyed Jonah and Sophia. We needed to check on Squeaks. "We think we might have answers to curing the plague. At least, Imogen did. We need to find out what she knew."

"Go," Cade told us. "Ezra and I won't leave her side."

"We'll be back as soon as we know anything," Sophia promised.

Squeaks had worsened by the time we made it back to the Anichi dorms. Feathers were coming off of her now in droves, and she was so weak now she could hardly move— just sprawled out on the rug, legs slightly twitching. Her eyes dropped big tears, as if she'd thought we'd abandoned her for good.

Jonah stumbled forward and fell at her side. He pulled himself across the rug and sat next to her. She was too tired to even lift her head, so Jonah picked it up and placed it on his lap for her. She sighed in contentment as he stroked her head feathers— as if all she'd been waiting for was for Jonah to get here, so she could die in peace.

"I'm sorry it took so long, Squeaky. But Imogen got hurt," Jonah said. Squeaks gave another rasping cough. It sounded way worse than the ones we'd heard earlier.

Sophia and I scattered the books across the table. Under her breath, Sophia asked, "Why is Squeaks worsening so quickly? Lindsey and Medusa contracted the plague weeks ago, and they're still alive."

"It has to affect various Familiars differently," I said. "Some of these creatures only have it for a week or so before they die. Remember Madame Chavis, the twin Elder from Koigni? She passed away in less than a week after her Familiar got the plague."

"Okay, but what's the difference? Why do some die quickly, and some linger forever?" Sophia asked.

"It's not unusual. Illnesses work like that all the time. Some people with cancer die in a couple of weeks; other people outlast it for years. Disease isn't a straight line," I told her.

I scanned the titles of the books quickly. *Curses of the Miriamic Coven. Miriamic Rituals and Practices. Spells of Miriamic Origin.*

What on earth would Imogen want with these?

Sophia came to my side and read the titles alongside me. "What's the Miriamic Coven?" she asked.

"They're a group of witches who live on the other side of America, in Connecticut. Part demon," I explained quickly. "But I don't know how they'd be connected to any of this. Witches and Elementai don't typically associate. They're enemies with the Arcanea, so we try not to talk to witches in the U.S. for fear of pissing off the sorceresses in Europe. Elementai don't like getting mixed up in international magical affairs."

"No shit," Jonah added meekly from across the room. "We've got enough of our own problems within the tribe."

"I don't know about this, Soph." I ran a hand through my hair in frustration. "This might be a coincidence. Maybe she was researching for a class or something. I don't know how you could connect a Familiar plague with the Miriamic Coven. They don't have Familiars."

"Imogen thought they were involved. So there must be an explanation," Sophia said firmly. "Let's start reading."

I sat down and opened a book. Jonah coughed again. It sounded like he needed a drink. Sophia hurried to grab a bottle of water from the fridge Jonah insisted we install up here. She knelt down beside Jonah and helped him drink.

"Man, this sucks," Jonah said, and Squeaks gave a weak coo. "I'm going to die. I'm not ready to die."

"You aren't going to die. We're going to save you," Sophia insisted.

Jonah looked down at Squeaks. He buried his hand in her feathers. "Do you know how Squeaks and I bonded?" he asked.

"I'm sure it's a very lovely story," Sophia said. "You wanna tell it to me?"

I was trying to focus, but the words blurred together in front of me at the sound of their soft voices. Right now, I was desperate to do something to save them. Anything.

"It was last year, the beginning of last summer," Jonah began. "Me and my dad got in this giant fight. Like, totally major. It was the worst argument we'd ever had."

Squeaks scraped her hooves against the floor, and Jonah hushed her so she'd calm down. "I burst out of the house and just ran for it," Jonah continued. "He came after me, but gave up after the neighbors saw him chasing. He had to keep up appearances, you know. Pretend like he was dad of the year, even though everyone in the neighborhood could hear him shouting at me night and day. Everyone knew that he loved Jenny and hated me. My sister always got all the love and attention. He and Mom made it clear I was the son they never wanted."

"Jonah..." Sophia whispered.

"I ran," Jonah said. "I ran so far into the woods I was pretty sure I'd gotten lost. But I didn't care. It wasn't safe for me to go back home, and I'd rather sleep in the woods than get hit again. So I just walked. I kept walking until the forest got really thick and I couldn't go through it anymore, so I had to turn around."

Jonah's voice got thick. "Then I heard chirping. I thought it was baby birds. I looked up and saw in this giant, massive tree there was a hippogriff nest. I was directly beneath it. The mother was there, but she did something horrible. She pushed one of her babies out of the nest."

"You're kidding." Sophia's voice was full of shock.

"Nope." Jonah shook his head. "She was the tiniest and weakest, so to save the others, the mom tried to kill it, so the others could survive. I heard this little chick's screams as she fell through the air. I ran forward out of instinct and dove to catch her. This little hippogriff landed in my arms, no bigger than a newborn foal. She couldn't have weighed more than a hundred pounds."

Squeaks sighed. Her eyes closed as she drifted into a peaceful rest. But I knew that if Jonah tried to rouse her, she wouldn't wake up. We were running out of time.

Jonah smiled. "I remembered I looked at her, and she looked at me. She was so excited that I'd saved her life. She acted like I was her new mama. She nuzzled my hair and cuddled up against me. Usually, people hear music, or smell things when they bond, but I didn't. It was like everything was complete silence, and calm. It was something I never had, growing up in a house that was always in turmoil. I tried to look for her name, ask her for it, but she didn't have one. Nothing popped into my head. Her mother didn't give her a name. She didn't think she was important enough to have one."

Jonah started to get choked up. "She just... she started making all these little squeaky noises, and I just thought... you know, Squeaks."

Jonah started to cry. Sophia rubbed his back and said, "It'll be okay, Jonah."

"What if it's not?" Jonah wept. Squeaks didn't stir.

"It will. Liam and I will find a way. You just rest."

Sophia got up to join me. Jonah closed his eyes and let his head fall back against the armchair.

I cleared my throat and focused back on the books. I skimmed through the pages, but these books were massive. There was just too much here.

"Liam, look at this," Sophia said. She pushed the notebook toward me. In Imogen's handwriting were page notations. I flipped to the first one and saw that a paragraph in the book had been highlighted.

"*For foes and fiends— there are few curses more powerful in a witch's arsenal than the Omnimotus Curse*," I read. "*Although it ceases to work against any member of the Miriamic Coven, it is valuable when targeting members of other magical factions. When performed properly, this spell will cause a person's magic to waste away inside of them, until it becomes poisonous and deadly to the victim. The curse has an added effect, as it mutates to become virally transmittable to other members of that faction's same species.*"

I sat back in the chair. "It... it sounds like a spell to steal someone's magic. Or at least, the curse attacks the magic until it turns against you. Like how an autoimmune condition works. The curse makes the body attacks itself until you eventually deteriorate, because it considers your powers a foreign entity."

"But why target Familiars? Why not Elementai?" Sophia asked.

"A Familiar *is* the source of an Elementai's magic, though," I said. "You don't get your powers until you're old enough to bond, and Familiars are easier targets. Animals transfer diseases much quicker than people do."

"So... the easiest way to take out someone would be to attack their magic, meaning you should attack their Familiar," Sophia mused.

"Right," I confirmed. "That has to be it."

"But an Elementai can't do this magic. They'd have to hire a witch," Sophia argued.

"Why wouldn't they? The Yapluma hired an Arcanea to bewitch the temple," I pointed out. "Who's to say someone wouldn't pay off a witch to cast a spell to make Familiars ill? Witches don't care about Hawkei politics."

Sophia reached out to stroke Esis' fur. "That makes sense why Esis can't heal them. If the body is already attacking itself due to magic, provoking it to do the opposite and heal won't do much good. But how do we stop it?"

I glanced at Imogen's notebook. I turned it around and read another annotation she'd written down. I grabbed a separate book, then flipped through it until I came to another highlighted paragraph.

"*The Omnimotus Curse can only be lifted in two ways, either by help of a witch...*" I shook my head. "Well, that's not happening."

"Go on!" Sophia insisted.

I continued reading. "*Either by help of a witch, or... the victim finds a way to restore and or replace the magic that has been infected.*"

I lifted my gaze. "That's it. That's the answer."

"What is?" Sophia asked. I got up from the table and rushed to Jonah. I kneeled beside him. He was almost out of it.

"Hey. Jonah, wake up." I slapped his face a couple of times. He barely roused.

"What is it?" Jonah asked weakly. He was barely conscious.

"You know how you draw power from Squeaks to do magic?" I asked.

"Yeah." His head bobbed. I slapped him again, to keep him awake.

"Try the opposite. Try pushing *your* power into Squeaks," I said.

"What?" Jonah blinked, as if confused. "What good is that going to do?"

"The curse can only be broken if you replace the magic that's already been infected. Jonah, you have to give Squeaks your magic. Then she'll be strong enough to push the curse out on her own," I told him. "Think of it like a blood transfusion."

He shook his head a couple of times to wake himself up. "Guess it's worth a shot."

Jonah laid his hands on Squeaks. He stared at her intently, as if he was focusing on putting all his effort into restoring her health.

Wind picked up in the room as Jonah channelled his Air magic. It ruffled Squeaks' feathers and made the notebook pages on the table flutter. An expression of surprise crossed Jonah's face. "Guys, I can literally feel the plague. It's inside her, blocking her magic. It's sucking the life out of her."

"Do you think that you can get it out?" Sophia asked.

"Yeah. I just have to push my magic toward it. Make it leave." Jonah's eyes narrowed, and his face scrunched up. He made a sharp grunt, and the wind in the room picked up again. Sweat beaded his forehead as he concentrated on his magic. Squeaks' hooves began to twitch, and her tail swished. We witnessed as a dark energy rose out of her form and twisted into the air— like some kind of smoke. It must've been the plague leaving her body.

"It's almost gone," Jonah gasped. He gave a final shock blast of Air, and the black smoke whisked away, vanishing for good.

Slowly, Squeaks began to stir. Her eyes fluttered open, and she lifted her head off the ground. Her expression brightened, and she gave a cheerful caw. I witnessed as the color of her feathers changed from a dull brown to a shining tawny.

Jonah gave a huge grin. "The plague's gone! It's not there anymore! I can't feel anything except her energy!"

Squeaks launched herself at Jonah and licked his face. Jonah laughed and flung his arms around her neck. "I'm so sorry, Squeaky. I was so stupid. I'll never abandon you like that ever again."

Esis was cheering, clapping his hands and jumping up and down. I glanced at my girlfriend. She had an ecstatic look on her face. We did it! We'd cured the plague! Now all we needed to do was tell everyone.

The thing was... who would believe us, and how could we tell enough people before it was too late?

"Soph, I think we need to use some of our celebrity status," I said as I rose.

"You're thinking exactly what I'm thinking," Sophia said as she got to her feet. Esis jumped, and she caught him in her arms.

"Hey, where you guys going?" Jonah asked as Sophia and I started for the door. Squeaks chirped happily in his arms. They still looked tired and hungry, but it was clear the plague had passed and they were on the upside.

"Turn on the news," I told him as we headed out. "Promise you'll see us."

Sophia and I took the carriage as fast as we could to the Elementai News Network station— the only one in Kinpago that provided 24/7 news broadcasting. We ran into the ENN lobby, holding hands, and *everyone's* necks craned our way. I swear that people stopped breathing as wide smiles lit up the faces of the reporters.

A million people were on us at once. They strode forward with cameras and notepads, pressing us against the wall with a million questions— Elementai and Familiars both. Sophia squeezed my hand as the crowd pressed in on us. I tried not to lose my cool and freak out about how claustrophobic they made me feel. Esis wriggled against Sophia and tried to avoid getting smushed.

One reporter muscled her way to the front. She had a smile like a snake oil salesman. A fat squirrel sat on her shoulder, chattering. "Mister Mitoh, Miss Henley," she said pleasantly. "I'm Amanda Sly, head anchor for ENN. I'm happy to see you've finally accepted my invitation to drop by."

"We want to go on air for an interview. Right now," I told them. "It's live, or nothing."

She was practically giddy with excitement. "Start up the cameras, boys!" she shouted as she grabbed both our arms and hustled Sophia and I into the newsroom. "We've got them!"

The group around us cheered. I sent an anxious look at Sophia. I didn't know if this plan would work, but it was the best we had.

We were shoved into chairs in front of a broadcasting table. Amanda Sly sat on the other side of Sophia and gave a fake grin the moment the red light for the cameras turned on.

"Good evening, Kinpago, and welcome to this special edition of Nightly News," Amanda began. "I'm your host, Amanda Sly, and we have a breaking new development in the interhouse scandal sweeping the tribe. In studio are the accused, Sophia Henley from Koigni, and Liam Mitoh from Toaqua, here to tell their side of the story."

Amanda shoved a microphone in Sophia's face. "Miss Henley, can we get an exclusive about your feelings on the upcoming trial?"

"Fuck the trial," Sophia snarled, and she grabbed the microphone, wrenching it out of the reporter's hands. Sophia looked straight into the camera and said, "Everyone needs to listen to me! The plague is caused by a curse. Whoever began it paid the Miriamic Coven to create it. But Elementai are the cure. You can use your elemental magic to push out the disease by filling your Familiar with your power. It's the same thing as your Familiar giving you their magic to help you become stronger, only reversed."

"Get her off the air!" I heard someone cry, but a producer shushed them, and Sophia blazed forward.

"You need to focus all your power on your creature. Imagine channeling your element into their body. You'll be able to feel the plague inside of them, and chase it out," Sophia insisted. "Their magic is what's making them sick, but you can replace it. It's the only way!"

Amanda gaped, but her expression was obviously gleeful. This was a far better story than she expected. I figured she thought we looked crazy.

"Are you two saying that you know who caused the curse? Did *you* have any involvement in bringing this plague upon the Familiars?" Amanda asked us.

Great, that's just what we needed. More propaganda. "Fuck no," I said. I probably should've used better language, since we were live on the air, but Sophia had already sworn, so too late now. Knowing we'd probably shot ourselves in the foot and already ruined the case, I plowed forward.

"What Sophia says is true. If you want to save your Familiars, you need to listen to her," I said. "It's the only way."

The doors banged open, and Task Force members swarmed inside the newsroom. ENN employees screamed and dove out of the way as law enforcement came sweeping into the room. They immediately headed for me and Sophia.

"Miss Henley and Mister Mitoh, you are under arrest," a Task Force member said from behind his helmet. They reached for us as Sophia and I backed against the wall. The camera was still on, catching everything for the broadcast.

"What are our charges?!" Sophia screamed.

"For inciting a tribe-wide incident, causing an intercity panic, and broadcasting a message that was not first approved by the Elders," a voice responded.

A tall man walked into the room, flanked by the Task Force. He was well put together, with a navy suit, slicked-back hair and narrow eyes. He was followed by Elder Poole and Elder Malison, both from Toaqua.

"We're trying to do good! We're trying to *save* people!" Sophia protested.

The man gave a delighted grin only vaguely disguised as a sneer. "This information was not formerly approved by tribal government. You have spread false and misleading information about this plague, and therefore, must pay the consequences. Telling lies about such a severe medical condition that affects the entire tribe is punishable by law."

"It's not a lie, it's the truth!" I shouted. The man didn't even glance my way.

"Elder Oleander, where do you want them?" a Task Force member asked as she approached.

"Take them to a holding cell. I don't want them going anywhere," he stated.

So *he* was Elder Oleander— the guy who'd replaced Baine on the Water Council. Baine had warned me about him. He was a fricken snake. I looked to Elder Poole for help, but he stared at the floor and kept quiet— spineless coward he was.

Elder Malison was grinning from ear to ear. He was thrilled that we were getting arrested. It was payback for me refusing to go through with the assassination contract last semester.

The Task Force grabbed the both of us and started hauling us out of the newsroom. Someone wrenched Esis out of Sophia's arms and shoved him in a little cage. He shook the bars in a feeble attempt to escape.

"Give me back my Familiar!" Sophia shouted. I smelled smoke as her hands started heating up, forming fireballs within her fingers.

"Sophia, don't struggle," I told her. "You'll only make it worse."

Sophia's magic slowly died, although she kept her eyes fixed on Esis. Great. Now we'd been dragged off camera by Task Force members on live TV. Our image couldn't possibly get any worse.

We were shoved into an iron carriage and taken downtown by Task Force members. They barely took our fingerprints before they tossed us into an isolated cell. Esis was carried off down the hall. He bit at the bars and screamed for Sophia before he was taken out of sight.

"Esis!" Sophia screamed. She created a large fireball in her hand and drew it backward, to fire it at the prison bars. I grabbed her wrist to stop her.

"Don't try it. Those bars are made of noxite," I warned her. "No way we're getting out."

Sophia gave an impatient yell and kicked the bars. "They can't just arrest us like this!"

"At least they put us in the same holding cell," I said hopefully. "We weren't separated. That's a good sign."

Sophia huffed. "We have to get to Esis. He's probably scared and all alone."

"Probably, but he's safe," I told her. "He's being held in a part of the building where they keep Familiars. If you attempt to bust out, Soph, who can say what's going to happen to him before we get there?"

Sophia's expression was still worried, but her shoulders fell. "You're probably right."

The cell only contained one small twin bed. I sat on it— I was so exhausted my legs were shaking. I didn't know if we were getting out of here. "We need to sleep. We've been up all night. We should get some rest— before whatever happens tomorrow."

Her eyelids drooped. "Guess we're not going anywhere else." She sat beside me. We curled up together on the small bed. I draped the rough blanket over both of us so we could stay warm. It was freezing in here.

Sophia nestled her head into my chest. "Do you think we made the right decision? Because right now, I think we screwed ourselves."

"We saved lives," I said. "Whatever happens now was worth it."

Sophia didn't reply, just pressed into me. Her fingers brushed against my jeans accidentally, and I snickered as a thought crossed my mind.

"What could you possibly be laughing about at a time like this?" she asked.

I grinned. "We could have prison sex."

A smile broke her lips. She laughed softly and said, "You know, that's not such a bad idea."

I kissed the top of her head and stared at the blank brick walls of our prison cell. If nothing else, we'd certainly given Amanda Sly one hell of a story.

THE TWO OF us were woken up the next morning by the screaming of a deranged woman. I could hear her all the way down the cell hall, from the main offices of the Task Force department.

"That sounds like Madame Doya," Sophia said. We quieted down to listen.

"I *demand* that Sophia Henley be released from his hellhole, or so help the ancestors, I'll *burn it to the ground!*" Doya screamed. Beside her, I heard Naomi let out an intimidating roar.

"Miss Henley, along with Miss Mitoh, have incited a panic within the city of Kinpago," the Task Force head told her calmly. "They are being held for a processing period of at least twenty-four hours."

"You call this a panic? People are celebrating!" Doya said. "The plague's been completely cured in a matter of a night. The deaths have stopped, and the quarantine is over. She *saved* your asses."

Sophia and I gave each other looks of relief. So the plan had worked, and we'd been right all along. At least now we wouldn't go down for nothing, and hopefully, the Elders couldn't charge us with spreading a false cure, along with everything else.

"Be that as it may, their message was not approved by any of the Elders, as Elder Oleander made clear last night," the chief responded.

"I'm an Elder, aren't I? I will not allow a student of my House to languish in some cell like a common criminal! Sophia still has three weeks until her trial date, and you will not hold her a second before then!" Doya replied.

"You forget Mister Mitoh is also being charged," he responded calmly.

"Keep the boy! I don't care if he rots!" Doya shouted.

I was really feeling the love from Doya right now. Beside me, Sophia scowled.

The cell block door leading to the station outside opened, and Vanderbilt was hustled through. Two Task Force members were at his side. They came to our cell and began shuffling through keys.

"You two have caused enough trouble," Vanderbilt seethed. "Now I'm left to clean up your mess. You pull a stunt like this, *now*? We have a month left before your court date!"

"We're well aware, Mister Vanderbilt," Sophia replied coolly. "So what's the deal?"

"You two are free to go, for the moment," Vanderbilt replied. "Your bail's been paid. Consider *inciting a panic* added to your long list of charges."

"Doya bailed us out?" Sophia asked, surprised.

"Well, Madame Doya paid *your* bail, Miss Henley," Vanderbilt said. "Though she refused to pay your boyfriend's. You owe me, Mister Mitoh."

"Tack it on your bill. I've got enough money," I told him.

We followed him out of the holding cells. Outside the block, in the offices, Madame Doya had her arms crossed and was tapping her high-heel against the floor impatiently.

She wouldn't even look at me. I had a rotten feeling she blamed me for everything bad that was happening to Sophia right now.

I kinda blamed myself, too. If I hadn't fallen for Sophia, she wouldn't be in danger.

"Esis!" Sophia cried when a Task Force member brought out the cage he was being held in. The cage was unlocked, and Esis scampered into Sophia's arms, quivering and upset. He'd hated being locked up by himself all night.

Doya sneered. "Vanderbilt? You picked *Vanderbilt* as your defense? Are you *trying* to get executed, Sophia?"

"Ah, Eleanor. You've always been fond of me," Vanderbilt said. He shut his briefcase and walked out of the station, as if he couldn't stand to be in Doya's presence a moment longer.

"He was the only one who took on our case," Sophia said firmly. "Now if you'll excuse me, we have to get back to school. There's someone who needs us."

Doya shook her head sharply. "Absolutely not. Although regrettable, I have spoken to Chief Mitoh, and you will be returning to his residence for the time being. And you *will. Stay. Put.*"

Doya hissed the last words at her, and Naomi growled. Sophia's face got red. "That's not fair! We have class, and Imogen—"

"When Miss Ahnild awakens, you will be informed. You shall be allowed to return to school in a few days, once things have calmed down," Doya snapped. "Do not make me force you, Sophia, because I will. And you will take my carriage— to ensure that there are no little stops along the way."

Sophia gave her a cold look. "Fine." She turned her back on Doya and stomped out of the station. Doya followed us, Naomi prowling behind her, as if she didn't trust us not to run off. She only left when the pegasus had carried us far away into the sky, high above the city of Kinpago.

The ride back home felt like it took forever. I was dreading walking through the door. My dad was gonna beat my ass when I got home for the stunt I just pulled, but it was worth it. At least the plague was over, though whoever had caused it still remained a mystery.

Sophia snuggled against me. "Do you think Imogen will be all right?"

I rubbed her arms. I wanted to tell her it would all be okay, but at the same time, I didn't want to lie to her if something happened. I wanted to prepare her for the worst. Imogen was in bad shape. And even with Esis' healing magic helping... I wasn't sure she'd pull through.

I gave the most honest answer I could. "I don't know, *pawee*."

Esis curled up into a ball on our laps. Sophia stared out the window of the carriage toward Orenda Academy, like she wished she could teleport there and be by Imogen's side.

I wanted to be there, too. Our friend needed us. The rest of Kinpago was okay, but Imogen was still fighting for her life.

sophia

EIGHTEEN

L iam and I ignored Madame Doya's instructions and returned to school the following day, since we wanted to visit Imogen after class. I was worried about facing Doya, as she had specifically told me not to return to Orenda until she deemed it safe, but when I entered her classroom I was relieved to find there was a substitute in her place... as well as curious. Where had she gone?

"Lindsey!" I cried. She was sitting at her desk, looking in peak health. Miranda had scooted her desk close to Lindsey. Their heads were close together, and they were talking quietly to one another. Medusa sat curled up at Lindsey's feet. No one else had arrived to class yet but the sub, so the three of us were alone.

Lindsey lifted her head to look at me, and her eyes brightened. "Sophia!"

She hopped out of her desk and held her arms out to me. I set Esis down on the nearest desk and pulled her into a hug.

"How are you feeling?" I asked, looking her over.

"Amazing, thanks to you," she said with a smile. "You're a hero."

I chuckled. "I'm not."

"You are," Miranda argued. "Didn't you see the reports?"

Miranda handed me a newspaper that'd been sitting on her desk. Across the top of the front page was a bold headline that read: *The Plague is Over!*

I began to scan the article.

Interhouse couple Liam Mitoh of Toaqua and Sophia Henley of Koigni are being heralded as heroes following the eradication of the Familiar Plague.

It was a welcome change to the rumors that had spread about our relationship, but I had a feeling the Elders weren't going to like this.

"Do you realize what this means?" Miranda asked enthusiastically.

"Everyone's cured?" I didn't know what she was getting at.

"Well, yeah," she said, "but I meant for you and Liam. Your trial. People are coming out to show their support. Here, let me show you."

Miranda grabbed the newspaper and flipped to the editorial section. "They're saying you should be pardoned, because you stopped the plague."

I froze, stunned. I could hardly process the words on the page. "I— I was just trying to help everyone. I didn't know it'd help the trial."

Lindsey bounced on the balls of her feet. "This is great news for you two."

"Wait," I said. "You aren't upset? About me and Liam, I mean. Because I'm really sorry about how everything went down, Lindsey. I didn't mean to—"

She held up a hand, cutting me off. "I'm going to stop you right there, Sophia. Don't *worry*. There are no hard feelings. There was someone I'd been wanting to ask out for a long time, anyway."

Her gaze traveled over to Miranda, and a blush rose to her cheeks. Miranda smiled as she entwined her fingers with Lindsey's.

"You two are dating?" I asked in excitement. I was happy for them.

Lindsey beamed. "Yes, and I seriously can't thank you enough for your help curing the plague. I thought I was going to die."

"I'm glad we found the answer in time," I told her.

It was then that Haley and Kelsey walked into the room. Haley took one look at Lindsey and Miranda's entwined hands and scoffed. She strolled over to her desk and tossed her hair over her shoulder, then mumbled a string of slurs under her breath to Kelsey.

"Ignore her," I said to Lindsey and Miranda.

Lindsey's eyebrows shot up. "Ignore her? Girl, we're going to give that bitch something to talk about."

Lindsey placed her hand on the side of Miranda's face, and Miranda leaned in. Their lips connected. I beamed proudly at them, and Esis clapped from his spot on the desk beside me. Haley was so shocked that she didn't make a sound.

Lindsey and Miranda returned to their seats with wide smiles on their faces. Lindsey turned around in her seat to whisper to me. "And that's how you deal with a Westfenix."

After class, I picked up Imogen's History of the Hawkei homework and met up with Liam in the hospital.

The hospital had completely transformed since we'd been here last. The beeping of machines and bustling of hospital staff had completely died down. The white curtain separating the quarantine area was no longer there, either. It was eerily quiet.

Liam was already in Imogen's room when I arrived. He was sitting at her bedside, stroking Sassy's fur. Sassy was back in her fox form and lying on Imogen's bed, though gauze was still wrapped around her middle. She seemed to be doing better. Sassy was awake and alert, but she kept her head low and rested it on Imogen's hand while she waited for her to awaken.

Cade sat slumped in a chair on her other side, holding her hand, but he was completely out of it. It was like he hadn't slept all night. He was even snoring a little. Arabelle slept at his feet. Esis hopped out of my arms and onto the bed, where he snuggled up beside Sassy and worked his healing magic on her and Imogen.

I pulled up a chair beside Liam. "Did you talk to the doctors?"

He nodded solemnly. "They said her vitals have stabilized, but they still don't know when she'll wake up."

I gazed down at her sleeping form. Her wounds were still tightly wrapped in bandages. Just thinking about what Renar did to her made me ill.

"I'm still trying to wrap my head around everything," I whispered. "The attack, the cure, that night in the jail cell... who was that prick that locked us away, anyhow?"

Liam frowned. "Elder Oleander. He's the guy who replaced Baine. Dad says he's just about as bad as Elder Malison."

"If your dad doesn't like him, why's he on the council?" I asked.

"I don't know," Liam admitted. "The chief gets final approval, but if Oleander was the only one eligible, my dad couldn't exactly say no."

"How do you get considered for the council?"

"You have to either do something good for the tribe or show great power," Liam explained. "Anyone with a seat on the Elder Council can nominate someone, and then the chief of that tribe must approve them. I guess Dad felt pressured to fill Baine's space on short notice."

I thought of something. "If you have to do something good for the tribe to get on the council, what did Doya do? She's so young for an Elder. She must've done something important."

"I've heard rumors, but I don't know if they're true," Liam said.

I raised an eyebrow. "Oh?"

Liam shifted in his chair to face me. "You know the riots that killed your birth parents?"

My guts twisted. The Toaqua had come into the Koigni Village the night after I was born, hoping to kill me so I couldn't fulfill the prophecy. "Yes, I remember the story."

"Well, after a bunch of people died, there was a lot of tension between Koigni and Toaqua," Liam said.

"There's *always* tension between Koigni and Toaqua," I pointed out.

He shook his head. "Not like it was. People were getting into fights and hurting each other even after the first riots were over. I guess Doya was instrumental in negotiating an agreement between Toaqua and Koigni to calm the tribes. She helped prevent a full-blown war, and everyone kind of forgot about the prophecy— until you showed up."

"Wow," I said, absorbing the information. "I had no idea. She must've been our age at the time. Can you imagine that the Elders actually listened to her?"

Liam chuckled. "I don't think it was easy."

"What's easy?" Jonah said cheerfully as he pushed his way into the room. He was carrying a large bouquet of flowers— every color of the rainbow— along with a dozen balloons that barely fit through the door, and a cup of coffee. Squeaks wore a saddle bag and held the door open with her foot while Jonah squeezed the balloons inside.

"Are we talking about Sophia?" Jonah asked with a wink when he turned to us. "Because I hear—"

"Ancestors, Jonah!" I threw my hands over my ears. "I do *not* want to know what you've heard."

I shot a quick glance at Liam. "Or do I?"

Liam chuckled. "Relax. He's just teasing."

Cade stirred awake at the sound of our voices. "Oh, hey. You... you brought flowers?"

"Yep, for you." Jonah held them out to Cade, who looked totally confused, but reached for them anyway. Jonah pulled back at the last second and laughed. "I'm only joking, man. But seriously, the coffee's for you."

Jonah handed Cade the cup of coffee, and he started sipping on it. Cade smacked his lips. "Oh, man. That's so good. Thank you."

"No problem," Jonah said. "You've been taking care of our Imogen. Someone needs to take care of you."

Jonah started digging through Squeaks' saddle bag. "I also went to the dining hall and got some takeout, plus packed a few mice for Sassy."

Jonah handed Cade two wrapped burgers, then opened a plastic container of dead mice and let Sassy sniff it. She wasn't as quick to scarf her mouse down as usual, but at least she was eating.

Jonah tossed a mouse to Squeaks, who caught it mid-air, then placed the top back on the container.

"That's really generous of you," Cade said kindly.

"That's not all," Jonah replied, like he was hosting some sort of game show. He returned to digging through the saddle bag. "I also picked up a going-home outfit for Imogen. She'll want to look fab when she finally gets out of this place."

He held up a pair of bright red tights and draped them over the bed on Imogen's legs, like he was trying to see how they'd look. On top of those, he placed a matching, pleated red skirt. He clapped his hands together. "See? She'll look gorgeous."

"Good God. I'll look like a walking tomato."

"Imogen!" I cried, shooting to my feet. I was beside her head in a split-second, as was Cade on her other side. Arabelle startled awake.

Imogen's eyes fluttered open. Cade pushed her hair back. "Babe, you're awake!"

He looked like he wanted to hug her and kiss her all over, but didn't want to hurt her, so he held back.

"It was either that or a heart attack," Imogen groaned. It didn't sound like talking was easy for her. "Get those off of me."

Jonah didn't listen. Instead, he threw himself at her feet and hugged her legs. "You're alive!"

"For now," she forced out. "Next time, get me rainbow tights."

"I don't care what you're wearing as long as you're alive. But noted." Jonah quickly removed the skirt and tights from the bed.

Liam stood beside me. "How are you feeling, Im?"

She took a moment to breathe. "Everything hurts, but I'll live."

"That's what's important," I said, feeling tears welling up in my eyes.

"You guys, the plague..." Imogen whispered.

"It's okay, Im. We figured out what you were going to tell us," Liam said. "It *was* the curse, but everyone's okay now, including Squeaks. The plague is gone for good. We cured it."

"Thank the ancestors." Imogen looked to Jonah, and she frowned. "Jonah, I have something to tell you about the attack."

"I know," Jonah said before she could explain herself. "I know Renar sicced Alvarice on you."

"He *what?*" Cade exploded. He started for the door, his hands fisting at his sides.

Jonah placed a hand on his shoulder to stop him. "Relax. It's been taken care of."

"What do you mean?" Cade snarled. "I'm going to kick his ass."

"Believe me," Liam said, "Jonah's already kicked his ass enough for the both of you."

"Yeah," Jonah said. "He'll be lucky to survive the tournament at this point."

"He won't if I have anything to say about it," Cade growled.

"Then let the tournament take care of him," Liam suggested. "You don't need to get yourself in trouble."

Cade backed away from the door, but he was still fuming. "I can't believe he would do this... all to get to you?" Cade looked to Jonah.

Jonah shrugged. "Something like that. All that matters is that it's over between us, and he won't be hurting any more of my friends."

"Thank the ancestors," Cade said, raking his fingers through his dark hair. "I just... I don't know how I'm going to compete in the tournament with him on my team, not after this..."

Imogen reached up and took Cade's hand. "Forget about him, babe. Just make sure that you come home alive."

Cade sank back into his chair, and his eyes glistened with tears. He looked deeply into Imogen's eyes, like they were the only two in the room. My heart broke just to see the look on his face. "Imogen, we've talked about this. I can't make any promises."

"Promise me you'll try your hardest," Imogen pleaded. "That's all I ask. There's still so much I want to do with you."

She wasn't just talking about sex, even though I knew they hadn't crossed that line yet. They were definitely at that point in their relationship, but Imogen said Cade was waiting until after the tournament. Just in case he didn't make it.

Cade hesitated. "Imogen, you know I'll always do what's best for the tribe."

She nodded. Tears rimmed her lower lid. "I know."

"I love you," he whispered, dipping his head to kiss her lightly on the lips.

A single tear streaked her face as he pulled away. "I love you, too."

"I DON'T THINK I'm ready for this," I told Liam as we entered the Nivita village two and a half weeks later.

"I know," Liam said, raking is fingers through his hair. "But there's no avoiding it. All of Kinpago is broadcasting the Elemental Cup this week. And to be honest, if something's going to happen to Ezra, I want to know right away. I don't want to have to wait."

"True."

We began climbing the steps to the Nivita treehouses. Imogen had been released from the hospital a few days after the attack, but she spent most of her time at her parents' recovering. Esis' abilities were helping speed up the process, but it'd been so bad that it was taking time for her to heal. I wasn't sure she'd have made it without Esis.

Liam and I visited Imogen's house most nights after class to study with her and Jonah for finals. Since Jonah was single now, he spent a lot more time around Imogen. He treated her like a queen, always making sure she was well taken care of and had enough blankets to keep warm. Cade came every now and then, but he spent a lot of his time with Ezra strategizing for the tournament and trying not to murder Renar.

Imogen was well enough to return to school for finals week, and I was pretty sure she'd aced everything— even her dance final, which she and Jonah had modified so she didn't have to move as much and risk injuring herself further.

For whatever reason, Doya hadn't paired me and Haley up for our final like she'd threatened earlier in the semester. I'd been paired with Ben instead, and we easily passed. I'd done well in my other classes, though Jonah and Liam had barely scraped by. They'd passed though, and that was all that mattered.

Finals were over, and we'd reached the week of the tournament. Since Imogen was still recovering, we agreed to watch the opening ceremony and following footage at her house. It was going to be a week-long party of junk food and chit chat while we waited for news on the Cup. Imogen said it was better if we enjoyed it together instead of getting all depressed over it. I figured it would keep her from worrying so much about Cade.

We reached Imogen's treehouse and knocked on the door. She was quick to answer. "Welcome!"

Imogen was looking better. She no longer needed the bandages, though there were still large scabs and pale pink lines where the wounds were once gashed open. It looked like Esis was helping enough that it wouldn't severely scar.

We stepped inside, and the smell of pizza hit my nose.

"I hope you're hungry," Imogen said. "Quick, grab some before Jonah eats it all."

Jonah was sitting in the living room with his feet propped up on the coffee table, scarfing down two pieces of pizza at once that were folded together like a sandwich. Squeaks lay in front of the TV, where pre-tournament commentary was playing. Old footage of the four of us winning the Cup from last year blazed across the screen, but we all ignored it. We didn't feel like champions or heroes. The Cup was an experience all of us just wanted to forget.

Sassy hurried over to us, and Esis jumped out of my arms to greet her. They sniffed each other playfully.

"Relax!" Jonah shouted with a full mouth. "There's enough to go around."

Imogen chuckled. "My family got tickets to the arena to watch the opening ceremony, so don't worry about leaving extra for them."

We entered the kitchen. I grabbed a plate and reached for a piece of pepperoni pizza.

"Hang on," Imogen said. "We ordered a special one for you."

Imogen opened a box of pizza on the other side of the kitchen, and I couldn't help but laugh. It was half supreme and half crust— no sauce, cheese, or anything. It was just like the one Liam and I had ordered my first semester at Orenda.

Liam smiled wide. "Seriously, guys?"

"What?" Jonah shrugged innocently from the living room. "It's perfect for you two. Total fucking opposites."

I laughed and reached for the supreme half. "You're right. It's perfect. Thank you."

Liam and I snuggled up beside each other on the couch with our food. "Did anyone place any bets—?" Liam started, but Jonah cut him off.

"Shh..." Jonah hissed. "It's starting."

Music played on the TV, and Head Dean Alric stepped out on stage. I felt like I was holding my breath the whole time as teams came up on stage to say their final words to the tribe before they were cast into the tournament. It was sick, really. For some of them, it would be the last thing their families ever heard them say.

The first team that came on stage— the Yellow Team— all looked like timid First Years. Their Familiars were small, like Esis, and didn't seem to possess any magical abilities. They kind of reminded me of us.

"I hope they all finish," I said.

Jonah shot me a skeptical glance, but he didn't say anything. He probably thought they would all die during the first task, but everyone had said the same thing about us. As long as they were smart and worked together, they'd make it. I was rooting for them.

The Yellow Team was ushered to the seating area on the edge of the stage, and another team came out. They kept coming, one right after the other. I recognized a few people from class, but it wasn't until I saw Lindsey come on stage that my heart began to pound nervously. At least she seemed to have a good team— including a griffin, hippocampus, and a lion-like creature on her team, along with her basilisk Familiar.

Kelsey's team came next, which included her jaguar Familiar, a sea serpent, and two different kinds of birds. I was sensing we were getting to the end of the lineup as more and more powerful Familiars were introduced.

My blood ran cold as the Green Team came on stage. Ezra walked out first, with Dyami at his side. The thunderbird looked bigger than ever. Alvarice strutted onto stage beside him, Renar looking confident on his back. He was still wearing two casts— one on his leg and one on his arm— so I was willing to bet he'd spend the entire tournament riding his Familiar. Renar raised his hand and waved to the crowd.

Jonah had just so happened to grab a handful of chips at that moment. He raised them to his mouth, but then the camera angle changed and focused on Renar's face. Jonah's hand clenched into a fist, and bits of chips sprinkled around his lap and the couch.

Cade and Arabelle came next. I noticed Imogen clutch Sassy a little tighter to her chest. Vanessa and Aisha stayed close to Cade as they walked on stage. Vanessa wasn't huge yet, but her baby bump was obvious in the tight uniform.

Alric gave them a short introduction, then said, "Is there anything you'd like to say?"

He handed the microphone to Ezra, who took it. Ezra opened his mouth to speak, but Renar leaned over from Alvarice's back and snatched the microphone out of his hand.

Renar looked at the audience like they were all beneath him. "I hope you bitches all bet on me, because only the *strongest* make it to the end. Enjoy the show."

His demeanor quickly changed. He smiled and waved to the crowd like he was a celebrity. He shoved the microphone back in Alric's direction, and Alvarice started toward the seats by the other teams. He didn't even give the rest of his team a chance to say anything.

Ezra leaned over to Cade and said something, but we couldn't hear what it was. I bet he was threatening to murder Renar as soon as they hit the course.

Two teams came after them, and then they filed into carriages and started toward the first task. Their carriages didn't fly like ours had, though. They rode through the forest, with the cameras and commentary following them the whole way.

Finally, they came to a stop beside a huge cave opening in the mountainside. It was large enough for at least three carriages to pass through side-by-side, but they didn't go in. They dropped off the contestants outside the cave, then continued into the forest.

Everyone stood around for a moment, gazing upward into the sky or deep into the depths of the cave, waiting for some sort of sign so they could form a plan.

Nothing happened until the Blue Team started into the forest. Fireballs rained down from the sky, forcing them back toward the cave. The Purple Team started to climb the rocks up the cave's side, but fireballs starting coming from all directions, and they had to retreat to avoid getting burnt to a crisp.

A few teams raced for the cover of the cave right away. I cringed. It was a stupid move, as they could get trapped in there— but it seemed to be what the Elders wanted. Renar didn't even glance at his teammates before he tried to fly Alvarice above the forest canopy. A fireball smacked straight into his side and knocked him out of the air before he could get far.

"Ha!" Jonah laughed with a mouthful of chips. "That's what you get."

Liam tried to hold in a laugh from beside me.

Ezra, Cade, and Vanessa joined hands and raced into the cave with their Familiars at their sides. They dodged fireballs the whole way. I let out a breath of relief when they all made it to the cave safely.

The camera angle switched to inside the cave, as if they'd set up cameras before the start of the tournament. We could no longer see Renar.

"Was that it?" I asked, a little baffled. "That seemed a lot easier than our Fire challenge."

Imogen shook her head. "I don't think that was the Fire challenge. I think this is—"

She cut off, her face paling. The cave began to shake, the earth groaning as rocks tumbled down the mountain. Screams filled the cave, and everything went dark as the entrance collapsed.

A horrified look fell across Imogen's face. "Earth."

For a moment, everything was dark, until Koigni on all teams started forming Fire in their hands to light the cave walls. The camera angle shifted again, and I noticed Renar and Alvarice beside the rest of the Green Team. Somehow, he'd made it before the cave-in. He was yelling at them, but there was so much chaos that we couldn't hear what he was saying. The earth continued to shake beneath their feet, and dirt rained down from the cave ceiling.

"We have to go. Now!" I could just make out Ezra's words as he took Vanessa's hand and followed the other teams deeper into the cave.

Large rocks three feet across started to fall from the ceiling. Cade raised his hands to try to deflect them with his magic. Several people from other teams screamed as huge boulders fell on them or their Familiars.

The camera angle changed again, and I couldn't look away soon enough. A boulder the size of Squeaks fell onto a feline Familiar, squashing it flat. Its Elementai didn't even have time to react to save it. Blood squirted everywhere.

I buried my face into Liam's shoulder, and he pulled me tighter to him. I couldn't block out the sound of the rumbling earth and crashing rocks— and the screams... so much screaming. Then... *bam!* The entire cave crumbled in on itself, causing a deafening roar as rock tumbled over rock.

I gasped, finally bringing my eyes back to the TV. The screen went black, then switched back to the commentary room, where the announcers from the opening ceremony were narrating the events of the first task.

"Unfortunately, that's as far as the cameras go," Eli the announcer said in a chipper voice. "But we'll see soon enough which teams made it through and which ones perished. Let's take a look at the scoreboard."

"That cave-in sounded insane," I said, horrified. "Do you think they made it?"

"They'll make it through," Liam assured me. I heard something in his voice, something that suggested there was no other way— like the Elders would never hurt everyone all at once, or they wouldn't have a show. I got that the Elemental Cup was tradition and all, but it still seemed horrible to me.

I shook impatiently as we waited for news on which teams had made it out. I knew it could be hours— or even days— but I wanted to know now. I *had* to know. Were my friends safe?

Imogen's family had returned from the arena by this time and were watching the TV as eagerly was we were. The program was filled with prior year recaps and commentary about this years' contestants.

I hated how all the commentators talked about were how Liam and I performed last year, along with notes about the upcoming trial. Couldn't they let it go? I just wanted to know if my friends were safe. Sitting here watching the Cup and being unable to do anything was ten times more tortuous than actually being in it.

We finally got word two hours later. An aerial camera circled an exit to the cave, and three members of the Purple Team came crawling out. They were covered in dirt, and one of their team members had a huge gash on their arm from the rocks. It would set them back to find plants and herbs to help the healing.

Another hour later, the Blue Team emerged from the cave, two members down. Twenty minutes after that, a member of the White Team. He was alone, and he still had three tasks left to go. I didn't think he was going to make it. He was already disqualified for being the only surviving member.

The Yellow Team emerged late that night with all four of their members and Familiars still alive. I felt a sense of pride wash through me, since they were the freshman team marked least likely to make it.

More and more teams made it out of the caves once darkness had fallen, but most were missing at least one or two members, and a lot of people were injured. I didn't know what had gone on down in those caves, but it seemed to be worse than what we went through during our Earth task.

"I don't remember so many people dying during the first task last year," I said solemnly.

"It gets harder and harder every year," Imogen whispered. She hadn't taken her eyes off the screen, as if holding her breath for the moment Cade would come back on.

Eventually, the Red Team— Kelsey's team— made it, with only three team members remaining. Not long afterward, Lindsey's team— the Gold Team— came out of the caves. They were only the second team who'd made it with all their team members still alive. I was relieved to see Lindsey and Medusa weren't hurt.

It was nearing midnight, and most of Imogen's family had gone to bed— all except her eldest brother, Soren. I was beginning to nod off, but I didn't want to sleep until I knew for sure what had happened to our friends.

"Maybe they're just waiting it out until morning," Liam suggested nervously. He couldn't take his eyes off the TV, and his hold on me had tightened. He was really worried about Ezra.

"Well, Eli," the second announcer, Louis, said. "It looks like the Orange Team and the Green Team didn't make it, but we'll have to wait until morning for confirmation—"

"Hold on, Louis," Eli said quickly, pressing his finger to his earpiece.

The camera switched back to the mountain, but Eli's voice continued over the video footage. A dark shadow moved through the narrow cave opening. "It looks like you might've spoken too soon. A member from the Green Team has just made it!"

We all let out a collective cry of relief. I suddenly felt very awake and alert. I straightened in my seat.

We couldn't make out much in the darkness of the night, but eventually, the figure emerged crawling. I couldn't tell who it was— except that it was one of the guys. A creature stepped out of the cave behind him, and I could make out the silhouette of the cockatrice.

Renar.

The blood drained from my face, and the room went silent as we waited. Finally, I couldn't take it anymore. "Wait. No. Where's the rest of the team?"

Imogen's bottom lip quivered. "Do you think...?" She choked up and couldn't finish the last of her sentence.

"It looks like this Green Team member might be alone," Louis said.

"Oh my God!" I cried, grabbing so tightly to Liam's hand that he gasped.

Another figure moved near the cave entrance. A beat passed, and then Vanessa stepped out of the cave with Aisha at her side.

"Yes!" I cried in relief. "She's alive."

Cade and Ezra came right after her, with their Familiars beside them. They looked exhausted, but they were alive. Ezra stomped up to Renar and shouted something in his face, but we couldn't hear it.

Eli chuckled. "It looks like we have some team drama this year. Of course, it wouldn't be the Elemental Cup without it."

Imogen started crying in relief, and Jonah quickly went to her side to console her.

"I really thought—" She could hardly speak past her sobs. "I thought they wouldn't make it."

"Shh..." Jonah encouraged. "They made it past the first task. That's always the worst. They'll make it through the rest."

I looked up to Liam and spoke lowly. "Do you think he's right?"

Liam looked nervous to answer the question. "I think they can all handle themselves out there... as long as Renar doesn't do something to get them killed."

I frowned. "Yeah. Let's hope not."

THREE DAYS PASSED. The tasks seemed even more grueling this year than the last, and people were dying in droves. In the Fire task, teams had been forced into a gorge and had to scale the steep rocks to escape the flames at the bottom.

I didn't want to watch the Green Team take on the task, but I couldn't look away. Renar had gone ahead, dodging fireballs as Alvarice flew up and out of the gorge. He used what Air he could as a shield. Meanwhile, Dyami was trying to carry everyone else out of the gorge, but his wing was hit by a rogue fireball. He couldn't fly injured with all that weight on his back, which left the task up to Vanessa. I was shaking the whole time, praying to the ancestors they'd make it. Vanessa had calmed the flames enough to give them some time, then Aisha scaled the rocky cliff to carry the rest of the team to safety on her back. I breathed a sigh of relief.

The Yellow Team had since lost two members, and the Gold had lost one, which meant that the Green Team was the only one left with all four members still alive. We'd spent almost every waking second at Imogen's watching the tournament... waiting.

On day three, Liam and I decided to take a break that afternoon, since it didn't look like any team was near one of the tasks. We walked hand-in-hand on the trail from the Nivita village toward Kinpago, which was a short, quiet walk. Esis rode on my shoulder.

"I don't get it," I said, gazing down at our entwined fingers.

"Get what?" Liam asked.

I kicked at a rock on the path. "How can the Elders keep allowing this? The Cup, I mean. It's so brutal. Half the contestants aren't even going to survive this year. It's a sick tradition."

"It's more than just a tradition," Liam said. "It's an important part of securing your bond with your Familiar. It puts the two of you through the worst together."

"Okay, I can accept that," I told him, "but everyone makes it sound like it wasn't always so bad."

"It wasn't," Liam admitted as we got to the outskirts of Kinpago. The dirt path turned to cobblestone, with small shops lining the street. "It used to be relatively easy. Almost everyone used to make it through."

"Then why have the Elders made it so hard?" I asked.

Liam sighed. "I don't know—"

He was cut off by the sharp sound of a slap. A woman let out a pained gasp.

"I'm sorry," she cried. I recognized the voice as Mia's.

"It's okay," a man said, shushing her to soothe her.

We were just passing a landscaping store with outdoor ceramic decor and working fountains out front when we rounded the corner to an alleyway. I stopped dead in my tracks. Mia was wrapped in Micah's arms, clutching the side of her face and holding back tears. Her canine Familiar, Taryn, cowered in fear of Micah's Familiar. The creature looked like a water serpent, but it was only the size of a young dragon. It had a serpent-like face, with spines coming out of its neck, and legs that reminded me of a lizard. Sharp, pointed scales stuck out of its back like some sort of torture device. I'd heard of these creatures before— it was a malerta. It stood over the canine, staring down at it threateningly so she couldn't step in and defend Mia. Mia caught our eyes, but Micah didn't see us there.

Micah ran his fingers through her silky dark hair as he cradled her close. "Now you know not to be late again."

Wait... did he just—? I'd had no idea... I felt terrible for Mia.

"What the hell?" I stepped forward.

Liam grabbed me by the wrist the same time Mia drew away from Micah and said, "Sophia, no!"

I struggled out of Liam's hold, but he held me tighter. "Drop it, Soph. Let me handle it," he hissed in my ear.

I ignored him and aimed my anger at Micah. I finally wrenched away from Liam. "You hit her, you asshole!"

Micah crossed his arms and smirked, like he was amused by my forwardness. "I fail to see how that's any of your business."

"Sophia, just go," Mia insisted. She dropped her hand, and I could see the welt forming on her skin. "I'm fine. It was my fault anyway."

My jaw dropped. "Your *fault*? Mia, he *hit* you!"

"Fuck off, *mopite*," Micah snarled.

Liam stepped in front of me, placing himself between me and Micah protectively.

"*Mopite?*" I asked.

"Slang term for interhouse couples," Liam whispered under his breath. I gritted my teeth.

Mia turned back to Micah. "You didn't have to call them that."

Micah grabbed Mia's wrist tightly and dragged her toward him. She struggled out of his hold, but he wouldn't let her go. He took his other hand and forced her to look at him. "Don't *ever* tell me what to do."

Mia's eyes filled with tears that she was desperately trying to hold back. That was it.

Liam and I both snapped at the same time. He stomped down the alleyway toward Micah, but I set Esis on the ground and pushed past Liam before he made it to Micah. I shoved Micah as hard as I could, and he stumbled a few steps, letting go of Mia. Esis held his fists up, like he was about to box with Micah.

"Leave her alone!" I shouted.

He turned to me with fury in his eyes. Mia threw herself between us and started crying as Micah advanced on me. "Please, Micah. Don't," she begged.

But I was already ready for him. I formed a fireball in my hand. Liam jumped in front of me.

"Take one step closer," Liam dared him.

Micah stopped and raised his hands in surrender. "Hey, it's all cool."

"It's is *not* cool," I growled.

Micah's lips twisted into a sneer. "You should learn to keep your girl in line," he said to Liam.

Liam opened his mouth to say something, but I spoke before he could. "Fuck you. Nobody owns me. And you don't own Mia!"

Micah raised his hand, like he was about to bring it down across Liam's face. Instead, he used his Water power to gather water from the gutters above our heads and whipped it at my face. It cracked across the side of my cheek, sending a stinging pain across my skin.

"Ow!" I screamed.

"Micah!" Mia cried, tears streaming down her face now.

Esis placed his paw in my leg, and the pain immediately eased.

Before I knew what was happening, Liam had lunged at Micah. He threw a punch, and the two ended up on the ground in a scuffle. Oh, shit! What had I done? Fists flew everywhere that I could barely tell who was punching who. Micah's Familiar let out a screech and snapped its jaws at Liam, but the two were moving so quickly that the creature nearly caught Micah with his fangs by accident.

Liam gathered water from the nearby fountains and shoved it up into Micah's face. Micah gasped for breath, but it was only a gurgle as the water moved in and out of his airways. Mia threw her hands over her mouth and wept in horror. Liam was drowning him.

"Liam!" I shouted, but he didn't seem to hear me. "You're going to kill him!"

I threw myself into the middle of the fight and dragged Liam off Micah. The effort made me trip. The water fell away from Micah's face, and he inhaled a deep breath. But he hadn't had enough. He threw himself at Liam again. Micah gathered the water into a ball in his hand and aimed it at Liam's face.

I reacted quickly and grabbed on to Micah's ankle. I called upon just enough Fire to hurt him, but not cause any permanent damage. Micah screamed and backed off, aiming his attention at me. He kicked out his other foot at my head, but I got to my feet and dodged out of the way just in time.

It was enough to distract him that Liam got free. Liam grabbed me and dragged me to my feet, pulling me several feet away from Micah.

Mia was at Micah's side in an instant. She knelt beside him and checked his injuries, then turned an enraged gaze up toward us. "What the fuck, Liam!?"

I could hardly believe my ears. After what Micah just did to her, she was still on *his* side?

Micah sat up, but he was too preoccupied with the burn on his ankle to pursue us. I was still too shocked to move.

"Just go, Liam," Mia whispered, while looking utterly concerned for her abusive ass of a boyfriend. The two of us hesitated, until Mia looked Liam straight in the eye and shouted, "Go!"

Liam had to practically drag me out of the alley while I watched Mia try to console Micah, who just shrugged her off and shot daggers my way. Liam finally let me go when they were out of sight. Esis jumped up my pant leg and crawled onto my shoulder. He checked the side of my face to make sure I was all right.

"Liam, we have to go back," I insisted, but he kept on walking. "*Liam.*"

He turned to me, looking distressed. "Look, Sophia, it's no use."

"Wait. You *knew* about this?" I demanded.

Liam sighed and dropped his shoulders. "It's why I was hanging out with Mia this semester. I was trying to help her. But no matter what I did, she always found a way to defend him."

My guts twisted. How could I have thought they were screwing around? He'd been trying to help Mia leave her abusive boyfriend. I was so stupid.

"She cheated on you with a guy who was abusive?" I asked, hardly able to believe it.

"Some people just don't know what's good for them, Soph," Liam said. "I don't think Mia really understands what love is. People go looking for the love they think they deserve. I treated her well when we were dating, but that probably felt strange to her. As sick as it is to think, Micah hitting her might seem... I don't know, normal to her."

"Ancestors, how long has this been going on?" I asked. "She needs to leave him."

"I know," he said solemnly. "I've told her that, but she just makes excuses. Nothing's going to work until she realizes for herself how bad he is."

My jaw dropped. "She could be dead by then."

Liam took my face in his hands and stared deeply into my eyes. "I know. Just promise me you won't get involved, Soph. Micah's dangerous, and I just can't... I can't stand the thought of him hurting you, *pawee*. I'd kill him."

"But don't you care about Mia?" I asked in a soft whisper. Even as I said it, I knew it wasn't true. He didn't care about her like he cared about me, but he didn't wish this kind of thing upon her.

"I do," he said. "I tried to help, but she still wants to be with Micah. She just wants him to change. And I told her that would never happen, but..."

I reached out to take Liam's hand. I could see the sorrow written in his face. He really had tried, but there was nothing more he could do if Mia didn't leave.

"Liam," I whispered. "I'm so sorry."

"I am, too." His voice cracked when he spoke, and I knew he meant it.

THE FINAL TASK arrived two days later. The Green Team had made it through the Air task, though not without hardship. The task had struck without warning. One second they were walking through the woods just fine, and the next, they were gasping for breath. The Elders had been trying to suffocate them!

Renar had gathered enough Air for him and Alvarice, then had flown ahead to get more oxygen for himself, the bastard. Ezra used his water power to gather water from a nearby steam. He used it as a force field to carry a large bubble of air over to each of them, which held them over until Dyami got high enough in the sky to force air downward with his wings so they could breathe again.

Now we sat in Imogen's living room with her family, on the edge of our seats as our friends reached the Water task alongside the Red Team. They stood at the edge of the ocean, staring up at a huge wall of water. It stretched up at least a hundred feet and was so long that the cameras didn't show the end of it. It was the only thing that stood between them and the finish line on the island out at sea.

Renar looked overly confident on Alvarice's back as they tried to fly up and over the water wall. But it didn't work. A long funnel of water stretched out and slapped them out of the air. Renar and Alvarice plummeted to the beach and rolled to catch their fall. I half expected Renar to stay down, but he pushed himself back up.

The cameras were high in the air, so we couldn't hear what was happening on the ground, but we could see Renar flipping off the ocean as if it were to blame. Meanwhile, Ezra, Cade, and Vanessa had their heads together, strategizing.

The two remaining members of the Red Team— Kelsey and a Toaqua guy I didn't know— had already decided what to do. Seeing as there was no way around it, they stepped forward to the wall of water. The guy's sea serpent Familiar swam up to meet them and stuck his head out of the wall. They climbed on its back, then the sea serpent carried them into the ocean. Though the wall looked calm on the outside, there was a raging current within, evidenced by the way the Red Team tumbled through the water. The Toaqua team member used his magic to right them, but the more they swam forward, the more invisible currents took them off course. It looked brutal inside.

"This looks impossible," I said. "Teams without Toaqua team members aren't going to make it."

"I could," Jonah said with a shrug. "I'd create a bubble of air around my head so I could breathe and bring an air pocket inside the water to rocket me to the other side."

"Shh," Imogen hissed, flapping her hand to keep us quiet. She was at the edge of her seat, holding Sassy so tightly she let out a squeak.

The Green Team faced the wall of water and stepped inside. They were mere shadows in the sea as the current caught them and tumbled them over and over again. Ezra used his magic to help Cade, Vanessa, and their Familiars escape the current, while Renar looked like he was trying to handle it on his own. Somehow, he got out of the current and started swimming alongside them again.

They all joined hands and rocketed forward, but another current swept past them. Cade's fingers slipped out of Ezra's, and he was dragged away from them, Arabelle at his side.

I found myself holding my breath so long as I watched that I felt like my lungs were about to explode. I couldn't imagine what they were going through right now. I wanted to turn my eyes away, but I couldn't.

Ezra used his magic to control the current and drag Cade back toward the team. He seemed exhausted already. I forced myself to take a breath, but it didn't seem fair— not when they were nearly drowning right now.

Another current swept through, but Dyami threw himself in front of it and blocked the flow of water with his wide wings while the others swam past. Aisha was at the front of their chain and used her wings to help pull the team through the water.

The Green Team was almost to the other side of the wall. *You're going to make it,* I thought.

But I spoke too soon. Another current came through to sweep the team away before Dyami could jump in front of it. Renar struggled to escape the current, kicking forward with everything he had. He had to try extra hard because of his one leg that was still wrapped in a cast. The three of them got out together, but Renar kept kicking, desperate to escape the water—

And he kicked Cade right in the face. My stomach plummeted to my toes. Across the room, Imogen sat straight up and whimpered, her eyes locked on the TV.

Cade and Arabelle went flying backward, straight into a passing current. They were both dragged down and down and down, far into the depths of the sea. Ezra went for them but was caught up by a second current, dragging him farther away from Cade.

My hands shot over my mouth, and my fingers trembled. Time altogether stopped as the room went dead silent. All we heard was the soft music playing on the TV. It all happened so fast. One second Cade was beside them, almost out of the task, and the next we couldn't see him at all. I wanted to scream, but I couldn't find my voice.

Ezra was only a dot in the ocean, but I could see him glancing every which way for signs of Cade. He was forced to make the toughest decision a person could make during the Elemental Cup. Did he go back and search for his lost teammate, or did he save the ones he knew he could?

Ezra hesitated, but he chose Vanessa.

"*No!*" Imogen screamed out in agony.

Imogen's parents and brothers were in complete shock, staring at the TV with open mouths. Their family was close to Cade's. It was like losing their brother Trace all over again.

I couldn't begin to pretend I knew what Imogen was feeling, but I felt the loss, too— even if it was only a fraction of it. Tears began to fall down my shocked face. Imogen's shoulders shook in heavy sobs on the couch beside us. Jonah pulled her into a hug, but she barely seemed to notice he was there.

My heart both broke and rejoiced when Ezra and Vanessa— along with their Familiars— broke the far edge of the wall. There was another camera on that side waiting for them. Renar and Alvarice had already gone ahead of them.

The camera angle changed to show Kelsey and her teammate arriving at the flag. They'd won.

In the background, we could see Alvarice racing toward the flag at the end with Renar on his back. Ezra and Vanessa were arguing on the beach, though we couldn't hear what they were saying. Vanessa grabbed Ezra's hand as he tried to go back into the wall of water. He ripped his hand from her grasp and went in, despite her and Dyami's protests.

"Ez, no!" Liam yelled at the TV.

Dyami dove into the water behind Ezra. He tried to get Ezra to come back with him, but he wouldn't. Ezra urgently searched for Cade in the water, but after a minute that felt like ages, the reality of the situation turned very real. Even if Cade and Arabelle were still somewhere out in the water, they both would've drowned by now.

It was clear what had happened. Cade and Arabelle...

They'd died.

Dyami dragged Ezra from the water, but they were alone. Ezra coughed and sputtered as he gasped for air. None of us could deny it any longer. Cade hadn't made it.

Imogen's sobs grew louder.

"Imogen," her mother said softly. She reached out for her daughter, but Imogen shrugged her off. The tension in the room was palpable.

"Mom, don't," Imogen snapped. Then she shot up from her seat and pushed Jonah off of her. "Don't touch me! I don't want *anyone* touching me!"

"Honey—" Jonah started.

"Stop! Nothing you can say can make this better!" she yelled. Imogen's voice had taken on a quality I couldn't even comprehend. It was worse than sorrow, or pain, or even grief. It scared me.

Imogen put a hand to her head and sobbed in despair. "I *hate* this society! I hate the Elders! I hate that we live in a tribe where we kill our own children! The colonizers should've wiped us out centuries ago!"

"Im," Liam said in a strangled voice.

She ignored him. I could barely understand her now through the tears. "Cade and I were supposed to have a future together. We were supposed to have *everything*. And it got taken away because this tribe is *fucked up*! I wish the ancestors would just hurry up and kill us all, because they obviously don't give a shit about what happens to us! I wish the Hawkei would just die out!"

Imogen raced out the front door, leaving Sassy behind where she sat. We all exchanged momentary looks of shock, then I sprang into action.

"We'll talk to her," I said quickly to her parents as I scooped up Esis and chased Imogen outside. Jonah, Sassy, Squeaks, and Liam followed close behind.

"Imogen!" I called, but she kept on running. I could hear her anguished wails all the way into Kinpago.

She didn't stop running until we were in the town square. She'd climbed up into the Blessing Tree and wept high in its branches.

"Imogen!" I called up to her, but she didn't answer. Liam and Jonah stopped beside me and looked up at her, but we were all clueless on how to help her.

Esis hopped out of my arms and scurried up the tree to her. Sassy barked at the base of the Blessing Tree, and Squeaks squawked, but Imogen ignored them all.

Jonah turned to us and sighed. "You guys might as well take a seat. This might take a while."

Jonah started climbing the tree, stopping to sit on a branch beside Imogen. He didn't say anything or try to coax her down. He was just there for her while she tried to deal with the weight of losing the man she loved.

I sank to the ground with my back to the large trunk. Liam sat beside me and wrapped me in his arms. My stomach felt heavy and empty all at the same time as I tried to understand exactly what Imogen was going through. I couldn't imagine losing Liam like that. It was unbearable to even think about existing without my true love.

And that was Imogen's new reality.

It took at least an hour before I heard Imogen speak. She was talking to Jonah, but I could hear her soft voice travel down to us on the ground.

"He kept telling me this could happen, but I didn't want to believe it actually would," she said thickly.

I glanced up to see Jonah rubbing her back. "No one can prepare for this kind of thing, Im," he told her.

They continued to speak in hushed whispers, while Liam and I shot worried glances at each other. My gut twisted even more. I felt awful for her.

Eventually, Imogen came down from the tree as darkness began to fall over Kinpago. She wiped at her red, puffy eyes. "I'm sorry."

"Don't be sorry, Im," I told her. "You cry all you need to."

She sniffled. "I wasn't ready to plan my boyfriend's funeral."

"You're never ready to let go of someone you love," Liam said gently.

Imogen tearfully nodded. "No. But thanks for being here for me. I don't think I could make it... make it through this without you guys."

"We'll always be here for you, Im," Liam said as he stepped forward and pulled her into a embrace.

She started crying again. All four of us and our Familiars wrapped her in a group hug.

Even after hours to process it, I still couldn't believe Cade was gone.

Liam

NINETEEN

The day of the trial had finally arrived, and I was pretty sure that I'd have a heart attack and die before I even got to the stand.

I'd been anxious in the days leading up to the trial, but was able to shrug the feelings off, because it wasn't here yet. Now that it was, I felt like I was gonna hurl, or jump out of my skin. If we lost today, we'd be going to jail... or worse. I almost wanted the worst to be here, just so it would be over. No matter what happened, it couldn't be as unbearable and torturous as this waiting was... not knowing was much worse than anything the Elders could do to us.

I hadn't slept well, and neither had Sophia. She was staring at me when I opened my eyes, as if she was trying to remember all the little details of my face, just in case this was the last time we woke up together. Esis was still sleeping, curled up in a ball by her head.

"It's here," she whispered. It was still dark in the room. It was going to be a long day.

"Yeah." I gave her a good morning kiss, then forced myself upward. "Let's get ready."

We took a shower together, though we didn't fool around. We were too somber. I put on my best suit, and Sophia had a modest dress. I wore a red tie, and Sophia's dress was blue. We were gonna show that the Elders couldn't push us around. We stand together until the very end.

Before we left my room, Sophia wrapped me in a hug. "We're going to win today."

"I hope so." I put my face in her hair. I didn't want to be ripped away from this— us. I'd lost so much in my life. I didn't know how much else I could lose. Esis was up by now. He sat on top of my head and hugged it, like he was confident, too.

"I know it," Sophia said. "I was right about winning the Cup, and I'm right about this, too."

I gave a humorless laugh and said, "Well, hopefully by the end of today you can say I told you so."

We headed downstairs, where Mom immediately pushed breakfast at us. "Eat," she said. "You're going to need your strength today."

Neither of us felt very hungry, but she was right, so Sophia and I forced ourselves to consume something anyway. Esis was the only one who swallowed eggs like he was starving. Dad had already left, to get ready for the trial. The rest of my siblings were all sleeping, except Ezra. He sat at the dining table and stared at his pancakes listlessly, like the thought of swallowing them was a huge ordeal. He'd been like that since Cade died.

Cade's funeral had been horrible. I'd been to a lot of funerals in my life, but his was one of the worst. Both his family and Imogen's were devastated. They couldn't accept the news that he was gone, and bitterly wailed that the tribe had taken away someone so cherished by them. The Elders had searched, but they'd never found the body. His and Arabelle's remains had been swept off by the waves, so we ended up putting two empty caskets in the ground.

I felt terrible for Imogen. She never got to say her final goodbye. She'd changed since Cade's death. She never smiled or laughed anymore, and the quirky parts of her personality were gone. It was like someone had taken all of her color and painted it gray. She wore sweatpants with t-shirts, a blank face and messy hair in the absence of her usual big dresses, flashy makeup and weird outfits. Her gaze was calculating... like she was contemplating on how she could get revenge on the Elders for taking away the love of her life.

Even Sassy was depressed. Her red fur had almost taken on a dulled tone. It was like the best parts of them had died along with Cade and Arabelle.

We all skipped the Elemental Ball. No one wanted to go without Cade. But as worried as I was about Imogen, I was more concerned about my brother. Even though Ezra was still alive, that didn't mean he hadn't died too and become someone else. He'd apologized over and over again, to Imogen, to me, to everyone that he'd let Cade die, even though we'd reassured him that it wasn't his fault.

His best friend had drowned in front of him, and he felt responsible. Ezra was jumpy, and on edge. He freaked out at loud noises and stayed away from the water completely. He refused to use his element. He lived with this constant haunted look on his face, like he was replaying Cade's death over and over again in his mind. At his side, Dyami often hung his head, and was losing feathers.

Ezra didn't even go out with girls anymore. He'd all but lost interest in dating. He wasn't the happy kid I once knew, and that shattered me. The Elemental Cup had changed him.

Yet secretly, I was selfish, because a part of me was glad Ezra hadn't found Cade. If he had, there was no way he would've been able to pull him out of the water in time. They both would've drowned. I couldn't have even saved him. Ezra was still alive, and I had Cade to thank for that.

Halfway through breakfast, Ezra left without a word. I wasn't sure where he was going.

"The carriage is outside, waiting to take you to the courthouse," Mom said. She brushed back my hair and kissed me on the forehead. "You'll be fine. Everything will work out."

I could see the crinkles of concern around her eyes. Mom never got worried. She handled everything in life like a warship. If she was concerned...

"We have to go. We have a half hour," Sophia said. She got up, and I followed her to the carriage.

We sat on opposite sides of the carriage and remained silent. Neither one of us were very touchy-feely today. I think both of us were too absorbed in our own thoughts on the price we'd pay if the Elders ruled against us.

"Liam?" Sophia asked after a time.

"Hm?" I looked up.

She didn't appear scared as she asked the question. "If we're ordered to be executed... how are they gonna do it?"

I paused for a long moment. "I'm not sure if I want to tell you."

"I want to know what I'm getting into," Sophia said firmly.

I sighed. I kicked the side of the carriage slightly and said, "When Elementai are executed, it's seen as a form of humiliation. You've brought shame onto your tribe and need to be made an example of. So you're usually killed by your opposite element. Yapluma are buried alive, or crushed— Nivita are either dropped to their deaths, or suffocated."

"So..." Her eyebrows knitted together.

I nodded. "You're right. If things go the worst possible way they can today, you'll be drowned, and I'll be burned alive. Our friends and families will be forced to watch."

She shook her head in disgust. "This society's barbaric."

"Well, that's why we're doing our part to change things. Right?" I asked.

Sophia gave a slight grimace, but I could see the realizations playing across her face. After all this time, she finally understood what I'd been getting at when I said we could lose our lives.

The carriage slowed as it landed on Kinpago's streets. The roads were crowded with people. When we got to the courthouse, my eyes widened in shock. Hundreds of Elementai were outside of it with their Familiars, protesting. People and magical creatures both held up signs and marched, shouting chants, phrases and slurs.

It seemed like the protestors were split into two sides. One side was the Interhouse Alliance.

Their signs read things like, *Interhouse couples deserve our respect*, and *Unify the tribe*. One big banner read, *They saved our Familiars, so we repay with death?* The Alliance protestors walked around with megaphones, chanting over and over, "Free our tribe, love is not a crime!"

The other side was obviously against us. Their signs were mostly derogatory, reading things like, *Keep the bloodline pure*, or, *Interhouse relationships are a sin*, and, *Do you want a mixed society?* I didn't care to repeat many of the things they were saying.

I never had imagined my love for Sophia would lead to this. There was so much hate. But positively, I noticed that the opposing side was much smaller than the Interhouse Alliance, which made me feel a little better. I'd noticed in the past few weeks even the people who didn't agree with our lifestyle had quieted down, because we'd eliminated the plague. Only the worst jackasses alive still thought we should be penalized for loving someone outside of their own House.

The media was having a field day. There were cameras and reporters everywhere. They swarmed around the edge of the courthouse, waiting for us to emerge from the carriage. Task Force members held back the mob, threatening protestors with shields and noxite guns.

Sophia looked at me. She extended her hand. "You ready for this?"

I grabbed her hand tightly in mine. "As ready as I'll ever be."

We stepped out of the carriage. A mix of boos and cheers met our ears as we proceeded up the courthouse steps. Esis sat proudly on Sophia's shoulder and puffed up his tail, like he knew all of our opposers were wrong and we were going to succeed. I kept Sophia close by my side and my eyes on the courthouse doors. Reporters screamed questions, but we ignored them.

Vanderbilt was waiting by the door. He guided us into a small, private room and said, "I've prepared your defense. What we've got here is the best we're going to get. Just let me do most of the talking, all right?"

"If you say so," I replied dully. It was quiet in the courthouse, compared to the raging noise outside, but for some reason it only made me more uneasy.

"Wait here. I'll come get you when the trial begins," Vanderbilt said. He left Sophia and I alone in the room. Esis squeaked, but that was the only noise that could be heard.

More waiting. I couldn't fucking take it anymore.

Sophia sat down in a chair and put her head in her hands. I put a hand on her shoulder, just because I felt like I had to comfort her. "At least we got a trial," I told her, but the positivity felt fake. "Most interhouse couples don't even get that."

She lifted her head. "I guess it's a good thing that they decided to try us together, too. I don't think I could take two court dates."

"Me either." The doors opened. We expected Vanderbilt, but we got Jonah, Imogen, Ezra, Vanessa, Lindsey, and Miranda. Their Familiars weren't here— most likely waiting outside in the halls, I supposed.

"What are you guys doing?" I asked. I knew Jonah, Imogen and Ezra were going to be at the trial for support, but I wasn't sure why the rest of them were here.

"Vanderbilt called some of us in as witnesses," Imogen said. "Though that's not the only reason. We're here for backup, just in case."

"You guys aren't going to jail," Jonah said darkly.

"And you're certainly not being executed," Imogen added. "If things don't rule in your favor, Jonah and I are willing to do whatever it takes to get you guys out of town."

"Exactly," Lindsey added. "If Miranda and I can be together, it's not fair you guys can't. We need to make a stand."

"Hell yeah, we do." Ezra cracked his knuckles. He looked ready for a fight— no, worse— like he *wanted* something to happen.

"Vanessa, you can't. You're pregnant," Sophia protested.

"I've talked to Bren, and we've decided together we don't want to raise our baby in a tribe that doesn't support interhouse couples," Vanessa said, laying a hand on Sophia's arm. "He and I will step in if it looks like the Elders are going to go with the death penalty."

"But you guys can't do that. You'll be fugitives," I protested.

"Fuck this society. I don't want to be a part of it if you guys aren't accepted," Imogen said violently.

"Me too," Jonah added. The rest of them had similar words of agreement.

"But you're only a few people. You can't take on the entire tribe alone," Sophia said.

"They won't be alone. They'll have the Alliance." Jaymin Riske had showed up out of nowhere. She was wearing a business suit, and looking fierce. She stopped before us and crossed her arms. "We have Nivita demolitionists on standby to start toppling buildings if worse comes to worse."

"Excuse me, what?" Sophia's eyes popped out of her head, and Esis peeped.

"You heard me, Sophia. I have Elementai from all houses stationed around Kinpago, waiting on my signal. If this doesn't go our way, we're going to start a riot, and it won't be a small protest," Jaymin said in a deadly tone. "We have to start fighting fire with fire."

"You can't do that. People will die on our behalf. We're not okay with that," I protested.

"I'm sorry, but this isn't about you anymore." Jaymin's eyes narrowed. "Hundreds of interhouse couples are depending on the outcome of the case. And we're willing to use any means necessary to get the Elders to change their minds on interhouse relationships. Even force."

I looked to the rest of the group, but none of them spoke up. Our friends didn't care about the rest of the tribe, as long as it meant getting us to safety.

"None of this is going to be necessary. We'll win our case," Sophia argued.

Jaymin gave a skeptical snort. "For your sakes, I hope so."

Jaymin walked out. She passed Vanderbilt on the way in— he barely acknowledged her as he stood in front of us. "Miss Henley, Mister Mitoh. It's time."

"See you guys on the other side," I whispered as I passed our friend group. They gave us lonely waves. Sophia and I glanced at each other as we made our way out. The same thought was on our minds. If we lost today, Jaymin and the Interhouse Alliance would turn Kinpago into a war-zone. Imogen and Ezra wouldn't mind helping. They were both loose cannons right now.

Jaymin Riske was the type of person who'd resort to terrorism to further the cause. She didn't care if people got hurt, as long as she got what she wanted.

Sophia and I *needed* to get a pardon. Otherwise, we wouldn't be the only ones to die today.

The courtroom was gigantic. It was circular, with twenty seats behind a huge bench at the head of the room where the Elders would sit. The entire room was made of white marble, and had wide wooden chairs that would sit at least three hundred Elementai and their Familiars. Columns were placed in organized rows, and windows that were set in the ceiling beamed light downward.

Vanderbilt took us to the defendant desk on the right side of the room. Sophia and I sat down, and she placed Esis on the table.

On the other side of the room, a lawyer gathered papers at the plaintiff station. He was attorney Greg Miller. He was middle-aged, stocky, and all business. He worked for the tribe prosecuting criminals, and hardly ever lost. I bet he had a ton of evidence stacked against us that he was going to present. A pitbull Familiar walked at his side and growled at us.

The wooden benches were crowded with people excited to witness the trial. This was the biggest case of the century. For Sophia and I, this was one of the worst days of our lives. For others, this was entertainment. Our friends sat in the closest bench behind us and waited. Sophia's grandparents and my mom took the seat behind them, along with Maddie. Mom had gotten a sitter for the younger kids at home. She didn't want them to see this.

Beside her sat Baine, who I supposed had showed up for moral support. You know, just in case he had to catch Mom after she fainted from me being sentenced to death.

I caught sight of Mia's face in the crowd. I was surprised Micah had let her come, but maybe she'd snuck out. She had a new bruise on her face. Mia waved and mouthed, *good luck.* At her side, her Familiar waved a tiny flag with the interhouse colors on it.

Well, at least it was nice Mia showed up to support us, even though we'd had a disastrous encounter with Micah the time we saw her last. It was like the Mia with Micah and the Mia without him were totally different.

I hoped she'd leave him soon, but I severely doubted it.

The trial was supposed to start at eight-thirty, but we waited for a half an hour and none of the Elders arrived. The crowds behind us began to whisper impatiently. What was taking so long?

Eventually, a security guard came into the center of the room and said, "All rise for the arrival of the Elder Council."

There was a lot of noise as people stood, and in entered the sixteen Elders from each of the respective Houses, along with each chief and chieftess. Toaqua took the left side of the room, with Nivita next to them, Yapluma in the middle, and Koigni on the far right side. Their Familiars joined the benches behind them— those that could fit, anyway. The bigger ones sat on the floor before the benches and observed. A couple of the Water ones were missing— they were still in the ocean.

I searched for Dad and found him sitting next to Chief Nahele from Nivita. Dad was stone-faced and calm. I resolved myself not to freak out unless I saw him losing control.

There were so many new faces on the council. I didn't know half of these people. Had the plague wiped out that many Familiars and their Elders that the council had basically been replaced overnight?

Elder Oleander was already giving us a scathing grin. I didn't have to guess what his vote was gonna be. He'd made up his mind before he got in here. The trial was just a formality to him.

Chieftess Annette was staring at Sophia like she couldn't wait to put her in her place. This would be payback for all the times Sophia had gone after Haley. Madame Doya's expression, on the other hand, was unreadable— she sat by the wall on the far side of the room and remained emotionless, like the trial already bored her. Naomi was still beside her, a cat waiting to pounce.

Sophia and I were made to take an oath to the ancestors that we would tell the truth before the charges against us were read. I hardly processed them. This still didn't seem real.

"Let's get down to business," Chief Nahele begun. He was leading the trial, because he was Nivita and a neutral party—as well as the oldest chieftain. "We'll start by examining Mister Mitoh, and move onward to Miss Henley from there."

There was a loud smacking sound against one of the windows. Someone was throwing things. A group of people outside were banging on the glass, trying to get in. They looked like Alliance members.

"Shut them up, will you?" Elder Oleander barked. "I've had enough of them today."

A few of the Task Force members inside the courtroom moved. A few minutes later, the protesters were dragged away from the windows. It clicked why the Elders had been late. Had there been fights outside the courthouse?

"Mister Mitoh, please proceed to the stand," Chief Nahele said.

I slowly stood up. My legs felt like they were going to collapse as I made my way to the stand, though I hoped I put on a good appearance of being undisturbed. I sat behind the large witness stand, and Chief Nahele began reading from a long list. "Liam Mitoh, you are hereby charged with high treason for having a romantic and intimate relationship with someone who is not from your House tribe. How do you plead?"

"He pleads not guilty, your honor," Vanderbilt spoke for me, rising from his chair as he did.

"Not guilty?" Chieftess Makawe, from Yapluma, asked curiously. "Is Mister Mitoh not publicly and romantically involved with this woman?" She gestured to Sophia.

"That he is, Chieftess, but we are making the motion that he is not guilty on account that interhouse relationships should be made legal within the tribal system," Vanderbilt began.

Shocked murmurs hovered around the courtroom. This was a bold move, but the only way Vanderbilt assured us we would win. There was too much evidence stacked against us. We'd only walk free if we could prove interhouse relationships should be legalized in the first place.

Chief Nahele raised his hands, and the room quieted. "Very well. If that is the stance you wish to take, Mister Vanderbilt, you may proceed."

Vanderbilt came forward. "Mister Mitoh, if you could please start at the beginning. Tell me how you and Miss Henley met, and how your relationship formed from there."

We'd rehearsed this yesterday night. I took a deep breath. "Last year, I was assigned by Head Dean Alric and the other heads of the four Houses from Orenda Academy to escort Sophia Henley from her home in Utah to Kinpago. She'd been sheltered from our society all her life, and didn't know anything about our world. The family that had raised her was Toaqua, so they thought I'd be a good choice in convincing them to allow Sophia to attend school here."

Something changed while I was telling the story. My eyes caught Sophia's, and the narration of facts became something stronger. "I'd liked Sophia from the moment I met her, but I didn't want to admit it. I knew interhouse relationships were forbidden. But the more I tried to pull away from her, the closer we became. We got paired up on the same Elemental Cup team, and from there, I knew I was in love with her. Our connection soon became something that was undeniable. We started dating formally in January, though we kept our relationship hidden."

Sophia was smiling at me like I was the only guy in the world for her. I gave her a reassuring grin back.

"So you didn't go into this relationship with the intention of starting some sort of revolution, or rebellion?" Vanderbilt asked.

"No," I said, shaking my head. "It was never my intention to overthrow the Elders. Or Sophia's. We just wanted to be together."

"And you tried to stop it, correct?" Vanderbilt asked.

"Yes," I said. "I broke up with Sophia in May of this year. We spent several months apart. But it didn't matter. I learned I couldn't be without her. We got back together in October, and agreed that we needed to go public with our relationship. We wanted people to accept us for who we were. We didn't want to hide anymore."

"And you think that good has come out of your relationship, yes, even that which is beneficial for the tribe? You did manage to cure the plague that was overtaking much of Kinpago only a few weeks ago," Vanderbilt persisted.

"Sort of," I said, and I shrugged. "We didn't find the cure for the plague. Our friend, Imogen Ahnild, did. We only spread the word, because she was in the hospital after being viciously attacked by a magical creature."

I eyed Elder Raviro, who gave me a cold stare back. Elder Raviro was Renar's dad. I wasn't sure if he wanted us to go down for this or not. I could see the questions burning in his eyes about the prophecy and what it meant— and he couldn't get answers if Sophia and I were dead, or out of his reach in prison.

But he couldn't interrogate us on the prophecy, either, not with all these people watching. It was supposed to remain a secret from the other tribes. If he didn't want to show his hand, he had to keep quiet.

"Ah. Makes sense." Vanderbilt turned to the council. "There you have it. The honest tale of two young people in love. Nothing more, nothing less."

"Nothing more, my foot," an Elder from Yapluma spoke up. "The way they look at each other is disgusting."

"Elder Wallace, please," Chieftess Makawe said. "Let's try to keep this civil."

"If you ask me, the fact that they were able to cure the plague at all is rather suspicious," Malison grumbled from his place next to Oleander. "All these Familiars get sick, then all of a sudden, when these two need to gain public favor, they're miraculously able to cure an illness our best alchemists and doctors failed to treat? I think they had something to do with the plague starting in the first place."

"Not to mention that many Familiars still remain missing. Many magical creatures were kidnapped, and so far haven't returned," Madame Chavis from Koigni spoke. She gazed at me with a cruel, narrow stare. I was betting she blamed Sophia and I for her twin's death.

Vanderbilt was starting to sweat, but Dad spoke up. "There is no evidence for either Miss Henley or Mister Mitoh's involvement in either of these cases," he said. "Let's get back to the facts, here."

"Easy for you to say. That's your boy being tried, Liwanu," Madame Chavis shot at him.

"With all due respect, I'd watch your tongue if I were you, Madame Chavis," Dad said lowly.

The Elders began to argue amongst each other, until Chief Nahele banged a gavel. "That's enough! We must keep proceeding. Mister Miller, you have the floor to cross-examine."

Miller got up and walked to the middle of the room, his pitbull following. He tugged on his suit jacket before he asked, "Mister Mitoh, I notice you're missing a Familiar today. But you competed in the Elemental Cup last year. Can you tell me where your Familiar is, currently?"

I knew they'd bring Nashoma into this. "He died."

"And how did he die, precisely?" Miller questioned.

I kept my curled fists hidden underneath the stand. "He died trying to protect me. It was over a year ago. Before I met Sophia."

"Hm. I see." Miller didn't look surprised at all. "But this is odd, you see, because as we all know, an Elementai can't survive without their Familiar. Can you tell me how you're still alive over a year later, Mister Mitoh?"

"Your guess is as good as mine. It's still a mystery to me," I said blandly.

"*Your guess is as good as mine.*" Miller repeated me, then turned to the audience with wide arms. "There seem to be a lot of things about this couple we *don't* know. Their involvement with the plague... the missing Familiars... even how Mister Mitoh is alive today."

"It's not a living you want. Trust me," I told him.

"What exactly do you mean by that, Mister Mitoh?" Miller raised an eyebrow.

"I have a rare disability. It became active after I lost my Familiar," I said.

"Do you have a name for this rare condition? It's not in your file," Miller said.

"It's undiagnosed," I said quickly.

He gave me a skeptical look. "An undiagnosed condition. Another unknown. How very convenient. This is all starting to sound very suspicious, Mister Mitoh. How do we know you are *actually* ill? You look fine to me," Miller said.

Sophia's look was pleading for me to calm down and not lose my shit. I took a steadying breath and said, "Well, there are plenty of disabilities you can't see. And it's very ableist to claim that just because you can't visibly *see* me suffering that I'm not."

"Is there anyone in this courtroom that can bring forth any sort of *facts* to this case, instead of just hearsay?" Miller asked loudly. "Some evidence would be nice."

Vanderbilt rose and spoke to the Elders. "We have a witness who can present proof that Mister Mitoh's health isn't as stable as Mister Miller would claim it to be. I would like to call Doctor Jacques Perot forward."

There was silence. I searched the courtroom for Professor Perot, who I was sure was sitting in the audience. We'd talked to him about being there only last week.

He wasn't there. I scanned the crowd three times, but there wasn't a sign of him, nor his peacock, Baxtor.

Where was Perot? He was supposed to be here. He was a key witness. Sophia looked just as panicked as I felt. Esis rose on his tiptoes to search for Perot, but he was nowhere to be found.

Vanderbilt looked embarrassed. Miller gave a smug smile and said, "It seems your witness has refused to come forward, sir."

My heart fell. It was obvious Perot wasn't coming. Why had he abandoned us when we needed him most? Our first witness had copped out on us, and one of the most important. We were totally going to lose.

"Chief Mitoh should be able to verify that his son's health isn't in optimal condition," Madame Wells spoke, tossing her long braid behind her. She sat on Dad's opposite side and was reserved and calm, as usual.

"Chief Mitoh will say anything to get his son off the death penalty," Elder Raviro snapped. "He's hardly a witness. It's a conflict of interest to even have him judge this case."

"All chiefs have the right to sit on trials of high treason, whether or not those accused are related, for House loyalty is considered to be thicker than blood relations," Dad said. I knew he was reciting word for word from the tribal book of law. "I will not say anything verifying or condemning my son's condition."

"That's all very well, Chief Mitoh, but perhaps someone in this courtroom can shine some light on how your son survived the Elemental Cup last year," Miller began. "Footage from the Cup showed that your son was very close to death, before Miss Henley showed up. He ended up crawling into a cave with severe injuries and burns, and walking out with nothing on him. Does anyone care to explain that?"

Shit. I didn't think that would come up. Sophia and I hadn't told Vanderbilt about Esis' healing powers, either, because we didn't trust him that far. There was silence in the courtroom for a few minutes, before Sophia stood up. "I can explain that."

Soph, what are you doing? She couldn't reveal Esis now. But instead, she grabbed the totem that hung around her neck and pulled it over her head.

The Spirit Totem. Fuck, she couldn't give that away. It was too valuable. But it was the only thing we had to barter with. Sophia displayed the totem to the Elders and said, "I found this during the Cup when I was wandering around by myself after the fire took over the forest. I thought it was just a cool carving, so I kept it. But after I found Liam in the cave, I gave it to him, and it healed him of his injuries. I think it might be an Anichi artifact."

Sophia handed the totem to Vanderbilt. He didn't know anything about this, but he acted like he did. "Elder Barron, you're an expert on Anichi lore," Vanderbilt said. "Would you mind taking a look at this?"

Elder Barron was from Nivita. His Familiar, a python that was over twenty feet long, snaked down from the judging stand and took the totem from Vanderbilt. She deposited the totem in his hand, and he studied it closely.

"This does look like an Anichi object," he said. "Though not similar to one I've ever seen. It's quite unique."

"Yes, but can it do magic?" Chieftess Annette asked impatiently. She looked at the totem greedily— like she wanted to get her hands on it.

"I've never known of Anichi totems that could heal," Elder Barron confessed. "But much of what we knew about the Soul tribe has been lost to history. Some magical races can enchant objects or infuse them with magic. I don't see why an Anichi couldn't transfer some of their healing power to an object. They kept many things secret from the rest of the tribe."

Elder Barron passed the totem down the line. Dad studied it closely, while the rest of the Elders talked in low voices.

"If this is true and this totem can heal, why didn't you turn the artifact into the Elders of your House immediately after the Cup was over?" Madame Chavis barked at Sophia. "Such possessions belong to the tribe."

"I showed the totem to Madame Doya," Sophia said. "But she said it wasn't anything special. So I just kept it as a souvenir from the tournament."

"Is this true, Eleanor?" Dad passed the totem to Wells and looked at Madame Doya.

Doya gave an impassive sniff and sat back in her seat. "It is true. Sophia did show me the totem, but I did not feel any sense of power when I held it. I mistook it for a child's plaything."

"Did she tell you that she used it to heal Liam Mitoh?" Elder Barron asked.

"Of course she did, but I didn't take her at her word. I hardly supposed such an insignificant little thing would be enough to save Mitoh's life, and brushed it off as the fanciful dreams of a First Year who knew little to nothing about our world," Doya said. Naomi growled in agreement. "There were many possibilities on how he could've survived the Cup, as being theorized at the time by the council. How was I to know Sophia was actually telling the truth? Not to mention that she couldn't *prove* the totem could actually heal at the time of her showing it to me."

I was shocked. When Sophia told Doya about the totem, Soph had made it clear to me that she hadn't told Doya about its magical powers— Soul or otherwise. Why would Doya lie on our behalf?

Sophia and Doya shared an impassive gaze that had the slightest undertone of an agreement within. It was clear. Doya still thought Sophia was the chosen one, destined to bring Koigni to glory. And Sophia couldn't very well fulfill the prophecy if she was in jail or dead.

Doya would lie all day if it meant getting Sophia off, so she could do her duty to her House.

"Forgive me, Madame Doya, but an object like this should've been brought to the attention of the council immediately," Elder Barron said. "It was foolish of you to disregard it."

Doya gave a cold laugh. "If you think I'm some sort of expert on magical artifacts, then you are sorely mistaken. I would be careful not to overstep, Elder Barron. I've been on this council a lot longer than you have."

Elder Barron turned pink, and there were a few insults mumbled by members of the Nivita House, which Doya shrugged off. The Elders weren't doing a very good job of interrogating us. If anything, they were confused and disorganized. Half of them couldn't get along well enough to cross-examine me.

"Can you give a demonstration on the totem's healing abilities?" Miller asked, crossing his arms.

Sophia shook her head. "No. I think the totem only had enough power for one healing. I couldn't get it to work after that."

"Of course not." Miller shook his head. "More circumstantial evidence."

Sophia blinked innocently. She was doing good at playing the part of the dumb little girl. It was clear Doya approved. I wondered if they'd talked about this before the trial...

Wait. *Of course* they'd talked about this. Before we left school, Sophia had told me she had a meeting with Doya about next semester. It was pretty clear now that meeting wasn't about signing up for classes and more about Doya giving Sophia acting lessons. I wondered what other tricks Sophia and Doya had waiting in the wings.

"The Elder Council will be confiscating this artifact, Miss Henley, to study it further," Madame Wells said, and she handed it off to a court official. "We thank you for your honesty."

The court official took the totem through a pair of double doors. There it went. We'd lost the Spirit Totem. That was a major blow. But if it helped us win this trial, it was a fair sacrifice.

Miller flipped through some files on his desk. "Well, as uncertain as the court is of your physical condition, Mister Mitoh, we *can* reach a conclusion on your mental state."

Oh hell to the fuck no. "What do you mean?"

Miller went to his desk and raised a file. "According to the records by your therapist's office, you had a recent suicide attempt no less than twelve weeks ago."

How the hell had they gotten their hands on those? They were supposed to be private and inaccessible to anyone whom I hadn't given permission to view. I supposed the Elders weren't opposed to using underhanded, illegal tactics.

I gave a stony face back and said, "That's private."

"There's no such thing as privacy when it comes to high treason, Mister Mitoh," Miller spat. "Tell us, did you or did you not try to take your own life?"

He had me cornered. But screw him. I was gonna fight back.

"Fine, you want to know the truth? I did try to kill myself. I was depressed," I said sharply. "But I'm getting better now, and it's because of Sophia. *She's* the one who made me go to therapy. *She's* the one who's been supporting me no matter what. *She's* the one who stopped me before I jumped off that bridge. So if you want the reason on why I'm still alive, there she is."

I pointed to Sophia. Esis clapped loudly, but he was the only one. Miller turned away from me— he was obviously done cross-examining.

"Elders, it's clear that this young man's mental health is unstable," Miller argued. "The stress from being in this interhouse relationship is obviously too much for him to handle. It could even be deduced that Miss Henley, as an outsider to our culture, manipulated Mister Mitoh into an interhouse relationship, and he fell victim to her control."

"Objection! This is getting absurd!" Vanderbilt shouted.

Miller ignored him, and instead turned to my father. "Chief Mitoh, as I understand it, your son was very much a law-abiding member of society. Even in line to be chief, before his Familiar died— everything a perfect Hawkei boy should be. Do you think his behavior has changed since Miss Henley came into his life?"

Dad looked uncomfortable. There really wasn't an answer he could give that wouldn't condemn me either way. "I, uh... can't say."

"There you have it. Is there really anything *more* to say, ladies and gentlemen?" Miller asked.

I didn't get why he was doing this. Sophia and I were both on trial. There was no way I was innocent when it came to me being with her.

Then I saw the eyes of Malison and Oleander eyeing Sophia greedily, along with a couple of others on various House councils. Then I realized this all led back to the prophecy. Doya was still fighting for the prophecy to come true, but other Houses were still trying to prevent it—and the Koigni Council no longer believed Sophia was the prophesied one, which meant they didn't care what happened to her either way. Sophia was their real target. I was just an obstacle in the way of the bigger picture. This was quickly becoming a witch hunt.

"Mister Mitoh, may I suggest that if you testify against Miss Henley, the court will understand your vulnerable position and significantly reduce your sentence?" Miller asked.

Fuck him. I'd burn at the stake first before I threw Sophia under the bus.

I raised the level of my voice so everyone could hear me clearly. "What you're trying to do isn't going to work. I'm not going to testify against my girlfriend. I made a decision to be with her willingly, of my own sound mind. And whatever punishment you're going to hand out to her, you're going to give me the same thing, because if her loving me has broken the law, I've done the same damn thing."

There were a few claps from the audience this time, which were quieted by Nahele. It was clear that Miller wasn't done with the Sophia-seducing-me angle yet, but he let it go to move on to something else.

"Very well," Miller said. He didn't seem bothered he couldn't pick at my health or sanity anymore, which meant he had something else up his sleeve. "Mister Mitoh, I would like you to answer this next question honestly. Have you and Sophia Henley had any sexual relations?"

"Objection!" Vanderbilt rose from his seat. "Elders, this goes too far!"

"On the contrary, Elders, it is the most crucial part of this case," Miller insisted.

"We'll allow it," Chief Nahele said, and he gestured to me. "Go on, son. Answer the question."

Everyone's eyes in the courtroom were on me. Ugh, Sophia's *grandparents* were sitting right there. Along with my own mom and dad. This was freaking embarrassing.

But you know what? Screw it. I wasn't going to be ashamed of having sex with Sophia. It was a way to express our love, and we both were of age. Nobody would think twice if we were banging and from the same House. It's what college kids did. We were in a committed relationship, and we cared about each other. We wanted to get married someday. Why was it such a big deal if we shared our bodies, anyhow? We weren't doing anything wrong.

I straightened up and said firmly, "Yes, we have."

The courtroom broke out into an instant uproar. Many people shouted in alarm and said things like *mopite* and *fornication*. Elder Nahele banged the gavel several times, but it took a while for everyone to calm down.

Mom and Dad didn't look surprised, nor did Sophia's grandparents. I figured they had to have guessed, anyway.

"Mister Mitoh, this is a very serious confession," Miller said slowly. "An interhouse relationship is one thing, but do you understand that having intercourse with Miss Henley could result in mixed-House children?"

I wanted to snap at him, *Well, duh,* but instead I forced out, "We're not trying to have a baby. We're using protection."

My words sounded so small and meek to me. I was losing my position.

"But accidents happen, don't they, Mister Mitoh? You do understand that if she was to conceive, you and Miss Henley would breed an interhouse child? One who has no place in this society?" Miller asked.

"Why wouldn't our child have a place here?" I said. I was almost shouting— I was getting pissed. "What's wrong with having a mixed-House kid, anyway? Why are they any different?"

Vanderbilt's face was horrified. He couldn't defend this. I was saying the exact opposite of what the Elders wanted to hear, and Vanderbilt wasn't sure if he could backtrack and recover from that. I wished he'd fucking step in and say something. He was supposed to be my lawyer. I wanted him to defend me, but mostly, I'd been defending myself.

"Mister Mitoh, mixed-House children are significantly weaker than children bred from parents of a singular House. If tribe lines were to disintegrate, we'd lose our culture and our way of life. The Elementai would die out," Miller argued.

"Show me evidence," I said. "Give me one fact that proves mixed-House children are weak, and I'll believe you."

Miller stared open-mouthed at me. I finally had him cornered.

"You can't produce any, because it's not true," I said. "The tribe used to interbreed for centuries before Anichi fell. The law against inter-house relationships hasn't even been around that long, except for the last few generations. And even though Sophia and I aren't trying to have a child, *any* baby we could make together is one I'd be proud of. I don't believe in throwing children away like the rest of this society does."

Surprised voices littered the courtroom. Miller saw an opportunity to advance and said, "That sounds like a challenge to the Elders, Mister Mitoh."

"There's no challenge. Just me wanting to protect my own," I said.

"At the start of this trial, you claimed you had no intention of starting a movement, a rebellion. But what you fail to realize is that you and Miss Henley have," Miller began.

"That's none of my concern. How people react to my relationship isn't any business of mine," I shot at him. "I'm doing my best to remain uninvolved."

"But you aren't uninvolved, are you, Mister Mitoh? The Interhouse Alliance has been using you as an example for furthering their cause," Miller shot at me.

"Big deal. It's not something I wanted," I said bitterly. Vanderbilt needed to get me off the stand, because I was only making things worse.

Just as I thought that, Vanderbilt practically jumped in front of Miller and said, "Are you done badgering my client, Mister Miller? Because your reaching has pushed this court to the point of being a circus."

Miller eyed Vanderbilt cautiously before he turned back to the Elders. "No further questions. For now."

Chief Nahele rubbed his face. He looked tired. "The court will take a short recess. We shall question witnesses and begin cross-examination of Miss Henley once we return. Court will resume in one hour."

He banged the gavel. The courtroom bustled with activity. I got off the stand and re-joined Sophia. She picked up Esis, and we followed Vanderbilt back to the private waiting room.

"What the hell was that?" I asked Vanderbilt the moment the door was closed. "Are you my lawyer, or are you gonna stand by and watch this go down?"

"I am rather out of practice," Vanderbilt said, and he frowned. "I haven't participated in an active trial in years."

"Then work on getting it together! We're getting massacred out there!" I shouted.

"Liam." Sophia put a hand on my shoulder. "Let's try to calm down. We aren't done for yet."

"Soph, they threw everything they had at me. They dug up stuff I didn't even think they could get their hands on," I said. "What do you think they're going to ask *you*? Because it's probably ten times worse."

Sophia gave a hardened look. "They can throw anything they want at me. I can take it."

She glanced at Vanderbilt. "Give us a minute."

He left, grumbling under his breath. Sophia forced me to sit down. "Liam, whatever comes up in that courtroom next, you can't explode. You can't show any emotion. Our lives depend on it."

I took a few calming, deep breaths. "Okay, but what do you expect me to do? Just sit there while they call my girlfriend a harlot? Because you know they're gonna do that. It's one of their angles."

"Yes. I can handle myself," Sophia said firmly. "Doya and I talked about this, and she has a plan. But you've gotta trust that we're gonna make it through this."

I forced myself to simmer. "Fine." I stood up. "I need some air."

"Don't take too long," Sophia said. She cuddled Esis to her as I slipped out the door. Cameras were everywhere, so I slipped into an isolated hallway and headed to the bathroom. It was thankfully empty. I didn't think the media was allowed this far into the courthouse. I washed my face, just to try and snap out of it. I needed to have a cool head. This trial was taking everything out of me.

On the way back, I heard hushed, aggravated voices coming from around the corner. One of them I recognized was Dad's.

The other had to be Oleander. I pressed myself close to the wall to listen in.

"I don't think you understand my meaning," Oleander said lowly. I had to strain to hear him.

"I understand *intently*," Dad said, his voice full of hatred. At his side, I heard Tatum give a low growl that was clearly an undelivered threat.

"This trial can go one of two ways. You don't want to lose my vote," Oleander said. His tone was filled with slightly suppressed glee. "If you want your son to walk out of here alive, you'll do as you're told."

"Understood," Dad replied.

I felt a chill go through me. What the hell? Dad didn't take orders, he made them. What was this about?

"Don't think that this deal ends once the trial is over. I've heard your boy's condition has managed to stabilize, but that doesn't mean he can't get sicker," Oleander threatened. "And very quickly."

"Leave my son out of this. He has nothing to do with what's going on in the council." Dad's tone was dark and intimidating.

"Your son will be fine, so long as you do what you're told," Oleander replied. "If you fail to follow orders, don't be surprised when your eldest ends up in the hospital— again. Or perhaps something more permanent. You've got an abundance of children to work through. I won't stop with just one."

Was this guy threatening my family? What a shithead! I was gonna kill him.

"My family is none of your concern. I inducted you into the Toaqua Elders, as you asked, and persuaded the other chieftains to choose who you wanted on the other councils," Dad said lowly. "If anything, you owe me."

"Oh, no, Liwanu. Our work together has just barely begun," Oleander practically sang. "I look forward to breaking the will of such a strong chief."

Dad laughed, and it was a scary sound. "One day you'll make a mistake, and the ancestors will make you pay for what you have planned."

"Perhaps. But I assume you'll meet your end far before I will. You've got an axe hanging over your head as it is." Oleander paused, then said, "You might want to get back to your little wife. She's waiting."

I'd heard enough. I pushed away from the wall and high-tailed it back to the waiting room.

Holy fuck. My dad had put Elder Oleander on the Toaqua Council because he'd threatened to hurt *me*. For once, Dad had actually put me ahead of the tribe.

Shit, this was my fault. If I wasn't such an easy target, Oleander wouldn't be on the council in the first place. And because I was vulnerable, that made Dad his puppet.

I must've looked freaked out when I came back, because Sophia popped right out of her seat when she saw me. "What's wrong?"

I quickly explained what I'd overheard. Sophia was fuming when I was done. "Oleander's extorting your dad to get the people he wants on the Elder Council? That's totally sick!"

"Yeah. And it makes sense why Oleander was mad we stopped the plague and arrested us for broadcasting the cure," I said. "The plague was actually working in his favor. It was taking out Elders and making openings so he could put the people *he* wanted on the different councils. People who are already working for him, or who are in his pocket."

She tapped her chin. "What if Oleander started the plague? All this seems to be working out in his favor. What if he's behind the missing Familiars, too?"

"I bet anything he is," I said lowly. "Who else is benefitting from all this chaos?"

Sophia shook her head. "This goes way deeper than we thought it did, Liam."

"I know," I said. "But you're right. We've got to stay strong. If Oleander is going to blackmail my dad like this, we've gotta at least make it worth it and win this case."

She looked at me. "What are you thinking?"

I was already coming up with a plan. "We've gotta fight back. Hard."

sophia
TWENTY

"Sophia Henley, to the witness stand."

My knees shook as I rose from my chair and stepped up to the witness stand, but I didn't let it show. I kept a firm mask of resolve on my face as the Elders stared me down. I carried Esis with me and set him in my lap. My gaze turned out the crowd, and shock riveted through me when I saw my sister's face staring back at me. I'd sent a letter about the trial, but Amelia had never said whether she could make it or not. I was glad she was here. It helped ease my nerves.

"Mister Vanderbilt," Chief Nahele said. "Your witness."

Vanderbilt stood and straightened his tie. "Miss Henley, do you love Mister Mitoh?"

Shit. It was starting already. I was nervous, but I was determined to do my best.

"Yes," I said honestly. "With all my heart."

"Did you have any intention of forming a relationship with Mister Mitoh when he arrived in Utah to escort you to Kinpago?" Vanderbilt asked.

"No." My tone was clipped, but confident.

"So it is as Mister Mitoh said? You two had no intention of falling in love, but you couldn't stay away from each other?" Vanderbilt raised an eyebrow.

"Correct," I confirmed.

"Miss Henley, is it true that you wish to have kids someday?"
Vanderbilt asked. We'd rehearsed this, and I knew exactly what to say.

"Yes, that's true," I told him.

A few people gasped, but other than that, the courtroom remained
silent. It was agonizing.

"You do realize that interhouse relations are banned due to the risk
of bearing interhouse children, don't you, Miss Henley?" Vanderbilt
pressed.

I knew he was only doing this to get ahead of the accusations Miller
would bring forth against me— he'd briefed me on that— but it felt like I
was being interrogated by Miller already.

"I do," I said.

"So, Miss Henley, how will you deal with these conflicts of interest?" Vanderbilt asked. "You simply cannot have both with how the laws
are currently written."

I took a deep breath. It killed me to admit this, but it was true. I'd do
anything to be with Liam. "I'm willing to give up having kids in order to
be with Liam Mitoh."

This time, there were a lot more gasps— like people couldn't believe
someone would give up something as precious as children for someone
they loved. Liam tried not to show his reaction, but I could see the tears
welling in his eyes.

"No further questions," Vanderbilt said. He returned to his seat, and
Miller stood.

My hands began to shake. At least with Vanderbilt, I knew what was
coming. Miller could throw anything at me. Esis placed a comforting
paw on my hand to calm me.

Miller cleared his throat and glanced down to a stack of papers in his
hands. "Miss Henley, how can we be confident that what you've just
said to the court is true?"

"I'm under oath," I pointed out, though my voice shook a little.
"You'll have to take my word for it."

"You did not grow up in this society, did you?" Miller asked.

"No," I said, gritting my teeth. What did this have to do with
anything? "But the court already knows that."

"Yes, of course," Miller said coolly. "When was the first time you
heard of the ancestors?"

"When I came to Orenda Academy," I answered. "Liam taught me about them."

"So you have spent most of your life ignorant to our religion?" Miller questioned.

Where was he going with this?

"Yes," I said calmly.

"Therefore, it's possible you have affiliations or loyalties to another god," Miller asserted.

There it was. He was questioning the validity of my oath.

"I don't," I said quickly. "My parents didn't take me to church or anything. I was never part of another religion."

"Your adoptive parents didn't even tell you about the ancestors?" he asked, turning to the Elders with raised eyebrows. "So you grew up without any religious affiliations at all."

"Yes," I said, shooting a nervous glance at Vanderbilt. He didn't show any emotion, though Liam looked peeved beside him.

"So your oath to the ancestors could mean nothing at all," Miller accused. "How do we know you're telling the truth?"

I gritted my teeth, but tried to stay calm. "I believe in the ancestors. I've seen them and spoken to them. I would never lie to them, especially under oath. I'm a Hawkei, same as you."

Miller ignored everything I said, except one part. "You've *spoken* to the ancestors? How is that so, Miss Henley?"

I gaped for a second. He was trying to make me out as a liar!

"I'm referring to my ancestral guides," I told him. "Liam is the son of a chief. He summoned them for me so I could meet them, and then I met them again at the time of my Naming Ceremony." I didn't mention the time I'd seen them during the tournament, or how I'd spoken to Showana on Ancestors' Day. "These types of encounters are not unusual, are they?"

Miller frowned, but didn't answer. He quickly moved on. "Miss Henley, you stated that you are willing to give up children to be with Mister Mitoh."

"Yes," I said calmly.

"And Mister Mitoh made it clear that the two of you were dating throughout the second semester of your first year at Orenda Academy. Is that true?" Miller asked.

"Yes," I answered.

He glanced down to his papers. "During this time, you prepared a presentation for your Hawkei Careers class that highlighted your desire to be a stay-at-home mother. Is that correct?"

Oh, shit. I knew where he was going with this.

I swallowed hard. "Yes, but I've since changed my mind."

"But you just said you and Mister Mitoh were dating at the time," Miller pointed out. "You must've realized then that you and Mister Mitoh would've had to conceive children for that dream to become a reality."

My hands were sweating against Esis' fur. It was true that I'd thought about having kids with Liam, but I also knew it wasn't realistic—not in this society.

"Yes," I answered honestly, then quickly added, "and that's one of the reasons why we broke up. We wanted different things."

"And do you still want children?" Miller asked, rather aggressively.

"I know I can never have children with Liam," I said.

"Yes or no, Miss Henley?" Miller shot back. "Do you, or do you not, still want children?"

I did. I *really* did, but I meant what I said that I was willing to give all that up for Liam. So if it meant that the only way I got to be with Liam was if I never had children, then the answer was no... I didn't want them anymore.

I answered honestly. "No. I don't."

Miller pressed his lips together and gazed down at his papers. "Interesting, considering you're majoring in Child Life Development."

I opened my mouth to protest, to say that had nothing to do with my desire to raise my own children. But the courtroom had already broken into protests.

"Order!" Chief Nahele shouted as he slammed on his gavel.

The courtroom quieted as Miller stepped closer to me at the witness stand. "You want children, Miss Henley," he accused, his voice rising. "You always have, and you still want them with Mister Mitoh. It's been your plan all along! You're trying to birth children from mixed Houses, even though they'll be weak!"

"That's not true!" I shouted back. "Mixed children are not weak!"

"Prove otherwise!" Miller demanded. "If you can present the court with a mixed House child whose powers have not taken a hit due to their ancestry, then perhaps the court will reconsider their position on this matter. But until then, the court's position remains. Interhouse children will not be tolerated!"

I shot a quick glance at Doya, and she sent back the smallest of nods. It was time to break out her plan. We hadn't told Vanderbilt, because we knew he'd protest. He wouldn't want his past being put on trial all over again. But Doya knew this might come up, and she knew this was the only way to contest these accusations.

"I *can* prove it," I said with stone cold resolve.

The whole courtroom went so quiet you could hear a pin drop. I raised my hand and pointed to a man sitting in the far corner of the front row. He wasn't much older than me, with dark black hair like his Nivita mother, and Vanderbilt's round eyes. A beautiful reindeer doe with golden fur and fire antlers sat beside him.

Vanderbilt stared at him, shell shocked, like he couldn't believe his eyes. I thought he might fall out of his chair. Half the Elders were frozen in shock, while the others were looking to each other like someone could explain what was happening.

Vanderbilt's son stood and held his head up proudly. "It's true. My name is Sean Andre, and I'm half Nivita, half Koigni."

"You were banished twenty years ago!" Elder Malison snarled. "You don't belong in Kinpago."

"For the ancestor's sake," Doya snapped, "let the man speak."

All eyes turned to Chief Nahele. He hesitated a moment, then said, "I'll allow it. Mister Andre, please make your way to the witness stand."

I breathed a sigh of relief as I stepped down and made my way over to Liam with Esis in my arms. Vanderbilt turned to me when I sat, and hissed, "What are you *doing*? You should have consulted me first."

"I knew you might not let him on the witness stand," I said regrettably. "But he can help our case."

Vanderbilt huffed, then turned back to look at his son. Liam leaned over and whispered, "How'd you find him?"

"I didn't," I whispered back, then shot a glance at Doya. Liam nodded. My message was clear. It'd all been Doya's doing.

"Mister Andre, can you tell the court exactly who you are?" Miller asked.

Sean adjusted his tie, then set his hand on the back of his Familiar's neck. "I'm Sean Andre, son of Alyssa Andre of Nivita."

"And your father?" Miller questioned.

Sean's gaze darted to Vanderbilt. It was clear he knew, though he didn't admit it. "It was never confirmed. All I know is that he was Koigni. When the rumors hit that I was interhouse, my mother and I were put on trial. I was six years old. My mother was put to death, and I was banished from the tribe, adopted out to a couple in Oregon."

"It appears that you've bonded, Mister Andre." Miller gestured to his Familiar beside him. "How is that possible if you were banished from the tribe?"

Sean spoke calmly. I admired him for that. "I was banished when I was young, but I was old enough to remember the Hawkei traditions. When I came of age, my magic appeared. I knew that I would have to bond in order to strengthen my magic and ensure my soul was whole in this life. So I came to the outskirts of Kinpago on my own and bonded with Nora in the woods."

"You do realize that taking a magical creature outside of Kinpago without the permission of the Elders is an offense punishable by up to life in prison?" Miller pointed out.

"Yes, but I never took her outside of tribal boundaries," Sean claimed. "I've been living by myself in the woods for some time now, just to be with her. And in that time, I've been teaching myself magic."

"Oh, really?" Miller asked curiously. "Do you care to show us that magic?"

Sean held his hand out in front of him, and his palm ignited. Fire shot up fifteen feet into the air, making the entire crowd jump back, before settling into a small flame in his hand. He closed his fist, and the fire died.

"Impressive," Miller said with raised eyebrows. "Now show us Nivita magic."

Sean hesitated. "I don't have Nivita magic."

"You don't?" Miller asked, like he was pretending to be shocked. "But you said your mother was Nivita."

"Yes," Sean confirmed. "But I only inherited my father's powers."

"This is absurd!" Elder Oleander burst. "For all we know, this isn't the child who was banished twenty years ago."

"Aye aye!" Elder Malison was quick to agree. "Even if he was, he's been banished! He shouldn't be allowed to testify, anyhow."

Elder Oleander pointed a bony, crooked finger at Sean. "You don't belong here!"

"Please, Elders!" Doya shouted. "Let him speak."

But by now, her pleas were almost inaudible beneath the rest of the crowd shouting. Elders were on their feet, yelling at each other to either take him off the witness stand or let him stay. Out in the crowd, people were chanting things like *Liar!* and *Take him away!*

Meanwhile, Chief Nahele pounded his gavel. "Order! Order!"

My jaw quivered. This isn't how this was supposed to go. They were supposed to believe him.

"Get him out of here!" Elder Malison growled to the nearest Task Force members. Since his voice was the loudest, it was him whom they obeyed.

Two Task Force members marched up to Sean and grabbed him by the arms, while two others took hold of his Familiar. Sean struggled, but he couldn't get free of them.

"It's true!" he shouted as they dragged him away. "I'm mixed house, and I am *not* weak!"

The Task Force members twisted Sean's arms behind his back until he was screaming in pain.

I shot to my feet and turned to Vanderbilt. Guilt assaulted me. "What are they going to do to him!?"

He threw his hand over his mouth and looked on the verge of tears. "I don't know, Miss Henley. He'll be lucky to get another trial."

"You're his father!" I exclaimed under my breath. "Do something!"

Vanderbilt grabbed my shoulders and dragged me down into my seat. "I am also your lawyer, Miss Henley, and if they hold me in contempt of court, you will have no one to defend you on this case. Do you *want* to lose?"

My lips trembled. "No."

"Then you do as you're told," he instructed. "I hope you don't have any other surprises in store."

"Stop!" Sean shouted. The Task Force members jumped away from him and screamed horribly, like they'd been burned. Sean aimed his hands at the ceiling, and Fire shot out of his palms. It was so intense and hot that I could feel it coming off him in waves. The entire room began to fill with smoke, and the ceiling was engulfed in flames.

Task Force members reacted quickly and shot Sean with a noxite dart. He crumbled to his knees and grabbed for his leg where the dart had sunk in. It must've had a tranquilizer in it as well, because his shouts died down when he was shot. Still, he wouldn't back down. Task Force members pursued him. He quickly used all the magic he had left before the noxite completely took over his body. He shot one last stream of Fire at the Task Force members who were restraining Nora. They jumped back from the flames, freeing her. It bought Sean enough time to crawl onto Nora's back. She took off running with Sean slumped over her. They burst through the doors near the Elder's table and kept going, never looking back.

The room was in total chaos. The crowd was on their feet, shouting a mixture of cheers and protests. A handful of Task Force members sprinted behind Sean and Nora, aiming their guns. By the way they shouted orders at each other, it sounded like Sean and Nora had escaped.

Meanwhile, the Koigni Elders were calming the flames. Scorch marks were left all over the ceiling, but the fire didn't burn long enough to cause any real structural damage. I couldn't read Doya's expression. Chief Nahele banged his gavel so hard I thought it might snap in half.

I looked to Liam with horror in my eyes. "I'm sorry," I whispered. "It wasn't supposed to go that way."

Liam took my hand under the table. "It's okay."

"Order! Order!" Chief Nahele shouted. The courtroom slowly quieted as the Koigni Elders killed the flames and the Yapluma Elders pushed the lingering smoke out of the room. "I will not tolerate such discourse in this courtroom. Sean Andre is not on trial here. The Task Force will deal with him. Let's move on with the trial at hand. Mister Vanderbilt, do you have any further witnesses to call to the stand?"

Vanderbilt stood. "Yes, several. The defense calls Lindsey Andrews to the stand."

Lindsey stood nervously but held her head high while she approached the witness stand. Medusa hung from around her neck. The courtroom had quieted. All I could hear was the sound of her heels clicking across the floor.

"Miss Andrews," Vanderbilt said kindly, but I could hear the slight shake in his voice. He was still hung up on what had just happened with his son. "Can you please describe your relationship with Miss Henley?"

Lindsey didn't sound nervous at all. "Sophia and I are friends. We've been in class together since our first year."

"Would you describe yourself as good friends with Miss Henley?" Vanderbilt asked. "Do you spend time outside of class together and talk about personal matters?"

"Yes," Lindsey said.

"What can you tell us about Miss Henley's character?" Vanderbilt asked. "Do you believe she would ever lie to you?"

"No," Lindsey said confidently. "Sophia has always been very honest with me. I don't believe she has it in her to lie to the court."

"Objection!" Miller yelled. "That was not the question Vanderbilt posed."

"Overruled," Chief Nahele growled. He was obviously starting to get very irritated with this case. "Please continue, Mister Vanderbilt."

"Miss Andrews, you know Miss Henley fairly well," Vanderbilt said. "Did you ever feel that she had plans to start a rebellion?"

"No," Lindsey replied. "I don't believe she even supports a rebellion. All she wants is to be with Liam."

"And what about children?" Vanderbilt asked. "Has she ever expressed interest in having children with Mister Mitoh?"

"No," Lindsey answered. "She never said anything like that to me."

"Miss Andrews, is it true that you were in the hospital for several weeks with the plague?" Vanderbilt asked.

Lindsey nodded. "Yes."

"Do you believe Miss Henley would withhold information about the cure at your expense?" he questioned.

"No," Lindsey replied. "I believe that Sophia came out with the information as soon as she found out. I told her I was sick before I checked myself into quarantine. She would've told me about the cure then, if she'd known."

Vanderbilt paced in front of the witness stand, looking pleased with her answers. "Miss Andrews, do you believe Sophia Henley loves Liam Mitoh?"

"Absolutely," Lindsey said. "I know she does. There's no question about it."

"And do you believe the two of them should be together?" Vanderbilt asked.

Lindsey took a deep breath, then stood from her chair. She stared out across the crowd, like she was addressing them all. "I firmly believe that love is love, no matter the age, gender, or House. So yes, I believe that Liam Mitoh and Sophia Henley should be allowed to be together."

"Thank you," Vanderbilt said as he sat. "No further questions."

"Your witness, Mister Miller," Chief Nahele said.

Miller stood with a smirk on his face. "Miss Andrews, you say you support love no matter the age, gender, or House. Would you agree, then, that pedophelia should be allowable in this society?"

Lindsey gaped, then said, "No. Absolutely not."

"But aren't interhouse relationships just as perverted?" Miller asked, looking out to the crowd. He was met with a chorus of mixed cheers and boos.

Lindsey turned to the Elder Council. "Chief Nahele, if permitted, I'd like to amend my statement to include only love between two consenting adults."

"I'll allow it," Chief Nahele said. He nodded to Miller to continue.

"Miss Andrews, you said you and Miss Henley were close friends," Miller asserted.

"Yes..." Lindsey confirmed, though she looked confused— like she didn't know where he was going with this.

Miller smiled and folded his hands in front of himself. "Is there a reason you left out the part about the two of you being romantically involved?"

My stomach sank. The crowd broke out into protest again.

"Why didn't you mention this?" Vanderbilt leaned over and hissed at me.

I stared wide-eyed at him. "Because I thought Liam and I were on trial, not me and Lindsey."

Chief Nahele banged his gavel. When the crowd finally quieted, he turned to Lindsey. "Answer the question, Miss Andrews."

The blood drained from my face. How did Miller even know? My gaze flickered up to the Elder Council, and I noticed the smirk on

Chieftess Annette's face. She was loving this. She must've heard about us from Haley and passed the information along to Miller to invalidate our case!

"I— I didn't think it was relevant," Lindsey stammered. "Considering it's over between us."

"Miss Henley's love life is on trial. It is very relevant," Miller pointed out. "Please tell the court when these relations took place."

Lindsey was starting to look as nervous as I felt. "I don't know the exact dates. It all happened early this semester, while Sophia and Liam were broken up."

"Why did you and Miss Henley break things off?" Miller questioned, looking positively pleased with himself.

Lindsey hesitated. "I was sick from the plague. I didn't want her to get hung up on me if I didn't make it."

"So she just moved on from you like *that*?" Miller snapped his fingers. "Doesn't that sound a little... heartless?"

"No," Lindsey insisted. Irritation entered her tone, and she shot me an apologetic glance. "I knew Sophia's heart still belonged to someone else. I encouraged her to get back together with him."

"If it's over between you two, how can you claim that you are still good friends? Are there no hard feelings that she left you to get back together with Mister Mitoh?" Miller asked.

"No hard feelings," Lindsey stated. "The breakup was mutual. Some people aren't so quick to hold grudges."

Miller huffed, but tried to hide it. "Why do you think Miss Henley turned to you for comfort after her breakup with Mister Mitoh?"

"I don't know," Lindsey said honestly. "I guess she was trying to get over him."

Miller raised an eyebrow. "And you don't feel bitter about that? About being *used*?"

"I never said I was being used," Lindsey snarled. She was getting more frustrated by the minute. "We were friends, and I comforted her. Is that a crime?"

"No," Miller said in amusement. "But it does suggest Miss Henley isn't as devoted to Mister Mitoh as she says."

Liam lost it. He shot up out of his chair and shouted, "That's a lie!"

But there were so many other voices ringing out over the courtroom that he could hardly be heard. The Elders were arguing again, and the crowd was mumbling amongst themselves.

Liam's dad was the one voice that stood out above all the others. "She's a teenage girl who was going through a wild and rebellious phase after her boyfriend broke up with her. That's not unusual."

I relaxed when Liwanu stood up for me. It was a relief to know he was on my side, even though all my dirty laundry was being aired.

Chieftess Annette scoffed and said, "My daughter's the same age, and *she* hasn't gone wild."

"Your daughter's a whore!" Miranda shouted from the audience.

Chieftess Annette shot a scathing glare out to the audience, searching for the source of the voice, but so many people were talking that she couldn't tell who said it. "At least my daughter's sleeping with people in her own house!" she belted.

"Order!" Chief Nahele shouted. The room quieted again. "Mister Miller, if you have no further questions, please call your next witness."

"Yes," Miller said with a nod. "I'd like to call Landon Barnes to the witness stand."

Landon Barnes? I didn't know who that was. He had to be some sort of expert witness or something. Lindsey came down from the stand, looking defeated. She mouthed a *sorry* at me as she passed.

And then I saw him stand in the crowd, and it hit me. Landon from the strip club. Shit. This couldn't be good.

Landon strutted up to the witness stand like he was coming to collect a lottery check. Miller had probably offered him something to get him on the stand. Who else would want to get involved in this shit?

Landon didn't have a Familiar at his side, and I realized I didn't know what he was bonded to— since he didn't have a Familiar by him at the club, either. Which meant it was too big to fit into the courtroom. The Elders were going to love this jackass.

"Mister Barnes," Miller said as Landon sat. "Can you please describe your relationship with Miss Henley?"

Landon leaned back in his chair and wore a confident smirk I would've liked to slap straight off his face. I couldn't believe I ever found this guy attractive.

"Sophia and I met at *Lucky Stars* a few months ago," Landon said.

"The strip club?" Miller asked, like he was shocked, but it was clear he already knew the answer.

"Yeah," Landon said with a shrug. "It was the end of September. She came in and got really drunk and danced up on stage. Her hands were all over the strippers, even though they don't let you do that. She had no respect for anyone else's boundaries."

I quickly leaned over to Vanderbilt and said, "He's lying."

"Objection!" Vanderbilt shouted quickly.

"Overruled," Chief Nahele said.

Miller smiled and continued. "Can you tell us what happened between the two of you that night?"

"Well, I was really drunk, so I don't remember a lot," Landon admitted. "But I do remember that Sophia came up to me at the bar and invited me to go make-out with her. We went out to my carriage and fooled around for a bit."

"He's lying!" I shouted, but Vanderbilt placed a hand on my shoulder to calm me.

Miller ignored my accusation. "Can you please be more specific, Mister Barnes?"

Landon sighed, like the answer didn't matter to him one way or another. "We had sex in my carriage."

The crowd gasped, and my skin heated. I turned to Liam and said, "It's not true, Liam. I didn't."

"I know," he said, but his hands were fisting in his lap. He looked like he was on the verge of choking this guy. Honestly, I was nearly to that point, too. And the worst part was that Landon looked like he believed every word he said. I was willing to bet he'd taken some other chick out to his carriage and was so drunk he forgot it wasn't me he'd fucked.

"Anyway, after that, Mitoh and his friends showed up and beat the shit out of me," Landon continued.

Miller stepped up to the Elders' table. "If the court would allow, I'd like to bring up evidence on the screen." He gestured to a large flat-screen TV near the witness stand.

Chief Nahele nodded, and Miller pressed a button on a remote he was holding. A picture of Landon's beat-up face came on screen. His eye was swollen, and there were bruises all around his nose. Miller clicked the remote again, and the image changed to another angle. The bruises on Landon's face were almost unbearable to look at.

I knew for a fact we hadn't done that much damage that night. Liam had walked away worse for wear than Landon. These pictures must've been from a different bar fight Landon had gotten himself into.

I quickly leaned over to Vanderbilt. "It's another lie."

"Objection!" Vanderbilt shot to his feet. "Where is the timestamp on these photographs? There's no way to prove these injuries occurred on the night in question."

"Sustained," Chief Nahele said, and I breathed a sigh of relief. "Mister Miller, without a timestamp, I'm afraid we're unable to accept this evidence."

Miller smirked. "Of course. Perhaps you'll accept this?"

He clicked another button, and the image changed to a video of security cam footage out front of the strip club. Liam and I were shouting at each other, surrounded by our friends. Liam's back was to the camera, so no one could see how beat up his face was. There was no audio, either. But one thing was very clear— the moment I pulled my dress down to flash the street. My breasts had been blurred out, but it was obvious what I was doing.

My hands shot over my mouth, and I felt completely mortified. How were they allowed to show this? I sank low in my seat as my cheeks turned bright red.

Liam squeezed my shoulder. "It's okay, Sophia. You didn't do anything wrong."

Tears pricked at my eyes. "Then why do I feel like I did? Liam, I'm sorry about that night."

"We were broken up," he whispered. "I don't hold it against you. I'm sorry, too."

Chief Nahele pounded his gavel again, and the courtroom silenced.

Miller turned to the Elders. "It's clear what we're dealing with here. On the one hand, we have a girl who can't keep her legs closed, and on the other, a boy who can't control his temper."

"Objection!" Vanderbilt shouted.

"Sustained," Chief Nahele said. "Mister Miller, I'm going to have to ask you to sit. Mister Vanderbilt, your witness."

Miller smirked as he returned to his seat, and his pitbull panted happily from beside him. He was pleased with the damage he'd done.

"Mister Barnes, you claim that you and Miss Henley engaged in sexual intercourse." Vanderbilt sounded a little flustered. Shit. "Do you have any evidence to prove this claim?"

"Hell no." Landon sounded disgusted, but it seemed like a show for the Elders. He definitely seemed like the kind of guy who would take nudes without asking first. "What kind of evidence are you suggesting I get? That shit's private."

"Yes, of course," Vanderbilt said. "No further questions."

My jaw dropped. That was it?

"Next witness, please," Chief Nahele said.

Jonah was called to the stand next. Vanderbilt questioned him on mine and Liam's character. It felt like the trial might be starting to turn around— until Miller got his hands on him.

"Mister Chanee," Miller said confidently. "You paint the defendants to be heroes, but you've had your own set of misdemeanors lately, haven't you?"

"I don't know what you're talking about," Jonah said. Squeaks huffed from beside him. "I've never been charged with anything."

Miller raised his eyebrows. "Was it not *you* that put Renar Raviro in the hospital shortly before he competed in the Elemental Cup?"

Liam and I exchanged looks of shock. Renar had never brought any charges against Jonah. We'd assumed he hadn't told anyone.

"I— I..." Jonah stammered.

"Answer the question, Mister Chanee," Chief Nahele encouraged.

Before he could answer, Elder Raviro slammed his hands down on the table in front of him and shot to his feet. "You broke my son's arm and leg! You should be in prison for battery, not on this witness stand!"

"Fuck you!" Jonah couldn't hold it in. He shot up and turned on Elder Raviro. "Your son is an emotionally abusive piece of shit who attempted to murder—"

"Order! Order!" Chief Nahele shouted, smacking his gavel.

"— My best friend!" Jonah continued without missing a beat. "He deserved far worse than he got. We should be prosecuting assholes like him instead of—"

Chief Nahele gave the order, and a Task Force member shot a noxite dart into Jonah's chest. Jonah took one look down at it, and his eyes rolled back into his head. He collapsed back into his chair. I heard Imogen let out a surprised scream from behind me. Liam's chair squeaked, like he was about to get up and fight the Task Force, but he thought better of it. Squeaks rose to her hind legs and squawked loudly in protest. She looked like she was about to cut a bitch, but she didn't even take a step before they'd shot a dart into her backside. She collapsed beside Jonah.

"Ancestors." My hands shot over my mouth, and my face heated from my Fire. I turned to Liam and desperately asked, "Are they going to be okay?"

"They should be," he said, but he looked worried.

"Take them to a holding cell until the trial is done," Chief Nahele growled. He placed his fingers to his eyes, like he was getting a headache, as Jonah and Squeaks were dragged away. "Please tell me we're almost done with these witnesses."

"No more witnesses from the defense," Vanderbilt said.

"What about Imogen?" I leaned over and hissed.

"Miller's turned around every character witness on us," Vanderbilt whispered back. "So unless you want to make it worse, we'll not be calling Miss Ahnild to the witness stand."

I was so fed up with this case already, and I wasn't letting Vanderbilt take away the last shred of hope we had at winning. I grabbed him by the tie and pulled him close to me. "You're a coward. You want to prove you have what it takes to win this case? You get Imogen Ahnild on that witness stand right now."

Vanderbilt looked totally shocked. I let him go, and he straightened his tie.

Chief Nahele raised his gavel. "If there are no more witnesses to question, the council will take a short recess—"

I elbowed Vanderbilt in the ribs, and he shot to his feet. "My mistake, Chief Nahele. The defense has one more witness."

Chief Nahele waved him to continue. "Let's just get this over with."

Vanderbilt straightened his suit coat. "The defense calls Imogen Ahnild to the stand."

Imogen strolled confidently to the front of the room, with Sassy holding her head up high at her feet. Imogen held a piece of paper and looked like she was about to lawyer this whole courtroom on her own. She barely looked like herself. She wore her hair down in waves, and had on a plain navy blue business dress and a single red bracelet.

"Miss Ahnild," Vanderbilt said, his voice losing all confidence. "Can you please describe your relationship with the defendants?"

"We were teammates during the Elemental Cup, and we've been friends ever since," Imogen said.

Vanderbilt went on to ask the same questions he'd asked our other character witnesses, and Imogen answered honestly and with poise.

Vanderbilt shot me a questioning look when he'd finished, as if to ask if that was acceptable. I nodded, and he returned to his seat. "No further questions."

As Miller stood, Vanderbilt leaned over to me and whispered, "I fail to see how Miss Ahnild is going to help win your case."

I smirked. Liam had spoken to her in our waiting room during the recess. Imogen knew what she was doing, and she'd spend the night in jail if she had to just for the chance to confront the Elders.

"Miss Ahnild," Miller started, "is it true that you discovered the cure for the plague that afflicted Kinpago these past few months?"

"Yes," Imogen said, with her head held high.

"And how did you discover the cure?" he asked.

"I knew that if this plague was magical, it must've originated outside our society, as the Hawkei don't have the power to create something like this," Imogen explained. "I used library books to research what other societies were capable of, and I came across the Miriamic Coven and the Omnimotus Curse."

"So it was you who single-handedly discovered the cure?" Miller asserted.

"I guess," Imogen said.

"So Mister Mitoh and Miss Henley had nothing to do with discovering the cure?" he asked.

"They helped," Imogen assured him. "I was in the hospital when they announced the cure to the public."

Miller raised an eyebrow. "So they just took credit for your discovery?"

"I wouldn't call it my discovery." Imogen's tone grew irritated. "They helped the tribe—"

"And yet they waited until you were unconscious and vulnerable to share the information with Kinpago," Miller accused. "You were in on this all along, weren't you? You were going to withhold information about the plague to make them look good."

"That's not true," Imogen stated, trying not to lose her temper too soon.

Vanderbilt whispered under his breath, "I told you this wouldn't go well."

I ignored him and watched Imogen.

"When exactly did you discover this information?" Miller questioned.

"The day I was attacked," Imogen answered. "November twenty-fifth. I have the library receipt to prove it."

She held out a strip of paper. A Task Force member came up to take it from her, then handed it to Chief Nahele.

"That shows the books I checked out that day," Imogen said.

Miller scoffed. "That doesn't prove that you didn't know about the cure before then. You could've researched elsewhere."

"He's right, Miss Ahnild," Chief Nahele said. "I'm afraid we can't file this with the evidence. If that is all, the Elders are ready to make a decision."

It was evident in their faces which way the council swayed. They wanted Liam and I to be put to death— to make an example out of us.

It was in that moment that Imogen lost it. She shot to her feet and snarled, "Do you want evidence? Take this for evidence." Her tone turned fierce— she would not back down. "Two days ago, I buried my boyfriend's casket."

The courtroom went silent in shock, but Imogen kept going, her voice wavering as she said the words. "Cade Garcia was a noble Nivita. He was full of love, spirit, and adventure. And you— the Elders— *murdered* him! Cade Garcia will never perform Nivita magic again. He'll never kiss me again. He'll never get to try out for the professional soccer team like he planned. He'll never play another game of ping pong in the Commons. He'll never see the sun again. And you know why? Because of your stupid tournament! When will the killing end?"

Chief Nahele banged his gavel as the courtroom burst into protest once more, but Imogen couldn't be stopped.

She raised her voice to be heard above the others. "If you kill any more of my friends, there will be hell to pay— because the Hawkei will no longer stand by and let you execute our own!"

"Miss Ahnild!" Chief Nahele shouted. "Sit down, or I'll be forced to order the Task Force to shoot you!"

She ignored his instructions and continued. I felt proud of her as her voice grew to such intense levels that she couldn't be ignored. "You know who else will never see the sun again because of you? My brother, Trace Ahnild. And all my classmates I watched die in the tournament this year!" Imogen looked down at the piece of paper in her hand and began reading off the list of names. "Avery Chase, Becca Smith, Alexis Brown, Casey Tyler, Sam Stone, Lauren Banks, David Chapman, Martin Patterson, Evan Baker, Eliza Brooks—"

Imogen hadn't even made it halfway through the list of names before Chief Nahele had enough. "Take her to holding!" he shouted.

A Task Force member shot Imogen with a noxite dart, and she collapsed onto the floor. Sassy rushed forward and pulled the dart out with her teeth, but they shot her, too. The Task Force proceeded to grab them and drag them away, the same way Jonah and Squeaks had been taken. The crowd was going insane. It was so loud that I could hardly hear the sound of the gavel slamming against the table. My Fire was about to escape if I didn't do something.

I got to my feet and continued shouting the names I remembered from last year's tournament. Tears began to fall down my cheeks as Imogen was dragged away.

"Isla Roberts!" I still remembered the lifeless look in the Toaqua girl's eyes after we'd found her frozen to death during the Cup. "Andy Henry! Taylor Curley!" I yelled. They'd been the two we'd found crushed by the landslide.

"Miss Henley!" Chief Nahele shouted.

"Rebecca Summers! Joseph Perry!" I continued shouting out all the names I could think of. After last year's Cup, I'd checked the list of those we'd lost to make sure I'd never forget them.

Liam stood beside me and began adding names to the list. "Kelly Catori! Cameron Wahkin!" They were the couple who'd been sentenced to death last semester for their relationship— the one with the young boy who'd been taken away.

Behind us, Lindsey and Miranda took hands and stood on their bench to get higher. They shouted names together. "Maria Hughes! Henry Gibson! Grant Duncan!"

"Order! Order!" Chief Nahele shouted. He was so angry that the veins in his neck were beginning to pop. The earth began to rumble beneath our feet. "Order!"

The crowd didn't seem fazed at all. Liam and I stood hand-in-hand, watching in wonder as more and more people stood on their benches to shout names. It became so overwhelming that I couldn't distinguish one name from another. But one thing was very clear: too many people had died at the hands of the Elders, and all of the Hawkei knew it. If the Elders didn't want a full-on revolt, they were going to have to think of a solution to calm the crowd— and fast.

Just as I thought it, the doors at the back of the courtroom burst open. It was so loud that everyone turned their heads and quieted.

A short man with tousled gray hair rushed down the aisle, waving a stack of papers in his hands. "Stop the sentencing!"

"Perot?" I glanced to Liam in shock. "I thought he bailed."

He looked equally dumbstruck. "Apparently not."

"I have new evidence to present!" Perot said quickly. He stopped at the front row of benches, breathing hard, waiting for Chief Nahele's signal.

"We've seen all the evidence!" Elder Oleander snarled.

Chief Nahele leaned over to whisper to the Elders on either side of him, then sat up straighter. "As long as the crowd can contain themselves, I'm willing to allow it. Should there be *one* more outburst, this court will adjourn," he threatened, wagging his finger. It was clear he was only allowing it to calm the crowd.

"Yes, Chief Nahele," Perot said with a bow.

The Nivita chief nodded, and a Task Force member ushered Perot to the witness stand.

"Your witness, Mister Vanderbilt," Chief Nahele said.

Vanderbilt stood, looking a little more confident. "Mister Perot, what's this evidence you speak of?"

"Well," Perot said, sitting straight up in his chair. "I've been running tests for many months now, to help diagnose Mister Mitoh's condition."

"Has this condition been diagnosed yet?" Vanderbilt asked.

"No," Perot said regrettably, "but I discovered something while running these tests."

I looked to Liam, like he could explain what Perot was talking about, but he looked just as clueless as I did.

Vanderbilt smiled, like he knew whatever Perot was about to say was good. "Mister Perot, can you please highlight your qualifications for the court?"

"Yes," Perot replied confidently. "I am a master alchemist and a professor at Orenda Academy. I'm also a certified M.D. by the Medical Board of California."

"Excellent," Vanderbilt said. "And what is this evidence you've come to present today?"

I held my breath. Perot held his papers out to a Task Force member, who brought them to the Elders' table.

Perot took a deep breath. "Liam Mitoh can't conceive children."

The entire courtroom shared a collective gasp. I turned to Liam breathlessly. "Why didn't you tell me?"

His face paled, and he couldn't take his eyes off Perot. "I— I didn't know. Perot never said anything."

"He must've just found out," I whispered. "And that's why he was late."

"Order! Order!" Chief Nahele banged his gavel. The courtroom quieted, and he turned to Perot. "Mister Perot, please explain what this data means."

"Certainly," Perot said. "As we all know, conception occurs when the sperm and the egg meet to form an embryo. However, I had to perform a variety of medical tests to narrow down what could possibly be affecting my patient, and results have concluded that Liam Mitoh's sperm is not viable. It's a side effect of his condition."

Vanderbilt beamed. He knew this changed everything. "Mister Perot, you're suggesting that Liam Mitoh is sterile?"

"Precisely," Perot said confidently.

"There's *no chance* that he could ever father a child?" Vanderbilt asked, making it very clear to the court.

"Correct," Perot answered.

"Chief Nahele." Vanderbilt turned on his heel toward the Elders' table. Chief Nahele was frantically checking the papers, before Elder Malison reached over and snatched the evidence out of his hands. Chief Nahele seemed to barely notice. He was too shocked. "Is it true that the laws currently in place forbidding interhouse relationships are there to prevent the birth of mixed children and the dilution of our magic?"

Chief Nahele pulled himself together. "I... I am not on the witness stand, Mister Vanderbilt."

"Answer the question!" someone from the audience yelled, and several others joined in.

Chief Nahele looked flustered, but answered anyway. "Yes."

"So if an interhouse couple were unable to have children, their relationship would not apply to current laws. Is that correct?" Vanderbilt asked.

"Uh..." Chief Nahele's jaw dropped, and he glanced to the other Elders for help. I could tell Elder Oleander was itching to burst out with an objection, but he also knew what that would do to the crowd. Vanderbilt had them cornered.

Vanderbilt grabbed a thick, leather-bound book from his stack of papers at our table. He approached the Elders' table with it in hand. "Elder Oleander, do you recognize this book?"

"Yes," he snarled, crossing his arms. "It is the *Hawkei Book of Laws*."

Vanderbilt held the book up for the court to see. "Precisely. Madame Doya, would you mind reading a passage for the court?"

Vanderbilt opened the book toward the end and placed it in front of Doya. He pointed to a spot on the page and said, "Beginning here."

She began to read aloud. "*Amendment K, subsection three. Written into law on August 13, 1906. Interhouse relationships are hereby banned on the basis of reproduction concerns following the fall of the Anichi House. Couples found in violation of this new law shall suffer no less than five years in prison and up to the death penalty.*"

Doya raised her eyes to the crowd. "It appears you're correct, Mister Vanderbilt. Interhouse relationships are only banned when the relationship may result in the bearing of children."

Vanderbilt smiled proudly and took a seat. "I rest my case."

"Mister Miller," Chief Nahele said breathlessly. "Your witness."

Miller's face paled. There was nothing he could ask Perot to turn this around. He remained seated. "No... no further questions."

"In that case, this court will take a short recess as the Elders convene for sentencing." Chief Nahele smacked his gavel, and the courtroom broke into chatter again as the Elders stood to go to a private room to talk.

Vanderbilt led us back to our waiting room. We barely made it inside before I'd flung my arms around Liam's neck. We just stood there in silence for a long time as everything that just happened sank in. Finally, I drew away.

"How did you know to use the *Hawkei Book of Laws?*" I asked Vanderbilt.

He shook his head. "I didn't, since I hadn't prepared this angle, but I always keep a copy with me to reference during a case."

"I'm so glad Perot made it!" I exclaimed.

"Don't get too comfortable," Vanderbilt warned. "The Elders have found ways to turn things around before. They'll do anything to make an example of you."

"But Madame Doya read the law right in the courtroom," I pointed out. "As long as we can't have kids, we're safe."

"I believe we've done all we can," Vanderbilt said, "but the Elders still have the power to change the laws."

Liam and I shared a look of disbelief, but it was he who spoke. "They can't change the laws and retroactively charge us, can they?"

"No," Vanderbilt agreed, "but they could prevent the two of you from being together in the future."

Liam looked horrified, as did Esis.

"They won't do that," I assured him. "The tribe would revolt if they did. They don't want a rebellion, so they have to take it into consideration."

At least, I hoped they would. It was the only thing that might save our lives.

A ruckus came from out in the hall, and I heard Amelia's voice shouting, "Let me through! I want to talk to my sister!"

Vanderbilt flung the door open and barked to the Task Force members, "Let her in."

Amelia rushed into the room and threw her arms around my neck. "Sophia! Ancestors, I missed you."

Kiwi flew around above our heads. Esis followed him with his eyes until he looked like he was going to get dizzy.

"Am!" I cried, squeezing her tightly. "I missed you. I thought you weren't going to make it."

She dashed tears from her eyes. "I wouldn't miss it for the world."

Amelia turned on Liam, pointing a finger at him. "You!"

Liam took an innocent step back.

"Am!" I grabbed her by the shoulder as she advanced on him, but she shrugged me off and stabbed her index finger into his chest. "You dirtbag! Do you know what you did to Sophia?"

"I—" Liam started, but Amelia didn't let him finish.

She stabbed him in the heart over and over again with her finger, even though he was half a foot taller than her and she was hardly intimidating. "You broke up with her, and she was devastated. *Devastated!*"

"Am, calm down," I insisted.

"No," Amelia growled. "I saw what you went through during your Naming Ceremony. I don't *ever* want to see you like that again."

"It's okay," I told her. "Everything's good now."

She narrowed her eyes at Liam. "It better be. Because if you break my sister's heart like that ever again, there's going to be hell to pay."

Liam remained calm, but I knew that Amelia meant it. She'd carve the skin off Liam's flesh if he left me a second time.

Amelia blew out a deep breath. "Wow. That felt good."

"Miss Henley, I think it's best if you leave," Vanderbilt suggested.

Amelia shrugged and started for the door. She pointed to her eyes, then to Liam. "I've got my eyes on you, Mitoh."

"It was great to see you, Am!" I called as she left the room.

Liam raised his eyebrows at me once she was gone. "Wow. Your sister's intense."

I shrugged. "She cares."

Hours passed. Liam and I were beyond anxious and both paced around the waiting room. Even Esis couldn't sit still. The wait was agonizing. It felt like we'd been in this room for days.

"This is a good sign, right?" I asked nervously. "It means some of the Elders are on our side."

"Yeah," Liam said, "but will it be enough?"

Liam and I sat beside each other, and he wrapped me in his arms. I tried to enjoy it— just in case it was the last moment we had together— but I couldn't get rid of the sinking feeling in my gut. What if we hadn't convinced them?

Task Force members came to escort us back to the courtroom after sunset. Liam and I walked slowly. We were both afraid of the outcome.

When we returned to the courtroom, it was as if no one had moved. The crowd looked eager to hear the sentencing, and the Elders sat up at their massive bench. I tried to read their faces, but each one wore an emotionless mask. I couldn't read them— not even Malison or Oleander.

"Please stand for sentencing," Chief Nahele said.

Liam took my hand and squeezed it tightly as we stood. I held my breath and pulled Esis closer to my chest.

"In the matter of Liam Mitoh and Sophia Henley versus the Hawkei tribe, we the Elders find the defendants..." Chief Nahele glanced down to a sheet of paper in front of him and let out a breath.

The following two seconds seemed longer than the hours we spent in the waiting room. My heart raced, and Liam's fingers tightened around mine.

"Not guilty," Nahele concluded.

Relief flooded through me, and my stomach felt a million pounds lighter. My mouth hung agape, and I finally took a breath.

Liam swooped me up into his arms. "We did it, *pawee!*"

The crowd cheered so loud it was deafening. I thought I heard a few protests in there, but they were nothing compared to the applause. Lindsey, Miranda, and Vanessa joined hands and held them up in the air in victory.

Chief Nahele banged his gavel. "Order! The sentencing hearing will continue without interruptions!"

The room went silent. Chief Nahele brought his paper back up to his face. "As I was saying, the Elder Council finds the defendants not guilty, due to their inability to bear mixed children. However, each will be fined one-hundred thousand dollars, for engaging in an interhouse relationship prior to having access to this knowledge."

A gasp traveled around the room, but I didn't care. It was a lot of money and would drain the remainder of our Elemental Cup winnings, but it was worth it to be with Liam.

"What does this mean for other interhouse couples?" a reporter shouted from the back of the room. The crowd began to murmur their support of the question, but they quieted to listen to Chief Nahele's response.

"Unfortunately, we can't answer that, as Liam Mitoh and Sophia Henley are the only two on trial today," he stated.

"If other interhouse couples can prove they can't reproduce, such as getting a vasectomy or tubal ligation, does that mean—?"

Elder Oleander stood and cut the reporter off. "We won't be taking any questions! Further issues on this matter will be taken up in their own cases. The Elders will convene to discuss an amendment to these laws."

"Is there an estimate on when—?" the reporter started.

"No further questions," Chief Nahele insisted. "Court adjourned!"

He smacked his gavel, and the Elders stood and filed out of the room.

The crowd began to buzz with chatter. Vanessa hurried up to us, with Lindsey and Miranda behind her. "Ancestors, I can't believe you won!"

Vanessa threw her arms around me, and I hugged her back tightly. "I know. I can hardly believe it, either."

I drew away, and Liam was there a second later. He grabbed me around the waist and picked me up, spinning me around. When he set me down, he took my face in his hands and kissed me in front of the entire crowd. "It's over, *pawee*! We get to be together now."

Tears streamed down my face. "I love you, Liam."

He began to cry and dashed the tears away. "I love you, too, Sophia."

"Out of the way, loverboy." Amelia came up to us and shoved Liam aside— though it was all for fun. She wrapped me into a hug and whispered, "I'm so relieved. Congratulations."

"Thank you," I said. "And really, you don't have to worry about me and Liam. We're good."

She drew away and wiped at her eyes. "I hope so."

"Thanks for being here, Am," I told her. "It means a lot."

People were starting to file out toward the back now, but reporters were pushing through the crowd to get to us. I could barely make out their questions over one another as they shoved microphones in our faces.

Vanderbilt threw himself between us and the reporters, holding his hands up to get them to back off. "No questions, please. If you'd like to speak to my clients, you can schedule an interview with them at a later time."

The reporters ignored him and continued to point their microphones at us while rattling off an endless list of questions.

Vanderbilt turned to Vanessa, Lindsey, and Miranda. "Excuse me, but I'd like to have a word with my clients."

We waved to our friends, then followed Vanderbilt toward a private hallway near the Elders' Chambers. Esis peeped from my arms. Task Force members let us through, then closed the doors behind us to block the reporters.

"I'm very proud of how you two handled yourselves today," Vanderbilt said once we were in the privacy of the hallway. "However, you got very lucky."

"That's a good thing, isn't it?" Liam asked.

"Yes," Vanderbilt said with a sigh, "but the Elders are going to be keeping an eye on you."

"That's nothing new," I scoffed.

Vanderbilt sighed. "The outcome of today's trial changes everything. You two truly have the power to start a revolution. I suggest you use that power wisely."

Liam and I exchanged a glance. Heck, we were already trying to stop the prophecy. We already had more power than he realized. We wouldn't screw this up.

"We will," I told him.

"You two should try to get some rest," Vanderbilt suggested. "It's been a long day. You should be able to meet up with your friends tomorrow, after they've been released from holding."

"Will they be okay?" I asked. "I mean, will the noxite cause permanent damage?"

"It will take some time to wear off, but they'll be fine," Vanderbilt assured me. "Try to keep a low profile until things calm down. There are a lot of people who would like to hurt you, and I can't help you if you're dead."

Shit. More ominous stuff. Vanderbilt was starting to scare me a little.

"We'll be careful," Liam said.

"I trust that you will," Vanderbilt replied. "If you ever need a lawyer again, you know who to call."

"Thank you," I told him.

He gave a polite nod. "Let's get you back to the carriage safely."

Vanderbilt, along with two armed Task Force members, led us out the back, where our pegasus and carriage were waiting. The street was quiet, but we could hear the roar of the crowd out front.

"Thanks for everything," Liam said to Vanderbilt as we climbed into the carriage. "We'll take it from here."

"Avoid the main roadways, or the media will be all over you," Vanderbilt instructed as he waved goodbye. "Good luck."

The carriage lurched forward, and I finally felt like I could breathe. I set Esis beside me, then flung my arms around Liam. I dragged his lips down to mine and kissed him with such passion that it made me tear up.

"I still can't believe it," I cried. It was all I could say.

Liam kissed me back, which sent heat to pool between my thighs. "Me either. We should celebrate."

I chuckled. "How? There's going to be media swarming everywhere."

He shrugged, but gave me a smile. "So we go somewhere private."

"Won't your parents worry?" I asked.

He pressed his lips together, then playfully said, "We'll make it a quickie."

I kissed the sensitive area behind his ear. "What about right here?"

"Not if the media might find us," he teased. "Do you want them to have another picture of your boobs on record?"

I placed my hand over my mouth to stifle my giggles. At first, I'd been horrified, but now that we'd won, I just found it amusing. "You're right. I don't want that. What about the cabin?"

Liam trailed kisses down my neck. "The cabin sounds perfect. Except— shit."

"What?" I asked in alarm.

"I don't have the key," he suddenly realized. "It's back in my dorm at Orenda. I never moved any of my shit out."

"So we go get it," I suggested. "The semester's over, so no one's there anyway."

"Good point." Liam instructed the pegasus to make a stop at the castle, and we arrived shortly after.

The castle was eerily quiet since the semester was over. We slipped inside the empty school and through the shadows. I'd never been inside the Toaqua dorms, but I wasn't surprised to see the common room was filled with multiple pools and wicker chairs— like some sort of spa resort. It was chilly, too. I stopped to stare, and Esis hopped out of my arms to rush over to one of the pools and run his fingers through the water.

I chuckled. "I think he likes it in here."

"He should," Liam said. "It's beautiful."

I poked him in the side. "Go get your key. I'll watch Esis, since he can't swim."

Liam gave me a peck on the lips, then started down a long hallway. I lowered myself to the floor beside Esis and watched the water ripple beneath his paws. It was so peaceful and quiet in here. I didn't even like water, but I couldn't get over how serene it felt to be alone in this big open space.

Alone... an idea suddenly struck me. I didn't give it too much thought before I stood and peeked down the hallway Liam had gone down. He wasn't in sight, so I figured I had at least a minute until he returned. I quickly stripped off my clothes and stepped down the stairs into the pool.

Esis gave a cat-call to me, and I splashed him. "Shut up," I said with a giggle. He got bored with the water and decided to go play with a bubble machine across the room.

The water was cool, so I called upon my Fire to help warm it. Bubbles sprang up on my skin, and the water started to boil around me. Steam rose up to fill my nasal passages. It felt amazing. I heard Liam's footsteps down the hall and pulled back on my Fire. I ducked down into the pool, until only my head stuck out.

"I got it—" Liam started, but he stopped dead in his tracks when he caught sight of my clothes lying at the edge of the pool. Esis chittered, then pointed to where I stood naked in the pool. Liam's jaw dropped. "*Pawee...*"

"Come in," I said, looking up at him past my lashes. "The water feels nice."

Liam glanced around the dorms, like he expected a Toaqua to jump out at any minute, but we were alone.

"What's wrong?" I asked smoothly. I stood up so that my breasts were out in the open. Water droplets dripped from my nipples.

Liam looked like he was about ready to drool. "N— nothing."

"Then come in," I encouraged, running my fingers across the surface of the water.

Liam quickly pulled his shirt over his head and kicked his shoes off. He fumbled with the button on his jeans for a second— since he couldn't take his eyes off me— then dropped his trousers. Heat spread all over my body as I drank him in. He was already hard for me, and he looked amazing.

He didn't go over to the stairs. He jumped right in from where he stood at the edge, but he barely made a splash. He was over by me in seconds, wrapping me in his arms and kissing me all over. Our bodies moved against each other as one. Ancestors, he felt amazing.

Liam spun me around slowly as we made out. He made the water swell around us, lifting us up until our feet were no longer touching the bottom of the pool.

Liam began to trail kisses down my neck. He spoke between each one. "Did you mean what you said about not wanting kids?"

"What does it matter?" I asked. "If you can't have them?"

Liam pulled away to look me in the eyes. "I don't want to take that away from you if it's what you really want."

I shook my head. "Liam, you're not taking anything away from me. All I want is you. I really meant what I said. If I have to give up kids to be with you, I'll do that. Besides, Esis is like a child himself, so we've already got one kid."

Liam chuckled. Esis raised a fist at me and shook it, obviously offended. Yeah, his horns were getting bigger and bigger, but he was still young.

"So... you're okay with me being sterile?" Liam asked.

"Yeah," I replied honestly. "It makes everything easier for us, I guess. We don't have to be so careful."

"True," Liam said with a shrug. He was acting like he didn't care, but I knew better. Liam had told me he'd always wanted kids, and now that had been taken away from him— and me, too. It'd been a good thing, because it was the loophole that enabled us to keep our lives, but at the same time, it was crushing to know we'd never get to have a family.

I decided to make the conversation lighter, and to try and take his mind off of it.

"So, how awkward was it?" I teased. "Jacking off into a cup for Perot?"

Liam got a horrified look on his face. "I'd rather not talk about it."

I laughed, and he joined in. "Good idea. I'm ruining the moment."

"Nah, nothing could ruin this moment," Liam said as he wrapped me closer. He glanced over my shoulder and began to run his fingers across my tattoo.

I shied away from him. I ran my hands through the water to drag myself a few feet away from him. "I thought you didn't like it. You acted that way when I got it."

Liam smiled. "That's not true. That was just me being an ass. I was pissed at you then."

I giggled, then splashed him. "Typical Liam."

He shrugged. "Hey, take it or leave it. You're stuck with me now."

He grabbed me by the wrist and pulled me close to him again. I wrapped my legs around him in the water. He gazed down at me with a sexy stare that made my mouth go dry. "If I'm being honest, I find it a little sexy."

My heart fluttered, but I tried not to let it show. "Sexy?"

"Yeah. I just want to... bite it."

I laughed so loud it echoed off the walls of the common room. "Bite it?"

Liam's hands ran up and down my body beneath the surface of the water. "I want my lips to touch every inch of you, Sophia."

Ancestors, the heat between my thighs was so hot that it must've been burning him by now.

"Okay," I said in a shaky breath.

"Okay, what?" he asked.

"Okay, touch me everywhere," I told him. "I want you to."

His eyebrows shot up. "Everywhere?"

I nodded. "Everywhere."

Liam gently guided me through the water until my back was to his. He wrapped his arms around me and slowly brought his teeth down to my shoulder blade. His bite was gentle, sensual. I wanted more.

I leaned my head back into him. "Touch me in other places."

"Like... here?" he asked as he cupped my breasts and squeezed them.

"Yes," I said in a begging tone.

"And here?" he continued as he grabbed my ass.

"Yes," I told him, a little louder this time.

"And... here?" Liam's fingers slipped between my legs.

"Yes!" I cried.

A water current moved past my legs, pressing into the most sensitive part of me over and over again at just the right amount of pressure.

"Oh, God, Liam," I moaned. "That feels so good."

"More?" he asked.

"More," I begged.

The current picked up, stimulating me over and over again. It didn't take long until I felt a glorious pressure building up inside of me, and then it burst in a beautiful display. I moaned loudly.

Water swirled around me, turning me around until I was facing Liam. I wrapped myself around him tightly, my legs circling his hips. He thrust up inside of me while I was still orgasming, making the sensation even more amazing.

Liam used the water current to continue stroking my front as he thrust into me over and over again. I was so overcome with emotion that my Fire began to heat the water again, which I could tell we both enjoyed.

"*Pawee*," Liam moaned as his mouth moved over my neck.

"What?" I asked breathlessly.

"This is amazing," he said. "My two favorite things together. Water and my *pawee*."

"I agree," I told him. "It's amazing."

Liam thrust upward again, then started moaning loudly. All around us, the water pulsed with waves as he reached his peak. The current rushed over me again, and I orgasmed with him.

Liam melted into the water when he'd finished. The two of us joined hands and floated on our backs beside each other, being supported by his magic. The water seemed to shimmer a brighter color. I was suddenly starting to like water a lot more now that I'd seen it in a different light.

"Liam," I said, barely able to catch my breath.

He had his eyes closed and looked like he was on cloud nine. I loved seeing him that way. "What is it, *pawee?*"

"I think everyone was wrong."

"Wrong about what?" he asked.

"Fire and Water," I said, and I smiled. "Turns out, they mix very well."

Liam

TWENTY-ONE

Life was absolutely perfect. Sophia and I were off the hook legally, and even better, we were allowed to be together. In public! We could be in a relationship, and there was nothing that the tribe or the Elders could do about it. We were completely free. A huge weight had lifted off my shoulders— it was nearly like I could feel myself floating. There didn't seem like there was anything to be afraid of anymore. From here on out, things were gonna be good.

On the last day of the year, I woke up earlier than Sophia did. I left her sleeping in my room and headed back to Orenda Academy. I had an appointment with Professor Perot, and I needed to thank him for what he did. His evidence had been crucial in setting Sophia and I free. Without it, I'd bet we wouldn't be alive today.

"Professor?" I slowly opened the door to the alchemy lab. I was shocked to see that everything was gone. Perot's desk was usually littered with papers and vials, but I didn't see a single alchemy instrument or sheet of potion recipes anywhere. It'd been completely cleaned out.

Except there was one letter on his desk, addressed to me and sitting on top of a large file holder.

Dear Liam,

Forgive me for parting like this. I despise goodbyes, although I hope that this is not so much as a goodbye rather than I'll see you again very soon. It grieves me to say Orenda Academy is no longer my home— nor is Kinpago. Baxtor and I have agreed it is best for us to move on. We've decided to go into hiding— I will not tell you where, for your safety as much as our own. This society is no longer welcoming to people like me, as you've experienced yourself.

Young people have an urge to right wrongs in society that us old folks have long given up on. You and Sophia have done no small thing in winning the case against you. I will not bother trying to convince you to run as well— I know both of you will want to stay and fight. I must warn you, however, that things are about to change here, and quickly. I wish I could tell you more, but at the moment, it would only put you in more danger.

I regret having to resign as your doctor, though it is clear you don't need me anymore— your little friend has shown he can provide far better care than I ever could. All your medical records are in the file I've left for you. I daresay it wouldn't be right for me to leave you after all this time without an official diagnosis. I've submitted a briefing to the Center for Magical Maladies, and they've agreed to include your condition in the universal manual of diseases.

Stay close to your friends. Only together will you stand a chance against the dark times that are to come.

Yours fondly,

Jacques

My heart dropped. Perot had left? He wasn't coming back to Orenda? Maybe it was Sophia and I's fault. He was probably receiving death threats for being a key witness.

I opened up the file holder and took out the briefing file. It was over twenty pages long, and filled with a lot of medical jargon I didn't understand.

But there, at the top of the brief, was something incredibly special.

Understanding variables in Combined Magical Suppression Syndrome (CMSS).

By Jacques Perot, M.D.

A name. It was more than anything I could've ever hoped for. Names of conditions in the hands of disabled people were powerful. It proved there was something wrong with you, told people you weren't actually crazy. Now if someone questioned whether or not I was truly sick, I had proof.

Perot hadn't left me with nothing. He'd given me the greatest gift he ever could, save for a cure.

I was bummed that Perot wouldn't be here next semester. I'd looked forward to our appointments. Out of all the teachers here, it was so obvious that he cared about his students. Orenda Academy was going to suffer a huge loss without him.

It was around lunchtime when I returned to the house. Sophia was up, and she was sitting on the porch swing with Esis, sorting seashells into piles the kurble had collected. She had the blanket I'd made her around her shoulders as she stared out to sea.

"Hey," she said. "How'd the appointment with Perot go?"

"He's gone," I said, and I sat beside her.

"What?" Her eyes widened. I handed her the letter. Her face grew confused as she reached the end of the note.

"But..." She bit her lip, and Esis started chucking the seashells he didn't like over the deck. "How could he just up and leave like that? Without a goodbye?"

"Something scared him, Soph. Maybe people have been going after him since the trial ended," I said.

She shrugged. "I don't know. Whatever he was talking about in the letter made it seem like it had nothing to do with the trial. It sounded... bad."

It really did. But after everything Sophia and I had been through, it was hard to imagine things getting worse. We'd already been through so much. I wanted to have hope that things would get better in this society, not worse.

"Even if things change, we'll survive it," I said, and I grabbed her hand. "We've already been through hell and back. What more can they do to us?"

Sophia grimaced. "Perot was right. We would stay and fight. We wouldn't want to accept that this world couldn't change."

"We did change it. It wasn't a lot, but it was a start," I said.

"It's still so hard to believe Perot left. What could've been so worrisome that he didn't want to stay?" Sophia asked.

"I know. It's confusing." I sighed. "But at least he didn't leave without giving my disease a name. Combined Magical Suppression Syndrome. Sounds complex, doesn't it?"

"Liam, that's so great." Her expression grew into a smile. "I know that was something you've been waiting for."

"For sure. It's a small answer in a very long line of questions. And now I have something to throw back at people when they tell me I'm not sick." I grabbed the file holder. "I'm taking this back up to my room. I'll go through it tomorrow. Now's a time to celebrate."

"What does the tribe do for New Year's Eve, anyhow?" Sophia asked. "I was with Imogen in Guatemala last year, so I never got to experience it."

"We have a powwow. It's called the Dance for the Ancestors," I said. "There's a huge party in Kinpago."

"I've never been to a powwow." She held her arms out to Esis, and he leapt into them. "I can't wait to see what it's like."

Sophia rose to her feet, and I slung an arm around her. "I wasn't here last year, either. Too busy doing tribe stuff with Dad. Now I get to spend one of my favorite holidays with my girl."

Esis chittered, and Sophia blushed slightly, giving a really cute smile. It was incredibly hard for me not to take her upstairs and have a quick round of really passionate sex. Now that we had the freedom to truly be together, I was growing more and more enamored with her every day.

She went to take the blanket off her shoulders, but I stopped her. "You should wear it," I said. "You don't have anything else for the powwow, and I think it'll fit nicely."

"What do you do at a powwow, anyway?" Sophia asked, and we left the front porch to walk toward the carriage that had just brought me back from Orenda. The pegasus snorted as we approached, stomping its hooves.

"Lots of things," I said. "There will be storytelling of Hawkei legends, and demonstrations on old tribal arts. Then there will be a ceremonial dinner. Later tonight, after the Grand Entry and honor songs, they'll have the contest dancing."

"Are you competing?" Sophia asked.

I smirked. "Yes. I plan to win."

"Of course you do." She tilted her head. "But shouldn't you be wearing your regalia?"

"Dad's already got my regalia at the ceremony site. Every year, Kinpago builds an authentic Hawkei village in the middle of the city for people to walk through and enjoy. My regalia is in the Toaqua plankhouse. I'll put it on before the nightly ceremonies begin," I explained.

Kinpago was already incredibly crowded when we arrived. People were dressed in a variety of different clothing, including everyday streetwear and authentic Hawkei regalia. I could already hear the music from the drums and flutes in the middle of the city. Esis perked his ears up and looked excited at all the activity, blue eyes shining with enjoyment.

A few people threw ugly sneers our way, or pleasant smiles, but we were mostly ignored. The excitement from the trial had died down, and most of the population had went back to ignoring us. The mystery of the missing Familiars had now taken precedence in the news. The plague had been eliminated, but there was still no answer on who had committed the kidnappings.

The center of the city had been transformed overnight. Long square buildings made of cedar planks, called plankhouses, were gathered in a circular fashion around the square. They had low roofs, and some were a hundred feet long or more. Totem poles with designs of magical creatures had been set up next to the plankhouses. Men and women in traditional Hawkei wear made of fur, shells, and cedar wood performed demonstrations outside in the square. They worked on constructing and painting long canoes, carved and crafted tools made of wood and stone, or crafted cups from horns of dragons. Their Familiars were beside them, their fur and scales painted with different designs and colors.

In the middle of the square, a large area had been cleared out to make way for the dancing tonight. The smell of cooking salmon had spread throughout the area, along with whiffs of fresh roasted corn. Tonight, over four-thousand people would be in the center of the square to take part in the powwow festivities.

I started pointing stuff out to Sophia and explaining as we walked.

"The original Hawkei were mostly fishers. They didn't need to plant agriculture, because seafood was abundant around the coast," I explained. "The cedar trees were especially important. They provided clothing, shelter, and canoes to hunt whales with. Their lives were mostly based around harvesting fish, and creating art from the landscape."

Professor Amber was weaving an intricate rug in the square next to a plankhouse, while her orangutan Familiar worked on a basket. I gave her a wave as we approached the Toaqua longhouse. The totem next to the door had depictions of an orca, a sea serpent, a leviathan, and a kelpie carved into the wood.

Sophia and I entered. Inside the plankhouse were a variety of bunk beds and shelves beneath them to store items. There were a collection of rugs and decorative items scattered throughout. My regalia was inside a trunk on the right side. I'd change into it after dinner.

Dad and Tatum were inside, along with Ezra and Dyami. They were setting things up for later. Dad was already wearing the traditional chief's wear of a long, otterskin robe, and buckskin cloth. Tatum wore a whale-bone necklace around his bulky form.

Ezra just had his normal clothes on and was goofing off with Dyami in the corner. They were having some sort of pushing contest, which Dyami was clearly winning. He just took his big wing and whacked Ezra into the ground each time he got back up. Despite getting his face smashed in, he was grinning. This was the first time I'd seen him have a smile on his face since Cade had died. We all needed this powwow, especially him.

"I'm glad you like eating dirt. It won't be so bad when you come in second," I told him as I approached.

"You'll be the one eating dirt when I kick your ass later," Ezra challenged. Dyami raised a wing to whack him down again, but Ezra waved him off.

"Ezra's competing against me in the men's fancy dancing tonight," I told Sophia. "He has yet to beat me."

"There are twelve other guys competing besides us. It's not always about you," Ezra shot back.

"Boys, get along," Dad called from the other end of the plankhouse. I snickered, and Ezra flipped me off.

Mom poked her head inside the plankhouse. My younger siblings, Katie and Christian, were at her side, while she balanced baby Jackson on her hip. Maddie was off with Drew somewhere. "Sophia, dear, would you mind helping me with something, please?" Mom asked.

"Coming," Sophia responded. She headed back outside.

Sophia had spent Christmas at my house. She was pretty much a part of the family now. It was crazy how well she'd integrated with the rest of us. Mia had never quite fit in, but with Sophia, it was like she'd always been there. Mom basically treated her like her own daughter. Even Dad, as standoffish as he was, had warmed up to her.

"Right," Dad said, and he turned toward me. "Now that your girlfriend's gone, I *please* ask that you and your brother stop using my hunting lodge as a sex cabin. I'm tired of finding condoms in the garbage."

Ezra bent over, howling with laughter. I let out an embarrassed chuckle and said, "Uh, those aren't mine. I don't use condoms."

Dad narrowed his eyes at me and said, "You're lucky you're shooting blanks, son. And you!"

He turned on Ezra. "How many girls do you need to be with in a week? You're going to be *chief*, for ancestors' sake."

"Not for a few more years," Ezra said. "And unlike my big bro, I know to wrap it before I tap it."

He high-fived me. Dad rubbed his eyes, and Tatum let out an unnecessary groan.

"Ancestors help me," he moaned. "Get out of here, you two. Enjoy the powwow."

Ezra and I punched at each other on the way out. Sophia was holding my little brother. She cooed at him and laughed as she tickled

Jackson's nose. Esis sat on the ground and stared up at the baby with a jealous expression.

It was hard seeing Sophia with a baby in her arms. It made my throat get a little tight. It reminded me that was something she could never have, because she was with me.

Sophia handed Jackson back off to my mother before rejoining my side. "Your baby brother is so cute," she said. "I can't get over how adorable he is."

"He is," I said quietly. It bothered me more than I let on that I was sterile. I felt like it was one more thing I'd taken away from Sophia. On top of it, I really wanted kids. I wanted to be a dad someday.

But beggars couldn't be choosers, and Sophia and I had barely escaped being killed for being together. It would be wrong to ask for more. A life with her was more than enough.

Sophia didn't seem to notice my melancholy nature, which was a good thing, because I didn't want to talk about sad stuff on a day we were supposed to be happy. We started wandering around the historical village. Esis hopped up on my head and sat there, as I was the tallest and he could see the most from that vantage point.

Eventually, we met up with Jonah and Imogen. They were watching the hoop dancers that were giving a demonstration in the square. Imogen was wearing a dress that portrayed all of the four tribes. It was made of buckskin and had red, blue, green and purple beads decorated in the designs of flames, water, leaves and wind. She also wore deerskin moccasins. Sassy had on a feathered headband.

It was the first unique outfit I'd seen her wear since Cade died. I was hoping she was starting to recover some of herself. She'd been isolated and quiet ever since the Cup was over. We'd had a hard time getting her to leave her house. I was surprised to see she was out today, even though her smile wasn't as big as I remembered it could be.

Jonah was wearing a t-shirt that commemorated this year's powwow, while Squeaks' feathers were streaked with purple paint. Sophia jumped on Jonah's back, thinking he would support her weight, but she caught him off guard. Jonah fell over, and Squeaks scrambled out of the way to try and save herself, but it was no use. Squeaks knocked into me, I tumbled into Imogen, and we all ended up on the ground.

"Agh! I'm being squished!" Sophia yelled. I could hear her muffled laughs underneath Jonah.

"Oh crap, I'm crushing you, sorry," Jonah hurried to apologize.

"Will someone *please* get Squeaks' ass out of my face!" I shouted.

There was a lot of pushing, and eventually, we all untangled. Poor Imogen had somehow gotten caught at the bottom and had to crawl her way out, gasping for breath.

"Stupid kids," an old man mumbled as he walked by, shaking his head. People moved away from us as we got up off the ground, like they were afraid they'd catch whatever made us weird.

"Where have you guys been?" Sophia said, and she brushed herself off. "We haven't seen you since the day after the trial."

"Recovering from the noxite," Imogen said. Her mouth was in a thin line. "We decided lying low was a good option."

"Yeah. Noxite is shit, man." Jonah shuddered. "I couldn't use my powers for like, a day after they shot me with those darts."

"Remind me never to get shot with those things," Sophia said. "You guys staying for the powwow?"

"All day," Imogen said. "I'm not participating in the competition, though. I usually take part in the jingle dress dancing, but..."

"We decided not to," Jonah finished for her. He eyed Imogen, and I pieced together that he'd opted out because Imogen didn't feel like it, and he didn't want to make her feel alone.

"That's okay. There's plenty to do," I rushed to say. "Let's just walk around."

We left the historical village and started wandering through the different alleyways of Kinpago. In front of the shops, a large variety of outdoor vendors had been set up. Wooden cedar masks painted in all sorts of colors were displayed on tables, along with white sage and other sacred herbs. Smudging wands and prayer feathers made from a variety of feathers and furs from magical creatures were sold beneath large dreamcatchers and woven baskets. There were other things— jewelry made of whale bone, large shells, and rare stones to be found around the area, along with grass braids, beaded bags, flutes, rattles, and drums.

There were even some ceremonial weapons on display. Bows and arrows lay next to knives, tomahawks, war clubs and spears.

Professor Baine was looking at the weapons intently. He gave us a kind, awkward wave as we passed by.

"Can you buy regalia here?" Sophia asked as we wandered through the marketplace.

I shook my head. "Regalia is made, not bought. A Hawkei assembles all the different pieces, and makes it with the help of his or her family. Each one is unique, and very special to the individual wearing it."

"So when Amelia gave me our mom's to borrow for my Naming Ceremony, she'd actually made it with the help of her parents?" she asked.

I nodded. "Correct."

She sighed. "I hope I get to make my own regalia one day. It sounds like fun."

"It is fun. But very time-consuming." Mine had taken years to make.

We spent the rest of the afternoon shopping and watching the exhibitions. When it was time to eat, we walked down the long path that led to the ocean shore, back into the forest. As the four of us reached the beach, we saw that it was filled with hundreds of tables, all laden with traditional food. There was fish, crab, clams, corn, fry bread, turtle soup, roasted cattail, and wild celery. Elementai and their Familiars swarmed around the tables, waiting to eat.

"Before the dancing begins, there's a ceremonial dinner," I told Sophia. "There are rules to how it goes."

"What are the rules?" Sophia asked.

"The men eat first, with their wives, girlfriends, or sisters behind them. Then the girls eat second," I said.

Her eyebrows knitted together. "Isn't that a little sexist?"

I shook my head. "The warriors eat first, and very quickly. Then the women are free to enjoy themselves while the men keep watch for enemies of the tribe. It's how things used to be."

"Oh, I see. That's actually rather sweet." She smiled.

"Yeah, but there's more to it," I teased. "But I think it's best if we leave that as a surprise."

We saw Bren and Vanessa at one of the nearest tables on the beach and immediately gravitated toward them. Lindsey and Miranda were with them, but I didn't recognize any other faces. I hadn't seen Ben and Marcee, or any other interhouse couples, since the trial. I worried about them. I knew a few other couples had gotten arrested, but their fate was still up in the air. I hoped they were okay.

I hadn't seen Jaymin Riske, either, which I was perfectly fine with. That woman was trouble, and I didn't want her anywhere near me, or my friends.

"Hey guys. Care to join us?" Vanessa asked. Aisha growled pleasantly behind her.

"Of course," Sophia said. Jonah, Bren and I sat down first to eat, while the girls stood behind us and chatted. There were canoe races out on the water as the dinner continued. People cheered for their favorite teams as the meal was switched over from the men to the women.

"Ancestors, I love food," Vanessa said. "I literally can't stop eating lately."

"Well, you *are* eating for two," Bren said. He kissed her cheek from where he stood behind her, and his chimera purred.

"What's your due date?" Lindsey asked. She and Miranda were holding hands as they ate and giving each other sultry looks. They were a cute couple, but damn, they sure loved PDA.

"May," Vanessa said. "We're hoping it's a boy."

"But we'll be happy either way," Bren said, and he gave Vanessa the most sickly sweet smile.

Sophia didn't say anything, just kept her eyes down. Lindsey's eyes flickered to us, and she changed the subject. "So, I hear Haley's participating in the women's fancy shawl dance tonight."

"Ick," Miranda said. "Now you've just ruined my dinner."

"I'll be competing against her," Lindsey said. "Wish me luck in kicking her ass."

"That's something we can all toast to," Imogen said. She raised a glass, and the girls clinked theirs against it.

I rubbed Sophia's neck and shoulders while she ate. Esis hadn't been happy about having to wait his turn to eat, and he devoured whole ears of corn in seconds. Sophia let out a soft moan of relief when I massaged a tender spot.

"Hey, no sex at the dinner table!" Jonah shouted. Imogen smirked, but didn't laugh.

"I figure they can have as much sex as they want, whenever they want, seeing as how they just told the Elders to go screw themselves," Lindsey added.

"Hear hear!" Miranda agreed loudly.

"I've always wondered about that," Vanessa said. "Was the sex better before or after the break-up?"

"Well, I was a virgin before we dated for the second time. And there were *conditions* for us getting back together," Sophia said coyly.

"I can imagine," Jonah began. His deep voice took on a higher pitch to mock mine as he said, "I agree to all your demands, Miss Henley. May we fuck now, m'lady?"

The table died laughing. "That wasn't quite how it went," I said.

"It was pretty much how it went!" Sophia shouted. She struggled to catch her breath in between giggles.

I opened my mouth to say more, but the sound of a war cry caught everyone's attention. We turned to look toward the tree-line. A line of male Elementai and their Familiars were charging toward us, faces painted and clothes smudged with leaves and mud from the forest. Ezra and Dyami were among them, hollering as they ran.

"Protect the women!" Jonah shouted, raising a fist to the air. He turned and jumped onto Squeaks' back, hurtling toward the mock battle full-speed.

I wiggled my eyebrows at Sophia and said, "This is the part where you run. Don't let them catch you."

I left her behind and ran after Jonah. Bren followed me. I hit the line of attackers and immediately harnessed water from the ocean. I sprayed several people in the gut and knocked them down while ducking a jet of fire from a Koigni dude and a blast of sand from a Nivita. Everyone started using their magic all at once, while Familiars tackled each other and rolled in the sand to fight.

It was all in good fun. Nobody was really trying to hurt each other. The rules were if you got hit in the chest with somebody's magic, you were considered dead and had to sit out and let the rest unfold— or, if you were a Familiar, got pinned and couldn't move.

Imogen had grabbed Sophia's hand and was pulling her into the woods. The two girls were laughing as they fled into the trees with Vanessa, Lindsey and Miranda, their Familiars behind them.

My heart pounded as the mock battle grew more intense and exciting. I had to duck and roll to avoid getting hit. Jonah was right next to me. He knocked a guy down with an Air blast before Ezra ran by and fired off a water ball. It knocked Jonah in the chest and flattened him to the ground.

"Aw shit, I'm dead," Jonah said from his place on the sand. Squeaks had gotten taken down by a griffin and was doing a spectacular job of playing dead, on her back with four legs up in the air.

"Hey, Liam, I've got your girl!" Ezra called from somewhere in the trees. I turned around and saw that Ezra was carrying Sophia, who couldn't outrun him. Dyami had Esis in his beak, who had crossed his arms and was looking pretty surly at getting caught.

"Not for long!" I shouted back. Ezra ran into the trees with Sophia, and I rushed to catch up with him. I heard Sophia's suppressed giggles and Ezra's quiet swear words as he struggled to carry her through the thick forest brush.

It was all too easy for me to catch up. I summoned a water ball and tossed it at Ezra's head. It made impact, and he tripped. Sophia squealed as she fell forward and tumbled out of his grasp.

When Ezra dropped Sophia, Dyami immediately let go of Esis. He coughed up white furballs and used his wing to wipe off his tongue. Esis, who was wet with bird spit, grumbled before he lowered his head and charged at Dyami's leg with his curled horns. He bounced off and tried again, but it failed to bother the large thunderbird.

I pulled Sophia up off the ground. "You're a terrible runner," I told her.

She snickered. "I'm better at standing my ground, I think."

Ezra's head was soaked. "I think I won. I caught her."

"Yeah, but I caught *you*," I said.

I reached out a hand to get him to his feet. Ezra brushed the dirt off him and said, "I need to clean up before the dancing begins."

"You should hurry," I said. "Grand Entry's about to start."

"Yeah. You'd better head back, too," he told me. Ezra climbed onto Dyami's back, and the two of them took off through a break in the tree-line.

I looked around and said, "Where's Imogen?"

"Over here!" Imogen called. She'd hidden behind a boulder about fifty feet away, and Sassy's head poked over it. "Come on, guys, we need to get Jonah and get going! The ceremony's about to start!"

Sophia and I headed toward her. Esis scrambled up Sophia's leg and tucked himself inside the blanket in the crook of her arm, seeming cross.

"Did you see where everyone else went?" I asked.

"Vanessa got taken by some Koigni guy. I think he's one of Bren's friends," she said, before she giggled. "I'm pretty sure Lindsey and Miranda slipped off to go bang in the woods somewhere."

"Oh, ancestors. Let's hope Ezra doesn't find them. That's like, his daydream." I rolled my eyes.

"So what's Grand Entry?" Sophia asked. "I know it's the start of the opening ceremonies, but what does it mean?"

I put my arm around her and drew her close as I said, "You're about to find out."

sophia
TWENTY-TWO

We returned to the square. It was packed with people and Familiars so tightly that I brushed shoulders with everyone I passed. Since Liam was competing in the dance, he had to leave to prepare for Grand Entry. Imogen, Jonah, and I pushed through the crowd toward the bleachers. They seemed endless, surrounding the wide dance area like their own arena. There was only a narrow strip of walkway between the back of the bleachers and the nearby buildings.

We were lucky enough to grab a seat in the front row. We sat at the edge so Jonah could sit beside Squeaks, since she didn't fit on the bleachers. The air was pleasant for New Year's Eve, though there was still a slight chill. I suspected the Elders were manipulating the temperature for the festivities.

"Your blanket's really nice," Jonah said while we waited. He smiled widely, though I didn't know why.

I stroked my fingers across the intricate design. Esis copied me from where he sat in my lap. "Thanks. Liam made it for me."

"Did he now?" Jonah wiggled his eyebrows.

"It figured I might as well dress up. It kind of works as a shawl, don't you think?" I paused to eye Jonah. "Why are you looking at me like that? Imogen, why's he acting weird?"

Imogen snickered. "Long ago, when a Hawkei man wanted to propose to a woman, he'd weave a blanket and place it around her shoulders. If she accepted, it meant they were engaged."

My jaw dropped in realization. "Oh my God. So Liam like, pre-proposed to me?"

Imogen just smiled and shrugged. My heart fluttered in a mix of nerves and happiness. I couldn't stop the wide grin that spread across my face. Liam Mitoh really wanted to marry me. It felt like all of my dreams were coming true.

Before any of us could say anything further, a voice came over the speakers. "Welcome, Hawkei! We are here to honor the sacrifices our warriors and ancestors have made for us. In honor and respect for our fallen forefathers, we ask you to rise at this time. Who's ready to powwow!?"

The crowd went wild as they rose to their feet. I quickly joined them, cradling Esis close to my chest. As the drums began to beat, the entire square went silent. All eyes turned down the street as a line of Hawkei dressed in regalia danced into the square like a parade. Familiars of all shapes and sizes followed. They chanted as they came in, with the beads on their regalia jingling to the beat of the drums.

One man walked at the front and held a large flag with all four House colors on it. Behind him, four others each carried a flag with their individual House colors and symbols on them.

Next came the dancers. I watched them in awe as they moved together as one.

"This is amazing," I said to Imogen.

She leaned over and whispered to me. "It's a high honor to carry one of the flags. They're honored warriors— or veterans. You see the guy and girl right behind them?"

I nodded as I watched the two people marching between the flag carriers and the dancers.

"Those are the Head Dancers," Imogen explained. "They basically direct the entire powwow."

The parade of honored warriors and dancers entered the empty cobblestone area in front of us. Liam caught my eye and shot me a smile. My heart warmed.

Liam's regalia was impressive, beyond anything I could imagine.

Endless blue feathers covered him from head to toe, with beads and ribbons everywhere. Long feathers were crafted in a careful arrangement behind his neck and at his tailbone, which reminded me of a beautiful bird. Beside him, Ezra wore similar regalia in yellow and black, but something about Liam's drew me in more than the others. They continued to dance around the square until the Head Veterans stopped at the center and the sound of the drums died down.

"They're going to sing the Honors songs next," Imogen explained to me. "The first is the Flag Song. It's like our National Anthem. The second is the Victory Song, which honors our veterans and ancestors."

"Shh!" Jonah hissed at us.

The drums began to beat again. There were at least ten drum players gathered around a huge drum, each beating their drumstick against it in time with each other. Even a koala-looking Familiar was playing alongside them.

First came only the drum beats as the crowd remained silent. Then came the sound of the drummers' voices. They didn't speak words— it was more a combination of "Hey!" and "Ho!"— but it was coordinated in perfect synchrony. It was like I could feel the ancestors with me. Tears beaded my eyes as I listened to the beautiful song. I'd never felt more connected to my tribe than I did in that moment.

When the songs ended, everyone sat. I turned to Imogen and said, "Wow! That was beautiful."

"I know," she replied. "Are you ready to dance?"

"Dance?" I asked in confusion.

"Yeah, intertribals," she clarified. "Everyone gets to dance while the competitors warm up."

The drums began to pound to a different beat, and the dancers in the square spread out.

"At this time, we invite everyone to come down from the stands to participate in the intertribal dance," the announcer said.

The dancers began to move in a circle around the square, bouncing on their toes and lifting one knee after the other. Familiars danced along, too.

"Come on," Jonah encouraged, tugging at my arm.

"Oh, I don't know," I said. "I kind of want to watch first."

"Squeaks and I aren't waiting around," Jonah said chipperly. "We're getting in there."

Jonah and Squeaks rushed into the middle of the square as more and more Hawkei joined the tribe. Jonah spread his arms out to the sides and twirled in circles as he bounced on his toes. Squeaks tried to copy him, but she ended up knocking over an juvenile alicorn and nearly squashing a small feline Familiar. Esis jumped out of my arms. He and Sassy rushed into the crowd behind Squeaks.

"I guess I better get out there," Imogen sighed, though she didn't seem too excited. She stood and followed behind our Familiars.

I couldn't take my eyes off Liam while he danced. He was beaming and looked like he was having the time of his life. I smirked. Liam told me at the Elemental Ball that he couldn't dance— and didn't like to. He was a filthy liar.

His eyes caught mine in the stands, and he started making his way over to me, dancing and smiling the entire time. He gestured for me to join him.

I shook my head and mouthed, *I want to watch.*

He faked a pout and fluttered his eyelashes. I threw my hand over my mouth because I couldn't help but laugh. When pouting didn't work, he pulled out the imaginary-lasso trick and started reeling me in. I mean, how could I resist that?

I stood and copied what everyone else was doing while I made my way over to him. I couldn't stop grinning as we joined the flow of dancers around the square. This moment was so powerful— it was like I could feel our ancestors here among us, celebrating. A deep connection to the Hawkei of the past resonated within me as we continued dancing our way around the square. This powwow seemed bigger than me— for the first time, the entire tribe seemed connected instead of divided.

"Having fun?" he asked as he took my hand.

"Absolutely," I replied with a smile. "Let's get up by Jonah and Imogen."

We increased the speed of our footwork until we caught up with them. Jonah was all over the place, while Imogen more or less walked to the pace of the moving crowd.

"Hey, slowpokes," Jonah joked as he continued to spin in circles. He started to shake his butt to show off, but Imogen smacked him on the shoulder.

"Ancestors, Jonah," she said. "A little respect?"

"Right." He stopped shaking his butt, but he was still going all out by kicking his legs high in the air and spinning as much as he could. Liam and I couldn't stop laughing while we watched him.

Esis stopped dancing beside Sassy and hurried over to Liam. He stretched his arms up high, and Liam bent to scoop him up. Esis pointed upward toward the sky.

"What is it, buddy?" Liam asked while he tickled Esis' belly. We continued dancing the whole time.

Esis threw his arms up above his head again.

"Oh, I see." Liam tossed Esis into the air, and Esis let out a gleeful cheer. Liam tossed him again and again as he spun around to the beat of the drums.

It was in that moment that the pure bliss sank in. Liam and I had won our trial— but more than that, we were happy.

I laughed, looking up at Liam beside me. "This is great."

"Isn't it?" he asked. He set Esis back on the ground, and Esis hurried back toward Sassy to join her again.

I noticed as the song continued that Liam was starting to slow down. He was taking it easy to save his energy for his competition.

Eventually, the drum beats ended, and the crowd returned to their seats. Liam headed off by the edge of the dance area to wait for his turn to compete, while Imogen, Jonah and I sat in the bleachers. The announcer made a short speech to welcome the first group of dancers. He called it the Women's Traditional category.

The women moved slower in this type of dance, but with the same enthusiasm as the intertribal dance. Most of their movements came from bending their knees, since they kept their feet on the ground. There were all types of Familiars dancing with them, but most were earth creatures, like deer and coyotes.

"How are the contests judged?" I asked Imogen. "They all dance so beautifully."

"They're judged on three things," Imogen told me. She began counting off on her fingers. "Their regalia, their dancing ability, and how well they know the song. For Women's Traditional, their feet should never leave the ground. It symbolizes their connection to the earth. That's why most of the women in this category are Nivita."

"Well, I'd hate to be one of the judges," I said. "It'd be so hard to pick."

The song finished, and the next set of contestants came into the square. The announcer called this dance the Women's Jingle Dress category. Imogen stared longingly at the dancers— like she kind of missed being out there.

The jingle dress competition was my favorite so far. The regalia was more extravagant than the other dancers', with layers upon layers of tassel-looking attachments all over their clothing... they somewhat resembled bells. The Familiars didn't wear the jingle regalia, but they moved in synchrony with their Elementai. The women jumped in circles to the beat of the drums and held feather fans that they waved while they danced.

"What's the significance of the fans?" I asked.

"This is traditionally a healing dance— usually performed by Anichi before they died out," Imogen said. "They would use the dance to send out prayers to the ancestors to heal a sick or injured Hawkei. See the metal cones on their dresses?"

I'd thought they were tassels or bells. It was hard to tell from a distance, but now that Imogen pointed out what they were, I could see they were made of metal.

"Each piece of regalia has three-hundred-sixty-five dancing cones to represent every day of the year," Imogen continued. "The Anichi would place prayers into the cones, and the fans were used to release those prayers to the ancestors."

"Wow," I said. "I had no idea these dances were so symbolic."

Jonah nudged me and teased, "It's like this is your first powwow or something."

I rolled my eyes at him playfully.

Following the Jingle Dress dance came the Women's Fancy Shawl category. I spotted Lindsey as the dancers came into the square, then noticed Haley. Haley had a smug look on her face, but I could already tell her step was off from the others.

I quickly had to take back what I said about the Jingle Dress dance being my favorite. The Fancy Shawl dance had more intricate footwork, and the shawls around the young women's shoulders accented their flowing movements. Haley's shawl was red with orange fringes and reminded me a little of Anwara's wings. Despite how much I hated Haley, I had to admit her regalia was beautiful. Lindsey's shawl was stitched with green and black diamonds, the color of Medusa's scales.

Haley looked kind of bored as she danced beside Anwara, until she spotted Lindsey and Medusa stealing the show with beautiful twists and turns. Haley quickly stepped up her game, but her movements didn't look as natural as Lindsey's. Lindsey didn't even notice Haley's eyes on her. She simply beamed and let the music take over her body.

"Is there significance to the shawls?" I asked.

"They're worn by young women to symbolize butterflies," Imogen answered.

When that dance ended, they switched over to the men's dances. The Men's Traditional was a lot like the women's, but the men wore more feathers and moved in sharp and deliberate ways.

The Men's Grass dance differed in regalia and symbolism. These outfits were more colorful, with long fringes. Imogen told me the dance was traditionally used to clear grassy areas for ceremonial purposes, and to represent the hunting that the ancient Hawkei partook in to provide for their families.

Finally came the Men's Fancy Dance, which was the last category and the one Liam would be competing in. Liam came into the square dancing alongside the others with the most amazing smile on his face. His eyes quickly found me in the crowd, and his smile grew wider. I clapped and cheered for him.

It was clear from the onset that the Men's Fancy was meant to entertain an audience. Their regalia was the most elaborate, and they moved quicker than the other dancers. The men jumped high to show off and spun whips around in their hands to add to the dazzling display.

I cupped my hands over my mouth and shouted, "Go Liam!"

He must've heard me, because he lit up. He started spinning faster and jumping higher. I knew he must've been pushing himself to his physical limit, but he didn't seem to care, since he was having so much fun.

Ezra noticed Liam stepping it up and started spinning his whips around faster to show off. Dyami quickened his step to keep up with

Ezra. The two brothers faced each other and mirrored each other's moves as they tried to show the other up. They were both beaming. It was all in good fun.

When the song ended, the dancers from every category were ushered back to the square so the winners could be announced. Liam looked wiped out. He leaned on Ezra while they laughed together.

"I'm glad Liam's having so much fun," Jonah said.

"Yeah," I agreed. "I haven't seen him this happy in... ever."

The three of us chuckled because of how ironically true it was.

The announcer stood at the front of the square with a microphone to announce the judges' decisions. I didn't know the first two winners of the women's categories, but I clapped anyway when they were announced.

I held my breath as the third category came up, then screamed in excitement when they announced Lindsey as the winner. She headed toward the announcer to gather her prize, while Haley huffed and stomped out of the square before they finished announcing the winners.

"*Someone* forgot to put on their big girl panties today," Jonah joked.

I chuckled. "You think she's wearing any?"

Jonah pretended to think about it. "Dunno. Wouldn't surprise me if she wasn't."

The announcements continued, until they reached the last category — Men's Fancy.

"Liam will win," I said with certainty.

"Ezra was pretty good, too," Imogen pointed out. "I think it's a toss up."

"And the winner of the Men's Fancy is..." The announcer paused to drag out the suspense. "Dunkan Rogers!"

"What?" I said lightheartedly. "Who's this Dunkan guy?"

"Apparently him," Jonah chuckled as one of the older men stepped forward to claim his prize.

Liam and Ezra both turned to each other and shared a friendly handshake. Ezra quickly turned it into a hug, which looked like it caught Liam off guard.

By the time the winners were announced, it was around ten o'clock. People began to climb down from the stands and dispersed.

"What happens now?" I asked my friends.

Jonah draped an arm around me. "We stay. We drink. We dance."

Imogen rolled her eyes at him. "The scheduled celebrations are over, but everyone will stay in the square until midnight. Now we just mingle and party."

Liam came up to the front row of the bleachers where we sat and reached out for my hands. Before I could grab them, Esis jumped into his arms.

I dropped my jaw playfully. "What a cock block, Esis."

Liam scratched his ears, and Esis purred. "What'd you think?" Liam asked as I stood beside him.

"I loved it," I said.

"I'm glad." He leaned over to peck me on the lips. "I'm going to change back into my street clothes, then we can hang out the rest of the night."

"We'll wait here for you," I said.

Liam handed Esis back to me, then headed back to the plankhouse to change.

"Let's get some drinks," Jonah begged.

"We will," Imogen promised, stoking Sassy's fur from where she was snuggling in her arms. "Wait for Liam."

"I'm no good at *waiting* when it comes to drinks," Jonah teased. Squeaks swished her tail in agreement.

Liam returned shortly after wearing his usual jeans and a light jacket. "Okay, should we start with—?"

Liam was cut off by the sound of battle cries coming from just outside the square. People screamed and jumped out of the way as heavy footsteps pounded across the cobblestone. I thought at first that this was some sort of mock battle display like earlier, until I saw the fallen expression on my friends' faces. The sheer terror in their eyes sent my stomach plummeting to my toes.

The source of the commotion finally came into view as the crowd jumped out of the way. Two men rode the biggest manticores I'd ever seen— creatures with a lion's head, bat-like wings, and scorpion tails. Their creatures were at least a thousand pounds each. They tore through the middle of the square like they were on a mission to the ancestors. The men dragged two women behind them with ropes secured to their wrists. The women's clothes were torn, and their faces were so bloody I could barely make out their features. Their Familiars were nowhere in sight.

The manticores slowed as the men reached the center of the square, screaming like warriors going into battle. The crowd went silent, too stunned to do anything but gasp. My friends and I inched closer to each other in fear.

Liwanu was the first to step forward. He was still dressed in his regalia and feathered headdress. "What is the meaning of this, Jonathan?" His voice boomed over the square.

"We caught them!" Jonathan shouted, holding the rope in his hand above his head like a victory flag. "These two were caught smuggling magical creatures out of town. They were behind the disappearances and plague all along!"

"Execution by element!" someone shouted.

The crowd responded with a mix of agreement and protests. I wasn't sure whether to be terrified or relieved that the criminals had been caught.

Liwanu held his hand up to quiet the crowd, but it barely helped. "If this is true, they deserve a trial!"

"If it's true, let them burn!" Elder Malison stepped forward and snarled. I hadn't even seen him come out of the crowd.

I grabbed on to Liam tightly, my knees quivering.

"Names!" a few people started chanting. "Give us names! Who's involved?"

Jonathan looked down to the women with pure and unadulterated loathing. Past the blood on their faces, I could see the pleading look in the women's eyes... eyes that I knew.

I inhaled a sharp breath. It hit me who they were a second before Jonathan spoke. I knew them from my Medical Care of Familiars and Unicornology classes.

Jonathan sneered their names like they were poison on his tongue. "Those who kidnapped the missing Familiars are none other than Professor Cynthia Costas, and Professor Brenda Fawn."

Liam

TWENTY-THREE

The square erupted. People tried pushing inward to get to the two professors. The Task Force had arrived on scene and created a square barrier around the two manticores and their Elementai. The professors stood in the middle of the square with their heads hung low, blood dripping down their faces. They'd been dragged to their feet.

My mind could barely process the information. *They* were responsible for the plague and the kidnappings? How could this be possible? I knew them. Costas and Fawn were good people. They were my *teachers*. I held Sophia even tighter to my side as the accusations grew.

The crowd parted as Elder Oleander emerged. He stood behind Malison and sneered at the professors with disdain. "Are these accusations true? Did you bring the plague upon the tribe, as well as kidnap and restrain various magical creatures?"

Professor Costas raised her head in defiance. "We will not deny it. We were responsible."

Angry shouts and slurs grew. The rage grew so loud I thought my ears might break. My body grew cold in denial.

"We have a confession! Execution! Execution by element!" someone in the crowd shouted. The mob around us vocalized their support for blood.

Elder Malison raised his hands, and the noise died down. "The tribe deserves to know *why*," he said, glaring at Professor Fawn. "We demand an explanation for these hideous acts."

Fawn's voice was trembling, but she spoke clearly. "We never meant for the plague to spread so far. The Miriamic Coven promised us that the curse that caused the plague could be easily contained. The sickness was only to target the Familiars of the Elders— so they would die, and new leaders could assume their place. We never intended it to wreak havoc upon the public."

Gasps spread around the square, and Malison's eyes widened. "How *dare* you question our power!"

Oleander held up a hand to silence Malison. "And the missing Familiars?"

"We initially took only unbonded magical creatures, to destabilize the region and cause distrust of the leadership within the tribe," Professor Costas spoke. Her tone was resolved and firm— like she'd already accepted her fate and was only using her last moments to defy the Elders. "As the plague spread, we intended to save as many bonded Familiars as we could, so we stole Familiars that we knew had contact with the diseased creatures. It was an elaborate plan that got out of hand."

"So you are confessing that all of this was a organized plot to bring down the Elders?" Oleander said.

Costas nodded. "Yes. We believed that if we disrupted the power system in the tribe, that a new government would take over. One that wouldn't be so cruel and unjust. Our plan wasn't to harm innocent people. It was to overthrow the Elders, and nothing more."

Oleander spread his arms out wide and turned to the crowd. "Is there anything more to investigate? It is clear that we have found the true perpetrators of this crime!"

"They deserve a trial!" a rebellious voice spoke out, but few voices rang out to agree with her. People were angry— very angry. Their faces contorted with hatred as they stared at the professors who'd caused so much pain and suffering.

"The trial has already been held," Oleander snarled. He faced Costas and Fawn. "We the Elders find you both guilty of high treason to the tribe. The sentence shall be public execution by element— carried out at once."

How could he do that? All the Elders weren't even here. I didn't know where they were. Oleander couldn't declare an official sentence without the approval of the other voters.

But the crowd didn't seem to care. They shook their fists and cheered in approval of Oleander's ruling. I looked desperately over the crowd. Where the fuck was Dad? He needed to stop this madness. I didn't see him standing with the other Elders. He'd been there only seconds before, then he disappeared.

Costas was Toaqua, and Fawn was Nivita. They'd be executed by their opposite element— Costas by Fire, and Fawn by Air.

"Bring in their Familiars!" Oleander shouted.

The mob roared, and our attention was diverted to a hydra and a unicorn being pulled on-scene.

Professor's Costa's hydra, Hera, was dragged out from behind a building by several large Familiars. A dragon, a wyvern, and a lizard that had to weigh a ton with razor-like spines on its back held ropes in their mouths that bound Hera's nine heads. Even though Hera was large and frightening, she seemed terrified. She pulled on the ropes and tried to get to Professor Costas. The Familiars holding the ropes bound her in place and prevented her from moving, except to drag her further into the square. She spat venom out of the poisonous spines on her back and used her tail to whip several Familiars behind her aside, but more just jumped forward to pin her down. Though she lashed out with her big claws, eventually, the weight of so many Familiars on her back caused her to collapse onto the ground.

Professor Fawn's Familiar, Sariah, looked worse for the wear. The unicorn's golden horn had been broken off, and long gashes along her sides poured blood onto her velvet fur. The whites of her eyes showed as they rolled backwards in her head. She struggled weakly at the ropes that were held by wolves and screamed for Professor Fawn. It was a haunting sound I feared I'd remember for the rest of my life.

Sophia let go of me and moved forward to do something, but I reached out and grabbed her shoulders to hold her back. "Soph, don't," I begged. There were four of us and hundreds of them. This was impossible.

"We have to stop this! If we just stand here and let it happen, we're just as responsible," Sophia protested. Esis squeaked in agreement from within her arms.

"Sophia, if you interfere, they'll kill you too," Imogen said worryingly. The four of us stared at the scene about to take place, feeling completely helpless.

Dad appeared suddenly in front of me, his face shadowed and dark. "Find your siblings, take your friends, and get out of here," Dad said to me. His tone was harsh and commanding.

"What do you mean? You can stop this, right Dad?" I asked weakly.

"Do as I say!" Dad fisted his hand in my shirt before pushing me, roughly. I staggered to the ground, and Jonah went to pull me up. My mouth hung open for a moment as I watched Dad stride away.

That got my attention. I immediately understood what was about to happen, and knew we had to get out of here before it did. I turned toward the group and said, "We gotta go. Now."

I grabbed Sophia's hand and started dragging her through the crowd. Imogen and Jonah closely followed, along with their Familiars. I searched the mob for Ezra and Maddie, but I didn't see them. There were just too many faces.

"Any last words?" Oleander called. The four of us skidded to a halt. I knew I needed to move, needed to get my friends out of here, but it felt like I was frozen, feet glued to the ground. I couldn't pull my eyes away from the scene. Neither could anyone else.

"It's okay, Sariah," Professor Fawn said gently. Tears ran down her quivering face as she desperately tried to comfort her Familiar. The unicorn snorted, blood drying on her inflamed nostrils.

Professor Costas' voice was cold as she spoke without mercy. "The ancestors will judge you for your cruelty, Elders. I know I will join my family in the afterlife. Can you say the same?"

Oleander narrowed his eyes and said, "I will hear no more of this slanderous talk from traitors. Let the execution commence!"

After he said those words, everything happened exceptionally quickly. Jonathan, the man who'd brought the professors in, stepped forward and whipped out his hand, creating a gust of wind that looked like a blade. His Air magic sliced against Sariah's neck, and the unicorn instantly fell, her arteries sliced.

"Sariah!" Professor Fawn screamed, her terrible yell cutting through the night. Sariah was down, her hooves desperately scraping the ground as she bled out. Jonathan then turned on Fawn and raised his hand. His fingers curled inward, and Fawn clutched at her throat. She gasped, her face turning blue as the oxygen was slowly drained from her body.

Nobody did anything. They just stood there and watched, some with horror and others with glee, as Professor Fawn struggled to breathe. Beside her, Sariah's legs twitched and went still.

Watching this was agonizing. Suffocation could take up to seven minutes. She'd suffer. Fawn's eyes pleaded for someone to have mercy and to help her. Jonathan smiled as he did it, as if it was pleasurable for him to take her life. He was dragging it out for as long as he could.

I didn't even think about it twice. I knew I had to do something. It was more of an instinct than anything else. I closed my eyes tightly and focused my magic on Professor Fawn. She was less than a hundred feet away, so she was still in my range of magic. The water in her blood was pumping furiously as it tried to keep her alive without oxygen.

It was just like killing a deer. I could feel her life be extinguished easily as I rushed the blood supply to her heart and it exploded inside her chest. I opened my eyes and watched as Fawn collapsed on top of her dead Familiar, one hand still clutched around her neck.

It was hard for me to comprehend that I'd taken Professor Fawn's life until I'd done it. My body went rigid with shock. I'd never killed a person before. Animals were different. I couldn't even understand what I had done, because I didn't believe it.

While I was still processing, the execution moved on. Oleander brought his hand down in an order, and Hera screamed in pain as the Familiars holding her tightened the ropes around her necks. Hera was slowly pulled apart by the various Familiars holding her ropes. They all went in different directions. I grabbed Sophia and pulled her face to my chest so she wouldn't see it, but she still could hear it. The sound Hera's body made as it was ripped apart was horrible. Blood went spilling in all different directions as her nine heads were torn from her torso. I could feel Esis' little claws scratching my stomach between Sophia and I as he scrambled to get free.

"*You bastards!*" Costas screamed in rage. She ran forward, her Water magic gathering in her bound fists.

Chieftess Annette, who'd been lurking behind Malison, strode forward. She threw out both of her hands, creating a Fire tunnel twelve feet tall that immediately engulfed Professor Costas.

Costas screamed in terrible pain as the Fire tunnel consumed her, flesh melting off her body. Her skin peeled away as the flames licked up her form. She staggered as her body turned immediately from human to charred ashes. Her charred husk fell to the ground in the fetal position, where her muscles contracted as the last of the flames died down from her form. I could smell her burning corpse from here as smoke rose over the square.

After Costas fell, Jonathan moved forward. He sliced with his Air magic, then held up Professor Costas' dismembered head for all to see.

The professors and their Familiars were dead before I could even comprehend it. The moment all four of them were gone forever, a cheer was raised, among violent shouts of protest.

Behind me, Jonah was throwing up. Imogen was crying. Sophia still had her face pressed into my shirt and was refusing to come out.

I was glad she hadn't witnessed.

"Justice has been served!" Oleander announced. There was scattered applause and cheering, though a lot of people, like me, stood in shocked silence. Nobody expected it to get that... brutal.

"No!" I heard the voice of Jaymin Riske escalate above the crowd. She was on top of a statue and shouting loud for all to hear. "The professors were right! The Elders have too much power, and they've just shown it today! Death! Death to the Elders!"

Jaymin had brought her army. The protestors among her raised shouts of approval at her words.

"Quiet down, or you'll be next!" Malison threatened. Worried murmurs scattered over the mob.

"That wasn't an execution! It was a slaughter!" Jaymin rebutted.

"I order you to stand down!" Oleander said. He moved forward with Task Force members behind him, approaching Jaymin at a high speed. The bodies of the dead lay in the square, and Oleander and the police stepped over them as if they didn't matter at all.

Jaymin didn't listen. "People of Kinpago, look at what happened! These good professors sought to make a change, and the Elders silenced their voices forever! The Elders no longer work for the good of the people!" Jaymin raged. "Are we going to sit back and do *nothing* about it?"

There was a divided yell of agreement and opposition. The Task Force members reached for Jaymin. They tried to pull her off the statue, but Jaymin's protesters fought back.

That's when everything dissolved into absolute chaos. The Task Force members raised their guns and began shooting noxite into the crowd. Jaymin's protestors or not, it didn't matter. A whole line of people was knocked down by noxite darts. Oleander lashed out at Jaymin with his Water, but Jaymin uprooted the ground out from under him using Nivita magic and caused him to fall over.

The mob divided into two sides— those who opposed the Elders, and those who thought that justice had been served. Elements started flying everywhere as screams lit up the night. A stampede erupted in the middle of the square as Hawkei started using their magic to hit anyone and anything. Things had gotten out of hand so quickly. The powwow had gone from a night of celebration to a desperate fight for survival.

"Guys, come on!" I screamed. I started pushing my way through the panic. All of our Familiars immediately went into protective mode. Squeaks shoved her way to the front and cleared a path for us. She bit into an Elementai's shoulder that stood in our way and tossed him several feet. Squeaks pushed back against people with her wings and trampled over people with her hooves that had fallen before us. She kicked a griffin in the face that had gone after Jonah and hissed before leaping onto him, ending his life with a quick blow to his neck.

At her side, Sassy had transformed into a kitsune. She used the vines on her back in a whip-like fashion to push and slap people out of our way. Sassy opened her mouth, and a beam of sunlight erupted from it. It blinded several people and Familiars, causing them to stumble back-wards. It cleared enough of a pathway that we were able to get out of the immediate area.

Once we left the square, the temperature immediately got colder. But the riot had spread to include the entire city. It wasn't just the Elementai that were losing it. Familiars fought each other as they tried to protect their Elementai from the chaos. Large Familiars, such as chimeras and elephants, squashed people underneath their giant feet while trying to escape. Dragons flew overhead and started lighting up houses. I caught sight of Jaymin's vigilantes and their Familiars destroying public property, toppling over statues and smashing buildings.

One Nivita, who I knew was on Jaymin's side, used his Earth magic to crumble a large office building to the ground. The four story building came falling toward us at a high-speed, looming overhead as it threatened to collapse on us. Jonah hurried backward the way he'd came with Squeaks, while Imogen, who was ahead of us with Sassy, darted ahead.

"Sophia, move!" I shouted. I pushed her out of the way, and ended up tripping. Sophia darted ahead to the right side and escaped the falling tower, but I didn't have enough time to get up and out of the way. The shadow of the tower loomed over me as the building approached. I was going to be buried alive.

I felt Air magic yanking me backward, and I skidded along the ground as if being dragged. I just got out of range of the falling building before it smashed into the pavement. Dust and debris kicked up and got into my eyes and mouth. I sputtered, trying to catch my breath as I staggered to my feet.

The building that had fallen over had killed dozens of people. Those barely alive moaned underneath the building, while limbs and unmoving bodies stuck out from under the crushed rubble. In the distance, I watched as several more buildings started crumbling down. Jaymin's people were demolishing the entire city.

My eyes hurriedly scanned the ruins. Where the fuck was my girlfriend!? "Sophia? *Sophia!*"

"Liam!" I heard Sophia scream. I caught sight of her over the ruins, mingling within the mob and holding on to Esis. Her head bobbed within the various faces of the crowd before it went under.

Complete panic overtook my body. I hurried to climb over the ruins and follow, but a lion knocked into me and sent me flying. I landed hard against the ground again. Several people stepped on me, and I screamed out in pain, though I don't think anyone heard me. A Familiar kicked my head, and my eyesight went hazy.

I was nearly trampled before I felt a brawny hand on my arm. Jonah yanked me to my feet before I could get crushed. A couple of people tried to push past us, but Jonah punched a particularly big guy across the face and sent him hurling backward. The crowd gave us space after that. I tried to stop the world from spinning as I wavered on my feet.

"I lost Imogen." Jonah's voice was totally freaked out. He turned in place, but even with as tall as he was, he couldn't spot her in the madness.

"We need to find the girls," I said breathlessly. My head was spinning. I couldn't keep up, but my body couldn't give out on me now. If it did, I'd die out here.

"Right," Jonah said darkly. Air magic filled his palms. "Let's fuck some shit up."

sophia
TWENTY-FOUR

"Liam!" I shouted. My heart slammed wildly against my rib cage as the crowd dragged me away from my friends. Esis clung tightly to my shirt. He let out cries of terror that sent my stomach plummeting. Someone's shoulder knocked into mine as they raced away from the rubble. I went tumbling backward.

I caught myself on the cobblestone, but a second later, someone's foot sank into my gut as they trampled over me. I held Esis and quickly got to my feet before anyone could squash him. I looked to where Liam had just been standing on the other side of the rubble, but he was gone.

Fuck!

I spun in circles, trying to find my friends. "Liam! Imogen! Jonah!"

Vanessa, Lindsey, Miranda, Ezra...

There were so many people here I cared about, and I didn't see a single one of them. Thank the ancestors my grandparents hadn't come to the powwow.

I aimed my palm toward the sky. Fuck it if anyone saw me conjure lightning. I had to signal to Liam where I was. But the lightning never came. My stomach dropped as I remembered I no longer had the Spirit Totem— the tool that had helped amplify my powers.

I couldn't conjure lightning without it. I was totally screwed.

The chaos around me didn't die down. If anything, it got worse. Rocks and rubble were flying through the crowd from Nivita magic. The main fountain was empty, since Toaqua were using the water to protect themselves. Whirlwinds swirled all around the square from Yapluma freaking out.

And then there were the fires. Buildings went up in flames, lighting the entire square against the dark of night. Screams filled the air from every direction. Above me, Familiars of all different sizes flew through the sky, some racing away from the riots, and others joining in. I couldn't find my bearings.

"Think, Sophia!" I chastised myself.

Instinct told me to run, to get out of here where Esis and I would be safe, but I couldn't go without my friends. I had to find them, and I wasn't going to find them standing here. My eyes turned upward toward the four-story buildings lining the square. I needed to get a good vantage point.

I started racing toward the nearest building. As I got closer, I saw that the entrance was crowded with people trying to push their way through the door to find shelter. A Yapluma shouted at the crowd to move faster. When he got impatient, he thrust his Air magic at the shop windows. They shattered, and nearby Hawkei screamed. One woman clutched her face. When she brought her hands away, tiny shards of glass were embedded all along her skin. Her face dripped with blood.

The Yapluma guy didn't even notice. He shoved her out of the way and jumped through the window to get inside. Several others followed, trampling her down. I pushed through the crowd to get to her, but before I could, a griffin had come to her rescue. She jumped on his back, and they took to the skies.

I turned back to the building entrance, but several fights had broken out in front of it. Blood splayed the cobblestone streets everywhere I looked. I thought I might be sick. I wasn't getting inside that building— and all the others looked just as bad. I needed another way to find my friends.

My eyes caught the narrow alleyway, and I started toward it. I had to elbow people out of the way if I didn't want to be trampled. It felt like I could finally breathe when I made it through the crowd and into the empty alley. I took a moment to catch my breath and tied the ends of my blanket tightly around my waist so I wouldn't lose it. I sprinted over to the fire escape on the side of the building, jumped on top of the nearby dumpster, and leapt toward the ladder to pull it down. Esis clung to me the whole time, leaving my arms free to climb.

My heart raced, and my breaths were heavy when I made it to the roof. By the time I looked over the edge, the chaos in the square was even worse. A dragon flew overhead and rained fire down upon a corner of the square. I could hear the pained screams of Elementai as the fire consumed their bodies. I couldn't bear to look.

I forced my gaze away and continued to scan the square frantically. It was almost impossible to make out any of the faces. I caught sight of someone familiar and had to do a double take. My heart skipped a beat. Across the square, Maddie and Drew— the Koigni I'd introduced her to months ago— were running hand-in-hand away from the dragon's fire. They ducked under a vendor booth to hide.

Stay put. I'm coming for you.

I continued to scan the square, my hands fisting at my sides. I didn't have time to stand here much longer! I had to find my friends— and I had to find them now!

Before I could get another thought in, the building began to shake beneath my feet. I spread my arms out to steady myself on instinct, but the shaking continued. Esis climbed up my shirt and crouched on my shoulder, tangling his paws in my hair to hold on. He whimpered quietly in my ear. Below us, hordes of people screamed and flooded out of the building they'd been hiding in. A Nivita below raised his hands, destroying the foundation.

"Fuck," I mumbled under my breath.

This building was going down, and I didn't have time to climb back down the fire escape. I glanced to the buildings on either side of me and quickly calculated the jump. It was too far.

My eyes caught sight of an incoming creature— one of the manticores, I quickly realized. It was going to fly straight past us. The building creaked and groaned beneath my feet, and I knew this was my one and only shot.

I backed up a few steps, took a deep breath, and said, "Hang on, Esis!"

Then I sprinted toward the edge of the building.

The brick gave way just as my feet left the edge. I soared through the sky with Esis hanging tightly to my shoulder... and landed on the manticore's back.

The manticore roared as it felt my weight land on top of it, and I breathed a sigh of relief. I quickly looked behind me to see the building crumbling to the ground. People screamed and ran out of the way, but others were crushed beneath the rubble.

"We did it!" I cried.

My relief only lasted a split second. This manticore was *so* not having it with me. It twisted its lion head back as we flew through the sky and snapped its terrifying jaws at my hands. I jerked away from where I was holding on to its fur until it couldn't reach me. It was so distracted that we nearly slammed into another building. Esis and I both screamed, and the manticore quickly corrected its flight.

Once we were steady in the air again, it lifted its barbed scorpion tail and aimed it at me. I grabbed tightly to its fur and dodged out of the way of the attack. I was hanging over its side now, my pulse pounding in my ears.

Fuck, fuck, fuck! I was barely hanging on and was going to fall!

I readjusted my hand on the manticore's back and pulled myself up with all my strength. It aimed its tail at me again. This time, I ducked my shoulder and wrapped my arm around its incoming tail, holding it in place. It roared in pain.

"Land," I commanded.

The manticore huffed in protest.

"Now!" I shouted, tugging harder on its tail.

The manticore swooped down out of the sky. It crashed so hard and fast on the cobblestone that Esis and I went flying over its head. I threw my arms out to catch myself. Esis rolled across the ground and came to a stop several yards away from me. He lifted his head and shook it, looking disoriented.

I barely had a second to glance at Esis before the manticore let out a loud, terrifying roar. A second manticore dropped out of the sky beside the first. They both bared their razor-sharp teeth at me and began to advance, like I was prey.

"Stay back!" I warned, but they continued toward me. I shot a blast of Fire out of my hands, but all they did was shake their heads, like it tickled them. Low growls bubbled up out of each of their throats.

Esis got to his feet and scurried in front of me. He lowered his head and aimed his horns at the manticores.

"Esis, no!" I scrambled forward and scooped Esis up, then took off running. I jumped over rubble and broken statues, my heart hammering.

The manticores pursued me. I could hear their roars from only feet away. When I glanced back, I saw that one of them was about to pounce. I threw myself to the ground at the last second, keeping Esis close to me so I wouldn't crush him. The manticore soared over me. It skidded into the base of a broken statue, its claws scraping along the cobblestone as it went. Its nose smashed into the stone, and it let out a whimper. Blood spurted from its face and dripped at its feet.

Behind me, the second manticore let out a primal growl. I rolled over just in time to see its sharp scorpion tail headed straight toward me. I kept rolling as quick as I could. Its tail pierced the ground right where I'd just been lying a split-second ago.

The manticore shot me a hooded look, then ripped its tail out of the ground. Dirt and stone went flying everywhere.

I jumped to my feet, and Esis hopped onto my shoulder again. I barely took a breath before the manticore with the broken nose lunged at me once more. I leapt out of the way, and it quickly whirled around to snap its jaws. Meanwhile, the second manticore had swiped its claws out on the other side. I ducked.

The two collided. One bit the other, while the second left deep claw marks in the first's neck. It barely slowed them down. Really, it only pissed them off. Shit. I couldn't outrun them, and they were too big to fight on my own.

They struck before I could come up with a plan. One aimed its tail at me, while the other snapped its jaws. I saw the solution in a split-second and took the opportunity before I could second guess myself. I ducked out of the way of the jaws, then spun and grabbed ahold of the other's tail. I yanked it forward and dragged it downward. The barb sank into the other manticore's neck. It reeled back on its hind legs and let out a pained roar as the venom entered its bloodstream.

Before the first manticore could yank its tail away, I brought Fire to my palms and let it burn as hot as I could manage. The manticore jumped away from me as its tail lit up in flames. The fire spread up its tail and to its body, quickly spreading to its wings. The manticore reeled on the ground in pain, while the other collapsed, dead.

I stepped back, breathing heavily and shaking at the knees. My flames consumed the manticore. It gave one last twitch, and then it went still.

Esis tugged on my hair and pointed. My eyes caught sight of a familiar couple. Ben and Marcee were running away from one of the fires. I took off sprinting toward them. They stopped when I crossed in front of their path.

"Ancestors!" I cried. "Are you two okay?" This was the first time I'd seen them all night.

Marcee was clutching her winged teacup pig in her arms, and tears were streaming down her cheeks.

"Sophia!" Ben said breathlessly. "You have to get out of here!"

"I know," I replied in a rush. "But I have to find my friends. Have you seen them?"

Marcee wiped at her nose. "No, we just got here."

"Just got here?" I asked. "Why'd you come?"

"We were trying to warn everyone," Ben explained quickly. "We knew Jaymin might start a riot tonight. She took Marcee's Familiar and threatened to hurt her if we told. We had to go find Daisy before we told anyone— to protect her."

"But when we got here..." Marcee trailed off and glanced around to the destroyed square.

I could hardly believe it. "Jaymin's taking this shit too far."

Marcee stroked Daisy's head and nodded in agreement.

"We'll help you find everyone," Ben promised. "Did you see where they went?"

"I don't know." I shook my head. "Last I saw, Imogen went that way, and Jonah and Liam—"

I was cut off when an arrow whizzed through the crowd and sliced straight into Marcee's stomach. Her eyes went wide in shock, and a chilling silence fell over the three of us.

"Ancestors!" Ben caught Marcee as she fell to the ground, letting out an agonized cry.

I quickly knelt beside them and frantically glanced around the crowded square. "What the fuck!?"

And then I saw it. A group of rioters had grabbed bows from a vendor stall and were firing the sharp-tipped arrows into the crowd.

"Shit." I turned back to Ben. "We have to get out of the square."

I couldn't find my friends anywhere. I hoped that meant they'd made it out. Either way, Ben, Marcee, and I had to get out of here if we wanted to survive.

"Agreed." Ben reached down for the arrow, but I stopped him.

"Wait," I said. "Pulling it out could increase the bleeding."

"Right, right." Ben sniffled as he stared down at the woman he loved. He was starting to panic.

I grabbed his wrist, forcing him to look at me. "Listen, Ben. Marcee's going to be okay. But we have to get her out of here."

This kind of wound would take time for Esis to heal. If we stayed any longer, another one of us could get shot. He could work his magic as soon as we were somewhere safe.

Ben nodded and wiped the tears away. "Okay."

He scooped Marcee up in his arms. She gasped in pain, but didn't protest.

"I've got her," he said. "Let's go."

Esis jumped off my shoulder and onto Marcee's stomach.

"Esis, no," Ben insisted.

"It's fine," I said quickly. "He can help."

Ben didn't question it. He carried Marcee and the two Familiars toward the edge of the square. We dodged arrows as we made a run for safety.

"I saw Maddie and Drew over there earlier," I said, pointing.

"Go get them," Ben instructed. "We'll meet you at the edge of the square."

"I'll be right there," I assured him as I took off toward the vendor table I'd seen Maddie and Drew hide under. I left Esis with them so he could heal Marcee.

But I didn't make it halfway there before I heard the sound of a dragon roaring above us. I whirled around to see a huge red dragon swooping down, aiming its talons straight at Ben.

"Ben!" I shouted.

He saw the dragon, but there was nothing he could do. The dragon curled its massive talons around Ben and Marcee. Esis squealed and jumped out between the talons and onto the cobblestone. His blue eyes went wide in terror as he watched Ben, Marcee, and Daisy being dragged away into the sky.

"No!" I screamed, my voice wavering.

Blood rained down into the square, and Ben and Marcee's screams echoed above me. Without warning, the dragon unclenched its talons, and the couple tumbled through the air, screaming as they clutched tightly to one another.

Nobody but Esis and I seemed to notice. Had a Yapluma seen, they might've been able to stop what came next.

I heard their bones crunch the same time their screams came to an abrupt halt. I let out a horrified shriek and slapped my hands over my mouth. Ben and Marcee were only yards in front of me, but I was completely frozen. I couldn't move as I took in their twisted limbs and lifeless stares. Blood splattered the ground everywhere, and a jagged broken bone stuck out of a raw, bloody wound in Ben's leg. Large gashes sliced across Marcee's side from where the dragon's talons ripped into her. Bits of insides that never should've seen the light of day leaked out of her. Even Marcee's Familiar was lying beside them, its skull crushed in and its eyes turned up to the dark sky. Their eyes still held terror as they gazed blankly up at the smoking sky.

My entire body shook, so much that I thought the ground was quaking again. Esis gently tugged on my pant leg. I tore my gaze away from the bodies, but it did nothing to remove the image from my mind. I didn't think anything ever would. I looked down at Esis, and he gave me a sad expression.

Without awaiting my instruction, Esis stepped forward and placed his hands on Marcee's stomach. The arrow had been broken off and shoved even deeper into her skin.

I finally found my feet and stepped up to their dead bodies. Tears welled in my eyes, but a searing burn in my face kept them back. "Esis..." I whispered.

He dropped his ears and looked up to me with watery eyes. It broke my heart. It was as if he was questioning why it wasn't working.

He didn't understand they were already dead.

I shook my head and swallowed the lump in my throat. "I'm sorry, buddy, but they're gone."

Esis furrowed his brow and turned back to Marcee. He resituated himself and stepped into the blood pooling between their bodies. He placed one paw on Marcee and another on Ben.

"Esis," I pleaded. "It won't work this time."

He blinked up at me. I could hardly bear it. Ben and Marcee were gone. And somewhere out there, a magical creature destined to bond with Ben— his literal soul— was dying and didn't know why.

A creature roared in the sky. I was too distracted to place what it was, but it snapped me back to attention.

I reached for Esis, forcing myself to pull myself back together again. It took everything I had. "Come on."

Esis clung to me and stared desperately after Ben and Marcee as I ran away. Blood coated my shirt from his paws, but I didn't care. I stopped beside one of the vendor tables and ducked down. Two terrified faces stared back at me as the Elementai clung to each other. Maddie and Drew.

I held my hand out. "We have to go!"

"Sophia," Maddie breathed in relief. She wiped her tears, and the two of them crawled out from under the table, their knees shaking. "Where's Liam?"

"We got split up," I said, taking her hand. "Where's Eira?"

"She's not here. She went hunting just before—" Maddie's voice cut off as a screech filled the air.

Above us, Eirakari dropped out of the sky. She landed with a hard *thud* in front of us and flung herself at Maddie, nearly knocking her over as she nuzzled her head against her shoulder. They both looked relieved to see each other.

"Get on!" I started ushering Maddie and Drew onto the ice dragon.

"No, wait!" Drew protested. "What about—?"

"You need to get somewhere safe," I insisted. "Meet us at the castle outside the southern tower on the third floor."

It was the safest place that came to mind.

Maddie pushed against me, but I shoved her harder onto Eirakari's back. "My brothers!" she shouted.

"I'll find them," I promised. "Get out of here. Now."

Maddie and Drew didn't have a choice. As soon as they were on Eira's back, she took off to the skies. I felt like a small weight had lifted off my shoulders now that I knew at least two people I cared about were safe.

Two down, about thirty more to go.

My eyes darted around the square. By now, the crowd had thinned, but the riots continued. It had only been minutes since all this started, but it felt like a lifetime. The sound of shattering glass came from all directions. People continued to fight one another, and magic of all kinds whipped through the square. The Blessing Tree was entirely consumed by flames, and it broke my heart. The fire was so big that I could feel the heat radiating off of it from twenty yards away.

What was fucking wrong with these people? And where were the Elders? It was like they'd all fled.

At least, I'd thought so, until I spotted Madame Doya and Professor Baine across the square. Doya was calming the flames raging through a shop, while Professor Baine was gathering what water he could find left in nearby fountains to clear a path for the people stuck inside. I could hear their screams from here. Naomi went full-on fire lion, then jumped through the flames into the open doorway.

Four other Koigni ran up to help. My heart lifted in my chest when I saw who it was: Lindsey, Miranda, Bren, and Vanessa. Their Familiars— Medusa, Kingston, and Aisha— were all beside them. The students lined up beside Doya and helped kill the flames.

I took off running toward them. Before I could get there to help, they'd killed the flames inside the building. Naomi walked out of the smoke in her regular form. In her mouth, she carried a baby swaddled in a blanket. The parents— Toaqua— rushed out behind her, coughing and sputtering. The smoke was so thick that they could barely breathe.

I arrived a moment later. "Guys!"

"Sophia!" Lindsey cried in relief. She threw her arms around my neck, squashing Esis between us. "You're okay!"

Doya whirled toward us, totally oblivious to our little reunion. "What are you all still doing here?" she snapped in the sharp tone she'd mastered. "All of you must leave immediately!"

"But we can help—" I started.

"You *need* to get to safety!" Baine roared in a tone I'd never heard him use. It was so commanding that none of us could argue with him.

"He's right," Bren said quickly.

Bren grabbed Vanessa around the waist and hoisted her up onto Kingston's back— his three-headed Familiar with a snake's tail and bat-like wings. Vanessa let out a surprised squeal.

"Let's go!" Miranda shouted.

We all glanced around, and the realization hit us at once. Between the fallen buildings and raging fires, the square was completely blocked off. Then I saw it— an alleyway that was burning with fire, but I could see to the other side. We were all Koigni. We could make it.

"There!" I pointed.

We ran toward the fire with our Familiars at our sides, leaving Baine and Doya behind. With five of us, the fire blocking our path was easy to calm. But what we found beyond it sent my stomach plummeting to my toes.

Imogen stood in the middle of the alleyway, looming over an old man who was cowered against the side of the nearest building. His Familiar was nowhere nearby. He held an arm up in front of his face, like he was trying to protect himself from her and Sassy, who was in kitsune form at Imogen's side. His leg was twisted, and his regalia was stained with blood. It looked as if his leg had been crushed by one of the falling buildings. He'd probably crawled into the alleyway, and Imogen had found him like that.

"Please," the man begged in a wavering tone.

"You killed him, Elder Poole!" Imogen shouted, taking another step toward the man. The murderous look in her eyes was enough to make anyone cower. "You designed the Water task that took Cade in the Elemental Cup!"

"Imogen!" I shouted from down the alleyway. I shoved Esis into Lindsey's hands and started sprinting. I couldn't get to Imogen soon enough. "No!"

Imogen never heard me. She gave the signal, and Sassy shot vines out of her back. They snapped at Elder Pool in the blink of an eye, wrapping around his neck tightly. He clawed at the vines and gasped for air.

My body slammed into Imogen's, and I tackled her to the ground. She stumbled over Sassy, who let out a high-pitched squeak and loosened her hold on Poole.

"What the fuck?" Imogen pushed me off of her. Her expression relaxed when she saw it was me. "Sophia?"

"Imogen, stop it!" I commanded. "You can't do this!"

We both got to our feet. Imogen's hands fisted at her sides, while her features contorted in fury. "I *can*! Poole and the Elders are responsible for too many deaths. Look what's happened here tonight!"

I grabbed Imogen by the shoulders and shook her. "You can't solve murder with murder! Killing Poole won't bring Cade back!"

Imogen blinked a few times, absorbing my words. Her chest rose and fell rapidly.

I softened my tone. "You're not a murderer, Imogen."

She didn't respond. She just stared Elder Poole down, like she wasn't sure whether she wanted to kill him or not.

"Imogen. Leave. It," I demanded. "We have to get out of here and find Liam and Jonah."

At the sound of Jonah's name, Imogen seemed to snap back to attention. She looked beyond me at the group and realized for the first time that Jonah and Liam weren't with me. Her face paled.

She turned to Poole and sneered, "I'll let you go today, but only because there's been enough death tonight. Mark my words, Elder Poole, the Elders' day is coming."

"Imogen." I pushed at her, but she kept her eyes on Poole.

Sassy ran ahead, and Imogen finally turned to follow her. She was fuming as she stomped out of the alleyway. I was just relieved she hadn't gone through with it. I took Esis back from Lindsey, and our group stepped out of the alley.

We didn't bother to help Poole.

Outside the main square wasn't the safe haven I'd been hoping for. Fires burned through the streets, though they weren't as large as the ones inside the square. The cobblestone had been upheaved in some places, and injured people were suffering on the edge of the sidewalks as other Elementai and Familiars tended to them. Voices overlapped as people cried out in pain or called for their loved ones.

"Jonah!" Imogen screamed.

"Liam! Jonah!" Bren cupped his hands around his mouth and called for them.

No reply.

My heart sank further and further as we walked through the streets of Kinpago without any sign of them. What if they were back in the square, buried under a pile of rubble? My chest ached just thinking about it.

No, I told myself. *They made it out. They had to.*

Still, a voice in the back of my head made my whole body shake. *But what if they didn't?*

We rounded a corner, and that's when my heart stopped. I felt both joy and utter despair all at once. Jonah and Liam were standing in the middle of the street, fighting a giant cobra as thick around as I was and at least fifty feet long. It bared its long fangs, then snapped its jaws toward Liam. He jumped out of the way and rolled across the cobblestone.

I threw my hand over my mouth and screamed. Liam gathered water from a nearby trough meant for horse Familiars. It smacked hard into the cobra's nose before it could strike again, and the creature reeled back, hissing.

Squeaks snapped her beak at the end of the cobra's tail, while Jonah swirled his hands above himself to stir up a wind storm.

"Liam!" I cried, rushing forward.

He turned to look at me while repeatedly spraying water toward the cobra's face. "Sophia!"

Jonah heard his cry. "Sophia! Imogen!"

Imogen ran beside me, the others close behind, as we hurried toward them. Liam ran out of water, and the cobra shook his head. He looked *pissed.*

"Back away!" I shouted as I stopped beside Liam. I held one palm up toward the snake, showing off my Fire. I didn't want to kill it, in case it was bonded.

Imogen didn't wait around. The earth shook, and plants pushed up through the cobblestone and wrapped around the cobra. But instead of holding it down, it quickly slithered out of the plants' hold. The snake was faster than Imogen. It circled around our group, causing us to back toward each other. Lindsey and Miranda shot fireballs at the creature, but it saw them coming and dodged around them.

"We've got this." Bren quickly helped Vanessa off Kingston and pushed her to Aisha's side. He stepped in front of her protectively, and huge streams of Fire rose up out of his hands. "Kingston, attack!"

Kingston lunged forward. His lion head snapped at the cobra, while the goat head aimed its horns at it and the dragon head shot fire.

Kingston barely made it three steps before the cobra had slithered out of his reach. The cobra lifted its head, then snapped forward toward Vanessa.

Vanessa screeched, but before the snake could get to her, Aisha had jumped in the way. She snapped her powerful dragon jaws at the cobra. Blood spurted out of the cobra's face and flew everywhere.

Bren lifted his arms to shoot Fire, but Vanessa grabbed him and said, "Don't! You could hurt Aisha!"

Aisha lunged again. Squeaks, Kingston, and Medusa all joined in to help her. They bit and scratched at the creature, scraping scales off as they attacked. Sassy whipped her vines out at the snake, leaving red, bloody marks behind. Medusa was less than half its size, but she slithered up its body and wrapped her own around it, squeezing hard. The cobra let out a low, growling hiss, then collapsed onto the street in a heap.

"Ancestors!" I cried as the street quieted.

Squeaks' clacked her beak and jumped around, pleased to see we were still alive. Esis struggled out of my arms and ran ahead of me. He jumped onto Liam's pant leg and climbed him until he was sitting on his head, giving him the biggest hug he could.

Liam and I collided like two magnets. He squeezed me so tightly I could hardly breathe, but I didn't care. They were okay, and that was all that mattered. Liam took my face in his hands and kissed me over and over again.

Beside us, Imogen and Jonah embraced, and Squeaks and Sassy rejoiced.

"You're alive!" Liam cried.

"I was looking for you." My voice cracked as tears started to stream down my face. "What happened?"

"*We* were looking for *you*," Liam said. "We saw the cobra's Elementai die, and he went full-on murder-crazy. He came after us."

I buried my face in his chest, and my tears soaked his shirt. "I'm so glad you're okay."

Just as I said it, a huge gust of wind swept through the street. It was so strong that Esis clung to Liam's hair to keep from getting swept away. His feet left Liam's head, and he waved in the wind like a flag. I jumped up to catch him, then cradled him to my chest. Our whole group huddled together, with the largest Familiars on the outside to protect us from the raging winds.

"It's not over!" I shouted above the deafening noise. "We have to get to the castle."

"The castle!?" Jonah shouted.

"I told Maddie to meet us there!" I yelled back. My hair whipped around my face. "It's the safest place right now. The semester's over. No one's there."

"Good idea!" Imogen shouted.

The winds began to die down, and we all parted.

Liam breathed a sigh of relief. "Maddie's okay?"

"Yes, Eirakari took her to the castle," I said. "We have to get there."

"What about Ezra?" Imogen asked.

"He's got a freaking thunderbird," Lindsey pointed out. "He'll be okay."

A loud screech came from the skies at that very moment. We looked up to see Dyami soaring overhead, lightning crackling around his form. Ezra leaned on his back, and they circled around to land in the middle of the intersection with us. The ground shook beneath Dyami's feet.

Ezra jumped off his Familiar's back and rushed over to Liam. I'd never heard him sound so worried. "I've been looking everywhere for you! Where's Maddie?"

"At the castle," Liam said. "We need to get up there."

"I saw a lot of people headed that way," Ezra said. "Do you think it's still safe?"

"We know somewhere that will be," I replied quickly.

Our group started down the street. It was a straight shot to the road that led to the castle. Liam walked in front, with Bren and Ezra on either side and Jonah at the back. The four guys were protecting us girls in the middle.

The further we got from the square, the quieter it became. It felt like we might actually be safe— until we reached the edge of town.

Task Force members were lined up along the road to the castle, blocking our route. They were spread out from the thick line of trees on one side of the road to the wide river on the other.

"What the hell?" Ezra exclaimed. "They weren't here when I was flying over before."

The Task Force caught sight of us, and three of them broke off and started walking our way.

I stole a glance at Liam. "Do we run?"

A muscle in Liam's jaw popped. "No. We stand our ground."

"You're to stay in the city limits!" one of the Task Force members demanded of us.

Liam stepped forward and raised his chin to the masked men. "No. Our family is out there. Let us through."

"We have explicit orders from the Elders to keep the Hawkei contained within the city," the Task Force member growled. "You're to return, or be marked as traitors."

"It's a bloodbath back there!" Jonah shouted.

Liam turned to him and calmly held up a hand, signaling for Jonah to let him handle it. He turned back to the Task Force. My heart pounded as I wondered what he was planning. I looked around for ideas, but there was only one way to the castle. Our airborne Familiars couldn't carry all of us at once, not to mention the Task Force was armed with noxite guns.

"Liam," I said, "maybe we should just go back."

There *had* to be other ways to the castle than the main road.

"No," Liam insisted. "I'm not leaving Maddie. So they're going to either let us through, or die."

The largest Task Force member— the one closest to us— scoffed. "You're all students. You really think you can take us on?"

Liam lifted his palms at his sides. "No. I *know* it."

I swore I could *hear* the smile in the Task Force member's voice, though I couldn't see it beneath his dark helmet. "Okay. Boys, take aim!"

"Now!" Liam shouted.

I barely knew what was happening. All at once, our group started to attack. Ezra gathered water from the river and started throwing balls of water at the Task Force, one after the other. Liam did the same, but with so much force that he knocked several on their asses. Lindsey, Miranda, Bren, and Vanessa shot fireballs in all directions. I quickly joined in, shooting fireballs at any Task Force member I could. Imogen rocked the earth beneath our feet, and Jonah sent the air raging around us until it was so loud I could hardly hear myself think.

Several men on the Task Force shot noxite darts at us, but they were carried away by Jonah's wind. Others dropped their weapons and used their magic to counteract ours. The earth shook a little less, and the winds died down. It was enough that they gained the upper hand and shot noxite darts into our group.

Lindsey gasped and grabbed her leg.

"Lindsey!" I cried, whirling around and rushing over to her.

She fell onto one knee and cursed under her breath. Miranda was a mess beside her, looking like she had no idea what to do. She held on to Lindsey's shoulder and said, "Shit, babe. Hold on!"

Lindsey ripped the dart from her leg and opened her mouth to say something, but she didn't get a word out before her eyes rolled back into her skull.

Everything happened so fast. I barely had a second to react before Bren shouted a curse. I looked over to see him ripping a noxite dart out of his shoulder.

"Bren!" Vanessa jumped toward him and caught him on the way down.

"Esis, help!" I shoved him toward Lindsey. I didn't know if he could do anything about the noxite, but maybe his healing abilities would help her magic work it out of her system faster.

"Fuck! Not this again!" Jonah shouted. The winds increased from his fury.

Only seconds had passed. The earth was still rumbling, and the winds were still swirling, but noxite darts were flying everywhere. My nostrils flared, and my whole body came alive with rage. I gathered all the Fire I could in my hands, then aimed them at the nearest Task Force member, who was laughing in joy as our friends collapsed on the ground.

Fire shot out of my palms like a flame torch, lighting the Task Force member up from his head to his toes. His laughter quickly turned to high-pitched shrieks. He dropped his gun and raced as fast as he could toward the river to extinguish the flames. He splashed around in the water frantically as the fire sizzled out.

A split-second later, a sharp pain shot across my belly. It felt like someone had pierced a needle through my guts. I felt my legs go numb, and the world began to blur.

All I saw was Liam's face contorted in fury before he let out a primal yell and I fell to the ground.

I heard Esis scream and the patter of his feet across the dirt, and then that was it. One second, I saw everything— heard everything— and the next, utter blackness.

It felt like I was only out a second before the world started to come back into focus again. The first thing I saw was Esis' white fur close to my face. I felt his warm paw on my cheek as he worked his healing magic to get the noxite out of my system.

And then I saw Liam. He'd totally lost his shit. He stood at the front of our group, his hands held in the air as he controlled the river beside us. But it wasn't a river anymore. The entire riverbed was exposed, and all the water within it swirled around the Task Force members, trapping them inside.

Liam threw his hands higher, and the water followed his command. It shot upward like a reverse waterfall, corkscrewing high into the sky. Against the moonlight, I could see shadows of the Task Force members inside the water. The massive water tower reached its peak, then started twisting downward again.

Just before it reached the riverbed, the entire river let go in an instant. Water rushed by so fast that it was like a flood coming down from the mountains. Task Force members screamed as they were carried downstream at record speeds, until we could no longer hear them anymore. All I heard was my ragged breathing as feeling returned to my extremities.

Liam collapsed to his knees.

"Liam!" I cried. I tried to push myself to my feet, but the noxite was still wearing off.

Imogen, Jonah, and Ezra rushed to his side.

"Dude!" Ezra exclaimed, laughing in a mix of exhilaration and disbelief.

"I can't believe you did that," Jonah said, clapping Liam on the back and helping him to his feet. "That was so badass."

Liam shrugged him off and stumbled back onto his hands and knees. "I've got this. Give me a minute."

He was a liar. His limbs were shaking, and there was almost no color left in his lips. What he'd just done took all his energy. It'd be weeks before he recovered.

"Liam." I finally got to my feet, though my knees shook.

Liam's head snapped up at the sound of my voice. He looked in my direction, but it was like he was looking *through* me. That magic had taken more out of him than I'd thought. He could hardly see straight.

"Let us help you," I insisted.

Esis hurried over and jumped on his back. He placed a paw at the exposed skin on Liam's neck. I could see Liam's entire body relax. His eyes finally focused on me as I knelt down beside him.

He sighed and collapsed into my lap, enjoying the feel of Esis' powers rushing over him. "Thanks, buddy."

"Now's not time for a nap, showoff," Ezra teased.

Liam kept his eyes closed and jabbed back. "I saved your ass, didn't I?"

Ezra chuckled, then quickly said, "No, but I'm serious. There could be other Task Force members out here. We can't wait around."

"He's right." Jonah stepped up and helped Ezra hoist Liam onto Dyami's back. Liam barely had control of his limbs— like they were made of dough.

"Guys, stop," Liam insisted. "I'm fine."

Even though he said it, he made no move to get off Dyami. In fact, he settled in and closed his eyes, stroking Dyami's soft feathers.

Esis jumped down from Liam's shoulders and into my arms. Lindsey was still passed out, since Esis hadn't had enough time to heal her, and Bren was out cold in Vanessa's lap.

Miranda stroked Lindsey's hair but gave me a confused look. "How — how did you do that? Are you immune to noxite?"

I glanced around the road for signs of incoming Task Force members, but we were alone— for now. "Let's get everyone to safety. I'll explain later."

I set Esis down and reached for Bren's legs. "Let's get him on Kingston's back."

"No," Vanessa said, grabbing my wrist to stop me. "Miranda's right. How did you do that?"

Her eyes filled with tears. I could sense the feeling of betrayal in her eyes. I glanced to Miranda, who wore the same expression.

My heart pounded at the thought of sharing my secret, but I couldn't keep it from them any longer. I wasn't going to let Lindsey and Bren lie here the rest of the night when I could help them. They'd know by the end of the night, anyway.

So I made a quick decision. My friends, or my secret.

The answer was obvious. I had to tell them the truth, just as I'd told Cade and Ezra when Imogen was in the hospital.

"Esis can heal," I said, dropping my head.

Vanessa blinked back my tears. "Why didn't you tell me?"

Fuck, now I was going to cry. Vanessa sounded seriously hurt.

"I was protecting him," I said. My throat closed up.

"He could've helped Aisha," she accused. She glanced to her Familiar with the twisted wing.

"I want him to." I sniffled. "But I thought people would notice. I didn't want anyone to suspect—"

"So we make something up," Vanessa insisted. "Say she got surgery or something. Do you know how much that could've helped us in the tournament? Sophia—"

"We can talk about this later," Jonah butted in. "We need to get up to the castle. Now."

Jonah and Ezra didn't wait for our permission. They hoisted Bren onto Kingston's back, then rounded the chimera to put Lindsey on Squeaks' back.

"I'm really sorry," I said to Vanessa as she climbed on to ride Aisha to the castle. "I'll explain everything."

Vanessa pressed her lips together and didn't meet my gaze. "Let's go."

We started up the trail to the castle, keeping watch for Task Force members the entire way. Somehow, amidst all the chaos, we made it to the castle without any further hiccups. We entered through a backdoor Ezra said he used to sneak out. Task Force members would for sure be swarming the Great Hall, and we had to get past them to get to Maddie.

We climbed the stairs to the third floor and found Maddie, Drew, and Eirakari sitting against a wall near the southern tower. Maddie shot to her feet and rushed over to us.

"Ez!" she cried, throwing her arms around her brother. She quickly turned to Liam. "What happened?"

Liam shrugged from where he lay on Dyami's back. "Used up all my magic in one go. I'll be fine."

"Liam," Maddie scolded.

"Come on," Jonah hissed. He unlocked the doors to the Anichi dorms and gestured for us all to follow him into the tower.

"I thought this tower was off limits," Miranda said as we stepped inside and started climbing the twisted stairs. "Are you sure this is safe?"

Jonah waited until everyone was inside, then closed the door and locked it behind us. "Safest place in the castle. No one knows about it."

"The school board lied to keep us out," Imogen explained from the front of the group. "The truth is, it's been abandoned so long because it's really—"

We reached the top, and Ezra gasped, cutting her off. "The Anichi dorms," he said in shock as the room came into view.

"The Anichi dorms!?" Vanessa exclaimed.

We all entered the vast common room. Miranda, Vanessa, and Ezra couldn't rip their eyes away as they took in the Anichi carvings along the walls and the high, ornate ceiling. Maddie's jaw dropped as she spun in circles, admiring it all. Drew's eyes locked on the huge fireplace, and a light smile spread over his face at the beautiful architecture.

"No one will find us here," Imogen said, sounding the most like herself all night. "Please, just don't tell anyone."

"We won't," Miranda promised.

"Let's get Lindsey and Bren to the couches," Imogen suggested.

Jonah and Ezra laid the two of them over the couches, and I stepped up with Esis in my shaking arms. Across the room, Dyami lay down with Liam still on his back. Liam stayed there with his eyes closed, looking comfortable, though I could tell he was still awake and alert. He was just waiting to get his strength back.

I placed Esis on Bren's stomach, and he got to work. I quickly untied my blanket from around my waist and draped it over Lindsey's legs. It was covered in dirt and blood, but I didn't care right now. All I cared about was my friends.

Now that things had calmed down, the weight of everything that had happened tonight finally sank in. I closed my eyes and pressed a hand to my mouth, trying to push the images out of my mind, but it didn't work. All I saw were the bodies, the fires, and the crumbled buildings. I saw blood everywhere I looked. Ben and Marcee's lifeless stares would forever be seared into my memory. I turned away from the group momentarily as tears streamed down my face. A heavy weight settled on my chest, and it took all I had not to let a sob bubble up and over the edge. My friends still needed me, and I had to be strong for them.

I quickly dashed the tears away and took a deep breath. It felt like an elephant was sitting on my chest, but I resolved not to let it show. I'd cry it out later— when I was alone.

I turned to Vanessa, who stood at the head of the couch to watch over her husband. Tears fell down her cheeks as she stared down at him, rubbing her swollen belly.

"Vanessa," I said softly, my voice cracking. "I'm so sorry I never told you. But you have to understand, if the Elders found out, they'd use Esis for their own personal gain."

She sniffled and wiped at her nose. "I'm sorry. I shouldn't have gotten so mad back there. It's just these hormones. They make me crazy."

She forced a chuckle, but it sounded pained. "I just... I can't believe you've had this healing power all this time and didn't..."

"Vanessa, we will," I promised. "Now that you know, we'll make sure Aisha gets her flight back."

"I won't tell anyone," she assured me. "I swear it."

"I know," I said in a small voice. "I'm really sorry. About everything."

She seemed to completely forget about me as Bren's eyes shot open. Vanessa threw herself at him. "Oh, Bren!"

He ran a hand over her back, looking confused. "Where are we?"

"The Anichi dorms," Vanessa cried into his shoulder.

Esis hopped over to the next couch to help Lindsey, while Vanessa continued to explain to Bren what happened.

Miranda looked up from where she was crouched at Lindsey's side. "Thank you for your help, Sophia."

I shook my head. "I'm not the one with healing magic. Esis is."

"Yeah, but you didn't have to tell us," Miranda pointed out. "You could've just let them ride it out."

"I can't do that," I told her. "You guys are my friends."

"Exactly," she said. "Which means your secret's safe with us."

I forced a smile. "Thank you."

Across the room, Liam coughed and pushed himself to a sitting position, stealing my attention.

"Give me a minute," I said to Miranda.

Liam slid off Dyami's back, but he wasn't standing for more than two seconds. He leaned against Dyami and slid to the floor, taking in deep breaths.

"Are you going to be okay?" I asked as I sat beside him. Being close to him helped ease some of the suffocating weight on my chest, but it was still unbearable.

He nodded. "It just took a lot out of me. You'd be useless too if you used that kind of magic."

I frowned. "You're not useless."

"I didn't mean that," he said, raking his fingers through his hair. "So, you told everyone? About Esis?"

"I had to," I said. "Even if we hadn't been knocked out, everyone still has scrapes and bruises Esis can help with. I don't want to hide him forever if he can help them. I only want to hide him from the people who would abuse his power."

Liam nodded in agreement. "Soph..."

"What?" I asked.

"I... I have to tell you something," he admitted. His voice sounded weird— it took on a quality I'd never heard before.

My heart sped up. It didn't sound good at all. "What?"

Liam rested his elbows on his knees and knotted his hands together. "I don't know how to say this, but it's kind of huge, and I can't keep it from you."

"What, Liam?" Ancestors, he was worrying me.

He took a deep breath, stalling. Across the room, Lindsey had woken, and Miranda was explaining to her what had happened. Esis moved on to Aisha, and her wing healed right before our eyes, straightening until it looked as if it was never broken in the first place. It was like the first time I'd seen it, when he'd healed her birth defect in Dragonology, right before the fall that had broken it and left it twisted again.

Vanessa sank to her knees and cried in joy as Bren wrapped her in his arms. Aisha flapped her wings and hopped around, rejoicing.

"I love you, Esis!" Vanessa exclaimed, scooping him up and giving him a kiss. Esis reached his paws out and hugged her back.

I turned my attention back to Liam. He swallowed hard. "What do you want to tell me?" I asked.

Water brimmed his lower lids, and his eyes burned red. "I— I killed Professor Fawn."

I gaped at him for a moment, before forcing out, "What?"

It had to be some sort of a joke. I'd been there. Those assholes had killed Fawn. Right?

He shook his head in regret, and the truth hit me hard like a punch to the gut. He was serious.

"She was suffocating, and I couldn't watch it." Liam's voice wavered. "I couldn't let her suffer like that. So I used my magic to— to stop her heart."

My blood ran cold. I could hardly wrap my head around what he was saying. Liam had killed someone tonight. It was in mercy, but still— he'd taken a life. And I could see on his face just how much it bothered him. He'd never be able to overcome the guilt.

"Liam," I whispered. I reached toward him and wrapped him in my arms. He rested his head on my shoulder, but he didn't move. He didn't make a sound.

Across the room, the group looked okay— as okay as they could be after a night like tonight. We were safe, and everyone was healed. But over in our corner, just Liam, Dyami, and me, it felt dark and depressing, beyond anything I'd ever felt before— even worse than the Cup. Yeah, we'd made it, but at what cost? So many people had lost their lives tonight.

Jonah and Imogen were still on edge. Imogen sat near the window, looking out toward the empty forest. It was like she was keeping watch, waiting for the Task Force or the Elders to swoop in for an attack. Maddie kept throwing glances our way, like she was worried about Liam. It was nearing midnight, and everyone was exhausted.

"I'm going to scope things out downstairs," Jonah announced as he and Squeaks started for the doors. "We'll make sure it's safe out there."

"I'll come." Bren started toward him, but Jonah held a hand up.

"The fewer who go, the better," he said. "I don't want anyone spotting us."

"Fair enough. Come back safe, man," Bren said, clapping Jonah on the shoulder.

He nodded. "I will."

Jonah started down the stairs, and I turned back to Liam.

"Liam... do we still want to keep doing this? Hunting down the pieces to the prophecy and everything?" I asked, so quietly that I wasn't sure Liam had heard me. I could barely speak past the lump in my throat. "I don't know if we can still save this society, or if it's too far gone."

Liam lifted his head to look at me. His face had fallen, but other than that, I couldn't read his expression. "That's exactly why we need to stick with it. We need to save the Hawkei."

"People are going to die in our name," I pointed out. "Is it worth it?"

Liam nodded. "With Oleander on the council, more people will die if we don't do anything. We need to stick this out."

I took a deep breath. Liam made a damn good point. We couldn't abandon the Hawkei when they needed us most. The prophecy was already coming true, and we had to find some way to reverse it.

"Okay," I said. "I agree, but if we keep doing this, we have to go forward knowing that after tonight, Orenda Academy will never be the same... *Kinpago* will never be the same. There's no coming back from what happened tonight."

Liam's expression was heartbroken. "I know." He reached out to wrap me in his arms.

I knew this was only the beginning. The Houses were turning against each other, and tonight had marked the beginning of even worse things to come. More people would die because of the prophecy— because of *us*. Nivita and Yapluma would soon choose their side, and we would have to find some way to change the future.

If we didn't, we were all fucked.

Footsteps on the stairs caught our attention. Jonah rushed back into the room, looking relieved. "Guys, it's safe to come out now. Head Dean Alric is in the Great Hall calling everyone down. Let's go."

Liam

TWENTY-FIVE

I felt numb all over as we headed down to the Great Hall in a collective group. My eyes couldn't focus on anything in front of me. I put one foot in front of the other, like I was compelled to do so. I didn't feel like I had any control over my body. All I could see replaying in my head was the sight of Professor Fawn collapsing on the ground, over and over.

Is this what it felt like to be a murderer?

Sophia caught my zombified gaze and slipped her hand into mine. She gave it a tight squeeze as she said, "Try not to think about it."

My mouth was dry. "I can't think about anything else," I whispered back quietly, so the others wouldn't hear. "I just killed somebody."

"You didn't have a choice. You spared Professor Fawn a horrible death," Sophia said. "It wasn't like it was murder. It was a mercy killing."

"How do you live with yourself after doing something like that?" I asked.

Sophia stared at me. "I don't know. You just go forward."

"But I don't know how," I said hoarsely. "How can I go on knowing what I did?"

"Professor Fawn would thank you," Sophia whispered. "There was no other way."

That much was true. Fawn's eyes were crying out for someone to save her as she'd gasped for air. She'd just watched her Familiar die.

535

There was no greater suffering than that. I knew. I'd done the right thing tonight, even though it'd come at a grave cost to my conscience.

Sophia wrapped her arm around mine and leaned against me. "Not a lot of people would be strong enough to do what you did. You're willing to make tough decisions. That's one of the reasons why I love you."

She didn't say anything more about it. Esis hopped from her shoulder to mine and settled in, wrapping his tail around the back of my neck.

There was a large group of people in the Great Hall, and not all of them were students. They looked like a collection of adults and children, pressed against the walls with their Familiars. Many people were injured or bleeding.

"Dad!" Ezra shouted. Relief flooded through me as I saw my father standing in the corner of the Great Hall. He was no longer wearing his headdress, and his regalia was stained with blood and dirt. But at least he was alive, though he looked terribly worried. Tatum stood at his side and let out loud rumbles, as if calling for us.

Ezra shoved his way through the crowd with the help of Dyami's big wings. We followed him. Ezra flung his arms around Dad the minute he was within range. Dad hugged him tightly before embracing me. Maddie was crying. Dad wrapped her in his arms and kissed her head. The worry on his face was replaced with ease.

"Thank the ancestors you're all safe," Dad said. "I've been looking for you for hours."

"Is everyone else okay?" Ezra asked.

"Your mother and the rest of your siblings made it home before the riots started," Dad said. "It's a miracle all of us made it out alive."

"Dad, how many people are dead?" Maddie asked.

Dad's expression hardened. "Maddie, you don't need to know."

"Dad, please." Maddie begged.

Dad looked to everyone's inquiring faces gathered around the group. He sighed and said, "Right now, the body count is somewhere around five-hundred. A thousand, if you count Familiars. Most people died when the buildings collapsed around the square."

Maddie started sobbing. Dad wrapped her in another hug. The rest of us stared at the carpet. I knew that hearing numbers of the dead made

Maddie upset, but I was honestly a little relieved. I figured the death toll would've been higher than that. There were ten thousand people in Kinpago at any given time, probably more than that tonight, since it was New Year's Eve and people were out celebrating. That the slaughter had been mostly confined to the square was a blessing.

"I should've been able to stop this," Maddie sniffed. "I could've prevented it."

"Maddie, you couldn't have done anything. What are you talking about?" Drew asked.

The rest of the group looked confused, but Dad, Ezra and I shared helpless glances. Maddie was a *naderei*. Of course she took it upon herself to feel guilty if she couldn't predict the future all the time, even if her visions didn't work like that.

"There's nothing you could've done. There was nothing that *I* could do," Dad confessed. "This has been coming for quite some time."

Maddie let go of Dad, and he looked at me. He seemed apologetic. For the first time, I noticed a trunk beside him, sitting between Tatum's big paws.

"Ezra, I managed to save your regalia," Dad started. "But Liam... I'm sorry, son."

Tatum pushed the trunk that carried my regalia toward me with his head. I kneeled down and opened it up. My heart dropped when I saw the mess of feathers, broken strings and beads, smeared with a collection of dirt and blood.

My regalia. It was trashed.

"It was ruined after the plankhouses were raided and torn down. Some of Jaymin Riske's rebels started destroying anything related to Hawkei lore. I'm sorry to say your regalia was part of it," Dad said heavily.

This had taken me years to make. I didn't even know how to fix it. I couldn't. It was completely ruined.

I swallowed the lump in my throat and shut the trunk. "It's okay. What matters is that we're all safe," I said finally. "Though I don't know what I'm going to do with it." It was beyond repair, but it meant too much to me to throw away.

"I'll take it for now," Imogen offered. I passed the trunk off to her, and she set it down beside Sassy.

I caught sight of Elder Oleander standing twenty feet away. He jerked his head, and Dad's face became stoic. "I have to go. There's an announcement to be made. Things are going to be all right, I promise."

Dad walked away. Sophia took Maddie in her arms instead and tried to calm her down. I observed as Dad and Tatum sullenly followed Elder Oleander like a dog on a leash.

When Dad said things were going to be okay, I heard the father in him, not the chief. Something was definitely wrong.

As time passed, more and more people kept pressing into the Great Hall. Our group was forced to span out in order to make room. I managed to stick with Sophia, Imogen, Jonah and their Familiars in the corner, while Maddie, Drew, Lindsey, Miranda, Vanessa, Ezra, and Bren lined the wall on the other side with their magical creatures.

There was muted conversation around the Great Hall as we waited for Head Dean Alric to make his announcement. Jonah leaned over Squeaks' back and stared at the carpet.

"Guys..." he started. "Was this our fault?"

No one answered right away. Imogen clung to Sassy, who was bundled up in her arms, and put her nose against the fox's ears. "I don't know."

"We're supposed to stop the war and reverse the prophecy," Jonah said. "And I don't even think we're close."

It was dangerous talking out in the open like this, but nobody was paying attention to us. The conversation around the room gave us an opportunity to speak without being overheard.

"How could we have prevented this?" I asked. "I don't even think the prophecy saw this coming."

"Your Dad did," Sophia pointed out. "He made it seem like the Elders were waiting for an opportunity like this."

We were quiet for a moment. Then Imogen said, "The Fire piece was a promise of what would come true if we fail. The Water piece was a warning of what would come before that happened. And the Earth piece is a turning point we still can't figure out how to stop."

"So what's the Air piece going to be?" I asked.

None of us had any ideas. "I don't know, but we need to find it as soon as possible," Jonah said. "Before things get any worse."

It was hard to imagine that happening. After everything we'd been through tonight, how could this society possibly get any *worse*?

"I'm the prophesied one," Sophia whispered. "This is my responsibility."

"It's all of ours. We're in this together," Imogen piped up, and Sassy yipped in agreement. "But we're running out of time. We have one more piece left to find. If we fail to stop whatever it's warning..."

Nobody wanted to finish the thought she'd left out in the open. All of us wanted to stop the prophecy, but we had no clues on where to begin searching for the next piece, or any idea on how to stop the events in motion. It's like we were completely helpless.

It was quiet between us for a few minutes or so. "This semester sucked," I said, abruptly and out loud.

Jonah, Imogen and Sophia all nodded solemnly. We'd all been through hell in the past four months. Break-ups, court cases, lost friends... the list went on and on.

"We need to take a break," I suggested. "Go on vacation."

"We can't go on vacation. The new semester is starting soon," Imogen said glumly.

"We don't have to be back until classes start on the thirteenth," I said. "We deserve this. Let's take a little trip."

"Yeah." Jonah was slowly brightening. "The *Hozho* is taking its yearly voyage to Europe. It'd be fun to go."

"Liam, the court fine and paying our lawyer ate up all our money," Sophia reminded me.

"Y'all know I'm broke," Jonah said glumly. He didn't need to add his parents had taken it all.

"I'll pay for you guys," Imogen said. "I've got more than enough left in my winnings. Liam's right. We need to step back from all this prophecy stuff and refocus. Maybe a bit of relaxation will help us find the next piece faster."

The chatter died down in the Great Hall. People looked upward as Head Dean Alric, along with Elder Oleander and Dad, took the balcony above the hall. Madame Doya was with them, along with Baine. I didn't see any other Elders among them. Alric raised his hands, and the room quieted.

"May I have your attention, please," Alric said firmly. "I would like to announce that the stolen Familiars have all been located, and will be returned to their rightful Elementai within the coming days."

A sigh of relief went up around the room. Alric grimaced, as if what was about to come next was nothing to celebrate. "I ask for everyone's cooperation. What the Elders are about to say is very important."

Alric turned toward Oleander and stepped aside. Oleander proceeded to the center of the balcony. His voice was commanding and firm as it rang out overhead. "What happened tonight can never happen again," he began. "We lost many of our own after justice was served to hideous traitors. Vile rebels who wish to overthrow the ways of our ancestors took to the streets with the intent to kill and destroy."

Every person was silent as they stared up at Oleander with a mixture of reverence, respect, and fear. "There are those within the tribe that seek to destroy our way of life," he went on. "Our heritage has been threatened. Who we are as a people is at risk. It is essential that the majority of us give up our personal rights and privacy in order to secure our future."

A growing horror began to overcome me as Oleander continued. "Our tribal security must come first and foremost, before any individual. It is essential for our children and for our race. The law of our religion and of our ancestors must be followed without question, or we cannot survive. Fealty to our tribal government, to our Elders, must come before all else. Before our family and friends. Before blood. It is the only way to preserve our survival. There can be no greater sacrifice for an Elementai to make than to be a loyal patriot to his tribe."

At a distance, Professor Baine stood behind Madame Doya, hands clasped and looking guilty. Had he regretted giving up his council position? He might've had a chance to stop this.

"There are those among us who are not *like* us!" Oleander bellowed. "We need to root out those who are threatening our nation. We are a superior race, but our livelihood is being threatened by certain individuals who pose a great threat to our people. They live beside us, pretending to be equals, yet they are surely the cause of so much division! We must unify against these dissenters and wipe them out!"

All around us, there were shouts of agreement and rage. So many people were buying into this. They were angry at what had happened tonight and needed someone to blame.

"How can this be happening?" Imogen whispered.

Jonah had his hands on her shoulders and was gazing up at Oleander with a grim expression, as if he'd expected this day would come. Sophia looked up at me with a terrified gaze, and Esis shivered on my shoulder. I put my arm around her and tried to remain calm.

"That is why," Oleander said, "the Elders have collectively voted to replace the four tribes with a better way."

My mouth dropped open in shock. They were abolishing the four tribes system? We'd lived this way for hundreds of years. Similar cries of surprise went up around the room. Oleander only raised his voice louder.

"No longer will you be known as Koigni, Toaqua, Nivita, or Yapluma," Oleander shouted. "From now on, our people will be sorted into *two* tribes. The Defortai— the strong— and the Biyami— the weak."

Some gasps went up, but among them were notes of approval. For a long time, the tribe wanted to change the four tribes system, to make it more fair and less divided. But this wasn't the right way. My insides curled at the use of the Hawkei words to name the new tribes. A *defortai* was practically a hero, someone chosen by the Great Spirit for greatness.

A *biyami*... a curse.

"Over the next coming months, every individual within Kinpago will be sorted into one of these two tribes," Oleander said. "Those who exemplify traits of loyalty to the Elders, of magical superiority, of clean heritage and of an allegiance to our master race shall be sorted into Defortai— the authoritarian Elementai, the true leaders of our people."

His tone held a warning... no, worse than that... a promise. "And those who show questioning toward the Elders— those who refuse to put our tribe first, those who cling to artistic expression instead of scientific proof, those who prove themselves to be weaker, magically or otherwise, than the pure bloodline of our ancestors— will be sorted into Biyami."

My stomach plummeted to the floor. The Elders needed a scapegoat, a group of people to blame for all the problems going on in our society. The Biyami would provide that easily.

I didn't need to guess what House I'd be sorted into. I already knew.

"Intertribal relationships are now legal," Oleander began. "There is no need to draw lines between elements. The only line that must be drawn is the one crucial to our world. There are only two sides now.

Those on the right side of history, and those who are doomed to destroy our tribe if we allow them to do so."

Oleander lifted his head high. He was working the crowd into a frenzy now, shouting into it like a wild man and raising his hands in an attempt to get the people to rise up. "Let our tribe rise to defeat the great threat against us, for if we do not stamp out and eliminate this threat, the blood of our infants will run through the streets, and massacres such as we experienced tonight will be held again!" Oleander shouted. "We must stick together and conquer over the weak— we must bind together and avoid destruction! The strong must survive!"

Many of the people and Familiars in the Great Hall were roaring with triumph, shaking their fists and screaming victory. Some people were starting to slip away quietly— others seemed nervous, or disapproving, shaking their heads, but no one dared to raise a voice against Oleander's tyrannical speech. Dad stood behind Oleander and said nothing, looking every part the broken man.

I hated what Oleander had done to my father. And on my life, I vowed to make him pay for it.

Oleander raised his hands to the ceiling. "Let the great awakening of our tribe begin, and may we move forward as a nation of peace!"

Several Task Force members behind Oleander stepped forward and raised their hands. Air magic blasted from their palms and carried toward the top of the Great Hall. Sophia gasped in horror as the large banners hanging from the ceiling of the Great Hall depicting the four Houses were torn in two and wrenched from their golden hangers. They crumpled onto the floor and over the crowd, where they were ripped off of shoulders and trampled underfoot, forgotten and fallen.

New banners unraveled from the golden hangers. In the place of the four Houses hung long, black banners with the depiction of two arrows crossing, the arrows stitched into the dark fabric with red thread the color of blood. With the arrival of the banners, the crowd chanted the same word over and over: *"Defortai, Defortai!"*

Those banners had been already made long before the riots began. Oleander had been plotting to usurp the Elders— probably for months. He had this planned all along.

The school bell then tolled, signaling the arrival of midnight and the passage of the New Year. It was an ominous, harsh ringing that signified we were too late.

The four of us thought we still had time. We figured there was a chance we could turn things around before the tribe dissolved into chaos.

We'd screwed up. Nivita had already chosen their side. We had failed to stop the prophecy the Earth legend forewarned would come true. We didn't think war would come so soon.

We were wrong.

War was already here.

END OF BOOK THREE

Turn the page to read a special excerpt from Book Four: *The Air Omen!*

HIDDEN LEGENDS

Read more from the Hidden Legends universe! Each Hidden Legends series takes place within the same world, but in separate and unique societies. Every series stands on its own, and they can be read in any order.

·

SHIFTERS, FAE, & SORCERESSES

University of Sorcery by Megan Linski

·

WITCHES, DEMONS, & REAPERS

College of Witchcraft by Alicia Rades

·

SUPERNATURAL PRISON

Prison for Supernatural Offenders by Megan Linski & Alicia Rades

·

Never miss a new release! Join our newsletter at www.hiddenlegendsbooks.com/fanclub/

THE AIR OMEN
CHAPTER ONE

Liam - *Fifteen Years Earlier*

"Do it again!"

Grandma and Grandpa lived in a cottage by the sea. The beach was their favorite place to be. Mine too. It was a sunny day and really hot. Grandpa stood in the ocean while his eagle Familiar flew circles overhead. Grandma weaved baskets on a bench in the sand and watched with a smile. We'd collected seashells this morning, and she was making the basket for me to take them home in.

Grandpa moved his hands in circles. The water in the ocean came out in two big strands and twisted together, creating loops and dips in the sky. The eagle flew through the loops and swirled in circles around the twisted strands. It looked like one really big rope. Grandpa was using so much water— much more than anyone else in the tribe could summon, even my Dad. Grandpa could do amazing magic. I could see fish swimming in the water high above me within the tunnels he had made. Grandpa lowered the rope, and out in the distance, a whale jumped out of the water and through one of the loops.

Grandpa made the water rope return to the sea. The water splashed past my knees, and waves crashed back and forth.

"Wow!" I said. "I want to do magic like that!"

"One day you will, my child. Be patient. You're only six." Grandpa raised his arm and called for his Familiar. Tinanco landed on Grandpa's forearm and shook his feathers.

I wrinkled my nose. "I'm seven now."

"That's right! I forgot." Grandpa winked. I think he was teasing me, but I worried he really had forgotten. Seven was much older than six.

Grandpa walked to a large rug spread out in the sand and sat down. I followed him. There were many bowls sitting on the rug, with strange powders of different colors in them. Beside the bowls was a large square piece of deer leather. Grandpa summoned water from the ocean and mixed it with the powder in the bowls. Tinanco jumped off his arm and stood on the blanket. His head tilted as he watched Grandpa mix the powders.

"Grandpa, why are we doing this?" I asked.

"Because this is our heritage. It's important you learn it before you become chief."

"But why?"

"You ask a lot of questions. A good chief stays silent, listens and learns. He rarely speaks his mind." Grandpa set the bowls in front of me. "Can you tell me what these are?"

I shook my head, and Grandpa said, "These are the sacred paints of our people. Red, white, blue, yellow, purple, and green."

"Why did you make red?" I scowled at the red paint. Red was for Koigni, and I didn't like them.

"A long time ago, before the tribes divided, we shared all the colors. We were one people and not four," Grandpa said. "Our tribe was not divided."

"It wouldn't be such a bad thing if things were like that again," Grandma said. Grandpa frowned like he was sad.

"Our paints are special, and they bestow powers and blessings onto those whom they are applied after they are prayed over," he said. "They are very sacred."

I got very serious. Grandpa uttered some prayers over the paints in our ancient language. I knew what he was saying, but it was hard to understand, because he used big words I didn't know.

When Grandpa was done, he said, "Each of the paints have a different meaning. They were once used for battle, but now are mostly used for ceremonies. It is said that each of the paints have a symbolic animal guarding over them, which gives the wearer the protection of that animal."

"I like wolves best," I said eagerly. I howled like one and laughed. Grandpa smiled.

"I know you do. Some of our bravest warriors used to paint their faces white in battle, to gain stealth and bravery from the wolf."

Grandpa took a scoop of white paint with his fingers and started putting it on my face. It felt thick and grainy. "White was not just the color of Anichi. It was the color of the original Hawkei tribe. It represented all of us in one, the people of the Great Spirit in unity."

I couldn't see what Grandpa was doing, but it felt like he was making shapes on my face. "Certain symbols have power. It is said that when some designs are drawn with paint on the bodies of Elementai, their magic is enhanced by these symbols."

"What do all the different paints mean?" I put one of my hands in the blue paint. I smeared it across Tinanco's beak, and he chirped.

"Red is for war. Blue is for peace, and for weddings. Green is for new growth and new beginnings. Purple is a rare color, and shows abundance. The paint signifies our connection with the earth, with our ancestors and with the Great Spirit."

"What about the black paint?" I asked.

"We never use black paint. Black paint is only for those who mourn and seek revenge."

"And yellow?"

"Yellow is for warriors who are ready to give their soul up to the Great Spirit." Grandpa stirred the paints again. On the leather, he began drawing symbols. They looked like birds, dragons, and other magical creatures. "These are our talismans. Each one has a different meaning when used with the paint. You will learn them all. The Hawkei had our own written language before the colonizers came to our lands. Many of our people have forgotten, but some still remember the old texts."

"How do we know the Great Spirit is *really* up there?" I asked. "How do we know the ancestors are really listening?"

"My child, the Great Spirit will always be there to guide you, if you ask for his teaching. Our ancestors are all around us, and they are here to help us down our path. You need only to believe and listen. The proof that the ancestors and the Great Spirit love you will be in your magic, when it comes."

Grandpa seemed so sure. I wanted to be sure, too.

Grandpa had me draw many symbols on the leather with the paint. I tried to make mine as good as his, but they weren't. I didn't think I'd ever be as great a chief as he had been. There were so many stories and lessons to learn. I worried I couldn't learn them all.

Grandma asked me if I was hungry. I shook my head.

"Are you not feeling well, *pawee?*" Grandma brushed my hair back.

"Yes. My tummy hurts." It had hurt since this morning.

"Hold on. I might have a plant that'll help."

Grandma was a medicine woman. She always had something. Grandma went inside the cottage and came out a few minutes later. She gave me some coast buckwheat to nibble on, and I felt a little better.

My tummy was always upset. I felt tired sometimes and wanted to take naps, but I didn't anymore, because I was supposed to be big now.

When the leather was full of symbols, Grandpa looked over them. "Very good! You did well for your first time. Your father will be pleased."

"Dad is always busy. He doesn't have time for me." I dropped my head. I didn't want Grandpa to show Dad my symbols. They weren't good enough.

"Your chief training will begin in a few years' time, then you'll always be with him. Have patience," Grandma said sweetly.

Grandpa looked at me, then scooched over to give me a hug. "You'll be a wise chief someday. Your father knows it. He's already so proud of you." Grandpa shook me.

I shrugged my shoulders. "I guess."

Dad was the best chief ever. I wanted to be like him, but didn't think I ever would.

It was late at night and really, really dark when I heard a tapping on my sliding glass window.

I woke up right away and sat upright. I thought the knocking had been a dream, but it continued. It scared me. I pulled my blanket up to my nose. What if it was a monster? Dad said he'd gotten rid of the one under my bed, but maybe it had just moved outside?

"Liam! Liam, let me in!"

I knew that voice. "Jonah?" I got out of bed. Standing outside *was* Jonah. He was dripping wet and shaking from the cold. I opened the glass door to let him in.

"Jonah, how did you get here? And how did you climb up to my room?" I asked. We lived on an island, and my room was on the second floor.

"I snuck on a boat. I kinda got wet." He shivered. "And then I climbed up the vines to your window."

Mom grew twisting flowers outside that grew up the side of our house, but I didn't know it was safe to climb them. I wanted to ask Jonah why he was here, but I didn't. Jonah ran away from home all the time. He usually went to the treehouse my Dad had built for us back on the mainland, near Grandpa's cottage. He'd never made it to my house by himself before.

Jonah was Yapluma. I knew I wasn't supposed to be friends with people from other tribes, but I didn't care, because Jonah was cool.

"Do you have any dry clothes?" Jonah asked.

I nodded. Jonah was the biggest kid in my school and my clothes wouldn't fit him, but Mommy had bought some extra clothes for him and kept them in my drawer, just in case he wanted to sleep over one night. I gave him what Mommy had bought. He changed out of them, and I put the wet clothes in the corner.

"Can I stay here with you?" he asked. He wasn't shivering anymore, but he still looked cold.

I nodded. "Yeah. But we have to be quiet."

"Okay."

I turned on the TV in my room and put the volume really low. Jonah and I played with my new PlayStation before we got mad we couldn't pass the next level and decided to watch cartoons instead. There weren't many kid shows on this late at night. I wasn't allowed to watch some of the shows that came on, but Jonah said it was fine, because his mom and dad allowed him to watch whatever he wanted.

Jonah started snoring when the clock said the number three. I got tired and fell asleep beside him.

Jonah was up before I was. He started shaking me when the sun came up. "Hey, Liam, do you have anything to eat?"

I rubbed my eyes. I was really tired. "Yeah. Come on."

We went to the kitchen. The cereal was up really high, and I couldn't get it. Jonah moved a chair across the floor, but I still couldn't reach. He tried putting me on his shoulders but that didn't work, either. We both fell down and made a loud noise.

"Liam, what are you doing up so early?"

We'd woken up Mommy. She was carrying my little sister, Maddie, and wearing her robe. Mommy still seemed sleepy. Maddie was only three and was still asleep on her chest. Mommy's eyes widened when she saw Jonah. "Jonah, dear. I didn't know you were here."

Jonah blushed. She looked at the chair, and us on the floor. "How about I make you boys some breakfast?"

Mommy cooked us bacon and eggs. Maddie sat in her high chair. Jonah and I played swords with our forks. It wasn't too long before Ezra came downstairs. Ezra was my four year-old little brother, and he always got up when he smelled food. He tried to get between us and play swords, too.

I mostly pushed my food around, but Jonah ate his really quick. Mommy gave him seconds.

"Now, I'd love for you to stay, Jonah," Mommy began, "but I do have a lot of errands to run today. I'm sorry to say we're running low on groceries. Otherwise, you know I'd love to have you."

Jonah looked sadly down at his plate.

"Can I go over to Jonah's house? Please?" I asked. It sounded more fun than going shopping.

Mommy frowned. She didn't like me going over to Jonah's house and didn't tell me why. "Are your parents home, dear?" she asked Jonah.

He shook his head. "No, ma'am. My sister's the only one home until dinner."

"Well, I guess that's all right, then." Mommy sighed and picked up the phone. "I'll give her a call. Your father will be by to pick you up in a few hours, Liam."

"I want to go, too!" Ezra shouted.

"No, baby, you'll stay here," Mommy said. "Let your brother go alone."

Ezra started to cry. I was glad. He was always copying me. It was annoying.

Before we left, Mommy packed a lunch and told me to take it with us. Mommy always packed extra food whenever I went to Jonah's house, even if I already ate.

Menilly was Mommy's Familiar. She was going to take Jonah and I to the mainland, where Jenny was waiting for us. Menilly was on the beach when we walked out. She was a kelpie— a sea horse. She walked on four legs and had green scales all over. Her mane and tail were made of seaweed, braided with seashells, and her hooves were the color of pearls.

Menilly lay down in the sand so we could climb on her back. I got on front, and Jonah sat behind me. She waded into the sea, and I hung on tightly to the seaweed in her mane as she swam forward.

Kelpies were fast. Menilly swam in the sea like she was galloping on land. Dolphins tried to keep up with her as the water fanned out around us on either side. My hair blew backward, and the wind made my eyes water. Nobody was quicker than Menilly in the water.

Jenny was waiting for us on the docks. She was Jonah's older sister, and a teenager. She made a face as we got off of Menilly. Menilly bobbed her head, and the water dried out of mine and Jonah's clothes magically.

Jenny grabbed Jonah's hand sharply. "Come on. Let's go."

Menilly turned and dove back into the water. I hurried to follow Jenny as she pulled Jonah through the streets. She acted like I wasn't even there.

We took a carriage to the Yapluma neighborhood. Jonah lived in a really big house, but it didn't have much furniture in it. I didn't know why.

Once the door was closed, Jenny turned on us. "Listen, you little brats," Jenny started. "I have a *very* important piano recital tomorrow, and if I blow it, Mom and Dad are going to be *pissed*. So you guys stay out of my way, and keep quiet. Don't you dare bother me for anything."

We nodded. Jenny stomped her feet as she walked away. She always had to be perfect in everything. I heard the sound of the piano coming from the living room.

We went up to Jonah's room. Jonah still looked hungry. He ate the extra sandwich my mommy packed for him. I gave him mine, too, because I didn't want it.

"I'll save it for dinner," Jonah said, and he hid it inside his drawer. "My mom sometimes forgets."

I thought that was okay, because the last time I was over and Jonah and I wanted snacks, the kitchen was empty.

"What should we do?" I asked. Jonah didn't have a lot of toys to play with. His room had a bed and his clothes, and that was it.

"Let's play Hippogriffs and Dragons," Jonah said. "It's my favorite."

I liked that game, because Jonah always wanted to be the hippogriff and he let me be the dragon. "Okay."

Jonah made a chirping noise and jumped at me. I roared like a dragon and tackled him. We fought back and forth like animals. It was hard to wrestle when you were trying to be quiet, but the sound of the piano muffled most of our punches.

After an hour of playing, we got too excited. Jonah jumped off his bed and landed on me. We made a loud crashing noise as Jonah accidentally knocked his lamp off the nightstand. It didn't break, but it created a loud *thump*.

The sound of the piano stopped from downstairs, and I heard the front door open. I think I heard the voice of Jenny's girlfriend. "You kids better be quiet up there!" Jenny called.

Jonah and I stopped wrestling. We shut our mouths and stared at each other. I had the thought that Jonah's house wasn't very fun. It probably would be if his sister wasn't around.

"We should go to the basement," Jonah whispered. "She won't hear us down there."

"All right." We tiptoed down the stairs to the main floor, then took the stairwell in the kitchen down to the basement.

Jonah's basement was dark and creepy. It was concrete floors and concrete walls. There were a ton of boxes down here. The basement was stuffed full. Some of the things in here were creepy. There were weird statues and old dolls that I swear kept giving me weird looks.

In the middle of the room was a huge square, at least six feet tall. I couldn't really tell what it was, because it was covered up by an old white sheet. It was the only thing down here not covered in dust. I wanted to peek under it and see what it looked like.

I went to look, but Jonah said, "Don't touch. It's a painting my Dad just bought. He told me not to play with it."

The boxes were towered up high. It didn't seem like a very safe place to play, but where else did we have to go?

There were loud noises coming from Jenny's room. I didn't know what they were doing up there. I asked Mommy once, but she told me it was adult stuff, so I just ignored it.

"We should play hide-and-seek," Jonah suggested. "There are tons of places to hide down here."

That was a great idea. "I'll seek, you hide."

It was too easy to find Jonah. I played seeker for an hour, but he was so big and so bad at hiding that it didn't take me very long to find him, no matter how long I counted or what he hid behind. Jonah was too good at getting caught.

"It's my turn to hide," I said. "We've been at this forever."

"But I hate seeking," Jonah whined.

"No fair. It's your turn!" I yelled.

"Shh," Jonah said, with a quick look at the stairs. "Okay, fine. I'll seek."

Jonah started counting. I looked everywhere for a spot to hide that he hadn't picked, and found a tall wardrobe in the far corner. I ran toward it and shut myself inside.

"Ready or not, here I come!" Jonah started looking. I pressed my hand to my mouth so I wouldn't laugh. I didn't want him to find me.

Then something happened. The room got... colder. And darker. We had the light on, but the bulbs broke. I heard the sound of glass breaking, and the only light that came into the basement were from the windows on the ceiling's level. The sunshine from outside went away... like there was a storm coming. I swear I heard the crackling of thunder, and it shook the room.

"What the hell? Power's gone out," I heard Jenny say from upstairs.

I heard something else. A low growl. From a very, very big animal.

Panic made it hard to breathe. It felt like the air was filled with static — we'd learned about that in school. It made my hair get all frizzy. I could almost hear a kind of sizzling popping in the air. Large footsteps thumped on the ground only a few feet away. What if some sort of monster lived in the basement, and we'd bothered it? It was going to eat us up!

"Liam!" Jonah was nearby. I opened the wardrobe door to see that he was crouched behind a pile of boxes, looking scared.

"In here!" I whispered. Jonah crawled to the wardrobe. I opened it up so he could squeeze himself in. We held the doors shut and held our breath.

"What is it?" I whispered. Jonah was shaking so hard I was afraid he'd tip over the wardrobe.

He shook his head fast. "I don't know. I didn't see it. I was trying to hide. All I saw were really, really big paws."

I gulped. This wasn't good. How had a big magical creature snuck into the house and knocked out all the electricity?

"Liam, it's coming this way," Jonah squeaked. I gasped. Jonah and I held the doors shut as something bumped against the wardrobe, knocking it back and forth. We leaned onto the wooden walls so we wouldn't fall over. There was a sniffing sound— the creature was smelling us.

Then it went away. I heard the footsteps retreating. When it had been quiet for a moment, I dared to open the doors back up, and I saw that the light from outside had returned. There was no monster outside — just a few fallen towers of boxes that it had knocked over on its way out.

"Shit!" I said as we hopped out of the wardrobe. "That was scary!" I wasn't supposed to say bad words, but I liked how they felt coming out of my mouth, and doing things I wasn't supposed to was fun.

"Oh no," Jonah said, pointing. "The painting!"

I looked. I noticed the painting that had been leaning up against the wall from earlier was gone. It had been there when we'd been playing, but now, it had disappeared.

"The monster must've took it with them," I said. "Though I don't know what they'd want with a painting."

"This is really bad." Tears dotted Jonah's eyes.

"What's the big deal?" I asked. "It's just a painting. At least we didn't get eaten."

"You don't understand. When my dad brought it home the other day, he told me *never* to touch it, or I'd really get it. It was super important." Jonah sniffed. "Now it's gone, and he's going to think I lost it."

"But you didn't. That monster came and took it," I said, confused.

"It doesn't matter. He'll think it's my fault." Jonah was really scared that the painting was gone. He was almost crying.

"Maybe my dad can help," I suggested. He was the Water chief. I bet he was boss of all the magical creatures in Kinpago. He could find the monster who took the painting and force it to give it back.

Jonah opened his mouth to respond, but then the basement door flew open. Jonah sank down. I looked up to see Jonah's dad at the top of the staircase.

And he looked really mad. His teeth were clenched, and he was breathing hard. His boots made loud, thumping noises as he came down the stairs. "What are you doing? Didn't I tell you not to play down here?"

Jonah was shaking. I don't even think his dad noticed I was there. Jonah's dad looked at him, and then at the empty wall. His eyes bulged out when he noticed the painting was missing.

"*What* the hell did you *do?*" he yelled. "Where's my painting?"

Jonah's dad must've spent a lot of money on that painting. He *was* really angry.

Jonah looked up at his dad with and started bawling. "I'm sorry! I didn't mean it!"

"Are you fucking kidding me?" Jonah's dad shouted. Jonah started screaming and apologizing over and over. I didn't know what to do.

"I... I can replace it," I stuttered. I'd probably get grounded, but at least my family could pay for it, and Jonah wouldn't get in trouble.

"That painting was *priceless*, you little bastard! Where did it go!?" Jonah's dad screamed. My lip wobbled. I wanted to cry, but didn't, because I was supposed to be brave for Jonah. I was the oldest, and Mommy told me the eldest always looks out for the younger ones.

"A monster came and took it," Jonah whimpered. Jonah's dad smacked him across the face, and he fell over. Jonah held a hand to his cheek and curled up into a ball as his dad stood over him. Jonah started to wail as a red welt formed across his cheek.

I was so shocked I froze. Jonah's dad wouldn't actually *hurt* us, right? My dad never hurt me.

When his dad raised his hand again, I ran to stand in front of Jonah. "He's telling the truth!"

Jonah's dad was shaking with anger. "I'll beat the truth out of you, you little shits!" Jonah's dad grabbed me by the shirt. He picked me up and threw me. I hit the ground hard. I think I scraped my elbow. Tears welled in my eyes, but I wouldn't let them fall. I had to be strong for Jonah.

Jonah and I looked at each other in fear. What were we going to do? We were just kids, and he'd never believe us. That monster had gotten us into a lot of trouble.

"That is *enough*."

A voice scarier than Jonah's dad echoed through the basement. I felt relieved as I saw my father standing only a few feet away. He was here to pick me up. He must've heard Jonah crying and came downstairs. Jenny stood at his side, looking helplessly between him and her dad.

Jonah's dad straightened up. "I don't believe I allowed you permission into my residence, *sir*." It sounded really disrespectful.

"I am a chief. I need no permission of yours." Dad pushed past him. He bent down and picked me up, holding me on his hip. I put my arms around his neck and held him really tightly. I was still really scared, but I didn't need to be anymore. My dad would protect me. Jonah's dad couldn't fight him.

"What I do in my own house is none of your concern," Jonah's dad said in a mean tone. "I am handling my business."

"My child doesn't belong to you. You put your hands on my son again, I'll prosecute," Dad threatened.

Jonah's dad didn't say anything more.

Dad's voice was flat as he said, "There will be a welfare check made here by the Yapluma Elders in a few hours. Mark my words."

Jonah's dad's face got a little white. Jonah was taking his chance to sneak away. He ran past us, up the stairs and to his room.

Dad turned his back and carried me up the stairs. "Come, son. Let's go."

My dad's Familiar was waiting for us outside of Jonah's house. The grizzly bear rumbled a friendly hello as we approached. Dad put me on Tatum's back before he climbed on behind me. Tatum started walking through the Yapluma village at a slow walk.

"Did he hurt you?" Dad asked, looking down at me.

"I bruised my elbow," I sniffed. *Now* I wanted to cry. It was like the time after the scary part was worse than it actually happening. I showed him my elbow. My shirt was torn, too.

"We can patch it up at home. Come now, chiefs don't cry."

I let out a few sobs and wiped my face with my shirt. Dad patted my back, and I felt better.

"Dad, can Jonah come live with us?" I asked.

Dad frowned. "I don't think that's possible, son."

I ran my hands through Tatum's fur. "I hope I see him a lot."

"He can come over as much as he wants. But you can never go back over there. Do you understand?"

I nodded. I didn't want to. But Jonah was still stuck there.

One day, I wanted to be just as strong as my Dad was. Everyone respected him. Once I was a great chief, nobody would push Jonah and me around. I'd make sure everyone was safe, and I'd use my magic to slay all the monsters. I promised myself to listen more closely to Grandpa and his teachings next time.

"I know what'll cheer you up. How about we stop for ice cream?" Dad asked. Tatum gave a happy growl. He loved sweets.

Ice cream got my mind off of it. "Sure."

I had almost forgotten about the monster that had stolen the painting, but watching Tatum's big paws roam over the pavement reminded me. I wondered. Why had that monster taken the painting, and why had it been so important?

Solve the mystery by continuing the series with The Air Omen!

BONUS OFFERS

Find coloring pages, games, quizzes, and bonus content at www. hiddenlegendsbooks.com

Join *Orenda Academy of Magical Creatures* on Facebook to talk to other Elementai about upcoming books in the Hidden Legends Universe!

Never miss a new release! Join our newsletter at

www.hiddenlegendsbooks.com/fanclub

Check out the *Academy of Magical Creatures Official Playlist* on Spotify!

ABOUT THE AUTHORS

Megan Linski (left) and Alicia Rades (right) are two best friends and the authors of the *Academy of Magical Creatures* series. Both are USA TODAY Bestselling Authors and award-winning novelists for teens and young adults. Megan Linski is a disabled author who loves laughter, adventure, and fantasy worlds. She is a proud member of Koigni House. Alicia Rades is a mother who enjoys exploring paranormal realms and trying new recipes. She is a champion from Toaqua House. Both girls love nature, animals, sexy romances, and eating cheese.